For Mum,
I miss your weekly calls checking if I'm alright...

Contents

Acknowledgement

This is a hard acknowledgement to write—*why?* It's because I lost my Mum while writing this novel.[1] She was perhaps one of the greatest supporters of my work—someone who would, without fail, try to attend any signings or book launches and always insisted her work colleagues purchased a copy—whether they wanted to or not. I miss her enormously, and I'm sure most of the jokes found in '*The Hero Interviews*' would have gone miles over her head—but she would have been so proud of it regardless. I want to thank my Dad for being there during the most challenging of times for us all. I'm indebted to my wife, Tash, who fell asleep every time she tried to proof anything for me but has kept everything ticking over while this book has absorbed my life. My kids, Zack and Neve—who never fail to put a smile on my face and continue to fuel my passion for writing. To Paul Martin, who has been there since the start of '*The Hero Interviews*'.[2] To the fabulous Erica Marks, marvellous Lisa Blackwell-Dickinson, and diligent Paul Devereux, who all donated their free time to give this a read—and gave me some much-needed feedback. To Matt Mastracci, who has been on hand for technical advice and continues to be an amazing friend. I also wanted to say a huge *thank you* to Conor Nolan for that awesome cover. To Guy Adams, Mark Bestford, June Courtney, Jodie Crump, David Devereux, Scott Donaldson, Alex Farnham, David Forrest, Mike Green, Sarah Griffin, Nichole Hanson, Paige Harris, Caroline Jenkins, Dennis Johnson, Duncan Jones, Ian Livingstone, Kenneth Mitchell, David Moore, Chris Norgate, Rhianna Pratchett, Nigel Rogers, Ben Shahrabani, Jim Strader, Alasdair Stuart, Lord TBR & the FanFiAddict crew, Jo Wain, Calum Alexander Watt, Matt Woodley, and all my friends and followers on Twitter *(there are a lot of you—so apologies if I missed anyone off)*, who have continued to be in my corner—I salute you all!

Finally, I wanted to acknowledge Sir Terry Pratchett, Rowan Atkinson (as Blackadder), and Douglas Adams, who inspired me to write a large part of what lies within these pages.

---

[1] *Several hours after my mother died from breast cancer, I returned to my parents' house and wrote a footnote in her honour. I know it probably seems strange to you, but I found comedy helped me through that difficult moment. So, I wanted to make a poignant mark in the novel that signified the exact moment my life changed forever. In case you're wondering, it was footnote 1660.*

[2] *Seriously, Paul, I owe you a massive debt of thanks, 'The Hero Interviews' is so much better for your hard work and insisting I push things further.*

A note from the Author

Hello—thank you for choosing to read 'The Hero Interviews'. It has been one unbelievable adventure getting to this point—so, I hope this book makes you smile as you discover the odd comedic gem buried within these pages. I want to let you know that there are numerous footnotes peppered throughout this novel—**<u>lots</u>** of footnotes, in fact. I humbly apologise. I hope you can keep going to the end; if it helps, think of this as a personal quest of your very own—minus the horde of Zombie Squirrels snapping at your heels…

To be a hero or not to be a hero
—that is the quest...

I was never destined to be a hero; the quill and parchment are my weapons—my sword and shield. I've always been interested in the art of adventuring, but partaking? Not so much. I wouldn't follow some fool's errand even if the realm's survival depended on it. Instead, I prefer to capture the experiences of those who have braved and survived, transcribing their adventures word-for-word as if one were right beside them, stepping into the unknown, weapons drawn, spells at the ready.

My name is Elburn Barr. I'm a Loremaster—a *Wordsmith* as my father calls it, although I suspect mine is not a profession[3] that makes him overly proud.[4] My family has always had a keen interest in adventuring; both my mother and father were reputable adventurers of note in their time. I can only imagine the deep-rooted disappointment they felt when I declared I wouldn't keep the hero tradition going and follow in their footsteps. However, for every black sheep, there is always a prize ram ready to step up when needed—and thankfully, that's where my older brother came to my rescue.

Aldon is the consummate adventurer—bold, good-looking, charismatic, and of course, he knows how to wield a sword, axe or anything else that inflicts pain.[5] While I spent most evenings practising calligraphy or had my head buried in *another* book, Aldon would stay up late, learning a new finisher move,[6] mastering the art of picking a trapped

---

[3] *I was lucky enough to choose my own profession; those less fortunate rely on a 'Careersmith'—a grumpy Gnome (who usually turns up with an even grumpier looking 'magical' Sorting Cap) to pick a profession for them. As much as I'm in awe of sentient, fate-deciding apparel, I don't want to entrust my future to a head covering in a foul mood and possibly fouler flatulence.*

[4] *I have a sneaking-suspicion my father wanted me to be a Wizard.*

[5] *This literally meant 'anything' my brother had in his hands at the time could be considered a deadly weapon—which made our youthful pillow fights somewhat of a one-sided and traumatic affair.*

[6] *That often required me to stand-in for demonstration purposes only.*

lock[7]—or honing his hunt and ambush skills.[8] Though we shared a passion for adventure, our pursuits of that passion could not have been further removed.

But, as they say, time and tide wait for no one; Aldon has been gone for ten summers now, following whatever epic adventure lands at his feet, no doubt searching for one quest-orb or another. I imagined I would remain at home till he returned, lest my parents are deprived of both sons. But I can wait no longer. The time has come for me to try and make my mark—not following fame and fortune but tracing the footsteps of those, like my elder brother, who strive so hard for both.

I've chosen to write a journal of my travels as I seek out those who could not resist the call to arms, the thrill of the quest, the perils and the potential rewards that a life of adventure entails. And not just them but also those they meet along the way, from the humblest Monk[9] to the most lauded Baron of the realm. My quill will take me far and wide, from arboreal forests to frozen peaks, as I seek to document tales of success, glory, failure, and possibly even death.[10] Perhaps along the way, I'll come to understand this 'hero' obsession my family has, or at the very least, shed some light on why my parents risked everything in the name of adventure.[11]

Elburn Barr, Loremaster.

---

[7] *Which bizarrely included an initial step of letting a nearby gullible Cleric attempt to pick the lock first.*

[8] *Being the youngest, it will come as no surprise that I often ended up as his unwitting quarry.*

[9] *Monks are usually humble, right?*

[10] *Hopefully not my* own *death, although I wouldn't be documenting this right now if I 'had' perished—unless I had somehow been resurrected by an evil Necromancer and forced to write this footnote for them. Let's hope not...*

[11] *And hopefully, find out where my errant brother is along the way!*

1. Dorn, the Barbarian

Whisper the word Barbarian, and I'd wager you would instantly picture a rage-filled, muscle-bound Warrior clad only in a fur loincloth fuelled by a love of spleen removal whilst drinking the nearest tavern dry of every alcoholic beverage sold. You can imagine my disappointment as I sit opposite a muscle-shy, pasty-looking 'Barbarian'. Dorn is the latest 'hero' to step out of the Heroes Guild, a polite man who seems eager to make a name for himself within the adventuring world. We've agreed to meet at Dorn's local tavern, The Spit & Spear, a favourite watering hole of heroes situated in the lively city of Tronte, a settlement plagued by wannabe adventurers hoping to be spotted by one of the Heroes Guild's numerous 'Scouts'.

The Spit & Spear is mercifully quiet, although I suspect the evening is still too young to attract the hardened drinker questing for the only elixir that matters in life. The tavern's only other patrons of note are a nearby Dwarven Fighter working his way through a flagon-orgy, and a Paladin, who is regaling the Barmaid with over-inflated tales of adventure. The young lady is so enraptured by the Holy Warrior's words she has failed to notice both the 'Barbarian' and I have been without a drink for a considerable amount of time.

Me: "Thanks for meeting me—"

Dorn: "My pleasure, it's not every day I get interviewed by a bona fide *Loremaster*—I suppose it's something I'm going to have to get accustomed to..."

Me: "Accustomed to?"

Dorn grins proudly as he turns the collar of his jerkin over; I catch sight of a flash of silver—a badge sits snugly underneath. I can make out a sword hilt etched into the design bisecting a large 'H' and 'G'.

Dorn: "I'm now *officially* a hero. Finally, I can follow in the footsteps of the greats, like Arin Darkblade[12] and Gilva Flamebeard!"[13]

Me: "*Erm...* I guess congratulations are in order?"

Dorn: "Thanks! To be honest, I'm still in shock; I have to punch myself to make sure I'm not dreaming."

Me: "Don't you mean pinch?"

Dorn: "*Rogues* pinch. *Barbarians* punch."[14]

Me: "Got it—"

As if to emphasise the point, the 'Barbarian' hits himself fully in the face—he shakes his head and looks around as if he's just woken up.

Dorn: "Nope, it's *still* real!"

Me: "You okay?"

Dorn: "Nothing a drink won't sort out—"

The 'Barbarian' waves trying to catch the eye of the Barmaid stood behind the bar without success.

Me: "Forgive me for saying, but you don't look how I'd imagine a Barbarian would look."

Dorn: "Really? What were you expecting?"

Me: "*Erm...*"

---

[12] *Renowned for being the meanest adventurer in the entire realm—and I don't mean in the 'never buys a round of drinks' kind of way, although I suspect he's never bought a round of drinks in his life either. No, Arin is an eye-patch wearing hero who has completed more quests and dispatched more monsters (and undoubtedly a few Paladins) than any adventurer in living memory.*

[13] *Gilva Flamebeard is a legendary Dwarven Cleric who has stepped back from the adventuring life to become a Hermit. As her name suggests, she sports a fiery red beard, which, by all accounts, contrasts sharply with an unusually calm demeanour for a Dwarf. Whether her given Dwarven clan name really is Flamebeard or not has been debated and argued in every tavern at some point or another.*

[14] *This is not strictly true; some Rogues <u>have</u> been known to punch, although I'm sure they'd prefer not to let their opponent know the blow was coming. While 'some' Barbarians have a bad reputation of unwanted pinching, usually of Barmaids' behinds.*

Dorn: "Perhaps you'd prefer it if I wore a fur loincloth?"

My cheeks flush red in embarrassment.

Dorn: "Sorry to dispel *that* particular myth! The truth is adventuring can get *awfully* cold. While I'm sure it has its place, a fur loincloth is impractical on so many levels.[15] If you want to survive on a quest, you need to be wearing layers, lots of layers—and I don't mean armour either."

Me: "Sorry, I just expected a bit more flesh on show."[16]

The 'Barbarian' gives me the strangest of looks.

Dorn: "Are you okay? Fighting in only a tight-fitting loincloth is… is a bit weird, isn't it?"

Me: "I thought that's the whole point of being a Barbarian? Attacking your enemies half-naked while lost in a furious battle-rage?"[17]

Dorn: "You've been hanging around with the wrong type of people if you think that's how Barbarians dress these days."

Me: "I'm only going by the legendary Warriors from days of yore."

I point to the wall of hero paintings on the far side of the bar, several of which are of muscle-mountains wearing only the tiniest fur loincloths.[18]

Dorn: "*Ha!* Those old Barbarians are so out of touch compared to the modern Barbarian of today. Nobody wears fur loincloths anymore— anyway, I prefer to leave my family jewels to the imagination if it's all the same to you…"

---

[15] *I guess on a frozen adventure, the loins would be nice and warm while the rest of the Barbarian's extremities would certainly be frozen solid—still, a warm groin is something not to be sniffed at (quite literally).*

[16] *Just to be clear, and as much as this may appear to the contrary, I wasn't trying to encourage the Barbarian into stripping for me.*

[17] *A rage possibly brought on by the recent discovery that someone had just stolen all the Barbarian's clothes.*

[18] *I 'hope' they're wearing loincloths; from where I'm sitting it could also be overgrown loin hair.*

He tries to catch the Barmaid's eye but misses once again—the 'Barbarian' thumps the table in frustration.

Dorn: "**Balls!**"

I feel the need to quickly change the subject away from the angry-Warrior's nether regions.

Me: "Did you *always* want to be a Barbarian?"

The angry-Warrior laughs at the absurdity of my question.

Dorn: "Me? No—never in my wildest dreams! I actually thought I was going to become a Wizard."

Me: "A *Wizard?*"[19]

Dorn: "I know, it's odd—but I was convinced to switch my focus to the Barbarian class[20] rather than follow a wizardry one. Besides, Wizards are generally frowned upon at the Heroes Guild."

Me: "Frowned upon—I thought the Heroes Guild would welcome Wizards with open arms?"[21]

Dorn: "Seems there's a long-running rivalry between the Heroes Guild and the Wizards Guild—in truth, they *hate* each other, but recently they've begrudgingly agreed on an uneasy peace..."

Me: "How did the feud come about?"

Dorn: "I don't think the Wizards Guild liked it when the Heroes Guild started recruiting Wizards to their cause—it resulted in *The Battle of the Blind Bowman*."

Me: "I've never heard of this battle."

Dorn: "That's because it happened one fateful afternoon in the middle

---

[19] *I'm glad my father isn't around to hear this—he'd never let me live it down.*

[20] *Also jokingly referred to (often out of earshot) as the 'angry-Warrior class' by non-Barbarians.*

[21] *As long as they had been patted down for any concealed spells or cantrips first.*

of a tavern—*The Blind Bowman,*[22] surprisingly."

Me: "They had a *battle*... in a *tavern?*"

Dorn: "I think I may have oversold the 'battle' part of this story—it was more of an untidy brawl with a lot of pushing, shoving and accusatory pointing."

Me: "Who won?"

Dorn: "Nobody; when the dust settled, *The Blind Bowman* was no more—the whole place had either been burnt down by a spell[23] or smashed into tiny pieces by the fist. The warring Guilds soon realised their mistake when they couldn't order another round of drinks[24]— and immediately held emergency talks in the ashes of the former privy.[25] The Heroes Guild agreed they wouldn't add any more Wizards to their numbers; in exchange, the Wizards Guild agreed to help them recruit more non-Wizard heroes to their cause."

Me: "So, Wizards *only* come from the Wizards Guild?"

Dorn: "Officially—yes."

Me: "*Unofficially?*"

Dorn: "I've seen a few robe-wearing, book-reading types walking around the Heroes Guild—but they *could* be Loremasters, I suppose."[26]

Me: "How *does* a Loremaster join the Heroes Guild?"

---

[22] *Named after a legendary blind archer who could hit any Goblin with unerring accuracy, a remarkable feat rendered useless if no 'actual' Goblins were in the area for the blind archer to shoot in the first place.*

[23] *I would bet my family's estate it was the Wizard's favourite go-to spell—Fireball.*

[24] *And the next nearest tavern was a three-day hike away across the foul-smelling waters of the Malodorous Marshes.*

[25] *I would love to have been a fly-on-the-wall that day—not that there were any flies left... or walls.*

[26] *I seriously doubt any of my profession would be interested in joining the Heroes Guild— the closest a Loremaster would ever want to get to danger is drinking a hot cup of tea too quickly and burning the roof of their mouth.*

Dorn: "If you get us a couple more ales, I'll put a good word in for you."[27]

I laugh at the boldness of the 'Barbarian'.

Me: "Fair enough—so the Heroes Guild made you a Barbarian instead? I mean no offence by this, but you don't look the angry-Warrior type.[28] Why do you think they wanted you to become a Barbarian?"

The 'Barbarian' narrows his eyes at me.

Dorn: "Isn't it obvious?"

Me: "Not really…"

Dorn: "They want me to revamp the Barbarian's stereotypical image. Usher in a new age of Warriors who don't go around smashing up taverns just because they're a bit angry about poor bar service. They want me to be the face of tomorrow's Barbarian—a thoughtful, calm Barbarian who has a bit of a sensitive side too."

The 'Barbarian' flexes an arm muscle. I can't quite see it, but I don't want to ruin Dorn's moment.

Me: "Impressive!"[29]

Dorn: "Yup, I'm the first in a new wave of approachable Barbarians; *less* rage—*more* brains."

Me: "The thinking man's Warrior?"[30]

The young hero slams the table with his hand before pointing at me excitedly.

Dorn: "The Barbarian with a heart of gold!"

---

[27] *If we could 'actually' get any service; the Barmaid still hasn't managed to drag herself away from the Paladin's vicinity—if I were the Landlord, I'd be asking some serious questions about her work ethic.*

[28] *Spoken like a true non-Barbarian.*

[29] **Loremaster Tip #1:** *Always tell a Barbarian what they <u>want</u> to hear—even if your whole being is screaming at you to do otherwise.*

[30] *Although I suspect every Paladin in existence will feel as if they have something to say about this.*

Me: "Catchy. So, have you been on any adventures yet?"

Dorn: "Only the training dungeons. They're pretty tough and can hurt if you're not careful—I mean, *really* hurt. I passed with flying colours, of course. Even resisted sitting on a trapped throne too—unlike the Ranger I was with."

Me: "What happened to the Ranger?"

Dorn: "He insisted on stopping to take the weight off his feet—and got his backside frozen solid as a consequence."

Me: "That's terrible."

Dorn: "I know; it took me ages to pull him free from the throne—when I finally did, he had a huge hole ripped in his breeches."

Me: "That must have been a bit awkward—?"

Dorn: "Yeah, I had to keep him behind me for the remainder of the adventure—there are some things not even a Barbarian should have to bare witness to."[31]

The 'Barbarian' looks again for the Barmaid, but she's still busy, lost in her Paladin-filled daze to notice him—I spy Dorn clenching and unclenching his fists as he slowly boils with anger.

Me: "How did you first get involved with the Heroes Guild?"

Dorn: "I was spotted."

Me: *"Spotted?"*

Dorn: "Yes, you know, *seen*—in this place actually, which is ironic if you think about it."

Me: "Why's that?"

The 'Barbarian' grinds his teeth and throws imaginary daggers in the Paladin's direction.

Dorn: "Because I *can't* seem to be seen right now, can I?! ***CAN I GET SOME SERVICE PLEASE!!***"

---

[31] *Spelt this way on purpose!*

The 'Barbarian' shouts at the top of his lungs, but he is still ignored by the Barmaid currently draped over the Holy Warrior.[32]

Me: "Who spotted you?"

Dorn: "A representative of the Heroes Guild—a *Scout*.

Me: "Where were you sat?"

I look around the bar and try to picture a nervous but excitable Dorn sitting around, waiting to be spotted by the Heroes Guild Scout.

Dorn: "Here!"

Me: "*Here?*"

I point to the table we're currently sitting at.

Dorn: "Well, not *here* exactly. More like over *there*."

The 'Barbarian' motions to a table next to us, occupied by a Dwarven Fighter polishing off his tenth flagon of ale—judging by the nine empty flagons sitting in front of him.[33]

I find myself staring at the inebriated Dwarf as he spills more beer on the table than into his mouth.

Dorn: "That's not the Scout, just in case you were wondering."

I nod and turn my attention back to the 'Barbarian'.

Me: "How did you find out about this place?"

Dorn: "I heard about *The Spit & Spear* from a friend. He told me the Heroes Guild Scouts frequented it—and if I wanted to be spotted, then this is where I needed to be."

Me: "What happens if you're lucky enough to be spotted?"

---

[32] *To be fair, the Paladin seems to be happily encouraging the Barmaid to do this.*

[33] *I have no idea how this Dwarf has managed to get served not once but TEN times—it is a miraculous feat that should be compared to Dragon-slaying with only one arm (the Dwarf, that is, not the Dragon—otherwise, that would be somewhat less impressive as a feat).*

Dorn: "If a Scout thinks you have potential to join the Heroes Guild, they employ a test—"

Me: "Test? What sort of test? Written?"[34]

Dorn: "No—practical. Sometimes it's a stolen coin purse, other times it's a spontaneous bar-fight—whatever it is, it is always designed to test a specific attribute."

Me: "What attribute did they test of yours?"

Dorn: "Why, my strength, of course.[35] Anyway, it so happened that I had struck up a conversation with the *very* Scout who had taken a keen interest in me."

Me: "What are the odds? So, what did you two talk about?"

Dorn: "*Oh,* this and that—he was especially interested in my family's estate on the far side of the Evergreen Forest. That seemed to give him the confidence that I had the right stuff to join the Guild. He said he saw enough potential in me to be one of the realm's greatest heroes!"

Me: "What did you say to that?"

Dorn: "It was Bardic music to my ears[36]—everything I wanted was being promised to me. But at the same time, I had to make an impromptu call to the privy, so I excused myself for a moment to tend to my pressing need. When I returned, I found this brute of a Half-Orc sat at my table, drinking my ale!"[37]

Me: "Who was he? What did you do?"

Dorn: "A stranger, it seemed he wanted a free drink. Honestly, it's a bit embarrassing to mention this, but—"

Me: "Go on..."

---

[34] *Which would be an overly cruel thing to do to any would-be Barbarian.*

[35] *Of course...*

[36] *This depends greatly on the Bard doing the 'music' in the first place.*

[37] *Something that is unlikely to happen again anytime soon—given we are <u>still</u> without a drink.*

Dorn: "I *barely* hit him. I guess I didn't realise I possessed such strength!"

Me: "You *hit* him?"

Dorn: "I knocked him straight out of my seat and across the tavern—which immediately started a mass brawl with some Gnomes sitting at the corner table. Once I had dealt with the Gnomes,[38] the impressed Scout clapped me on the back and signed me up, there and then!"

Me: "And that's when you became a Barbarian?"

Dorn: "He said I was a natural—that I had untapped raw power in my fists!"

Me: "Untapped raw power—and you *believed* him?"

Dorn: "Why wouldn't I? I had just seen what I could do with my own eyes! But I still held a strong desire to be a Wizard..."

Me: "I guess he explained the problem with that?"

Dorn: "Indeed he did—we had a good chat about it, and I agreed to give up my dream of wielding magic in favour of wielding an oversized sword.[39] Anyway, Barbarians have better perks in the long run.[40] Sure, there's a clause in the contract, but the Scout said that it was just a standard—"

Me: "Wait a moment—a clause? What clause?"

Dorn: "He promised me it was all just legal mumbo-jumbo. The Scout called it a *'Death in Service'* clause—If you want to join the Heroes Guild, you have to sign the clause, <u>no</u> exceptions."

Me: "What does the clause do?"

Dorn: "For me? —Nothing... but for the Heroes Guild—they end up

---

[38] *As much as this sounds unimpressive, fighting something that stands at waist height is extremely dangerous for tall combatants—and their extremities (frozen or not).*

[39] *The weapon of choice for any self-respecting Barbarian—closely followed by an oversized axe, oversized spear, and finally an oversized fist...*

[40] *For starters, Barbarians get served first in any tavern keen to avoid spending a large amount of coin on urgent repairs twenty-four hours later.*

owning my family's estate in the event of my death."

Me: "That sounds a tad unfair."

Dorn: "Apparently it's standard stuff that every hero signs. But you needn't worry; it won't ever happen, not to me. The Scout explained there's a sizeable risk in retrieving a hero's fallen body from a failed quest, not to mention all the funeral arrangements and possible lost equipment—some of which are magical and very expensive. The *'Death in Service'* clause covers all damages, repairs, and replacements. It's pretty thoughtful if you think about it."

Me: "I see—what else did the Scout say?"

Dorn: "He said he had never seen such a natural athlete—the *complete* hero he called me! Said he wanted to send me on a Category Five[41] adventure after I had completed all my training dungeons."

Me: "What's a Category Five adventure?"

Dorn: "Only a quest meant for the hardiest of adventurers—certain death assured!"[42]

Me: "Aren't you worried? You might, you know—*die?*"

Dorn: "Nah, you're talking to the realm's next greatest Barbarian;[43] I laugh in the face of death—"

High-pitched laughter breaks out from the Barmaid sitting in the Paladin's lap; Dorn suddenly kicks back from the table and stands with purpose and drive.

Dorn: "Although the Guild's next greatest Barbarian is **STILL** thirsty. Time I finally got that drink—wait here, I'll be right back."

I watch as Dorn the 'Barbarian' storms over to the Paladin and the

---

[41] *I'm not sure what this means, but the fact there are four categories before it cannot be a good thing.*

[42] *See, I was right!*

[43] *The realm's last greatest Barbarian was Thrux the Biter, who expired after a fight with a group of drunken Gnomes and ended up ironically bitten in the groin and bleeding to death—perhaps not quite the glorious way he had imagined bowing out. I can only assume Thrux was pretty tall...*

Barmaid to make his displeasure known. Not wanting to be caught up in the approaching *Battle of The Spit & Spear*, I decide to leave this interview post-haste.[44]

---

[44] *I did leave a polite note explaining my departure, blaming it on a sudden urge to drink elsewhere—specifically a place with good bar service and less chance of seeing spilt blood...*

2. Morgan, the Wizard

The weathered castle has undoubtedly seen better days. In its prime, it would have been a sight to behold—a thin spear of architecture thrusting skywards from the cliff-face that overlooks the tempestuous waters of the Dauntless Sea far below. But both time and tide have ravaged the foundations; brick and mortar have eroded away to leave a solitary gnarled finger gesturing defiantly at the rest of the realm. The steps leading up to the castle's main door require the lightest of touches, lest I risk sending the entire structure crashing down into the sea. The platform I'm on creaks ominously underfoot, threatening to give way at a moment's notice. I'm here to meet a former hero, and now permanently retired Wizard, who stopped adventuring at the height of his career. I'm curious to know why someone who basked in the light of fame would suddenly step back into the shadow of obscurity.

The wooden platform continues to protest under my weight as I reach the castle entrance and hammer the door hard with the base of my fist. A metal lock slides free as the door opens by an inch or two, and a scrawny face appears in the gap.

Wizard: "Whatever you're selling, I don't want it!"

Me: "Morgan the *Magnificent?* I sent word of my arrival?"[45]

The stern face stares at me in confusion as it struggles internally to recall our *arrangement*—before suddenly brightening.

Morgan: "Of course, come in, come in! Though do watch your step; some of the floorboards in this place can be fatal."

I stare with increasing concern at the uneven floor.

Me: "Are they trapped?"

Morgan: "Trapped?"

Me: "Yes, trapped—to deter would-be thieves?"

---

[45] *Sending 'word' involves visiting a local 'Barker' and paying them to shout very loudly to the next nearest 'Barker' within earshot. This communication is then shouted from Barker to Barker until the intended recipient finally hears the original message. The whole process can take over a month, and it's not uncommon to discover the innocuous word of an impending arrival has somehow morphed into an open declaration of war—or worse...*

Morgan: "*Oh,* no, no, no, no—traps? *No,* the floor is rotten; I would hate our conversation to be interrupted so soon by your sudden disappearance and subsequent realisation that you can't fly as you hurtle towards the rocks below."[46]

The Wizard notices the colour draining from my face and pats my shoulder reassuringly as he smiles.

Morgan: "But that probably won't happen. I'll tell you what—let me lead the way. Walk where I walk, and I'm sure you'll be fine."

I nod with relief.

Me: "Thanks."

Morgan: "Don't mention it—but if you fall, *also* don't mention it."[47]

I follow the Wizard for what seems like an eternity as he carefully tiptoes and skips along an invisible pathway that only makes sense to him. Slowly, we negotiate our way toward a large oak door, which the Spellcaster gingerly opens before lightly stepping through. We find ourselves in a surprisingly cosy room. There's a large bearskin rug[48] covering much of the wooden floor,[49] and an orange glow from the open hearth warms the two seats awaiting us.

Morgan: "Can I offer you a drink?"

Me: "Do you have any water?"

The Wizard cocks a quizzical eye in surprise.

Morgan: "Are you *sure* I can't tempt you with something a little stronger?"

Me: "You can tempt all you like. I'm more worried about making the

---

[46] *As would I—although I'd hope the Wizard would be good enough to cast a Levitation spell if that <u>did</u> happen!*

[47] *I'm now convinced I'm going to die here.*

[48] *With a slightly annoyed-to-have-ended-up-like-this expression on its face...*

[49] *Given the size of the room—that was one BIG bear!*

return journey to your front door in one piece."

The Spellcaster nods his head with sage approval.

Morgan: "*Ah,* yes, of *course*—water it is then."

The Wizard leans over and picks up a small, unassuming stick from the side table; he waves it with a flick of his wrist—a glass unexpectedly appears in my hand, filled to the brim with a pale orange liquid. The Wizard looks a little embarrassed by this mistake. A second flick of his wrist removes the drink from existence—but not before a few drops of liquid spill into my lap.

Morgan: "Damn, sorry about that—this thing can be a little temperamental, especially if I've ignored it for a while."[50]

Me: "Ignored it?"

Morgan: "All wands have a personality—this one in particular likes to be the centre of attention."

I always knew Wizards treated their wands like a beloved family member, but am I hearing this right—wands have personalities? I'm slightly concerned the Wizard's isolation has pushed him closer toward insanity. I watch as he taps the wand on the side table several times as if trying to knock the Gremlins out of it,[51] before trying once more— this time, a glass filled with a cold clear liquid appears in my hand. I tentatively sip at it, just in case it's something that will put hairs on my chest[52]—but it's only water, mercifully.

Morgan: "*Ah,* now it decides to work. I sometimes wonder why I bothered to make this thing; it's always playing up—"

Me: "Wait—you made that wand?"

---

[50] *A temperamental wand? Whatever next—A moody orb? An emotional robe? A hot-headed staff?*

[51] *Gremlins are small mischievous critters that go around unfastening the straps on any unsecured armour, unscrewing the stoppers on potions, or sabotaging wands to explode unexpectedly on use.*

[52] *Not that I don't already have hairs on my chest, it's just I don't want to risk drinking something that turns me into a rug that's more pissed-off looking than the one currently beneath my feet.*

The Wizard beams with pride.

Morgan: "Of course! Making magic items is my speciality!"

Me: "Forgive me; I thought you made your name as an adventurer, *not* a creator of magical trinkets?"

The Wizard's demeanour sours slightly as he *'tuts'* at my comment.

Me: "Did I say something wrong?"

Morgan: "I haven't adventured in a looooong time. To be honest with you, it's not a period in my life that I'm proud of—or want to be remembered for."

Me: "But the saga of your heroics in the Caves of Rebulung is the stuff of legends![53] What could possibly make you turn your back on something most of us can only dream of?"

The Wizard sucks in his breath and holds it for a moment. He waves his wand once more; this time, a stiff drink appears in his hand—he downs it in one swift motion and quickly summons a refill.

Morgan: "There was an *incident*..."

Me: "An incident?"

Morgan: "Okay—an *accident*..."

Me: "Were you hurt?"

Morgan: "Me? *No*, I escaped relatively unscathed..."

Me: "What about the rest of your adventuring party?"

The Spellcaster does not meet my gaze, choosing instead to stare deep into the flames of the fire burning in the hearth.

---

[53] *The Caves of Rebulung were home to the much-feared 'Bunjee', a type of Giant Spider that would leap from the rocky ceiling on stretchy webs before hoisting unsuspecting victims off the cave floor and springing back to the ceiling to consume them. Unfortunately, the near-blind Bunjee would often misjudge the velocity of their ascent and impact hard into the ceiling's surface (together with their screaming victim), resulting in a rather sticky splat. Fortunately, Morgan's panache for Fireballs saw the much-feared Bunjee wind up on the endangered monster list—only whispered by tired parents to unruly children who refuse to go to bed: 'If you don't go to sleep, the Bunjee will jump down and splat you into the ceiling!'*

Morgan: "They weren't so lucky…"

It is now my turn to look away, ostensibly for a sip of water to soothe my dry mouth. I feel the Wizard's eyes upon me, unhappy about reliving the past.

Morgan: "Ask your question, Loremaster."

Me: "What happened?"

The Wizard visibly shakes as he quickly downs his second drink and summons a third.

Morgan: "There was a crypt… I forget the name now—they all seem to roll into one these days."

Me: "*We?* Who was with you?"

Morgan: "Let me think… there was a Paladin, a Fighter, a Rogue, a Cleric—and the legend himself, Arin Darkblade."

My eyebrows rise at the mention of Arin's name.

Morgan: "I take it you've heard of him."

Me: "Who hasn't heard of Arin Darkblade—the realm's most successful hero."[54]

Morgan: "And the realm's most dangerous too, don't forget that—he once stole my shoes after I accidentally knocked his arm as he was drinking his ale."

Me: "If I'm being honest, that doesn't sound *too* dangerous."

Morgan: "Really? Well, let's see how *you* cope with bare feet and the ground covered in *Tickle Thorns*.[55] It took me nearly an hour to finally crawl out, by which time my eyes were red from the tears of laughter I

---

[54] *It's worth noting that 'success' in the adventuring business is usually measured by whether you're still breathing after completing an adventure. Those who aren't successful typically wind up dead.*

[55] *Tickle Thorns may sound unimpressive as a form of torture—but no other punishment comes close to the effectiveness this bothersome plant can deliver. It's so potent many torturers wear a vial of Tickle Thorns around their neck to break in case of emergencies… such as a particularly stubborn prisoner.*

had shed."

Me: "*Ah,* I see... but your adventuring party must have been filled with confidence nonetheless, knowing Arin Darkblade's sword was with them."[56]

Morgan: "Nope—it just made us all nervous as anything. I mean, here was this famous hero who was in *our* adventuring party—being honest, we all felt a little out of our depth."

Me: "He's just a man, just a normal man. Granted, not like you and me. But he's only flesh and blood all the same."

The Wizard chuckles to himself.

Morgan: "*Hmmm... just* a normal man—anyway, I can still recall that fateful morning, we had camped on the hill overlooking the crypt; a dark sense of trepidation fell over the group as we began to make our descent into that unholy catacomb. Maybe it was the smell of death that filled the air, but most of us experienced the feeling of dread—as if something wasn't quite right about this particular quest. Only Arin and one of the younger Fighters seemed unaffected—I can't remember his name, but he was a new recruit on his first or second adventure. If I close my eyes, I can still see his face, full of life and nervous excitement as we ventured deeper into that unholy tomb."

Me: "When was this?"

Morgan: "Oh—let me see... eight—maybe, nine summers ago now."

Me: "When Morgan the Magnificent was at the height of his legendary fame—"

The Wizard *'tuts'* scornfully.

Morgan: "That name died with my companions in that crypt—there was nothing 'magnificent' about what I did to them..."

I was scared to ask my next question, so grave an air had the Wizard assumed. But I knew I must.

---

[56] *A point of clarity for those not familiar with my writings, I don't 'just' mean Arin's sword here—otherwise, I can imagine the grizzled adventurer being somewhat perplexed on his next adventure when he goes to draw his weapon only to discover it missing...*

Me: "What did you do to them?"

There's a tear hidden behind the Wizard's weary eyes; it finally breaks rank and rolls down his worn cheek, disappearing in a crease of facial skin only to emerge on the point of his chin a heartbeat later.

Morgan: "I *burnt* them, turned them to ash. Their screams pleaded with me to stop the inferno. But I couldn't—it was too late. Far, far too late."

Me: "An inferno? What? H—How did that happen?"

Morgan: "It was that *damn* Warlock Lich's fault—it appeared out of nowhere! I—I just cast it instinctively..."

Me: "Cast what?"

Morgan: "A *Fireball*[57]—a bloody *Fireball!* I thought we were a safe distance from its blast radius, but I was wrong... *so, so* wrong. I had badly miscalculated the size of the room we were standing in at the time..."

Me: "Everybody died?"

Morgan: "Only Arin Darkblade *and* I walked away from it unscathed..."

Me: "What—What did he *say* to you?"

Morgan: "What *could* he say? It was an unfortunate accident that left a permanent scar on both his memory and mine—I'm pretty sure he may have sworn at me—*yes,* now I recall, he definitely swore at me; it wasn't a nice word either."

Me: "What did you do about the quest—or the Warlock Lich?"

Morgan: "It had sensibly fled deeper into the crypt, and we weren't in any position to give chase—so we abandoned the quest. Arin helped me scrape what was left of our companions into a sack, and we got out of there quick. It wasn't my proudest moment, but what else could we do?"

---

[57] *It should come as no surprise that 'Fireball' topped the Wizarding Spell List for the most frequent spell to be cast this summer. Second place went to the increasingly popular 'Firebolt' spell, closely followed by the heartburn-inducing 'Fireburp' in third place. Why Wizards have such an affinity for fire-based spells is beyond me. Perhaps behind every pointy hat with a spellbook is a pyromaniac with a pointy hat wanting to watch the realm burn?*

Me: "What happened afterwards, when you were safely away from that place?"

The Wizard sucks in his breath and holds it for a few beats before exhaling.

Morgan: "We did what any hero would do—we buried them. They had adventured together, so it was only fitting that they should be laid to rest together. We found a quiet spot on a hillside overlooking a river by a crossroads. I think the Cleric would have approved of the view, the Paladin... probably not so much.[58] We dug a small hole and dropped the sack in. I mumbled a few apologetic words—I'm pretty sure Arin swore at me again. Then we left... I haven't been back since."

Me: "What happened when you returned home?"

Simply Morgan shifts uncomfortably in his seat.

Morgan: "Yeah, that was a difficult time. Both Arin and the Cleric were members of the Heroes Guild. I assume you know of them?"

Me: "My mother and father were both members. They still attend its annual banquet[59] though both retired from adventuring a long time ago. I understand the Guild likes to take care of its own, or so my father always told me."

Morgan: "Quite. So, you can understand why then when one of their heroes didn't return, questions were asked—awkward questions. The Heroes Guild were understandably alarmed that one of their number had fallen. Fortunately, being a Heroes Guild member, Arin managed to smooth the incident over. He calmly told them it was a freak accident caused by the Rogue, who had set off a trap that unfortunately incinerated most of the party—"

Me: "He lied—why did he do that?"

---

[58] *I still don't understand why a Cleric and Paladin would go on an adventure together—they're practically the same hero doing the same thing!*

[59] *I'm being a little generous by calling it a 'banquet'; it's actually an excuse for my parents to meet up with some old adventuring buddies at The Dunkin' Witch Inn, get blind drunk and start singing loudly about the lost Orc of Arrowmire (spoiler alert, the Orc was never found).*

Morgan: "Arin didn't want to be associated with a botched quest—he also knew the guilt of my mistake weighed heavily on my conscience. He convinced me that shifting the blame onto the dead Rogue was best for everyone—I protested, of course, said I had to face the consequences of my actions. But Arin insisted on pointing the blame at the poor thief. I mean, it's not as if he could complain about it much anyway—and *nobody* argues with Arin Darkblade. I swallowed the truth and buried my guilt along with the fried remains of my comrades."

Me: "But that still didn't sit well with you?"

Morgan: "I swore I would never go on another adventure ever again—that would be my punishment."

Me: "Did the Heroes Guild believe your ruse?"

Morgan: "Arin's word carries a lot of weight at the Heroes Guild. Nobody questioned it when the report was finally passed onto the Tallyman."[60]

Me: "They never questioned *you* about it either?"

The Wizard stares into the spluttering flames in the hearth.

Morgan: "Never questioned—nor ever spoken about it since."

Me: "Why are you trusting me with this information—aren't you worried the Heroes Guild will find out the truth about what happened in that crypt?"

Morgan: "Maybe it's time that the truth came out. I'm old, too old to worry about what may or may not happen to me. I'm ready to face my demons... time is not on my side. I don't want to spend my last days with this remorse weighing me down. I like the look of you, Loremaster—for whatever reason, I trust you to bring a little more truth into this realm."

Me: "What about Arin Darkblade? What will happen when this revelation is exposed?"

---

[60] *Tallymen are employed by the Heroes Guild to write up reports for every adventure and adventurer, be they successful or not. I would imagine the paperwork needed here would require a forest-sized number of trees alone.*

Morgan: "He'll be fine—he's too embedded in the Heroes Guild for this to damage his reputation. Sure, he'll probably swear a bit more—I take that back, he'll probably swear *a lot* more—but nobody will dare cross swords him. Not *even* those running the Heroes Guild are that foolish."

Me: "Have you seen Arin since the *incident?*"

Morgan: "No. But I know he also stepped back from adventuring after that fateful day—he's more of a figurehead at the Guild now. An adventuring siren, luring the next wave of heroes through their doors."

The Wizard rises from his seat and walks over to the dying embers—a few well-aimed prods with a poker encourages the fire to stay alive a while longer.[61]

Morgan: "I was a *great* Wizard, you know—powerful, knowledgeable, a force for good in this realm. Look at me now... spending the rest of my days in this crumbling stronghold, creating magical trinkets to scratch a living. All that studying, all that potential, what a waste... still it could be worse, I could be like that old goat Inglebold, traversing the Merchant's Road, peddling so-called 'potions' to any fool with coin to lose, be they peasant or Paladin. At least I became a *Certified Supplier* for the Heroes Guild—I may not be active anymore, but I've not fallen far from the adventuring tree."

Me: "Certified Supplier?"

Morgan: "Of magical trinkets and objects—I have probably created most of the magical items a Heroes Guild member carries on any given quest. My wares are all made here in my castle, away from prying eyes."

Me: "Prying eyes?"

Morgan: "My competitors..."

Me: "You mean Inglebold?"

Morgan: "He has become something of a nemesis of late. A Potioneer who believes potions are the future. I, on the other hand, believe he's an idiot."

---

[61] *I wonder if a few of the Wizard's more 'rebellious' wands have found themselves used as makeshift kindling?*

Me: "Why?"

Morgan: "My magical items don't have any hazardous side effects,[62] unlike Inglebold's potions."

Me: "Why, what do his potions do?"

Morgan: "You'll have to ask him, I'm afraid—just *don't* drink any of the wretched concoctions he offers you; you may find yourself transformed into some kind of hideous abomination with a taste for horseflesh, *then* you'll be screwed! Every adventurer in the realm will be hunting the bounty on your head—and you *won't* want that!"

I shiver at the thought as I look around the room, taking in the tired décor.

Me: "You live here alone?"

Morgan: "Does it *look* like I employ a maid? No, I'm happy in my own company, living out my days in this retirement castle by the sea—that's more than enough for me."

Me: "You never wanted to share your life with anyone?"

Morgan: "No, never, and certainly not now—I'm too long in the tooth, too set in my ways to spend the little time I have left with someone. They'd never last anyway."

Me: "Why?"

Morgan: "They'd probably forget to mind their step and fall through the floorboards into the sea below—I couldn't have another death on my conscience."[63]

Me: "Fair enough. But at the peak of your adventuring fame, you must have received many offers."

---

[62] *I think my drink-soaked lap would say otherwise!*

[63] *I had forgotten this little 'detail' about Morgan's death-trap castle; now my mind is scrambling like crazy as I imagine myself plummeting towards the sharp sea rocks below. I wince and try to banish the image from my consciousness—my brain has a delightful habit of doing this just when courage, a steady nerve, and a steadier footfall is needed.*

Morgan: "From all genders and species alike."[64]

Me: "But no one special?"

The Wizard stares wistfully off into the distance.

Morgan: "Once—but that was long ago."

Me: "What happened?"

Morgan: "The magic didn't last."

Me: "*Ah,* I hear that's something that can happen in relationships over time—"

Morgan: "No, I mean, the magic *'really'* didn't last."

Me: "What? I don't understand."

Morgan: "When I was with her—I couldn't perform, you know—"

Me: "Sexually?"

Morgan: "No, you fool, *not* sexually—**magically!**"

Me: "You became spell-impotent?"[65]

Morgan: "Don't laugh, but I couldn't get a single cantrip right when she was around."

Me: "What did you do?"

Morgan: "What do *you* think—it was either the magic *or* her."

Me: "So, you chose your spells."

Morgan: "You don't see any wedding band on my finger—do you? Which reminds me, I have something for you..."

The Wizard digs into his pocket and draws out a small object—a ring. He throws it to me and grins. Holding it up in my fingers, I marvel at the intricate wave pattern etched into the surface.

---

[64] *A curious part of me wants to dig deeper—but the sensible part of me knows to leave this question well alone.*

[65] *Although, I guess a hastily cast Levitation spell could have helped in <u>this</u> emergency too...*

Morgan: "Here you go."

Me: "T—Thanks… what *is* it?"

Morgan: "It is a gift—a Ring of Water Breathing."

Me: "Water Breathing?"

I give the Wizard a confused look as I turn the trinket over in my fingers.

Morgan: "Yeah—just in case you misplace a step on your way out."[66]

---

[66] *I really hope I don't end up in a watery grave!*

3. Gwenyn, the Farmer

The village of Wendle is on the Serpent River, a river that strikes out east from the Doom Mountains and snakes away for as far as the eye can see. Wendle is a picturesque hamlet, predominately populated by Farmers and Farmhands working hard to produce seasonal root vegetables and meats for the nearby city of Tronte. It's a tough life here at the best of times, made more challenging by the occasional wandering monster seeking an easy meal. After receiving 'word' from a Barker,[67] I've arrived in Wendle to meet with one such Farmer, Gwenyn Plow, who has seen her livestock numbers steadily dwindle after a series of monster attacks. I'm eager to hear first-hand from someone in the local community who appears in desperate need of heroes to protect them.

Me: "Nice place you have here."

I point to the view overlooking Gwenyn Plow's homestead, a joyous vista of rolling hills and lush green meadows that disappear into the valley in the distance. This place could potentially be the most idyllic spot in the entire realm—if it weren't for the thick plume of black smoke spewing from the fields west of Gwenyn's abode. I frown as I feel a burning question about to erupt from my lips.[68]

Gwenyn: "It was a Dragon, in case you were wondering."

Me: "A Dragon?"

Gwenyn: "Happened last night. I was awoken by screams coming from the herd in the field—"

Me: "Screaming cows?[69] That must have been terrifying."

Gwenyn: "Sure, but not as terrifying as it was for the cows themselves."

Me: "I've never heard a cow scream—is that *even* possible?"

---

[67] *I'm thankful I've actually turned up to the correct place—I have to assume the Barker's 'word' didn't have very far to travel.*

[68] *A burning question that is wondering what else is burning over yonder...*

[69] *Not to be confused with 'steaming cows', which are angry bovines that wander the grassy plains in herds, seeking retribution against their former owners. Although, I'm also pretty sure those same cows were literally 'steaming' after being turned into a hot snack during the Dragon attack too.*

Gwenyn: "Sure is, Loremaster. Tell me, have *you* ever stared into the eyes of pure evil as it rushes towards you or smelt death as a monstrous maw widens to unleash an inferno to scorch the very soul from your body?"

Me: "Thankfully, I can't say I ever have."

Gwenyn: "Then I pray you never do. Trust me when I say this, be you human or livestock, *everything* screams in the face of terror like that—I mean *everything*."

Me: "Does this happen a lot—the Dragon attacks?"

Gwenyn: "Harvest time is generally the worst for us; the overgrown lizards come swooping down off the mountains in search of easy pickings. We're the first thing those monstrosities encounter before following the river east and beyond."

Me: "What lies to the east?"

Gwenyn: "The Dragon breeding grounds."

Me: "So, your cows..."

Gwenyn: "Are a pre-coital snack before the seasonal Dragon orgy, yes."[70]

Me: "So, every summer, you have to try to protect your livestock from horny and hungry Dragons? How long have you had to endure this?"[71]

Gwenyn: "For as long as I can remember—and I was born on this farm. My parents and my grandparents had to struggle through this. Now the farm is mine; it's my turn."

Me: "How many cows do you think you lost to the Dragons?"

Gwenyn: "Seven this time, but it depends on how hungry and horny the buggers are. Some summers have been a lot worse. I remember we lost forty-five heads on one particularly hot and sticky night..."

---

[70] *'Dragon' and 'orgy' are two words that should <u>never</u> appear together in the same sentence.*

[71] *Sadly longer than five fumble-filled minutes...*

Me: "That's terrible! Can't anything be done to stop these creatures?"

Gwenyn: "What do you suggest—we're Farmers, not Fighters!?"

Me: "Couldn't the other Farmers help? What if you worked together to come up with a solution?"

Gwenyn: "Don't you think we've tried that? We even pooled all our hard-earned coin to build a state-of-the-art watchtower complete with an alarm bell and part-time Halfling Archer once..."[72]

Me: "Really?"

I scan the nearby area, searching for any sign of the structure.

Me: "I don't see it—"

Gwenyn: "It's gone."

Me: "Gone?"

Gwenyn: "Burnt to the ground."

Me: "And the Archer?"

Gwenyn: "Probably ended up as a toothpick to dislodge a piece of stuck cow..."[73]

Me: "Isn't there anything else you can do?"

Gwenyn: "What do you suggest, Loremaster?"

Me: "What about hiring a hero or two to take on the creature?"

The Farmer gives a derisory snort in retort.

Gwenyn: "No thanks."

---

[72] I think I can see where this is going.

[73] I subsequently discovered the Halfling Archer actually survived the Dragon attack and had quit his post to pursue his dream of becoming the town's drunk. Even though he was always in a constant state of intoxication, I also have it on good authority that the Halfling Archer's skill with a bow improved considerably with his self-imposed drunken demotion—this obviously speaks volumes about the often forgotten power of alcohol.

Me: "I don't understand? Heroes are trained for this sort of situation; they could protect your community from this habitual Dragon threat and ensure your herd is left to graze in peace."

The Farmer's face darkens.

Gwenyn: "You know how much it costs to hire a Dragon-slaying hero from the Heroes Guild?"

I shake my head.

Gwenyn: "A lot more than one ex-watchtower and one half-eaten Halfling Archer..."[74]

Me: "Couldn't you ask one of the up-and-coming heroes to do it for free? Perhaps to help grow their reputation?"

Gwenyn: "My father taught me that you always get out of life what you put into it. If you're only paying a Dwarf in crumbs, then you're only going to end up with a pissed-off Dwarf who is _still_ hungry."

Me: "There are other ways of paying for a hero."

The Farmer looks at me aghast.

Gwenyn: "Just because I'm a Farmer doesn't mean I don't have morals!"[75]

Me: "No—I didn't mean—I meant some heroes are happy enough with a comfortable bed[76] and a hot meal on the table."

Gwenyn: "They can go to the local tavern to get that sort of thing for all I care."

Me: "I don't understand why you're so against them."

Gwenyn: "It's simple—I don't trust heroes."

---

[74] _Which would technically make this particular Halfling a Quarterling..._

[75] _Is there such a thing as an immoral Farmer? I wonder what form an immoral Farmer would take? Maybe they'd do something questionable, like using an unstable Potion of Giant Growth to win first prize at their local Cor!-Look-At-The Size-Of-That-Giant-Vegetable! competition._

[76] _A single bed!_

Me: "Don't trust them, but why—?"

Gwenyn: "You want me to explain? Then follow me…"

The Farmer marches purposefully down the hillside, leaving me to follow in her wake. She opens a gate and heads through a small herb garden filled with numerous plants growing in abundance. As we pass through the rear-most gate, we head towards the rising smoke from the scorched field just ahead.

Gwenyn: "Take last night's attack—"

Me: "The Dragon attack?"

Gwenyn: "We were asleep at the time; the first we knew something was wrong was when we heard a rushing of wind followed by a bright light which lit up the night sky. Then we heard the ungodly screams coming from our herd… and that smell—that *damn* smell…"

Me: "What was it—the smell?"

Gwenyn: "Death—the unmistakable stench of death."[77]

Me: "What did you do? You *must* have all feared for your lives!"

Gwenyn: "Yes, but everyone knows what to do in the event of a Dragon attack on our farm. We've even gone as far as constructing a Dragon shelter in the hillside behind you—buried deep where the heat can't touch us. Our children were scared—I could see the panic in their eyes, but they were as good as gold and so brave; they knew how dangerous a Dragon could be. They ran quickly and quietly to the shelter, just like we had practised so many times in the past. Anyway, as we were halfway to safety, I heard another scream—"

Me: "Another cow?"

The Farmer looks at me as if I'm trying to make a bad joke.[78]

---

[77] I'd imagine this smelt like soured milk after it had been used to wash an Ogre's sweaty armpit. Not that I have ever smelt anything like that—my mind just concocted this as the worst possible stench on the legendary Scale of Pongs. I also pity any fool who tries to point out this stomach-turning hygiene 'problem' to 'Death' too…

[78] A comedic bloodline runs in our family, and I wouldn't be surprised if this makes more of an appearance throughout this journal—so I'll now apologise for any misplaced mirth.

Gwenyn: "No—it wasn't a cow; it was a woman's voice."

Me: "A *woman?* Who did it belong to? Was it a neighbouring Farmer?"

Gwenyn: "No—it was a *bloody* hero!"

Me: "A hero? I thought you said you didn't trust heroes, nor had the coin to hire one to help you either?"

Gwenyn: "Both of those statements are true, *this* one decided to throw her Fireballs where they weren't welcome—for free."

Me: "Fireballs? Was it a Wizard?"

Gwenyn: "Worse—a *Sorceress*."

Me: "How could you tell the difference? She *may* have been a Wizard—"

The Farmer shakes her head in disappointment at my error.

Gwenyn: "You're not much of a Loremaster if you don't know the difference between Wizards and Sorcerers. Wizards use spellbooks; Sorcerers do it *all* from memory."[79]

Me: "You didn't see a spellbook?"[80]

Gwenyn: "No—but I *did* see the destruction she was unleashing in the middle of my turnip field. She was throwing Fireballs like she was in a snowball fight with a bunch of unruly Elves.[81] Everything was ablaze, including my field *and* my herd—everything but the damn Dragon."

Me: "How did the Dragon respond to this Fireball frenzy?"

Gwenyn: "It was understandably peeved—all it wanted to do was eat a few cows and get down to the business of propagating,[82] but now it had

---

[79] *This probably explains why some Sorcerers cast the same spell over and over, again and again...*

[80] *In fairness to the Farmer, it was probably still dark...*

[81] *Who have just thrown off the chains of oppression and broken free from the workshops where they are forced to fashion all manner of unwanted gifts for their heavily encumbered yet jolly master.*

[82] *Once a Farmer, always a Farmer...*

something else to deal with, something that wielded fire *exactly* like a Dragon."

Me: "Wait! Are you telling me it mistook the *Fireballs* from the Sorceress as a horny rival's challenge—?"

The Farmer nods slowly in agreement.

Me: "But Dragons are huge in comparison—shouldn't it have noticed the tiny figure flinging balls of fire at it wasn't a rival?"

Gwenyn: "You'd think that, but you have to remember this unfolded in the middle of the night. Even though Dragons can smell a gold coin from thirty miles away, they have terrible eyesight at the best of times—*and* it was pitch black. Come to think of it... Dragon eyesight is *so* bad it probably explains why it's easy for bumbling heroes to waltz into their lairs undetected..."[83]

Me: "So, the Dragon fought the Sorceress thinking it was a rival—did she die?"

Gwenyn: "If she had, that would have been the end of it. Instead, suddenly there's a whole lot more of them buzzing around."

Me: "More Dragons?"

Gwenyn: "No—more *bloody* heroes."

Me: "Where did they all come from?"

Gwenyn: "Damned if I know—it was like this poor Dragon had just woken a whole nest of the heroic irritants, and now they were attacking it in droves!"

Me: "You talk of heroes as if they are annoying pests—"

Gwenyn: "Annoying pests? That's *precisely* what heroes are. Do you know how often I've woken up to find a so-called 'hero' rummaging around my cupboards searching for something valuable to steal or eat?"

Me: "*Erm*—"

---

[83] With all those huge piles of loose coin sitting around, I would have thought a Dragon's lair would be the <u>last</u> place a 'bumbling hero' would want to dance around.

Gwenyn: "*Too* many times! I've had more apples, potatoes, and pies pinched from my kitchen than I can count—if it's not food, it's my clothes. I've lost countless tunics, shoes, hats, and smalls[84] to those bastards. They even took my *best* dress. It may have been a simple patchwork gown—but it was *mine!* I mean, come on, who breaks into someone's house *just* to steal a dress? Look at me; it's not as if I'm dripping in wealth, am I? I can barely afford to clothe my own children, yet it's perfectly fine for a well-to-do 'hero' to walk in unannounced and take what they want without so much as a please or thank you!"

The Farmer sighs as we reach the stile leading into the smoking field.

Gwenyn: "Heroes? *Bah*—I'd rather have the Dragon any time; at least it's only doing what it needs to survive. I can respect that."

Me: "Couldn't you say the same about heroes?"

The Farmer turns and stares coldly at me.

Gwenyn: "No, I could not."

Me: "So, what happened when the rest of the heroes turned up to fight the Dragon?"

Gwenyn: "I didn't stick around to find out—we kept running for the shelter and waited until morning when it was safer for us to survey the damage."

Me: "What did you find?"

Gwenyn: "Our humble home had been ransacked, picked clean of anything of value—they *even* stole the eggs I was saving for the children's breakfast in the morning."

Me: "What about the Dragon?"

Gwenyn: "*Oh*—they left that behind, of course."

Me: "What do you mean?"

We clamber over the stile and into the scorched turnip field.

---

[84] *Just to be clear, say 'smalls' to a Dwarf and you're going to get a severe case of axe-to-headitus. It is also worth remembering that Dwarven 'smalls' will come up big on any Gnome or Halfling who has stolen them.*

Me: "*Oh my—*"

Gwenyn: "*Oh my* wasn't exactly the first words that sprang to mind…"

Lying in the centre of the turnip field is the smouldering husk of what remains of a once-mighty Dragon. The body is still smoking where numerous Fireballs have ripped right through its chest. A large flock of carrion are perched on the exposed white ribcage, picking off any cooked flesh they can find.

Me: "They just left it here… like *this?*"

Gwenyn: "You seem surprised—they never clean up after themselves! Look at the state of this place! I've burnt craters in this field—<u>and</u> the next. Not to mention all the livestock that have either fled or have been reduced to piles of ash!"

I can feel the fury burning brightly within the Farmer's small frame, almost as if a raging Barbarian was about to break free and hunt down the nearest Cleric to punch.[85]

Me: "I don't know what to say. I didn't realise they were so many thoughtless adventurers these days."

Gwenyn: "Thoughtless? That's putting it mildly. These bastards are a heroic pain in the arse. My turnip crop is ruined! How am I supposed to recover from this?"

Me: "I—I don't know…"

Gwenyn: "That's not even the worst part of it. The worst part is knowing that while I'm here picking up the pieces of our life, the 'heroes' responsible are probably patting each other on the back as they head off to celebrate their success by getting blind drunk in the nearest tavern!"[86]

Me: "I'm *sorry—*"

---

[85] *It is well documented that Barbarians and Clerics don't play well together. Although Clerics always tend to come off second-best if the ensuing argument leads to fisticuffs.*

[86] *As the nearest tavern is a good five-day ride from Wendle, across the dreaded Swamp of Absolute Despair, it's safe to assume any hero brave enough to attempt such an arduous journey is probably allowed to let their hair down a little and slap a few backs in return.*

Gwenyn: "Why are *you* apologising? It's not *your* fault; you're not one of those hero types, are you? It's not *your* mess that was left here to rot. What am I supposed to do with a giant Dragon corpse? You think I've got it bad now, just wait another week—the stench from that thing will be almost unbearable. We'll be forced to move away until the next summer at the earliest—that's a large portion of our coin for the season lost to these so-called heroes."

Me: "Why?"

Gwenyn: "I told you already—Dragons have a keen sense of smell. It won't be long until the rotting stench reaches the peaks of the Doom Mountains—when it does, then we'll be in trouble. This place will be swarming with Dragons drawn to its fetid corpse."

Me: "Where will you go now?"

Gwenyn: "Well, I've already complained to the Heroes Guild—"

Me: "Has it done any good?"

Gwenyn: "To be fair to them, they were extremely alarmed by this news. They promised to look into the matter—see if any of this had anything to do with their heroes."

Me: "What happens if it turns out these heroes *are* affiliated with them?"

Gwenyn: "Then the Guild promised I would receive some form of compensation for the distress and damage caused. They've even agreed to relocate my family to another village."

Me: "How long for?"

Gwenyn: "Until it's safe to return, I suppose."

Me: "At least that's something."

Gwenyn: "It is—but it still won't stop us from losing the harvest for this summer. That's a heavy blow to our livelihoods."

Me: "Surely the reparations from the Heroes Guild will go some way to softening that?"

Gwenyn: "Only if it can be proved those responsible came from the Heroes Guild, and as I said at the start—*I don't trust heroes.*"

Me: "And if they *aren't* affiliated with the Heroes Guild?"

Gwenyn: "I don't know. Our future rests *solely* on the idiots responsible being members of the Heroes Guild—it's not a position adventurers should *ever* put common folk like us in. We're the innocent bystanders in this sorry tale—yet we stand to lose *everything* because of their selfish actions."

Me: "If you ever saw the Sorceress again, what would you say to her?"

The Farmer thinks carefully before turning away from the rotting Dragon corpse to speak one last time to me.

Gwenyn: "I'd say... *GET AWAY FROM MY DRESSES, YOU BITCH!*"[87]

---

[87] *This isn't quite what the Farmer said—her 'actual' words are unrepeatable and should never be heard or read by anyone—especially minors (the small children kind, not the Gnomish cave-loving kind, although I guess that <u>could</u> include small Gnomish children who love caves).*

4. Yarna, the Mime Warrior

My following interview is a little strange to say the least—through my study of tomes, scripture, legend, and folklore, I have made myself familiar with most professions, such as Fighters, Clerics, Wizards, Bards, and alike. But Yarna comes from a new wave of adventurers answering the hero's call—for she is the first officially recognised Mime Warrior to set foot in the realm. 'But, Elburn...' I hear you ask, 'what is a Mime Warrior?' To answer that question, I'm standing in the shadow of the Goblin-infested Halgorn Crags, waiting to find out from Yarna herself.

My senses are primed as the crags loom ominously above me; I'm more than aware of the reputation of this dangerous place—and I don't fancy becoming target practice for any arrow-happy Goblins lurking out of sight.[88] But, as I round the first large stone boulder and begin the arduous hike, I spy a solitary figure sitting patiently upon a large flat rock. She's stoic—almost statuesque as she sits in perfect silence. A handful of stones scatter behind me as I try to scramble up the incline towards the woman's position. In a flash, her head turns in my direction, revealing a shocking white face with thick black lines daubed across her eyelids and lips—her hand goes to her hip to grasp the pommel of a sword that isn't there.[89]

Me: "Y—Yarna? Yarna the *Mime Warrior?*"

The woman smiles warmly before standing on her rocky perch and bowing low.

Me: "I'm Elburn... Elburn the *Loremaster*..."

The Mime Warrior gives a thumbs-up and leaps from the rock before beginning a jaunty little walk towards me. Suddenly she stops as if blocked by an invisible barrier, forcing her to feel her way around an obstacle I cannot see. Finding an edge, the Mime Warrior begins to slowly navigate through the transparent maze. I witness this bizarre spectacle unfold for a full ten minutes as she frustratingly hits dead-

---

[88] *Goblin Archers are awful shots, second only to Halfling Archers. Halfling Archers are so bad they have been known to shoot themselves, rather than their notched arrow at an enemy. For some reason, I find the image of a surprised Dragon turning to see an even more surprised Halfling hurtling towards it at high speed highly amusing.*

[89] *A point of clarity for those still not familiar with my writings, this time I do 'just' mean the Mime Warrior's sword...*

end after dead-end—until mercifully, she finally finds her way out of the unperceivable labyrinth.

Yarna: "Sorry about that, one of the many downsides of my profession—the *Unexpected Maze.*"[90]

Me: "Unexpected *what?*"

Yarna: "Maze—yeah, they're a problem for any Mime Warrior[91] and can spring up when least expected. When they do, I have no choice but to find the exit or be forever trapped inside. Have you ever tried navigating your way through an Unexpected Maze? Thankfully, it's just a bit of an annoyance more than anything else—and don't even get me started on the *Unexpected Locked Door!*"

Me: "I can imagine that to be as equally vexing?"

Yarna: "More so, especially if you can't find the *Invisible Key* that unlocks it!"

Me: "*Ah,* yes, I can *see* how that would be problematic..."[92]

I walk forward with my hand extended, trying to touch the Unexpected Maze for myself.

Yarna: "*Erm...* what *are* you doing?"

Me: "Trying to feel for the invisible wall."

Yarna: "You'll have a job—it's already vanished. Unexpected Mazes and Unexpected Locked Doors are like that, always doing things you never anticipate. But I wouldn't ask for anything less—"

Me: "Why?"

Yarna: "Because it keeps me on my toes—helps me sharpen my skills. Trust me, being a Mime Warrior means it's *always* worth putting in the extra training wherever and whenever you can."

---

[90] *I've been told that nobody expects the Unexpected Maze.*

[91] *If any other Mime Warriors actually existed, of course.*

[92] *Unlike the Invisible Key and the Unexpected Locked Door in question.*

Me: "I've seen Mime Artists in places like the Tronte Fete[93]—they're highly amusing with their invisible medley of situational tricks. But it's only recently that I heard of a Mime *Warrior*."

Yarna: "Those pretenders you see make a mockery of our profession—they are fools who do not understand the *power* they have in their hands. I'm almost embarrassed to admit I used to be *just* like them."

Me: "You mean *you* were once a Mime Artist?"

Yarna: "Yes, for my shame. I was so misguided back then; I thought I could earn my fortune by making people laugh at my attempts to push a stubborn unseen balloon or by eating an imperceptible banana—only to slip on the banana's invisible skin moments later.[94] I thought I was at the pinnacle of my career—I had no idea I was about to become something far more important, something nobody in this realm had *ever* seen before."

Me: "How did you happen upon the path of the Mime Warrior?"

Yarna: "I didn't—*it* found me."

Me: "I don't see—"

Yarna: "That's because the answer you are searching for is much like the sword that hangs from my waist—"

I stare at the Mime Warrior's waist—true to her word, I still see nothing but a belt.

Me: "But nothing *is* hanging from your waist—"

The Mime Warrior smiles as if I had just fallen into her carefully laid trap.

Yarna: "Spoken like a *true* disbeliever—your eyes *lie* to you, Loremaster..."

---

[93] *Not so much of a Fete, more of a rag-tag collection of Rogues dressed up in brightly coloured clothes while looking for easy pickings. It's a rite of passage for attending revellers of the Fete to complain bitterly about the cost of the food and entertainment, completely unaware they are being robbed from the moment they pay the extortionate entrance fee.*

[94] *I bet that would have been a hilarious spectacle to see!*

The Mime Warrior grabs the imaginary pommel of her sword and draws out... *nothing*. I *still* cannot see the weapon she claims to wield. In an effort to convince my eyes that they have been deceived, the Mime Warrior twirls her sword several times before launching into a series of dramatic slashes. So forceful is the motion and so credulous does she appear of her own actions, I swear I can almost hear the slash of the non-existent blade as it slices through the air.[95]

Yarna: "Just because you can't *see* it... it doesn't mean it does not exist—or do you need me to free you of an eye as further proof?"

I instinctively cover both eyes with my hands but risk a peek through my fingers.

Me: **"NO—NO—I BELIEVE!"**

The Mime Warrior waves her make-believe sword menacingly in front of my face. I find myself stepping backwards; I'm still not convinced there is any chance of being maimed—but I don't want to tempt fate in case I'm gravely mistaken.[96]

Me: "Okay, okay—do you mind if you put that mighty weapon away now?"

She nods as she sheaths the unperceivable blade back in its equally unperceivable scabbard.

Me: "How did you become a Mime Warrior? You mentioned earlier the path *found* you—what did you mean by that?"

Yarna: "I had come to the end of my usual daily performance in Tronte. As expected, the crowd were already disappearing quicker than a heavily encumbered Halfling Paladin in quicksand—when I spied an old man in dusty robes waiting patiently to speak to me."

Me: "What did he want?"

---

[95] Although 'technically' that sound could also have come from a wayward arrow fired by one of the Goblin Archers hidden in the crags, or a lost Halfling Ranger—we will probably never know...

[96] And end up looking like Arin Darkblade's less threatening younger brother.

Yarna: "He asked me for directions to The Endless Desert."[97]

Me: "*The Endless Desert?* That's just a story told to children to make them put on a hat and slap on some Wyvern cream so they don't end up with sunstroke—it doesn't exist."

Yarna: "That was my exact reaction too. I told him he was looking for the impossible."

Me: "What did he say to that?"

Yarna: "He laughed and asked me if I thought my audience believed my routine to be possible?"

Me: "What did you say?"

Yarna: "I said of course not—I make it *look* possible, but it's all part of the act."

Me: "How did he react?"

Yarna: "He just winked and told me he knew a way to make the impossible... *erm*... well... *possible.* I said *that* was impossible, but he dismissed me with a wave of his hand."[98]

Me: "Had this fellow escaped from the care of the *Sisters of Perpetuity?*"[99]

Yarna: "No—he introduced himself as the realm's only *Mime Grandmaster;* he proclaimed he was on a life-quest to find the *One True Chosen One.*"

Me: "That sounds a little mysterious."

---

[97] *The Endless Desert is not 'endless' as one would assume—it is, in fact, a round desert. It gained its reputation after a doomed expedition got lost and wound up walking in circles until they got sand-madness and buried each other in the golden soil—it is also a complete myth and has never once been proven to exist.*

[98] *Thankfully, otherwise this disagreement could have possibly gone on for an impossibly long time.*

[99] *The Sisters of Perpetuity are an all-female volunteer order made up of former Clerics, Herbalists, and bloodthirsty Barbarians who believe the best medicine includes shouting very loudly and vigorous exercise on a 'Wheel of Pain' to cure any ailment. Their order's chapels are spread out across the realm, offering sanctuary and wellness to unfortunates (and by 'unfortunates', I mean injured adventurers and heroes, not commoners like you and I).*

Yarna: "He also said he had made it his mission to discover the first truly recognised Mime Warrior to grace our realm. He was convinced I had the potential to be one of his *Chosen Ones*..."

Me: "Hang on? Don't you mean the One True Chosen One?"

Yarna: "*Ah—no*, you see, before we can *become* the One True Chosen One, one must become the Chosen One *first*... understand?"

I struggle to follow the Mime Warrior's logic before quickly deciding it's probably best not to test her patience any further than necessary—unless I want to risk losing a very real eye to an imaginary sword.

Me: "Did you believe him?"

Yarna: "No, it sounded ludicrous; I certainly wasn't hero material—and I knew nothing about adventuring. I thought he was a crazy old man who had taken a shine to me. But then he did something that I *still* struggle to believe to this day."

Me: "What did he do?"

Yarna: "He cast an *Invisible Fireball* right there in the town square!"

Me: "An *Invisible* Fireball?"[100]

Yarna: "It was spectacular to behold."

Me: "*Invisible*... Fireball...?"

Yarna: "I knew straight away I was in the presence of *true* power!"

Me: "What... *erm*... exactly happened to the... *ah*... *Invisible* Fireball he cast?"

Yarna: "It landed in the square."

Me: "Did anyone notice?"

Yarna: "Notice? *Everybody* noticed! That's when the screaming and writhing in agony started—but the people caught in the fiery blast didn't understand why they were spontaneously combusting!"

---

[100] *To any Wizards reading this, please don't get any bright ideas about casting 'Invisibility' on your next 'Fireball' spell—the usual 'visible' ones are bad enough.*

Me: "Because they couldn't see the flames?"

Yarna: "It was the most bizarre experience, watching people melt before your very eyes for no tangible reason they could fathom—I couldn't help but stare, mesmerised by it all unfolding before me."

Me: "Sounds horrific!"

Yarna: "Yes—I guess it was kind of horrific too. That's when the City Guard showed up. Understandably, they took a dim view of their citizens being burnt by an Invisible Fireball. Fortunately, the Mime Grandmaster had planned an escape using some *Mime Rope!*"

Me: "Mime Rope...?"

Yarna: "It's like normal rope, except only Mime Artists like myself can use it. Together we scaled the city walls with ease and evaded capture."

Me: "Where did you go once you were clear of Tronte?"

Yarna: "Everywhere! The Endless Desert was surprisingly difficult to find."[101]

Me: "How long did you search for it?"

Yarna: "Four summers; we finally discovered it after a chance meeting with a well-travelled Potioneer who told us of a secret southern pass on the far side of the Shadowlands—it led us all the way to the edge of The Endless Desert."[102]

Me: "That's remarkable—what did you see when you found it?"

Yarna: "Nothing... there was nothing but sand for as far as the eye could see..."

I stare in disbelief at the Mime Warrior.

Me: "*Nothing?* You went *all* that way for... **NOTHING?!**"

Yarna: "You misunderstand—to a Mime Warrior, *nothing* is *everything!*"

---

[101] *Which is to be expected with something that only exists in fables.*

[102] *Not to be the eternal sceptic, but it also could have been a desert that just* looked *endless—which most deserts, I find anyway, do...*

Me: "Please... I beg of you, just make one grain of sense..."

The Mime Warrior stares impassively at my pleading. She waits a full minute before drawing in a breath to speak again.

Yarna: "We discovered the fabled lost *Mime Temple of Gesture*..."

The Mime Warrior pauses, her eyes glazing over as she slips back into a halcyon memory.

Me: "Mime Temple of *Gesture?*"

She snaps out of her cosy daze and stares back at me.

Yarna: "The last resting place of the long-forgotten *Mime God-King.*"[103]

Me: "I've never heard of him."

Yarna: "You wouldn't—only those who have studied *the Way of the Empty Hand* know of his existence... well, and you now, of course..."

Me: "What did this temple look like?"

Yarna: "It was... *indescribable.*"

Me: "Because its beauty was beyond comprehension?"

Yarna: "No, because I couldn't see it—remember, you experience the world through what you can *see*... that's not how a Mime Warrior works; we do not look—we only *feel.*"[104]

Me: "That seems so frustrating. I would have wanted to see it with my own eyes."

Yarna: "I didn't need to see it to appreciate its exquisite artistry. There was something so pure about it, so right—I still remember walking around the temple feeling the ancient stone under my fingertips."

Me: "What was that like?"

---

[103] *I'm slightly unnerved by the thought of an omnipresent being ruling through the medium of mime—mind you, on the other hand, being on the wrong end of 'gesticulated' wrath is probably better than being on the wrong end of 'actual' wrath...*

[104] *Most of the Mime Artists I have ever witnessed usually 'feel' via their noses first, which probably explains why most have large red conks and suffer from throbbing headaches...*

Yarna: "Like nothing I had ever felt before. Even though the temperature in The Endless Desert was unbearably hot, the stone of the temple was ice cold to the touch—it was a sheer pleasure wandering around the place having already endured the punishing heat outside."

Me: "How long did you stay at the temple?"

Yarna: "Five summers."

Me: "Five summers? Just *you* and the Mime Grandmaster?"

Yarna: "Actually, there were three other Chosen Ones—fellow candidates the Mime Grandmaster had summoned to the temple."

Me: "Five of you? Together in the temple?"

Yarna: "Yup."

Me: "Inside an *invisible* temple?"

Yarna: "What's your point?"

Me: "Wasn't there—you know, certain problems with that *arrangement?*"[105]

Yarna: "Problems? Problems like what?"

Me: "Privacy for one?"

Yarna: "Bodies are just bodies—we all respected one another's space and never directly stared at someone when they needed some alone time."

Me: "That's a relief. What about accidents?"

Yarna: "Just because we're all former Mime Artists—doesn't mean we're not toilet trained!"

---

[105] *At the end of a long day of Loremastering, I am grateful that I can always retire to a local inn, close the door, take off my clothes, relax in a hot bath, and enjoy the quiet in relative solitude. There is <u>nothing</u> worse than trying to do that while being watched as everyone else goes about their 'business'...*

Me: "No, I mean accidents such as banging into invisible chairs that haven't been put away properly or falling down a flight of stairs you forgot were there?"

Yarna: "*Ah*—I see... we believe problems such as these are just daily obstacles *all* Mime Warriors must overcome if they are to prove their worth; living in the Mime Temple elevated our senses to new untapped levels."

Me: "So, what happened after the fifth summer? Did you all leave to become Chosen Ones in different parts of the realm?"

Yarna: "No—there was one more twist in the tail. The Mime Grandmaster revealed that only *one* of us could progress to become the One True Chosen One."

Me: "What happened to your rivals?"

Yarna: "We all knew that to become the *One True Chosen One,* we would need to find a way to eliminate each other. On the final day of the fifth summer, the Mime Grandmaster gave us one last test to overcome, *The Mime Warrior's Trial...*"

Me: "The Mime Warrior's Trial? That sounds dangerous."

Yarna: "That's because it *is*—it is the final obstacle all Chosen Ones must overcome. The Mime Warrior's Trial is an invisible maze filled with all manner of deadly mime traps and invisible monsters designed to push our physical and mental abilities to the limit."

Me: "I take it you emerged victorious?"

Yarna: "Indeed—I did."

Me: "What happened to the other Chosen Ones?"

Yarna: "One fell into an invisible spiked pit—you could even see *right* through his body where the invisible spike had skewered him. Another ended up inside an invisible Gelatinous Cube—it was quite terrifying seeing her bones floating in mid-air."

Me: "And the last one?"

Yarna: "We had to fight to the death in a final arena battle—both wielding *Mime Daggers.* He was good—but not good enough to defeat me."

Me: "That must have been difficult for you."

Yarna: "You have no idea—for we were also lovers as well as Chosen One rivals."

Me: "I'm sorry—hang on, you were *lovers?*"

Yarna: "Yup..."

Me: "*Lovers* in an *invisible* temple?"[106]

Yarna: "You know this already."

Me: "Don't you see the problem?"

Yarna: "No."

Me: "Never mind..."

The Mime Warrior gives me a puzzled look.

Yarna: "We had grown close during our five summers together; it was a difficult decision to end his life—but a necessary one. With my rivals and former lover vanquished, the Mime Grandmaster declared I was the One True Chosen One."

Me: "It sounds like it would have been far easier if you had become a Wizard or a Paladin instead."

The Mime Warrior mimes a yawn.

Yarna: "*Boring.* Everyone nowadays is a Paladin or a Wizard, but how many can say they're a Mime Warrior? **None!** That makes me different, makes me *unique.* Mark my words, Loremaster, Mime Warriors are the future—one day soon, I can imagine locals cheering our great deeds or having our own range of articulated figurines that can be positioned in different mime poses, such as *Brushing the Step*[107] and *Walking the Hell Hound*[108]—"

---

[106] *(See footnote 105) I take it back—THIS IS WORSE!!*

[107] *Complete with a surreptitious welcome mat lift...*

[108] **Loremaster Tip #2:** *Never do this to a real Hell Hound; it won't end well for you if you do—also, they defecate pure evil!*

Me: "But if there are *more* Mime Warriors, won't you cease being the One True Chosen One?"

The Mime Warrior seems caught off-guard by this minor flaw in her plan.

Yarna: "Well, they would only be… *erm*… Chosen Ones… because… I would still be the One True Chosen One…"

I try to spare the Mime Warrior's non-imaginary blushes and swiftly change the subject.

Me: "Can I ask how many quests you have been on since you became a fully-fledged Mime Warrior?"

Yarna: "Actually, this is my first quest; Guildmaster Toldarn *personally* asked me to stop the Goblins of Halgorn Crags from entering Greenvale Forest."

Me: "Who is Guildmaster Toldarn?"[109]

Yarna: "Why, only the highest-ranking Guildmaster in the Heroes Guild!"

Me: "Had Toldarn ever seen anyone like you before—a Mime Warrior, I mean?"[110]

Yarna: "No—but after I gave him a demonstration of my sword-twirling abilities, *well*, he practically handed me a contract right there and then!"

Me: "*Ah*—so I'm guessing you also signed a *'Death in Service'* clause?"

Yarna: "I did—and I signed it straight anyway!"

Me: "*Erm*… without reading the small print first—isn't that a tad foolish?"

The Mime Warrior grins mischievously.

Yarna: "I used a Mime quill!"

---

[109] *I'll be honest here—I do actually know who Guildmaster Toldarn is, but I wanted to see how Yarna answered this question.*

[110] *Outside of the Tronte Fete…*

Me: "A *Mime* quill?"

On cue, the Mime Warrior begins to mime the act of writing—she even adds a dip into a non-existent inkpot. I stare at the Mime Warrior, unsure if she's joking or a genius.[111]

Me: "Why do you think Toldarn tasked you with clearing out the Goblins here?"

Yarna: "He probably realised the importance of Mime Warriors. Toldarn even promised he would team me up with an Elven Battle Dancer on my next adventure[112]—I cannot wait!"

Me: "And how have the Heroes Guild been towards you?"

Yarna: "I've found them nothing short of inspirational. They have been so supportive in everything I do; they crafted the sword I carry by my side, given me free food and lodgings—they have really gone the extra mile to ensure I have felt part of the Heroes Guild."

Me: "Did you expect such good treatment from them?"

Yarna: "I had secretly hoped but made no assumptions. I feared some would dismiss my credentials and suggest I become yet *another* Fighter—or worse, a Cleric. But I had nothing to worry about; everyone has been genuinely curious about my craft—it's refreshing to be among such open-minded heroes."

There's a high-pitched screech from somewhere deep within the Halgorn Crags. In a flash, the Mime Warrior spins around, a hand on her imaginary pommel.

Yarna: "If you would excuse me, Loremaster—it's time I started earning my coin."

Me: "I only have one last question for you; being a Mime Artist—*sorry*, I mean *Mime Warrior*, shouldn't you be silent?"

The Mime Warrior turns back and winks.

Yarna: "That's my secret, Loremaster—I'm *always* silent…"

---

[111] *I'm still none the wiser.*

[112] *First Mime Warriors—now Battle Dancers; what happened to the good old days of simple Fighters and… erm… simpler Barbarians?*

There's a blur of movement as the Mime Warrior charges up the incline towards the crags above—before suddenly slamming face-first into an Unexpected Locked Door. The Mime Warrior rubs her swelling nose and begins fishing around for an Invisible Key in her pocket. I'm torn between wanting to see how this encounter with the Goblins plays out and making myself scarce in case several misplaced arrows hit me.[113] Just as the Mime Warrior finally manages to open the Unexpected Locked Door, I decide to hurriedly depart southwards and head for the nearest tavern with a door I can clearly see.

---

[113] *Even though the odds of actually being hit by a Goblin Archer's arrow is incredibly low— it is never zero...*

5. Nibb, the Dungeonmaster

I have to be honest with you; a dark, dank dungeon wasn't on my list of the ten-most-popular-places-to-hold-an-interview, but that's precisely where I find myself right now. Mercifully, I'm not on some foolhardy quest to retrieve a mysterious orb, but I'm here at the behest of the dungeon's owner, Nibb the Dungeonmaster. I'm not entirely sure what a Dungeonmaster actually 'does' beyond forcing heroes to jump through hoops[114] while sitting at a table, so I'm hoping to dig a little deeper into this unusual role.

The corridor ahead of me reverberates ominously with the sound of approaching footsteps. My leg muscles tighten, expecting a hideous monstrosity to appear at any given moment. Instead, a white-haired Gnome dressed in what seems to be a robe made from bright red lichen greets me. She raises her lamp and peers through a strange brass-rimmed seeing-device that sits neatly on the end of her bulbous nose.

Nibb: "You must be the Loremaster?"

I nod in reply.

Me: "And I assume you're the—*erm… Dungeon… mistress?*"[115]

The Gnome smiles warmly.

Nibb: "Sadly, Dungeonmistress conjures up all manner of sordidness—so, Dungeonmaster it is. Are you ready to head further in?"

Me: "Is—Is it safe?"

Nibb: "Of course it's safe. Besides, you're with me—so you've *absolutely* nothing to worry about…"

She turns back to look at me with a mischievous glint in her eye.

---

[114] *'Hoops' is a Gnomish word meaning 'Wheel of Death'—not to be confused with a Barbarian's 'Wheel of Pain', which is considerably less fatal but <u>will</u> leave you with a severe case of crushing lamentation.*

[115] *I can feel myself turning a shade of red that threatens to put the Gnome's robes to shame.*

Nibb: "Just *don't* wander off where I can't see you..."[116]

We pass through dimly lit room after dimly lit room, occasionally sidestepping at odd angles, avoiding what I can only guess is some kind of devious floor trap. Nibb says nothing. She walks with assured purpose without delay or hesitation.

Me: "How do you remember where to go?"

Nibb: "I've owned this dungeon for over twelve summers now. I know every flagstone and archway as if I built the place myself."

Me: "Forgive me; I thought you created this dungeon."

Nibb: "This place? No—I'm only the latest proprietor; a few others have held the title of Dungeonmaster."

Me: "Would you have done anything differently if you had the chance to build it yourself from the ground up... *erm*... down?"

Nibb: "*Hmmm...* I would have designed the whole thing as a spiral."

Me: "Why a spiral?"

Nibb: "Would make getting to the dungeon's heart a lot quicker for a start!"

Me: "Why? What's at the heart of the dungeon?"

Nibb: "*Shhh*—you'll spoil the surprise..."[117]

We pass under an archway with a glaring stone face carved into it—its mouth wide open as if in the middle of a scream—or a belch.

Me: "Anything I should worry about?"

Nibb: "Only if you put your hand inside. Dart trap—catches out the curious ones who should really know better."

Me: "Curious ones?"

---

[116] *I'm now shadowing the Gnome as if I'm a Rogue about to go in for the backstab...*

[117] *I'd imagine 'surprises' in a place such as this are quickly followed by pain, then inevitably, a lingering death.*

Nibb: "Rogues mainly—they can't resist sticking their hands in holes that don't belong to them."[118]

I shiver at the thought and leave the open-mouthed stone face behind me as I hurry after the Dungeonmaster, who has almost diminished into the darkness ahead.

Nibb: "Keep up!"

Me: "How did this dungeon fall into your care?"

Nibb: "I won it."

Me: "Won it? As a reward for completing some impossibly difficult quest?"

Nibb: "No—nothing so poetic. I won it in a card game."[119]

Me: "A *card* game—you're joking, right?"

The Gnome laughs.

Nibb: "If only I were—it's the straight-up truth. I was playing against this Cleric—"

Me: "A gambling Cleric—that sounds like a bit of a contradiction?"

Nibb: "Well, if you think about it—religion as a whole is one big gamble."

Me: "I don't follow."

Nibb: "Tell me, are you a spiritual man, Loremaster?"

---

[118] *I'm fairly certain there's an eye-watering story behind that revelation.*

[119] *There are many card games in the realm, but by far the most popular is 'Fellowship'; a game where players are dealt nine cards, one of which must not be taken by an opponent— players must use the other eight cards in their hand to protect it at all costs. Fellowship games have been known to go on for nearly a summer with the eventual winner crying out, 'IT IS DONE!' before collapsing into an exhausted heap on the floor and refusing to budge until a rather large eagle has turned up to carry them away...*

Me: "Not especially."[120]

Nibb: "What do you think happens when you leave this life?"

Me: "Not a lot."

Nibb: "What do you think a Cleric believes?"

Me: "Some kind of Holy nirvana awaits them?"[121]

Nibb: "What if *they* are right and *you* are wrong?"

Me: "I'm probably in a lot of trouble."

Nibb: "What if they are wrong and you are right?"

Me: "Nothing—I guess…"

Nibb: "Your average Cleric prefers to stack the odds in their favour."[122]

Me: "I see…"

I ponder the Dungeonmaster's words.

Nibb: "Anyway, this particular Cleric thought he could gamble with the coin from his collection box—then threw in the deed to this dungeon when their luck ran out."

Me: "I bet there were a few red faces after he lost."

Nibb: "I made myself scarce pretty quick. There's nothing more unnerving in this realm than a Cleric who just lost everything and is looking for someone to smite."

Me: *"Smite?"*

---

[120] *I don't believe in any sort of 'Supreme Being'—the idea that a God demands a lifetime of devotion and worship in exchange for a seat at the top table feels a little too shifty for my liking.*

[121] *Most professions have a God they believe in. Paladins follow a Holy Warrior God; Wizards follow a Magical God; Barbarians follow a short-tempered God—Rangers, on the other hand, follow a 'bush' God who likes to hide in overgrown shrubbery and jump out at people when they least expect it.*

[122] *It is well known that Clerics are poor gamblers; the fact they are making a bet they feel they cannot lose should put the fear of… erm… God… into their congregation.*

Nibb: "Supposedly it's a punch that has the weight of their Deity behind them;[123] Clerics prefer to give the act of physical harm a Holy name—I assume to make them feel superior."[124]

Me: "I guess I'd better not play cards with any Clerics in future."

Nibb: "Not unless you know what's good for you!"

Me: "But you won your game."

The Gnome taps her temple.

Nibb: "Ah, the trick is always making sure they're slightly drunk beforehand."

Me: "Drinking and gambling—so much for dedicating a life to abstinence."

Nibb: "Most heroes have a hidden vice or two—Clerics are nearly always at the top of that list."

Me: "Nearly always?"

Nibb: "Paladins are worse."

The Gnome stops as the corridor abruptly comes to a dead end. There seems to be nowhere for us to go but back the way we came.

Me: "Perhaps we took a wrong turn."

The Gnome raises her lamp and continues to study the wall.

Nibb: "Perhaps—but unlikely."

The Dungeonmaster puts her hand against the stone and follows the smallest of cracks. There's a soft *'click'* as she presses her finger into a recess. The wall shakes and rumbles as stone grinds against stone and an entrance slowly reveals itself. The Dungeonmaster steps through and flicks another switch on the other side of the wall—the door

---

[123] *I wager a Deity who has been at the 'All-You-Can-Eat Deity Banquet' will probably deal a lot more 'crushing' damage than a Deity who has been on an Omnipotent Diet.*

[124] *It's worth noting that Paladins also like to 'smite'—although with Paladins, you're more inclined to believe any incoming slap will hurt a lot more than one from a Cleric.*

immediately rumbles again; this time, it begins to close at speed. I hesitate for the briefest of moments—unsure if I should follow.

Nibb: "You not coming?"

The fear of being alone compels me to leap through the rapidly closing gap before it seals itself shut.

Me: "Sorry, I don't know what came over me."

Nibb: "Understandable. You're a surface-dweller. It's not natural for you to be down here for any great length of time. But, as I'm a Gnome, I find I'm more at home here than I am up there—although the lack of a tavern does force me to venture out into the open from time to time."

Me: "You live here?"

Nibb: "Yes—this place is probably the safest place in the entire realm."[125]

Me: "How can it be safe?"

The Gnome stops at a heavy-set door and pulls out a ring of iron keys. She quickly settles on one and places it into the lock. One weighty *'CLUNK'* later and the door opens. She gestures for me to step inside—I hesitate again, not wishing to put a foot wrong or wind up trapped somewhere with no hope of escape.

Nibb: "Because I say it is—fortune favours the brave, Loremaster."

I nod and take a deep breath before stepping into the Dungeonmaster's private quarters. A bizarre forest of ropes and pulleys immediately greets me; I can't help but notice some have obscure little coded notes attached to them. I grab the nearest rope and examine the handwritten parchment secured to it.

Me: "C4?"

Nibb: "It's a small firetrap awaiting anyone foolish enough to take the stairs down to the third level—only burns your boots, though."

---

[125] *Actually, the safest place in the entire realm is the town of Viscid, where the ruling Baron has decreed that all sword tips, axe blades, and spear points must be coated in a strange gelatinous mixture that makes each weapon bounce off whatever they hit without harm. This makes for an amusing evening's entertainment when the inevitable bar fight breaks out. However, it's worth noting that Viscid has never once successfully defended itself from heavily armed non-Viscid raiders.*

Me: "CO2?"

The Gnome chuckles to herself.

Nibb: "A personal favourite of mine—*an ice-trapped throne.* Anyone who feels the need to rest their weary backside on such an auspicious seat will find their rump stuck solid in place—there is nothing worse than enduring a frozen backside!"[126]

Me: "These ropes are all attached to a trap somewhere in your dungeon?"

Nibb: "I wouldn't be a very good Dungeonmaster if they weren't."

Me: "How do you know when to activate a trap at the right time?"

The Dungeonmaster claps her hands excitedly.

Nibb: "*Ah!* I'm glad you asked!"

The Gnome pulls a lever in the centre of the room, summoning a strange, tubed contraption, which drops from the ceiling with a solitary glass lens protruding from it.

Nibb: "Here! Here! Look through *this!*"

Cautiously I place my eye against the lens and peer inside. Suddenly I find myself staring at a deathly pale, toothless face that gazes back at me. I scream and fall backwards in shock. Confused, the Gnome takes a look through the mechanical device herself.

Nibb: "*Ah,* those damn Zombies—always getting in the way! Hold on, let me try another mirror."

The Gnome pumps a handle on the strange device and rotates the lens one complete turn.

Nibb: "Look now…"

I gingerly get to my feet and cautiously peer through the lens once more. This time I see the same Zombie but from another part of the

---

[126] *Having once sat for over an hour on a metal bucket when I went 'ice-fishing' with my father, I can safely say I can easily imagine the pain of anyone unfortunate enough to sit on that trapped throne.*

room. It continues to stare at the hole in the wall, oblivious to my presence.

Me: "What magic *is* this?"

Nibb: "*Magic?*"

The Gnome spits in disgust.

Nibb: "No magic here—just mechanical mastery."

Me: "Mechanical?"

Nibb: "It's all engineering... smoke and mirrors... well, mirrors—the smoke is activated by that rope over there."

The Gnome points to a heavy rope with the words 'SMOK' written below it on a sign.

Me: "I think you spelt 'smoke' wrong..."

Nibb: "That's how us Gnomes spell it—why? How do you spell the word?"

Me: "With an 'E' at the end."

The Dungeonmaster scratches her head in thought.

Nibb: "Smok—e? That means 'cheese' in Gnomish—I don't think cheese would be useful in a dungeon situation? Unless you were trying to use it to tempt a Druid into a large trap..."[127]

I nod in thought.

Me: "These ropes all look new—did you add them yourself?"

Nibb: "I may have made a few tiny modifications for the better—a Gnome always makes a home their own, *even* when that home is a dungeon. After I took ownership of this place, I spent a lot of time and coin adding features that said something about me."

Me: "But it's now a dungeon filled with dangerous traps!"

---

[127] *I'm guessing this would only work if the Druid had previously transformed into a cheese hungry rodent.*

The Gnome winks at me.

Nibb: "I prefer to think of it as *a surprise around every corner—*"

Me: "—you mean a *lethal* surprise around every corner."[128]

Nibb: "Oh no, no, no, this isn't a *hard* dungeon like that—it's a *soft* dungeon."

Me: "What's a *soft* dungeon?"

Nibb: "It's a safe space."

Me: "If it's a safe space, won't most heroes avoid it?"

Nibb: "*Good!* I don't want any high-level adventurers descending into my dungeon and slaughtering the carefully curated Zombies I have here—or destroying all the hand-built traps just because they're too experienced and can't be bothered to disarm them correctly."

Me: "Forgive me, but if your dungeon isn't meant for hardened heroes and adventurers—what's the point of it?"

Nibb: "As I said before, it's a *soft* dungeon."

Me: "But what does that *mean* exactly?"

The Dungeonmaster kicks a pedal, and the optical device disappears back into the ceiling—she turns on her heels and sits on a stool that suddenly sprouts out of the floor.

Nibb: "Look, this dungeon has been designed with newly qualified adventurers in mind. It's a safe place to train, to learn the ropes of their profession. Most of the traps in here aren't lethal—they just... you know... *hurt* a bit."

Me: "But the Zombies?"

Nibb: "There are only Zombies in here—why? Because they are so resilient! You can hack away at them all day long, and they can keep on going! They literally work for food..."

Me: "Yeah—although it's usually raw food that once was a person."

---

[128] *I want to refer you back to footnote 117 here—just for the record!*

Nibb: "Granted—I give you that. But to be honest, if you're going to get bitten by a Zombie, you have to ask yourself if you're *really* cut out for the adventuring life."

Me: "What happens when a Zombie can't keep going, and you need a new one?"

Nibb: "I have an *arrangement* with a local Gravedigger…"

Me: "What sort of *arrangement?*"

Nibb: "He has a backlog of fallen heroes to put into the ground—so sometimes this Gravedigger sells me the corpses of his… *ah…* overflow."

Me: "You buy *dead* adventurers!?"

Nibb: "Trust me—they'd rather spend their days wandering a cold dungeon floor than being stuck in a cold box for all of eternity."

Me: "I suppose—but how do make them… *erm… not* dead?"

Nibb: "I have another *arrangement* with a Necromancer. He brings the dead back to life for a small fee. Well, not *exactly* 'to life'—but you know what I mean."[129]

Me: "That's quite clever—morally dubious mind, but clever nonetheless."

Nibb: "In a matter of hours, I can repopulate this place with fresh Zombies and reopen for business."

Me: "But can't Zombies make more Zombies by biting and infecting the living?"

The Gnome taps her head.

Nibb: "I tell the Necromancer to remove their teeth beforehand. No bite means no infection. Although sometimes a few teeth get missed—but

---

[129] *I have no idea why Necromancers have such an obsession with bringing dead things back to life. I can only assume that they looked after a friend's pet dog and accidentally killed it at some point in their youth. So, rather than coming clean about the unfortunate accident, they searched high and low for a way to defy nature and bring the poor creature back from the dead to spare them an awkward conversation about it over dinner.*

that's life!"[130]

Me: "Seems you've thought of everything. How do you attract new adventurers to your dungeon?"

Nibb: "That's where the Heroes Guild comes in. I have an—"

Me: "Let me guess—another *arrangement?*"

Nibb: "You catch on fast!"

Me: "I'm starting to see a pattern forming..."

Nibb: "To be a successful Dungeonmaster, you need to have a lot of *arrangements* in place—otherwise you won't last a summer in this job before running out of something."

Me: "Like what?"

Nibb: "*Everything!* Dungeons don't magically refresh themselves. Someone has to take stock of any expired monsters and replace them with new 'wandering' ones. All the traps need to be checked and, in some cases, refilled with their payload. Even the dungeon's loot needs to be constantly sourced and replenished."

Me: "I didn't realise how much goes on behind the scenes to keep a dungeon functioning properly."

Nibb: "You see, the whole place would grind to a halt without these little *arrangements*. That's what makes the difference between a successful, repeatable dungeon and a one-adventure wonder."

Me: "Ingenious!"

Nibb: "Not only that, The Heroes Guild pays me an eminently reasonable fee for every new recruit entering this place. In return, I guarantee their heroes will survive—although some will leave with a few new cuts and bruises to remind them of their time down here. I like to think of it as a heartfelt kick up their heroic behinds."

---

[130] *Or, in an unlucky adventurer's case—undeath...*

Me: "Hence a *soft* dungeon."[131]

Nibb: "The Heroes Guild don't want to lose their fledgling heroes before they've reached their potential—think of the coin they'd waste if their brand new adventurer died moments after stepping foot in here. There's a sizeable investment involved where each hero is concerned; bed and lodging costs, training costs, equipment costs, magical item costs, armour costs, and weapon costs, not to mention body retrieval costs if the unthinkable *should* happen—it all adds up. The Heroes Guild would much prefer it if their adventurers paid their debts back way before checking out early to some minor mishap on a low-level quest. At least my dungeon gives those hapless fools the experience they desperately need without the threat of death lurking around every corner or haunting every bad decision they make."

Me: "That's quite progressive of the Heroes Guild."

Nibb: "You have to give them credit—when it comes to adventuring, they know what they're doing."

Me: "It certainly appears so."

A bell suddenly chimes from somewhere in the room. Nibb rubs her hands eagerly in anticipation.

Nibb: "*Aha,* you're in luck—the day's first customer!"

One pulled lever later, and the optical device drops from the ceiling once more—the Gnome leaps at it as she peers into the lens before it's even had a chance to come to a stop.

Nibb: "Bugger, a Barbarian... I _HATE_ Barbarians..."

Me: "Why Barbarians in particular?"

Nibb: "They break everything they touch, guaranteed to leave such a mess—*Oh,* but this one is already heading straight for the throne room! What an idiot—so predictable! Barbarians just can't resist sitting on a golden throne and pretending like they are the *King or Queen of the*

---

[131] *I wager that in the future, some bright spark will have the idea to turn this 'soft' dungeon into somewhere for younglings to run around unsupervised. While, at the same time, tired parents who are supposed to be watching their offspring 'play' sit next to other tired parents to complain bitterly about their lives as they drink overpriced non-alcoholic beverages—it's a chilling thought.*

Barbarians!"

The Dungeonmaster looks over at me with a wicked glint in her eye.

Nibb: "You want to pull the rope marked CO2?"

Me: "No, I don't think so—"

Nibb: "You sure? You're missing out—it's *so* much fun."

I find my hand rising, fingers twitching with electricity as they hover by the rope marked CO2. The Gnome grins at me with undisguised glee. But I cannot bring myself to activate the trap. A Loremaster's sworn duty is to observe and record *without* involving themselves in what they witness—this is the path I have chosen to follow. I turn away, much to the Dungeonmaster's evident disappointment.

Me: "No, I'm sure—I'll pass..."[132]

Nibb: "Suit yourself."

The Gnome's attention remains locked on the lens of her optical device.

Nibb: "He's sitting down... 1... 2... 3... ***NOW!***"

The Dungeonmaster yanks on the rope. A few seconds later, a high-pitched scream can be heard from somewhere deeper within the dungeon, causing the Gnome to chuckle with childish delight—she claps her hands with glee.

Nibb: "That gets me *every* time—*I LOVE THIS JOB!*"[133]

---

[132] *As tempting as it was, I know fate has a strange way of balancing out misdeeds. I don't want to know what payback I'd owe for freezing an angry Barbarian's backside to a golden throne.*

[133] *I think the Gnome enjoys her Dungeonmaster role a little more than I'd consider 'healthy'...*

6. Thorde Ironstein, the Forgemaster

At 98, you'd be forgiven for thinking that Thorde Ironstein was well beyond his prime to be running a busy forge—but as Dwarves age five times slower than humans, in their world, he is only nineteen. The young Forgemaster took over the family business after his father hung up his tools to enjoy his beloved rock collection in relative peace and quiet.[134] It was a proud moment when Thorde was finally handed the ancient cross peen hammer that has been in the Ironstein family for seventeen generations. The latest Ironstein Forgemaster has embraced his new position to the full and already drawn up ambitious plans to drag the venerable business, The Hammer & Tongs, kicking and screaming into the present.

The heat from the smouldering forge hits me in the face like a warhammer—staggering me backwards, forcing me to shield my face from the blast momentarily. I can taste iron in the air, which leaves an unpleasant tang on my tongue. The sound of heavy metal striking even heavier metal reverberates all around as I head deeper into the forge, trying to locate the Forgemaster through the steam. There's a sudden hiss as metal rapidly cools in what I assume is a barrel of water somewhere behind the wall of impenetrable condensation. I see a shadow moving through the vapour as a sweat-covered Dwarf emerges, holding a bright orange blade of superheated steel. Looking up, he thrusts the metal back into the water barrel before wiping his palms on his leather apron. He holds a hand out for me to take—I hesitate for the briefest of moments, a pause that doesn't go unnoticed by the Forgemaster.

Thorde: "Not one for dirt and hard work then, Loremaster?"

I smile weakly and grasp the Dwarf's hand.

Me: "Forgive my rudeness—"

The Dwarf pulls my hand in tight, flips it over and studies each one of the tips as if they contain the answer to life's greatest vexing question.[135] The Forgemaster grins as he finally releases the grip on my hand.

---

[134] *Rock Collecting is the number one Dwarven pastime, closely followed by Axe Collecting, Empty Flagon Collecting, and Excessive Facial Hair Collecting.*

[135] *The greatest vexing question is: 'What is the point of having a Paladin AND a Cleric on the same adventure?'*

Thorde: "Your thumb, middle and index fingers have tiny callouses; pressure points from where you hold a quill, I wager—and your hand edge is smooth where it constantly moves across a sheet of parchment. But the rest looks as fresh as a newly born bairn."

Me: "You got me there—the curse of my trade."[136]

The Forgemaster shows me his hands in return—they're blistered and cracked, baked and battered from the constant heat.

Thorde: "Mine haven't been the same since I started working here."

Me: "That looks painful."

Thorde: "Thankfully, they look far worse than they feel. The heat killed the nerves ages ago—I can barely sense anything in my fingers these days, not unless I hit them *really* hard by mistake…"

Me: "I guess that can come in handy."

Thorde: *"Eh?"*

Me: "Your dead nerves, for when you mistime a hammer blow."

Thorde: "Aye—but those heavy ones still hurt like buggery. However, there are generations of Ironsteins coursing through my veins—I can't let them down by screaming out in pain, can I? Tell me, Loremaster, what brings you to my forge?"

Me: "I'm on a quest—"

Thorde: "So, you need a weapon? Say no more! You've come to the right place—"

Me: "Sorry, not *that* kind of quest—what I seek is information."

Thorde: "Information? I don't know much about the adventures that go on around here, only rumours that I pick up from passing trade—"

Me: "No, my apologies for the continued confusion; my quest is to find out about heroes, discover what drives them, why they do what they do—talk to the people who help them achieve greatness, people like *you*…"

---

[136] *Along with wrist cramps, grammatical headaches, crippling self-doubt and an unfathomable thirst for tea…*

Thorde: "Why?"

Me: "I come from a family of heroes—the pressure to follow in their footsteps is immense."[137]

Thorde: "*Ah,* family—and how do they feel about your undertaking?"

Me: "They don't understand why I have this burning need for answers."

Thorde: "I take it you haven't found all the answers you seek?"

Me: "Not enough to call my quest complete."

Thorde: "Maybe your parents believe you're not up to the task?"

Me: "They have no idea what it was like growing up, not knowing how to slay a Dragon or walk safely through a monster-filled dungeon as if it were a jaunty little stroll in a peaceful forest.[138] The weight of expectancy was too much to bear for one whose greatest adventure was reading a book while on the privy."

Thorde: "Aye, I understand all too well the pressures of keeping a family tradition going. This forge's future must be carried on my shoulders alone—you and I are not so different."[139]

Me: "My parents only ever wanted me to become a hero and follow in their footsteps—just as my brother did."

The Dwarf looks me up and down, even stepping to the side as he sizes me up.

Thorde: "You were wise not to follow in their footsteps."

Me: "You think so?"

---

[137] It's worth remembering that I come from a long line of ancestral adventurers and heroes; practically 'everyone' in our family has done a spot of questing at some point or another. Even my Grandmother was a Cleric who sought out the undead and laid them to rest, which was ironic considering she eventually married my Grandfather, a closet Necromancer. He used to reanimate the same 'dead' undead solely to annoy her—theirs was a strange relationship, but somehow it worked for them.

[138] A 'jaunty' little stroll that features spring-loaded spike traps, flame pits, a plethora of angry monsters baying for your blood, and a sarcastic Dungeonmaster to commentate on your woefully inept attempts to pick a lock while under pressure...

[139] Figuratively speaking...

Thorde: "Aye—I've kitted out enough adventurers in my time to spot the ones who aren't destined to become a returning customer of mine. I'd bet my whole forge on you being a *one-er*."

Me: "A one-er? What's that?"

Thorde: "One quest and out—never to be seen again."[140]

Me: "My brother would be laughing right now if he heard you say that."

Thorde: "Where is your brother now?"

Me: "I don't know—I've not seen him for ten summers."

Thorde: "What's his name—this brother of yours?"

Me: "Aldon Barr."

Thorde: "Aldon Barr...? Aldon *Barr*...?"

The Dwarf scratches his head to see if the name connects with a distant memory.

Me: "Do you know him?"

Thorde: "I'm sorry, that name doesn't ring any bells, I'm afraid—but that doesn't mean I don't know him."

Me: "What do you mean?"

Thorde: "No offence, but the name *'Aldon Barr'* doesn't exactly sound 'heroic'—if I were your brother, I'd have paid a visit to the Heralds Guild to register something a little more inspiring, or even feared.[141] Say, there's a thought. If you ever find yourself in Tronte, why not visit them and see if he passed through their halls—The Heralds Guild may hold a clue to his whereabouts?"

Me: "I'll do that—thank you."

---

[140] *Either the Dwarf is referencing an Invisibility Potion here, or things have just taken a rather dark turn.*

[141] *Knowing my brother, he would have chosen one of the stupid pretend adventuring names from when we were kids, like Naug Skullcleaver or Ricardo Stagaxe. I, on the other hand, always went with the nom de plume of Mister Underheel...*

Thorde: "I never once deviated from the path my father set out for me."

Me: "How do you feel about that?"

Thorde: "I've grown used to it. At first, I wanted to see the world and adventure, but I soon realised I wasn't cut out for a heroic life—"

Me: "Why was that?"

Thorde: "Truth be said—I never really enjoyed fighting.[142] Destroying things always seemed to be a bit soulless for my liking. Instead, I found I enjoyed making things, crafting the finest weapons—that's what *really* fills me with a sense of purpose. Knowing legendary heroes will one day wield my artistry in combat. So, I'm not cut out for the adventuring life—but I *do* like the idea of being an integral part of a hero's one."

Me: "I understand your forge has become increasingly popular with newly qualified adventurers since you've taken charge."

Thorde: "It's good to see *The Hammer & Tongs* doing so well with the new wave of adventurers coming through the ranks. It wasn't always that way—my father fought hard but could not stop the steady decline in the business."

Me: "How have you managed to turn this forge's fortunes around where your father had failed?"

Thorde: "My father was old-fashioned—he would spend weeks on a single blade, folding the metal repeatedly, beating it until it was as hard as Dragon scale. He would be at his whetstone for days, sharpening the blade until it could cut the air in two with a deft flick of the wrist."

Me: "Sounds impressive—that must have been some blade to wield?"

Thorde: "*Oh,* it was, for the one lucky adventurer it was meant for—but

---

[142] *Somewhere deep in the ancestral Dwarven burial halls, the sound of a thousand Dwarven Warrior corpses turning in their graves can be heard...*

for the other twenty or so heroes who were *still* waiting their turn for a blade to be forged, it was unbearably frustrating."[143]

Me: "So, he couldn't keep up with the increasing demand for weapons?"

Thorde: "The fewer weapons he sold, the more expensive his weapons became as he tried desperately to cover the forge's spiralling costs. When I finally took over as Forgemaster, I needed to rethink everything from the ground up—"

The Dwarf stops and gives me a wary look as if waiting for me to make a joke—but I remain impassive and interested. Satisfied, the Dwarf continues with his trail of thought.[144]

Thorde: "If the business was to survive, it needed *quantity* over *quality*..."

Me: "So, you refocused the forge toward creating inferior weapons?"

Thorde: "*Now*—you're putting words in my mouth. I didn't *say* they were inferior; I just didn't want to spend four weeks making one blade when I could spend one week making four instead."

Me: "Hence *quantity* over *quality*."

Thorde: "Which in turn became *profit* over *poverty*."

Me: "So, you don't craft weapons that could... you know... slay a Dragon?"

The Forgemaster picks up a newly finished sword and feels its weight in his hand.

Thorde: "Take this sword—who is to say that this blade won't go on to slay a Dragon during its next adventure? It's well balanced and has a fair chance of piercing Dragon hide. Remember, it's not the sword that

---

[143] I'd imagine this wouldn't be an issue for the usually stoic Paladins, but any Barbarians waiting this long would be foaming at the mouth—I wouldn't fancy being the unlucky adventurer sat next to an agitated Barbarian in the forge's waiting area.

[144] My father would be proud of me for holding my tongue—my Uncle Bevan Barr (the Gods rest his soul) would be kicking me with his oversized boots for this missed golden comedic opportunity.

kills the Dragon—it's the hero at the other end of the pommel, holding it."[145]

Me: "What if the Dragon kills that hero?"

Thorde: "Blame the hero, blame the training, but *never* blame the weapon. My creations can be trusted to do the job they were made for."

Me: "Do you think your customers trust your weapons?"

Thorde: "Well, I can't remember the last time I had a complaint. But as I've always said, those who *do* have a complaint seldom return alive to do anything about it."

The Forgemaster laughs.

Thorde: "I'm joking—I have complete faith in the weapons I make, so much so that *every* weapon I sell comes with a lifetime guarantee."

Me: "What does that lifetime guarantee *actually* mean?"

Thorde: "It means '*if*' a weapon breaks in combat, then I promise to replace it with a brand new one—just as long as that hero can bring back the broken weapon in one piece."

The Dwarf grins.

I stare at the Forgemaster, unsure if the paradoxical conundrum is an attempt at another joke or if he's serious. After an awkward silence, I decide to press on with the interview.

Me: "Are you worried about your competition? There must be other Forgemasters trying to entice your customers away from you."

Thorde: "No, not at all—I've always encouraged healthy competition from the other forges. I know *my* forge is the best in the realm. I've modernised the entire operation—even gone as far as to hire a Gnome architect to construct a mechanical production line, complete with gears and pulleys. It's quite something to see it in action."

Me: "What does the mechanical production line do exactly?"

---

[145] *Do heroes kill monsters, or do weapons kill monsters? It is a question that has vexed the greatest scholars since the previous vexing question about the wisdom of having both Paladins and Clerics in the same adventuring party.*

Thorde: "In layman's terms,[146] it moves the metal further along the forge without the need to move from one spot."

Me: "I don't see how that can be of any use."

Thorde: "Positioned along the mechanical production line are my apprentices. They all have one part of the weapon-making process to complete, only one—the same one, which they repeat time and time again."

Me: "Sounds a little monotonous, if I'm being honest."

Thorde: "Aye—but it accelerates the weapon-making process exponentially."

Me: "Is it possible to see your mechanical production line working?"[147]

The Dwarf shakes his head.

Thorde: "I'm sorry, but that's one trade secret that I cannot share—you understand."

Me: "Of course—you can't be too careful with the competition sniffing around. So, where are you exactly when the production line is in full swing?"

Thorde: "Waiting at the end of the line to apply a finishing touch to the forging process; stamping *The Hammer & Tongs* maker's mark onto the weapon itself."

Me: "How efficient has this mechanical production line been?"

Thorde: "Extremely—it's increased our output tenfold. Name me one forge this side of the Doom Mountains that can make forty good quality blades in a week!"

---

[146] *A layman is a Gnome who refuses to do any work until they have been paid, not to be confused with a laywoman, a female Gnome who gets half the amount of a layman for doing twice the same job.*

[147] *Although, it's almost impossible to see anything in this steam-filled place!*

Me: "I struggle to think of one."[148]

Thorde: "Add to that a flawless health and safety record, and you can see how I've managed to turn the fortunes of *The Hammer & Tongs* around in a little under a summer."

Me: "Health and what?"

Thorde: "*Safety.* You have to remember that forges are dangerous places, far more dangerous than any Goblin-filled dungeon.[149] There is always an accident or two waiting to happen, but with the correct training and certifications from the Heralds Guild, I'm delighted to say we've been 'serious injury' free since I took over the place."

Me: "That's good to know."

Thorde: "It's just another reason why we've managed to convince our bigger clients, such as the Heroes Guild, to kit out their new recruits with only <u>our</u> wares."

Me: "You're not the first individual I've spoken to who has had dealings with them. That must be a pretty lucrative *arrangement.*"

The Dwarf shrugs.

Thorde: "I like the way the Heroes Guild operates. Their adventurers are highly trained—and they always pay on time and without fuss. That's why I always go the extra mile for any Heroes Guild member—regardless of their badge colour."

The Dwarf holds up a little card with *'The Hammer & Tongs'* logo printed at the top; underneath are eight circles lined up in two neat rows of four.

Me: "What's that?"

Thorde: "I call it a loyalty card."

Me: "What's a loyalty card?"

---

[148] However, had I guessed at 'The Anvil & Hammer', 'The Tongs & Hammer' or 'The Hammer & Anvil', I'm pretty sure one of them would have hit the proverbial nail on the head.

[149] Unless those Goblins had taken up archery lessons, I'm sure any dungeon filled with them would be reasonably safe to traverse.

Thorde: "Every time a Heroes Guild member buys a weapon from *The Hammer & Tongs*, I punch a hole in one of these little circles on the card."[150]

Me: "Then what happens?"

Thorde: "When all eight circles are punched, the hero can choose their next weapon free of charge. Then the whole process starts again with a new card."

Me: "That's ingenious! But what's to stop a hero punching the hole out for themselves—or claiming your best weapons for free?"

Thorde: "I use a specially shaped puncher—impossible to replicate. There's also some small print on the reverse of the card, which they have to adhere to even if someone *does* manage to punch all the holes out for themselves."

Me: "Small *what?*"[151]

The Forgemaster narrows his eyes and taps the diminutive lettering on the reverse of the card—it's so small I can barely make out the words printed there.

Thorde: "Print."

I peer closer at the card's reverse to read the tiny line of text: *No weapons of plus one grade or higher.*

Me: "*Plus one*—what's that?"

Thorde: "Weapons that are a wee bit better than the regular weapons I sell."

Me: "But what does the plus one bit *actually* mean?"

Thorde: "It means I worked one extra hour over what it normally takes for me to make a regular weapon."

The Dwarf walks to a large drape that covers the far side of the forge.

---

[150] *Not literally—unless the Dwarf has really tiny fists.*

[151] *Honestly, I'm <u>not</u> trying to make a joke here—no matter how it looks otherwise.*

He yanks at a dangling rope as a heavy sheet rolls back to reveal rows and rows of weapons, all neatly stacked and clearly marked. I can't help but marvel at the sight as I peer closer to look at the different signs hanging above each row.

Me: "I suppose plus two means two extra hours? While plus three means three extra hours?"

Thorde: "Aye, you got it."

Me: "The signs stop at eight—but in reality, how far could it go up to?"

Thorde: "Eleven."[152]

Me: "Eleven?"

Thorde: "The end of a full working day—beyond that, and the weapon just doesn't pay for itself."

Me: "Where are the plus eleven weapons kept?"

Thorde: "Under lock and key, they're way too valuable to leave out on display. Too tempting a target for a Rogue with sticky fingers[153]— especially those weapons that have had *magic* added to them."

Me: "Magic?"

Thorde: "I don't pretend to understand the arcane ways. The Heroes Guild wanted us to supply magical weapons for their higher-level heroes, so they put us in touch with an old Wizard living in a castle by the sea. We usually leave the weapons at the foot of his abode; I daren't risk carrying such weight up to his front door—those old wooden steps are a fatal accident waiting to happen."[154]

Me: "You leave him to carry all those weapons up on his own? That must be an arduous task for one so frail."

---

[152] *I've subsequently found out every other forge only makes weapons that go up to plus ten. I have to assume that 'The Hammer & Tongs' just wanted to go one number bigger.*

[153] *I've discovered some Rogues like to wear Gelatinous Cube-covered gloves that allow them to steal objects with ease—the only downside to this is that the Gelatinous Cube's ooze eventually burns through the glove, dissolving any exposed fingertips in the process.*

[154] *And don't I know it! I still can't quite believe I escaped that death-trap castle without making an impromptu drop into the ocean.*

Thorde: "He doesn't carry them—he uses his magic to move them."

Me: "How?"

Thorde: "He probably wields one of his wands or a ring—honestly, I don't stick around to find out. Although it's not completely fool proof, he always seems to drop one or two weapons into the sea in the process. It's annoying to lose good quality stock, but it's an acceptable loss considering the profit we make overall..."

Me: "Makes sense—then what happens?"

Thorde: "We wait twenty-four hours. By morning, he returns the magically imbued blades to us in the same spot and collects his fee."

Me: "How does he put his magic inside your weapons?"[155]

Thorde: "I don't know—and I'm not stupid enough to find out either. Magic doesn't sit well with me, but I don't want to let the Heroes Guild down. These magically imbued weapons are reserved for their heroes only—I don't sell them to anyone else."

Me: "I think I may know this Wizard you speak of,[156] is he called Mor—?"

The Forgemaster holds up a hand to stop me mid-sentence.

Thorde: "**Don't** tell me his name—I don't want to know."

Me: "Why not?"

Thorde: "Deniability. If I don't know his name, then I can't be held accountable for any errors in his work."

Me: "Why, is there anything about his work a hero needs to be concerned about?"

Thorde: "I told you already, I don't *trust* magic, and I trust the people *behind* magic even less. The Heroes Guild has reassured me this particular Wizard's magic is the best—although I don't want to risk any comeback upon my forge if that's not the case."

---

[155] I have no idea why that sounds very wrong.

[156] I had already figured out 'who' this was from the description of the death-trap wooden steps earlier.

Me: "Surely you have a responsibility to your customers' lives to ensure those magical weapons are safe to wield?"

Thorde: "Aye, but I can only trust what I can *see*, what I can *feel*—iron, steel, hardened wood. I know the craftsmanship of any weapon simply by picking it up. But magic? I can't see it; I can't feel it—it's just not my area of expertise, and I can't afford to be held responsible for anything that goes wrong due to a wayward spell inside a magical blade.[157] So, all enchanted weapons sold by me are sold without a lifetime guarantee—if anyone has a complaint about it, then I'll happily point them towards the Heroes Guild for answers."

Me: "That's fair enough, but your magical weapons *do* sound a little risky—"

Thorde: "Look, Loremaster, no offence, but adventuring as a *whole* comes with a fair amount of risk involved.[158] Suppose a hero wants to charge into a monster-filled dungeon with a magical sword they've never used before—good luck to them, I say. They're all big enough and ugly enough to understand the dangers associated with that. What happens next is not my concern."

I nod, but deep down, I have to disagree with the Forgemaster's mercenary ethos.

Thorde: "Now, if you don't mind, I have a busy schedule to keep. Today, we're adding a new weapon to the mechanical production line—Holy swords!"

Me: "Holy swords—I assume for Paladins?"

Thorde: "No—Clerics."

Me: "Clerics? I thought they were only allowed to use blunt weapons—like maces and warhammers?"[159]

Thorde: "*Pfft!* You really need to keep up with the times. Clerics relaxed their weapon laws last summer. Since the temples agreed to expand the weapon list to include 'slashing' weapons, I've been inundated with

---

[157] *I wager my whole inheritance this 'wayward' spell includes the words 'fire' and 'ball'...*

[158] *The sweaty Dwarf has a valid point here.*

[159] *Or shields—that Clerics are often known to hide behind.*

Clerics wanting Holy swords instead of boring old maces to wield. It seems they've *really* taken to the idea[160]—I guess that's what happens when you've been denied something you've wanted to do for *so* long."[161]

Me: "How do you make the swords 'Holy'—it sounds complicated?"

Thorde: "Well, first, I'm going to have to break one of my health and safety rules."

The Forgemaster places his finger on the blade of a sword and grabs his ancient cross peen hammer.

Me: "What are you doing?"

Thorde: "Swear words contain great power—I just need to say one each time I make a sword."

Me: "You put a *swear* word into a sword?"

Thorde: "Aye."

Me: "How many have you got to make?"

Thorde: "Twenty or thirty blades a week."

Me: "A *week?*"[162]

Thorde: "The things I have to do in the name of profit."

The Forgemaster winks at me as he lines up the hammer with his finger.

Thorde: "You may want to look away for this bit..."

I can't bring myself to watch as the hammer begins to fall—but I still hear the sickly blow land and bellowed cuss that follows.

'THUNK!'

---

[160] *I have long suspected that inside every Cleric is a repressed Barbarian waiting to unleash their inner fury. Religion has a lot to answer for.*

[161] *Like stabbing Barbarians...*

[162] *I know a certain Paladin who would probably fill that quota in a single breath...*

Thorde: *"**HOLY SHI—!!**"*[163]

---

[163] *I shall never look upon a Holy weapon the same way ever again.*

7. Balstaff, the Merchant

Often cut off by severe snowstorms that block the only passage south, Port Salvation, and the locals who live there, have learned to cope with the cold, harsh conditions by becoming a close-knit community.[164] I've come to meet one of these hardy residents, Balstaff, a Merchant who peddles a rather unusual commodity from his frost-battered store.

Entering *'Ye Olde Hero Shoppe'*, a small bell rings out, publicising my arrival as I stamp my feet to shift the ice from my boots. Waiting patiently for the Merchant to appear, I can't miss the trove of colourful heroic trinkets, posters, and souvenir swords on display.

Balstaff: "Hello? Can I help you?"

Me: *"Balstaff?"*

Balstaff: "Yes? *Oh*—you must be Elburn…"

The Merchant welcomes me with the warmest of embraces.[165]

Balstaff: "What do you think of my shop?"

I stand back to admire the wall of banners, flags and drawings, all created in honour of the many heroes found across the realm. There's something oddly nostalgic about the shelves and wall space crammed with heroic memorabilia—a poignant reminder of home and my absent brother.[166]

Me: "It's a little different to what I was expecting, if I'm honest—I think I imagined a lot less… stuff. Can I ask, how did all this begin?"

---

[164] *Meaning the locals frequently huddle together to knit warm clothes on bitterly cold evenings.*

[165] *Given how cold I am, I'm tempted to embrace Balstaff a little longer than what's acceptable.*

[166] *In his youth, my brother had a large drawing on his wall of a scantily clad Barbarian fighting a fierce Dragon—the giant flying lizard probably burnt the angry-Warrior's clothes or something equally foul.*

The Merchant laughs and pours us both a hot cup of tea.[167]

Balstaff: "I fell into it by accident. I had actually planned on opening a clothes shop, selling heavy furs, winter boots, and warm knitwear—but, as I found out, what Port Salvation doesn't need is yet *another* Merchant selling weather-appropriate attire."[168]

Me: "How did you fall into this exactly?"

Balstaff: "*Quite literally!* Dejected with my prospects, I had taken it upon myself to trek along the Western Peninsular to clear my mind when I fell through the ice into a deep cavern. When I woke, I found I had badly injured both ankles in the fall—I thought I was done for."

Me: "That's terrible! What did you do?"

Balstaff: "To begin with, I just laid there and tried to keep warm. I knew the locals would eventually notice I was missing. I just hoped someone would come to my rescue before I froze to death—or worse."

Me: "What's worse than freezing to death?"

Balstaff: "Being eaten alive by hungry Snow Wolves."

Me: "Okay, that *is* worse. The fact you're talking to me today, I have to assume someone found you."

Balstaff: "I was near-death when a figure emerged out of the gloom—at first, I thought it was my father's spirit, appearing to escort me to the *Great Beyond*.[169] But then I realised it couldn't be my father because the figure was way too short, had a giant red beard—and like my father, was very much alive."

Me: "So, who was it then?"

Balstaff: "A Dwarf."

---

[167] *For once, I'm going to throw caution to the wind and drink this steaming hot beverage as quickly as possible!*

[168] *Whenever a specialty shop opens its doors, three more specialty shops are guaranteed to spring up selling the exact same wares. Why this happens is a complete mystery—even the Merchants involved are as baffled by this strange phenomenon as anyone.*

[169] *More on the afterlife a little later—I'm not quite sure I'm ready to go there right now (figuratively speaking).*

Me: "Did you recognise him?"

Balstaff: "*Her*[170]—she was a Cleric who had heard my cries and come to my rescue."

Me: "Wow, that *was* lucky—what are the chances of that?"

Balstaff: "The Gods certainly smiled down at me that day—I can tell you! I was almost frozen to the core; thankfully, the Dwarf realised I didn't have long and immediately set about creating a *Sanctuary* before the cold could finish me off for good."

Me: "A Sanctuary—what's that?"

Balstaff: "It's a little difficult to explain unless you see it for yourself. A Sanctuary is a place a Cleric can create using the magic from their Deity—it's a warm space that protects those within from the dangers outside. That Cleric saved my life more than once that day."

Me: "What do you mean?"

Balstaff: "Not only did she keep the cold at bay, but she also single-handedly defeated a pack of hungry Snow Wolves who had been drawn by the smell of blood—I owe that Dwarf *everything*."

Me: "That must have been quite something to witness."

Balstaff: "She wielded her warhammer like a crazed Barbarian[171]—slaying Snow Wolves left and right. When the beasts were all dead, she skinned their fur and made a warm blanket for us both to share."

Me: "How long were you stranded in the cavern?"

Balstaff: "For nearly three days we were alone together—the Sanctuary gave out on the evening of the last day. As the temperature plummeted, we had to strip naked and press our bare bodies together to survive. I never realised Dwarves were *so* hairy—yet *so* soft and comforting. This

---

[170] *Female Dwarves can grow beards as equally impressive as male Dwarves. The greatest Dwarven beard ever recorded belonged to Hildar Hammerstone, a rebellious princess who would dress in white robes and twist her beard hair into two giant 'chin' buns before chastising a nearby Dwarven Guard for being too short.*

[171] *A Barbarian, who has been waiting too long for their sword to be forged by a Dwarven Forgemaster, so picked up the nearest warhammer to swing around instead.*

far north, we have a saying, *'if you can't find the heart of a warm woman, then find a warm woman'*[172]—in that ice cavern, I found mine."

The Merchant looks wistfully away into the distance, lost in the moment of a cherished memory.

Balstaff: "On the morning of the fourth day, the storm had subsided enough to attempt the journey back to Port Salvation."

Me: "But your ankles—?"

Balstaff: "They had been healed thanks to Cleric's potent magic."

Me: "I see. Did the Dwarf return with you all the way to Port Salvation?"

The Merchant looks crestfallen.

Balstaff: "No, we were within sight of Port Salvation's frozen wharf when she stopped and turned back."

Me: "Why did she do that?"

Balstaff: "She didn't say—I got the feeling she was trying to run away from something."

Me: "What was she running away from?"

Balstaff: "I know this sounds strange—but I think she was running away from herself."

Me: "Herself?"

Balstaff: "Maybe it was the way she avoided talking about her past—now I come to think about it, she never spoke about anyone at all during our cold nights together..."

Me: "What was this Dwarf's name?"

Balstaff: "Gilva Flamebeard."

---

[172] *The female half of Port Salvation has a slightly darker saying: 'if your idiot ends up frozen in the snow dunes, get yourself another idiot.'*

Me: "*The* Gilva Flamebeard—the *same* Gilva Flamebeard who faced the Midnight Army of Lord Zolar and sent them crawling back into the abyss?"[173]

Balstaff: "Yes—unless there's another Gilva Flamebeard I don't know about."[174]

Me: "But she disappeared from the adventuring scene many summers ago—did she ever say why?"

Balstaff: "I did try to ask her just as she turned to depart."

Me: "How did Gilva reply?"

Balstaff: "She simply smiled and beckoned me to kneel before her."

Me: *"Kneel?"*

Balstaff: "To place the gentlest of kisses upon my brow. I wept as I bowed my head and thanked her from the bottom of my heart."

Me: "What else did she say?"

Balstaff: "Nothing—when I finally looked up, she had already disappeared back into the swirling blizzard."

Me: "What a tale to tell! What happened when you finally reached town?"

Balstaff: "There was relief from the locals, of course—everyone had assumed the worst. A few had even started to earmark some of my combustible possessions for firewood."

Me: "That sounds a little extreme."

Balstaff: "It's a Port Salvation tradition—heat is the main currency in these parts.[175] I would have done the same if the circumstances were different."

---

[173] *Given Gliva's height, I can only assume she dealt a lot of leg damage, explaining the 'crawling' part.*

[174] *Unlikely—although Wizards are known to cast duplication spells for kicks and giggles...*

[175] *Wizards would make a <u>fortune</u> in Port Salvation.*

Me: "Did you tell them about Gilva?"

Balstaff: "I told them *everything!*"

Me: "Did they believe you?"

Balstaff: "The legendary Gilva Flamebeard *here? In Port Salvation?* Not to mention being saved by her? *No*—they laughed at me and said I was suffering from snow-madness. The more I tried to persuade them it was the truth—the more they mocked me. In the end, I stopped trying."

I can see how much hurt the Merchant carries behind his eyes.

Me: "You survived—that's all Gilva wanted from you."

Balstaff: "It's not enough; she deserved better than that. Gilva saved my life and won my heart in the process—I needed to do something to acknowledge that, *even* if it was only to myself."

Me: "Like what?"

The Merchant opens his arms wide and gestures to the shop interior.

Balstaff; "I opened *'Ye Olde Hero Shoppe'*—a shop that would honour our heroes. Heroes like Gilva Flamebeard."

Me: "How did you afford such a place?"

Balstaff: "It wasn't easy—I had to sell my home and my parents' home first."

Me: "I bet they were pleased."

Balstaff: "*Delighted.* Especially as the first they knew about it was when the new owners showed up to use the bed they were sleeping in at the time."[176]

Me: "I suppose you're not on speaking terms with your parents anymore?"

Balstaff: "Not at the start, but when the profits began to roll in, I bought them a beautiful retirement watermill just a mile south of Tronte as a way of an apology."

---

[176] *That could have been awkward...*

Me: "Did it work?"

Balstaff: "Not really—they're *still* angry with me, but at least they are furious in a place where they can get some uninterrupted sleep."

Me: "Parents can be awkward like that."[177]

Balstaff: "I guess it's every parent's right to be disappointed with their children."[178]

I nod in sympathy, knowing deep down how painful that feeling is.

Me: "So, now you sell figurines of heroes as souvenirs…"

The Merchant pulls out a Gilva Flamebeard figurine and carefully strokes her beard as he stares deep into the toy's eyes.

Balstaff: "I wanted to do something for Gilva—to hold a little piece of her, even if it is only one-eighteenth of her actual size."[179]

Me: "How did the locals in Port Salvation take to your idea?"

Balstaff: "Surprisingly, they embraced it; I think deep down they appreciate the thankless task heroes have[180]—even heroes like Gilva Flamebeard. Since opening, I've seen a steady stream of trade flow through my door."

I pick up one of the figurines and look for a maker's mark.

Me: "Who creates these?"

Balstaff: "I signed a five-summer deal with the Gnomes out east; they produce all the figurines I design to the highest of standards *and* for a competitive price too—check this one out."

---

[177] *Especially when they've just been woken by a Half-Orc family standing at the foot of their bed.*

[178] *For the record, this can go both ways.*

[179] *I'm not going to work out if the Merchant's maths is correct; otherwise, I might discover that Gilva is really a nine-foot-tall Dwarven Giant!!*

[180] *Either that or they're just relieved 'another' cold-weather clothes Merchant didn't set up shop in town.*

The Merchant hands me a 'Gilva' figurine; it's meticulously detailed with an interchangeable beard and detachable warhammer.

Balstaff: "I've had six different versions of her made in case the Dwarven Cleric does something unexpected with her facial hair."

I cock my head at Balstaff.

Me: "*Six* versions... of the *same* Dwarf?"

Balstaff: "There's *Rescuer Gilva, Sanctuary Gilva, Snow-Wolf Slayer Gilva, Brow-Kiss Gilva,* and *Warm Bedroll Gilva.* The one you're holding is *Hairy Gilva*—"

Me: "*Hairy Gilva?*"

Balstaff: "If you take her clothes off, you'll find a silky-smooth hairy layer underneath. I've *even* tried to replicate her peaty aroma as close as possible—why don't you give her a sniff?"[181]

Me: "I'll take your word for it."

I hand the figurine back to the Merchant, who tweaks her chin whiskers before carefully placing the figurine underneath the counter.

Me: "What other heroes do you have?"

Balstaff: "I hoped you'd ask me that—take a look at *this* one!"

The Merchant unlocks a heavy cabinet and carefully takes out another figurine that even a non-collector like me would admit to being in awe with. This impression is due not so much to the detail of the toy (which is admittedly elaborate, even down to a removable eye-patch) but the sheer power and presence captured within its miniature form. Yet even though the figurine appears to hold a frozen, *happy* expression,[182] something about its grimacing smile still makes me feel uneasy.[183]

---

[181] *Somehow, I'm pretty confident the 'real' Gilva Flamebeard would disapprove of me doing that.*

[182] *The sort of fixed 'happy' elation a homicidal axe-wielding maniac has during a blood rage.*

[183] *The figurine looks like it has stepped in something rather unpleasant or is imagining what it is like to choke the life out of me while I sleep.*

Balstaff: "This is the *Limited Edition Laughing Arin Darkblade* figurine, perhaps my most prized figurine in existence."

Me: "*Arin* Darkblade..."

Balstaff: "You recognise the name?"

Me: "Of course. But I would imagine a hero of his standing has inspired innumerable imitations of his likeness—what makes this one so valuable?"

Balstaff: "Why, because he's laughing, of course!"

Me: "I suppose that does run rather contrary to his humourless reputation."

Balstaff: "True, Arin isn't exactly the cheeriest of heroes. It's even rumoured he's only ever laughed *once* in his whole life."

Me: "I wonder what monumental event amused him so?"

Balstaff: "No doubt something to do with a Wizard and a misplaced Fireball spell.[184] Those Spellcasters always make me laugh with their absentminded bumbling and haphazard ways."

As the Merchant chuckles at what seems to be the thought of a calamitous Wizard setting fire to themselves—I remain unusually silent.

Balstaff: "Well, whatever it was, I decided to commission this figurine in his honour as a one-off."

Me: "Why only a one-off?"

Balstaff: "Making more would risk incurring the wrath of the Heralds Guild and their Arcane Copyright magic... or worse, Arin Darkblade *himself*."

Me: "Does the Heroes Guild ever give you any trouble?"

Balstaff: "Not at all—the Heroes Guild are more than welcome to browse my wares, just *not* this particular piece. That's why I keep it

---

[184] *I'm glad the Merchant finds this funny—I'm not sure anyone else in a ten-foot radius would be as amused.*

under lock and key and hidden well out of sight."

Me: "How have you found the Heroes Guild?"

Balstaff: "A little mercenary—but isn't everyone?"[185]

Me: "Mercenary? With their approach to quests and heroes?"

Balstaff: "No—*no,* just in business. The Heroes Guild expects all Merchants to give their members a sizable discount on any sold wares."

Me: "How sizeable *is* the discount?"

Balstaff: "A full third off the advertised price—in exchange, the Heroes Guild helps spread the word throughout the rest of the realm of any establishments who look favourably upon its members. It's a pretty good deal—their numbers and reach are considerable."

Me: "Out of curiosity, how much is the *Limited Edition Laughing Arin Darkblade* figurine?"

Balstaff: "One thousand gold coins."

I stagger backwards.

Me: "One *thousand* gold coins?!"

Balstaff: "I told you—it's one of a kind."

Me: "Who would ever want a figurine that costs one *thousand* gold coins?"

Balstaff: "There are plenty of die-hard hero fans out there who are willing to pay *twice* that if they could."

Me: "I don't understand the obsession? What are they getting—in reality? It's just a representation of their hero—"

Balstaff: "*Ah,* but for some, it's not just about owning a representation of their favourite hero—there's a huge secondary market of collectors out there, all buying and selling the rarest of my figurines between one another."

---

[185] *Especially Dwarves...*

Me: "Really—I wouldn't have thought there would be much interest in second-hand goods?"

Balstaff: "You *must* be joking; there are some collectors who'd happily pay through the nose just so they can send an exhausted Halfling courier halfway up the Deepening Mountain, dragging behind them a chest filled with their prized figurine collection."[186]

Me: "Why would they pay some poor Halfling to go to all that trouble?"

Balstaff: "To freeze the figurines in the Mountain's fabled *Pool of Preservation,*[187] of course."

Me: "That sounds like an awful lot of effort to ruin some perfectly good figurines."

Balstaff: "Submerging them in the pool doesn't ruin the figurines—they encase them in the Pool's magical waters."

Me: "Encase?"

Balstaff: "The water is *so* cold it literally freezes anything dropped into it—including the figurines."

Me: "Why do that?"

Balstaff: "The frozen water protects the figurines from the ravages of time, increasing their value exponentially. You should see some of the prices my figurines fetch *after* they are encased—it would literally turn your hair white in shock."

Me: "Can't you do anything about that?"

Balstaff: "Why should I?"

Me: "Because they're probably making more profit from this than *you!*"

Balstaff: "I need a secondary market to thrive. It creates a huge demand

---

[186] *Half-Time Delivery™ is a company run by a group of dedicated Halflings who claim they'll deliver any package <u>anywhere</u> in the realm in half the time it would take you to do it if you had delivered it yourself—or half your coin back. This deal does not extend to Wizards, Sorcerers, or those with teleportation, flight, or access to a flying mount, disk, carpet, mat, rug, or similar household floor covering—it also doesn't apply to Gnomes.*

[187] *Not to be confused with the Pool of Petrification, which works <u>very</u> differently...*

for some of my limited releases. Sometimes I'm selling out of figurines before I can put them on the shelf—it's almost unbelievable! What happens afterwards isn't my concern; I've made more than enough in the first instance."

Me: "How do you know what heroes to sell next?"

Balstaff: "*Ah*—that's the *real* trick, understanding which adventurer is going to be a future hit."

Me: "How do you find out?"

Balstaff: "I listen to what the 'Barkers' have to say about the hottest heroic exploits—"

Me: "Barkers? *Really?* I heard their information is a little unreliable at the best of times..."[188]

Balstaff: "*Bah,* rubbish—Barkers are a great source for adventuring information. I like to listen to their bellowed messages, scouring for clues in anything I overhear. Once I catch a hero's name who I think is on the up, I immediately put an order in with the Gnomes—I'm seldom wrong."

Me: "So, who, in your opinion, do you think is going to be the next big hero to listen out for?"[189]

The Merchant leans closer and whispers into my ear.

Balstaff: "I've heard nothing but good things about *Born the Fartarian.*[190] Mark my words, that one is *destined* for greatness."

Me: *"Really?"*

Balstaff: "Trust me—he's going be a big noise in the realm!"[191]

---

[188] *Who can ever forget when the under-siege Baron of Grondor famously called for 'aid' and somehow ended up with a digging implement hurriedly being hand-delivered instead?*

[189] *And by 'big', I don't mean a 'heavily encumbered' hero who is so laden with loot they're easily overtaken by a snail who just slithered through a spilt Potion of Slowness.*

[190] *Poor Dorn—those <u>bloody</u> Barkers!*

[191] *Like any true Fartarian!*

Me: "Funny enough, I recently met... *erm... Born*—"

Balstaff: "You *met* him!? What was he like? Is he as legendary as the Barkers would have me believe?"

I cannot bring myself to shatter the Merchant's hopes with my own doubts and fears.

Me: "He <u>is</u>—*and* more..."

The Merchant punches the air in delight.

Balstaff: "I *knew* it! I *must* send word to the Gnomes and increase my initial order of his figurine."

Me: "Is it just successful adventurers you deal in?"

Balstaff: "No—those that continually fail are also in high demand— more often than not for their comedic value, though."

Perhaps there's hope for Dorn's figurine after all.[192] Another thought crosses my mind.

Me: "I don't suppose you have a figurine of Aldon Barr?"

Balstaff: "Who?"

Me: "Aldon Barr—he's my brother. He left home to become an adventurer—I just wondered if you had come across his name?

The Merchant blows the dust from the cover of a large, hefty tome.

Me: "What's that?"

Balstaff: "My *Hero Ledger;* I write the name of every hero and heroine I hear through the Barkers inside this."

After several minutes of thumbing pages, the Merchant stops at one entry and scans the page with his finger; he looks up at me—my heart almost skips a beat.

Balstaff: "*Aldon Barr*—you say?"

_____

[192] **Loremaster Tip #3:** *Barbarians are always funny; just never let them spot you laughing at them unless you want your spleen viciously removed and fed to your horse—which the Barbarian <u>will</u> find highly amusing.*

Me: "Yes…"

Balstaff: "Is that 'Barr' with one 'R' or two?"

Me: "Two…"

Balstaff: "And 'Aldon' is spelt with an 'A'?"

Me: "How else do you spell Aldon?"

My stomach is doing somersaults in nervous anticipation—but the Merchant suddenly slams the tome closed with an ominous *'THUD'*.

Balstaff: "Nope, sorry—I don't have anything on him. Maybe he changed his name? I mean, 'Aldon Barr' doesn't sound much like an adventuring name, does it?"[193]

Me: "You're the second person to say that to me."

Balstaff: "Then there, I'm afraid, is your answer—I'm so sorry."

I had a feeling the Merchant would draw a blank, but the disappointment still cuts deep. I'm keen to move the conversation away from the edge of this pit of despair.

Me: "What about figurines of Evildoers and monsters? Do you sell them?"

Balstaff: "What?"

Me: "Evildoers and monsters—surely you have a range of them to purchase?"

Balstaff: "Why would I sell *them?*"

Me: "Don't you want your customers to recreate their favourite adventures? I'm sure some would like to imagine their heroes fighting a foe?"[194]

The Merchant looks at me in utter disbelief before throwing his arms around me and squeezing with all his might; for a split second, I have a

---

[193] *Given Balstaff's reliance on using 'Barkers', I didn't really hold out much hope here.*

[194] *Rather than pretending the Barbarian is thumping the Cleric—over and over again.*

glimpse into what it must have been like in that ice cavern, our bodies wrapped around one another for warmth.

Balstaff: "By the Gods—that's **inspired!** How did I miss this opportunity!? I will put an order in with the Gnomes immediately for a new range of Evildoers and their minions! This idea is going to make me a fortune! I have to get this down on paper, quick! If you would excuse me..."

The Merchant ushers me towards the exit. As I go to leave, Balstaff puts an object into my hand. I look down with trepidation and stare into the grimacing face of the *Limited Edition Laughing Arin Darkblade* figurine.

Me: "What? What's *this*—?"

Balstaff: "A gift—"

Me: "But I can't accept this—it's worth a *thousand* gold coins!"[195]

Balstaff: "You have probably just made me ten times that today with your idea! I can't let you go without paying you for it. Besides, I can always ask the Gnomes to make another one on the quiet..."

The Merchant gives me a wink as he shuts the door of *Ye Olde Hero Shoppe* behind me before turning the sign over in the window to read 'Closed'. I take a last look at the Arin figurine in my hand; I can't help but find his face slightly disagreeable but compelling at the same time.[196] I shiver and place the miniature-scaled adventurer-cum-pirate carefully in my bag before drawing my tunic tightly around my neck. I dread the idea of being stuck in this inhospitable place without any hope or Sanctuary to keep me safe from the punishing elements. On cue, the cold begins to bite as I head towards the stables, searching for a ride south towards warmer climates.

---

[195] *If I fail to make my fortune as a Loremaster, I can always sell this to keep the proverbial Snow Wolves from the door.*

[196] *I'm convinced the figurine's scowl has deepened since it was handed to me.*

8. Redmane, the Paladin

His plate armour shining in the sunlight, a huge plume of Oric feathers sprouting from the top of his helm[197], Redmane the Paladin cuts an imposing, stoic figure as he stands surveying the horizon from his watchtower. On his hip hangs his ancestral blade, an ornate sword which has slain countless foes. His eyes remain fixed on the Southern Pass leading towards the ShadowLands, scouring the skyline for any approaching evil that would threaten the good people of this land.

I feel humbled in the Paladin's presence, unsure if I should be troubling him with my trivial questions. As I begin to summon the courage to speak, the Paladin breaks the enduring silence for the both of us.

Redmane: "Tell me, *Loremaster,* do you know *why* I stand here—at this watchtower?"

Me: "Keeping an eye out for bandits and marauders?"

Redmane: "Do you think I would stand to watch for petty thieves and criminals?"

Me: "Erm—*Dragons?*"

The Holy Warrior snorts with derision.

Redmane: "I stand here because it is my sworn duty to do so. I am a protector of the weak and helpless—*this* is what it means to be a Paladin."

Me: "Who would you consider weak and helpless?"

The Paladin growls as he keeps his eyes fixed firmly on the horizon.

Redmane: "People like *you.*"

Me: "*Me?* I'm not weak—I admit I'm not much of a Fighter, but I'm not completely helpless!"[198]

---

[197] *Orics are flightless birds that are flightless because they have had all their feathers stolen from them to make Paladin helms. Needless to say, most Orics are pretty annoyed by this, especially as they've had to resort to walking everywhere.*

[198] *I like to think I'm about as handy with a sword as any Cleric or Wizard—just don't expect me to charge headfirst into a monster-filled dungeon anytime soon (much like the aforementioned Cleric or Wizard).*

The Holy Warrior turns to briefly regard me before returning his gaze to patrol the distance.

Redmane: "Trust me—*you* are."

I quickly check my immediate surroundings—satisfied I'm safe, I turn back to the Paladin.

Me: "I'm pretty sure I'm not in any danger at the moment."[199]

The Holy Warrior sneers at me.

Redmane: "Your type will *always* be in danger."

We stand in silence for a moment.

Me: "What about adventuring?"

Redmane: "What about it?"

Me: "Don't you ever go on adventures? I thought that's what Paladins were supposed to do? Go searching for trouble and 'smiting' it—rather than waiting around all day for it to show up first?"

Redmane: "Are you suggesting I'm lazy?"

Me: "N—No, but there has to be more to life than standing in one spot all day?"

Redmane: "I gave up on adventuring a long time ago."

Me: "Gave up? Why?"

The Paladin sighs heavily.

Redmane: "The need for heroes has dwindled as of late. It appears we are no longer in demand."

Me: "How can that be?"

Redmane: "Too many heroes—not enough quests."

Me: "The competition must be tough."

---

[199] *For starters, nobody appears to be forcing me to drink an overly hot cup of tea...*

Redmane: "*More than you realise.* I was once a popular figure on adventures—when I walked into any town, the locals would throw roses before my feet, and maidens would kiss my cheek and weep in thanks at my arrival. Nowadays, I'm lucky if I can walk anywhere without having a bucket of slop thrown in my direction or being spat at by a bitter old hag."

Me: "Why is that? Surely Paladins are the most respected out of all the hero types?"[200]

Redmane: "Not anymore.[201] Sadly, the Paladins of today are not forged from the same steel I came from; they are poor imitations of what we used to be. Honour and sacrifice mean nothing to them. They aren't Holy, they aren't chivalrous, they never fight for good—only for coin."

Me: "Where have they come from—these Paladin pretenders?"

Redmane: "I do not know—all I do know is the realm is filled with these *'pretenders'* as you call them. Their actions tarnish the hard-earned reputation of true Paladins everywhere. I fear for our Order. These fools don't just damage us—they damage those we are trying to protect."

Me: "I sense this wound cuts deep."

Redmane: "*More than you realise.* How would you feel if you trained for countless summers with a sword, sat through endless sermons about righteousness, endured the trial of vices, stood motionlessly staring for months on end from the top of a watchtower, only for an *'unofficial'* Paladin to come along and get all the plaudits?"

Me: "I find it a miracle you're not screaming with rage right now."[202]

---

[200] *As heralded in a recent article, 'Paladins & Pedestals', which appeared in the 'Paladin Times' (a bi-monthly journal put together by Paladins, for Paladins).*

[201] *Strangely, in another survey run by 'Barbarian Weekly' (a bi-monthly journal put together by Barbarians, for Barbarians), Paladins came in second-to-last, just above Clerics. As to why Clerics came bottom of this list is anyone's guess. Even Necromancers ranked higher—and they 'literally' steal dead bodies to bring them back to life. Even more peculiar was how 'Barbarians' topped the poll, leading some to question the validity of the entire survey. Some even went as far as to claim the results had been skewed by a legion of scantily clad, muscle-bound readers and the publication's large-print format.*

[202] *I know one short-tempered adventuring type that would be if this had happened to them—and I don't mean Monks.*

The Holy Warrior looks at me again for the briefest of moments.

Redmane: "That is because I am trained to keep my emotions in check."

Me: "What would I need if I were to become a Paladin—hypothetically speaking?"

Redmane: "To answer your highly-hypothetical question: *Stoicism, Sacrifice* and *Selflessness;* we call them the four S's."

Me: "I only count three—what's the fourth 'S'?"

The Paladin glares at me as if I'm asking a trick question. I glance at the Holy Warrior's pauldron symbols, where four interlocking S's form to make an ornate geometric symbol of his Order. It's clear the Paladin isn't going to dignify my question with an answer—feeling foolish, I decide to change the subject.

Me: "I get the impression you're struggling to find your place in today's realm."

Redmane: "*More than you realise.* I have become a stranger in this land. It matters not if I have saved its people countless times. I am more alone than I have ever been—and that's coming from someone who grew up in near solitude."

Me: "What about those you adventured with? Your comrades in arms?"

Redmane: "What about them?"

Me: "Do you not count them as friends?"

Redmane: "No hero worth their salt should *ever* make friends out of comrades—it's the fastest way to the grave."

Me: "I don't understand."

Redmane: "Friends have a habit of putting themselves in harm's way—yet it is always the Paladin who must put their life on the line to save them."

Me: "Forgive me, but isn't that one of your four 'S's—*Sacrifice?*"

The Paladin glares at me once again, accompanied by an alarmingly large nostril flare.

Redmane: "Sacrifices should *only* be offered—*never* demanded.[203] I have distanced myself from those who enjoy dancing with death on a daily basis."

Me: "I guess that includes Battle Dancers and Rogues."

Redmane: "A Paladin would *never* make friends with a Rogue."

Me: "But you must have adventured with a few Rogues in your time?"

Redmane: "Of course—they have their purpose, just like Barbarians and Wizards. It doesn't mean I'm suddenly going to welcome them with open arms…"

Me: "What was it like working with those of ill repute?"

Redmane: "Difficult; I could never turn my back for a second. Sleeping in camp was practically impossible—I would just sit and stare at them until dawn."[204]

Me: "That sounds exhausting."

Redmane: "Stoicism is another trait we Paladins excel in."

Me: "And another one of your four 'S's—if I'm not mistaken?"

Redmane: "Indeed…"

Me: "Did you ever try talking to any of the Rogues when you were adventuring together? Perhaps if you got to know a few, you wouldn't see them as a threat."

Redmane: "There were some occasions where we shared a few choice words. I would, of course, choose my words carefully and considerately."

Me: "And the Rogue in question?"

---

[203] *Tell that to the Watunabe Tribe Elders, who frequently demand a ritual sacrifice from their people—although, as nobody has actually <u>ever</u> stepped forward to offer themselves up to be sacrificed, the Watunabe Tribe Elders are in a perpetual state of disappointment along with their unsatisfied Gods and exceedingly unhappy volcano.*

[204] *I imagine that would have made it remarkably difficult for those being stared at to sleep soundly too.*

Redmane: "Less so, it was not uncommon to hear a profanity or two uttered from their devious lips."

Me: "So, general small-talk did not go well between you?"

Redmane: "Not well at all. More often than not, I would discover they had daubed a rude word on the back of my armour[205]—how, I do not know, as I never took my eyes off them for a moment, not even to blink."[206]

Me: "What did the rude word say?"

Redmane: "I shall never repeat it—to do so would be unbecoming of a Paladin."

Me: "I take it you don't swear at all—*ever?*"

Redmane: "Never."

Me: "What if you hit your finger with a hammer?"[207]

Redmane: "I would not be so foolish as to do that."

Me: "But say you did—wouldn't the anger take hold of you in your moment of pain? What if nobody was around? Don't you even swear to yourself—under your breath?"

Redmane: "No—my Deity forbids it—for they hear all."[208]

Me: "Isn't religion about forgiveness? Surely your Deity is the forgiving type? Especially in a moment of weakness."

---

[205] *I have to take my hat off (if I owned one) to the Rogue who had the sheer audacity to deface Redmane's armour while the Holy Warrior was still wearing it.*

[206] *Although I'm pretty sure the Paladin's back was turned whenever he used the privy. But how a mischievous Rogue managed to daub a rude word on the Holy Warrior's back whilst he was otherwise engaged will forever remain a mystery.*

[207] *Thinking back on it, unless the Paladin was spending time learning how to forge his own Holy sword—I doubt something like this would ever happen in reality.*

[208] *I sincerely hope not, as I've said a few things in my time that no Deity should ever hear— thank the Gods I don't believe in them!*

Redmane: "My Deity only cares about two things—*smiting* and *redemption.*"[209]

Me: "Okay, but what about temptation or vices? Surely nobody can be *that* pure of heart?"

Redmane: "Nobody but a Paladin."

Me: "To go through life without any vice must be incredibly sad."

Redmane: "Do not pity me, Loremaster—I was taught the evil of temptation from an early age and how to focus the mind on the horizon whenever it rears its ugly head."

Me: "I notice you stare at the horizon a lot."

Redmane: "Indeed I do."

There's another awkward pause as we both stare off into the distance.

Me: "What would you do if a Merchant gave you too much change from a purchase you had just made?"

Redmane: "I would notify them of the error and return the extra coin forthwith."

Me: "What about finding a gold coin on the floor in a tavern."

Redmane: "I would donate it to the local temple."

Me: "But that coin belonged to someone else—why should the temple get it?"

Redmane: "The temple would do good with the donation—a tavern's patron will only spend it frivolously away without a moment's thought on alcohol."

Me: "What about temptations of the flesh?"

Redmane: "Paladins are celibate."

---

[209] *Basically, this boils down to 'hitting things' and then feeling so bad about it you're compelled to make amends somehow—call me cynical, but I don't think these should be the two moral pillars to build a religion on.*

Me: "Really? *All* Paladins are celibate?"[210]

Redmane: "Yes—*ALL* Paladins. Desire is a weakness of the weak."[211]

Me: "Is there anything you do that's fun? Because as far as I can see, being a Paladin means you don't get to enjoy life as much as others."[212]

Redmane: "Silence."

A stillness falls over me—the silence drags deeper until falling into an uncomfortable vacuum of nothingness.

Redmane: "W—What are you doing?"

Me: "You said—"

Redmane: "I said *silence* as in, I *enjoy* the silence—not *keep* silent."

Me: "*Oh*, my mistake! So, you enjoy 'silence'—is there anything else you like to do?"

Redmane: "Yes—standing stoically in silence."

Me: "Isn't that just silence again, but this time standing up?"

Redmane: "No—it is different."

Me: "Besides silence and standing stoically—is there anything else?"

The Paladin thinks for a moment; he turns from his horizon-obsessive stare and furrows his brow—deep in thought. After a few minutes, he speaks again.

Redmane: "No. That is it."

---

[210] *Something about this bothers me—however, I can't quite put my finger on why. It'll come to me in a minute...*

[211] *I'm unfamiliar with the temptations of the flesh—the closest I've been is when I've swiped an extra sausage off the family table before everyone had a chance to sit down to eat.*

[212] *By others, I mean Barbarians—who, when they aren't hitting things, are usually laughing at the things they've recently hit.*

Me: "I guess while you're standing here, stoically and in silence—this must be peak excitement for you?"[213]

Redmane: "This is as close to nirvana as one can get…"

Me: "So, why *this* particular watchtower, when there are numerous watchtowers up and down the border?"

Redmane: "This was my father's watchtower, and my father's, father's watchtower before that—it is my honour to follow in their footsteps[214] and take my rightful place here."

Me: "Were they both Paladins?"

Redmane: "Yes."

Me: "I assume they both followed the Paladin code?"[215]

Redmane: "What sort of question is that? Of course, they did—they carried out their duties to the letter. I intend to do the same until I earn the right to take my place in *The Heroes Hall of Legends*."

Me: "The place for old and vulnerable adventurers?"[216]

Redmane: "Yes—it's where all the great heroes go when they eventually retire from day-to-day adventuring. My grandfather spent his last summers there until he passed to the *Great Beyond*."[217]

Me: "I assume that's where your father will go when it's his time to hang up his blade?"

Redmane: "No—my father died on a quest; it has been nearly ten summers since his passing."

Me: "I'm so sorry for your loss—may I ask what happened?"

---

[213] Or there would be silence if I weren't here, of course…

[214] Stoic footsteps, of which there would have been very few…

[215] I can feel it on the tip of my tongue—what is it about this line of question that vexes me so?

[216] I suppose this could mean Wizards and Clerics of any age.

[217] Not to be confused with the 'Great Behind', which is where everyone believes Elves go when they 'die'.

Redmane: "I still do not know the full truth of the matter. There was a rumour he fell to a Wizard's spell that went awry,[218] but I have no proof of that. I asked the Heroes Guild, but they could not help me."

Me: "I'm surprised they could not give you the answers you sought—I understand their influence is significant."

Redmane: "All I know is, my father had made an *arrangement* with the Heroes Guild, an *arrangement* that ultimately cost him his life."

Me: "Do you blame the Heroes Guild for his death?"

Redmane: "No, I do not. My father trusted the Guild's leaders when they said they shared his desire to bring stability and security to our Order's future; he believed that in time, only officially recognised Paladins would be allowed to call themselves Paladins."

Me: "But that never happened—why?"

Redmane: "His dream died with him on his first quest as part of the Heroes Guild."

Me: "That must have been a huge blow to you and your Order..."

Redmane: "*More than you realise*—but that's not the worst part; the worst part is I don't even know *where* my father's body is buried. Can you imagine not being able to visit his final resting place to say goodbye properly?"

There's another awkward silence—this time from me. I know I shouldn't say what I'm about to say, but there has been something the brooding Paladin has said which has left me confused.[219]

Me: "If your grandfather and father were both Paladins—and they both followed the Order's code to the letter... how was it your father was *born*... or even *you* in that matter?"

The Paladin stares at me as if I had just landed an unexpected mortal blow. The colour drains from his face as he struggles to find a suitable answer that sits well within him.

---

[218] *No prizes for guessing what particular spell went 'awry'...*

[219] *A Wizard's Light spell has just illuminated the darkest corner of my mind...*

Redmane: "Well, I... *er*... they must have... *ahem*... well, it's difficult to say *exactly*... no... I—I..."

Me: "I mean, we both know *how* babies are made—"[220]

Redmane: "Yes—of *course!* I—I'm not an idiot!"

Me: "Which means somewhere along the way, there must have been someone *who*—"

The Paladin takes his helmet off; his hair is as red as his name suggests; he runs his fingers through it nervously as he licks his dry lips.

Me: "Are you still in touch with your mother?"

Redmane: "*Mother?* I—I never *had* a mother—"

Me: "You must have had a mother at *some* point—even if she was only there for the birth?"

The Paladin shakes his head—trying to work out this thick paradoxical conundrum now swirling in the air.

Redmane: "Those *lying shi*—"[221]

Me: "Wait! You just <u>swore!</u>"

The moment the profanity leaves his lips—the Paladin's hand goes to cover his mouth as he stares at me in horror. He slowly withdraws his fingers and unleashes another forbidden word in my general direction.

Redmane: "*FU—!*"[222]

---

[220] *Although in this realm, 'babies' can be made in various 'unique' ways, including 'Wish' spells and pacts with Demonic entities. However, like any birth from a mystical source, the innocent and loveable summers swiftly pass and are soon replaced by the difficult 'rebellious' ones. Gone is that loveable bundle of joy—in its place is a stroppy adolescent who stomps moodily around their bedroom, claiming dominion over everything while simultaneously eating all the food in the pantry.*

[221] *Just in case any of my younger readers are reading this, I shall endeavour to shield some of the profanity from your eyes—lest your parents send word of their 'wrath' via a local Barker (who would probably change the final word to 'bath' anyway, leaving everyone involved very confused but considerably cleaner in body, if not in spirit).*

[222] *Wow, that was a BIG one! Fortunately, I'm on hand with my quill to spare you from your blushes.*

The Paladin's eyes widen in shock as the swear word floodgates suddenly burst.

Redmane: "*FU—! FU—! FU—! FU—! FU—!*"[223]

Me: "You're *still* swearing!"

Redmane: "*PISS OFF!*"[224]

Me: "You look like you're enjoying it too—"

Redmane: "*FU— YOU, LOREMASTER!*"[225]

The Paladin storms down the steps of the watchtower—leaving me to call out after him.

Me: **"Where are you going? Aren't you supposed to be watching out for evil?"**[226]

The Paladin doesn't even look back to reply.

Redmane: ***"FU— THAT! I'M OFF TO THE NEAREST BAR WITH THE PRETTIEST BARMAID!"***[227]

I shout back one last time to the rapidly retreating Holy Warrior.

Me: **"I didn't know Paladins liked to drink?"**

Redmane: ***"MORE THAN YOU 'FU—KING' REALISE!"***[228]

---

[223] *I now like to think of myself as the quickest quill this side of the Dauntless Sea!*

[224] *That one is a bit tamer—you're safe to try that one out on your parents.*

[225] *I fear I may have unleashed a 'profanity' monster. My mother would be so disappointed in me; Uncle Bevan Barr, on the other hand...*

[226] *I don't really have a clue what 'evil' Redmane was keeping an eye out for—so, it's probably best I don't stand here for too long in case it makes an appearance.*

[227] *What is it with Paladins and Barmaids—it's almost as if they're somehow inexplicably drawn to one another?*

[228] *Oops—my apologies, that one almost got through!*

I watch as Redmane the Paladin disappears into the distance, leaving me alone at the watchtower[229] to take over his vigil, albeit temporarily—I last a full five minutes before feeling a little vulnerable, and choosing to hastily follow the departed Paladin's (less than stoic) footsteps.

---

[229] *It's worth noting that Baron Dumpfh once gained power by convincing an entire kingdom that he would build an impassable wall to keep the bandits and marauders of the ShadowLands from crossing the border into their realm. Sadly, Dumpfh was a bit of a narcissist who bankrupted his kingdom and was kicked into the very exile he sought so hard to contain. Consequently, all of Dumpfh's lavish properties were taken down brick by brick and used to construct the numerous watchtowers now dotted along the border. The last anyone saw of Baron Dumpfh, he was living in a cave and still insisting his right to rule was illegally 'stolen' from him.*

9. Bergenn, the Ranger

Greenvale Forest has become a feared place; the once idyllic woodland is now home to Goblins from the Halgorn Crags, who lay in wait to ambush travellers heading along the only direct road to the city of Heartenford. The alternative to the Goblin-infested route is a three-day hike around the woodland domain via the Merchant's Road—but that journey is also plagued with danger, mainly from the Heartenford Guards who patrol it. These 'Guards' are nothing more than bandits with uniforms who expect a small donation from passing Merchants to ensure nothing of value mysteriously 'disappears' from their wagons en route. But recently, one hero, Bergenn the Ranger, has made it her quest to deal with the Goblin threat once and for all by driving the evil menace out of Greenvale Forest. I've agreed to meet Bergenn at a prearranged spot to talk about her life as a Woodland Warrior.

I'm waiting patiently by a small bush at a crossroads where the northern path to Heartenford meets the Merchant's Road before disappearing into the depths of the Greenvale Forest. The agreed time of our rendezvous has come and passed with little sign of the Elven Ranger. Fifteen minutes later, and I'm beginning to wonder if I should give up on this interview before an opportunistic Goblin starts taking pot shots at me,[230] when the nearby bush starts talking.[231]

Bush: "You must be the Loremaster—*Elburn?*"

Me: "*Erm... yes? Hello?*"

Bush: "Forgive the subterfuge; it *always* pays to be careful in my experience."

Me: "Bergenn? Is *that* you?"

Bergenn: "Indeed it is—well met!"

Me: "*Ah... yes... it's a pleasure to meet you too—if I could actually *see* you, that is.*"

---

[230] *If I'm being honest, the bush sitting next to me is in more danger of getting hit than I— but I would still rather not be around when the arrows begin to fall in my general direction.*

[231] *Surprisingly, talking bushes are not uncommon in the realm; however, those that 'do' talk seldom have a good word to say about anyone or anything—especially the Heartenford Guards, whom they consider to be among their greatest nemesis.*

Bergenn: "You like my disguise?"

Me: "It's certainly good; I had no idea that was you—how long have you been here?"

Bergenn: "Since last night."

Me: "Last *night?* You have been sitting in that bush for nearly a day?"

Bergenn: "You speak as if you do not believe me."

Me: "No—I'm just a little shocked, that's all. Did anything out of the ordinary happen while you were undercover?"

Bergenn: "A Heartenford Guard passed this way during the early hours."

Me: "Did they see you?"

Bergenn: "For a moment, I thought they had when they stopped their horse and walked straight for me."

Me: "Had they?"

Bergenn: "No—fortunately, they were only answering the call of nature and decided I looked like a good privy spot."[232]

Me: "That must have been slightly disconcerting."

Bergenn: "Just don't, whatever you do, step anywhere behind me."

Me: "Thanks for the warning."

The bush suddenly lifts itself off the ground as it sprouts a pair of legs and steps towards me. I recoil slightly—I was expecting the Elf to materialise from the foliage; instead, it soon becomes clear that the Ranger is wearing some kind of bush-like armour as her disguise. I go to shake the Elf's hand, but the bush outfit makes finding one a near-impossibility. I settle instead for grasping a large protruding branch and hope for the best.

Me: "That's some disguise. Is it heavy? It *looks* heavy..."

---

[232] *For some inexplicable reason, even in the middle of the wilderness with nobody around for as far as the eye can see, it's impossible to actually 'go' without first finding a nearby bush for some privacy.*

Bergenn: "Maybe for you."

Me: "What does that mean?"

Before I can react, a bushy twig grabs my arm and reveals an unimposing bicep.

Bergenn: "No offence, but you look like someone who has been pushing a quill for most of their life—rather than an oversized Wheel of Pain."[233]

I pull away and cover my mortally wounded right arm.

Me: "Hey, no fair, I've dedicated my life to honing the mind rather than the body."

Bergenn: "Why didn't you hone both?"

Me: "My brother was more than physical enough for the both of us."[234]

Bergenn: "Maybe *he* should be interviewing me rather than you?"[235]

Me: "Why do you say that?"

Bergenn: "It's dangerous to be this close to Greenvale Forest without a sword."

Me: "I doubt the Merchants who pass this way carry any weapon of note—nor have the stomach for a fight."

Bergenn: "True—but those who *can't* fight generally hire someone who *can*."

Me: "Perhaps I should hire myself a Ranger for protection?"[236]

---

[233] The 'Wheel of Pain' was voted the number one exercise by the large-print readers of 'Barbarian Weekly'; second was the 'Wheel of Woe', closely followed by the 'Wheel of Mild Annoyance' in third.

[234] Aldon developed his own 'Wheel of Rain' exercise regime that was so intense, I had to bury my head in my books just to protect myself from being covered in my brother's secondary sweat.

[235] My brother's questions would probably focus on what the Ranger ate for breakfast, the Ranger's favourite Bard, and how many Goblins the Ranger had killed while dressed as a bush.

[236] Although I'm not paying extra for the Ranger's leafy attire...

Bergenn: "You'll be lucky to find a Ranger who is up to the task nowadays."

Me: "Why's that?"

Bergenn: "We are a fading profession."

Me: "I would have thought there would be lines of eager heroes itching to become Rangers and embrace the great outdoors."

Bergenn: "Sadly, the wilds are under attack, not from Goblins and Orcs, but from something much closer to home—something *far* more fearsome."

Me: "What *is* this mysterious beast you speak of? What manner of creature could fill the bravest of Elven hearts with such dread?"

The bush leans closer and drops her voice to a dramatic whisper.

Bergenn: "It is called *Progress*—and it is far more dangerous than any beast..."

I blink several times in confusion.

Me: "What is this abomination called *Progress?* Is it winged? Does it have scales? Does it breathe fire?"[237]

Bergenn: "It is no creature you can fight with sword or bow—it is the sprawling community that has awoken. Stinking towns have been hastily erected across the realm, bringing choking smoke that burns for weeks as woodlands are chopped down and turned into poorly fitting doors and rickety floorboards..."[238]

Me: "*Ah*—so it's not an *actual* monster then?"

Bergenn: "No—but it is no less terrifying. I have seen first-hand the trail of destruction it leaves behind, from the forests that have fallen foul of it to the earth it has blackened and scorched in its name. All the different races are... *erm*... in a race to expand their districts using whatever natural resources they can mine, chop-down or refine. Our

---

[237] *Does it have an irrational love of Gold? If so, I think 'Progress' might actually be a Dragon...*

[238] *Floorboards that could give way at a moment's notice and drop an unsuspecting Loremaster like a stone into an angry sea.*

environment is diminishing at an alarming rate—as a result, the number of Rangers coming through the ranks has fallen drastically too."

Me: "How do you know?"

Bergenn: "*Excuse* me?"

Me: "How do you know the Ranger numbers are dropping due to this thing you call *Progress?*"

Bergenn: "Because as we are Rangers, we are in tune with one another—just as we are in tune with nature. When one Ranger falls— we *all* feel their pain."[239]

Me: "What does that feel like—I mean, when you lose one of your own?"

Bergenn: "Something like... *ARGGGGHHHHH!*"[240]

Me: "That must be... *disconcerting.*"

Bergenn: "That's nothing—imagine feeling that pain when you're otherwise indisposed;[241] it's not a pleasant experience, I can tell you."

Me: "I shudder to imagine."

Bergenn: "The shudders usually follow afterwards."

Me: "I have another question for you; if you're always dressed so... *erm*... organically, I'd imagine you're quite conspicuous wandering around town."

I point towards the Ranger's bushy attire—she laughs in response.

Bergenn: "We don't *only* wear foliage; we *do* wear normal adventuring clothes from time to time. When we're away from nature we are the

---

[239] *This begs the question: if a Ranger falls in a forest, does another Ranger in a bush far away make a pained sound?*

[240] *Comedic timing from the Ranger that would get Uncle Bevan Barr's seal of approval.*

[241] *The bizarre thought of a 'bush' suddenly caught short and hurrying to relieve itself by ducking behind 'another' bush pops into my mind.*

118

ones usually dressed in green and carrying a bow."[242]

Me: "I take it you also don't choose to wear something natural when you're relaxing at home?"[243]

Bergenn: "*Ha!* No, can you imagine the mess if I did? I only wear it out here, in the open. It's actually quite comfortable—I could happily sleep in it too."[244]

Me: "*Really?* It looks a little—you know, restrictive? I always thought Elves were fleet of foot? It doesn't look like you can move far without making a lot of leafy noise if I'm being honest."

The bush remains perfectly still.

Bergenn: "Listen..."

I strain to hear anything of the note.

Bergenn: "What do you hear?"

Me: "Not much?"

Bergenn: "Close your eyes and try to unlock your senses."

I nod and obey the Elf; this time, I can hear the leaves in the distance as the passing wind caresses them—I open my eyes in realisation.

Me: "Rustling."

The bush shakes excitedly.

Bergenn: "The *exact* same sound I make when I move. Do you think you could tell the difference?"

I shrug my shoulders.

Bergenn: "When I move, it's like the wind is gently blowing the leaves on the trees. Nobody can hear me coming—trust me."

---

[242] *Not to be confused with a Goblin—who IS usually green and carrying a bow...*

[243] *Not to be confused with 'Oh, Natural', which is Gnomish for 'naked'.*

[244] *Just expect to be woken by the sound of birds chirping in your earhole first thing in the morning.*

The bush stares into my face and catches the faintest whiff of disbelief.[245]

Bergenn: "You don't look convinced."

Me: "I didn't say that."

Bergenn: "Close your eyes again and keep them closed."

Me: "Why?"

The bush stares at me like a predator sizing up its next kill.

Bergenn: "Close. Your. Eyes."

I shut my eyes as instructed. There's a moment of silence, broken only by the soft rustling of leaves all around me—it *could* be the Elf moving, but then it *could* just be the sound of the trees in the distance.

Me: "H—How long do you want me to keep them closed?"

The Ranger shouts something at me; I can tell she's moved further away from my position—I hazard a guess that she wants me to open my eyes. So, I blink several times and look around. The only bush in view now sits about three hundred yards further along the path.

Bergenn: (incomprehensible noise)

Me: ***WHAT?***

Bergenn: ***DID. YOU. HEAR. ME. MOVE?***

Me: ***NO—I DON'T THINK SO!***[246]

The distant bush suddenly sprouts legs and hoists up its lower branches before running back toward me.

Bergenn: "Told you! I *knew* you couldn't tell the difference. Now imagine we repeated that inside Greenvale Forest—you would never hear me coming."[247]

---

[245] *Although it 'could' have something to do with the Heartenford Guard from earlier in the day...*

[246] **Loremaster Tip #4:** *Always tell <u>any</u> hero what they want to hear—it will save you a lot of awkward exchanges later on.*

[247] *Or, in this example, going...*

Me: "I bet that comes in handy in your fight against the Goblin hordes?"

Bergenn: "Those Goblins don't stand a chance. You can keep your metal armour—give me a bush any day of the season."

Me: "Speaking of 'seasons', what do you do about your bush then?"

The bush looks at me in confusion.

Bergenn: "Whatever do you mean?"

Me: "In autumn, do you change its colour to match the surroundings? What about in winter—do you strip your bush bare?"

The bush shakes in agitation—leaving me to wonder what I've said.

Bergenn: "Do you not *know* your bushes, Loremaster?"

I can feel the heat in my cheeks as they turn red with embarrassment.

Me: "I must admit my knowledge is somewhat lacking in the flora area."

I notice the leaves of the bush slightly sagging in disappointment.

Bergenn: "I am an evergreen—which means I don't need to change my attire as it stays like this regardless of the season."

Me: "*Ah,* very clever—do you find it's trickier hunting for Goblins during winter time?"

Bergenn: "The snowy season is usually quiet for us—as the Goblins retreat back to the warmth of the caverns[248] dotted around the Halgorn Crags."[249]

Me: "Why do you think the Goblins are invading Greenvale Forest?"

---

[248] *Warmth in the metaphoric scene, not literal; caves and caverns are not warm by any stretch of the imagination—even the ones kitted out with a state-of-the-art fire-pit and toasting fork to toast baby Gelatinous Cubes (Which is a highly sought-after Goblin delicacy that I'm told will dissolve a tongue if it's not quickly washed out with a mouthful of alkaline rock salts).*

[249] *Contrary to local opinion, Goblins don't hibernate in winter; they just sit around complaining bitterly about how bitterly cold it is while drinking warm mushroom bitter with a twist of bitter lemon.*

Bergenn: "I'm not sure; I heard a rumour that a *'Dark Power'* was calling out to them, luring the wretched creatures down from their rocky domain to torment the good people of this land with the promise of precious gems, fresh meat and free archery lessons."[250]

Me: "A *'Dark Power'?* Who or what do you think it is?"

Bergenn: "I've yet to find the source—but I intend to. Whatever it is, it's just the tip of the arrow. Goblins have been sighted on the outskirts of several settlements in this area; more worryingly, Dragons from the Doom Mountains have been attacking the local farms far more frequently than ever before—*something* has gotten these creatures hot and bothered."[251]

Me: "I heard—"

The bush seems suddenly agitated and rustles her leaves angrily.

Bergenn: "**What?** What have you heard?"

Me: "Just... someone mentioned how there are now too many heroes and not enough quests to go around—if that's true, surely there are plenty of adventurers kicking their heels, eager to deal with this Goblin menace for a fair price?"

Bergenn: "And who exactly would pay these layabout heroes for their time? *Me?* I suggest you stop listening to idle gossip and open your eyes a little wider, Loremaster. If there was this *'supposed'* quest shortage, why would I be here, dressed as a bush, searching for Goblins—do you think I'd be doing this for the good of my health?"[252]

Me: "I suppose not. Can I ask why you have a deep-rooted hatred of Goblins?"

Bergenn: "I don't *hate* Goblins... in fact, they're my *favourite* enemy."

Me: "Favourite? What does that mean?"

---

[250] *Okay, I made that last one up...*

[251] *Probably a voluptuous Dragon putting out all the right signals...*

[252] *Although deep down, I have a feeling the Ranger would probably still be here, dressed as a bush—regardless of any Goblin threat or not.*

Bergenn: "It means I get a warm fuzzy feeling inside when I kill one."

Me: "How many Goblins do you think you've slain in your time?"[253]

Bergenn: "*Oh,* I don't know—a lot. I just love the way they *'pop'* when they die[254]—it's just so *satisfying,* you know."

Me: "I'm not sure I do; I've never killed anything before—"

Bergenn: "We could hunt one together if you want? Take my word for it; once you start *popping,* you won't be… *erm… stopping.*"

Me: "Thanks all the same, but I think I'll pass."

Bergenn: "Well, you know where to find me if you change your mind."

I gesture to the Ranger's bushy disguise.

Me: "*If* I can find you, of course…"

The Elf bursts into laughter.

Bergenn: "Alright, yeah—you got me, *that* was a good one."

Me: "I thought you'd appreciate the—"

There's a snapping of twigs just inside the edge of Greenvale Forest— Bergenn spins on the spot and freezes.

Me: "What is—?"

Bergenn: "**_Shhhhhh!_**"[255]

I stay perfectly still and watch the treeline, heart in my mouth. A deer suddenly bolts out of nowhere and spies the solitary Loremaster

---

[253] *Did I really stoop to ask a question that I would expect from my brother?*

[254] *This is due to the gases built up from the copious amount of warm mushroom bitter Goblins like to drink (with a twist of bitter lemon) and one baby Gelatinous Cube too many that's swirling around their potted bellies.*

[255] *I've always thought it's a bit peculiar to make one <u>really</u> loud noise to hear one <u>really</u> faint one.*

standing next to an innocuous-looking bush[256] before deciding to dart back into the safety of the forest. I can sense the pseudo-bush next to me relaxing a little.

Bergenn: "I feel a little exposed out here.[257] Could we perhaps continue this conversation somewhere where there are a few more nearby trees?"

I know the Elf means for us to go further into the foreboding forest. But I can't help but imagine the plethora of unseen beasts waiting to pounce from the undergrowth.

Me: "You know what, I think I've got everything I need right now. Perhaps if you're ever in town—we could meet up again?"

Bergenn: "Unlikely—even though I own a house, I rarely leave the woodlands."

Me: "*Really?* How do you stock up on supplies?"

Bergenn: "Look around Loremaster; the great outdoors provides everything I need to survive."[258]

Me: "I don't think I could live outdoors without some of my luxuries—"

Bergenn: "Being around nature is the only luxury I need."

Me: "Do you go on any quests not set outside in the wilds?"

Bergenn: "No, I'm not interested in anything but protecting forests like Greenvale—although I do take the odd side-quest when winter finally comes."

Me: "What sort of side-quests?"

Bergenn: "Outdoor ones."

---

[256] *Thank the Gods I wasn't caught short; otherwise, that could have been embarrassing for all three of us.*

[257] *I don't think the Elf means this in an 'Oh Natural' way—or at least I hope not.*

[258] *I feel this is somewhat being oversold. Where are my modern comforts? Where are my crisp white bedsheets? My fluffy pillows? Or the strange chest sat in the corner of an Inn's bedroom that 'could' be a sleeping Mimic or 'could' just contain random clothes left behind by a previously guest (who may or may not have been eaten by a Mimic).*

Me: "Isn't it frightfully cold, though?"

Bergenn: "You'll be surprised how warm it can get inside this bush—especially if a Heartenford Guard pays a visit beforehand."

Me: "Why endure all that hardship? Why not bask in the comfort of the great indoors once in a while?"

The bush shakes its leaves nervously.

Bergenn: "I—I don't like going inside; it makes me feel trapped."

Me: "Are you claustrophobic?"

Bergenn: "Chronically so, the moment I lose sight of the sky, I begin to panic—my palms start sweating, and I get the shakes."[259]

Me: "That must be debilitating for you."

Bergenn: "In a dungeon environment, it could cost me my life; that's why I only choose to adventure out in the open."

I nod sympathetically.

Me: "Did you ever adventure with members of the Heroes Guild?"

Bergenn: "Not usually—the Heroes Guild are quite particular about who joins a party. If I *must* adventure with someone, I'd rather they weren't affiliated with the Heroes Guild if at all possible."

Me: "Why is that?"

The bush moves closer and whispers.

Bergenn: "Too many dungeon-loving types."

Me: "Do you know of any Rangers who work with the Heroes Guild? Or are members themselves?"

Bergenn: "I don't know of any."

Me: "Is that a bit strange?"

Bergenn: "As I mentioned before—the number of active Rangers is

---

[259] *But, thankfully, not the shudders...*

dwindling rapidly. Perhaps the Heroes Guild is partly responsible for that."

Me: "How so?"

Bergenn: "There was a time when a Ranger was the first name on an adventuring sheet—we were the Trackers, the Ambushers, the Archers, the Scouts, and the Guides all rolled into one. But then the Heroes Guild came along, and things changed for the worst. They split our roles up and gave them away to the other hero types. You want someone good at ambushing? Then you hire a Rogue. You want someone who is good with arrows? Then you hire a Fighter who can shoot straight.[260] You want someone who is good at hiding? Then you hire a Cleric—"

Me: "A Cleric?"

Bergenn: "At the first sign of trouble, they *always* run a mile.[261] Anyway, almost overnight, we became surplus to adventuring requirements..."

Me: "I thought you said *Progress* was responsible for the dwindling number of Rangers?"

Bergenn: "The two are intrinsically linked. When a new settlement is established, the Heroes Guild is at the fore, ensuring their presence is felt from day one. That can only mean one thing—less work for Rangers."

Me: "While the Heroes Guild is attracting every other adventuring type in the immediate area to them."

The bush nods in agreement.

Me: "It almost sounds like the Heroes Guild is targeting Rangers on purpose."

Bergenn: "I wouldn't put it past them. Part of me believes the Heroes Guild are phasing out wilderness adventures altogether."

----

[260] *Just not a Goblin Fighter... or a Halfling one...*

[261] *I've since discovered the actual average distance travelled by a Cleric looking for somewhere to hide is closer to forty-five feet—I guess running in heavy armour will make forty-five feet _feel_ like a mile...*

Me: "But why?"

Bergenn: "I'm guessing they see little reward in outdoor quests; they would rather put their energies into lucrative dungeon-delving adventures where the rewards are guaranteed to be higher."

Me: "So, they see no long-term value in Rangers at all?"

Bergenn: "I think they believe we are nothing more than a forest Fighter who likes swinging a sword surrounded by trees or a woodland Rogue who enjoys shooting arrows from a bush."[262]

Me: "Surely the Heroes Guild don't think *that* little of your profession?"

The bush sighs deeply and kicks a stone onto the Merchant's Road.

Bergenn: "Let me ask you this—why choose to bring a Ranger on an adventure when you could bring both a Fighter *and* a Rogue?"

Me: "But you could do both professions equally well—why the need for two heroes instead of one?"

Bergenn: "Because *two* heroes would always return from a successful quest carrying *twice* the amount of one."

I slowly follow where the Ranger is going with this thought.

Me: "—And the Heroes Guild obviously takes a percentage of that loot..."

Bergenn: "Two adventurers are always better than one..."

Me: "I see!"

Bergenn: "It's simple economics—having a Ranger on an adventure reduces the amount the Heroes Guild can take at the end of it. We're not profitable to the Heroes Guild. That's why I think our days are numbered. Mark my words, Loremaster—give it a few summers, and there won't be any of us left in the realm."

Me: "Any that you can *see*, at least..."

From inside their bush, I know the Ranger is grinning from Elven ear to Elven ear.

---

[262] *Unlike Goblins, who often end up unintentionally shooting arrows <u>into</u> a bush...*

Bergenn: "Spoken like a *true* Ranger!"

I watch as the bush jumps for joy.

"SQUELCH!"

Bergenn: *"Oh..."*

Me: "What? What's wrong?"

Bergenn: "I think I just stepped in whatever that Heartenford Guard left behind from *their* behind..."[263]

---

[263] *I think that's my cue to leave.*

10. Holtar, the Necromancer

I walk through the graveyard on the outskirts of Rotford with growing trepidation, heading toward the last house before the endless swamps take hold. It's a dark and depressing walk, illuminated only by the occasional lantern that hangs from a metal pole, guiding my footfalls along a path away from the relative safety of the town fading behind me. I try to bury my fears and carry along the trail, convinced a Zombie is waiting to pounce on me at any given moment.[264] In the distance, I can make out the dark shape of my destination, a solitary dwelling built on stilts with a wooden staircase leading to the entrance. As I ascend, the wood protests ominously beneath my feet, threatening to give way under my weight at a moment's notice[265]—almost instantly, the front door creaks slowly open in reply. My consciousness screams at me to run from this unholy place. But if I am to achieve my goal of understanding the realm's heroes, I must be brave enough to walk in their footsteps, no matter where that leads me.

Unseen Voice: "Welcome to my humble abode, *Loremaster...*"

As I step through the doorway into the gloom of a dimly lit interior, I see a figure sitting with their back turned away; all I can make out is a lithe frame tightly-wrapped in a heavy cloak to shield them from the cold. The figure has its hood up, obscuring any discernible features.

Me: "Holtar? Holtar the *Necromancer?*"

Holtar: "Are you expecting someone else? Please, do not stand on ceremony on my account—*sit.*"

I close the door and edge closer through the shadows to the empty seat opposite my host.

Holtar: "Forgive my lack of illumination; I find light to be a bit of a nuisance."

Me: "Why is that?"

Holtar: "A curse from my racial heritage, or a gift—depending on how

---

[264] *Although, 'pounce' might be giving the Zombie in question a little too much credit.*

[265] *Thankfully, the drop would only be a few feet into a foul-smelling swamp rather than a few hundred onto sharp, sea-battered rocks...*

you see it."

I take the seat as instructed and look straight into the pale eyes of a Dark Elf.[266] His black beard neatly follows his jawline, making Holtar look more like an Evildoer than a Necromancer.[267] The Dark Elf even has a suitably macabre artefact staring across the table separating us— a grinning skull.

Holtar: "Can I offer you some refreshment?"

Me: "Anything to take the chill away from my bones."

I catch a hint of a smirk from the Necromancer at the mere mention of 'bones'. The Dark Elf withdraws a delicate bell from his cloak, which he dutifully rings with a flick of his wrist. In reply, a figure emerges from the darkness, shuffling and groaning as it comes closer to the light.

Me: "That's a Z—"

Holtar: "A Zombie—yes. Although it *was* a corpse until I raised it from the Great Behind."[268]

Me: "B—But... isn't it dangerous? I mean, doesn't it eat brains[269] or have an infectious bite that turns you into one of them?"

The Necromancer grins as he turns to talk to his unholy Butler.

---

[266] So-called because Dark Elves say things that are considered a little 'darker' than what other Elves would say—for example, a High-Elf would bid farewell to someone by saying: 'May the Grace of Terendull keep you safe from the Great Behind. Whereas a Dark Elf would say: 'May the Grace of Terendull lead you safely into the Great Behind." As you can see, it's almost the same thing, but said just that little bit 'darker'.

[267] Although many in the realm believe the difference between the two is like trying to argue whether Gnomes are taller than Halflings or not, whereas, to everyone else, they are both small.

[268] The 'Great Behind' is what the Elves consider their afterlife—which many, especially the Dwarves, jokingly refer to as the 'Huge Backside'.

[269] There has been a tremendous amount of debate as to why Zombies have an inexplicable desire to eat brains. Some believe Zombies can detect the memories in others and are gripped by an insatiable hunger to savour those precious moments once again. While others believe Zombies are so enraged by their own stupidity that they eat anything smarter than them.

Holtar: "Be a good chap and go make us both a cup of *Sigh* tea, please."[270]

The animated corpse groans in acknowledgement before shuffling back into the darkness.

Holtar: "It won't hurt you; it is completely under my control. It does everything I tell it to do—within reason, of course. There are certain limitations, as you can imagine."

Me: "How long will it stay like that?"

Holtar: "I'm not sure exactly—it could be days, it could be minutes. That's the problem with Necromancy—it's not what you call 'reliable' magic. Fingers crossed it manages to bring us our tea first; I really do hate making it myself or having to clean up any unplanned mess."

I wait until the Zombie has shuffled entirely from view before speaking again.

Me: "Can I just pick up on something you said earlier—you find 'light' a nuisance? Isn't that a strange thing for an adventurer to say? Don't most heroes prefer light—especially when it comes to monster-filled dungeons or trap-filled crypts?"

Holtar: "Light expedites the rotting process and decomposes corpses faster—it's a constant thorn in the side of any Necromancer worth their salt."

Me: "So, you'd prefer to adventure in the dark?"

The Necromancer gestures to his eyes.

Holtar: "My eyes allow me to see in the void as if it were clear as day."

Me: "Infra-Vision."

Holtar: "Please, Infra-Vision is what those rock-loving Dwarves and daylight-loving Elves have. I use *Holtar-Vision*™—it's something I

---

[270] *'Sigh' tea is so-called because after you make a cup, someone immediately asks you to do something that makes you forget you've made it in the first place—only to discover the beverage several hours later, cold and horrid.*

pioneered myself using my arcane dark arts."[271]

Me: "How does that work?"

Holtar: "Infra-Vision uses heat to show up the living, but Holtar-Vision™ uses the cold to see *everything* else. It's also good for pinpointing corpses buried deep in the ground."

Me: "That must come in handy; what with you being a Necromancer and all?"

Holtar: "It's invaluable."

I catch sight of the skull on the table; I swear the fixed grin on its face has widened since I last glanced at it; my eyes wander over to the bowl of human teeth sitting next to the skull[272]—repulsed, I quickly turn away.

Holtar: "You *really* shouldn't stare."

Me: "I—I'm sorry, I didn't mean to—"

The Necromancer shakes his head and holds up a hand.

Holtar: "I wasn't talking to you."

I glance down at the skull in my confusion.

The Necromancer reaches over to the table and spins the skull in a half-circle to glare at it, eye-to-eye socket.

Holtar: "We talked about this—didn't we?"

The skull doesn't reply.[273]

I'm concerned the Necromancer may have stared too deeply into the abyss.

---

[271] *I subsequently found out that Holtar had registered the name Holtar-Vision™ with the Heralds Guild, hence the legal requirement to add a trademark symbol next to it. If you're wondering, the trademark symbol is a magic glyph that prevents it from being written down or spoken about in idle conversation without Holtar's express permission.*

[272] *Teeth that have clearly never been near a Toothsmith...*

[273] *Honestly—as if I was expecting that it would!*

Holtar: "I'm not putting up with this attitude—apologise _NOW_ for staring."

The skull still stubbornly refuses to talk; the Necromancer's eyes narrow as they turn into ominous slits.

Me: "It's fine; honestly—it wasn't the skull's fault—"

Holtar: "_No_—he knows better than to do this."

Me: "I think I should just be leav—"

Skull: "Alright! I'm **_SORRY_**—you happy?"

My mouth opens and shuts in disbelief.[274]

Holtar: "Not to me—to _our_ guest."

The Necromancer spins the skull around so it can emotionlessly glare at me once more.

Skull: "I'm—**_SOR—REE!_**"

Holtar: "See, that wasn't so bad—was it?"

Skull: "_Humpf—he_ was staring at me first—"

Holtar: _"Seymour..."_

Me: "You have a talking skull?"

Seymour: "I'm not **_his_**, you clot!"

Holtar: "Seymour—**_manners!_**"

Seymour: "Well, he asked for it."

Me: "Sorry, I—I'm just struggling to understand what's going on right now."

Seymour: "Why do you want to talk to this guy again? He's not that bright."

---

[274] _Almost mirroring what the skull is doing—except I still have my skin, hair, lips, nose, ears, and eyeballs, thankfully._

Me: "Is it—I mean, is Seymour a *he?*"

Seymour: "I *was* the last time I checked. *Ah*—I hark for those days when I had something to idly scratch. It's always the *little* things you miss…"

Me: "What happened?"

Seymour: "What do you *think* happened?"

Holtar: "There was an unfortunate *incident.*[275] Seymour and I were on an adventure."

Me: Forgive me, but what was Seymour—in terms of his profession and race?"

Seymour: "*Oh*, I love this game—*guess!*"

Me: "*Erm*—a Dwarven Fighter?"

Seymour: "Do I look like I have a beard?"[276]

Me: "*Erm*… no, I guess not. What about an Elven Cleric?"

Seymour: "Do you think I'm the type destined for the *Great Behind?*"

Holtar: "Seymour…"

Me: "A Gnome Monk?"

Seymour: "Are you blind?!"

Holtar: "Seymour!"

Seymour: "<u>Look</u>—this is *all* I have left in life to look forward to, Holtar!"

Holtar: "He was a Human Rogue—although, I say *'Human'* in the loosest sense of the word."

---

[275] *Aren't all incidents 'unfortunate'?*

[276] *I'm now hugely tempted to ink a beard and moustache combo onto the skull's 'face' to see how he would look.*

134

Seymour: "Gee—thanks for stealing the wind out of my gale."[277]

Me: "How did you end up like this?"

Seymour: "It was my reward for completing a quest successfully..."

Me: "I suspect that may not be the truth."

Seymour: "I *told* you he was a clot."

Me: "He always like this?"

Holtar: "Yes—*always.*"

Me: "How did he die?"

Seymour: "Hey! I am still in the room, you know—even if it *is* only part of me."

Holtar: "Fine, do you want to tell him our story then, or should I?"

The skull sighs, which is quite an achievement, given he doesn't have any lungs.

Seymour: "We were high up in the Doom Mountains, inside the citadel—"

Me: "What citadel?"

Seymour: "Do you always interrupt when someone is trying to talk? It was the *Dragon Lord's* Citadel if you must know."

Me: I'm guessing this Dragon Lord rules over all Dragons found within the peaks of the Doom Mountains?"

Seymour: "You guess correct—although the Dragon Lord wasn't *exactly* a proper Dragon Lord to speak of."

Me: "What do you mean?"

---

[277] *This saying originates from a drunken Rogue who once proclaimed, many summers ago, that he was so stealthy he could literally steal the wind from a Wind Elemental. Sadly, when this boast was put to the test, the Rogue was caught mid-pinch and launched by the Wind Elemental into an angry maelstrom—needless to say, the drunken Rogue was never seen again.*

Holtar: "It was more of a self-appointed title. In truth, the Dragon Lord was *just* a common farmer who got tired of his turnip fields being turned to ash, so decided to do something about it."[278]

Me: "A common farmer? How did a common farmer end up becoming a much-feared Lord of all Dragons?"

Seymour: "That's *Dragon Lord* to you—I heard he convinced all the other Farmers in his hamlet to pool their coin together so they could buy something to help them stop the frequent Dragon attacks."

Me: "What did he buy?"

Seymour:" Something magical—a helm... of *Dragon* Control."

Me: "A Helm of Dragon Control? How did he obtain such an item?"

Seymour: "I don't know, but if I had to hazard a guess, I'd start by looking up someone like Thorde Ironstein—he owns *The Hammer & Tongs* forge."

Me: "We've met—he said his magical items come from a Wizard of the coast."[279]

Seymour: "That wouldn't surprise me—there's plenty of Grey Magic still active in the realm.[280] When this Farmer finally had the magical helm in his turnip-stained hands, he set off at once for the Doom Mountains. After an arduous climb, the tired Farmer finally stumbled across the ruins of the citadel that overlooked the entrance to the Dragons' lair."

Me: "Did he use the helm to stop the Dragon attacks as planned?"

Seymour: "Not exactly. You see, the helm was *cursed*—sure, it *controlled* Dragons, but it also made the wearer *forget* why they were

---

[278] *The lengths Farmers will go to protect their turnips are staggering.*

[279] *I have this strange feeling that if there were more than one Wizard of the coast, this would send shockwaves through the Heralds Guild Arcane Copyright department.*

[280] *'Grey Magic' includes old Wizards, Sorcerers, Warlocks, and anyone else who would throw a Fireball at you for accidentally walking through their prized herb garden unannounced or wandering noisily past their abode late at night. Most of these veteran Spellreaders have retired to dribble into their arcane spellbooks in peace. However, a few still find ways to make themselves some spare coin to spend on the odd flagon of ale.*

controlling Dragons in the first place."

Holtar: "The wretched soul forgot about everyone and everything when he put that cursed helm on. He forgot he was a Farmer, forgot he was supposed to stop the Dragons, he *even* forgot about the turnips that were in fiery peril—"

Me: "That's a pretty big problem."

Seymour: "You don't say! And remember—he had just spent the entire hamlet's coin on this accursed thing too."

Me: "That still doesn't quite explain how he wound up as the Dragon Lord."

Seymour: "Well, the helm didn't just *control* Dragons—it *talked* to them too."

Me: "So, the Farmer was able to understand the Dragons?"[281]

Holtar: "And they—him. The cunning Dragons must have quickly realised he wasn't cut out to be a real Dragon Lord and persuaded him that they weren't the problem here. Instead, they pointed the clawed finger of blame squarely at the Farmers in the valley below."[282]

Me: "So, the Dragon Lord—?"

Seymour: "—Ordered *more* Dragon attacks on the unsuspecting farmsteads."

Me: "Where do you two fit in this sorry tale?"

Seymour: "We were tasked with sorting this mess out."

Me: "Who hired you?"

Holtar: "The Heroes Guild. We were both fully qualified members at the time, and they came to us with the quest."

---

[281] *It does make you wonder what their conversation was like. I can't imagine there's a lot of common ground between a Farmer and a Dragon—unless the Dragon fancied chomping down on a side order of turnip with their steaming cow.*

[282] *Isn't that 'just' like a Dragon—taking advantage of a situation. They put some Rogues to shame with the depths of their deceitfulness. I'm thankful the oversized lizards aren't into backstabs.*

Seymour: "They offered a sizeable reward too."

Me: "Why did they give this quest to the likes of you?"

Seymour: "What are you suggesting?"

Me: "A Rogue and a Necromancer, it doesn't seem like a well-balanced party to me? No Fighter? No Paladin or Barbarian—forgive me, but wouldn't it have made more sense to add an experienced sword or two to your quest."

Holtar: "That was my concern—"

Seymour: "It was just one turnip Farmer, not an Evildoer[283]—it was *supposed* to be an easy quest! Once we had the Helm of Dragon Control in our hands, the Farmer would realise his mistake, and things would go back to relative normality."

Holtar: "Or so we thought."

Me: "But things didn't go back to relative normality."

Seymour: "We badly underestimated the size of the quest."

Holtar: "We didn't underestimate anything. See—I *told* you it was a mistake accepting that quest without a recognised Fighter by our side."

Seymour: "Here we go again with the '*Why didn't we hire a Fighter to join our party?*' moan."

Holtar: "Well—we didn't."

Seymour: "Don't you think I know that? I'm the one who has to lament over the folly of that decision *every… single… day…*"

Me: "What went wrong?"

The Necromancer scratches his temple nervously.

Seymour: "Sneaking into the citadel was easy. There were no Guards to speak of, no traps that required—"

He glances over at the skull.

---

[283] *Just an innocent turnip Farmer—with an army of horny Dragons under his command!*

Seymour: "It's okay, just say it."

Holtar: "*Disarming*—sorry…"

Seymour: "It's fine; I'm over it."[284]

Holtar: "The Dragon Lord had *no* idea how to prepare his stronghold for adventurers. Even before we had completed the quest, we were already discussing how we would spend our reward when we had returned to the Heroes Guild safely."

Seymour: "Then there it was, the Helm of Dragon Control—all we needed to do was grab it and get out."

Me: "Where was the Dragon Lord?"

Seymour: "Nowhere to be seen—snoozing probably. As Holtar said, the Dragon Lord really didn't have the first idea how to keep heroes like us out."

Me: "But…?"

The Necromancer coughs with embarrassment.

Seymour: "*One* of us got distracted while the other one was about to get their hands on the Helm of Dragon Control—didn't they, *Holtar*?"

Holtar: "I couldn't help it—it was just too good an opportunity to pass up!"

Me: "What was?"

Seymour: "He found a corpse, but not just any old corpse—*noooooo!* Holtar here found a big old *Dragon* corpse."

Holtar: "You should have seen it! It was magnificent—and in perfect condition. All I had to do was animate it to see it live once more."[285]

---

[284] *Even though the skull cannot visibly express emotions, Seymour appears far from over it.*

[285] *Having experienced first-hand how unsettling a Dragon corpse is—the thought of one coming back to life is the stuff of nightmares.*

Me: "You reanimated a Dragon's corpse?"[286]

Holtar: "How could I not?"

Me: "So, what happened?"

Seymour: "*Everything* happened."

Holtar: "As the undead beast rose, it was a sight to behold. I swear I had a tear in my eye as it lifted itself off the citadel floor and stretched out its decomposing wings."

Seymour: "So, imagine my surprise as I turned with the Helm of Dragon Control in my hands to stare into the rotten eye sockets of an undead Dragon staring right back at me."

Me: "What did you do?"

Seymour: "I screamed and dropped the helm on my foot, causing one of the horns to pierce my boot, leaving me in absolute agony and unable to walk."

Holtar: "Meanwhile, it took all my unholy strength to keep the undead Dragon under my control. I had never reanimated something as powerful as this before. I had vastly underestimated how much dark magic it would drain from me. I collapsed to my knees under the sheer force of will the beast still had clinging to its bones."

Seymour: "That's when the Dragon Lord showed up."

Me: "Bet he wasn't pleased to see you two."

Seymour: "You *think?* He just walked in to find an animated Dragon corpse stumbling around his great hall, a magically drained Necromancer on his knees and a Rogue rolling around holding a bloody foot!"

Me: "That must have been a bizarre spectacle to witness—what did the Dragon Lord do?"

Seymour: "He grabbed the helm—pulled it out of my boot and placed it upon his head. In a battle of wills, he eventually managed to wrestle the undead Dragon's corpse from under my control."

---

[286] Even *I* know that wasn't going to end well...

Me: "But it was *your* spell?"

Holtar: "But it was _his_ dragon—besides, I wasn't in any fit state to do anything about it. I could only watch as the Dragon Lord turned the lumbering corpse on poor Seymour here. It gobbled him up with one rotten bite!"[287]

Me: "That must have been awful."

Seymour: "Awful is an understatement—the undead Dragon was missing quite a few of its teeth. The last conscious memory I have is slowly being 'gummed' to death; it was the worst way possible to go—I wouldn't wish that fate on my worst enemy."[288]

Me: "Then what happened?"

Holtar: "The Dragon must have sucked Seymour's head clean off because it suddenly bounced towards me. All I could do was dive and catch it before it flew past. I summoned my reserves, hauled myself to my feet, and bolted out of the citadel before the Dragon Lord could turn his attention on me."

Me: "Why didn't the undead Dragon chase you down?"

Holtar: "Fortunately, I always carry a few Potions of Invisibility for such emergencies. I remember downing my entire stash before fleeing back to town with Seymour nestled in my armpit."[289]

Seymour: "But you didn't think to give *me* any of it, though, did you?"

Me: "What good would *that* have done?"

Seymour: "It would have stopped that poor Potioneer jumping out of his skin in fright. I can still see the look of horror on his face as I floated past, screaming."

Me: "Screaming?"

---

[287] *(See footnote 286) I told you so!*

[288] *Who, to the former Rogue, would probably be a morally uptight Paladin who caught Seymour daubing rude words on his beloved armour.*

[289] *I'm not sure who that would have been worse for, the Necromancer or the severed head of the Rogue.*

Holtar: "Indeed he was."[290]

Seymour: "If I remember rightly, I didn't stop screaming until we had reached the safety of our local tavern."

Holtar: "It's a sound I'll not forget in a hurry—so high-pitched."

Seymour: "Alright, let's see how you sound after your head has been used as a boiled sweet."[291]

Me: "How was Seymour still alive?"

Holtar: "You see when the undead Dragon 'killed' Seymour..."

Seymour: "...the Dragon Lord was in control of it..."

Holtar: "...but it was born out of my spell..."

Seymour: "...which found its way into me the moment I died—trapping my lifeforce in a Mortality Loop."[292]

Holtar: "As long as the Dragon Lord continues to use the Helm of Dragon Control to keep the undead Dragon alive—Seymour will forever remain stuck in this undead form."

Me: "What if someone were to kill the undead Dragon or steal the Helm of Dragon Control from the Dragon Lord?"

Seymour: "Then potentially it's *goodnight* from me."

Me: "That must be a constant cause for concern—knowing you could be gone in a blink of an eye... *erm*... socket..."

Seymour: "Why? Where am I going?"

Holtar: "I think the Loremaster means *'death'*, Seymour."

---

[290] *Although judging by Holtar's expression, I'm pretty sure the Dark Elf found this exceedingly funny at the Potioneer's expense.*

[291] *Boiled sweets are a rare delicacy in the realm. They are only ever in possession of Witches, who use them to entice plump children into their homes. Mercifully, Witches have all but died out thanks to their trusting nature and the popularity of large Witch-sized ovens to be pushed into when 'innocently' asked how big the oven is.*

[292] *Not to be confused with a 'Mortality Hoop', which is a cursed Gnomish item that kills you unless you continuously gyrate it around your hips.*

Seymour: "Death doesn't scare me; I've died once already and lived to tell the tale."

Me: "Aren't you worried the Heroes Guild will send more heroes back to deal with the Dragon Lord?"

Holtar: "Hopefully not with an undead Dragon now guarding the citadel—there aren't many heroes on the books who could get into that place without being spotted."

Me: "I thought you said the Dragon Lord *wasn't* a proper Evildoer? That he didn't know *how* to defend his stronghold? Perhaps one of the new recruits, like Dorn the Barbarian, would be able to get inside undetected and steal back the Helm of Dragon Control?"

The Necromancer and the skull exchange glances.

Me: "What did I say?"

Holtar: "There's no need to worry; I've returned to the Dragon Lord's citadel to add magical wards—there's no way anyone will get inside without considerable risk to their health."[293]

Me: "Why would you do that?"

Seymour: "Why do you think?"

Holtar: "I owe Seymour this—it's the least I can do to protect him."

Me: "What if the Heroes Guild finds out about your meddling?"

Seymour: "Let them find out. We were kicked out from the Heroes Guild when we returned empty-handed from the original quest anyway—"

Me: "Kicked out?"

Holtar: "Yup, right after they tried to use the *'Death in Service'* clause to claim Seymour's estate."

Seymour: "Except I could prove I wasn't technically *dead* by the mere fact I could still hold a meaningful conversation. They had no choice

---

[293] *Unless the Heroes Guild sends a Titan of Thunder or something equally as impressive to deal with the Dragon Lord—but seriously, what are the chances?*

but to leave empty-handed—a fact that did not sit well with them."

Holtar: "They revoked both our memberships as a consequence. Overnight we lost our only source of income. Fortunately, Seymour had some coin stashed away that we used to buy this place."

Seymour: "I told you it would pay to save for a rainy day!"[294]

Me: "But the Dragon Lord remains free to unleash his Dragons upon the realm?"

Holtar: "Yes—but deep down the Dragon Lord is *just* a Farmer trying to do the right thing albeit the wrong way—does that make him an Evildoer? Like all of us, he's another person struggling to find his place in this realm."

Me: "What are you going to do to make coin now you're not affiliated with the Heroes Guild anymore?"

Holtar: "*Oh,* there are always some small side-quest or another that needs doing. Simple things like finding a lost Merchant or killing a bunch of rats in a cellar.[295] The pay is insultingly low, but it's welcome coin nonetheless."

Me: "Do you go on any adventures alone?"

Holtar: "*Oh no*—Seymour *always* insists on tagging along…"

Seymour: "I'm *still* a hero! I *still* want to go questing! Just because I'm a decapitated skull doesn't mean I don't have my uses."[296]

Me: "Like?"

Seymour: "I'm the master of distraction."

Me: "Distraction?"

Seymour: "Where's your bag?"

---

[294] As rainy days go and given the Rogue's decapitated state, this must be considered the tsunami of rainy days…

[295] And 'raising' them again to keep the side-quest going—if the Necromancer has anything to do with it.

[296] Perhaps as a novelty candlestick holder or talking doorstop?

I instinctively go to check my side and find it missing. Panic fills me—before I suddenly spy the Necromancer waving it from his seat.

Me: "*Ah*, I see—very clever."

The Necromancer hands my bag back to me.

Holtar: "Of course, that's the not extent of Seymour's abilities—he's great for external, internal monologue."

The skull's voice suddenly takes on a slightly ethereal tone.

Seymour: *"Is this what you want to do? Perhaps you should re-evaluate your life choices, Loremaster..."*

Holtar: "It's a clever ruse we employ for messing with an impressionable mind."

Seymour: "Not to mention I'm fantastic at jump scares—nobody, and I mean *nobody*, expects a skull to speak."

Me: "That all sounds very useful, but surely you can't continue being trapped in this form—don't you want this ordeal to end?"

Seymour: "I promise you when you're given a second chance at life—no matter how different it is, you do everything to hold on to it with both hands."

An awkward silence falls over the three of us.

Seymour: "—if I *still* had any hands, of course."[297]

There's a groan from the darkness as the animated corpse reappears, carrying a tray with two cups of tea on it.

Holtar: "*Ah!* Finally, the refreshments have arri—"

But before the Necromancer finishes that sentence, the reanimated Butler violently shakes, sending the tray clattering to the floor. Cups smash, and the 'Sigh' tea spills everywhere as the Zombie disappears in an explosive dust ball. Holtar splutters and coughs as he tries to clear the air with his hand.

---

[297] *I think my Uncle Bevan Barr would have gotten on very well with the skull.*

Holtar: "Well, that's just perfect—*dammit!*"

Me: "W—What happened?"

Holtar: "What does it look like?"

Me: "It looks like your Zombie just spontaneously combusted."

Holtar: "A pretty accurate guess given the evidence. When one of my spells expires, the corpse in question ages so fast it practically explodes into dust."

The Necromancer gets up from his seat and brushes down his cloak before heading towards the front door.

Me: "Where are you going now?"

The Dark Elf doesn't even turn around to reply as he picks up a well-worn spade.

Holtar: "I'm going to dig up another corpse so I can get a decent cup of tea. I'll bid you farewell now, Loremaster. May the Grace of Terendull lead you safely into the *Great Behind*."[298]

Perplexed, I watch as the Necromancer steps out into the night—leaving me alone with the grinning skull.

Me: "Do you have any regrets?"

Seymour: "Only one..."

There's a pause as the skull stares back at me impassively.

Seymour: "That I don't have any-*body*."

The Rogue grins as I burst into unexpected laughter.

Seymour: "That's a good one, *huh?* You liked that—didn't you?"[299]

---

[298] *See, I <u>told</u> you Dark Elves were dark...*

[299] *I'm glad the decapitated skull still manages to see the bright side of life—although, I suspect after a sustained period of 'body' jokes, even my Uncle Bevan Barr would find Seymour's humour starting to wear a little thin.*

I say my farewells to the skull before taking my leave—I can't help but admire Seymour's ability to remain positive despite his unfortunate predicament; perhaps being 'dead' isn't as bad as I've been led to believe.[300]

---

[300] *Although I still prefer the alternative.*

11. Tendall Fleetfoot, the Rogue

The Dancing Dragon Inn is your standard hero-tavern filled with the kind of adventurers you'd expect to find in the last 'friendly' town before the foreboding Doom Mountains dominate the skyline as far as the eye can see. I say 'friendly' with a thick sense of irony; since sitting here, I've witnessed three backstabs[301] and a bar fight between a drunk Dwarven Barbarian and an even drunker Elven Cleric.[302] Yet, for all the rowdiness and brashness going on in the tavern, I still feel relatively safe in this sea of heroes. Perhaps it's because I'm sitting opposite a sharp-eyed adventurer who appears to be keeping watch for any unwanted attention headed our way. Tendall Fleetfoot is a Halfling Rogue who carries a grudge big enough to dwarf a Storm Giant,[303] which is somewhat prophetic considering there is a storm brewing both inside and outside The Dancing Dragon Inn.

Me: "Can I buy you an ale?"

The Halfling regards me suspiciously for a moment before nodding.

Tendall: "Sure, a—"

There's an awkward pause between us.

Tendall: "—*small* one…"

He watches for the faintest of smirks; like a true professional, my face is utterly statuesque, as if a Gorgon had frozen my expression in place.[304] The Rogue nods again and relaxes back into his seat as I order

---

[301] *That's three different backstabs perpetrated by three different assailants on three different victims, not three different assailants backstabbing the same victim—that would be unfortunate indeed.*

[302] *If the Elven Cleric's not careful, they're going to discover what lies inside the Great Behind…*

[303] *The smallest of the Giant types, but the one with the biggest temper—or should that be 'tempest'.*

[304] *Contrary to legend, Gorgons don't turn their victims to stone—they actually only freeze their victim's face into a hideous grimace that often leaves those who are unfortunate enough to catch a glimpse of it with a frozen grimace of their own. Those afflicted with this curse have to wear a bag over their head for the rest of their days or risk spreading it to everyone they meet.*

our drinks from a passing Barmaid.[305]

Tendall: "I assume you're some kind of *Loremaster?*"

Me: "What gave it away?"

Tendall: "The frightened look in your eye—it's like you're expecting a dagger in your back at any moment."

Me: "Is it that obvious?"

Tendall" "Right now, you look like an easy meal—or a *side-quest-giver*, one of the two."

Me: "A side-quest-*what?*"

Tendall: "—giver. Most side-quests get picked up from weary souls troubled by problems so petty they prefer to drown their sorrows in the local tavern and wait for an adventurer to turn up rather than deal with it themselves. You look like a guy who has a vexing rat infestation problem in their cellar—from a *certain* angle."

Me: "I'll take that as a compliment."

Tendall: "*Don't*—it's not."

Me: "So, why do you think I look like someone with a rat infestation problem?"

Tendall: "It's the stench of helplessness you give off."

A rousing cheer from the other side of the tavern interrupts us; looking over, I can see the drunken Elven Cleric is now riding the less than impressed Dwarven Barbarian.[306] As the Halfling turns to watch the spectacle unfold, I surreptitiously sniff my clothes—I can't discern anything but the dusty road I've travelled on all day. There's a heavy **'THUD'** as I assume the Cleric is now on first-name terms with the tavern floor.

Me: "Do you mind if I take down some notes while we talk?"

---

[305] *Mercifully, there's no nearby Paladin to distract this particular Barmaid.*

[306] *It's common knowledge that Barbarians do not react well to being ridden by Clerics, or by <u>anyone</u> for that matter—the fact this is an Elven Cleric riding a Dwarven Barbarian is even worse.*

Tendall: "Sure."

As I go to grab a quill from my bag there's the unmistakable sound of a multitude of blades being hurriedly drawn. I freeze in panic—the Halfling jumps to his feet and tries to calm the agitated crowd down.

Tendall: "Relax—he's just a Loremaster."

I slowly withdraw my hand and hold up the quill for the jittery bar patrons to see. A multitude of blades being quickly sheathed becomes the most beautiful sound I've ever heard in my life.[307] I turn to whisper to the Halfling.

Me: "Why's everyone so jumpy?"

Tendall: "It has been this way since the adventuring work started to run dry."

Me: "Work?"

Tendall: "Aye, you don't think we go questing for our health, do you? Life on the adventuring road is a hard path to tread..."

There's another rowdy cheer from the bar as the Cleric 'blesses' the Barbarian by connecting an ale bottle with the short-tempered Warrior's brow—only to be knocked down to the floor again.

Tendall: "As a result, mistrust is rife within the adventuring community. Double-crossing and backstabbing are commonplace—even amongst Paladins."

Me: "Paladins? I thought they were filled with stoicism, sacrifice and selflessness?"[308]

Tendall: "Paladins are the *worst*. They have all that repressed pent-up aggression swirling inside; it just takes the wrong word for them to break their oath and unleash their inner rage.[309] You do know that Paladins are just Barbarians who prefer to hide their modesty and have

---

[307] *Second only to the sound of my mother shouting up the stairs that supper is ready, of course...*

[308] *I know there's a fourth one, but as of yet, I've not found out what that is.*

[309] *There's a pang of guilt as the image of a swear-filled Redmane suddenly pops into my mind.*

a higher forgiveness threshold, right? But you didn't come here to this place to talk about Paladins; why are *you* here, Loremaster?"

Me: "I want to talk to adventurers about their experiences."

Tendall: "*Ha—experiences...* I could tell you a few stories; mark my words."

Me: "Then do! I'm interested in the tales you have to tell."

Tendall: "Why? What is it to you?"

Me: "I come from a family of adventurers, my father, mother and brother—"

Tendall: "—But not you?"

Me: "My brother's ambition to become a hero casts a shadow from which I fear I will never emerge. Better to accept my limitations and follow the path that suits me, which has turned out to be writing down adventuring experiences for others to enjoy."[310]

Tendall: "*Enjoy...*"

The Halfling almost spits the word at me in disgust.

Me: "Do I detect a hint of disdain in your voice?"

Tendall: "It's more than a hint. I think you're on a fool's errand, Loremaster. Take my word for it—you're chasing something that does not exist."

Me: "But you're a hero; why would you say that—?"

The Rogue holds his hand up as if to stop me.

Tendall: "Don't do that. Don't *ever* use the 'H' word around here—"

Me: "What? Hero—?"

The Halfling winces as if I had just landed a mortal blow and leans closer to whisper angrily across the trestle table.

Tendall: "Are you *trying* to get us both killed?!"

---

[310] *Which is as close to 'actual' adventuring as I'm ever going to get...*

Me: "What did I say wrong?"

The Rogue continues to whisper at me with urgency.

Tendall: "Around here, being a 'hero' is *not* something you shout about. You ever met a Rogue who thought they were heroic?"[311]

Me: "No, but that doesn't mean you're not—why would you ever contemplate going on an adventure otherwise?"

Tendall: "One word—*coin.*"

Me: "Surely the pursuit of coin can't be the *only* reason?"[312]

Tendall: "It's not—but it's the only reason that matters to me."

Me: "What about the other members of your party?"

Tendall: "What about them?"

Me: "Why do they do what they do?"

Tendall: "You'd have to ask them—but I'd wager Fighters and Barbarians probably do it for the thrill of the fight, Rangers and Druids do it for nature, Monks do it for inner peace, Wizards, Warlocks, and Sorcerers undoubtedly do it for power,[313] while Clerics and Paladins do it for their Sky God—whoever or whatever that is..."[314]

Me: "That must make for some interesting personality clashes."

Tendall: "If I had it my way, I wouldn't go with any of them, but needs must—we all have a role to play."

---

[311] *That depends—does a decapitated talking skull count here...*

[312] *It's worth pointing out here that I'm earning nothing for this work. All these interviews, all these journeys, all these risks are for you, dear reader—although, if there's a Publishing Guild reading this who is interested in offering me payment for this journal to appear in print—then get in touch (just please don't use a 'Barker' to send word first).*

[313] *I notice that Necromancers aren't included in that list—although I suspect they'd happily do it for a corpse or three.*

[314] *Even though I'm not religious in the slightest—I want it on the record that I've never called any omnipresent being a 'Sky God' before—although I can't promise I won't start using that term in future.*

Me: "What's your role?"

The Rogue sits back and sucks in his breath.

Tendall: "We do the stuff the others can't or won't do; picking locks, disarming traps, finding secret doors. Can you imagine the Barbarian trying to disarm a trap? That muscle-bound dolt would lose their temper after the first failed attempt and start hitting things—hard. I've learned, over the many summers, that violence and trap-disarming usually make for a fatal combination."

Me: "If you despise the other classes, why not go on Rogue-only adventures?"

Tendall: "You're *joking*, aren't you? Could you imagine—a bunch of us Rogues all on the same quest and trying to work together towards the same goal? We'd all backstab one another before we've had a chance to leave the tavern!"

Me: "I suppose there are no *heroes* amongst thieves—"

There's a **'THUD'** as a pint and a half lands heavily between us. I look up at the gruffest of Barmaids, a muscled Half-Orc who probably puts in an evening shift as the tavern's no-nonsense bouncer. I can't miss the irony of the tattoo inked onto her eye-popping bicep, which boldly states 'Desire'.[315]

Me: "T—Thanks..."

I slide two silver coins across the table towards her. They are quickly snapped up and disappear in the Barmaid's enormous fists.

The Halfling leans closer and hisses.

Tendall: "*I told you about using that word in here!*"

Me: "Sorry—it was a slip of the tongue."

I notice a few unsavoury types glancing at our table; the Halfling looks up at me in alarm and hisses another warning.

Tendall: "Keep on using it, and your tongue will do more than slip—it'll be cut out and used to string you up by the neck."

---

[315] *At least the tattoo doesn't say A.C.A.B.—which stands for 'All Clerics Are Blasphemers'.*

Me: "That's a pretty messy way to go."[316]

Tendall: "If you're not careful, this crowd will do a *lot* worse to you."

Me: "I understand the lack of quests is causing tensions to rise, but I'm still struggling to see why there's so much animosity towards heroe—"

'THUD!'

I'm stopped from completing my question as the gruff Barmaid slams a foaming flagon on the table next to us,[317] where a weary adventurer sits brooding in silence. The Rogue says nothing more until the Half-Orc is safely out of earshot.

Tendall: "There are many who believe adventurers cause as many problems as they solve."

Me: "Can you give me an example?"

The Halfling takes a sip of his drink and wipes his top lip with the back of his hand.

Tendall: "Let's go back to your rat infestation problem."

Me: "But I don't *have* a rat infestation problem—"[318]

The Halfling waves away my protests.

Tendall: "Humour me. You're a Farmer; you're starting to lose a fair bit of grain to this rat infestation. But it's not going to change your way of life overnight—not straight away."

Me: "Agreed."

Tendall: "Now throw some adventurers into the mix, adventurers who are keen to get a quick result."

Me: "Why quick?"

---

[316] *Not to mention totally impractical—unless you're a Dragon with an exceptionally long tongue—but even then, that has got to be some gallows to take the weight of the unfortunate beast.*

[317] *If this is how 'gruff' the Barmaid is—imagine how 'gruff' the Landlord has to be!*

[318] *That I know of!*

Tendall: "Plenty of reasons; perhaps they're worried about a rival adventuring group coming in and completing the same quest before them? Or worse, they miss out on a well-paid quest because they're stuck clearing out the rats from your fetid cellar."

Me: "I see… so my rat infestation *has* to be completed with speed."

Tendall: "Which means they'll happily cut corners to complete it."

Me: "What do you mean by cut corners?"

Tendall: "Maybe the Wizard casts spells that get the job done faster; maybe they start throwing Fireball spells around like it's happy hour at the Weendale Straw Festival."[319]

Me: "So, cutting corners ends up with my rat infestation going—"

Tendall: ***"BOOM!"***

Me: "Ouch…"

The Halfling **'chinks'** his flagon against mine in agreement.

Tendall: "Exactly!"

Me: "So, any side-quests…"

Tendall: "—are being completed far too quickly. The… '*H*' Guild… are picking the realm clean of every adventure from here to the Forgotten Marshes."[320]

Me: "But if the land is cleansed of these Evildoers—isn't that a *good* thing?"

Tendall: "Maybe in the short term, sure, everything is rosy and peaceful for a while—but adventurers still need to earn coin to live. How can they support a wife and three screaming kids when there are no well-

---

[319] *The Weendale Straw Festival is famed for some of the most intricate effigies in the entire realm; huge straw monstrosities are constructed as part of a summer-long festival, culminating in the festival-goers jumping into a huge pool of highly flammable alcohol before lighting an enormous Halfling-rolled woodbine.*

[320] *Which is somewhere far away—not that anyone can remember. The 'Forgotten' Marshes are not to be confused with the 'Unforgotten' Marshes, which are difficult to forget in a hurry.*

paid quests left to feed or clothe them? What work is there for an ex-adventurer?"[321]

Me: "I didn't think Rogues would ever come up short on coin-making schemes."[322]

The Halfling blows out his cheeks and sits back in his seat.

Tendall: "Not *all* Rogues are thieves and pickpockets. Some, like myself, are good honest adventurers who just happen to know how to survive a trap-filled dungeon—our skills aren't designed for making a quick coin."

Me: "Sorry, I wasn't suggesting you were *that* kind of Rogue. But, forgive me for saying this, if you have no coin, isn't it normal for you to take it from those who do?"

Tendall: "And as I said before—I'm _not_ that kind of Rogue."[323]

I stare at the Halfling, unsure if he's being serious or not.

Me: "Why do you think there's been a sudden rise in the number of adventurers appearing across the realm?"

My interviewee looks left and right, making sure there are no nearby earwiggers,[324] before leaning closer and answering in a hushed voice.

Tendall: "The 'H' Guild."

Me: "You mean the *Heroes* Guild—?"

The Halfling winces in pain at me—I notice there are more than a few scowls thrown in our direction from the nearest patrons.

---

[321] *An interesting question, I'm guessing many fall into Bodyguard roles (not to be confused with Bodyguard rolls, which is a favoured delicacy of bad-tempest Storm Giants).*

[322] *Halfling, Gnome, and Dwarven Rogues excluded.*

[323] *I'm just wondering if there's another kind of Rogue I don't know about?*

[324] *Earwiggers are a type of Gnome with a notorious reputation for listening in on private conversations—they also like to dig into sleeping adventurers' ears, looking for tasty earwax to snack on in the middle of the night. Needless to say, they're seldom invited on any group adventures.*

Me: "*Sorry*—why don't you simply join the '*H*' Guild then? I hear they have the lion's share of profitable quests in the realm."

Tendall: "Look at me, Loremaster—what do you see?"

Me: "*Erm...*"

Tendall: "It's not a trick question."

Me: "A Rogue?"

Tendall: "What else?"

Me: "A... *Halfling* Rogue?"

Tendall: "Precisely! I'm *never* going to be quest-giver *facing*."

Me: "Quest-giver facing? What's that?"

Tendall: "Okay, I want you to imagine we're at a lavish banquet thrown in honour for my successful questing—then imagine the look on the quest-giver's face as they're forced to hand over a large sack of coins in payment for my *particular* set of skills."

I scrunch my face at the thought.

The Halfling slams the table and points in my direction.

Tendall: "*Ha*—that's *exactly* the same look the quest-giver would give me!"

Me: "But doesn't it take all sorts to become a h—"

The Halfling glares at me as he takes a swig of ale. He wipes the foam from his mouth with the back of his hand before speaking again.

Tendall: "That's the 'H' Guild talking—in truth, those bastards wouldn't let me within a thousand feet of any post-quest celebratory party. That's only reserved for the ones dripping in charisma[325]—certainly not for the likes of me."

Me: "That seems a tad unfair."

---

[325] *Paladins or Bards—although I doubt any party where both a Paladin AND a Bard are present at the same time would be worth attending.*

Tendall: "Unfair, maybe, unethical, almost certainly. Remember, this is the same 'H' Guild that operates with a 40% tariff on *any* loot obtained—65% if you're a Rogue. And if you're unlucky enough to be a Halfling Rogue, you'll be paying upwards of 80%. They term it an *'Honesty Tax'*—can you believe that?"

Me: "80%? That's steep. Why would you have to pay a higher rate for being a Halfling?"

Tendall: "Halflings don't have the greatest of reputations at the best of times. Other adventurers are quick to judge us."

Me: "Who?"

Tendall: "Generally anyone taller than us.[326] Many think that just because we're head-height to a coin purse, we can't be trusted near one. Paladins are the worst; they're *always* watching us when we're out in the adventuring field together."[327]

Me: "So, the 'H' Guild taxes you for being a Halfling *AND* a Rogue? In my travels, I've heard accounts of the Guild's efforts at modernisation and expansion. Might your circumstance just be some arcane bylaw that will be changed as part of that process?"

Tendall: "Changed? *Huh,* not so long as Bartlet has his say."

Me: "Who's Bartlet?"

Tendall: "A Tallyman with a grudge—he *hates* Halflings with a passion.[328] What's worse is that he has the ear of Toldarn, the Guildmaster."

Me: "Why would a Gnome hate a Halfling? Aren't you both cut from the same cloth?"

The Rogue eyes me suspiciously.

Tendall: "What do you mean?"

---

[326] *Which may or may not include Gnomes.*

[327] *Probably making sure the Rogue doesn't daub rude words on their prized armour when the Paladin's back is turned.*

[328] *I suspect the Tallyman feels Halflings would generate twice the amount of official paperwork a Gnome would make for the exact same quest.*

I suddenly fear I'm about to insult the Rogue—possibly not for the first time.

Me: "Just... you're both of similar stock—"

The Halfling puts his hand up again and shakes his head.

Tendall: "Let me stop you right there. Halflings and Gnomes are *nothing* alike. For a start, we are at least a hand taller than those cave-hugging fools."

Me: "Nonetheless, it would appear to an outsider that both your races face many of the same challenges."

Tendall: "Like what?"

Me: "*Erm...* things being placed too high and out of reach? Chairs that must first be climbed upon before being sat on?"

The Halfling stares at me before roaring with laughter.

Tendall: "You're funny, Loremaster—has anyone told you to give up your writing and become a Joker?"[329]

Me: "A few have mentioned it—*yes...*"

Tendall: "You should have listened to them when you had the chance, Loremaster—you would have made a fortune by now."

The Halfling takes another swig of ale.

Me: "Would a common approach between Halflings and Gnomes not further both your interests?"

Tendall: "A common approach? Listen, do you see any Gnome Rogues being taxed as much as us?"

Me: "Well... *erm...* I don't know the answer to that—are there any Gnome Rogues in the 'H' Guild?"

Tendall: "None."

---

[329] *By sheer coincidence, my recently departed Uncle Bevan Barr was a 'Joker'—a professional funny man who would go around making Barons laugh for coin. As I had refused to follow in my parents' adventuring footsteps, he had tried unsuccessfully to convince me to follow in his 'oversized' comedic ones.*

Me: "What about Gnome Rogues outside the 'H' Guild?"

The Halfling shakes his head.

Tendall: "The point stands. It's not my fault they're too busy tinkering around with their pointless inventions to go on a proper quest."

Me: "What's the purpose of the *Honesty Tax* anyway?"

Tendall: "It's to cover any shortfall that <u>blasted</u> Bartlet finds in the loot total."

Me: "Why would there be a shortfall? Wouldn't you truthfully declare whatever haul you returned with?"

The Halfling shifts uncomfortably in his seat.

Tendall: "I would declare whatever I *thought* the 'H' Guild deserved. Let me ask you this—do you think it's right that a Paladin, dressed in full plate armour and carrying a sword twice the size of this table, should pay **<u>less</u>** loot tax than me? Who do you think steps into an unexplored room first or checks for traps in the darkest of corridors? Who is expected to pick a lock that could inflict a lethal dose of poison when opened? *Clerics?* Those self-righteous fools are always trying too hard to impress their Sky Gods[330] rather than get their hands dirty. *Wizards?* All they care about is unleashing their next spell to impress any nearby Barbarians.[331] *Paladins?* They are so morally superior they just want to rub your nose in it. No, I'll tell you who gets to do it—me, or at least someone else like me. The way I see it, the small amount I skim off the top is only danger coin I'm owed."

The Halfling sits back with visible relief as if a heavy burden has been lifted from his shoulders.

Tendall: "Now tell me, how I'm supposed to survive when the last time I earned any coin was three weeks ago? Do you want to know how much I made back then?"

I shake my head.

---

[330] *If a Sky God is somehow reading this, that was Tendall's words—not mine!*

[331] *Those 'pretty lights' a Spellcaster musters will happily distract your average Barbarian for hours on end...*

Tendall: "Ten measly silver coins, *after* tax, of course…"

Me: "I thought you said you weren't in the 'H' Guild?"

Tendall: "*Oh,* I'm not—but if you go on a quest, the chances are the adventurer standing behind you *is.* The Guild collects their tax from *all* adventurers—be they members or not. That *arrangement* is non-negotiable if you know what's good for you."

Me: "What does that mean?"

The Rogue drains the contents of his tankard and doesn't seem keen to follow it with another.

Tendall: "It means you don't measure a Dragon's bite by sticking your hand in its mouth.[332] Look, I don't claim to be a shining light of perfection; I've done some less than honourable things in my time."

Me: "Like what?"

Tendall: "Well… I—I've sold my body to a Necromancer for one."

Me: "You sold your body to a Necromancer? But you're *still* alive!"

Tendall: "It's one of those *'In the unfortunate event of death'* kind of *arrangements*—until then, it's all mine."[333]

Me: "That doesn't sound wholly ethical."

Tendall: "Maybe not, but is it really any worse than what the 'H' Guild is doing? I don't think so—at least this way, I'm still making some coin."[334]

The Halfling thinks for a moment before speaking again.

Tendall: "Tell me, why didn't you follow your family's path and become an adventurer?"

Me: "My father doesn't believe I have what it takes to step into the unknown."

---

[332] *Or if you're Seymour, your whole body…*

[333] *Somehow knowing this isn't making that 'fact' any better.*

[334] *What are the chances there's a small clause that reads 'Payment only upon delivery of the body'.*

Tendall: "Take my word for it; your father is right. He is only doing what any parent would do in his situation—keeping you safe."

Me: "If that is true, why did he let my brother go off to adventure?"

Tendall: "Don't take this the wrong way, but did your father hold your brother in high regard?"

Me: "Of course he did—Aldon was his favourite, the one destined to carry the family's adventuring name into the future."

Tendall: "Perhaps it was *you* who was the favourite, not your brother."

I stare at the Halfling in confusion as thoughts of home fill my head.

Me: "I don't understand? *I* was his favourite? How can that be?"

Tendall: "You're not the one trying to survive a monster-filled dungeon to impress him. Maybe you should ask yourself why that is?"

There's an awkward moment of reflective silence, mercifully broken by cheers coming from the bar—the unconscious Elven Cleric has awoken from his floor slumber and is buying the Dwarven Barbarian a drink.[335]

Me: "What lies further along the road for Tendall Fleetfoot?"

Tendall: "I've heard about a rare spellbook in Meepvale that could fetch a handsome price to the right buyer—*if* I can get my hands on it, that is."

Me: "A rare spellbook? I doubt that will come cheap."

The Halfling grins as he winks at me.

Tendall: "I'll get it for *a steal*, I'm sure."[336]

I'm suddenly aware of a figure standing behind me—the Rogue falls silent. I turn to see the tired-looking Fighter staring expectantly.[337]

---

[335] *The Barbarian is taking it in good spirits by ordering one of <u>every</u> spirit from the shelf behind the bar.*

[336] *Once a Rogue—<u>always</u> a Rogue...*

[337] *The Fighter watches me like a dog, salivating with expectancy while watching their master polish off a plump steak without offering them a single morsel.*

Fighter: "Are you a quest-giver?"

Me: "A quest-giver—*me?* No—"

Fighter: "Forgive me; you look like someone who has a severe rat infestation in their cellar..."[338]

The adventurer spins on his heels and disappears into the sea of heroes. I hear a squeak of a chair as the Halfling gets up to leave, a wide grin fixed upon his face.

Tendall: "See—told you. Thanks again for the drink and the company..."

The Rogue fishes around in his pocket before placing a coin on the table and sliding it toward me. I put my hand up to stop him.

Me: "It's okay, you don't have to repay me—"

The Halfling shakes his head and turns to leave.

Tendall: "I *only* take what I need and *need* what I take. Farewell, Loremaster. Watch your back *and* your coin purse—especially in this place."

The Halfling's sharp eyes look back and hold mine before he too disappears into the crowd behind him. Alone and surrounded by an angry sea of heroes, I suddenly feel adrift in dangerous waters. I quietly leave without touching a drop of the ale that has been sat in front of me the entire time—a travesty, I know, but a necessary one if I want to live to see another day.[339]

---

[338] *This is absolutely not true—for starters, I do <u>not</u> own a cellar.*

[339] **Loremaster Tip #5:** *Sometimes, it's better to leave a full flagon rather than risk not leaving at all.*

12. Lance & Holden, the Castle Guards

Situated on the top of a high bluff, Castle Verdale is an impressive feat of architecture that overlooks the namesake town of Verdale, located on the shores of Lake Verdale far below. I regret my decision not to dedicate more time in my youth to building up my stamina as I slowly ascend the single steep road that winds its way to Castle Verdale's foreboding portcullis. More than once during the arduous climb, I'm forced to stop to catch my breath, pausing to look down upon the town of Verdale as locals go about their daily business blissfully unaware a Loremaster is watching them like an omnipresent voyeur. I'm hoping to speak to the Guards who keep a constant watch over the lake town from the castle's impressive ramparts. I intend to find out what the average local thinks about the notable increase of adventurers who now spend their days frequenting the town's only tavern—The Armed & Armless.[340]

As I near the closed portcullis, two Guards suddenly sprint from their posts and level their crossbows at me. I instinctively raise my hands to show them I carry no threat about my person.[341]

Me: "H—Hello!"

Moustached Guard: "What do you want? Where's your gold badge?"

Me: "What gold badge?"

Non-Moustached Guard: "We should just shoot him!"

Moustached Guard: "No gold badge? No entry—!"

Non-Moustached Guard: "There's no loitering, running or petting either!"[342]

Me: "W—Wait! I—I just want to talk to you!"[343]

---

[340] *So-called in honour of a local Paladin who forgot to take his sword on a particularly brutal adventure—as the tavern's name suggests, it did not end well for the Holy Warrior in question.*

[341] *Although I could probably jab someone in the eye with my quill if my life depended upon it...*

[342] *Petting? I don't even own a pet, or a Familiar of note!*

[343] *Without getting shot.*

Moustached Guard: "If you ain't got a gold badge, we're under orders to put a crossbow bolt between your eyes."[344]

Me: "What If I'm a 'Barker' carrying an important message for the Baron?"

Non-Moustached Guard: "Well—*are* you?"

Me: "No, *but*—"

I'm suddenly staring straight at the *'business end'* of a crossbow bolt.[345]

Me: "I—I'm a *Loremaster!* I just wanted to talk to you both about all the adventurers gathered around here—I'm here to interview you both!"

The crossbows are slowly lowered as the two Guards exchange looks.

Non-Moustached Guard: "What? You want to talk to *us?*"

Me: "Yes, for the journal I'm writing—"

Moustached Guard: "You mean we'll be *famous?*"

Me: "Why not—*yes*, I suppose you *could* be."[346]

Both Guards relax and hoist their crossbows over their shoulders as they step closer toward me. I'm still visibly shaking from the thought of nearly becoming a human pincushion as the first Guard introduces himself.

Moustached Guard: "I'm Lance; this here is Holden."

Holden: "That's spelt with *two* 'N's."

Me: "Two 'N's—got it."

Lance: "You *really* a Loremaster?"

---

[344] *If the two Guards were Halflings, I wouldn't be too worried by this—but as they're not, I'm taking this threat <u>very</u> seriously.*

[345] *A Gnomish phrase meaning 'the exact point where there's a sudden and painful death— namely yours'...*

[346] *It's said that 'success is relative' when it comes to selling a journal—I assume <u>that</u> means how many of my relatives end up buying a copy will undoubtedly decide whether it's a success (or not).*

Me: "Yes—why do you ask?"

Lance: "Just we get *all* sorts trying to sneak in here—"

The Guard gestures to the imposing castle standing behind him.

Lance: "—some go over the walls."

Holden: "Others try and bluff their way past us..."[347]

Me: "Who would do that?"

Holden: "Adventurers."

Me: "Adventurers? *Really?* Are you sure?"

Lance: "Positive. We've had all sorts try and get inside—Rogues, Rangers, *even* had the odd Paladin or two—but they're really easy to spot."[348]

Me: "Really? Why?"

Holden: "Noisy buggers."

Me: "Noisy?"[349]

Holden: "Plate armour. It may stop a spear or sword, but it's not the subtlest of choices when it comes to sneaking into places. Have you ever heard someone in plate armour trying to scale a wall? They make so much noise they could wake the undead!"

Me: "Why are these adventurers so determined to get inside?"

Holden eyes me suspiciously.

Holden: "Are you *sure* you're a Loremaster? Shouldn't you be writing all this down or something?"

I tap my temple reassuringly.

---

[347] As Castle Verdale is built on a bluff, I suppose technically this can be called a 'double-bluff'...

[348] Maybe the sound of their huge ego scraping against the sides of the castle walls gives them away?

[349] Maybe it *is* the sound of their immense ego after all...

Me: "On the road, this is all I need."[350]

Holden narrows his eyes suspiciously.

Holden: "So do *Wizards*. They need excellent memories to remember all those spells—you *sure* you're not a Wizard?"

Me: "I thought Wizards relied on their spellbooks rather than their memory?"

Lance: "He's right, Holden..."

Holden: "What am I thinking of?"

Lance: "Sorcerers?"

Holden: "Yeah, Sorcerers, not Wizards—are you *sure* you're not a Sorcerer?"

Me: "I'm not magically inclined—*I swear!*"[351]

Holden: "Watch this one, Lance—he's probably got a Fireball up his sleeve."[352]

Lance raps Holden on the arm.

Lance: "Stop being an idiot—does he *look* like a Wizard? Where's his Wizard robes or pointy hat? He doesn't even have a long white beard—"

Me: "You know that's a cliché you've described, don't you?"

Holden: "No, it's a Wizard—and I know what I'm talking about. You *stink* of magic; we should put a bolt in him, Lance—before he turns us into piles of hot ash."

---

[350] *This is true to a point, I do have a good recall for detail, but I still like to commit some of my experiences to paper—just in case a mischievous Wizard decides to cast 'Befuddlement' on me for the fun of it, rather than their go-to 'Fireball' spell...*

[351] *Although the longer this interview goes on, the greater the chance I'll perform a spontaneous disappearing trick.*

[352] *I hope whoever came up with the name 'Fireball' used an Arcane Copyright spell on it—because if they didn't, then someone just missed out earning a potential fortune every time someone says it.*

I roll my eyes skywards.

Me: "Please pick another spell!"

There's a beat of silence as I can see the Guard struggling to name another spell.

Holden: "*Firesphere?*"

I shake my head in disbelief.

Me: "You just made that up!"

Holden: "No, I didn't!"[353]

Me: "Look, I'll just go and leave you two to it—"

Lance: "NO, WAIT! Don't go! Holden is just being—*Holden*. He doesn't mean it... it's just that he's been burnt a few times—"

Me: "Was it a Wizard?"[354]

Holden grabs his crossbow and levels it at me once more—but Lance is quicker and thankfully pushes it away.

Lance: "Go ahead and ask your questions, Loremaster."

I nod and glance at the glaring Holden before continuing.

Me: "Why do heroes want to break into this castle so badly?"

Holden coughs conspicuously as Lance drops his voice to a whisper.

Lance: "The Baron who lives here... *well*—he's not exactly a *good* Baron, if you know what I mean."

Me: "Is he an Evildoer?"

---

[353] *I have subsequently found out that there is a spell called 'Firesphere', which is a cheap knockoff of the infamous 'Fireball' spell. It was renamed 'Firesphere' to get around any unseen Arcane Copyright spells—although it also has a reputation of burning away the Spellcaster's clothes too...*

[354] *Sorry, I couldn't resist.*

Lance: "*Oh,* I wouldn't go *that* far. On the *Scale for Evildoers*,[355] the Midnight Army of Lord Zolar[356] would be at one end, while our Baron would be *waaaaaaaaay* down at the other—"

Holden: "—right next to *Wizards*..."

Me: "But *is* he bad?"

Lance: "Look, he pays us well, takes care of our families, and gives us sick days off when we're unwell. He also throws a great end-of-summer party held in the castle's Grand Hall that includes free food and drink. Now—does that *sound* bad to you?"

Me: "No, it sounds pretty good—I see how working for the Baron could be an attractive proposition to some."

Lance: "There you go!"

Holden: "Although... he *does* rule his domain with an iron fist and executes anyone who defies his command. He has also taxed his people to the brink of starvation whilst sitting on a mountain of stolen gold— but those parties are to *die* for!"

Lance: "Don't forget the *Survival Bonus* in our monthly pay—which comes in handy."

Holden: "Yes—how could I forget the *Survival Bonus!*"

Me: "So, these uninvited adventurers then—?"

Holden: "Annoying buggers. If one of them got in and, the Gods forbid, *killed* the Baron, we can kiss goodbye to our extra pay and fun parties. That's why it's our sworn duty to keep *all* adventurers out."

Me: "All of them?"

Lance: "No exceptions."

Holden: "Well, *except*—"

---

[355] *I really hope there is a Scale for Evildoers—with dramatic pipe organ music that grows more menacing the further up the scale you go.*

[356] *Contrary to popular opinion, the 'Midnight Army' were so-called because they took so long to mobilise, it was the middle of the night before they were finally ready for battle.*

Lance fixes Holden with a hard stare.

Lance: "Look—there are a select few who are allowed in."

Me: "I'm confused. Shouldn't you be stopping *every* adventurer from getting to the Baron?"

Holden takes out a pipe and taps the end several times on the stonework before stuffing it with a generous amount of tobacco from his pouch.

Lance: "You have to understand there's a perfect equilibrium at work here; any adventurers we let in on purpose *aren't* hired to take the Baron down."

Holden grabs a long twig off the floor and ignites the end on a nearby fire pit. He puffs several times—making sure the tobacco is fully ignited before taking out his pipe and releasing a large plume of smoke through his nostrils.

Lance: "Verdale isn't exactly knee-deep in quests. Where will the next main quest come from if the Baron is vanquished? The nearest one must be over forty-five miles away and probably involves clearing a rat infestation in some poor soul's cellar, no doubt."[357]

Me: "I still don't understand—if the Baron is the cause of all the suffering and misery in Verdale; why don't the locals pay for a hero to remove him for good? Wouldn't everyone in the area prosper from his fall?"

There's a splutter from Holden as he almost chokes on his pipe smoke.

Holden: "That's what you think! The truth of the matter is, Verdale *needs* a steady stream of adventurers passing through so the locals can earn enough coin to pay the heavy tax demanded of them. Why would any hero turn up in Verdale if the Baron were already dead? Verdale would become an inconsequential blot on the landscape overnight,

---

[357] *Though technically, I believe this is regarded as a side-quest, not a main quest.*

avoided by everyone except Gravediggers and Necromancers."[358]

Me: "Wait, let me get this right—the Baron taxes the locals to the brink of starvation—then adventurers are hired by the populace to steal back the coin from the Baron?"

Lance: "—Who taxes the local residents to the brink of starvation once again."

Holden: "—Meaning another batch of heroes can be hired."

Lance: "I told you—there's a perfect equilibrium at work here."

Me: "It's the quest that never goes away."

Lance: "I like to call it an *Endless Quest...*"

Holden: "Destined to repeat itself!"

Me: "But how do you know who the right adventurers are to let in and who isn't?"

Holden: "That's where the Heroes Guild comes in handy."

Lance gives a rueful headshake at his colleague's looseness of the tongue.

Me: "Why would the Heroes Guild involve themselves in something like this?"

Holden: "They have an *arrangement* with the Baron. He stays alive and gets what he wants, while the Guild's adventurers get what they want—a quest and ample reward—everyone wins."

Me: "Everyone except for the locals of Verdale, it seems."

Lance: "*Really?* They have a town full of adventurers eager to spend their hard-earned coin on food, drink and distractions."

---

[358] *There has been a long-standing rivalry between Gravediggers and Necromancers, each accusing the other of getting in the way of their hugely important work. Often the two rivals will bury and dig up the same corpse in an endless cycle of one-upmanship. However, a few shrewd Gravediggers see Necromancers as a coin-making opportunity in the waiting and vice versa.*

Holden: "*Everyone* wins."[359]

Me: "Unless a non-Guild adventurer turns up and takes out the Baron, of course."

Both Guards suck in their breath in wide-eyed shock and turn deathly white.[360]

Lance: "Well, it's our job to make sure that doesn't happen."

Me: "How do you do that?"

Lance: "The Baron has a permanent number of Guards with him at all times."

Me: "At all times?"

Holden: "At *all* times. There isn't a moment he is left alone—not for a heartbeat."[361]

Me: "The Baron has no privacy at all?"

Holden: "None, whatsoever—in fact, if you've ever upset the Baron, chances are you'll end up guarding him through privy duty."

Me: "That's an unpleasant thought."

Holden: "Not as unpleasant as when the Baron has eaten spicy buttered goat and washed it down with several flagons of Bigblow's Bowl-Basher Bitter."[362]

Lance: "We usually put a number of '*Token*' Guards on privy duty."

Me: "What are 'Token' Guards?"

---

[359] *I sense this was said as a threat, more than a statement.*

[360] *Both looking a little like a Mime Warrior trapped in an Unexpected Maze.*

[361] *I'm not sure I would be happy watching someone every second of the day—or the one being watched, for that matter.*

[362] *Bigblow's Bowl-Basher Bitter has an unenviable reputation of passing through a typical digestive system in under a minute. It's even rumoured to be the preferred poison of the much-feared White Porcelains—a secret order of Assassins, who lie in wait for their victims to rush to the privy before striking mid-flush.*

Holden: "They are drafted locals who were lucky enough to be picked for Guard duty through the Baron's fair-but-firm *'Token' Lottery.*"[363]

Me: "I've never heard of a 'Token' Lottery before—how does it work?"

Lance: "It's quite simple—if you have the Baron's 'Token' shoved under your door, then you are expected to show up the next morning at the castle, where you are given a five-minute sword-handling demonstration, and one of those inferior swords we buy in bulk from Thorde Ironstein. However, those who would rather hide under their bedrolls are quickly rounded up and put on privy duty."[364]

Holden: "They really have nothing to worry about. They're just there to offer any 'official' adventurers found inside the castle walls what we like to call *'Token' resistance.*"

Lance: "We can't make it *too* easy for them."

Holden: "We also give clear instructions to any visiting adventurers that our 'Token' Guards must *not* come to any harm—it's all part of the *arrangement* we have with the Heroes Guild."

Lance: "But accidents *do* happen from time to time."

Me: "Are the locals aware of your *arrangement* with the Heroes Guild?"

Lance: "They don't need to know all the details; it would only make them worry."

Holden: "Which would only lead to them doing something that'll get them killed."

Me: "Are the locals happy being part of this 'Token' Lottery?"

Holden: "As long as it keeps the coin rolling in for them—they're happy."

---

[363] *Apparently, there is a big ceremony where the names of the locals are written on the surface of a chicken egg. All the named eggs are then placed inside a huge Gnomish contraption called a 'tombola'. Once the eggs are added, the Baron rotates the tombola before plucking the (un)lucky named egg out to become the next 'Token' Guard. The whole ceremony is done with the utmost care lest the Baron ends up with scrambled egg on his face.*

[364] *They should rename this the 'Taken' lottery.*

Lance: "But it's not as if they have any actual choice on the matter."

Me: "Have any non-Guild members ever managed to sneak inside the castle?"

Holden: "Only one—a blind Elven Monk. She somehow skulked past us undetected. The Elf almost got to the Baron too, but her attack missed at the crucial point, and she drop-kicked another Guard out of the privy window to his death—Doogan, poor blighter, what a messy way to go."

Me: "Messy?"

Lance: "He landed in the privy tank directly below the window. A Turd Lurker ate him."

Me: "What's a Turd Lurker?"

Holden: "Imagine your worst nightmare, then cover it in human excrement—*that's* a Turd Lurker!"[365]

Me: "And this 'Doogan' was a friend of yours?"

Lance: "More of a professional acquaintance—I mean, we never got drunk together or anything like that—he was just another face in armour around here."

Me: "How did he end up on privy duty?"

Holden: "Unfortunately, he had incurred the wrath of the Baron the night before when he giggled as the Baron sat down in a noisy chair. Poor blighter, he was a decent lad, always making people smile, never had a bad word to say about anyone. He ended up leaving a wife and three kids behind. I still remember their little faces when I gave them the news; it broke my heart telling them about his final poop-filled scream as that fetid Turd Lurker dragged him under."

Holden: "The Baron did right by Doogan's family though; even paid out on the '*Death-during-Service*' contract the Guard had—<u>and</u> he always makes sure the kids never go hungry. He also arranged for Doogan's

---

[365] *I've since discovered that there are numerous types of 'Turd Lurkers', from annoying 'Wall Clingers' and the lethargic 'Surface Floaters' through to the stubborn 'Impact Stainers' and the terror-inducing 'Recurring Bobbers'. If you encounter one in a dark privy, make sure you have plenty of parchment and a very large brush to tackle the foul-smelling monstrosity.*

body to be fully fumigated before the cremation; that sort of thing really shows how much he cares about us."[366]

Lance: "Aye, he's good like that."

Me: "How do you know the Monk was blind?"

Lance: "She was carrying a long white stick."

Me: "How do you know it wasn't some kind of *exotic* weapon?"[367]

Lance: "I don't, but how do you explain mistaking Doogan for the Baron? They couldn't be less alike; Doogan is over six feet tall and hairier than a naked Dwarf, while the Baron is four foot three and bald. The Monk *had* to be blind; it's the only explanation that makes any sense."

Me: "What happened after that?"

Lance: "The Guard's turd-filled cries disorientated the Elf long enough for the Baron to escape. We immediately ran to investigate, but the Monk had fled back over the castle wall and into the night."

Holden: "Poor Doogan—it could have been any of us."

Lance: "The Baron understandably took his frustration out on the locals."

Me: "It wasn't their fault, was it?"

Lance: "No, but he has a reputation to uphold, so..."

Me: "What did he do?"

Holden: "He set some of the homes in the poorer quarters on fire—as punishment for not warning us about the Monk."

---

[366] *I've heard that some 'Grey Wizards' earn extra ale coin cremating bodies with a well-placed Fireball. Mind you, the recommended safe distance for any mourners attending the cremation is about half a mile from the deceased's body.*

[367] *Exotic weapons are usually forged by tropical-based Forgemasters—like blow darts, boomerangs and nunchakus (a type of Holy weapon designed to launch multiple 'Nuns' at a foe). Not to be confused with 'Erotic Weapons'—which is something completely different and probably banned in most places in the realm.*

Me: "I'm guessing there hasn't been a repeat of the incident since?"

Lance: "Not yet—"

'CLANG! CLANG! CLANG! CLANG!'

There's a loud ringing from the alarm bell deep within the castle grounds. Both Lance and Holden jump out of their skins and turn in shock.

Me: "Wha—?"

Holden: "I'll be a Goblin's mother—"[368]

Me: "What's happening?"

Lance: "The intruder alarm! It's another non-Guilder trying to get to the Baron—it better not be that bloody blind Monk again."

Holden: "One silver coin says it is."

Lance: "You're on!"

The pair spit into their hands to seal their bet with a liquid contract.[369]

Holden: ***"RAISE IT! RAISE IT!"***

The heavy portcullis starts to rise slowly off the ground.

Lance: "There's going to be trouble in Verdale tonight…"

He turns back to me with a growled warning.

Lance: "Loremaster, I wouldn't stay in town if I were you…"

---

[368] *This is a popular saying in these parts—elsewhere, the phrase morphs from region to region. In the north, they say: 'I'll be a Snow Wolf's Uncle', while in the south, they prefer to use 'Orc's Second Cousin—twice removed'. Why these phrases have evolved in such a way is a mystery. I like to use the term 'Troll's Auntie', although I have to be careful there are no Trolls or Aunties within earshot of me using it.*

[369] *A liquid contract is even <u>more</u> binding than a written one, especially if one of the dealmakers is a Gelatinous Cube—although do expect your hand to dissolve shortly after 'shaking' on it.*

Holden: "Unless *you* want to end up burnt, which would be a novel change, *huh*—wouldn't it, Wizard?"[370]

Me: "I'm not a Wiz—you know what, thanks for the warning; I'll make sure I leave at the earliest opportunity."

Lance: "Good man, and remember we both want a signed copy of your work when you're finished scribing it."

Me: "It's the least I can do."[371]

I watch as the portcullis finally reaches the pinnacle of its ascent; Lance runs through, crossbow at the ready. Holden stops briefly and turns to shout in my general direction.

Holden: *"JUST REMEMBER, IT'S HOLDEN WITH TWO 'N'S!"*[372]

---

[370] Wishing I <u>did</u> know Fireball, so I could throw one in Holden's direction.

[371] Small point of clarification, but 'not' giving them both a copy is undoubtedly the least I can do...

[372] Yes, yes, two 'n's—I know! It's not as if that's going to be an easy mistake for me to ma— oh, <u>bugger</u>...

13. Silvanna, the Sorceress

A bathhouse in Tronte isn't exactly a place I frequent, so I'm not entirely sure what to expect from my next interviewee. I'm sat opposite Silvanna, an Elven Sorceress who has magic coursing through her veins. Being a Sorceress, she does not need to carry a spellbook or tome; her power is ready to be unleashed with a simple snap of her fingertips or whispered word.

I find myself a little self-conscious as I sit in the same room as the Sorceress while she bathes in a warm bathtub; a thick layer of bubbles mercifully covers her modesty like a soft foamy blanket. The Elf notices my awkwardness and grins playfully as she slowly lifts a leg above the surface to wash her calf with a Gelatinous Sponge.[373]

Silvanna: "What's wrong, Loremaster? Does my lack of grace disturb you?"

Me: "I freely admit I'm a little more accustomed to talking to people with their clothes on rather than off."[374]

The Sorceress lowers her leg beneath the bubble blanket and splashes warm water over her shoulders.

Silvanna: "There's nothing like a long hot bath after completing a quest to wash away all that dungeon filth from my skin. I believe one should take a moment to cleanse the mind and free the body from the toils and stresses that come from every adventure."

The Elf gives me a mischievous wink.

Me: "I sometimes forget that quests can be mentally tiring just as much as they are physically demanding."

Silvanna: "You are, of course, correct. It's not enough to have a strong body and heart; to truly be a hero, your mind needs to be unbreakable,

---

[373] *A Gelatinous Sponge is a smaller distant cousin of the Gelatinous Cube; that dissolves dirt rather than Rogues and heavily encumbered Clerics.*

[374] *The exception here being Barbarians, who usually enjoy wearing clothes that wouldn't keep a Gnome warm on a bitterly cold night.*

like Dwarven stone.[375] You cannot step into the unknown without believing you can survive both the seen and unseen. A sword can give you courage—but fear can stop you from drawing it. I've witnessed the mightiest of Barbarians wailing like a newborn once they're within spitting distance of a friendly tavern.[376] I've known powerful Wizards unable to turn a single page of a spellbook without 'Familiar' assistance.[377] The right sort of quest will certainly *make* a hero, while the wrong one will almost undoubtedly *break* them."

Me: "How do you choose between the right quest and the wrong one?"

Silvanna: "Carefully! When you take your first step into an adventuring life, you don't know what to do; you'll take *any* and *every* quest that comes your way. I mean—you don't want to turn down the next quest only for a rival hero to complete it and find a much-coveted Ring of Power.[378] So, until you start to get a feel for questing, it's all a bit of trial and error. You're going to make a few mistakes—mistakes that, with luck, don't leave you a warm corpse on a cold dungeon floor for an opportunistic Necromancer to find. Hopefully, you'll begin to recognise the quests that will pay out handsomely versus the ones that end up being a complete waste of time."

Me: "But how can you know any of that before you've even started the quest?"

Silvanna: "It all begins with the *quest-giver*—"

Me: "The person giving you the quest..."

Silvanna: "Nothing gets past you, Loremaster. Do you mind passing me the soap?"

---

[375] *Until recently, it was believed that Dwarven stone was the hardest of all the natural minerals until the legendary stone fortress of the Dwarven King, 'Hammer' Hammerstone, was quickly reduced to rubble by a Storm Giant with bad flatulence. As a result, Dwarves now tend to get a little jumpy if they hear thunder rumbling in the distance.*

[376] *I'm now starting to understand why some Barbarians like to walk around with nothing but a fur nappy on.*

[377] *No doubt a 'Familiar' with opposable thumbs is required for this impressive feat.*

[378] *There are many Rings of Power in the realm. Why they are considered 'powerful' is anyone's guess. Countless Kingdoms and lives have been lost over these annoyingly addictive magical trinkets. By now, you'd think someone would have the bright idea to create the one 'true' ring to rule them all and be done with it—I can but only hope.*

Me: "*Huh?*"

Silvanna: "On the table—to your right."

I dutifully pick up the bar of soap as requested before holding it out for the Sorceress to take whilst averting my eyes skywards—this makes the Elf burst into fits of laughter.

Silvanna: "How sweet. You need to get a bit *closer*—I won't bite."

Me: "*Erm… sorry…*"

I lean forward with my hand outstretched—silently hoping the Sorceress will save me from embarrassment and mercifully take the slippery object from me. There's a sudden spark of electricity from the Elf's fingertips as she softly plucks the bar from my grasp.[379] I beat a hasty retreat and sit back on the bench.

Silvanna: "Where was I? *Oh yes*—quest-givers. To begin with, I make sure of their credentials and standing. Farmers and peasant folk are never usually blessed with considerable wealth; their quests are low-paid, menial, and time-consuming. Hunters are slightly better; they often require your services to help defeat a legendary creature that has been stalking a family estate or threatening the livelihood of a town. You have to consider each hunt carefully, mind—the less organised a Hunter appears, the more likely you'll end up wading waist-deep through swamps and marshlands on some Wild Goose chase,[380] whilst literally trying to avoid being bogged down."[381]

The Sorceress pauses to gently wash her arms—I stare at my worn boots while I wait for the Elf to finish.

Silvanna: "Merchants are even better; you occasionally get lucky with the odd magical-item quest that can prove lucrative. Although, more often than not, you'll be tasked with finding a missing delivery cart that

---

[379] *If there's one thing I know about magic—electricity and water do not play well together.*

[380] *A Wild Goose is a much-feared creature that likes to bully unwary travellers into handing over their breaded lunches by honking aggressively until they get what they want.*

[381] *Not a pleasant way to go—second only to being devoured by a hungry Turd Lurker.*

failed to show up on time.[382] Then there are Nobles; they pay well but have *very* specific requirements. Sometimes it's retrieving a stolen heirloom from the Thieves Guild or removing a restless spirit from a family crypt—it's tough work but usually pays well enough to make all that extra effort worthwhile. Finally, we get to the most profitable of quest-givers, the Barons; they usually have one huge quest that's made up of a plethora of smaller quests, all connected by some obscure plot thread or another. Their quests can be anything you can imagine, from defeating an undead army of mice[383] to closing an evil portal that has annoyingly sprung up in the middle of the Baron's castle."

Me: "Are all portals evil?"

Silvanna: "Well, I've never encountered a portal that *wasn't* evil."

Me: "Why do you think that is?"

Silvanna: "Because nothing 'good' wants to leave their world behind just so they can find another world to portal-crash. Think about it, if you were content in your realm, would you go to such lengths to leave it for another?"[384]

Me: "I guess not... so how often does a Baron-level quest come along?"

The Sorceress lifts her foot from the water and watches as the bubbles slide down her ankle.

Silvanna: "Once in a lifetime if you're lucky—but if you complete it successfully, you'll make enough coin to buy a little retirement castle by the sea."

---

[382] *Nine times out of ten, the errant driver has gotten himself so drunk and disorientated he eventually turns up in the wrong town wondering why everyone is as confused as he is about his sudden appearance. The odd time a cart has <u>genuinely</u> gone missing, it's undoubtedly the fault of a joyriding Barbarian—who has taken great pleasure in stealing the passing cart with the sole aim of leaving chaos and mayhem in their wake.*

[383] *An undead army of mice that wants to eat your grains...*

[384] *This is true; I'm struggling to imagine a horde of overly helpful Clerics emerging from such a portal, insisting they use their Holy healing powers on those who need it the most. Come to think of it, such an event would be horrific—I'd imagine most locals would prefer a huge squid-like entity to appear rather than a bunch of self-righteous priests with either a complex God or God complex.*

Me: "Do you only accept a quest based on how well off the quest-giver is?"

Silvanna: "I know it sounds a little mercenary, but I have a target I need to hit; the small stuff is, well, you know, just that—*small.*"

Me: "Is that a Heroes Guild target by any chance?"

Silvanna: "No—just my own. Any hero worth their salt should always have a target wealth in mind for when their adventuring days inevitably draw to a close. Otherwise, you could find yourself doing this job until your final moments alive—who in their right mind wants that?"

Me: "So, you wouldn't take on a job that didn't help you achieve your target? What if you saw someone in trouble, but they looked unprofitable? Would you not stop to help them?"

Silvanna: "I don't know—it *depends*..."

Me: "Depends on what?"

Silvanna: "Depends if doing the deed will increase my exposure or not."

Me: "*Erm*... Exposure?"[385]

Silvanna: "Yeah, you know—my reputation.[386] Sometimes it's not just about earning coin; sometimes it's about how well received you are by the locals."

Me: "Why would you care what others think?"

Silvanna: "*Ah*—remember, a good reputation will open a door, while a bad one will see it slammed in your face. With the right amount of exposure, you can gain a plethora of free stuff or attract a better quality quest-giver. Did you hear about the Dragon that was terrorising the hamlet of Wendle recently—?"

Me: "Yes, this adventurer turned up and killed it. I heard they left behind a real mess—"

---

[385] *Well, unbelievably, this has become even more awkward than it already is...*

[386] *Phew, as you were.*

182

Silvanna: "I never earned a single coin for slaying that beast—yet that feat has travelled the length of the realm and ended up on your lips.

You can't put a price on that kind of limelight."[387]

Me: "*You* were the one who killed it!?[388] Wait—I thought some other adventurers turned up to help you defeat it?"

Silvanna: "*Oh,* there were some Heroes Guild types who tried to steal my glory—but by the time they finally showed up, the overgrown lizard was already a smouldering corpse."

Me: "Didn't you leave the Dragon's remains for the locals to deal with?"

Silvanna: "Do I look like a Necromancer to you? What good is a Dragon corpse to me? I had already spent considerable time and effort dispatching that monstrosity for them—and for free, I may add. The least they could do is mop up the mess and quit their bellyaching."[389]

Me: "I get the impression the locals didn't see it that way."

Silvanna: "The locals should count their blessings that this Elf was on hand to save the day; I'd imagine one smouldering Dragon corpse is far better than a smouldering field and cowherd, don't you think?"

Me: "I guess..."

Silvanna: "Remember, even though quests make a hero, it's a reputation that keeps them there—that and their fans, of course."

Me: "Fans?"

Silvanna: "Yeah, you know—common folk who run to greet you the moment you step into a new town. I call them the *Great Unwashed.* Their grubby little faces filled with awe as they clamber over one another to shake your hand."

---

[387] *Limelight is a glowing lantern carried by cave-dwelling Gnomes to stop them from tripping over their sleeping relatives in the dark—unsurprisingly, the primary fuel used is limes.*

[388] *I'm now hoping a 'certain' Farmer never sees this interview—if you 'are' reading this, Gwenyn, I strongly advise you to skip to the following interview...*

[389] *Please tell me you're still looking away, Gwenyn.*

Me: "Does this happen everywhere you go? Isn't that kind of annoying?"

Silvanna: "Yes—which is why you also need a good scrub in a hot bath after meeting them too. It's quite sweet, really, but they'd happily sell their kids to grab an autograph or buy a souvenir from you; it's a humbling experience."[390]

Me: "I wouldn't know; I've never had anyone greet me with anything more than growled acknowledgement when I've walked into a tavern before."

Silvanna: "I have to say it's certainly one of the perks of being a hero. I cannot buy a drink anywhere without someone else wanting to pay for it instead. Those autographs? I charge a silver coin for each one—gold if they look well-to-do. I don't just turn up unannounced at any random tavern; I make certain *arrangements* beforehand..."

Me: "What do you mean?"

Silvanna: "If a tavern wants to see a sizeable increase in their profits, they *arrange* for me to turn up 'unexpectedly'. An adventurer of my standing will always attract a large crowd eager to loosen their purse strings in my honour. The tavern in question will happily pay a fee for such an *arrangement*. It's a win-win agreement for both parties—the tavern makes coin from the large crowd, and I make coin from both. Remember, Loremaster, when you're a somebody, the coin *always* finds you—but when you're a nobody, the coin will *always* find somebody else."[391]

Me: "Not every adventurer can be doing this, surely? With the number of active heroes out there, wouldn't they bleed the locals dry of coin before the end of the summer?"

Silvanna: "Undoubtedly. Thankfully, I only know a handful of shrewd adventurers with the same vision—those with an *exit* plan. Luckily, the Heroes Guild doesn't allow their members to make coin on the side; otherwise, the realm *would* be in financial trouble."

---

[390] *Humbling isn't 'exactly' the word I would use here...*

[391] *I prefer the old Dwarven saying: 'Riches cannot buy you happiness, but it can certainly make those who don't have either <u>extremely</u> miserable.'*

Me: "What exit plan do you have?"

Silvanna: *"Five and out."*

Me: "Five and *what?*"

Silvanna: *"Out*—I'm limiting myself to five more summers before I'm done adventuring. By my calculations, I should have enough coin in the coffers to retire for good without needing to work ever again."

Me: "But if you're still making good coin, why not just carry on?"

Silvanna: "Everything has a finite amount of time—myself included. Adventuring is getting harder by the day. I don't want to give it any more time than absolutely necessary. I'm technically immortal,[392] so you can imagine the sizeable amount of coin I would require to live in peace without the need to worry. Besides, if the coffers *do* run dry, I can always reappear at a tavern and sign a few more autographs."

Me: "Where will you go when you finally do call time on adventuring?"

Silvanna: "I'll get that retirement castle by the sea I mentioned earlier—somewhere I can look out beyond the horizon and enjoy the tide rising and falling every day."

Me: "What about the Heroes Guild?"

Silvanna: "What about them?"

Me: "With their hero numbers rapidly rising, won't it affect your exit plan? I've heard that even side-quests are becoming harder and harder to find these days."

Silvanna: "I'm not worried—I'm confident I'll always be in demand. Besides, the Heroes Guild doesn't have any of our kind within their ranks."

Me: "Why is that?"

Silvanna: "Because Sorcerers and Sorceresses know better than to trust their magic to anyone but themselves. We're not even in the

---

[392] *Contrary to what the Sorceress says, Elves only 'appear' immortal thanks to their rigorous moisturising routine using copious amounts of Wyvern Cream. Most live in a perpetual state of youthful disdain before getting bored and wandering off towards the 'Great Behind'.*

Wizards Guild—those old fools only care about their spellbooks;[393] they do not understand the true power of *raw* magic."[394]

Me: "What if you found yourself competing for a quest with a Heroes Guild adventurer?"

Silvanna: "It wouldn't bother me; they would be no match for this Sorceress."

Me: "But what if you were up against one of their big-name heroes? I hear Arin Darkblade still works for them."

The Elf's eyes glow purple as bubbles start to break from her bathwater—I'm left speechless as I struggle to think of anything other than the obvious joke forming on my lips.

Silvanna: "Sorry, my water was cold—I just needed to warm it up a touch."

Me: "Did you do that with your magic?"

Silvanna: "No, my backside."

The Elf grins mischievously as I feel my cheeks glowing with embarrassment.

Silvanna: "I'm just playing with you. It was a simple cantrip[395]—even a Wizard could do it[396] if they could find the damn thing in that dusty tome of theirs. Anyway, you were saying? *Oh, Arin Darkblade,* well, I'm not scared of anyone. I've fought fire-breathing Dragons and lived to tell the tale, so be it the Heroes Guild's star adventurer or even one of their Enforcers—it matters not to me."

Me: "Enforcers?"

Silvanna: "You *do* know what an Enforcer is?"

---

[393] With a step-by-step guide on how to cast 'Fireball' written inside like a twisted cookbook...

[394] Which is the <u>exact</u> opposite of 'cooked magic'...

[395] This Sorceress is certainly keeping me on my toes today!

[396] I'm pretty sure a Wizard would add more flames, burning, and screaming—lots and lots of screaming.

Me: "Y—Yes—of course... they are hired muscle."

Silvanna: "Correct. Well, regardless who their muscle is, they will suffer the same fate as any who have crossed me before."

Me: "Which is?"

The Elf's eyes flare purple again, almost teasingly.

Silvanna: "Why, a painful death—*silly*..."

The Sorceress stares at me coyly as she begins to rise from her bath. I quickly avert my eyes and politely shield them from the Elf's sudden nakedness.[397]

Me: "*Oh...*"

Silvanna: "Did I startle you?"

Me: "I—I had anticipated you staying in your bath for a bit longer—at least until we had concluded our conversation and I had left. Didn't you just warm your water up?"

Silvanna: "I did, but I also have a free meal being prepared for me by the *Dancing Dragon's* kitchen staff. I can always ask them to rustle up another—would you care to join me?"

I turn my back, allowing the Sorceress some privacy to towel herself down.

Me: "Sadly, I have a prior *arrangement* that cannot wait..."[398]

Silvanna: "That's a shame. Another time, perhaps?"

I nod, waiting patiently for the Sorceress to dress.

Me: "Of course, that would be most agreeable."

A few more heartbeats of silence pass before the Elf speaks again.

Silvanna: "You can turn around now."

---

[397] *We've just passed the awkwardness event horizon.*

[398] *I'll think of something—anything.*

Me: "Okay—"

I stop, the words failing to tumble from my lips. I was expecting Silvanna to be wearing battle-ready adventuring robes—but instead the Elf is dressed in an unassuming patchwork dress. She rotates her hips to swish the hem about her, smiling as it hangs with perfection. For a brief moment, I forget she's a dangerous Sorceress; she looks—well... *normal*.[399] No one would ever guess by looking at her that there is raw magic coursing through her veins.

Silvanna: "It's a pretty little thing, don't you think?"

Me: "Very nice—where did you get it from?"[400]

Silvanna: "I picked this up on an adventure—I forget where. Finding clothes is easy when you're a hero. People literally leave them around for you to take—it's *so* considerate. I love rummaging through chests, cupboards, and drawers, searching for new things to wear."

Me: "Perks of the profession, I suppose."

The Sorceress goes to leave, stops, and picks up the half-used soap, sponge, and damp towel off the rail. I can't help but say something as she drops them into a large sack.

Me: "Are you taking those?"

Silvanna: "When you're a hero, you never leave anything behind—no matter how small. There is always someone willing to pay good coin for it. I'm forever taking half-used trinkets and selling them on to Merchants looking to turn a profit from hero souvenirs—"

Me: "But... it's... just... soap!"

Silvanna: "*Ah,* but this isn't *just* soap, it's soap that a legendary hero has used—*Silvanna the Sorceress,* to be precise. I know quite a few die-hard fans who would pay handsomely to get their eager hands on this

---

[399] *I'm not saying that a Sorceress doesn't look 'normal' in the conventional sense—I just mean, right now, the Elf seems like someone who isn't about to unleash bolts of purple lightning from her fingertips.*

[400] *I know the answer to this—as does 'Miss V. Angry from Wendle'.*

slippery thing."[401]

Me: "You're turning your seconds into coin—isn't that a little mercenary, even for you?"

The Elf leans closer to whisper into my ear.

Silvanna: "Nobody can survive on *exposure* alone..."

I feel a faint crackle of electricity jolt through my fingers as a piece of parchment is pressed into my hand. I look down and see a remarkable illustration of Silvanna dressed in simple robes.[402] Signed with her name and several 'X' marks—it's quite a captivating picture.

Silvanna: "*Shhhh*—don't tell anyone I gave you that for free."

Me: "*Erm*... T—Thank you..."

Silvanna: "See you around, Loremaster. If you ever find yourself passing a castle by the sea—maybe drop in to see if I'm at home..."[403]

I watch as the Elf departs for her next coin-making opportunity, leaving me to wonder if I'll take the Sorceress up on her tempting offer one day.[404]

---

[401] *No doubt, for some, it will be the closest they will come to 'actual' washing.*

[402] *Probably stolen from some poor local—sorry, Gwenyn.*

[403] *If the castle used the same carpenter that constructed the rickety stairs leading up to Simply Morgan's abode, the only 'dropping in' I'll be doing will be from a great height into the rough seas far below.*

[404] *And also wondering if Gwenyn will ever get her favourite dress back from the Elf too...*

14. Otto, the Landlord

Located at the heart of Tronte's market square, The Green Goblin tavern is popular with a large number of Heroes who frequent the city in search of their next quest. It seems I've become far too familiar with such raucous establishments of late; I know my parents would be disappointed to learn how often I find myself in one.[405] Taverns have become an excellent source of information for me, and a steady stream of ale is the perfect way to loosen any stubborn tongue. Every inn I frequent is different, each with its own distinct aesthetic—from locally sourced wall memorabilia to the colourful locals found within. Yet despite the rich and varied nature of taverns, one thing is <u>always</u> constant—a gruff Landlord who runs the place.

As I step into *The Green Goblin,* my senses recoil, stung by the smell of hops mixed with the stale sweat from the last party of adventurers to stagger through the establishment's doors.[406] Otto Golôth cuts a lonely figure as he mops up what *could* be blood from his wooden floor—but equally could also be a spilt condiment from a clumsy patron. The weary look on the Half-Orc's face tells me it's not the first time he's done this. As I wait patiently for the Landlord to finish swabbing the offending spot, Otto looks up and points towards the bar.[407]

Otto: "You want a drink, Loremaster?"[408]

The Landlord has an eloquent tongue, unusual for a Half-Orc; most tend to drop as many letters from their words as they can until nothing is left but a steady stream of barked grunts and growls—which probably explains why Half-Orcs make excellent 'Barkers'.

Me: "I prefer to keep my wits about me—what's the weakest beverage you can muster?"

---

[405] *I can feel my liver breathing a heavy sigh of relief, knowing I'm only here to ask questions and not for the ale.*

[406] *Creating a potent cloud of heroism that makes you feel like you could take on the realm—but will also leave you drunker than a teetotal Paladin drowning their sorrows after breaking their sacred oath for the first and only time.*

[407] *Rather gruffly, as is the norm with Landlords in everything they do.*

[408] *I wince in pain as my alarmed liver flinches at the mere mention of alcohol.*

The Landlord's hand pumps a lever before handing me a full flagon—I take a sip.

Me: "It's water…"

Otto: "You asked for the weakest thing I've got—*well…* you got it."

As I take another sip, I look around the tavern interior; broken tables and chairs dominate the eyeline.

Me: "Seems like you had a rough night."

Otto: "The life of a Landlord."

Me: "What happened?"

The Half-Orc snorts as he recounts the tally from the evening's chaotic revelry.

Otto: "Forty-five flagons, six windowpanes, four broken limbs, two concussions, one death, and most of the furniture in pieces—*happened* here…"

Me: "*Death?* Did someone die?"

Otto: "A Monk… or was it a Cleric—yeah, probably a Cleric…"

Me: "A Cleric—how?"

Otto: "Same old story. Adventurers with too much time to kill—and not enough monsters. Throw in several flagons of ale, and you're on a well-trodden path that leads only to trouble. This time, one party of adventurers didn't take kindly to a second adventuring party showing up. Some deeply offensive things were said—then *someone* made the mistake of shoving the Barbarian…"

Me: "So, the Barbarian was responsible for *all* this?"

Otto: "I'd be so lucky. In fact, the Barbarian was the tamest of the lot; he even tried to stop the whole thing from escalating into a pitched battle."

Me: "If the Barbarian was trying to be the peacemaker, then who caused all this wanton destruction?"

Otto: "A damn Paladin! He appeared out of nowhere, swearing and cursing like a Blue Goblin.[409] I have never seen anything like it. He strode through the arguing parties and sent the Barbarian flying. Both adventuring groups turned on the Holy Warrior when **WHAM!** He started hitting everybody—*anybody*. That's when this place turned into a mosh pit."[410]

Me: "A *Paladin* started it? I thought they were supposed to be the most restrained and disciplined of us all?"[411]

The Landlord spits in an empty flagon and wipes it clean.[412]

Otto: "Not this one; this one was the worst."

Me: "I'm sorry, I'm really struggling to picture a Holy Warrior doing this amount of damage without good cause."[413]

Otto: "You'd be surprised. They are *always* doing stuff like this. Can you read the sign above the bar?"

The Half-Orc jabs a thumb over his shoulder towards a chalkboard: *IT HAS BEEN '0' DAYS SINCE THE LAST ADVENTURER DIED HERE!* I rub my chin with a faint whiff of scepticism.

Me: "Aren't you currently cleaning up from a recent incident—that sign could already have been changed?"

Otto: "But I haven't touched that sign for weeks—not once."

Me: "That's rather troubling to hear. Why do you think that is?"

---

[409] *'Blue Goblins' are so-called because they frequently have their winter clothes stolen by their stronger cousins, the Green Goblins. As a result, the cold seasonal air turns their naked skins blue, which is ironic as they usually turn the 'air' blue with their foul language and frozen curses.*

[410] *Mosh pit is Gnomish for 'small space crammed with smelly Halflings who can't stop jumping on each other's toes'.*

[411] *So much for the four 'S's... unless they stand for 'Shove, Swear, Smite, and Smash!'*

[412] *Clean in spirit—although I suspect it would take a different kind of spirit to remove the Half-Orc's saliva from the inside of the flagon. It leaves me staring at my own flagon with growing suspicion.*

[413] *Well... maybe there's <u>one</u> Paladin I could imagine doing this—and he certainly wouldn't need a cause, regardless of whether it was good or not.*

The brusque Landlord picks up the recently 'cleaned' flagon and pours himself a drink from a beer casket sitting behind the bar—he downs the contents in one impressive swig.

Otto: "Heroes get bothersome unless they have a quest to keep them occupied. They need a constant distraction—if they don't get it, they get bored, and bored adventurers are bad news for everyone else. Once you have a tavern filled with bored adventurers, it only takes one pissed-off Paladin to start something that ends badly."[414]

Me: "Has it always been this way?"

Otto: "Nope. At first, only one or two of them were coming in here hassling my patrons, asking all their bloody questions."

Me: "What sort of questions?"

Otto: "The usual. *Where's the nearest main quest? Got any spare side-quests? Have you got a cellar? Has it got a rat infestation problem?*— That sort of thing. But the ensuing *Quest Drought* has hit everyone hard.[415] Now heroes aren't just asking for quests; they're *demanding* them off my customers—even patrons who don't have a quest to give!"

Me: "But how can they expect someone to give them something they don't have?"

Otto: "You tell me? Most quest-givers avoid this place like the plague. They're either too poor to hire a hero or too scared..."[416]

Me: "So, quest-givers don't frequent *The Green Goblin* anymore?"

Otto: "The last quest-giver I remember in here was at least a summer ago."

Me: "But that still doesn't stop any heroes pestering your patrons for work?"

---

[414] *Especially for any nearby Clerics, it seems.*

[415] *A 'Quest Drought' conjures up the image of a desperate Barbarian, doffed loincloth in hand, moving from tavern table to tavern table, growling as they hunt for any scrap of quest information they can get.*

[416] *A near-naked Barbarian angrily demanding a side-quest is enough to put anyone off their stiff drink.*

Otto: "Nope—and you'd better watch your back. If you're not careful, you're going to have a steady stream of them asking if you know of any kidnapped Barons who are in need of rescuing."[417]

Me: "What do you think is responsible for all the quests drying up?"

Otto: "I dunno—you hear things, but nothing set in stone."[418]

Me: "What sort of things."

Otto: "Just things. But if I had a coin for every rumour that turned out to be true, I wouldn't be here mopping up some poor Cleric's blood off these floorboards."[419]

Me: "Try me."

The Landlord sighs as he pours himself another ale.

Otto: "Word is, a nearby main quest got completed."

Me: "What main quest?"

Otto: "Beats me, but it probably involves a *Ring of Power*."[420]

Me: "A Ring of Power? Why a Ring of Power specifically?"

Otto: "I dunno—I thought a main quest *always* had a bloody magical ring at its heart."

Me: "Why would a completed main quest bring so much turmoil to all the other quests?"

Otto: "Because main quests aren't supposed to be completed—not for a long time, and sometimes *never*."

Me: "Why—what happens if a main quest is completed?"

---

[417] *From an invasion of overzealous Clerics who arrived through a mystical portal, and who are now trying to wrap anything with a pulse in bandages.*

[418] *Certainly not Dwarven Stone.*

[419] *So it's not an accidental condiment spillage, then—at least that's now cleared up, unlike the Cleric's blood that's currently spread across the tavern's floor.*

[420] *Another Ring of Power?! Someone should really bind these bloody things together—it would certainly make them easier to find in the darkness...*

There's an awkward moment of silence before the Half-Orc opens his arms and gestures to the damage still evident in his bar.

Otto: "I suppose *this* is what happens."

I give the Landlord a confused look.

Me: "A bar brawl?"

Otto: "Look beyond the carnage, Loremaster—this place is filled with a lot of heavily armed egos, all anxious to know where their next adventure is coming from. As I already told you, heroes *need* a distraction, and a main quest is perfect for that. Now broaden your imagination and picture this in every tavern, town, and corner of the realm."

Me: "That's a lot of broken tables and chairs."

Otto: "All because some *solo* decided they would complete the main quest for themselves—it has left every adventurer looking at an empty coin pouch as a consequence."

Me: "*Solo?*"

Otto: "Yeah—an adventurer who goes questing alone."

Me: "Why is that a problem?"

Otto: "Adventuring parties have debates about *everything*. They argue amongst themselves for hours before finally coming to a majority decision—a solo doesn't have that burden. That means they often go on gut instinct, which can be dangerous for everyone."[421]

Me: "I see..."

Otto: "There's a certain unspoken rule about main quests. For starters, it's a matter of courtesy to *always* inform those on the smaller, connecting quests of your intentions to complete it. Main quests are made overly complicated for good reason—it gives everyone else a chance to earn a huge amount of coin from it. The coin should always trickle down from the main quest and spill into the smaller ones, in a way that benefits everyone."

---

[421] *Especially the 'gut' in question...*

Me: "*Everyone*—you mean heroes, right?"

Otto: "Not *just* heroes. You have to realise there's a whole chain of people who rely on that main quest—Merchants, Guards, even Landlords. But this solo just rushed in like an unexpected squall in a sleepy port and finished it without even breaking into a sweat—in an instant, he threw the *entire* area into chaos."[422]

Me: "I guess if the main quest is complete, a few of the connecting quests vanished overnight."

Otto: "A few? Try *hundreds*..."

Me: "*Hundreds?* Does anyone know who this solo was?"

Otto: "No—some say it was a Barbarian;[423] others say it was a thin, pasty-looking guy.[424] Whoever it was, they left me with a massive headache and a lot of cleaning up to do each night."

Me: "So, this *solo* is responsible for almost singlehandedly *increasing* the number of heroes in these parts while simultaneously *decreasing* the number of quests available?"

Otto: "Yup. I'll wring their scrawny little neck if I ever get my hands on the fool."

The Landlord slowly clenches and unclenches his hands to emphasise his fury.

Me: "Could this solo have anything to do with the Heroes Guild?"

Otto: "What do you mean?"

Me: "I heard they are growing as an influence—this could be an area where they are making their presence felt."

Otto: "What'd be in it for them?"

---

[422] *I can imagine the solo shouting something like: "Time's up—let's do this!" at the top of his voice before leaping into the fray.*

[423] *No, it couldn't be...*

[424] *Oh, it bloody well could—Dorn! Although I'd use the word 'Barbarian' loosely here...*

Me: "The pursuit of wealth is often a leading factor to drastic change. Perhaps this is part of a larger plan to charge adventurers for going on future quests?"

Otto: "Charging adventurers to go on an adventure—how would that work?"

Me: "I don't know—maybe the Heroes Guild will ask adventurers to make a monthly donation for free access to as many quests as they can handle?"

Otto: "This is dangerous talk, Loremaster. If you want to continue along this path, I will have to insist you do it elsewhere. Cleaning up a nightly brawl is one thing, but this kind of gossip could seriously endanger *The Green Goblin*."[425]

Me: "If the hero business is causing you *that* much trouble, why not deny adventurers entry to *The Green Goblin?*"

The Half-Orc roars with laughter.

Otto: "If *only* it were that easy! Don't you think I've *tried* banning heroes from coming in here? I lasted one day before some grizzled muscle showed up, urging me to change my mind and lift the ban."

Me: "Did you recognise them?"

Otto: "Sure, I had seen him around Tronte. He was a dark and brooding type, wore an eye-patch, had this death stare from his one good eye that filled you with dread."[426]

Me: "It's hard to imagine a Half-Orc like yourself being intimidated by anyone."

The Landlord draws himself up to his full stature—an imposing sight for any drunk, let alone one still as sober as I.

Otto: "Look, I know how to handle myself in a fair fight. But I could tell straight away that a fair fight was *not* something he was prepared to

---

[425] *In which case, I'd suggest banning Paladins, Clerics, Barbarians and Wizards from the establishment too.*

[426] *Unlikely to be a Pirate this far from the coast unless someone in town stole his beloved ship…*

give me."

Me: "Who sent him?"

Otto: "He never said. I have my suspicions—"

Me: "The Heroes Guild?"

Otto: "*You* can say that—but not me."

Me: "If the Heroes Guild *were* behind it, what reason could they have for insisting you open your doors to adventurers again?"

Otto: "Well... if I *had* to guess... to continue making coin for them."

Me: "How?"

Otto: "Any Landlord who allows a Heroes Guild member to drink in their establishment must pay an *Appearance Tax* for that privilege—a 12% cut of all takings."

Me: "12% sounds steep—does that mean you're making a loss?"

Otto: "Not usually, in fact, we would *still* be making a healthy profit even with the Heroes Guild taking their cut."

Me: "Then I fail to see the problem."

The Half-Orc gestures once more to the carnage he's been busy cleaning up this evening.

Otto: "*This* is the problem—my business can only survive if I'm free from the daily grind of repairs and replacements I'm forced to make. Every time there's a fight, my spare coin disappears quicker than a Cleric in a Necromancer-only party.[427] One thing is for sure, the local carpenter is currently making a small fortune out of me."

Me: "What's the answer?"

Otto: "I don't know—unless there's a sudden glut of new quests, I'll be forced to shut the doors and sell the deed to this place by next summer."

Me: "Then what?"

---

[427] *Seems it's a tough time to be a Cleric right now...*

Otto: "I suppose I'll have to go back to adventuring."

Me: "Wait—you used to be one of them?"

Otto: "I was a Fighter. That's how I managed to buy *The Green Goblin* in the first place—it was part of my exit plan. Looks like my retirement is going to have to wait for a while now..."

Me: "But without any quests—what's the point of going back out there?"

Otto: "I know some people who owe me a few favours from when I was active; they'll have a few low-level side-quests I can do on the quiet, I'm sure."[428]

Me: "Why not petition to join the Heroes Guild? I believe their members are still being given a few well-paid quests?"

Otto: "No chance. I wouldn't join them even if they begged me."

Me: "Why not?"

Otto: "Because I want to keep what I earn, not give it away to line the current Guildmaster's pocket. Given a choice, I'd rather join the Thieves Guild. At least they know how to treat their own. Sure, you could end up with a dagger lodged in your back, but only if you 'really' deserved it[429]—I can respect that."

Me: "But you're a Fighter, not a Rogue—?"

Otto: "Haven't you heard of *multi-classing?* It's never too late to learn a new skill—but even joining the Thieves Guild isn't an option for me now..."

Me: "Why not?"

---

[428] *'On the quiet' means clearing out a rat-infested cellar without making a single sound—a feat that is as difficult as asking a drunk Barbarian to walk past a camel without punching it.*

[429] *It's difficult to quantify if someone was deserving of a dagger in the back or not—unless, of course, they're a Bard who hasn't stopped their infernal warbling from the moment they left the tavern. Then they thoroughly deserve the 'Business End' of a sharp blade.*

Otto: "Because the Thieves Guild in Tronte mysteriously vanished without a trace."[430]

Me: "Isn't that the point of the Thieves Guild, though? Never knowing where they are? I thought they lived for operating in the shadows, a world filled with cryptic passwords and secret handshakes."[431]

Otto: "Maybe, but there's been a noticeable drop in muggings and pickpocketing around Tronte of late."

Me: "Isn't that a good thing?"

Otto: "No, far from it. No crime means there's an even *larger* threat brewing in the shadows, and the Thieves Guild left Tronte before it was too late."

Me: "Do you *know* what this trouble is exactly—that they ran from?"

Otto: "The sort of trouble you can't talk about in my tavern."

Me: "The Thieves Guild and... *erm,* this *trouble*—are they at war with one another?"

Otto: "I wouldn't say war exactly, not yet—but there's certainly no love lost between them."

Me "Why do you think that is?"

Otto: "I heard the *trouble* was stealing Thieves Guild members and adding them to their own ranks[432]—you can imagine what the Head of the Thieves Guild thought about that!"

Me: "What about the other Guilds? How did they react to the sudden disappearance of the Thieves Guild?"

Otto: "Sheer panic, probably—some openly suggested that the *trouble* was behind the Thieves Guild's sudden disappearance. But I don't have

---

[430] *They didn't even leave a forwarding address or cancel their weekly milk order. The first anyone knew about the missing Thieves Guild was when a City Guard tripped over seven crates of curdled milk, neatly stacked outside their not-so-secret-anymore entrance.*

[431] *This is what's known as 'Cloak & Dagger', although I suspect there's a lot more 'Dagger' than 'Cloak' going on.*

[432] *Oh, the sweet irony of this statement!*

any proof beyond idle gossip and whispered conspiracy theories. I know an uneasy truce exists between the *trouble* and the Wizards Guild, but how long that will last is anyone's guess. I have a bad feeling in my gut[433] that tells me the realm is heading towards its first *Guild War.*"

I finish my flagon of water and hand back my empty, closing my journal as I do. Otto spits into the flagon and gives it a token wipe with a rag.

Otto: "Another one for the road?"[434]

Me: "Thanks, but I'd better not—I'll only have to find a bush to go behind the moment I step out onto the path.[435] But before I depart, I just want to say I don't know where you find the inner strength to keep going like this. I think I would have given up a long time ago if our circumstances were reversed."

I offer the Landlord my hand to shake.

Me: "I do hope you find a way to survive…"

The Half-Orc grins as he takes it.

Otto: "Thanks—who knows, maybe I'll find my own Ring of Power to give me the strength I need to keep going…"[436]

I hold the Half-Orc's gaze for a moment as I try to tell if he's serious or not—it's impossible to read the gruff Landlord, and I'm left none the wiser. Without another word said, I turn and make my way towards the exit, hoping I can leave quietly, without being harried for a side-quest by an inebriated adventurer.

---

[433] *Could it be from the winds of war, or could it be just wind from the ale the Half-Orc chugged down?*

[434] *I can feel my liver going cold at the mere thought of another free drink—even if it is only water.*

[435] *Hopefully not a bush with an Elven Ranger hiding inside it…*

[436] *One made by a Wizard who doesn't have a precarious cliff-face staircase riddled with woodworm!*

15. Flintlok & Brin, the 'Entrance' Planners

I'm glad the weather has been kind to me as I walk in the afternoon sun towards a large crimson tent pitched outside the market town of Cloverton. With a carved sign welcoming those who enter, Cloverton is a popular destination for newly qualified heroes eager to make a name for themselves—and those looking to make easy coin from the latest batch of fresh-faced adventurers to set foot in town. From Potioneers peddling homebrewed concoctions,[437] to Heralds offering to 'protect' an adventurer's name with their Arcane Copyright magic,[438] a newly qualified hero could do worse than browse the many wares Cloverton has to offer. But none of these distractions can compare to the unique service Flintlok & Brin provides for those new adventurers who stumble into their tented abode.

As I step through the fabric doorway, I see a solitary seat positioned neatly in front of an empty stage—the rest of the tent is eerily quiet; there's no sign of either proprietor. Behind the stage background, I can just make out another large doorway masked by a black curtain. A string of lamps evenly lines the stage, illuminating the edges. I feel compelled to sit and wait for either Flintlok or Brin to make an appearance.

Me: "*Erm*—Hello?"

As I settle down into the chair, the lamps suddenly extinguish—plunging the whole area into darkness, disorientating my senses.

Unseen Voice: "Ladies and Gentlemen, Elves, Dwarves, Halflings, *and* their slightly smaller cousins, the Gnomes[439]—may I present to you, the **GREATEST** Wizard in the entire realm... **FLINTLOOOOOOOK!**"[440]

WOOOOSH![441]

---

[437] *Which will probably turn your body green rather than anything else it promises (this will only be popular with very cold and very angry Blue Goblins).*

[438] *Arcane Copyright magic is renowned for summoning a bad-tempered 'Fair-Use Ogre' when called upon.*

[439] *I'm pretty sure every Gnome in the realm would take umbrage at this.*

[440] *Do not fear, dear reader; I am keeping a sharp lookout for any wayward—*

[441] *—Fireball!*

I instinctively duck as a sudden burst of flame erupts skywards from the stage, accompanied by a loud blast of music, possibly from a mortally wounded pipe organ. The black stage curtain is thrown aside by an elderly Wizard, his chest puffed out proudly like a love-struck rooster, struts out onto the stage. He waves his hands in the air and magically brings the stage flame to life with intricate hand gestures—creating a huge flaming serpent that hisses menacingly before disappearing in a puff of orange smoke. I freely admit it's one of the most spectacular things I've ever witnessed in my entire life. I clap—partly in awe, partly in fear the Wizard's performance may not be entirely over.

Flintlok: "Thank you, *thank you*—you're *too* kind!"

He smiles smugly and bows low.

Flintlok: "And *that's* how you make an entrance..."

Me: "It was most... impressive!"

The flames inside each lamp flare briefly before returning to their original illumination. I notice more movement from behind the curtain as a second figure attempts to join the Wizard on stage but is thwarted by the weight of the fabric. Eventually, after much consternation, an elderly Bard hobbles out and stands next to Flintlok; he has a sizeable pipe organ strapped to his chest with a row of keys resembling a Barbarian's smile after a fierce barroom brawl.[442]

Bard: "I'm Brin—"

Flintlok: "—and *I'm* Flintlok! *Together* we are **Flintlok & Brin— entrance extraordinaires!** We will use our considerable skills to design you an arrival *so* extravagant they will be talking about you for generations to come!"[443]

Me: "I'm s—sorry, you seem to have me confused for a hero."[444]

---

[442] *Undoubtedly started by a Paladin who just broke their oath—then the Barbarian's jaw.*

[443] *The only 'arrival' I'm concerned with right now is the hasty apology trying to escape from my lips—I expect a certain amount of disappointment when they learn I'm not here to hire their services.*

[444] *Ensuing disappointment arriving in 5... 4... 3—*

The Wizard leaps from the stage and lands neatly beside me—although I cannot mistake the cracking sound coming from his knees as they protest at the unexpected impact.

Flintlok: "Nonsense, my boy, why, you—**ow**—*are* a hero!"

The Wizard holds my arm up to pose me like a Barbarian drying his armpit hair.

Flintlok: "Do mine own my eyes deceive me—are these not the arms that could vanquish a bloodthirsty Troll?"

Me: "No—they are not."

Brin: "—And do my mine own ears betray me, are these not the— *AAK!*"

The Bard's words are cut cruelly short as he leaps from the stage, catches his organ strap on a lamp hook and is violently catapulted backwards—the organ blares in low C like an ominous death knell.

Flintlok: "You clot!"

Brin: "Don't call me a clot—your flames nearly set fire to the tent again!"

Flintlok: "Why *you*—!"

Me: "Please, gentlemen! There's no need to argue—I'm not a hero, honest!"[445]

The Wizard stops bickering with his dangling associate and stares at me with growing suspicion.[446]

Brin: "*Ahem?* Can I have a little help—please?"

Flintlok hurries to support Brin while I quickly grab my chair for the stricken Bard to stand on.

Brin: "Thank you, I was starting to lose the feeling in my legs—"

---

[445] *Not to be confused with 'I'm not an honest hero', which is another way of saying you're a Rogue.*

[446] *—2... 1... you have now arrived at your 'ensuing disappointment'...*

Me: "You're welcome."

Flintlok: "You're *still* a clot—"

A poignant glare from the Bard quickly silences the Wizard's grumbles.

Brin: "Hero or *not*—we treat *all* who enter our tent with the same level of professionalism—"

Flintlok: "*Humpf!*"

The Wizard crosses his arms in defiance.

Brin: "You must forgive my associate. He can get a little grouchy around non-heroes—especially ones just browsing."

Me: "It is *I* who should be apologising—I should have sent word of my arrival; allow me to introduce myself properly. I am Elburn Barr, a *Loremaster*—"

The Wizard suddenly brightens upon hearing my introduction.[447]

Flintlok: "A *Loremaster,* you say? What brings a Loremaster to Cloverton?"

Me: "In truth, you—well, *both* of you, to be precise. I'm writing a journal about heroes—and I was wondering if I could take a moment of your time to ask you some questions?"

The Wizard's face explodes into an excitable grin, his aged and crooked teeth suddenly pushing through his wiry beard like long-forgotten headstones rising above the thicket of an overgrown graveyard.

Flintlok: "Of course, of course—we'd be *more* than delighted to talk to you. Be mindful of spelling our names correctly, though. I've heard Loremasters can be notoriously careless with details—"

Me: "I shall endeavour to be as careful as a Wizard with a Fireball spell."[448]

---

[447] *You'd be surprised how many people are wary upon first meeting me, only to warm up once they realise what I can do for them—I guess this is what it feels like to be a Cleric...*

[448] *That felt exceedingly good to say.*

I feel a sudden chill run down my spine as the Spellcaster fixes me with a deathly stare before *'tutting'* tersely.

Flintlok: "How *reassuring.*"

Brin: "Ignore him; he's still sore he did all that entrance magic for nothing."

Me: "Magic?"

Flintlok: "The flames, *you fool!* Don't tell me you didn't take stock?"

Me: "Sorry, my mistake—I thought you were using some kind of Gnomish contraption[449]—"

The Wizard stares at me in disbelief.

Flintlok: "Gnomish contraption? Good Sir—you *insult* me! I wouldn't trust those diminutive idiots to light my fart—let alone dabble with this level of intricate spellcasting!"

The Bard circles around me, playfully caressing the keys on his pipe organ.

Brin: "While I accompany that magical display with a rapturous tune—and not just *any* tune, but an inspirational one-of-a-kind melody that captures the adventurer's essence in question to perfection."

Me: "I know this may seem a strange thing to ask—but why go to so much trouble?"

I can tell my query has irked the Wizard somewhat.[450]

Flintlok: "Because it beats sitting around waiting to take my last breath, *obviously.*"

Brin: "Forgive him, Loremaster—I understand what you're trying to ask. To give you a satisfactory answer, we must start at the beginning..."

---

[449] I <u>know</u> it was magic, but I don't want to give the Spellcaster the satisfaction of my knowing.

[450] My father warned me <u>never</u> to play with fire—especially magically created fire from a slightly miffed Wizard.

I look at the Wizard suspiciously.

Me: "You're not going to cast another spell, are you?"

Flintlok: "Not unless you *want* me to?"

Brin: "You have nothing to fear, Loremaster—we'll do this the old-fashioned way. *Once upon a time, there were two very successful adventurers, a grumpy Wizard—*"

Flintlok: "—very funny."

Brin: "*—and an extremely talented Bard. The pair had quested countless times together and had forged a friendship that could never be broken—*"

Flintlok: "—although it had been tested numerous times, including right _now_."

Brin: "*But nothing lasts forever—as time eventually crept up upon the pair of heroic friends. Their bodies now felt the burden of their many adventures, their dependable bones creaked, and their impressive muscles ached.*[451] *So the Wizard decided he would close his spellbook—*"

Flintlok: "*Close?* If you remember, it was *lost* when I had to come to your rescue again; the Warbling Caves, if I recall—"

The Bard hisses at the Wizard.

Brin: "You're *ruining* the story!"

The Spellcaster waves the Bard away.

Brin: "*So, they both retired from the adventuring life to spend the rest of their days in peace.*"[452]

Me: "Sounds like a warming story—"

Flintlok: "It's not over yet! We're getting to the good bit!"

---

[451] *The Bard is clearly overstating the truth here.*

[452] *Choosing to retire to a tent in a field, rather than buying a dilapidated castle by the sea.*

Brin: "*But soon the itch of adventure called out to them once more, luring them back to the depths of the abyss with the promise of riches and fame…*"

Me: "But you didn't come back—well, not in a way familiar to you both."

Flintlok: "That is true; we may be old—"

Brin: "—but we're certainly a *lot* wiser. We realised the adventuring scene had changed, and we needed to change with it. We both knew we wouldn't last five minutes in a modern dungeon."

Me: "So, you decided to set up *Brin & Flintlok?*"

Flintlok: "That's *Flintlok & Brin*, Loremaster!"

Me: "Sorry—my mistake, *Flintlok & Brin*…"

Brin: "We didn't want to give up on adventuring altogether. We felt we still had something to give, but we didn't know *what* that something was."

Me: "So, what happened?"

Brin: "We were enjoying a drink at *The Giggling Giant*,[453] the main tavern in Cloverton, when this young Fighter tiptoed in. I remember he looked so scared but desperate to make a good impression with the rest of the drinking patrons."

Me: "What did he do?"

Brin: "He coughed a lot."

Me: "Did anyone say anything?"

Brin: "Nothing—not a single person batted an eyelid. Although, eventually, a concerned Cleric thought he was ailing and offered some 'healing' assistance."

---

[453] *Named after a Storm Giant who got so drunk he tried to fit inside the tiny drinking establishment. The inebriated Titan failed miserably and flattened every single one of the evening's patrons in the process. It was a horrendous incident that left the Giant giggling like an idiot before being arrested and put into Giant-sized-foot stocks that were once the city's main bridge.*

Flintlok: "How humiliating."

Me: "Why didn't anyone take any notice of the Fighter?"

Flintlok: "Because heroes are ten a copper coin these days—especially in Cloverton."

Brin: "This place is a crossroads town. It sits precisely where four different provinces meet.[454] The ruling Barons of each principality despise one other, and as a consequence, many heroes are hired to bring mischief and mayhem to their rivals."

Flintlok: "And there are rumours of a '*Dark Power*' rising in the south, which is *also* getting the heroes around here considerably agitated too."

Me: "I've heard of this '*Dark Power*' in the south—what do you know of it?"

Brin: "I think it's a Warlock."

Me: "Why?"

Brin: "Whenever there's a '*Dark Power*' threatening the realm, there's *always* a sneaky Warlock with a very small beard behind it all."[455]

The Wizard shakes his head.

Flintlok: "It's not a Warlock—it's worse."

Me: "What's *worse* than a Warlock?"

Flintlok: "A Warlock Lich…"

Me: "What's a Warlock Lich?"

Flintlok: "The *worst* of both worlds—undead *and* a Spellcaster; a nasty mixture that would make your toes curl if you ever encountered it in the flesh."

---

[454] *Not to be confused with Brundale, which is the realm's smallest kingdom—more on that later.*

[455] *I can't imagine a Warlock being 'sneaky'. Rogues? —Yes. Warlocks? —Not unless they're the type of Warlock who goes around lifting the hem of their arcane robes to tiptoe around whilst laughing mischievously.*

Brin: "Which is unlikely as Liches don't have any flesh."

Flintlok: "You know the only thing people despise more than a Lich? A pedant!"

Me: "What do you think it wants?"

Flintlok: "What do *all* undead want?[456] To feed off the flesh of the living[457]—"

Brin: "Of course, this could all be a ruse designed to scare the Noobs."

Me: "*Noobs?*"

Brin: "They are new inexperienced adventurers yet to attempt a quest."

Me: "Why do you call them Noobs?"

Brin: "It's a Gnomish word—it means *soon to be dead*."

Flintlok: "When we were younger, it took us a few summers of training before we attempted our first adventure—but nowadays, all these modern heroes want everything handed to them on a plate the moment they are given a sword."

Me: "I take it that's what the Fighter in *The Giggling Giant* was—a Noob?"

Flintlok: "He was desperate to be noticed, but as I said, *nobody* paid him an ounce of attention. That's when the idea hit me—"

Brin: "No—that's when *I* did; you were about to take a swig from my flagon, remember? I was also the one who suggested the lad needed a themed entrance!"

Flintlok: "Poppycock![458] Anyway, I called the Fighter over, sat him down, and bought him a drink before pitching my vision to him."

Brin: "*Erm,* I think you'll find *I* paid for the drink!"

---

[456] *Not to be undead?*

[457] *My mistake.*

[458] *Which is Gnomish for 'your mother was a Halfling and your father smelt of old canaries.'*

Flintlok: "Using the coin you borrowed from *me*—"

Me: "What did you say to the Noob?"

Flintlok: "I promised him an entrance that would make *everyone* sit up and take notice, an entrance that nobody had ever seen—"

Me: "What did this Fighter think of your idea?"

Brin: "He was sceptical at first, but we made him a guarantee—if it didn't work, we wouldn't charge him a single coin."

Me: "A fair offer—did he take you up on it?"

Flintlok: "Do you think we would have this place if he turned us down? We brought the Fighter to this empty field, and I ran through a few different spells until the Noob settled on one he liked."

Brin: "I, on the other hand, worked on a tune that captured this young lad's persona to perfection."

Flintlok: "We instructed him in the art of entrances and made him practise it until the Fighter could do the routine with his eyes closed. The next day when he stepped into the tavern, we were convinced he would bring the house down."[459]

Me: "Did it work?"

Brin: "Like a charm. As the Fighter strode through the door, the whole place erupted with lightning bolts, leaving the patrons speechless in shock[460]—they had never seen anything like it before. The entire tavern flocked around the Fighter as if he were a legendary hero returning from a recently completed main quest."

Flintlok: "—And thus *Flintlok & Brin* was born. With our first coin earned, we bought a tent and pitched it in the field. We have never looked back since."

Brin: "Word spread through Cloverton. Soon heroes from every corner of the realm were seeking us out, each one of them wanting a bigger

---

[459] *This is Wizard-speak, meaning maximum carnage with minimum effort.*

[460] *That must have been a hair-raising experience for them—sorry, I couldn't resist.*

and better entrance theme than the last hero to grace *The Giggling Giant.*"

Flintlok: "Our tent has been overflowing with them ever since..."[461]

Me: "With so many customers coming to your tent and endless spell casting, isn't there a greater risk of an accident occurring? I've heard a rumour that a Fireball can be fatal in enclosed spaces."[462]

The Wizard stiffens.

Flintlok: "*Never* blame the spell, *always* blame the Spellcaster!"

Brin: "We also have a bucket or two of water on standby, in case of any spell emergencies—you can never be too careful."[463]

Me: "Sounds like you've both landed on your feet."[464]

Brin: "You want to know the best thing about all of this?"

Me: "What?"

Brin: "We're helping adventurers, making a lot of coin, and doing it without any risk or danger to ourselves—isn't that something?"

Me: "Surely danger is half the attraction of being a hero? Without danger, isn't all *this* a tad, well—*boring?*"

Flintlok: "You have a lot to learn about adventuring, Loremaster. Danger is just death's distant cousin once removed—many an adventurer has fallen foul of it."

There's a polite cough behind me; I turn and see a face I instantly recognise.

Me: "Dorn?!"

Dorn: "*Oh hey,* Loremaster, it's *you*—how are you doing?"

---

[461] *Except for today—it must be dungeon-changeover day or something.*

[462] *Less of a rumour—more of a certainty...*

[463] *Handy versus Fireballs, practically lethal versus Lightning Bolts...*

[464] *The Wizard at least—I suspect the Bard caught his pipe organ on something on the way down.*

Me: "I'm good, thanks. Although I wish the same could be said for you—that looks like a nasty bruise you have there."

I gesture towards the black eye he's sporting. Dorn touches it ruefully and grins.

Dorn: "Got into an altercation with another Paladin, didn't I..."[465]

Me: "Did you win?"

The 'Barbarian' looks hurt.

Dorn: "Do you *really* need to ask that? I kicked that Holy Warrior's backside, of course!"[466]

Me: "What brings you to Cloverton?"

The 'Barbarian' nods in the direction of the Wizard and Bard.

Dorn: "I have an appointment with these two fine gentlemen—they're going to create an entrance theme for me."

The 'Barbarian' leans closer to whisper.

Dorn: "I've asked for a giant Hydra to appear behind me with a thumping musical accompaniment that will shake the foundations of the tavern in Cloverton and the one in Bellhurd several hundred miles away!"[467]

I turn to look at Flintlok.

Me: "You think the Wizard can cope with a Hydra?"

Dorn: "I'm sure a Spellcaster of his ilk can muster up something like that—if not, I'll ask for a Dragon with nine heads."

Me: "Isn't that just another way of describing a Hydra?"

---

[465] Hopefully, this one wasn't wearing a smitten Barmaid at the time.

[466] Not while the Paladin was wearing their Plate Armour, I hope—not unless Dorn wanted to risk a broken foot.

[467] Considering that Bellhurd is located high up in the snowy peaks of the Saltor Mountains, wedged on a narrow precipice where avalanches are a daily hazard—I assume this would not be a welcome sound to the locals living there.

Dorn: "Yeah, but he probably doesn't know that. Just look at him—I doubt he's even *seen* a Hydra before in his life."

The Wizard *'tuts'* and gives me the faintest of sneers, which I take as my cue to leave. But before I depart, I have one last question for Brin.

Me: "Your musical organ—did you always take it on your adventures?"

The Bard grins at me.

Brin: "The one I used back then was a fair bit larger and on wheels, which made navigating dungeons a lot easier—"

Flintlok: "Unless you encountered any stairs, then it was a musical pain in the backside—"

Brin: "Yeah, stairs were always a bit of a problem—and cliffs or ravines too, but it was an excellent workout for the core muscles!"

Flintlok: "I *hated* your bloody organ!"[468]

There's a polite cough from the waiting 'Barbarian'.

Dorn: "Sorry, but can we get started? Just I have a *'Dark Power'* in the south that needs my urgent attention."

The Wizard bites his top lip as the Bard blows out his cheeks and widens his eyes in disbelief—the awkward silence is almost palpable.

Brin: "Well, we'd better create a suitable entrance theme for you then—by the way, we're doing a discount on funeral exit themes if you're interested?"

The 'Barbarian' thinks a moment, mulling the offer over.

Dorn: "Sure, why not!"

I thank Brin & Flintlok[469] for their time and bid the smiling Dorn a fond

---

[468] *I suspect the Wizard's hatred has been boiling away for some time—I'm surprised he didn't incinerate the infernal instrument in an impressive inferno while the Bard's back was turned.*

[469] *This should have been written as Flintlok & Brin, not Brin & Flintlok—I wish to thank the Herald's Guide for bringing this to my attention with one of their Arcane Copyright spells— mercifully minus the 'Fair-Use Ogre' that often accompanies it.*

farewell. I'm unsure if this will be the last time our paths will cross, but regardless, it has been good to see the young 'Barbarian' again.

16. Sister Agatha, the Healer

The Sisters of Perpetuity have been around for as long as anyone can remember. A profoundly religious group, they have dedicated their lives to the art of healing and helping those unable to heal themselves. Their chapels can be found scattered across the realm, but most are situated only a stone's throw from any densely populated 'hero' town. Last summer, the Sisters of Perpetuity started an outreach program to help smaller, isolated settlements that don't have a large neighbouring township to lean on. These vulnerable hamlets are often on the wrong end of a Goblin raid or plagued by the occasional passing Dragon.[470] As a result, the Sisters of Perpetuity have seen a steady increase in the number of half-dead adventurers needing their 'gentle' touch.

Determined to dig a little deeper into their work, I find myself in Wolfsberg, a small hamlet close to the edge of the Unmistakable Marshes[471]—where wounded heroes seeking urgent healing are common. Sister Agatha, one of the longest-serving of her Order, greets me as she descends the steps of her outreach chapel.

Sister Agatha: "Welcome, *Loremaster* Elburn—I have been expecting you."

Me: "It's kind of you to meet me, Sister, but there was no need to wait outside for my arrival."

Sister Agatha: "It was a pleasure rather than a chore. It is a beautiful day to enjoy—one could almost say it is divine..."

She smiles sweetly, warming my soul and sparking a memory within me of a childhood in the company of now much-missed elders.[472]

Me: "Sister Agatha, may I ask, how long have you been in the Order exactly?"

Sister Agatha: "Nigh on forty-five summers now..."

---

[470] *Hopefully, not a horny Dragon in need of a quick post-coital snack...*

[471] *More on this place later...*

[472] *Grandmother Barr was a kind and loving soul who would often regale us with tales from her adventuring days—back when she was a mace-wielding Cleric. Even though time and tide had caught up with her, she could still strike fear into anyone foolish enough to steal her apple and cider tart.*

Me: "Forty-five summers? That's quite an achievement—it must be a hugely rewarding role."

Sister Agatha: "Spiritually, *yes*—financially, it's a bit of a mess, I'm afraid. These days we usually have to rely on donations and the gratitude of strangers to make ends meet."

As if to reinforce her answer, Sister Agatha takes out a small collection box and shakes it under my nose—I feel a burning obligation to find a spare coin and drop it into the box's hungry maw.[473]

Sister Agatha: "Bless you, my child—follow me."

The Sister turns and heads towards the white double doors of the chapel, adorned with an interlinking moon crest and sun motif. I point at the carved symbols as we approach the entrance.

Me: "The sign of your Order?"

Sister Agatha: "For as long as the moon follows the sun, and the sun follows the moon—the Sisters of Perpetuity will continue."

The chapel doors are thrown wide open, and we step into a long hall filled with neat rows of beds, each separated by insect netting and a discretional curtain. At the end of the hall is a statue of a woman holding the sun in one hand and the moon in the other, illuminated by a spear of light from a stained glass window high above.

Me: "That is breathtakingly beautiful—"

Sister Agatha: "I take it you were expecting something a little more rudimentary?"

Me: "If I'm being honest, I was expecting somewhere for the congregation to sit—not lie."

There's a titter of laughter from the Sister.

Sister Agatha: "This isn't a place of worship—not in the conventional sense of the word."

I stare at her in confusion.

---

[473] *My choice of words here is no accident; there's a strangeness to this box, almost as if it's alive and waiting to be fed.*

Me: "Forgive me, I thought this was a Holy Chapel?"

Sister Agatha: "It is—but its main purpose is not reverence, rather rest and recuperation. Come, let me show you."

The aroma of medicinal salves and pungent ointments fills the air. Sister Agatha notices my face recoiling at the overbearing odour.[474]

Sister Agatha: "It's from our sacred Fillomore plant[475]—we distil the roots and use its potent healing properties to cleanse any infected wounds."

I'm led to the bed of a patient wrapped head-to-foot in bandages; their arms are suspended in the air, making them look like some kind of macabre mummified puppet.

Sister Agatha: "This is Regalast—he's a Wizard."

Me: "What happened to the poor fellow?"

Sister Agatha: "He arrived a month ago almost burnt to a crisp. It seems Regalast here got into a fight with a Dragon and unwisely chose to cast a Fireball at it."

Me: "Why was that unwise?"[476]

Sister Agatha: "Because fire-breathing Dragons *eat* Fireballs for breakfast. This one *spat* the offending spell straight back at the Wizard—with a considerable amount of molten heat added for good measure..."

The bandaged Wizard suddenly coughs as he senses our presence.

Regalast: "It... came off the... Doom Mountains... looking for food... I

---

[474] *It's hard to describe the smell succinctly, so I shall endeavour to make a descriptive noise that encapsulates the sensation I am now experiencing—**HUUURRRRGHHH!***

[475] *Fillomore is a unique plant found only in the Unmistakable Marshes. Highly sought after for its powerful healing properties, it does come with one notable side effect, a distinct and potent odour—in fact, it is the sole reason the 'Unmistakable Marshes' came by its name. Many adventurers who have fallen foul of the marshes have taken that repugnant stench to their grave.*

[476] *I probably already suspect I know the answer to this question—but I'm curious to see what the Sister says.*

tried to stop it... but I forgot the golden rule..."

Me: "What rule was that?"

Regalast: *"Never fight fire... with fire..."*

Me: "Does it still hurt?"

Regalast: "Only when I laugh—so please... no jokes."

Me: "No jokes, got it. Is there anyone I can send word to—friends or family perhaps?"

Regalast: "Friends? Family? **Hahaha—OW!** I said 'no jokes' for good reason... No, I have nobody... not even the Heroes Guild... know... I am here..."

Me: "You're in the Heroes Guild? I thought they had an *arrangement* with the Wizards Guild not to take Wizards into their ranks?"

Regalast: "I—I was working with the Heroes Guild outside of... the Wizards Guild's knowledge..."

Me: "Isn't that forbidden—?"

Regalast: "Don't you think... I know that? If either Guild ever found out I was here... I'd be in a world of hurt..."

Me: "You look like you're already in a world of hurt."[477]

Regalast: "What? *Oh* yeah! **Hahaha—OW! DAMMIT!**"

Sister Agatha: "I've told you before, Regalast, all our patients here are under our protection—you have nothing to fear."

Me: "Can I ask, what were you doing working for the Heroes Guild?"

Regalast: "I—I was on a quest... a well-paid for one too, much better than the Wizards Guild ever pays... b—but my encounter with the D—Dragon ended my chance to secure the loot I had hoped to claim..."

Me: "Surely escaping with your life is all that matters?"

---

[477] *Uncle Bevan Barr would be cheering from the Great Beyond for that well-timed quip.*

Regalast: **"N—NO! YOU DON'T UNDERSTAND... I _HAVE_ TO RETURN WITH LOOT... I _HAVE_ TO!"**

Sister Agatha: "Settle down now, Regalast. Forgive him, _Loremaster_—it's the pain; it makes him delirious."

Regalast: **"OW!"**

The Sister puffs up Regalast's pillow a little too rigorously for the Wizard's liking.

Sister Agatha: "We should move on—I'll get one of the orderlies to give him a Fillomore essence bath."[478]

Regalast: **"Not the bath, anything but that—OW!"**

We leave the bandaged Wizard's protests behind us as we continue along the rows of beds towards the next patient.

Me: "Do you have much to do with the Heroes Guild, Sister?"

Sister Agatha: "Of course—they are our _main_ sponsor, but it does not mean we answer to them. We are free to run our affairs as we see fit."

Me: "_Sponsor?_ What's that?"[479]

Sister Agatha: "Someone who gives a sizeable contribution to our cause but doesn't like to get their hands dirty, so to speak. The Heroes Guild's monthly donations ensure we remain focused on our mission to help others."

On cue, the collection box makes another appearance, pressuring me to delve into my coin purse once more in response. I swear I hear a hungry growl from the box's depths as the coin is quickly gobbled up.

Me: "Why would the Heroes Guild help you?"

The Sister looks puzzled, as if I'm asking a question that needs no answer.

---

[478] _Hopefully, when I'm safely out of nose-shot!_

[479] _I've subsequently discovered that the word 'Sponsor' is Gnomish for 'Big Pockets—Little Ability'._

Sister Agatha: "There are a large number of heroes and adventurers in this realm. The Heroes Guild wants to protect its members and give them the best chance of recovery if the unfortunate should ever occur—it's a tough world out there, Loremaster; *anything* can happen to those who go looking for trouble."[480]

Me: "Can any injured hero turn up and ask for the Order's help?"

Sister Agatha: "We are not a tavern; we do not want *everyone* to limp in here with a minor ailment, my child—we need certain assurances our work is going to genuine heroes and *not* someone who stubbed their toe on a hoe[481] and expects it to be healed for free. That's why we ask for proof whenever an injured soul turns up at our doors."

Me: "How can someone prove they are a genuine hero?"

Sister Agatha: "Those who belong to the Heroes Guild always wear an official badge—that is usually enough to alleviate any doubts."

Me: "What if someone stole a badge and tried to pass themselves off as a hero?"

The Sister looks shocked and hurriedly makes a sun and moon gesture with her hands, while keeping her eyes firmly closed.

Me: "What was that?"

Sister Agatha: "It is our sacred Order's mark; we use it to ward away Evildoers, Gnomes, and Barbarians.[482] To answer your question, who would claim to be that who was not? *Hmm?*[483] No, the Heroes Guild would ensure such deceit could never happen."

Me: "You say the Heroes Guild does not hold any sway here, but I assume you notify them if any of their members are admitted through your doors?"

---

[480] *Why does this feel like a thinly veiled threat from the Sister?*

[481] *I'm fairly positive if this were the 'other' hoe variety, you'd be left with more than a bruised toe to worry about.*

[482] *Or even Evildoing Gnomish Barbarians—if there were such a thing.*

[483] *Just a wild stab in the dark here, but perhaps those 'untouchable' Rogue types?*

Sister Agatha: "We are not peons, Loremaster—we do not answer to anyone *but* our faith."[484]

Me: "What about non-members? Adventurers not affiliated with the Heroes Guild?"

Sister Agatha: "If they can prove they can afford our treatment, then who are we to deny them the help they desperately seek?"

Me: "And how much does this 'help' cost?"

Sister Agatha: "That all depends on the wound we are dealing with. Although they can get that price down *if* they are willing to part with more than just coin."

I sense the Sister's collection box glaring in my direction at the mere mention of the word 'coin'.

Me: "Like what?"

The Sister's eyes light up in excitement.

Sister Agatha: "Like *information!*"

Me: "What sort of information?"

Sister Agatha: "The questing kind of information—anything that can point the way for others to follow. That type of information will *always* take the sting out of a final bill."

I scrunch my face up, slightly perplexed.

Me: "What use is this information to you? You're not adventurers."

Sister Agatha: "No, we are not—but certain people we deal with *are*."

There's a moment of clarity as I suddenly realise what Sister Agatha is implying.

Me: "You're giving this knowledge to the Heroes Guild—aren't you?"

Sister Agatha: "Such news is of little use to a non-member—especially one so badly injured, don't you think? Without a properly trained hero attempting it, that quest would only leave another poor soul crawling

---

[484] *And a hungry collection box, obviously.*

222

through this chapel's doors. I don't think any of us would want that. No, it's much safer if a qualified adventurer took on such a task—a hero from the Heroes Guild, no less."

Me: "That sounds a little unethical? What about patient confidentiality?"

Sister Agatha: "We don't divulge anything personal to the Heroes Guild about our patients—only the quest that left a patients' bodies battered and broken. This is just a way to reduce further pain and suffering of those who think they are ready for adventure but are sadly not."

Me: "Aren't you worried the Heroes Guild would use this information for their own ends?"

Sister Agatha: "You'd have to ask them, I'm afraid. I wouldn't want to hazard a guess as to what they do with the information we provide; as I say, we are trying to stop the wrong people from ending up in our care."

Me: "Don't you think taking quests from non-members will only increase the risks they face once they have sufficiently recovered—they still need to earn an honest coin, or even a dishonest one if they're a Rogue?"

There's another hungry growl coming from the collection box trembling in Sister Agatha's hands—I try my best to ignore it.[485]

Sister Agatha: "The Order's view is unwavering. If a non-member has ended up in one of our beds, they're certainly not suited to a life of adventure. I strongly suggest they find an alternative profession, one that does not include dungeons or dragons."[486]

Me: "What happens if any of your patients cannot pay in coin or information?"

Sister Agatha: "Then they have to look for help elsewhere, I'm afraid."

Me: "You'd turn them away—in their moment of need?"

---

[485] Did I just see drool coming from it?

[486] Another uneasy feeling falls across me as if a 'Fair-Use Ogre' somewhere suddenly cracked their knuckles in preparation for an Arcane Copyright spell coming my way.

Sister Agatha: "The needs of the Sisters of Perpetuity *must* come first—it **cannot** be burdened with the debt of others. Otherwise, all our hard work will be for nothing."

Me: "When was the last time you turned a hero away?"

The Sister stops to think for a minute.

Sister Agatha: "A few days ago. There was a Halfling Rogue. He turned up looking like someone had just thrown him through a brick wall—which was quite astute as that's *precisely* what had happened to him."

Me: "He had been thrown through a brick wall?"

Sister Agatha: "Seems it was a shop quest that went *very* wrong *very* fast. The poor fellow was in such a state. We did as much as we could for him, but it turned out he didn't have a single coin to his name, nor did he seem willing to tell us what he thought was so precious in that shop that it almost cost him his life..."

Me: "What did you do?"

Sister Agatha: "We allowed him to stay for the night before encouraging him to make alternative *arrangements* in the morning."

Me: "How did he take that?"

Sister Agatha: "Surprisingly well, especially when he discovered the Heroes Guild was interested in talking to him. He practically walked out unaided—it was a miracle to behold!"[487]

Me: "Were they interested in talking to him?"

The Sister titters politely.

Sister Agatha: "No, poor chap—but it helped *'encourage'* him to crawl further down the road to become someone else's problem."[488]

---

[487] *Especially considering he was probably strung up like a bandaged puppet at the time.*

[488] *As the local tavern is the only other building of note in these parts, I doubt the Halfling found the kind of medicinal aid he was looking for. Although I'm sure after a few swift ales, he discovered the pain 'miraculously' dissipating.*

We stop by another patient, a nervous-looking Dwarf who has his hands and arms heavily strapped up. He sits up and stares at me with concern written across his face as we near.

Sister Agatha: "Calm yourself, Master Yarl. My associate is only a Loremaster writing about all the good work we do here."

The Dwarf's relief is almost palpable.

Yarl: "M—My apologies; for a moment, I thought you were someone else—"

Sister Agata: "Master Yarl is a Cleric."

Me: "What happened to your hands?"

Yarl: "I misjudged the radius of my *Protection from Evil* spell. I was using the sphere to keep an unspeakable foe at bay—but I stupidly forgot about my hands and left them hanging outside the aura. By the time I realised my mistake, the unholy abomination was draining the life out of them."

Me: "That sounds terrible!"

Yarl: "I got lucky—"

Me: "*Lucky? Lucky how?*"

Yarl: "This evil creature seemed hesitant to capitalise on my predicament and momentarily withdrew—presenting me with an opening to slip away from the unnatural monstrosity. I was in a painful daze, but somehow, I managed to stagger through the wilderness until I reached this very chapel. I remember slamming my withered hands against the doors, trying to get the attention of someone within. Fortunately, Sister Agatha answered and saw my desperate plight; she immediately set about tending to my wounds and nursing me back to health.[489] I survived—*just.* But it's safe to say I won't be multi-classing as a Bard anytime soon."

Me: "A Bard?"

---

[489] *After ensuring the poor Cleric was either a bona fide Heroes Guild member or could afford the final medical bill, no doubt.*

Yarl: "Yes, before I became a Cleric, I had a dream to play an instrument. The pipe organ—but not just any pipe organ, *a Holy* pipe organ."

Me: "I've never heard of a Holy pipe organ before."

Yarl: "It's a legendary instrument that my Deity, *Ham-Fist the Head-Splitter*,[490] constantly played before the people of the realm finally revolted against his musical rule and threw him *and* the Holy pipe organ on a great bonfire.[491] Fortunately, the instrument proved to be resistant to fire—my Deity less so..."

The Cleric holds up his bandaged stumps for me to see.

Yarl: "The only things I'm ever going to play now are drums."

Me: "*Ba dum tsss...*"[492]

Regalast:**"OW!"**

There's a yelp of pain from the Wizard several beds away.

Regalast:**"I SAID STOP WITH THE JOKES!"**[493]

Yarl gives me a weary shake of his head. I glance over at Sister Agatha, who is in a deep conversation with an orderly.

Me: "When we first met, you thought I was *someone* else—who did you think I was?"

Yarl: "One of *them*..."

Me: "Who?"

Yarl: "An *Enforcer*. The Heroes Guild is known to sometimes send a hound, harrying late payers who've failed to meet their monthly

---

[490] *So-called because his right hand was inexplicably large, and he could probably split a skull in two like a three-summer-old walnut with a flick of his oversized wrist.*

[491] *I'm pretty sure Ham-Fist the Head-Splitter AND his Holy pipe organ deserved it.*

[492] *I'm not destined to enjoy the nirvana waiting for me behind the Great Beyond at this rate...*

[493] *I admit that one was on purpose.*

quota."

Me: "Wait up a second—monthly quota?"

Yarl: "The amount you need to earn for the Heroes Guild each month."

Me: "And how much *is* that?"

Yarl: "Depends on your profession and how experienced you are. The more quests you complete, the more you earn—but the larger your monthly quota becomes."

Me: "What's *your* monthly quota?"

The Cleric flashes me a look; Sister Agatha is still locked in conversation with the orderly.

Yarl: "Three thousand gold coins."

Me: "Three *thousand* gold coins? That's how much you have to pay them?"

Yarl: "By Ham-Fist's Headache[494]—*No.* That's how much I *need* to have in my coffers by the end of the month. The Heroes Guild takes a cut and gives me the good grace to live off the rest."

Me: "What happens if you don't make their target?"

Yarl: "That all depends on how short I am[495]—if the difference is *too* great, I could wind up having my membership revoked."

Me: "They'd kick you out of the Heroes Guild?"

Yarl: "Ha! That's *if* I'm lucky…"

Me: "What if you're unlucky?"

The Cleric sucks in his breath.

Yarl:" Maybe I'll lose more than just my membership…"

---

[494] *Which, by all accounts, was 'splitting'.*

[495] *This is one of the hardest phrases for a Dwarf to say—and just as hard for me to keep my mouth straight while the Dwarf is saying it.*

Me: "That's appalling—why would anyone ever want to join the Heroes Guild in the first place if there's so much pressure placed upon them to complete quests?"

Yarl: "You must remember that being a member of the Heroes Guild has its benefits. For starters, you're part of a group that's always looking out for one another. You also get heavily reduced prices from Merchants and Landlords, such as *The Hammer & Tongs* or *The Green Goblin*. The Heroes Guild never seems to be short on quests either—"[496]

Me: "Funny that."[497]

Yarl: "They also have fresh fruit delivered to the kitchen area twice a week."

I shoot Sister Agatha a sideways glance; her conversation appears to be drawing to a close.

Yarl: "Look, I'm not saying the Heroes Guild is *bad*, far from it. They just have a particular way of doing things. Sometimes that involves making unpopular decisions—as a Cleric; I can respect that."[498]

Me: "Surely they can't expect you to make your monthly quota now you've been maimed."

Yarl: "I'm confident they'll understand my situation. Unless, of course, they decide to send Arin Darkblade—that's who I thought you were earlier. Not some bumbling quill-pusher, no offence."

A hand softly touches my arm as Sister Agatha politely interrupts our conversation.

Sister Agatha: "Forgive my rudeness, some clerical matters that could not wait. I trust you've had a good chat with this clerical *master*, though?"

Me: "Thank you, yes—it was extremely illuminating."

---

[496] *Dwarves are extremely sensitive to words like this and will only use them as a last resort to make a point.*

[497] *The situation being explained, not the subtle joke in the previous footnote.*

[498] *Apparently, Clerics are always making unpopular decisions with locals / congregation / adventurers / the entire realm (feel free to amend or add to this list where necessary).*

I turn to the recumbent Cleric.

Me: "Thanks for your time."

I go to shake Yarl's hand but realise my mistake. He looks at me with an ironic grimace as he holds up his stumps again. There's distant mocking laughter coming from behind Wizard's discretional curtain.

Regalast: ***"HAHA—OW! DAMMIT!"***

The Sister escorts me toward the doors leading out of the chapel.

Sister Agatha: "I'm afraid that's all I can do for you today—I hope it has given you a small insight into the good work we are doing here?"[499]

Me: "Thank you, it has. Clearly your Order has a lot to offer those unfortunate enough to end up here."

Sister Agatha: "The urge to adventure is strong in Wolfsberg; it calls out to those poor heroic souls—like a siren, luring sailors to the rocks. Our mission is to mend the broken bones of those who stumble in the darkness and help them eventually stand again in the light."

Me: "I can't help but feel heroes like Regalast and Yarl are being forced to take bigger and bolder risks with each passing quest. Not to mention the '*Dark Power*' in the south rumoured to be calling the Goblins down from the Halgorn Crags—are you concerned that we may be standing on the edge of worrying times?"

Sister Agatha: "Forgive me, Loremaster Elburn—but I think you're being somewhat overly dramatic. You forget I've been doing this for nearly half a century, and I have heard it *all* before. If I had a coin every time someone mentioned a '*Dark Power*' in one compass direction or another, I would have enough to fix the leaky roof of this chapel—"

Me: "Is the chapel roof in need of repair?"

Sister Agatha: "No, but it *always* pays to be prepared—don't you think?"

I'm suddenly aware the Sister is holding out her ravenous collection box again—I feel helplessly compelled to drop another coin into its

---

[499] *I suppose in this instance, 'good' is relative—and by 'relative', I mean a dodgy-looking distant cousin nobody trusts being left alone with the youngsters.*

salivating maw. There's an audible '*gulp*' as it disappears into the blackness.[500]

Sister Agatha: "Bless you, my child."

As we step through the chapel doors, I turn for one last question.

Me: "Do you ever remember if a hero named Aldon Barr was ever admitted here? He's my brother—I'm trying to track down his whereabouts."

She shakes her head sadly.

Sister Agatha: "I remember the names of all those who have been carried through our doors. I'm sorry, but your brother is not one I'm familiar with. Take it as a good sign and pray it remains that way, Loremaster. That said, I cannot speak for the other chapels. Perhaps you will have more luck with them—or if you are passing through Tronte, you could try the Heralds Guild; they may hold a clue to his fate."

Me: "Thank you, I may do that."

Sister Agatha smiles sweetly as she hands over a small bundle wrapped in a white handkerchief.

Sister Agatha: "Bread and cheese for your onward journey."

Me: "A most thoughtful gift. Thank you again, Sister—"

As I go to leave, the ominous collection box growls at me one last time. There's an expectant grin fixed on Sister Agatha's face.

Sister Agatha: "It's all for a good cause!"

I'm encouraged to make one last donation to the Sister's eagerly awaiting collection box. With slight trepidation, I withdraw my hand from my pouch— when the wooden case suddenly leaps forward and swallows the coin before I've even had a chance to see its denomination.[501] Sister Agatha smiles and pats the collection box as

---

[500] *I have no idea exactly how Sister Agatha plans to retrieve all these coins from her collection box—I suppose she could always wait for Mother Nature to take its course...*

[501] *I found out later that it wasn't one of my cheaper coins.*

she bids me a fond farewell.

Sister Agatha: "I do hope your path continues to be safe, Loremaster Elburn..."[502]

As I descend the chapel's steps, I turn and wave to the Sister with one hand while holding on tight to my coin purse with the other. I catch a glimpse of the collection box snuggled deep in the crook of Sister Agatha's arm—it 'burps' a final satisfied goodbye as I depart.

---

[502] That was _definitely_ a threat.

17. Hagworl, the Shovelsmith

Regardless of the reason, this is the one place in the entire realm where I'd rather not be.[503] Yet, as the sun begins its inevitable descent towards the horizon, I find myself standing opposite the locked gates of a graveyard. Turnwall is a private plot of land; set away from the local graves of those wealthy enough to avoid the pauper pit. It is a quiet spot solely dedicated to those brave souls who have perished mid-quest—a suitable resting place for heroes who have fallen into the darkness.[504]

I stare at the ranks of gravestones within, wondering how many heroes lie unseen below the surface. The clanking of keys snaps my attention back to the present. A gaunt man wearing mud-stained overalls unlocks the wrought-iron gates barring my way.

Me: "Are you *Hagworl?*"

The gate hinges squeak in protest as the grubby workman pulls them inwards and nods solemnly.

Hagworl: "You see another Shovelsmith standing around here? I take it you're the Loremaster."

Me: "*Elburn Barr,* a pleasure to meet you."

Hagworl chuckles at my reply.

Me: "Something I said?"

Hagworl: "It's not often someone is pleased to meet a Shovelsmith,[505] not while they *still* have breath in their lungs, that is."

Me: "I suppose the living prefer to avoid anything associated with death."

---

[503] *Although happy hour at 'The Raging Rag' is a close second, an establishment favoured by short-tempered Barbarians who enjoy ordering the tavern's signature punch, 'Lamentation on the Beach'.*

[504] *Such as Clerics who are too preoccupied looking up at their Sky God to notice they are about to step down into a bottomless pit.*

[505] *The Gravediggers Guild coined the name 'Shovelsmith' in an attempt to give their somewhat grisly image a much-needed boost. Sadly, almost everybody else still refers to them as 'Gravediggers'.*

Hagworl: "Yet death is always close—it could be a hidden chicken bone in the hot broth you're about to scoff down, a rickety old staircase that gives way under your weight,[506] or even a cold dagger in your back after walking down the wrong alleyway. Death is always there, waiting to appear just when you *least* expect it."[507]

Me: "That's slightly disconcerting."

Hagworl: "It is—but it's also strangely reassuring."

Me: "Reassuring?"

Hagworl: "Because *everything* must end—which means mercifully, one day, I won't be needing to do this job anymore."

Me: "Don't you enjoy your work?"

Hagworl: "Enjoy isn't *exactly* the word I'd use, but it pays well enough for me to continue to do it. But enjoy? No—my enjoyment is buried alongside the poor souls you see here."

We follow a meandering cobbled path around a plethora of gravestones and tombs until stopping at a mighty oak tree overlooking the outer wall. The sheer number of dead here is staggering.

Me: "Are *all* these heroes?"

Hagworl: "*Were*—they won't be swinging a sword or throwing a Fireball anytime soon."[508]

Me: "—and they *all* died adventuring?"

Hagworl: "Not all—some died of old age or ill health. Others died as a result of their own stupidity."

He gestures towards a nearby gravestone; I turn to read the words

---

[506] *It's fortuitous I decided against wearing a heavy hat when visiting Simply Morgan's abode.*

[507] *Unless your head is on the chopping block—then it's not going to take a Divination Spell to work out precisely <u>when</u> 'death' will make an appearance.*

[508] *Not unless a particularly twisted Necromancer turned up and reanimated the Wizard's corpse with the sole purpose of casting that flaming spell in the smallest of rooms—just for the hell of it.*

carved into the granite headpiece.

Me: *"Sinlow the Cleric—fell to the darkness after trying to 'turn' the undead without a suitable light source."*[509]

Hagworl: "In truth, he was 'backstabbed' in the tavern privy after drunkenly mistaking the grubby-looking Rogue next to him for an undead abomination. The pious fool even tried to 'turn' the thief while he was mid-stream, so to speak—very messy."

Me: "What about that one?"

I point to another headstone and read aloud the words carved into it.

Me: *"Perrival the Bard, sung his last song as he bravely fought a swarm of Giant Spiders."*

Hagworl: "He had an orgy with his own 'Mirror Image' and died of exhaustion four days later."[510]

I nod towards the next headstone along.

Me: "And I suppose Blarn the Barbarian didn't really die fighting a Dragon swarm?"

Hagworl: "Actually, he did—but he was drunk at the time and thought he was about to fight a bunch of angry butterflies."[511]

Me: "Why do all these heroes have different descriptions than how they actually perished?"

Hagworl: "Because they have it written into their contract with the Heroes Guild.[512] In the unlikely event of their death, the unfortunate hero may have their epitaph written to reflect the kind of hero they *want* to be remembered as, not necessarily the kind of hero they *were*."

---

[509] *Not the smartest of ideas—even for a Cleric.*

[510] *I think even within Bardic circles, this probably raised a few eyebrows.*

[511] *This should be a stark warning to those who consume too many glasses of 'Lamentation on the Beach'—at some point in your inebriated state, you could mistake butterflies for Dragons that are really, really, far away.*

[512] *Although technically, it's a footnote in the 'Death in Service' clause, which is imaginatively referred to as the 'Death in Stupidity' clause...*

Me: "I've noticed the Heroes Guild has pretty comprehensive contracts."

Hagworl: "That they do—drafted by the best Heralds coin can buy."

Me: "It seems like a lot of hard work and toil for nothing."

Hagworl: "Not every hero gets to bow out fighting beasts and Evildoers; some expire in the most embarrassing of ways, like showing off their transformative abilities by turning themselves into a mouse— only to be eaten by a passing cat."[513]

Me: "So, the Heroes Guild ensures nobody ever hears about these mishaps?"

Hagworl: "Can you imagine the reaction if everyone realised heroes die in the stupidest of ways? There would be pandemonium!"

Me: "Pandemonium from the locals?"

Hagworl: "From *adventurers!* Do you believe if everyone knew the truth, they would become a hero? Not likely—"

Me: "Surely any wannabe hero would be encouraged by these failures? They would see an opportunity where the ranks had been thinned enough to make their mark in the realm—even complete a quest or two without looking over their shoulder for the competition?"

The Gravedigger scratches his head ruefully.

Hagworl: "You reckon they would be willing to accept that those who fell were simply unworthy fools destined for the grave—unlike them?"

Me: "Why wouldn't they?"

Hagworl: "An interesting theory, but I disagree—"

Me: "So, what? You're saying those who die in such circumstances only serve to tarnish the reputable image of the Heroes Guild—"

Hagworl: "Not *just* the Heroes Guild..."

I blink several times in confusion.

---

[513] What would be even <u>more</u> embarrassing is if the cat was called 'Mr. Jingles'...

Me: "Who else then?"

Hagworl: "Ask yourself this, who stands to lose from this knowledge being made public?"

Me: "I'm struggling to think of anyone?"

The Gravedigger shoots me a knowing look.

Hagworl: "*Evildoers...*"

Me: "*Evildoers?* I don't understand—what do *they* care if a hero dies? Aren't they in the business of killing heroes?"[514]

Hagworl: "Take my word for it; they care plenty enough. For example, this '*Dark Power*' rising in the south—"

Me: "—The one rallying the Goblins?"

Hagworl: "The very same. I can guarantee it *doesn't* want any adventurers bowing out in this comedic fashion before they've had a chance to enter their shadowy domain."

I cannot believe what I hear—the Gravedigger must be mistaken.

Me: "Why? Isn't one dead hero just one less hero to worry about?"

Hagworl: "Yes, but what's better for an Evildoer's reputation? A hero who is slain attempting their dungeon? Or a drunk hero who dies falling from a tavern window before the adventure has begun?"

Me: "Wait, you mean Evildoers don't *want* adventurers to die—unless it's specifically by their hand?"[515]

Hagworl: "I didn't say that exactly, but what an Evildoer does want more than anything is *fear*—fear is a weapon, fear can be tempered, it spreads through every living thing, rotting all hope in the process. An Evildoer *needs* a hero to try to thwart it—because there's nothing more satisfying than crushing them in the process and letting the entire realm know about it. If an adventurer dies before they've even set foot

---

[514] *Wouldn't be much of an Evildoer if they weren't. They would probably be less of an Evil 'doer' and more of an Evil 'procrastinator'...*

[515] *Or by claw, poisonous breath, razor-sharp teeth, a flaming sword, death-stare, or even absorbed by their wobbly gelatinous insides...*

in a dungeon, what use is that to an Evildoer? It's the kind of revelation that will only serve to reduce the number of adventurers applying to the Heroes Guild next summer. If that were to happen, *everyone* loses. So, the Heroes Guild *occasionally* embellishes the true nature of an adventurer's death, substantially increasing the infamous reputation of the Evildoer in the process, while attracting more and more new heroes to their cause—all of whom are eager to prove themselves worthier than those who perished before them."

Me: "So, a mutual *arrangement* exists between the Heroes Guild and the Evildoers its members have sworn to destroy? It sounds almost too fantastical to be true."[516]

Hagworl: "It does—but I can assure you this <u>is</u> the truth."

I sit by the tree, trying to comprehend everything the Gravedigger has revealed to me.

Me: "How do you know all this?"

Hagworl: "Heroes aren't the only ones who belong to a Guild."

Me: "You mean the Gravediggers Guild."

Hagworl: "You catch on quick—but we prefer to call ourselves the *Mort-Men*."[517]

Me: "The Mort-Men? How many of you are there?"

Hagworl: "Well, there's at least one in every town from here to the Dagger Coast."

Me: "That must be over a hundred villages and towns—"

Hagworl: "One hundred and forty-five to be exact."

Me: "Are there really *that* many fallen heroes to bury?"

Hagworl: "In truth, we're stretched to breaking point and need more Shovelsmiths. Heroes are falling faster than we can put them in the

---

[516] *Along with self-driving carriages, Merchant-less shops, and portable Bard-playing devices, some things simply defy belief!*

[517] *Somehow, I doubt those Gravediggers who aren't male rate the name 'Mort-Men' much...*

ground—it's a sad fact that sometimes we have no choice but to bury two in the same grave to save on time and space."[518]

Me: "How come so many are dying?"

Hagworl: "Ain't it obvious?"

Me: "Not to me."

Hagworl: "The ones that wind up dead simply aren't cut out for a heroic way of life."

Me: "But I thought new heroes were supposed to be thoroughly trained to survive anything a quest throws at them—or at least that's what the Heroes Guild *Welcome Parchment* promises?"[519]

Hagworl: "Yeah, *saying* and *doing* are two different things. The majority of the poor buggers don't have the *first* clue about the craft of adventuring. I swear most are walking straight out of the tavern and straight into their grave plot."

Me: "Shouldn't they be attempting lower-level quests? I heard they are generally safer and easier to complete?"

Hagworl: "Nice idea—but it's an idea that relies solely on an abundance of low-level quests to begin with. Sadly, that's not the reality. New heroes are faced with sniffing around for side-quests for the rest of their days or attempting a dungeon way out of their league—those who choose the latter don't tend to come back—and in some cases, they don't come back from the former either..."

Me: "What happens to the bodies of those who fall mid-quest?"

The Gravedigger scratches his chin nervously.

Hagworl: "*Ah* well... you see... we have an *arrangement*."[520]

---

[518] *This indignity is compounded by the thought of a recently deceased Gnome being buried alongside a heavily encumbered Half-Orc, or worse—a heavily encumbered Halfling...*

[519] *With its glossy cover of a scantily clad, well-oiled Elven Barbarian standing next to a scantily-clad well-oiled Dwarven Barbarian, while in the background a scantily clad, well-oiled Sorcerer throws Fireballs at a scantily cad, well-oiled Gelatinous Cube—I assume the cover artist wasn't very good at drawing clothes.*

[520] *It seems everyone has an 'arrangement' these days—everyone but me...*

Me: "An *arrangement*—with *whom?*"

Hagworl: "Now, don't panic when I tell you—"

Me: "With **whom**?"

Hagworl: "Evildoers…"

Me: **"WHAT?!"**

The Gravedigger laughs nervously as my eyes nearly pop out of my skull in disbelief.[521]

Me: "You've got to be joking, right?"

Hagworl: "I wish I were, but I'm not making this up—Shovelsmiths are allowed to deal with the cadavers of any dead heroes who perish while attempting a quest with an Evildoer at the heart of it."

Me: "How can this be?"

Hagworl: "I can tell you're struggling to understand this—that's okay; it takes a while to see the bigger picture. Sure, we *all* know Evildoers are bad; everyone knows that, right? But even a deadly shark needs its teeth cleaned once in a while[522]—that's where we come in."

Me: "Even where this '*Dark Power*' in the south is concerned?"

Hagworl: "Yup, even there."

Me: "Then you know who it is!"

Hagworl: "No, don't be foolish, I may deal with death, but I don't have a death wish. Everything is done anonymously. That way, there's no risk to either party."[523]

Me: "But, how can you find any hero who dies mid-quest?"

---

[521] *This would amuse Seymour no end.*

[522] *This is a vexing riddle to test the wisest in the realm—on the one hand, I wouldn't want to be the one cleaning a shark's teeth, while on the other, I don't think I want to be eaten by a shark with bad breath either.*

[523] *Just the adventuring party…*

Hagworl: "We don't. Look, when an adventurer, *you know*—"

The Gravedigger thumbs across his throat and dangles his tongue out awkwardly from one side of his mouth.

Hagworl: "Their body, or whatever remains of them, will be left on the outskirts of the nearest town. When some luckless local eventually discovers the corpse, we are called in to take care of it, which includes figuring out who they were and how they died. Sometimes, if the Evildoer is particularly thoughtful, they'll even leave a polite note with the dead hero's name on it—or at least what profession they were before they expired."

Me: "A polite note?"

Hagworl: "Yeah, it doesn't happen a lot, in all honesty—but some of them *do* appreciate how difficult a job we have. Once we know an expired hero's profession, then we can contact a relevant Guild or even the Heralds Guild to begin formal identification."

Me: "What if they weren't members of any Guild?"

Hagworl: "Then we have to pray they have an identifying mark or carry personal effects that can give us a clue as to who they were. Failing that—they are buried with a Phoenix symbol on a headstone together with the recorded date they were found."[524]

Me: "What does the Phoenix symbol mean?"

Hagworl: "It signifies a hero with *no* known name."

Me: "I heard there are some opportunistic Necromancers interested in the bodies of unclaimed heroes."

He eyes me suspiciously.

Hagworl: "What do you mean exactly?"

Me: "*Erm…* well, I'd wager they'd happily take them off your hands before you bury them."

Hagworl: "Shovelsmithing is one of the oldest and noblest professions

---

[524] *Maybe this is an ironic joke within the Gravedigging community?*

in existence.[525] Even if someone cannot pay for the plot, we *never* leave a body uncovered. I cannot believe for one instant that any of the Shovelsmiths I know would stoop so low—*who* told you this?"

Me: "Just… a… *Necromancer*…"

Hagworl: "*Bah*—they're *worse* than Paladins! I wouldn't trust a single word from their corpse-loving lips. They'll say anything to sully the name of our reputable profession—anything to throw controversy on our hard work. You want to know why they do it? I'll tell you, so they can steal a body from under our noses while everyone else is pointing the finger of blame at us—well, **not** on my watch!"

Me: "*Sorry*—I had to ask…"

Hagworl: "You're a Loremaster; it's in your blood to ask the awkward questions."

A thought suddenly crosses my mind.

Me: "Do you remember if you've ever buried someone called Aldon? *Aldon Barr?* He's my brother—he left home ten summers ago, and we've not heard from him since."

The Gravedigger thinks for a moment before slowly shaking his head.

Hagworl: "I've laid thousands to rest in my time; I can't remember them all. But that's not to say he's not here somewhere, buried with a Phoenix symbol to mark his final resting place. I'm sorry, but I can't help you."

Me: "I know… it's okay… I don't believe he's dead. I think I would have felt it—deep down. For now, I have to keep hoping he's alive and well somewhere, probably entertaining a crowd with his tales of adventure."[526]

Hagworl: "Hold onto that thought tightly in your heart, and you'll see

---

[525] *The actual oldest non-Guild profession known is, in fact, 'street-walking', an ancient role performed by women that involved assisting a drunken soul back to their home and ensuring they are safely tucked into their own bed—for a pre-arranged fee, of course.*

[526] *That's not to say my brother is a braggart, but he does love the sound of his own voice.*

your brother soon enough—take my word for it."[527]

I nod in thanks and look out across the graveyard's outer wall. The rolling hills offer a calming view, inciting a sense of natural serenity that not even the distant outline of the Doom Mountains can disrupt. This is a perfectly peaceful vista; one any hero would be happy to spend their eternal rest in the shadow of—perhaps it's time I started to take risks on my quest to find Aldon. So far, I have played it relatively safe. Maybe I should push my luck further; I know it's what he would have done if things were different.[528]

Me: "You think you can help me get in touch with the '*Dark Power*' in the south? To talk to, I mean?"

Hagworl: "Now, why would you want to do something as foolish as that?"

Me: "If there's a chance of discovering what happened to my brother, I owe it to him to try."

The Gravedigger thinks for a moment.

Hagworl: "I've buried so many young heroes; it would be a shame to add your name to the list of the dead here. You're a good brother, but you should leave this one well alone."

Me: "*Please,* I have to see this journey through to the end—to whatever end that may be."

The Gravedigger holds my gaze; a silent understanding passes between us.

Hagworl: "It's your funeral—leave it with me; I'll send word when I have some news."[529]

---

[527] For some reason, I find the Gravedigger's words slightly disconcerting.

[528] My brother was always the risk-taker. When we were younger, he was always the first to climb the tallest tree or jump into the fastest-flowing river. On the other hand, I had a hard time separating bravery from stupidity—much to my brother's mocking chagrin (as he was carried over the onrushing waterfall or fell from a great height hitting every branch on the way down).

[529] Just don't send word via a 'Barker'—I don't want to end up a with a random garden implement being delivered instead...

Me: "Thanks."

As I stand, Hagworl turns to talk to me one last time.

Hagworl: "Pick a spot."

Me: "I'm sorry?"

Hagworl: "A plot—pick one."

Me: "I thought this place was reserved for heroes only?"

Hagworl: "Aye, so pick a spot before I change my mind."

I think for a moment as I look across the graveyard—sitting between the plethora of graves already occupied, a number of empty plots await their turn to be filled with the bones of unfortunate adventurers.

Me: "The one next to this tree, with the view of the hills and mountains in the distance…"

Hagworl: "A good choice. I'll put it aside for you."[530]

I get up to leave and shake the Gravedigger's hand.

Me: "I hope you don't think me rude, but I do hope we *don't* meet again—at least, not here, in this place."[531]

The Gravedigger grins a toothy grin.

Hagworl: "Me too, Loremaster—me too. Good luck with your onward journey. I hope you find your brother."

I head out of the graveyard with purpose, keen to put as much distance between my potential final resting place and myself as possible.[532]

---

[530] *Thanks—I think…*

[531] *And if we 'do' meet again, I don't want to be alive to know anything about it unless, of course, we both happen to be passing in the street or spy one another in a local tavern— then I'd much prefer to remain alive at that point of meeting.*

[532] *Though it does now leave me wondering what happens if I were to walk over my 'own' grave, however, after a brief moment of contemplation, I've decided I don't want to know…*

18. Kara Rocksplitter, the Heroes Guild Scout

The Golden Golem tavern is a destination frequented by both adventurers and fans of adventurers alike. Situated in the heart of Loroton, nestled between the local Heroes Guild and Wizards Guild, the drinking establishment has an unenviable reputation of being more than a little 'lively' on any given night. The Golden Golem is also popular with the Heroes Guild 'Scouts'—specialised individuals trained to spot and convince any potential up-and-coming adventurer to join the Heroes Guild's fold. I've arranged to meet one such 'Scout'—Kara Rocksplitter, in the hope of understanding her small yet vital role in finding the heroes of tomorrow.

The smell of hops is strong as I take a careful sip from the flagon of ale in my hand. I find myself momentarily distracted by an argument between a Barbarian and a Wizard on the far side of the bar.[533] But my attention quickly snaps back to the Dwarven Scout sitting opposite me. Even before I've asked my first question, I can tell Kara's eyes are everywhere, scanning the sea of patrons around us, searching for that heroic treasure in the deep.

Me: "Are you working right now?"

Kara: "Sorry, a force of habit, once you start looking, it can be pretty hard to stop—if you know what I mean?"

Me: "In my world, looking for anything too long often leads to trouble."[534]

Kara: "Trouble is *exactly* what I'm looking for."

Me: "I thought you were supposed to be looking for heroes?"

The Dwarf looks me up and down like I'm an inexperienced Noob.

Kara: "You should know, Loremaster, trouble *always* attracts heroes..."

Me: "But how do you spot someone who has heroic potential?"

---

[533] *Weirdly, the argument between the pair seems to be over each other's choice of attire—with the Barbarian insisting the Wizard is wearing a dress while the Wizard is questioning the Barbarian's decision to wear a dead rat as a codpiece. All I know is I want to be as far away from here as possible when the Fireballs and oversized swords start flying.*

[534] *Or, to be more precise, trouble comes looking for _you_...*

The Dwarf smiles at me from behind her flagon of ale.

Kara: "*Ah*, that's the real trick—to spot a potential hero, you need three things—"

The Scout's fist uncurls one solitary digit.

Kara: "First, you need courage—you can't charge into the unknown without having the biggest balls of steel around.[535] I don't care if you have pushed a Wheel of Pain around for most of your life[536]—unless you're ready to jump into the metaphorical jaws of death at a moment's notice, your destiny probably lies at the bottom of a cold empty grave or a spiked trap under a dungeon floor."

The Dwarf uncurls a second digit.

Kara: "Next—you need determination. As a hero, you'll encounter low points, moments where you're on the floor dying, too exhausted to pick yourself up and charge back into the fight. Without determination, you're not going to make it to the next room, let alone the end of day one."[537]

She uncurls a third and final digit.

Kara: "Any guesses as to what the last quality is?"

Me: "Loyalty?"

Kara: "Nope."

Me: "Sacrifice?"

Kara: "Not even close."

Me: "Silence?"

Kara: "What?"

---

[535] *I'm assuming the Dwarf is referencing some kind of 'exotic' weapon here.*

[536] *The Wheel of Pain is actually more of a square—not a wheel. Making the task of 'wheeling' more arduous and unbearable for the trainee Barbarians attempting it, and even more so for those wearily cheering this rite of passage on from the sidelines.*

[537] *Although if the next room contains a very hungry Dragon, I* still *think your chances of making it to day two are pretty slim...*

Me: "Sorry, private joke. Fortitude? Skill? Cunning? Compassion? Honesty? Valour?"

Kara: *"Wealth..."*

Me: "What? That can't be right—"

Kara: "It is. You see, I *always* look for those who are rich over those who are poor."

Me: "That doesn't sound like a particularly defining quality needed to be a hero."

Kara: "On the contrary, being rich means you have more to lose. What's the point of a hero who has nothing—where's the risk for them? If they die, they've only lost their lives. But if they're rich—well, they've not only lost their lives, but the *wealth* they've amassed too—what better motivation is there than that?"

Me: "What about doing it for your loved ones? Surely that's greater motivation?"

The Dwarf downs her ale in one fell swoop and burps loudly before catching the eye of the Bartender for another.

Kara: "A noble cause for sure—but you'd be surprised how many would feed their loved ones to the beast rather than be consumed by it themselves. Riches and fortune, however—now that's *always* worth dying for."

'CLUNK!'

A new flagon of ale is planted next to the Dwarf without the customary gruff enquiry about payment—the Scout spies my quizzical look and grins.

Kara: "Perks of the job, although not a perk you'd want to get *too* acquainted with if you catch my drift."[538]

There's a loud shout and a sudden blast of foul-smelling air as the Barbarian is sent flying in our direction. He slides on his face to a

---

[538] *I sense my liver nodding furiously in agreement.*

squeaky stop right under our table.[539] Everyone turns to stare at the red-faced Wizard, who stands defiantly, waiting to see if anyone else wants to pass judgement on his choice of attire. I carefully lift my feet to avoid kicking the prone angry-Warrior in the ear.

Kara: "Idiots... wasting their energy fighting one another when they should be out there fighting Evildoers."

Me: "Isn't it normal for Barbarians and Wizards to clash? Better in here than out there, mid-adventure, surely?"

Kara: "True, but Evildoers don't care—they *want* chaos. Heroes killing one another saves them a lot of time and effort."

Me: "But with so many adventurers operating across the realm, it's not really going to change much in the long run—is it?"

Kara: "Spoken like someone who has *never* been on an adventure— look, the lifespan of a hero isn't great; there are few who go the distance and buy a little retirement castle by the sea.[540] Perhaps a handful will even get lucky enough to live out their days in *The Heroes Hall of Legends*. Most, however, will end up as worm food—we call them the '*Thirty Suns*'..."

Me: "Thirty Suns?"

Kara: "Thirty Suns—the average number of sunrises a hero sees before they... you know... *die*..."[541]

Me: "I don't remember anyone *ever* mentioning that bit of crucial information."

Kara: "Are you surprised?"

Me: "Yes. Hugely. Thirty Suns? That's terrible—"

Kara: "No—that's *business,* and the Heroes Guild is the *master* of business."

---

[539] *I later discovered the Barbarian was hit by a spell called 'Bobbet's Blustery Belch', a foul-smelling cantrip that lingers in the air long after being cast.*

[540] *Whoever is selling retirement castles by the sea must be losing a fortune.*

[541] *The best-case scenario for this is an adventurer lost in the Timeless Desert—where, by a quirk of fate, one whole day lasts an entire summer.*

Me: "But why are you telling me this? What if this sort of information became public knowledge—wouldn't it damage the Heroes Guild?"

The Scout creases her brow as if wrestling with an inner conflict.

Kara: "'Damage them? Take it from one who knows, they won't care a jot about anything I say, or what you write down in your little book of words."

Me: "Even if that little book of words suddenly became public knowledge?"

Kara: "I still doubt they'll care much—they have more pressing matters to deal with."[542]

Me: "Like?"

Kara: "What am I to you—a Dungeonmaster?[543] *You* figure it out."

The Scout quickly polishes off the second ale before ordering another on the house.

Me: "Isn't it a challenge to find a wealthy hero willing to sign up? I can't imagine there would be many who would risk their lives on some dungeon romp?"[544]

The Dwarf takes a swig from her third drink. She gasps with satisfaction, leaving behind an impressive frothy white moustache in the process.

Kara: "Coin buys you infamy, not fame. The rich are bored of their lives, bored of having everything handed to them on a plate, bored of counting their coins. They want more—they want to be recognised as heroes, to have songs sung about their adventures by common folk. They covet this more than anything."

Me: "That sounds a little shallow, if I'm honest."

---

[542] *'Pressing matters' is Gnomish for 'crushing traps'.*

[543] *In a certain light, I must admit, a Dwarf could easily be mistaken for a Gnomish Dungeonmaster—but as you can appreciate, I'm a little hesitant to point this out to the terse Scout.*

[544] *And put their substantial fortune on the line at the same time...*

Kara: "Let me ask you this, what do you think matters more to the locals in this tavern, how much a hero earns, or what that hero has done for them?"

Me: "Well... when you put it like *that*..."

Kara: "Don't forget—a hero isn't allowed to use their own wealth to get by. It's frozen the moment they sign up to the Heroes Guild."

Me: "Frozen?"

Kara: "Yup, by one of their *'unofficial'* Spellcasters; a guy with a grey beard and blue wand. He literally freezes any assets a new hero has, effectively stopping them from using their funds while adventuring."[545]

Me: "But why?"

Kara: "Why do you think? All heroes start at the bottom—with nothing but their adventuring name. To be a hero means crawling inch by inch up the adventuring ladder until you finally reach the top."

Me: "Why start them with nothing?"

Kara: "Because heroes must come from *nothing* before becoming *something*, and they can only achieve that by completing quests. Remember, all their lodgings, food, drink, adventuring supplies, new weapons, repairs, magical items, healing potions, training—are paid for in advance by the Heroes Guild."

Me: "But won't they just end up owing the Heroes Guild a sizeable amount of coin?"

Kara: "Precisely. The cost of being an adventurer is huge—mentally, physically, *and* financially. That's why I prefer to put forward 'heroes' with substantial assets the Guild can reclaim in the *unlikely* event something unfortunate should happen to them.[546] Do you know anyone willing to give an adventurer credit? They're the least likely to repay any accrued debt and almost certainly won't be returning any goods in one piece—if at all."

---

[545] *I'll be disappointed if this Spellcaster didn't utter a clever pun or two while using their wand—something like "Now that's n-ICE", "Let's leave this to chill for a while", or "That was Free-zy!"*

[546] *Coincidentally, 'unlikely' is Gnomish for 'almost certainly'.*

The Dwarf leans back, finishes her third ale, and waves for a fourth.[547]

Kara: "Being rich means you are responsible—and a responsible adventurer has the greatest chance of returning from a quest in one piece. Unlike a poor adventurer, who usually ends up in pieces so small even I would dwarf them."[548]

I find myself ill at ease with the Scout's pragmatic logic.

There's a groan beneath the table as the Barbarian staggers to his feet. He rubs his head and tries to focus once more on the laughing Wizard by the bar.

Me: "This doesn't look promising—shouldn't someone do something?"

Kara: "In my experience, it's usually best to leave them to it."

The Barbarian bellows with rage and charges the Wizard, poleaxing him as he leaps forward, catching the Spellcaster in the torso with his collarbone. The Wizard vanishes as the Barbarian continues on his horizontal trajectory and slams headfirst into the hardwood bar, knocking himself out cold. There's a rousing chorus of approval from the other Wizards in the tavern as flagons are held aloft in the victor's honour. The conquering Wizard reappears, standing with one foot on the unconscious Barbarian's back—almost as if he's just completed an arduous journey to the summit of this man-mountain.[549]

Me: "What can you tell me about the 'Death in Service' clause found within a Heroes Guild contract?"

Kara: "It's all standard legal stuff—it's there to protect the hero signing it as much as the Heroes Guild themselves. When the Heroes Guild takes in a new recruit, they are gambling a huge amount on that adventurer being a resounding success. The 'Death in Service' clause is the only way the Heroes Guild can guarantee any return on their substantial investment. Put it this way, if your hard-earned coin was on

---

[547] *I have a feeling the Dwarf could drink a Barbarian under the table, which is ironic as there is one currently lying unconscious beneath ours at this* exact *moment.*

[548] *Ten house points to the Dwarf slipping that gem of a pun in!*

[549] *The only thing missing is a fluttering flag adorned with the Wizard's insignia planted in the Barbarian's muscular behind.*

250

the line—wouldn't *you* want some assurances you'd get it all back if things took a turn for the worse?"

Me: "Yes, I guess I would..."

I take another sip from my ale; strangely, I'm finding the taste has soured slightly on the tongue.

Me: "What about the '*Death in Stupidity*' clause?"

Kara: "What's there to say? Adventurers do stupid things from time to time—the '*Death in Stupidity*' clause means we can keep that stupidity from becoming common knowledge, sparing the fallen adventurer's family from ridicule—*and* the Heroes Guild from being seen in a less than favourable light."

Me: "How often, would you say, the '*Death in Stupidity*' clause is used?"

For the first time this evening, the Dwarf fixes me with a deadly serious stare.

Kara: "A lot..."

The Golden Golem is awash with people coming and going; raucous laughter and loud voices dominate the air. I decide to steer the conversation away from the talk of the Heroes Guild.

Me: "How is it possible to spot *anything* in this crowd?"

Kara: "The trick is looking with your ears."[550]

Me: "Pardon?"

Kara: "Precisely—you need to listen first, then look."

Me: "You listen for suitable candidates? What are you listening for in particular?"

Kara: "A well-spoken voice, someone who has had an educated upbringing, lived well—not just lived. I'm looking for a candidate who can think for themselves, who knows their own mind. Someone with a bit of charisma—"

---

[550] There is a monstrous creature called a 'Behearer', which is a giant floating ear covered with a plethora of smaller ears on tentacles. It often sneaks up on loud adventurers before shhh-ing them and asking if they could keep the noise down a bit.

Me: "Why charisma in particular—why not strength or dexterity?"

Kara: "Would you let a hero regale you with tales of their dungeon-delving if they had a personality of a Turd Lurker?"[551]

Me: "I—I guess not..."

Kara: "There's more to being a hero than simply swinging a sword or casting a spell—a hero *must* be entertaining, charming, and inspire their fans. This is why only adventurers with strong personalities and an estate to match are welcomed in by the Heroes Guild nowadays."

Me: "What else do you look for?"

Kara: "Strong wrists."[552]

Me: "Excuse me?"

Kara: "For signing—heroes are expected to make frequent appearances around the realm, scrawling their signatures on whatever merchandise the Heroes Guild can sell. Fans will queue up for days for a chance to ask their favourite adventurer to sign a wooden flagon with that hero's likeness etched into it."

I look around the bar; the tavern is now thick with potential candidates. How the Scout can find a hero in this rough sea of hopefuls is beyond me.

Me: "Okay, say you hear a potential recruit, then what?"

Kara: "Next, I look at what they are wearing, at every tiny detail—the rings on the fingers, the family heirlooms they wear around their neck. I look at how fine the quality of their clothes are, if their hands are clean and soft, or if they have toiled too hard in the pursuit of coin."

Me: "Say all the signs look promising—what next?"

Kara: "Next? Next, we test them..."

---

[551] *I don't know any Turd Lurkers to confirm if this is a bad thing or not, but judging by the reputation of their stench alone, I would have to assume the worst.*

[552] *If you could see my face right now, you'd know this isn't quite the answer I was expecting.*

Me: "Test them *how?*"[553]

Kara: "I usually find a spontaneous bar-fight between a Barbarian and a Wizard works wonders..."

I stop and look over at the Barbarian still out cold by the bar.

Me: "Wait, you mean—?"

The Dwarf laughs and holds up a hand to stop me.

Kara: "That one *was* real—but yeah, *that* kind of test. If prospective candidates want to join the Heroes Guild, they need to be ready for any situation, including an impromptu bar brawl."

Me: "If, for example, this *was* a proper test, who would you expect the prospective candidate to side with? Should they help the Wizard or the Barbarian?"

The Scout cocks an eye.

Kara: "You tell me—who would _you_ side with?"

I think for a moment about the conundrum.

Me: "The Wizard obviously knows magic and could *easily* cast a lethal spell, but—"

Kara: "But...?"

Me: "The Barbarian *should* have the strength and speed to beat him *if* he can avoid his magic, so—"

Kara: "So...?"

I look around the bar at the aftermath of the recent fight. The Barmaid is busily mopping up the broken glass while the Landlord is buying drinks for those caught up in the melee. I turn back to the Dwarf with my answer.

---

[553] *I suspect this test does not include a theory section.*

Me: "I'd fight *both* of them."[554]

The Dwarf nods and leans back in her seat with a grin spread across her face.

Kara: "Your reason being?"

Me: "They are both a problem for the locals; *they're* the ones who need saving."

Kara: "Well said. Perhaps there *is* a hero somewhere in you after all."

Me: "What happens after the candidate passes your test?"

On cue, another free flagon of ale is planted on the table between us— the Dwarf gestures towards it.

Kara: "Then I try to break the ice between us. I find ale is the perfect tool for the job."

The Scout takes a deep quaff of her beverage and belches with satisfaction.

Kara: "After an evening of being plied with drinks, they're usually ready to sign anything put in front of them."

Me: "You get them drunk before they sign—isn't that a little immoral?"

Kara: "Drink fills them with the courage they need—while the Heroes Guild ensures it never runs dry. All I'm doing is giving them a little push out the door and in the right direction."

Me: "Hypothetically speaking, what adventuring role would you say *I* would be best suited for?"

The Scout laughs and slaps the table in glee.

Kara: "An **excellent** question! Now let me think…"

The Dwarf's red eyes glisten as they study every pore of my face in meticulous detail.

---

[554] *Hypothetically speaking, of course, there's no way in this realm I'm going to fight a Wizard _and_ a Barbarian at the same time—not without an expeditious escape plan and a brand new identity in a realm far, far, away….*

Kara: "I would say..."

There's a pregnant pause while the Dwarf makes some final adjustments to her prediction.[555]

Kara: "A Wizard."

Me: "A Wizard? Really? But the Heroes Guild doesn't hire Wizards[556]— it's part of their *arrangement* with the Wizards Guild."

Kara: "*Ah,* that's correct, but to navigate around that *arrangement,* we tend to call Wizards something else."

Me: "What?"

Kara: "Spellcasters."

Me: "Isn't that just another fancy word for Wizards?"

Kara: "Of course, the *arrangement* we have with the Wizards Guild is that we don't hire Wizards—it says nothing about Spellcasters..."

Me: "What if the Wizards Guild found out?"

Kara: "What could they do? We have the legal paperwork to back us if any dispute broke out between us again."

Me: "I'd wager paperwork is no match for a Fireball..."

Kara: "Maybe not—but then a Fireball is no match for Arin Darkblade."

We stare at one another in silence.

Me: "So, you think I'd make a good Spellcaster then?"

Kara: "You appear well educated; you carry a journal around with you, probably couldn't lift anything heavier than a dagger. Yeah, I'm positive, a Wiz—*I mean,* Spellcaster. Why, what were you hoping? A Cleric?"

I recoil at the thought.

---

[555] *I guess this is what it would be like waiting for a Careersmith to mull over my future profession. I can imagine my look of horror as his 'magical' Sorting Cap squats on my head and blurts out its answer before angrily breaking wind.*

[556] *Officially speaking.*

Me: "No, I'm not at all religious—I'd take a Spellcaster over a Cleric any day."

The Scout laughs.

Kara: "I'll be sure to let them know down at the Heroes Guild."

I go deathly pale at the thought.

Me: *"Oh no,* I—I don't want to be a hero; we were just talking—"

The Dwarf turns suddenly as her ears prick up at the sound of a light, well-spoken voice floating above the furious din of the tavern's noisy patrons. She scans the tempestuous crowd once more—stopping only when she locks eyes on a well-dressed Elf sitting at a table, slowly sipping at a flagon of ale.

Kara: "Relax, Loremaster, you really aren't what I'm looking for."

Me: "That's a relief—"

Something tells me that the Scout has already left our conversation, in spirit at least.

Kara: "Thanks for the chat—and good luck with the rest of your journal. Now, if you don't mind, I've got to see an Elf about a contract..."

The Scout snaps her fingers and points in the Elf's direction. There's a sudden roar of anger as a nearby loincloth-wearing Barbarian sends an elderly Wizard sliding towards the Elf at high-speed.[557]

The Elf springs to his feet and hurls the prone Wizard from his table. He twists on the spot in a flash, landing a well-timed boot in the Barbarian's fur-covered nether regions[558] before bowing gracefully in front of the tavern's cheering crowd.

The Dwarf grabs two recently poured pints from a passing Barmaid and jumps off her seat. She turns one last time to grin at me.

Kara: "I like this one already!"

---

[557] *All without the aid of a 'Greased-Up' spell...*

[558] *On closer inspection, what I first thought was fur, is, in fact, still attached to the Barbarian's groin.*

I watch on in admiration as the Scout disappears into the tavern's heaving crowd. I can just make out the Dwarf's topknot bobbing through the sea of patrons, heading with purpose towards what might be the Heroes Guild's next big name.[559]

---

[559] *And that's my signal to leave—I'd rather not sit through a Barbarian Vs. Wizard rematch.*

19. Raglan, the Druid

On the outskirts of the Village of Bode-and-Wells sits a small copse of trees no wider than a thousand feet. Situated at the heart of this diminutive woodland is an ancient oak, a towering tree with lower branches that dwarf its nearest rival by a considerable amount.[560] Like a wooden beacon, the ancient oak dominates the horizon as far as the eye can see[561]—even diminishing the mighty Doom Mountains to the north.

A storm is brewing, sending a howling wind to whip around my body as I slowly walk towards the monolithic oak. Nearing, I can't help but peer skywards, marvelling at the sheer size of this woodland giant looming over me. Only now, as I examine its enormous trunk, I notice the myriad of windows cut into its bark, curling upwards as if some strange spiral room lies undiscovered inside. A creak of wood-on-wood leads me to an impressively carved door on the far side of the trunk, piquing my curiosity further.

I knock on the door several times and wait without reply. Left with no other choice, I take a deep breath and grip the large walnut handle before pushing it open. As I step inside, my initial fears are immediately replaced with sheer awe—the interior of the oak appears to defy logic, bending space to appear larger on the inside than physically possible. Before me is a grand hall beautifully carved from a single piece of wood. To my left is a twisting staircase that disappears into the darkness of unseen upper levels—punctured only by sporadic daylight from the same windows I had already noticed from the outside.

Me: *"Hello?"*

My voice is lonely and confused as it reverberates around the grand hall—it's met only by silence.

Me: "I'm supposed to be meeting Raglan—Raglan *the Druid?*"

---

[560] *The actual origins of the ancient oak are a mystery; many believe it was a gift to the Druids from their Nature Gods, while others insist a Giant Squirrel once ruled the entire realm and buried a large acorn one harsh winter before forgetting about it. It's also worth noting the second group also vehemently believes it's their divine right to bear arms—why they want huge hairy limbs is anyone's guess, but each to their own, I suppose.*

[561] *Although, if asked, I'm sure everyone in the surrounding area would prefer if this particular 'beacon' weren't set alight as a last resort to call for aid.*

My ears prick up at the subtlest of sounds—a pitter-patter of tiny feet from a critter drawn towards my presence.

Me: "I—I'm Elburn... *the Loremaster?* I'm supposed to meet Raglan here for an interview?"

The scampering noise increases in volume as I just make out a small shape emerging from the gloom—it appears to be a rodent of some sort.[562] Never one to completely trust *anything* in this realm, I look around for something suitable to defend myself with. My hand grasps a nearby hoe leaning against the wall.[563] In a flash, it's raised above my head with the sole purpose of dispatching the foul creature before it can attack.[564]

The rodent, a mouse of some sort, skids to a halt at my feet—emitting a cry of terror as I tower over it with the hoe raised like a sword, poised to strike.

Mouse: "I hope you're not thinking of using that on me!"

I blink several times in disbelief, unsure if my ears were mistaking the shriek for words. My muscles tighten as I opt to deal with the critter now rather than wait for it to stuff my corpse into its tiny hole later. Sensing my decision to slay rather than stay my hand, the mouse shouts again in desperation.

Mouse: "***STOP!***"

There's a sudden flash of light as the mouse disappears, only to be replaced by a cowering old man in a long white robe. He holds his hands up defensively, expecting the fatal hoe blow to fall.[565]

Me: "By the Gods—"

---

[562] *Hopefully, it's just a mouse and* not *a rat scout for an advancing rat army silently scurrying toward me. Even though a rat infestation is considered relatively 'easy' in the Scale of Side-Quests chart, I don't fancy putting that theory to the test right now.*

[563] *The gardening tool variety, not the other kind...*

[564] *And deliver twitchy-nosed death unto me.*

[565] *To some immoral types, this sounds like the perfect way to shuffle off this realm towards the Great 'whatever'...*

The hoe clatters to the ground as I stagger backwards in surprise. I peer closer at the cowering man when a sudden realisation strikes me.

Me: "Raglan? Raglan the *Druid?* Is that *you?*"

The old man peers up at me through his fingers.

Raglan: "W—Who *else* were you expecting?"

Me: "I'm sorry, I—I thought you were an angry rodent—"

Raglan: "Y—Yes, I am—*erm*—well, *was*, although angry is perhaps too strong a word for it—I prefer *inquisitive.*"

Me: "I didn't realise you could turn yourself into a mouse."

The Druid gets to his feet and dusts his robes down. I can't help but notice his nose is still twitching a little unnaturally as he sniffs the air in front of him.

Raglan: "Druids can turn themselves into any animal they wish—do I detect the subtle aroma of cheese upon your person? You aren't carrying any, are you?"

I can't miss the hint of desperation behind the Druid's eyes—I find myself gripping my bag a little tighter, trying to quell the faint whiff from the last of the cheese given to me by Sister Agatha.

Me: "Sorry, I don't."

Raglan: "What's in the bag?"

Me: "Just my journal, several quills and a few bottles of ink…"[566]

The Druid's eyes narrow—leaving me convinced that Raglan can see through my deception. I try to lead the conversation away from the wedge of cheese still wrapped tightly in a handkerchief and buried deep in the recess of my bag.

Me: "Why the sudden need for cheese?"

Raglan: "*Hmm? Oh*—sadly, it's an unwanted side effect of my transformative power. I occasionally bring back the odd animalistic

---

[566] *And a Limited Edition Laughing Arin Darkblade figurine—but somehow, I doubt the Druid would care much for it unless it was yellow and melted on toast.*

quirk—with mice, it's an insatiable desire for cheese. Fortunately, it usually wears off after an hour or so, but some of the quirks can be *really* annoying—if not a little socially awkward; double-so if I change into a non-cheese eating animal again shortly afterwards."

Me: "Are there any other awkward quirks you can recall?"

Raglan: "Let's just say it's been a long time since I been a lion—it's generally frowned upon to eat raw meat in public, especially when the raw meat in question is still kicking and screaming."

Me: "Anything else you avoid changing into?"

Raglan: "Cats, I don't do cats."[567]

Me: "Any particular reason why?"

Raglan: "I hate the aftertaste of mouse—it can stay on your breath for days."

Me: "You've eaten a mouse?"

Raglan: "Just one—that was a _big_ mistake."

Me: "Beyond the obvious, can I ask why?"

Raglan: "Because the mouse I consumed was *another* Druid who had transformed into the damn thing earlier in the day—it was hugely embarrassing for everyone, an unfortunate error of judgement that I have regretted every day since."

Me: "*Oh my—another* Druid? That's horrible! Did you know them?"

Raglan: "No, but that didn't make the fact any better; I had eaten another person; someone with friends and family. After that costly mistake, I swore <u>never</u> to transform into *Mr. Jingles* ever again."[568]

Me: "So, what animals *do* you transform into?"

---

[567] *Isn't a lion just a big cat guaranteed to react badly to impromptu tummy tickles?*

[568] *I have a slightly disturbing thought—what if the consumed Druid returned to their original form whilst slowly digesting inside Ralgan's stomach? I suspect he probably wouldn't need Elevenses if _that_ happened.*

Raglan: "*Oh,* the usual. Mice, hamsters, rabbits. But I have to say squirrels are probably my all-time favourite—they're just fabulous creatures."

Me: "Why's that?"

Raglan: "They're completely bonkers, that's why. There's nothing quite like the thrill of leaping about from tree to tree at high speed—it's pure joy!"

Me: "What about fish?"

Raglan: "Nope, I'm always paranoid I'll wind up on the wrong end of a hook."

Me: "Snakes?"

Raglan: "They eat mice…"

Me: "*Ah* yes, I see—"

Raglan: "No spiders either. The last time I did that, I passed silk threads for a whole week—<u>never</u> again."

Me: "So, it's only mammals."

Raglan: "You got it."

Me: "Not birds?"

Raglan: "I have a fear of flying—"

Me: "But what about squirrels?"

Raglan: "What about them? Do you know something I don't? Have you ever seen a squirrel fly?"

Me: "Not personally, no. But they *can* climb pretty high—"

Raglan: "I said I was afraid of flying, not heights."

Me: "*Ah,* apologies, my mistake."

The Druid wanders towards the staircase.

Raglan: "Right, as it's clear you're not going to dash my brains across the wooden floor—do you want a quick tour of the place?"

262

Me: "*Erm... sure...*"

For nearly twenty minutes, we climb the stairs, stopping only to peer from one of the numerous windows looking out above the trees far below. It's an impressive view. Through the whipping rain outside, I can make out the distant walls of Tronte. The city's colourful flags are fluttering angrily in the storm's wind.

Raglan: "This sacred oak has over three hundred rooms, each stacked on top of one another."

Me: "So, you're saying you could do with some kind of Gnomish contraption to aid your journey to the higher ones?"

The Druid furrows his brow.

Raglan: "I would never let a Gnome set foot inside this place—not even a single nasal hair from under their bulbous noses."[569]

Me: "Really?"

Raglan: "They rely too much on their precious metal; that's a big 'no' where Druids are concerned."

Me: "Why's that?"

Raglan: "Metal attracts lightning, lightning causes fires, and this tree is made from wood. Fire burns wood—you can probably see where I'm going with this..."

Me: "Fire burns a lot of things."[570]

The Druid stares at me with a noticeable degree of disdain.

---

[569] *Gnomes are the most prolific inventors in the realm—but also the most unreliable when it comes to their inventive contraptions. Unbelievably, their creations have caused more damage and chaos to the realm than all the Evildoers combined. Thankfully, heavy regulations have been put in place to ensure that any Gnomish contraption is checked and approved before use. This hasn't stopped some unscrupulous Gnomes from bypassing these regulations and selling their dangerous creations to as many unsuspecting Halflings as possible. Gnomes also have huge noses.*

[570] *Fireballs burn even more.*

Me: "But, I can understand you'd prefer it if this ancient oak didn't attract an unexpected bolt out of the blue."[571]

Raglan: "You could say that."

Me: "How can such a place as this exist? I mean, it's *so* big—I can't understand how there's so much space inside here? I know it's big on the outside, but this simply defies logic."

Raglan: "What you actually mean is it defies *simple* logic. Your brain is trying to fit everything into what you know is to be real—but you're missing the obvious."

Me: "What's that?"

Raglan: "The room isn't bigger on the inside."

Me: "It's not?"

Raglan: "No—it's *you* who is smaller..."

The Druid waits for his words to sink in. I stare at the bark, letting my hand run over the surface—only now do I notice the grain is large, much too wide to be natural.

Me: "How—how is this possible?"

Raglan: "Druid magic, or *Oh, Natural* magic if you prefer.[572] This oak is the oldest in the realm; we call it the first oak[573]—it's the source of power for every Druid in existence, not just those found around here."

---

[571] *The actual saying is: 'an unexpected bolt out of the Blue Goblin', which came about after a clueless Blue Goblin drank what it 'thought' was a Potion of Warmth but turned out to be a Potion of Lightning Storm. The pitiful creature was farting lightning bolts for hours on end—from out of their end.*

[572] *Pronounced in a kind of nonplussed way: 'Oh, 'Natural' magic...' by scornful Wizards.*

[573] *Imaginatively named—although it would be a bit embarrassing if the 'first' oak turned out to be the 'second' oldest oak in the realm or even the 'third'....*

Me: "What about outer-realm Druids?"[574]

The Druid gives me a puzzled look.

Raglan: "*Ah*—well, not *those* ones, obviously…"

I stare intently at my hands; a worry line creases deep across my brow—the Druid notices it too.

Raglan: "Don't fret; you'll return to your usual size when you step back outside."

Me: "That's amazing—truly it is."

Our ascent comes to an end as we step out on a new level. There's evidence of this being the Druid's living quarters; there's a bed, chamber pot[575] and a plethora of incense paraphernalia on a nearby desk. There's also a white robe thrown over a chair and another white robe hanging from a nearby modesty screen.[576] Beyond that, the room is a little rudimentary but perfectly functional.

Me: "Are you a member of any Guild?"

Raglan: "Guild?"

Me: "Like the Heroes Guild?"

Raglan: "No. I'm probably not the right kind of adventurer for them."

Me: "Right kind?"

Raglan: "I'm not interested in chasing coin or desperately seeking fame."

Me: "Why not?"

---

[574] *'Outer-realm Druids' are exuberant and over-the-top Druids from other dimensions who enjoy popping in for a visit from time to time and transforming themselves into some hideous monstrosity from their home-realm. These visits are usually unannounced and occur at the most inconvenient moments possible for everyone concerned—like during the middle of a family funeral or while you're trying to get an order of drinks in before a gruff Landlord calls 'time'.*

[575] *Hopefully empty.*

[576] *I'm not exactly sure why a modesty screen is here—unless the Druid is worried about being spied on by peeping-tom cats.*

Raglan: "Life is not about how much you can take from it—it's about how much you can put back; I'm not a huge fan of their *Welcome Parchment* either."

Me: "Why? What's wrong with it?"

Raglan: "Have you *seen* the cover? It's practically obscene! Why do they have to put all that flesh on display?"[577]

Me: "Perhaps you can ask them to put a Druid on a future cover?"

The Woodland Wizard laughs at my words.

Raglan: "Never going to happen—Druids aren't considered a glamorous adventuring profession. We're a little too weird to be popular; most think we just go around hugging trees and talking to animals all day.[578] No, a Welcome Parchment is the *last* thing we'd appear on the cover of. But to be honest with you, that's probably for the best... I've heard the complimentary food in the *Welcome Basket* is woeful. It doesn't even come with any cheese—makes you wonder what kind of idiot is running the place?"[579]

My mind wanders back to the leftover cheese hiding at the bottom of my bag.

Me: "Indeed... as you're not affiliated with the Heroes Guild, talk me through what it's like going on an adventure with you?"

Raglan nestles into a comfortable-looking oak chair and brings out a wooden pipe. He carefully fills it with tobacco and lights it before

---

[577] I later discovered, after numerous complaints, the Heroes Guild Welcome Parchment had a new cover commissioned. This new illustration featured a semi-naked Dwarven Barbarian being tossed by a semi-naked Elven Barbarian at a Gelatinous Cube containing a semi-naked Wizard whose clothes have been dissolved by the wobbly beast—I guess drawing clothes is tougher than it looks. I'm also beginning to suspect the Heroes Guild has an unhealthy obsession with sending their heroes off to adventure wearing as little armour as possible for some strange reason.

[578] Better than going around talking to trees and hugging animals all day, which is definitely weird...

[579] The Druid wouldn't say that if Arin Darkblade were standing next to him—or at least he wouldn't be saying that for long before a dagger rudely interrupted him mid-sentence.

sucking a huge lungful of the smoky vapour into his body[580]—he exhales slowly before staring wistfully into the void above us.[581]

Raglan: "It's different, that's for sure. I'm not too fond of swords or spears; I don't carry shields or wear any armour. I prefer to enter a dungeon only with my *Oh, Natural* magic on display—if you catch my meaning?"

Me: "*Wait*—does that mean you go dungeoneering naked?!"

The Druid coughs and splutters on his pipe in shock.

Raglan: "No, no... *erm*, no, I'm not into *streaking*[582]—I don't do that! Who said I did that? Was it that bloody Paladin, Redmane? He's such a pompous arse. Just because he wears plate armour to avoid injury, it doesn't give him the right to besmirch those who are class restricted or choose not to wear armour out of choice. It was *just* that one time, the Dragon's lair was hot—I mean **really** hot. My robes were sticking to my skin and getting dirty from the soot; I had to take them off— "

Me: "N—Nobody said anything; I—I just got confused when you said entered a dungeon *Oh, Natural*. I didn't mean anything by it—"

The Druid stares at me with his cold, glaring eyes.

Raglan: "Well, it <u>never</u> happened. Are we clear?"

Me: "Crystal—"

Raglan shifts uncomfortably in his seat.

Me: "What happens to the clothes you're almost definitely wearing when you change shape?"

---

[580] *I suspect the tobacco in his pipe contains something stronger than Oh, Natural magic— probably something closer to Ohhhhhh, Natural magic...*

[581] *I really hope the Druid doesn't start doing something weird like blowing a smoke ship at me—or worse, a smoke ship manned by a motley crew of smoke rodents...*

[582] *After spending a week in the company of Gnomes, I later discovered 'streaking' is a Gnomish word to describe a hero who runs through a monster-filled dungeon whilst wearing as few clothes as possible. The sole purpose is to complete the quest in the fastest time without being attacked by the dungeon denizens startled by a bare-arsed hero bolting past—I'm also expecting this image to appear on the cover of a Heroes Guild Welcome Parchment in the near future.*

Raglan: "They morph with me to form my fur and skin."

Me: "And any weapons too?"

Raglan: "All of it."

Me: "Probably a good thing you don't use a sword or spear."

Raglan: *"Huh?"*

Me: "The idea of something sharp and pointy merging into my body doesn't fill me with excitement."

Raglan: "*Ah*—you really don't notice it, especially when all manner of spells and swordplay is going on around you."

Me: "That's something I was going to ask about—what good is a mouse or a rabbit in a life or death fight?"

Raglan: "Have you ever been bitten by a rage-fuelled mouse or kicked in the groin by a slightly miffed rabbit?"

I shake my head.

Raglan: "I advise you to reserve judgement until you have. Remember, the *smaller* the teeth, the more *painful* the bite."

Me: "Do you ever change into anything bigger?"

Raglan: "Of course—I'm more than capable of turning into something larger."

Me: "Have you ever become a horse?"[583]

Raglan: "No."

Me: "An elephant?"

Raglan: "No."

Me: "A camel?"

---

[583] *I'd imagine if the Druid <u>were</u> to change into a horse, this would only serve to annoy the 'real' horses in the adventuring party.*

Raglan: "No."[584]

Me: "What's the largest thing you've turned into since you gave up lions?"

The Druid ponders the question for a moment before answering.

Raglan: "A skunk."

Me: "That doesn't sound that big."

Raglan: "There's a noticeable size difference between a mouse and a skunk!"

Me: "But how effective is a skunk in a fight?"

Raglan: "Extremely—everything I encounter tries to run away from me the first chance they get, which suits me fine. Although, when I've returned to my human form, I found the other adventurers in my party usually give me a wide berth for some strange reason."

Me: "You don't say. Besides fighting, can you give me some examples of how your animal form can be useful on an adventure?"

Raglan: "Let me think… as a mouse, I can gnaw through rope. As a mole, I can dig under most obstacles. As a pig, I can lure enemies away—that's especially handy against Goblins and Orcs who are easily tempted by my mouth-watering rump."[585]

Me: "What about your adventuring party?"

The Druid's eyes narrow sharply.

Raglan: "I should think they know better than to eat me unless, of course, I'm adventuring with a Barbarian—those types eat anything."[586]

---

[584] That's probably a good thing, especially if there's a punch-happy Barbarian in the group.

[585] I'm not sure what compelled Raglan to give his backside a hearty 'slap' here—a slap that was probably heard all the way to Tronte…

[586] Anything except hamsters—as I soon discovered…

Me: "No, I mean, what do they think of your ability to transform into various animals?"[587]

Raglan: "I—I don't know, I haven't really asked them."

Me: "Do you feel they don't take your power seriously—perhaps not giving you the dues you clearly deserve?"[588]

Raglan: "There are always a few in any adventuring party who like to ridicule me—"

Me: "What do they say?"

Raglan: "*Oh,* you know—ask me if I want to chase a stick, sniff a backside, or if I've got a furball whenever I suddenly cough. It's pretty unimaginative stuff."

Me: "Who in the group mocks you?"

Raglan: "Fighters, Rangers, Clerics, Rogues, Paladins—sometimes the odd Wizard, Warlock, Necromancer, Sorcerer, and Bard. Even the Monks have been known to crack a joke or two at my expense—"

Me: "That's pretty much everyone!"

The Druid thinks for a moment.

Raglan: "Barbarians weren't on that list, were they?"

Me: "No."

Raglan: "Every Barbarian I've ever met always takes a keen interest in my ability to change into an animal..."[589]

Me: "*Why?*"

Raglan: "I don't know, but they always ask me to change into the same thing."

---

[587] *Albeit a relatively small circle of animals here—quite literally!*

[588] *It always pays to massage an ego—even if that ego can transform into various critter types.*

[589] *Barbarians are easily entertained by anything magical—often demanding more and more tricks from a spell-weary caster who is rapidly approaching the end of their tether.*

Me: "Excuse me?"

Raglan: "Barbarians—they want me to turn into a bloody hamster."

Me: "Do you?"

Raglan: "What do *you* think? I prefer my limbs still attached to my body and fully functioning—thank you very much!"

Me: "Why do they want you to turn into a hamster?"

Raglan: "I can't explain it. All they ever do is sit there stroking me—it's a little disconcerting if you ask me, but who am I to judge?"

Me: "Sounds awkward."

Raglan: "You're telling me—I can't even look at them after I've changed back."

The Druid coughs several times before putting his pipe to one side.

Raglan: "Are you *sure* you don't have any cheese?"

I sense my grip instinctively tightening on my bag.

Me: "Positive—can I ask how many quests you have been on?"

Raglan: "Too many to mention. They all seem to roll into one these days. I've lost count of how many Rings of Power I've had to retrieve,[590] Barons' daughters I've rescued, or Evildoers I've had to vanquish—"

Me: "By vanquish, I assume you mean *kill?*"

The Druid suddenly looks evasive and shifts uncomfortably in his wooden seat.

Raglan: "I don't know."

Me: "What do you mean, you don't know?"

---

[590] *Someone should really hire a Ring-bearer to keep track of all these bloody powerful rings.*

Raglan: "Putting Evildoers to the sword is usually left to the Barbarians or the Paladins in the group... sometimes even the Clerics too, I suppose[591]—lest you forget, I don't use *a* sword, spear, axe, or anything with metal in it."

Me: "Because a Druid's magic can attract the occasional lightning bolt—"

Raglan: "Precisely. It doesn't help that everyone around me is carrying something metal; some are even dressed head-to-toe in the bloody stuff."

Me: "Why's that a problem?"

Raglan: "Because, collectively, they look attractive to a bolt of lightning."[592]

Me: "That sounds bad."

Raglan: "It is—for them; I've been hit by so many lightning bolts I practically look forward to it. But it's *fatal* to the metal-obsessed hero next to me."

On cue, there's an ominous rumble outside as the storm arrives at Raglan's little patch of woodland.

Me: "What's it like—being hit by a lightning bolt, I mean?"

Raglan: "It's a bit like—**ARRRRGHHH!** But with more smoke and flashing lights."

Me: "Isn't it dangerous?"

Raglan: "As I've already said, only if I'm carrying anything metal.[593] Otherwise, it just passes harmlessly through."

Me: "Really?"

---

[591] *I've been reliably informed that 'Evil' Clerics are far more willing to do this than 'Good' Clerics.*

[592] *Attractive as in 'I _really_ want to pass through you' kind of way—not 'I think we should start courting' kind of way...*

[593] *Or standing under a tree—or sitting _inside_ one a hundred floors up when it suddenly catches alight...*

Raglan: "Of course, my *Oh, Natural* resistance protects me from harm. That and my robes—they're purposefully designed to absorb lightning strikes."

Me: "I see..."

Raglan: "Although they do have a habit of combusting afterwards, which can be quite revealing..."[594]

Me: "Going back to the Evildoer for a moment—have you ever seen what happens to one when they've been finally defeated?"

Raglan: "No."

Me: "Aren't you curious to know?"

Raglan: "Nope."

Me: "Why not?"

Raglan: "I prefer to avoid the gory details. I don't have the stomach for it—I'm a pacifist at heart."[595]

Me: "That must be pretty difficult to maintain as an adventurer."

But there's no reply. Instead, the Druid suddenly sits upright and twitches his nose again before pointing a crooked finger accusingly in my direction.

Raglan: ***"LIAR! YOU <u>DO</u> HAVE CHEESE, I KNOW IT—I CAN SMELL IT ON YOU!"***

Lightning flashes outside as the sky rumbles along with the Druid's accusation.

Me: "Honestly, I don't have any chee—"

Raglan leaps at me from his chair, but I grab my bag and run for the stairs. The cheese-obsessed Druid licks his lips, his beady black eyes locked onto me.

---

[594] *Not to mention a little chilly.*

[595] *Contrary to whatever anyone says, Pacifism and Heroism seldom go hand-in-hand together.*

Raglan: *"GIVE ME YOUR CHEESE!"*

Me: "I—I think I *really* should be going—"

Raglan:*"IT'S SO TASTY! I LOVE THE WAY IT MELTS IN MY MOUTH—GIVE IT TO ME, I WANTS IT! CHEESE IS MY TASTY PRECIOUS!"*[596]

The Druid begins to transform before my eyes—his body folding in on itself as hair sprouts across his back and arms. His teeth sharpen and merge into two giant front teeth that gnash excitedly in anticipation. A big bushy tail erupts from his behind, thrashing in agitation.[597] But I'm already running down the endless stairs, trying to make the descent in seconds rather than minutes. I'm too scared to look over my shoulder even though I can hear excited chattering from somewhere above. Several times I almost lose my footing and tumble down the staircase in haste, desperate to escape the cheesed-obsessed Druid-cum-squirrel I know is in pursuit.[598] I finally reach the ground floor and race to open the oak door. I rush through without a second's thought—back into the woodland outside. I stare momentarily at my hands, relieved to discover that I've returned to my normal size. Overhead, a dark cloud clears its throat as I turn to see the squirrel leaping straight at me. I brace myself and prepare for the worst, just as a flash of lightning floods everything with a blinding light.

Raglan: *"OWWWWWWWWW!"*

I blink several times, trying to clear my vision. I'm suddenly aware of a familiar figure spread-eagled on the floor—it's Raglan, back to his normal form, albeit minus his clothes. I peer over him.[599]

Me: "You okay?"[600]

The Druid groans as he raises his hand and gives me a stunned thumbs-up.

---

[596] *Thank the Gods he's still a Druid—imagine if he changed into something faster-moving, like a squirr—*

[597] *Me and my big mouth!*

[598] *But squirrels don't eat cheese—why is this happening to me?!*

[599] *Though making a conscious effort not to let my eyes wander needlessly.*

[600] *This may seem a bit of a pointless question, given that the Druid has just been struck by lightning—but I can't stop myself from asking it anyway.*

Me: "*Erm*—your robe appears to have vanished..."

Raglan: "The lightning... burns it off... don't... worry... I've got another..."

Me: "Can I do anything? Do you need help?"

Raglan: "It's fine... I just need to... rest here... for a while..."

Me: "You might want to get back inside. That storm doesn't look like it's abating any time soon."

Raglan: "I find the rain... nice and... relaxing... Zzzzzz—"

The Druid's snores are joined by the sound of thunder as it rumbles overhead once again. The rain begins to fall on the leaves above us—but the dense foliage appears to be keeping us both dry for the moment.

I wait, unsure what to do—in the end, I choose to quietly leave this place before a second lightning strike decides to target the non-Druid out of the two of us. Before I depart, I gently place my final piece of cheese next to the recumbent *Oh, Natural* Druid snoozing safely under the canopy of the ancient oak[601]—it's not much of a gift, but at least I feel a little better about leaving the Druid out here alone, exposed to the elements.[602]

---

[601] *I'd hate for a vicious predator to find him like this, or worse, a rival squirrel foraging for nuts. But I feel strangely reassured about withdrawing from this place; almost as if the ancient tree towering above is silently watching over the Druid—Oh, Natural magic indeed!*

[602] *Whilst exposing <u>himself</u> to the elements...*

20. Vanuska, the Fighter

The watermill wheel turns slowly on its axis, cutting through the breakline with reassuring regularity. I'm sitting on the bank of a river, looking out across this calmness, marvelling at the sheer tranquillity unfolding before me; life is reassuringly slow here. No monsters lurk in the shadows; no storm threatens to unleash its fury on those wandering beneath it—there is only peace and the occasional angry buzz of a passing insect.[603] A faint rhythmic chopping noise can be heard in the distance as an unseen axe begins to bite into a stubborn piece of wood.[604]

I gather to my feet and follow the hacking noise until I stumble upon a muscular Elf cutting heavy logs in a nearby woodland clearing. She stops and looks at me, sizing how much of a threat I carry before deciding to wipe her brow on a nearby cloth and leaning against a stack of recently dispatched trees.[605]

Woodcutter: "You look confused; what's the matter? Have you never seen an Elf chopping *down* a tree before—or did you think we only hugged them?"[606]

Me: "Forgive me, I wasn't sure what to expect—I just followed the sound, and it led me here."

Woodcutter: "I'm sorry to disappoint you."

Me: "I'm not disappointed in the slightest—in fact, do you have a moment to talk?"

The Woodcutter extends a hand for me to shake—as I take it, a firm squeeze leaves me in no uncertainty of the impressive strength the Elf possesses under her slight frame.

---

[603] *Hopefully, the buzzing critter isn't the angry equivalent of a short-tempered Barbarian of the insect world.*

[604] *Either that or a Treant is doing something it really <u>shouldn't</u> be doing somewhere out of sight. It also begs the awkward question, if a Treant gratifies itself in a forest, does it make a sound?*

[605] *By her reaction, I have to assume she believes I carry as much threat as that passing insect did to me only moments ago—although, in my defence, that insect was big and looked like it knew how to handle itself in a 'swatting' duel.*

[606] *Which would instantly make this Elf a <u>really</u> weird kind of Druid.*

Woodcutter: "Well met—*I'm Vanuska.*"

Me: "Elburn the Loremaster. Pleased to make your acquaintance."

The Woodcutter cocks a quizzical eye at me.

Me: "Something I said?"

Vanuska: "You're a long way from home, Loremaster. Shouldn't you be safely tucked up in a library next to your parchment, quill, and a bottle of ink?"[607]

Me: "Usually, yes—but I'm on a quest... of *sorts.*"

Vanuksa: "You? A *quest?*"

Me: "Okay, I perhaps made that sound grander than it really is. I'm travelling the realm, gathering stories and experiences from heroes and those who surround themselves with the adventuring type."[608]

My eyes dart to the glinting ornate blade partially hidden by a heavy cloak on the ground next to the Woodcutter's backpack—the Elf follows my eyes.

Vanuska: "*Heroes?* You won't find any heroes around here—you will probably have better luck trying Tronte or even Cloverton."

Me: "I've been to both, but I wanted to widen the field a little and visit some of the more remote places—places where the average hero seldom treads."

Vanuska: "In that case, try the ShadowLands; perhaps on second thoughts—<u>don't</u>; you probably wouldn't last a hundred yards before a bandit took an unhealthy liking to you..."[609]

---

[607] *Contrary to popular belief, libraries are as dangerous as any monster-filled dungeon in existence. They are an endless maze of shelves designed to confuse those foolish enough to search for an obscure tome in the darkest of corners; additionally, they have a cryptic filing system that can only be deciphered by the most intelligent in the realm. Each library is also home to a fearful ancient guardian, eager to hunt down anyone who makes too much noise, dog-ears pages, or dares to bring back their borrowed books after the stipulated deadline.*

[608] *And those who chase after heroes hoping to loosen a coin from them—such as beggars and collection-box-carrying Clerics...*

[609] *Or worse, an angry Paladin who has just discovered a rude swear word daubed on their beloved armour—just as they turn to see me innocently holding an ink-soaked quill...*

Me: "Thanks for the advice."

I watch as the Woodcutter walks over to her belongings and quickly pulls her cloak across to cover her ornate blade.

Me: "That's a pretty impressive sword you have there."

Vanuska: "You saw that, *huh?*"

Me: "Sorry, nothing much escapes me."[610]

Vanuska: "That's Loremasters for you, I suppose—always with one eye on the smaller details."[611]

Me: "I wager you're a hero then?"

Vanuska: "You may be an astute Loremaster, but you're a poor gambler—I *was* a hero—I am no longer."

Me: "No longer? Why is that?"

The Woodcutter sighs—there's a sadness etched into her face.

Vanuska: "I realised there was more to life than fighting and drinking."[612]

Me: "Such as?"

Vanuska: "Living, Loremaster—*living…*"

Me: "Forgive me, surely being heroic means you <u>are</u> living a life that others can only dream of?"

Vanuska: "True, but it takes more than completing a noble cause to give my life purpose. You have to understand, being a hero is a

---

[610] *We're talking information and detail here—I'm not some overzealous jailer who would chase down a flight-risk prisoner as if their life depended upon it.*

[611] *Loremasters are better listeners than observers—I blame all that writing by lamplight. I'm fortunate I've not yet needed a Gnomish seeing-device to aid my craft. However, I suspect it can only be a matter of time before I would come to depend on such a contraption and invite even more ridicule from my brother—if he ever returned. Now I think about it; if I <u>were</u> to rely on a Gnomish seeing-device, I fear I would be in a state of constant concern that said contraption would spontaneously combust while perched on the bridge of my nose—inviting more mirth and ridicule from my errant brother.*

[612] *Unless you're a Barbarian—when this is considered the absolute pinnacle of your profession.*

nightmare; I'd had enough of the constant need to succeed—I wanted to get out."

Me: "What happened? Did someone you care for die? Did you fail an important quest?"

Vanuska: "You always ask so many questions?"

Me: "I wouldn't be very good at my task if I didn't."

Vanuska: "Spoken like a true Loremaster! To answer your question— no, nothing like that. There was no real reason to speak of; no death devastated me, no critical realm-dependant mission failed, no untold evil I was forced to watch triumph over the weak. To speak plainly... I just grew so damn weary of it all."

Me: "What do you mean by that?"

Vanuska: "It all—from start to finish and everything in-between."[613]

Me: "But why? Were you not successful?"

Vanuska: "I had my share of successes and failures like any adventurer—although I like to think I had a little more success than most if I'm perfectly honest. But I had to weigh up what a quest was doing to my body and mind. I lost count of the times I had to drag myself off the dungeon floor to stay in the fight. Even afterwards, when I was back in the safety of my home, I'd find myself listening out for every unexpected creak coming from a distant floorboard, checking and rechecking every corner for hidden monsters, or testing every footfall for traps. I became a nervous wreck—I was constantly imagining trouble where there was none, sensing danger *everywhere*. It became impossible to shut off."

Me: "I can imagine that must have taken a toll on you."

Vanuska: "The day I hung up my sword was a bittersweet day."

---

[613] *The 'in-between' can either be construed as everything that surrounds an adventure except the 'actual' adventure itself or the literal midpoint of an adventuring journey (which is usually the bit where everyone is grumpily camping outdoors, trying to stay warm and dry while tediously keeping guard in hourly rotational shifts throughout the night). As I hate camping with a passion, I will assume the Elf means the latter, although you, dear reader, will undoubtedly assume she means the former.*

Me: "Bittersweet? I thought you said the burden of success was too much to bear? Surely your retirement was a moment of happiness for you—a weight finally lifted?"[614]

Vanuska: "To begin with—yes, the joy I felt was immeasurable. It was a relief waking up in the morning knowing I wasn't about to put my life on the line at some point later in the day. Having that pressure removed was like nothing I had ever experienced in my life before. I remember I just sat down and wept."

Me: "Wept? Tears of joy, surely?"

Vanuska: "Guilt."

Me: "Why guilt?"

Vanuska: "I don't know; maybe I felt bad for those who still needed my help, the quests I wouldn't go on to complete, or the lives I would never be there to save. I've seen *so* much death, Loremaster, it was becoming difficult to know right from wrong. Was I a hero? Or was I slowly becoming one of the monsters I had sworn to defeat?"

I nod slowly in sympathy.

Vanuska: "You want to know the worst of it? I never once felt like a hero, just someone who got paid for chaos."[615]

Me: "How did the people closest to you take the news of your retirement?"

Vanuska: "They were sympathetic, of course, said I had to do what was right. But..."

Me: "You didn't believe them—"

Vanuska: "—it wasn't that, not exactly. I think some of them were actually glad I had put my adventuring days behind me—my parents

---

[614] *I don't mean 'I was so heavily encumbered I was reduced to walking everywhere at a snail's pace' kind of weight, either.*

[615] **Loremaster Tip #6:** *Don't ever say something like this to a Chaos Knight; those unholy creatures work for free and would not be happy to find out they were entitled to some form payment for their brand of mayhem. Also, this sounds suspiciously like something a Barbarian would say...*

seemed encouraged by my decision to give up..."[616]

Me: "Did they not support your decision to become a hero in the first place?"

Vanuska: "They were extremely proud of what I had become; they would delight in recounting tales of my exploits to any in their community who would unwittingly lend them an ear. But I guess they started to see that my heart wasn't in adventuring anymore—and that saddened them more than anything."

Me: "How could your parents tell your passion for adventuring had waned?"

Vanuska: "They recognised the signs; noticed I had become withdrawn, that I avoided talking to them directly about anything to do with my quests. They commented how I had become increasingly evasive, even angry, whenever they asked about my latest exploits.[617] In truth, I found it impossible to look them in the eye whenever they asked if I had saved anyone lately. It became painfully obvious that *something* wasn't right."

Me: "How did that make you feel?"

Vanuska: "Worse, I didn't want to let my family down, but I knew I would be letting myself down if nothing changed. I stopped taking risks, that's for sure. I used to be quick on the draw, the first to get my sword out and start hacking away at anything that deserved my wrath.[618] But towards the end, I stayed my hand more times than my companions liked—it was a choice that would come with certain repercussions."

Me: "You mean within your adventuring party?"

Vanuska: "Yes—they began to see me as a liability, someone who would be slow to react. I can't blame them—I know I wouldn't want

---

[616] *I know exactly how this feels. Growing up, I never went on any wild adventures to speak of, which seemed to put my parents at ease for some strange reason.*

[617] *The Elf honestly sounds more like a Barbarian than a Fighter. Although, let's be honest for a moment, there's only a short fuse and a lack of clothes difference between a Fighter and a Barbarian anyway...*

[618] *See! I was right—she is a Barbarian!*

someone like that by my side when things got *very* real, *very* fast. It would only be a matter of time before my actions got someone hurt, or worse."

Me: "Did anyone get hurt?"

Vanuska: "Only my pride—*oh,* and my rump."

Me: "Your rump?"

Vanuska: "My companions literally kicked me out of the party <u>and</u> from the cart we were heading out to adventure on. The bumpy landing was a painful reminder of how far I had fallen."[619]

Me: "What did you do after that?"

Vanuska: "I picked myself up and dusted myself down—"

Me: "I mean, after that, what did you do? Did you try adventuring alone?"

Vanuska: "No, even though my party had kicked me out, they had given me the greatest reward of all—*freedom.* I had put some coin aside for my retirement—it wasn't much, but enough to buy a place here, in a quiet corner of the realm where I could chop down a few trees without being haunted by my guilt or the past."[620]

Me: "You seem at peace with your decision."

The Woodcutter smiles as she picks up her axe and brushes the dirt from the blade.[621]

Vanuska: "I am—completely. The only thing I hit these days are tree trunks—do you want to know the best thing about that?"

Me: "Sure."

---

[619] *Around five-foot in literal terms—but probably way further figuratively speaking...*

[620] *But not enough to buy a retirement castle by the sea.*

[621] *Barbarians love axes, so much so that some have even been known to marry them—although, I'd imagine any subsequent wedding night would be fraught with danger. Even worse would be the fallout if, many summers later, the Barbarian in question was caught red-handed by their spouse fumbling with a two-handed sword behind their back...*

Vanuska: "They don't try and hit you back."

Me: "Unless you chop down a Treant by mistake, of course..."[622]

The Woodcutter laughs and brings the axe down with a **'THUD'** into the nearest log, splitting it in half easily. I'm left speechless in admiration.

Vanuska: "That would be my luck."

Me: "Do you miss it?"

The Elf shakes her head.

Vanuska: "No, not really. I miss the coin; I mean, who wouldn't—woodcutting is hardly the lucrative career I need it to be."

Me: "What do you miss most from your adventuring days?"

There's a moment's silence while the Elf mulls the question over in her mind.

Vanuska: "The camaraderie, the unspoken bond between groups of heroes who adventure together. Yeah—I miss that, the moments of laughter between the screams and cries."[623]

Me: "I can appreciate that—I used to fight with my brother when we were younger, but we could still laugh at one another when something funny happened."[624]

Vanuska: "You speak as if your brother is gone from this world—did he die?"

Me: "N—No, I hope he's very much alive. But I haven't seen him for ten summers now. I just miss him, you know..."

Vanuska: "Why did he leave?"

Me: "To follow in our parents' footsteps—he left to become a hero."

---

[622] *Or worse, a Treant who was having some 'personal time', if you catch my meaning...*

[623] *From the Clerics in the group, no doubt...*

[624] *Usually, my brother breaking wind on my head; sure, it was unpleasant, but it was also highly amusing, especially when our mother walked into our room and immediately walked straight out in disgust—her nostrils burning from the stinking cloud my brother's backside just cast.*

Vanuska: "Another fool following the great lie.[625] What is his name?"

Me: "Aldon—Aldon Barr. Have you heard of him?"

Vanuska: "Can't say that I have—but I've been away from the adventuring business for a while now. Is he a member of the Heroes Guild?"

Me: "I don't think so... what am I saying? I—I really don't know if I'm being completely honest; I'm struggling to pick up his trail. I'm sure his path would have crossed with the Heroes Guild at some point on his travels."

The Woodcutter nods.

Vanuska: "I'm sorry I can't help you much. I never managed to get on with the Heroes Guild myself."

Me: "How so?"

Vanuska: "When I started out in the adventuring business, I made preliminary enquires with the Heroes Guild about potentially joining their ranks. We agreed to meet at a tavern, *The Spit & Spear*, I think— anyway, one of their representatives *ambushed* me before our prearranged time."

Me: "What? They ambushed you!?"

Vanuska: "*Ha,* sorry, no—not like that! He hadn't waited in the shadows to strike, although he had caught me a little flatfooted as I left my room."

Me: "Why did he do that?"

Vanuska: "I think he wanted to see how I'd react to the unexpected."

Me: "And how did you react?"

Vanuska: "I punched him—although, in my defence, I had reacted instinctively."[626]

---

[625] *I don't think my brother is a fool—a little stubborn, maybe, but a fool he certainly is not. On the other hand, Uncle Bevan Barr was paid to entertain locals with his jovial mishaps and comedy japes—he <u>was</u> a fool, and a professional one at that!*

[626] *Now, this <u>is</u> something a Barbarian would do.*

I cock an eyebrow in surprise.

Me: "You *punched* him!"

Vanuska: "In his one good eye."

Me: "One good eye? *Erm...* this *representative* wasn't Arin Darkblade by any chance, was it?"[627]

The Elf looks sheepishly at me.

Vanuska: "You've heard of him?"

Me: "Who hasn't? His reputation is legendary—not to mention dangerous. What did he do after you punched him?"

Vanuska: "That's the weirdest part—he just stared at me and said one word."

Me: "What word?"

Vanuska: "No."

Me: "*No?* No—what?"

Vanuska: "Just—no..."[628]

Me: "What did you think he meant by that?"

Vanuska: "I guess he didn't think much of my chances of joining the Heroes Guild."

Me: "Did he say anything else to you?"

Vanuska: "I didn't wait around to find out. Once I realised who it was and what I had done, I ran back into my room, locked the door, grabbed my gear and leapt out of the window."[629]

---

[627] *If he ever found out about this, I'd imagine Balstaff would commission a new Limited Edition Arin Darkblade figurine sporting an impressive shiner.*

[628] *That doesn't sound too bad unless 'No' was quickly followed by '...more breathing for you!'*

[629] *I take it back; Barbarians would not do this—Clerics definitely would, but Barbarians? Never, maybe the Elf is secretly a Cleric?*

Me: "Did your paths ever cross again?"

Vanuska: "No—of course, I ran into a few adventurers who were members of the Heroes Guild, but I never saw Arin Darkblade again—thankfully."

Me: "Do you regret that punch?"

Vanuska: "Part of me does—part of me thinks if I had impressed Arin enough, I'd now be regarded as a legendary hero rather than a reasonably successful yet anonymous one. But deep down, I know I would have lost more than I would have been willing to give. I'd *still* be trapped, desperate to leave the hero business far behind me—but *still* expected to step into the unknown in the name of adventure."

Me: "It seems fame comes with a heavy price."

Vanuska: "Looking back on it, punching Arin Darkblade was probably the best decision I ever made; it led me to where I am now rather than down another monster-filled dungeon that needed clearing."[630]

Me: "At least you appear to be enjoying your retirement in peace."

Vanuska: "—And at least I survived adventuring long enough to enjoy retiring. Many don't make it this far."

Me: "So, what's next for you?"

Vanuska: "Right now? I have no idea—and that suits me just fine. The most challenging quest I want these days is wondering what I will have for lunch."[631]

---

[630] In my days of youth, I would read a series of adventure books called 'Accountants & Administrators'. These were fantastical stories where, as the reader, you could choose which page to turn to as you venture through a 'corporate' story towards the final battle with the end 'boss'. I remember using all my fingers and thumbs to bookmark a section, just in case I made a poor decision about 'company mergers' and needed to backtrack fast to pick an alternative path. Needless to say, there was much consternation from the ancient library guardian, who kept an ever-watchful eye out for any dog-eared shenanigans going on. That's probably the closest I ever got to 'dungeon clearing'—or 'workload clearing' as the adventure books called it.

[631] My stomach growls at the mere mention of food, reminding me I must soon feed the beast unless I want it to rage like an oath-broken Paladin on a swear-filled whistlestop tour of the realm.

The Woodcutter grins; she pulls another log off the pile and places it on the chopping block. She lines up her axe and strikes the wood, splitting it in half satisfactorily.

Vanuska: "That's more than enough adventure for this former Fighter."[632]

Me: "Well, I think I'll leave you to it—thank you for your time today."

Vanuska: "No problem, safe onward travels and good luck finding your brother, Loremaster—keep your eyes sharp and your wits about you. The unexpected waits around every corner."[633]

I bid the Woodcutter farewell and head back to the river—the sound of the Elf's axe continues once again, chipping away at nothing more terrifying than wood and bark, a far cry from the days when it was monstrous flesh and bone.

---

[632] *Who may or may not really be a Barbarian, a secret Cleric, or a weird tree-hugging Druid.*

[633] *Like invisible mazes, woodchopping Elves or self-satisfying Treants...*

21. Talbert, the Herald

Of all the Guilds found within the bustling city of Tronte, the Heralds Guild is perhaps the most extravagant. Situated east of the main gate, with its distinctive redbrick exterior, the Guild is set slightly away from the cobbled streets of the raucous Merchants' Quarter.[634] The polished roof tiles are adorned with a plethora of coloured flags fluttering in the wind like puffed-up stallions vying for attention—each one bears an intricate crest of a current legendary hero.[635] I walk the short distance to the entrance, past two impressively crafted topiary lions that sit on either side of a heavy oak front door.[636] The Heralds Guild is synonymous with Arcane Copyright spells—but they're also the only place in the realm where a new adventurer can obtain an 'official' heroic name.

I'm conscious my presence here somehow diminishes the impressive décor surrounding me. I quickly pull down on a metal lever I hope is some kind of announcement contraption rather than a fiendish trap designed to keep the waifs and strays from the Guild's door.[637] I exhale with relief as I hear the shrill ringing sound from somewhere deep inside the building. Placing my ear on the wooden surface, I listen for any hint of movement—when, without warning, the entrance unexpectedly swings inward, causing me to almost topple over in the process. A stern-looking woman greets me; she peers over her round, thick-rimmed Gnomish seeing-device and regards me from head to toe in utter disdain—her demeanour is anything other than welcoming.

Stern woman: "Yes? Do you have an appointment?"

Me: "Talbert the Herald is expecting me—I'm Elburn, *the Loremaster*."

---

[634] *Like a Bard edging away from a pox-riddled fan who wants to shake their hand enthusiastically.*

[635] *There's even a flag here for Dorn the 'Barbarian', complete with a Wheel of Pain symbol being eternally pushed by a skinny man in a loincloth—although I'm not entirely convinced he would be pleased with the scrawny depiction of himself embroidered onto the standard's surface.*

[636] *I wonder who crafted these impressive leonine bushes.*

[637] *Tronte has so many waifs and strays that some Guilds have taken to kitting out their entrances with non-lethal Gnomish traps to deter such undesirables from darkening their doors. These traps include spring-loaded 'welcome' mats, teleportation doors, and knockers of minor shocks (although the latter is rumoured to be only used by the Bards Guild).*

The stern woman glares at me, her disapproval almost reaching boiling point before she smartly turns on her heels.

Stern woman: "*This* way."

My prickly host leads me along a spacious hall filled with rows of leather-bound tomes, each painstakingly lettered in gold leaf on the spine. She notices my interest and acts quickly to cauterize any curiosity I may hold with a threatening lip curl and raised eyebrow combo.

Stern woman: "It is forbidden for outsiders to touch *The Ledgers of Heroes.*"

Me: "I was just admiring their beauty—"

Stern woman: "It is *also* forbidden for outsiders to <u>admire</u> *The Ledgers of Heroes.*"

Me: "I'll just look straight ahead then, shall I?"

Stern woman: "Yes—that would be preferable."

I can't tell how genuine this woman's threat of physical harm is, but I suspect that behind her stiff pent-up exterior beats the heart of a short-tempered Barbarian or a *really* annoyed Paladin.[638] Although, even with the growled word of warning, I still risk an opportunistic glance at the auspicious tomes as I'm led past. We continue the rest of the short journey in silence until finally reaching our destination—a set of gold-leafed double doors. The stern woman knocks twice before turning the handle and walking straight in. I go to follow, but she stops and glares at me with eyes so wide I swear they almost rolled straight out of their sockets and onto the floor.[639]

Stern woman: "*You...* wait here."

---

[638] *As to which of the two professions would triumph in combat if pitted against one another has been the subject of many a drunken debate (usually by groups of inebriated adventurers nearing the end of an evening's heavy drinking session). On the one hand, the Barbarian would appear to be the clear favourite—using his superior strength, speed and burning fury to overwhelm the Paladin. However, there are others who believe a Paladin's plate armour, training, and out-of-the-blue language would catch the Barbarian off-guard long enough for the foul-mouthed Holy warrior to land the killing blow. Whatever the answer is, I'm certain I wouldn't want to be around to witness the final outcome unfurl.*

[639] *A feat that would have certainly unnerved Seymour...*

Not wanting to risk my chaperone's wrath any further, I obediently wait outside as instructed. The stern woman shuts the door with a considerable amount of force. I carefully press my ear to the cold surface and can just make out the muffled voice of two people talking before the door suddenly springs open once more—this time nearly taking my nose clean off.

Stern woman: "You may enter—but do not touch ***anything***."

I nod as I step into the chamber. My nerves tingle as I feel the stern woman's glare burning a hole into the small of my back. There's a sharp click of a lock as the door behind me closes—lifting the tension considerably now the unwelcome harpy has retreated to her nest. I peer into the gloom towards a solitary lamplight no further than twenty feet away.

Me: "H—Hello?"

Sitting at a desk, I see a smartly dressed High-Elf wearing an ornate floral waistcoat. He appears preoccupied with scribing words into a tome—a tome similar to the one I dared to glance at earlier in the hallway. The High-Elf doesn't look up as he continues to transcribe whatever it is he is busily copying into his book.[640]

The Herald: "Hi[641]—the name's Talbert."

Me: "Elburn, Elburn *Barr*..."

Talbert: "A pleasure to meet you, Elburn Barr."

Me: "Likewise."

Talbert: "I hope our Guild Warden, *Miss Riler,* gave you a warm welcome."

---

[640] *There are four threads of thought as to why High-Elves are called 'High' Elves. The first thought is that High-Elves consider themselves morally superior to all others (highly likely, but reasonably dull). The second thought is that High-Elves hark from a floating island in the sky (highly unlikely but incredible if true). The third thought is that High-Elves are hugely addicted to a locally procured herb, which they insist is for purely 'medicinal' reasons (which could also be the reason how the second thought came about). The final thought (and the most ridiculous) is that High-Elves say 'Hi'—a lot...*

[641] *Perhaps the final thought is not as ridiculous as 'I' initially thought.*

Me: "Warm? She made me feel like a heavily encumbered Halfling who stumbled into an Orcs' banquet just as the ravenously hungry horde discovered the highly-anticipated 'off' meat was *also* 'off' the menu."

The Herald chuckles softly as he looks at me from over a myriad of lenses strapped to his face—I'm unsure which eye I should be looking at, given the sheer number of refracted eyeballs I can count staring back at me.

Talbert: "You must forgive her gruff manner. The Heralds Guild needs someone of Miss Riler's disposition; she keeps everything in order and in its proper place. Our tomes are precious, and it takes a guardian like her to ensure the safety of our work. A Guild Warden has a sworn duty to protect *The Ledgers of Heroes* from falling into the wrong hands— and I don't doubt she would willingly kill for them if she had to or die if *absolutely* necessary."[642]

Me: "Die? Why would Miss Riler be willing to die for these ledgers?"

The Herald flips a small lens down that instantly converges the myriad of eyeballs into one giant eyeball, which stares at me with intense scrutiny.

Talbert: "I thought you were a Loremaster of note?"

Me: "I am—"

Talbert: "Then let me ask you this, *who* benefits from knowing the true identity of a hero?"

Me: "*Erm...* Evildoers?"

Talbert: "And why is that?"

Me: "Because... they... will... know... their family name... and if they know that... they might... hurt the people heroes care about?"

The Herald flips up his seeing-device from his eyes and smiles at me knowingly.

Talbert: "*Bravo,* Loremaster! You see, the Heralds Guild offers its members and their loved ones a certain amount of protection from

---

[642] *Now ask me who would win a fight between a Barbarian, a Paladin, and Miss Riler—I know whom my coin would be on.*

Evildoers who seek revenge—like those who just had their prized dungeon cleansed or seen their favourite monstrous pet slain.[643] A new hero's name isn't something to be thrown around a tavern to impress the locals, *oh no*—a new hero's name gives our members <u>total</u> anonymity."

Me: "And how much does this anonymity cost?"

Talbert: "That depends. Usually, it's a hundred coins for the first summer—increasing by a hundred every summer after that."

Me: "Isn't that going to prove quite expensive over time, even for a veteran hero?"

Talbert: "If an adventurer is serious about adventuring, then the fee should be a small drop in an extremely wealthy sea to them."[644]

Me: "And if they're not?"

The Herald dips his quill in a pot of ink and continues scrawling into the open ledger in front of him.

Talbert: "Then they should think about a permanent career change by picking a far less demanding profession—something like turnip farming.[645] Plenty of heroes have made a name for themselves, heroes such as Rexar the Fearless,[646] The Crimson Shadow,[647] and Dorn the

---

[643] *I'm guessing this won't be a dog—but feasibly, it <u>could</u> be a cat.*

[644] *Or in Wizard denomination, a medium-sized Loremaster...*

[645] *I'm pretty confident Gwenyn Plow would take umbrage with the Herald here, especially as she has to deal with horny Dragons, ex-horny Dragon corpses, scorched fields, and steaming cows on any 'less-than-demanding' day.*

[646] *Rexar earned his name after mistakenly failing to spot he was fleeing straight <u>into</u> an advancing army of Ogres rather than <u>away</u>. So perplexed by the sight of a screaming Halfling Cleric running toward them, the Ogre Warlord suspected a trap and ordered his troops to retreat to the safety of their swampy domain—leaving the stunned Cleric to return to a hero's welcome.*

[647] *The Crimson Shadow is so-called because she usually dispatches her victims from the darkness—leaving a sizeable bloodstain behind on the floor; unsurprisingly, she is also considered a nemesis to Landlords, Mopsmiths, and Raghands everywhere.*

Barbarian[648]—they've all come through our doors looking to make a name for themselves. Admittedly a name 'we' gave them, but a name nonetheless."

Me: "Wait—*all* those names are made up?"

Talbert: "The Crimson Shadow—*really?* You think that's a real name?"

I look a little sheepish.

Me: "Okay, perhaps not *that* particular name—but the others?"

Talbert: "Yes, all the others. Each one is a fully paid-up member of the Heralds Guild."[649]

Me: "Let me ask you this—what happens to a hero's name if they can't afford to pay their fees anymore?"

Talbert: "Then that particular name *is* 'regrettably' removed from the coin-short hero and put back into the pool."

Me: "The pool?"

The High-Elf grins at me with impish delight.

Talbert: "Do you want to see it?"

Flicking through the stack of papers on his desk, the Herald spots what he is searching for.

Talbert: "*Aha,* perfect—*this* one will do nicely!"

He proceeds to cross-reference his find with the ledger, his finger slowly sliding down the page until eventually coming to a stop. He draws out a thin knife from deep within the cuff of his robe—then, with a deft flick of his wrist, he slices a section of the page out of the book and closes it shut.

Me: "*Erm...* won't that leave a hole in your book?"

---

[648] *There seems to be no stopping Dorn at the moment. Like the waifs and strays of Tronte—he's everywhere (thankfully minus the overbearing smell of rotting cabbage).*

[649] *I'm clearly in the wrong business—I should be using my considerable writing talents to come up with hero names from the safety of home, not trek around the realm searching for heroes for free.*

The High-Elf gives me a knowing wink.

Talbert: "Troll Flesh."

Me: "Sorry?"

Talbert: "The pages are made from Troll Flesh—it regenerates over time. By morning the hole will have repaired itself, and I'll be able to write on it again."

Me: "That's astounding—if not a little disgusting."

The Herald grins at me mischievously.

Talbert: "That's not even the best bit—*follow me*."

The High-Elf stands and heads towards a small alcove that pulses with a strange blue luminance. Sat at the heart of the alcove is an ornate font, a pool of bright liquid swirls ominously in a slow anti-clockwise motion.

Me: "What is this?"

Talbert: "*The Mythical Pool of Naming*."[650]

Me: "Couldn't you come up with a better title for it? I don't mean to sound rude; *The Mythical Pool of Naming* sounds a little unremarkable. Isn't this your particular area of expertise?"

Talbert: "It's an age-old problem—we have no issue coming up with names for other people, but when it's a name for ourselves, we can never settle on anything we all agree upon."

Me: "So, tell me about this *Mythical Pool of Naming*—I feel foolish almost asking, but what does it do?"

Talbert: "What—you mean you couldn't guess what it does from its name?"

Me: "Humour me."[651]

---

[650] *Not to be confused with the Mythical Poo of Shaming, which is something else altogether.*

[651] *Uncle Bevan Barr would disapprove of me saying this—he always felt the best jokes were the ones you never asked for but got anyway.*

The Herald sighs wearily.

Talbert: "Very well—this pool is where *all* the available hero names found within our Guild exist."

Me: "Exist? But I thought they were all written in your precious ledgers?"[652]

Talbert: "That's where they end up, but every name needs a beginning—the pool is that beginning."

Me: "How?"

Talbert: "It's probably easier if I show you. First, we'll add the *free name* I cut out from the ledger and drop it into the pool."

Me: "Free name?"

Talbert: "A free name is one that has yet to be attributed to a new hero."

Me: "I don't understand—"

Talbert: "*Hmmm...* let me ask you this then—how did you come by the name Elburn?"

Me: "I'm sorry?"

Talbert: "Your name, Loremaster—how did you come by it?"

Me: "M—My parents gave it to me when I was born."

The High-Elf nods with approval.

Talbert: "This is no different. When the hero is 'born', it is our task to suitably name them—the pool does that for us."

The Herald drops the small square of Troll Flesh into the water—the letters quickly dissolve from the skin's surface and disappear into the pool's depths. Talbert waits several seconds before fishing out the

---

[652] *(See footnote 640) That came across a little more sarcastic than I had intended it to sound. Fortunately, the High-Elf chose to ignore the misplaced tone—unmistakably putting the 'High' into 'High-Elf' and making a solid case for the first 'thought' to be the true origin behind the name...*

blank skin with a pair of metal tongs and setting fire to it. The High-Elf catches my confused face.

Talbert: "Troll Flesh has a nasty habit of regenerating at great speed; I need to make sure the damn thing doesn't sprout legs in the middle of the night and wander off to cause some mischief for Miss Riler to find in the morning."[653]

The Herald looks at me expectantly, with the floating skin now a black gooey mess.

Me: "What should I—"

Talbert: "Place your hands in the water, if you would—"[654]

As soon as my fingertips touch the surface, I feel a cold, tingling sensation coursing through them as the magic from the pool takes hold. I push my fingers further into the swirling depths, and the pulsing glow of the pool suddenly intensifies—the High-Elf looks at me in alarm.

Talbert: "Not *that* deep!"

I instinctively snatch my hands back and stare at the Herald in shock— he grins at my reaction.

Talbert: "I'm just kidding, sorry, bad joke[655]—go ahead, put them back in."

Me: "Very funny."

The High-Elf holds his hands above mine, inches from the pool's surface. He closes his eyes and begins to chant softly under his breath.

Talbert: *"Curnish... Felontus... Macramatus... Decardo... Golumpus...*

---

[653] *I concur—although I think it would be highly amusing to watch the regenerated Troll give Miss Riler the run around for a while. But I know, inevitably, the Guild Warden would catch the poor creature and unceremoniously dispatch it with extreme prejudice (hopefully not before the Troll had thumbed through her sacred ledgers and dog-eared some of the pages for good measure).*

[654] *I'm suddenly reminded of Miss Riler's stern warning not to touch __anything__...*

[655] *Uncle Bevan Barr __would__ approve of this, however...*

Telkenikus! Walanus... Fastrix... Fustoon... Fustoon..."[656]

The words sound impressive enough, even though I have absolutely no idea what they mean—the pool, however, reacts to the High-Elf's voice, swirling faster around my fingers. The pulsing maelstrom finally reaches a watery crescendo.

Me: "What do I do now?!"

Talbert: "Keep your hands perfectly still! *The Mythical Pool of Naming* is about to speak—"

A deep and mysterious voice calls out, reverberating around the alcove.

The Mythical Pool of Naming: "*Devlin Stormwind!*"

My eyes widen with a sense of impressive wonder.[657]

Me: "*Devlin Stormwind?* You know what—I *like* it!"

Talbert: "Good. Now, for a hundred gold coins, it's yours—"

I cough in shock at the mere mention of the exorbitant price.[658]

Me: "A *hundred* gold coins? I—I don't carry that kind of amount around!"[659]

The Herald throws a hand towel in my direction.

Talbert: "It's a gift—you can keep it for thirty days. After that, if you haven't paid us our fee, the name goes back into the pool—no hard feelings."

For a split second, my brain tries to determine if I can afford to pay for

---

[656] *I'm trying my hardest <u>not</u> to burst into spontaneous laughter at this point.*

[657] *This was said in a far more officious way than a Careersmith's 'magical' Sorting Cap, which just gruffly coughs out a profession as if it had been smoking forty Halfling-rolled woodbines a day.*

[658] *Now 'I' sound like I've been smoking forty Halfling-rolled woodbines a day!*

[659] *Especially after I've already lost most of my wealth to Sister Agatha's coin-hungry donation box.*

this name before the deadline expires, but I quickly dismiss the idea as I dry my hands.[660]

Me: "Thirty days it is—thank you."

Talbert: "The pleasure is mine."

A sudden thought crosses my mind.

Me: "Can a new hero use a name they've come up with themselves—rather than leaving it to the Mystical Pool of Naming to decide?"

The High-Elf looks disapprovingly in my direction.

Talbert: "I find most heroes lack the creativity required to generate a suitably heroic name—but there are *always* a few exceptions. For such a request, we charge a premium fee of a thousand gold coins—"

Me: "A *thousand* gold coins!? I'd be surprised if anyone would pay that kind of amount!"

Talbert: "Exactly."

I shake my head in disbelief as I think further upon my new 'heroic' name.

Me: "Do I get any official paperwork for *Devlin Stormwind?*"

The Herald pulls out a rolled-up parchment from the cuff of his robe before handing it to me. I unroll and stare at the official document—the name *Devlin Stormwind* is emblazoned across the bottom, next to a red wax seal with the Heralds Guild crest pressed into it.[661]

Me: "What? That's imposs—? When did you do—?"

---

[660] *Loremasters sit just above Turnip Farmers, Landlords, Merchants, and Potioneers in 'Farbe's: Get Rich Quick' list, but a long way below Rogues, Clerics, Barbarians, Monks, Fighters, Paladins, Rangers, Wizards, Sorcerers—and even Necromancers (who have the luxury of using animated corpses to haul any loot back to their abode, saving the Dead-Collector valuable backpack space in the process). Strangely, for some reason, Druids earn on average as much as Loremasters do...*

[661] *The Heralds Guild crest is a picture of the Heralds Guild crest inside another picture of the Heralds Guild crest, which, remarkably, is inside <u>another</u> picture of the Heralds Guild crest. The whole thing is slightly hypnotic to look at and could easily entertain a bored Barbarian for hours on end or freak out any High-Elf who stares at it for too long after enjoying some dried herbs (purely for medicinal reasons).*

Talbert: "I've been doing this for so long; I can practically do it in my sleep."

The High-Elf turns on his heels and returns to his desk, leaving me to finish drying my hands. As I neatly place the hand towel to the side of the font, I catch myself staring into the pool's depths once more.

Me: "Does that mean any expired name could end up being given to someone else to use?"

Talbert: "Of course."

Me: "Doesn't that get confusing—what if another new hero with the original name came along and was mistaken for the original hero?"

Talbert: "That doesn't really happen. There's a cooling-off period with hero names; they are only added to the pool two summers after being returned to us."

Me: "Why two summers?"

Talbert: "Our research showed that commoners usually forget a hero's name after two summers. Most remember *someone* came along in that time and killed a legendary Dragon, or whatever—but rarely *who*."[662]

Me: "What if a hero becomes *so* popular everyone remembers them?"

Talbert: "*Ah,* in those rare occasions, a name is retired for good—for a nominal fee, of course."

Me: "How much is nominal?"

Talbert: "Ten thousand coins—and for that, we'll agree never to add that particular hero's name back into *The Mystical Pool of Naming.* Thus, allowing them to become the stuff of legends!"

Me: "Ten thousand—that's pretty steep!"

Talbert: "We believe it's a fair price for ensuring legendary status."

I try to process everything the Herald has revealed to me while sitting back in my seat. I can't help but stare intently at the official document,

---

[662] *Ask most commoners, and they usually only remember what a hero wore, like plate armour, Wizarding robes or a stolen patchwork dress, but not their name.*

my mind distracted by an ever-growing list of questions.

Me: "Who had this name before me?"

The Herald smiles and reaches for an unremarkable black book sat just to the right of his elbow.

Talbert: "I thought you'd ask that…"

The Herald flicks pages at speed until stopping suddenly at a particular entry.

Talbert: "Thimble Groin."[663]

Me: "Excuse me?"

Talbert: "*Thimble Groin*—the original hero, who was subsequently reborn as Devlin Stormwind."

Me: "Let me get this right, Devlin Stormwind was really a man called Thimble Groin?"

The High-Elf double-checks the written entry in his black book.

Talbert: "Dwarf."[664]

Me: "Huh?"

Talbert: "Thimble Groin was a Dwarf—not a man."

Me: "What happened to Thimble… *erm*… Groin?"

The Herald reads the footnote at the bottom of the page.

Talbert: "Unfortunately, he aged rapidly and turned to dust."[665]

Me: "That doesn't sound like a particularly pleasant way to go."

Talbert: "I guess the lesson here is *never* fight a Warlock unless you're

---

[663] *A most unfortunate name—one I would pay almost <u>any</u> amount to the Heralds Guild to change for the better.*

[664] *I imagine most of Thimble's enemies saw his name as a gift that needed to be unwrapped and mercilessly mocked on a near-daily basis.*

[665] *I'm guessing whatever remained of Thimble probably could fit inside his former name.*

better prepared—"[666]

My ears prick up at the mention of a Warlock.

Me: "*Warlock?* Does it say if this particular Warlock was a Lich in your book?"

The High-Elf scans the written entry one more time.

Talbert: "No, sorry."

Me: "What about a name for this Warlock?"

Talbert: "I only log the heroes, not the Evildoers—you're better off talking to the Tallyman if you're searching for any information on them."

Me: "This Tallyman—he wouldn't happen to be called Bartlet by any chance, would he?"

Talbert: "You know him?"

Me: "By reputation alone."

Talbert: "Then you know he works for the Heroes Guild, logging every detail of every quest—even the failures."

Me: "So, Thimble Groin was a member of the Heroes Guild?"

Talbert: "Apparently so—and that's about as much as I can tell you, I'm afraid."

The High-Elf shuts his black book with a level of finality.

Me: "Thank you—I appreciate your time."

Talbert: "Not at all; it's the least I could do. Is there anything else I can help you with today?"

There's a moment of silence before I finally muster the courage to ask the question that has been burning on my lips since the moment I walked through the Guild's doors.[667]

---

[666] *And wearing some form of 'Protection from being rapidly turned to dust' ward...*

[667] *No, it's not the one asking who the person responsible for the topiary lions is...*

Me: "Actually, are you able to look someone up for me?"

Talbert: "I'm afraid not—we have a strict privacy policy, you understand. I told you about Thimble because you now *own* his hero name—Why? Whom were you interested in?"

Me: "My brother, Aldon Barr... my family hasn't heard from him for ten summers."

The High-Elf studies my face for a moment before speaking again.

Talbert: "*Hmmm*... wait here a moment."

The High-Elf pushes himself from his desk once more and turns to the row of books behind him. He pulls at a metal lever, and there's a sudden heavy **'clank'** of a mechanism as the entire contraption begins to rotate hypnotically.[668] There's another heavy **'clunk'** as the mechanical spectacle slowly spins to a stop. The Herald quickly scans the spines of the revealed tomes until he locates a heavy emerald green one edged in silver leaf. Pulling it from the shelf, he blows the dust from the cover and places it open on his desk in front of him.

Talbert: "*Barr... Barr... Barr...* here we go, *Aldon Barr—*"

My heart leaps at the mention of Aldon's name—but quickly drops again when I spy the High-Elf's smooth brow turning into a frown.

Me: "Something wrong?"

The High-Elf spins the book around so I can see the entry for myself; Aldon's name is there, but the subsequent Troll Flesh page has been ripped out and cauterized—the one with his current hero name.[669]

Me: "It's missing—why is it missing?"

The High-Elf shakes his head slowly, his expression completely dumbfounded.

---

[668] *I hope this isn't a Gnomish contraption—otherwise, I'd wager a large fire could be looming on the horizon...*

[669] *There's a frosty chill in the air as if a billion Guild Wardens suddenly cried out in thunderous rage—and then fell silent. I fear for those who committed this heinous vandalism act when Miss Riler eventually finds out what has happened to one of her 'precious' ledgers...*

Talbert: "I don't rightly know; I've never seen anything like this before—it is most irregular…"

Me: "What do you think it means?"

The Herald leans closer to me, flipping his lens to stare into my eyes with a large solitary eyeball again.

Talbert: "Somebody doesn't want your brother to be found and is making damn sure they cover their tracks in the process."

Me: "Who would do this?"

The High-Elf shakes his head.

Talbert: "I'm not entirely sure. Only a handful of Heralds and Guild Wardens have access to these tomes—myself included. But we have all sworn a binding oath to protect these ledgers. The miscreant, whoever they are, must have sneaked in here somehow to perform their foul act. Whatever the truth is, it seems your destiny lies out there, Loremaster…"

Me: "But—"

Talbert: "*Devlin Stormwind,* it looks like you're about to embark on your first adventure as a hero…"

I look down at the official document with Devlin's name etched onto it.

Me: "But I'm not a hero…"

The High-Elf grins as he holds his hand out for me to shake. I grasp it with a sense of trepidation.

Talbert: "I'll let you in on a secret; if I've learned one thing in my time—it's that *nobody* starts as the hero they eventually become.[670] If you find your brother—say *'Hi'* from me…"[671]

---

[670] *Although some don't end up as the heroes they <u>believe</u> they'll become either…*

[671] *Spoken like a true 'Hi' Elf.*

There's a stern cough behind me as I sense another person in the room[672]— I know without turning it's Miss Riler who has come to escort me out. I nod at the High-Elf one final time and leave under the watchful eye of the Guild Warden. I don't want to be around when the Herald finally informs her that one of her pages is missing.

As I hurry past the topiary lions[673] and down the steps to the exit, I find myself saying the name *Devlin Stormwind* repeatedly in my mind. I may have entered this place as a lowly Loremaster, but by some quirk of fate, I think I've just left as a rising hero...[674]

---

[672] *For a split second, I could have sworn it was the Careersmith accompanied by his gruff 'magical' Sorting Cap, returning to say they made a mistake and I should have been a Cleric all along.*

[673] *Who did create these bizarre creations?*

[674] *A hero by name only, I may add!*

22. Axel-Grind, the Bard

I'm on the outskirts of Silver Pond, a picturesque hamlet whose residents pride themselves on their unique export, Argent fish—a highly-valuable catch sought after for its precious silver scales.[675] As one would expect with such a rare commodity, Silver Pond is plagued by poachers eager to make their fortune off the back of this prized aquatic creature. I walk along a narrow path that bisects Lakemere, where I assume the Argent Fish reside. I'm also acutely aware of the small army of crossbow-carrying Guards who patrol the water's edge.

I nod and wave as I pass these heavily-armed fish guardians, trying my best to appear as innocuous as possible and certainly not carrying any form of fishing rod or giant net hidden about my person. Lakemere's surface vibrates hypnotically to a faint beat I can hear emanating from beyond the hamlet's outer wall. The beat steadily increases to a pumping pulse, followed by a huge cheer that suddenly erupts ahead of me. Confused and eager to discover the source of this commotion, I step through the hamlet's gates and straight into a throng of excited locals. I call out to anyone listening who is within earshot as I struggle to push my way through the layers of peasant folk.

Me: "What's going on?"

Someone in the crowd: "It's Axel-Grind—he's due to appear on stage soon!"

Me: "Axel-*who?*"

Someone else in the crowd: "Axel-Grind, only the greatest Bard in the entire realm! Where have you been living all this time—the Caves of Rebulung?"[676]

I push myself towards the head of the herd and suddenly find myself eye-to-belly button with a stern-looking Ogre who leers over me. The

---

[675] *Each Argent fish is carefully hallmarked, meaning they are placed in Silver Pond's Great Hall and 'stamped' on the head using a pair of heavy Silver Pond-branded boots.*

[676] *Now the Caves of Rebulung are free from the dreaded Bunjees—a thriving Gnome community has taken over ownership of the caverns. The new residents have even found a use for the plethora of sticky strands still hanging from the cave's ceiling; they've been hiring them out as part of an intensive training regime for highly-strung Barbarians with a desire to be highly strung for real.*

warty creature stares at my pitiful form, arms crossed, as he sneers at my unwelcome appearance.

Ogre: "No. Entry."

Me: "I'd like to talk to Axel-Grind—"

The muscle-bound brute leans closer and growls a little louder through his pursed yellow lips, in case I missed it the first time.

Ogre: "So, does everyone—but I said. **NO. ENTRY.**"

Me: "I'm a Loremaster—"

A light yet sharp voice interrupts the awkward exchange.

Half-Elf: *"Loremaster?"*

I peer around the warty yellow mountain of blubber to locate the owner of the harmonious voice—an exceptionally well-groomed Half-Elf steps out from the Ogre's immense shadow to address me in person.

Half-Elf: "You said you were a Loremaster—is that true?"

Me: "Last time I checked."

Half-Elf: "If I may be so bold, you look a little like a Wizard—"

Me: "I assure you I *am* a Loremaster—and not a Wizard."[677]

The Half-Elf nods, although I'm not entirely sure he believes me.

Half-Elf: "Stand aside, make way, Donk[678]—let the Loremaster through."

The Ogre grunts as he allows me to pass before slamming his body shut just as a tide of opportunistic locals tries to follow in my wake. I look back at the sea of panicked peasant faces, unable to stop themselves

---

[677] *Why are people confusing me like this? I don't even have a white beard and crazy teeth—nor do I smell of burning balls of fire!*

[678] *Ogres have a fondness for naming their newborns after onomatopoeia, which can no doubt be slightly confusing when the real onomatopoeia occurs in close proximity to the creature's namesake.*

from crashing into Donk's sizable gut—it's an ungodly sight, one I wish I hadn't witnessed first-hand. The Half-Elf leads us towards an impressive-looking tent, which appears to be the focal point of attention in Silver Pond—calling everyone to it like some kind of bizarre red and white striped siren.

Half-Elf: "So, tell me, what is a Loremaster doing in this part of the realm?"

Me: "To be honest, I was looking for a place to stay before heading on to Port Ardor—I wasn't expecting to come across all *this*."

I gesture at the crowd, some of which are still trying to extract their faces from the Ogre's belly blubber.

Half-Elf: "What business do you have in Port Ardor? It's not exactly the most hospitable of areas in the realm. There are rumours the Sharks Guild is circling the area.[679] Certainly not somewhere a Loremaster should wander about alone, or at least without a hired sword to watch their back."

Me: "It's all part of my research; I'm writing about adventurers and their adventures. I go where my work leads me—even if it does mean visiting disagreeable places such as Port Ardor."

Half-Elf: "Writing about adventurers? Well, this is your lucky night— you're about to meet the legendary Axel-Grind and the Bardettes!"

Me: *"Bardettes?"*

Half-Elf: "They're the rest of his musical companions. Axel-Grind has only one requirement for anyone joining his adventuring party—they must be able to play an instrument. Can you play an instrument, Loremaster?"

Me: "Not really."[680]

---

[679] *The Sharks Guild is a coin-lending Guide that 'literally' takes a bite out of those who fail to pay up on time. They're easily identified by the fin-like helms their members wear on their heads and the loud 'dur-da... duuur-daaa... du-du-du-du...' tune they hum ominously before walking into a room.*

[680] *Not strictly true, I have been known to play forks—which are a little like playing spoons, but with a slightly greater risk of serious knee injury.*

Half-Elf: "That's a shame."

Me: "Sorry, *who* are you again?"

Half-Elf: "Of course, where are my manners—I'm *Vero*."

Me: "What's your role here?"

Vero: "Why—I'm Axel-Grind's Manager."

Me: "And what does a Manager do exactly?"

Vero: "All sorts of things—I handle everything, from book appearances and performance fees to signings and damage mitigation.[681] I tell Axel where he needs to be and what he needs to do—like a Dungeonmaster but a lot taller and without any of those irritating dungeon overheads, I suppose..."[682]

Me: "And I assume you must charge a fee from Axel for all this personal service?"

Vero: "No, I do it for the love of the job—"

I look in surprise at the Half-Elf.

Me: "*Really?*"

Vero: "No! What do I look like to you? Of course, I charge a fee—and a competitive one at that too! I get 15% plus an additional 5% of adventuring profit after costs. *Aha*—here we are!"

The tent entrance is thrown wide as Vero holds the canvas door open for me. I step inside and immediately recoil from the pungent aroma of herbal smoke as it leaps down my throat, forcing me to cough involuntarily.[683] I wave my hand in front of my face, trying to brush the

---

[681] *Being a legendary Bard means there are times when everyday objects inexplicably break for no good reason (everything within a ten-foot radius, that is). Anything from bedrolls to broomsticks can suddenly snap in two without a moment's notice. This, I've been reliably informed, is a little-known curse all successful Bards experience from time to time called 'Trashed'—it's Vero's task to ensure fair payment is made for any 'unforeseen' inanimate damage.*

[682] *I suspect Vero means costs here and not some cleverly constructed ceiling traps.*

[683] *Making me sound like a forty Halfling-rolled woodbines a day 'magical' Sorting Cap...*

air clear so I can find something still alive in this choking hell. Through the parting vapour, I spy an unkempt man sitting on a stack of velvet cushions; his hair sprouts in a multitude of directions without a single care for his exasperated parting.[684] He looks up at me with his tired, red eyes as he fiddles with the strings on his lute simultaneously.

Axel-Grind: "Who's this then? The warm-up act?"

Vero: "May I present, *erm*— sorry, I appear to have forgotten to ask for your name."

Me: "Devlin—*no*, I mean, Elburn, *Elburn Barr*."

Vero: "Very good. May I present Elburn Barr, *Loremaster* extraordinaire."

The Bard perks up at the mention of my profession as he nods and beckons me to sit on a cushion next to him. As I take a seat, I notice a glint of gold from something buried deep within the folds of the Bard's tunic.

Axel-Grind: "Loremaster, are you? Take the weight off your feet then— Vero, be a good Half-Elf and get us some beverages?"

Vero: "The usual?"

Axel-Grind: "Yeah, but make it a triple this time; the stuff they serve in this place wouldn't floor a tee-total Cleric, let alone a Bard of my reputation..."[685]

Vero nods and departs from the tent. Axel stares at me as he takes the longest of inhales from the woodbine before offering it to me through an exhaled cloud of smoke.

Axel-Grind: "You want a toke?"[686]

Me: "*A toke?*"

---

[684] *That is frantically waving a few white hairs in surrender...*

[685] *Most of the Clerics I've encountered look like they sneak a few sips of the Sacramental wine when nobody (except their disapproving Deity) is looking.*

[686] *'Toke' is a Gnomish word meaning '...to smoke without inhaling'.*

Axel-Grind: "Yeah, from this Ice-Sativa woodbine. I can't perform without taking a hit—although it's for medicinal purposes only, you understand."[687]

Me: "Of course—I understand."[688]

I politely decline the offered woodbine. Axel-Grind shrugs his shoulders and continues fiddling with his lute string.[689]

Me: "Tell me about yourself? How did you come to be here?"

Axel-Grind: "We took a wagon from Tronte to—"

I hold up my hand to stop Axel from finishing his reply.

Me: "Forgive me, it seems there's a need to keep one's wit sharp around you—I mean, how did you become the legendary Bard sitting before me now?"

Axel-Grind: "*Ah,* sorry man, *yeah*... well, I've always been into my music, even from an early age. My mum swears blind I was banging out the tunes when I was still in her womb—though my old man says that was down to the copious amount of Buttered Beans my mum ate when she was pregnant.[690] Growing up, I was never far from a lute—I was practically raised with one in my mouth.[691] I guess my mum always knew I was destined to be a Bard of note."[692]

Me: "Did your parents support you in your decision to follow your love of music?"

Axel-Grind: "My mum seemed genuinely pleased—she always encouraged me to sing to her of an evening—"

---

[687] *No doubt obtained from a very High-Elf...*

[688] *I understand ALL too well...*

[689] *I'm no musician, but even 'I' know a lute isn't meant to be played that way.*

[690] *Buttered Beans are so-called for the noise it makes when it comes out of one's backside; sold with the popular slogan, 'Butt-ered Beans make your butt-heard and the wind blow hard—the more you eat, the more you parp!"*

[691] *Perhaps not the best way to play a lute...*

[692] *As opposed to an off-key one...*

Me: "And your father?"

Axel-Grind: "He hated *everything* to do with music—even broke my lute once in a fit of rage."

Me: "*Ah,* he disapproved of your talent—"

Axel-Grind: "Not so much that. I think he was still sore I didn't want to follow him into the family business."

Me: "What was he—a Barbarian?"

Axel-Grind: "Nah, he just sold any old shit—"

Me: "So, he was a Merchant of numerous wares?"

Axel-Grind: "Of sorts... he sold old shit, *actual* old shit—he was a Dung Merchant. Didn't matter what kind. Elf,[693] Human,[694] Dwarf,[695] Halfling,[696] Gnome,[697] Cleric,[698] Barbarian[699]—he sold any he could get his hands on."

Me: "A Dung Merchant?"

Axel-Grind: "My old man sold the best shit in the entire realm. He was really good at it too—everyone wanted a piece of whatever shit he had on him at the time; his punters couldn't resist his stash."

Me: "Why would anyone want sh—?"

Axel-Grind: "*Erm... hello?* Because it's so versatile! You can build with it... you can cook with it—*hell*... I bet you could *even* smoke it if you

---

[693] *Thinks it's superior to all other shits.*

[694] *Standard shit that has no discerning features or abilities of note...*

[695] *Usually hard as stone—probably explains why they are grumpy all the time.*

[696] *Very small—easily mistaken for rabbit droppings, which in turn could actually belong to a wild-shaped Druid caught short while adventuring.*

[697] *Still insists it's bigger than a Halfling's turd.*

[698] *Often followed by the phrase 'Holy Sh—' when someone clasps eyes on it.*

[699] *Usually appears midway through a screaming rage before destroying whatever it lands in.*

really wanted to. Sure it's not the most glamorous of professions, and the smell takes a lot of getting used to—but my old man made us enough coin to put me through Bard School."

Me: "I thought your father didn't approve of your music."

Axel-Grind: "He saw I wanted more for myself than spending my time elbow deep in other people's dung. He didn't like it, but he realised he couldn't stop me either."

The Bard strums his lute as its harmonious chords waft over me. I find my consciousness rising above a mythical floating island populated by morally superior High-Elves with a Halfling-rolled woodbine addiction—a group of smoking Elves point at me and call out in unison as I slowly glide past.

High-Elves: "*Hiiiiiii—!*"

As the tune abruptly stops, my mind stretches and snaps backwards towards reality.

Me: "What did you do just then, t—that music was almost hypnotic!?"

Axel-Grind: "Chill, it was a simple Charm Spell. I was, you know, just showing off my powers a little. Works wonders with the yokels— especially when we need to shift a few more Axel-Grind posters and figurines after a performance."[700]

Me: "You charm your audience with your music?"

Axel-Grind: "Am I charming them? Or are they just feeling the vibes?"

Me: "Having experienced your music first-hand, I'd say the former— but why the need to do it?"

Axel-Grind: "Why do you think? Those post-show autographs and figurines won't sell themselves. Remember, life as a successful Bard doesn't come cheap—and it's a hell of a lot quicker than seducing every

---

[700] *The Bard points to a figurine of himself (complete with a tiny woodbine in one hand and a lute in the other) relaxing next to me on a side table. These are clearly inferior Halfling-created figurines rather than the ones the Gnomes make for Balstaff—some of the limbs have been put on backwards, while Axel's sculpted features looks suspiciously like he just shaved his face with a Gelatinous Cube.*

potential customer first."[701]

Me: "Did you learn your Charm spell at Bard School?"

Axel-Grind: "No, everything I learned was self-taught; Bard school ended up being a huge waste of my time and effort."

Me: "But you said—"

Axel-Grind: "I was too good for that place, *too* gifted to learn anything of value from those backwards-thinking clowns. I dropped out before graduating—but as you can see, I've done pretty well for myself since."

Me: "Dropped out? Why?"

Axel-Grind: "I'm not good with rules—I always want to break them.[702] Besides, school couldn't teach me more than I already knew. They certainly would have kicked me out if I hadn't dropped out."

Me: "How did your father react to that?"

Axel-Grind: "By then, he didn't give a shit.[703] Instead, I bounced from town-to-town for a few summers, performing small gigs at any local tavern that would welcome me. I even had a few invitations to go adventuring, but I never found the right party that *really* got me. There was always someone in the group who said it was a 'no' from them whenever I suggested a song."[704]

Me: "Like whom?"

Axel-Grind: "A stuck-up Paladin or jealous Cleric usually—those guys need to learn how to chill out—they are _way_ too serious."

Me: "That must have been difficult for you creatively?"

---

[701] Although, being a Bard, I bet they wouldn't let that stop them from trying.

[702] Along with the Cleric's donation box, Ranger's bedroll and Wizard's Scrying Ball, no doubt...

[703] Although he would have happily sold it...

[704] No matter how good you are something, there's always one outspoken critic determined to bring you down—almost as if it's their _own_ quest to do so.

Axel-Grind: "It was a complete nightmare—for example, the Wizard kept casting *Silence* on me whenever my back was turned."[705]

Me: "So, you decided to form your own group—how did that come about?"

The Bard smiles as he takes another deep puff of his woodbine.

Axel-Grind: "It was no secret I wanted to be a hero—but not just *any* hero, I wanted to be the first hero of a Bard-only group. I paid a visit to the Heralds Guild and procured myself a new heroic name. Then I stopped off at the Bards Guild and advertised for some auditions. I whittled down the prospective candidates from the thousands[706] who answered the call until I was left with those you now know as the Bardettes."

Me: "How did you decide who was good enough to become a Bardette?"

Axel-Grind: "It was as easy as falling into a spiked pit[707]—I only chose the *best-looking*, *best-sounding*, and *best at partying as if there was no tomorrow* to join my musical adventuring group. We were an immediate hit and exploded onto the hero scene like a Fireball in a ten-by-ten room."[708]

Me: "Why were you such a success compared to any regular Bard of note?"

The Bard smiles as he flicks the ash from his woodbine into an ornate bowl.

Axel-Grind: "*Ah,* you see, the difference was—we *knew* how to put on a *real* show. When we returned from some mundane side-quest or another, we reimagined the tale to be a realm-threatening quest we had just completed, rather than letting on it was another boring rat-

---

[705] *It could have been worse; it could have been a 'Silent Fireball' instead.*

[706] *Bards have a reputation for embellishing the truth—so I'm taking several zeros off this number.*

[707] *Especially easy if you're a Cleric...*

[708] *Hopefully without incinerating some unlucky bystanders in the process.*

infested cellar that needed clearing.[709] In doing that, we captured the imagination of our audience with our musical tales and never once looked back. Word spread of our feats, and we quickly realised we had something special on our hands..."

Me: "How special?"

Axel-Grind: "Just take a look around—*this* is special, don't you agree?"

I take a moment to examine all the luxuries sat inside the tent:[710] cushions, soft towels, fresh fruit, and enough alcohol to satisfy a parched Barbarian who has just finished pushing their Wheel of Pain around[711] and is now in need of lubrication. Speaking of which, our drinks have finally appeared, served by the ever-smiling Vero.

Vero: "Two triple Dragon-gins, as requested—"

I can't help but notice the beverage is glowing ominously with a pair of yellowed eyes.

Me: "I—I didn't request a triple."

The Bard looks at me unimpressed as Vero smiles at me expectantly.

Axel-Grind: "Come on, don't disappoint me now, Loremaster."

I nod and take a sip—a sip that almost ignites my breath. I cough so hard I break wind loudly, forcing me to stare at Bard in abject horror.

The Bard roars with laughter as he knocks back his drink in one go and releases a bowel belch of his own that nearly blows Vero out the tent door.[712]

---

[709] *Boring, but one* most *adventurers get to walk away from unless you're particularly unlucky...*

[710] *Well, from what I can just make out through the hazy smoke.*

[711] *And for the majority of the time, uphill, no less...*

[712] *Forget the Buttered Beans—a* new *champion is laying claim to the Horn of Blasting crown! Arise, Sir Dragon-gin, King of the breeches blowers!*

Axel-Grind: "*That's* the spirit! Dragon's-gin is syphoned from the fermented juices of Dragon's gut—it's impossible to drink without letting rip from one's behind."

Me: "Can I ask—how did you and Vero meet?"

Vero: "I used to be a Talent Scout for the Tronte-Fete when our paths crossed.[713] I arranged a meeting to discuss their immediate future after hearing Axel and his Bardettes sing one evening at *The Green Goblin* tavern."[714]

The Bard raises his empty glass to salute his Manager.

Axel-Grind: "Fortune smiled on us that day!"

Me: "Can I ask what you talked about?"

Vero: "Plans."

Axel-Grind: "*Big* plans!"

Vero: "Axel wanted the group to put on appearances and shows across the *entire* realm—visiting towns, hamlets, cities, and castles from the Dagger Coast to the Western Peninsular. I arranged for Axel to perform for every Baron in the land. His group have even played for the odd Evildoer or two."

Me: "You've played music for an Evildoer?"

Vero: "They enjoy a good song just as much as anyone else—plus they usually pay a bit more for the privilege too."

Axel-Grind: "Not forgetting the pre-performance *arrangements* we always insist upon[715]—no death or imprisonment of any of the performers—"

Vero: "<u>Or</u> backstage team!"

---

[713] *Ah, so <u>this</u> is the fellow responsible for all those annoying Clowns, calamitous Halfling Acrobats, and frustrating-to-watch Mime Artists.*

[714] *A place that does not welcome Blue Goblins, foul-mouthed comments, downbeat views, and spontaneous nakedness...*

[715] *Including Non-Dismemberment, Non-Disintegration, and Non-Disemboweling clauses.*

Axel-Grind: "The usual small print stuff we put into any contract agreement."[716]

Me: "What Evildoers have you performed for?"

Axel-Grind: "By the Gods, I can't remember their names; I've done so many concerts I can't even remember what town we're in now—"

Vero: "Silver Pond."

Axel-Grind: "The one with the shiny fishes, right?"

Vero: "That's the one."

The crowd outside suddenly goes wild with anticipation as a harried-looking Dwarf rushes into the tent carrying a piece of paper.

Dwarf: "Two minutes, Mr Grind..."

The Bard nods and gathers to his feet as the Bardettes begin to warm up their vocal cords in an unseen tent nearby.

Axel-Grind: "Sorry, my public cannot wait."

Me: "No problem, just one or two more questions before you leave?"

Axel-Grind: "Shoot."

Me: "Where do you get your inspiration for your songs?"

Axel-Grind: "Most come from our experiences from when we used to adventure together. Songs like *The Cleric is Dead—go get another one, Barbarians rage against the Gnomish Machines* and the fans' favourite, *Toss a Dwarf—but don't tell the Elf.*"[717]

Dwarf: "One minute, Mr Grind..."

Me: "Don't they get old? I mean, if you play them so often, doesn't it get a little repetitious for everyone—including you?"

---

[716] *Usually written up and triple-checked by seeing-device wearing Gnomes—much to the bemusement of Halflings everywhere.*

[717] *I cannot help but notice the nearby Dwarf wincing at the mention of this song title.*

Axel-Grind: "That's why we try to come up with new material from any new experiences we have together. I have to keep one step ahead of the competition."

Me: "What competition?"

Axel-Grind: "There are a lot of Bards who regard us with envy—any one of them could pull a group of Bards together in an attempt to steal our thunder. I'm not about to give all this up without a fight."

The sound of clapping and rhythmic chanting grows from the crowd waiting impatiently outside—the Bard gives me a knowing grin.

Axel-Grind: "Hear that, Loremaster? That's *my* crowd—they are the ones who keep me doing this."

The worried-looking paper-carrying Dwarf leans over to whisper into the Bard's ear.[718]

Dwarf: "It's time, Mr Grind..."

Axel-Grind: "Let's get this show on the Merchant's Road..."

Me: "Good luck—and thank you for talking to me."

Axel-Grind: "No problem at all."

As he goes to leave, the Bard turns back to me with a wink.

Axel-Grind: "Who knows, maybe our next song will be called *"The Loremaster parps like Dragon-gin spirit."*

My sphincter immediately hides in fright at the thought of another round of that accursed beverage. Axel-Grind chuckles as he grabs his lute before disappearing through the tent door to rapturous applause—leaving me alone with the Bard's Manager.[719]

---

[718] *Who, I now suspect, is hoping they won't be tossed during the final encore...*

[719] *I'm conscious, dear reader, that I have perhaps let my professional standards slip with the amount of 'bottom' references and gags peppered throughout this interview—I shall endeavor to do better and avoid such gutterball reporting in future (I mean, it's not as if I'm going to be holding an interview in a privy or underground sewer anytime soon).*

Vero: "Thanks for your time, Loremaster. I trust you'll send us a copy of your work when it's finally published?"[720]

Me: "*Erm*—Sure... no problem, where shall I forward the copy to?"

The Half-Elf hands me a small card with an address written in fancy bronze lettering.

Vero: "Send it on to my abode in Tronte—if you would be so kind."

Me: "Will do."

I stand to leave and find myself swaying slightly from the potent Dragon's gut juice, now fermenting in my own.

Vero: "You okay, Loremaster? You seem a little shaky..."

Me: "Nothing some fresh air won't remedy."

I grab my bag and head out of the tent towards the wall of noise.

Vero: "Why don't you stick around for the show? There's usually a great party afterwards if you're interested?"[721]

I turn back to the Half-Elf with a slightly inebriated grin.

Me: "Well, I always wanted to join a party..."[722]

There's a massive fanfare of noise as Axel-Grind begins belting out his opening number. I should try and get some sleep, but the chance to see Axel-Grind performing in the flesh is too good an opportunity to miss. I may regret the outcome when the sun rises once more, but that's a problem for tomorrow.[723]

---

[720] *Ah, the irony of that question won't be lost on any Loremaster reading this.*

[721] *I'm sure there was another question I would ask the Bard—oh well, it's slipped my mind for now.*

[722] *The great Doctor Frodoian, a noted Moralist and part-time Halfling adventurer, would undoubtedly have something profound to say about this sudden admission.*

[723] *Maybe I'm going to be the one needing a certain 'medicinal' herbal remedy in the morning...*

23. Inglebold, the Potioneer

The wheels grind and creak as a weary dapple-gray mare strains to move the weathered old cart it's hauling behind it. Potion bottles rattle and clink together in their boxes while the wagon meanders along the worn tracks of the heavily traversed Merchant's Road. The old man sitting at the reins pulls his carthorse to a halt as he notices me up ahead on the road. His eyes dart nervously, scanning for any hidden accomplices while hurriedly digging into his robes to withdraw an ornate glass bottle. One spat-out cork later, and the old man is standing as he points at me with a gnarled finger—the other arm is pulled back, ready to launch the potion in my direction at the first sign of trouble.

Inglebold: ***"Stay right there—I have a Potion of Fireballs[724] in my hand, and I'm not afraid to use it!"[725]***

Me: "Please, I mean you no harm—"[726]

Inglebold: "I doubt you could do me any harm, sonny. You don't look the type. But then you're probably just the patsy in this pitiful ambush attempt. Tell your friends to come out where I can see them, with their weapons raised—and no funny business!"[727]

The Potioneer widens his eyes and feints a throw, causing me to duck in panic.

Me: ***"I'm alone! There is <u>no</u> ambush, I swear! My name is Elburn. I'm a Loremaster, I—I was given your name by Morgan—<u>Simply Morgan!</u>"***

---

[724] *Fireballs? Plural? As if one wasn't bad enough...*

[725] *The feasibility of putting Fireballs inside a tiny glass bottle is so staggering I cannot even begin to comprehend the 'why' of doing it, let alone the 'how'—of course, the old man could be lying. Still, I don't think I want to put the contents of his fiery-looking potion to the test just yet.*

[726] *Especially as I'm still nursing the remains of an Ogre-sized three-day-old hangover...*

[727] *This would break Uncle Bevan Barr's heart to hear this; he is an enthusiastic supporter of the 'funny business'... well, he was, till he died of an ill-timed heart attack while performing one of his comedy routines. I've subsequently been told that many a Joker has 'died' on stage—but none so 'literal' as my poor Uncle Bevan Barr!*

The Potioneer laughs and picks up the stopper from the wagon's floor—mercifully sealing the volatile potion shut and rendering it safe.[728]

Inglebold: "*Ah, Simply* Morgan—what did that old fool have to say about me?"

Me: "He mentioned something about his items not having any hazardous side effects—"

The Potioneer jumps down from his cart like a winter chicken.[729]

Inglebold: "*Ha!* I also bet he forgot to mention that most of *his* items are cursed—?"

I find myself nervously twiddling the *Ring of Water Breathing* on my ring finger.[730]

Me: "Cursed? Are you sure?"

Inglebold: "I've no idea—but who am I to get in the way of a good rumour?"

I silently scold myself for letting the Potioneer's words trouble me so easily.

Inglebold: "Where do you hark from, young Loremaster?"

Me: "Fellmoor."

The Potioneer raises an eyebrow.

Inglebold: "*Ah*, I believe they make a superb Wasp's Milk Wine in

---

[728] *For now...*

[729] *A winter chicken with a pronounced limp, one eyeball larger than the other and a crooked back...*

[730] *My mind is racing, imagining the possible curse hidden within this ring. Maybe it'll turn me into a fish or summon a hungry shark to eat me—I silently send an unpleasant curse of my own in the Wizard's general direction. But then I remember the Potioneer is a business rival—and this could just be an imaginative attempt at tarnishing the Spellcaster's reputation... I hope.*

Fellmoor.[731] You're a long way from home, Loremaster—I hardly think I warrant such an undertaking."

Me: "I'm afraid it's not just you that brings me this far."

Inglebold: "**What?** You mortally wound me, Sir—I want nothing more from you or this conversation—goodbye!"

Startled by the Potioneer's directness, I begin to apologise, only to catch the old man grinning at my obvious discomfort.

Me: "Okay, you *got* me."

The Potioneer lets out a hearty guffaw, wiping a tear of mirth from his eye.

Inglebold: "You have to forgive my twisted sense of humour; it's been a while since I've had a good laugh.[732] The Merchant's Road can be lonely, leading you to some really dark places."

Me: "I take it you don't mean that literally?"

Inglebold: "I'm afraid I do mean it literally. The Merchant's Road *will* eventually lead you to some pretty dark places—especially if you go beyond the Heartenford Falls."

Me: "Why? What lies beyond the Heartenford Falls?"

Inglebold: "Trouble, if you go looking for it—which is quite a difficult thing to do, *Loremaster,* given how dark it is. But something tells me that is precisely what you're looking for, *trouble*—am I right?"

Me: "I go where the story takes me."

---

[731] *This is true—although the taste of Wasp's Milk Wine is an acquired one. It has a distinct after-sting that will stay with you unless you first batter your taste buds with a rolled-up parchment. Also, the task of actually 'milking' a wasp is not an easy one—it's common for a Wasp 'Whisperer' to be repeatedly stung before they've even squirted out a thimble's worth of the stuff.*

[732] *Even now, I can feel Uncle Bevan Barr's comedic spirit joining in with the Potioneer's chortles.*

Inglebold: "And what story would that be, my friend?"

Me: "A story filled with adventurers and adventures. I'm researching heroes and those behind the heroes—people like your good self."[733]

Inglebold: "Researching heroes? Why the interest in those poor souls?"

Me: "My brother left home to become one—"

Inglebold: "*Ah*—and now you feel you must follow in his footsteps?"

Me: "Actually, I'm trying to find my brother and convince him to return home."

Inglebold: "Can I ask your brother's name?"

Me: "Aldon, Aldon Barr—have you heard of him?"

Inglebold: "Can't say I have, but then I only sell potions; I don't usually stick around long enough to swap life stories."

Me: "Isn't interacting with people something you need to do, you know... building a rapport with your customers, so they return with more coin?"

Inglebold: "There are two schools of thought—those who believe in spending the time to really get to know their customers, and then a small minority of one, who believes they don't."

Me: "Let me guess, you're the one."

Inglebold: "In my line of work, being the one is generally seen as a good thing."[734]

---

[733] *Eccentric types who would happily lob a 'Potion of Fireballs' at anyone who looks like trouble...*

[734] *Unless you're the 'one' being sacrificed to appease a bloodthirsty God.*

Me: "Am I also to assume owning a shop isn't a wish of yours either, then?"[735]

Inglebold: "The realm is a large place. Why should I chain myself to one spot when I can visit them all? Besides, deep roots mean you can't pull them out in a hurry when the Snow Wolves are at your door."[736]

Me: "Why would you need to do that?"

Inglebold: "No reason, no reason at all[737]—hold that thought."

The Potioneer walks to the rear of his cart and checks his wares are tightly secured.

Inglebold: "Can never be too careful. There are plenty of Halfling Rogues about who would love to get their grubby little hands on my *Lucky Potions.*"[738]

Me: "I'd have thought Rogues would have preferred a Potion of Lockpicking?"

Inglebold: "Who needs a Potion of Lockpicking when a Lucky Potion will do that *and* much, much more?"

The Potioneer throws back a tarp and rummages deep in a box before suddenly pulling out a potion tied with an orange string.

Me: "It sounds potent—"

Inglebold: "*Potent?* This potion is practically lethal! You give this to a

---

[735] *Wishes come in two forms, either out of a bottle (Inglebold will no doubt have secreted a few of these about his person) or by stealing the tears of a Genie (not an easy task, given that it's the responsibility of the Wish-Seeker to make the Genie cry in the first place). From Halfling butt-burns to Gnomish insults about a lack of legs, there are only a few ways to make a Genie blub like a Wizard in a fistfight. Those who fail to make the Genie's tears flow like the Ascension Falls on a rainy day often find themselves 'wished' away—four miles up in the air without a Flight spell, potion, item, scroll, or magic rug to save them from the effects of gravity...*

[736] *Or members of the Sharks Guild following the smell of blood in the metaphoric water...*

[737] *Even a brain-shy Barbarian would suspect this to be a lie.*

[738] *Rogues really need to rethink their whole hand wash routine.*

Halfling Rogue, and he'll be backstabbing Giants for breakfast.[739] Four towns have already banned anyone from carrying this stuff about their person."

Me: "Isn't that a bit of a problem then? I mean, what good is it if you can't sell it?"

Inglebold: "Who said I couldn't sell it? I just can't be *caught* selling it. This sort of notoriety creates demand—and demand always attracts a large amount of coin. This is liquid gold, and it fetches a princely sum on the Back Market."[740]

The Potioneer walks from the rear of his cart and hands me the *Lucky Potion*.

Inglebold: "Think of it as a gift."

Me: "I couldn't—"

Inglebold: "I insist. Besides, you never know when you'll need an extra bit of good fortune—especially in the dark places you're bound to visit..."

I quickly tuck the bottle into my bag—keen to hide it from any envious Halfling eyes.[741]

Me: "Thank you."

Inglebold: "A pleasure—anything else I can do for you?"

Me: "There *was* something I wanted to ask you about. Have you had much contact with the Heroes Guild on your travels?"

Inglebold: "Some..."

---

[739] And still have room for 'Elevenses'.

[740] So-called because everything on sale is usually sold out the back of a wagon with the horses fed and watered for a speedy escape. Not to be confused with the 'Black Market,' which will sell you anything your heart desires, as long you're okay with it coming in <u>black</u>.

[741] Which are bigger than their two-breakfast stuffed bellies...

Me: "I've heard their demand for heavy discounts from vendors makes it difficult for honest Merchants to earn a coin?"[742]

Inglebold: "They've never asked me for a discount. In fact, when we've done any business, they've always paid whatever price I've given them—haggling with me is pointless."

Me: "Do they buy a lot of potions from you?"

Inglebold: "*Oh,* around three or four hundred bottles each summer— I heard they like to give them away to new heroes in their complimentary *Welcome Baskets.*"

Me: "Do you know what other items they give away in their Welcome Baskets?"

Inglebold: "Just the standard stuff, rations, bedroll, bandages, maybe a novelty Heroes Guild branded quill,[743] even a magic ring with the low-grade curse from that idiot Wizard we both know—and of course a potent potion from yours truly."

Me: "A tidy haul[744]—are there any of your Lucky Potions included in that trove?"

Inglebold: "Are you mad? I don't give them the premium stuff—*oh no,* I usually sell them Minor Healing or Stamina Potions. I have plenty of those lying around collecting dust—it's almost a *pleasure* to get rid of them."

Me: "I can't believe the Heroes Guild don't make any extra demands from you—"

---

[742] *Leaving the not-so-honest ones to make a tidy profit while their backs are turned.*

[743] *When I first heard this, I wondered if they were trying to recruit Loremasters to their cause, but then I remembered the Heroes Guild has a 'love' of asking their recruits to sign contracts. My Grandmother always said to be wary of any deal that includes a free gift of a quill—only now do I finally understand what she meant by this.*

[744] *Although the Welcome Parchment alludes to a slightly more impressive haul of gifts than it actually delivers—including a +2 Sword of Belittlement (that mocks every missed swing or thrust with a sarcastic 'Oooo—so close! Maybe you should try actually 'hitting' it next time!' quip), a Shield of Deflection (that tries to shrug off any incoming blows by changing the subject entirely), a Cloak of Ghosting (that doesn't acknowledge you after you've put it on), and a Helm of Puzzlement (that leaves you wondering where the last attack came from).*

Inglebold: "What are you suggesting they want—sexual favours? I'll have you know my reputation is far better than you give me credit for! No—no extra concessions made or given."

Me: "Forgive me; I didn't mean to offend. You mentioned the Back Market earlier—"

Inglebold: "No, I didn't."

Me: "Yes, you did—"

The Potioneer looks visibly nervous and puts a finger to his lips as his eyes continue to scan the bushes on either side of the Merchant's Road.[745]

Inglebold: "The first rule of the Back Market is—we *never* talk about the Back Market."

Me: "But *you* mentioned it first!"

Inglebold: "Did I? In that case, the second rule of the Back Market is, *always* deny everything if you accidentally mention the Back Market first."

Me: "Dare I ask—if there is a third rule?"

Inglebold: "Yes, *never* eat red snow. It means there's been a fight nearby, and someone is bleeding profusely."[746]

Me: "Before, you referred to heroes as 'poor souls'—was there a reason behind this?"

Inglebold: "Because anyone who is forced to buy my potions to survive a dungeon or two has my deepest sympathies and utmost respect. Chances are they will be attempting a quest that will probably end their lives—my concoctions are a final throw in *The Last Chance* tavern for many."[747]

---

[745] *Ever since my encounter with Bergenn the Ranger, I have a deep mistrust of bushes...*

[746] *Aha—finally, a rule to live by or (if you're the one bleeding profusely) die by!*

[747] *This is the name of an actual tavern near the ShadowLands border. It's run by a perpetually gruff Half-Orc Landlord who always gives his patrons one final chance to pay an outstanding bar tab before taking matters in hand—and breaking someone else's hand as a consequence. Because of the Landlord's direct approach towards late payers, The Last Chance tavern has always been coin-rich since the Half-Orc took over ownership.*

Me: "You make it sound like your potions are a little unstable—"

Inglebold: "Unstable? You've been hanging around that Wizard too long—or that wretched Herbalist."

Me: "What Herbalist?"

Inglebold: "*Zillith.* She owns an unremarkable herbal store in Tronte that sells all manner of *Oh, Natural* remedies to the weak-willed. I wouldn't pay too much attention to her unorthodox ways *or* consume anything she gives you to sample either—if you ever have the foolish notion of visiting her, that is."[748]

Me: "Is she a rival?"

Inglebold: "Of sorts; the Wizard—I can respect, but the Herbalist? I prefer my luck to come from a bottle, not from some dried-up old seed you need to smoke."

Me: "Surely only a few would ever seek out this herbalist—and certainly not enough to threaten your livelihood?"

Inglebold: "You'd be surprised how popular she has become of late. I blame the younger generation of heroes coming through the ranks; they're always looking to be controversial by finding new and exciting ways of gaining an edge to impress their companions. High-Elves seem especially keen on the Herbalist's wares for some strange reason[749]— it's almost as if they're addicted to her plants. I haven't sold a single potion to a High-Elf for at least a summer or two now."

Me: "Why is that?"

Inglebold: "I suppose they can't get what they need from the bottom of a bottle."

Me: "But that's just High-Elves—surely they only make up a small number of your customer base."

Inglebold: "You'd think, but these days everyone wants to copy whatever the stuck-up High-Elves are doing. The only thing worse than

---

[748] *I hadn't—but now my interest is piqued...*

[749] *Why does this not even remotely surprise me?*

a High-Elf is a Bard."[750]

Me: "What's wrong with a Bard?"

Inglebold: "Two words: Horny. Noise. Always bloody warbling an annoying tune or trying to bed something—*anything*. You know how often I've had to turn down a Bard's advances?"

Me: "Excuse me—*what?*"

Inglebold: "Too many times—and usually when they're only fishing for a big discount. But I see through their ridiculously good looks and mesmerising charisma[751]—*bastards*, every single one of them."

Me: "What about High-Elven Bards?"

The Potioneer looks aghast and circles his chest for protection.[752]

Inglebold: "Never mention those fiends in my presence ever again— they're the *worst* of both worlds!"

Me: "Sounds like you've had your fair share of bad luck with a minstrel or two. Maybe you should take one of your own Lucky Potions next time?"

Inglebold: "What? Never! I don't drink any of my own concoctions!"

Me: "Not even when you're brewing them? Surely you need to taste your wares to ensure it will do whatever it's supposed to do?"

Inglebold: "*Ahem!* I _know_ what my potions are supposed to do. I've spent endless summers in my field, understanding the finer arts of home brewing.[753] I don't need to wound myself to test if a Healing potion works the way it's supposed to; I _know_ it works the way it's supposed to, that's good enough for me, and it should be good enough for any damn hero who buys it too—*even* High-Elves, Bards, _and_ High-Elven Bards-*tards!* When I said earlier that anyone drinking my potions

---

[750] *This doesn't surprise me either…*

[751] *Albeit aided by a Charm spell—or should I say 'song'…*

[752] *Which looks more like he's trying to winch his crooked back into shape.*

[753] *From the tell-tale stench on his breath—I do not doubt this.*

had my sympathy, it's because I know my potions offer something a hero doesn't want—but desperately needs."

Me: "What's that exactly?"

Inglebold: "*Salvation in bottle form.* The moment an adventurer breaks that wax seal—a small part of me dies. Do you want to know why? Because both that hero and I know, deep down, they had to seek extra help when everything else had failed them. Whatever it was, their strength, sword, or magic, it couldn't save them—but do you know what could? My potions! Using an elixir of mine is an admission that a quest has gotten the better of you. That's why I pity any hero using my concoctions and why I do what I do. It's the sole reason I keep travelling this realm—so I can help as many adventurers as possible. I don't have the luxury of owning a shop and waiting for them to find me... I have to find them first before it's too late."

Me: "To help as many adventurers as you can?"

Inglebold: "It sounds a whole lot better than me saying that more customers lead to more coin, doesn't it?"[754]

Me: "I guess so, but doesn't it also mean you have to traverse the Merchant's Road more often—isn't that dangerous?"

Inglebold: "Everything in this realm is dangerous, Loremaster—you should know that. You could go to your local tavern and run into a short-tempered Barbarian with an axe to grind.[755] I'm in no more danger on this road than you are walking about town.[756] Besides, I have a surprise or two in my robes if I ever run into trouble."[757]

The Potioneer flashes open his robes and shows off a multitude of potions, all tethered to his body by pieces of coloured string.[758]

---

[754] But it wouldn't be any less true.

[755] Or a Dwarven Barbarian, which could mean running into a short, short-tempered Barbarian...

[756] This depends on the town, obviously.

[757] Hopefully, the old Potioneer is talking about his Potions again...

[758] Phew, it *is* Potions! I've since discovered that Inglebold uses coloured string to help identify each potion in question; However, I've also discovered that Inglebold is, in fact, colour-blind...

Me: "What do they do?"

Inglebold: "*Oh,* all manner of interesting stuff—I've everything from Potions of Stinking Cloud,[759] Speed, Invisibility, to Potions of Healing and Transformation."

Me: "Sounds like you're well-stocked for any eventuality."

Inglebold: "Too right, on the Merchant's Road, you have to be ready for the unexpect—"

'*THUD!*'

A crossbow bolt suddenly protrudes from the side of the cart, cutting the conversation short—the Potioneer shifts on his heels to face the figure riding hard towards us.

Inglebold: "You'd better get out of here."

Me: "Bandits?"

Inglebold: "Worse—it's a *Heartenford Guard.*"

Me: "Surely they're here to *protect* Merchants from marauding bandits?"

Inglebold: "You're joking, aren't you? These guys _are_ the bandits! They take a cut from every Merchant traversing the Merchant's Road. They call it a *Safe Passage Tax,* but it's practically legalised theft. They're Rogues with badges—*quick,* get out of here unless you want to lose coin you can ill afford!"

Me: "What about you?"

Inglebold: "*Oh,* don't worry about me; I have my own way of dealing with them—a Potion of Charisma works like a charm every time."[760]

I duck into a hedge and keep out of sight as the Potioneer digs into his robes and pulls out a green-stringed potion bottle. He quickly cracks

---

[759] *Brewed using a barrel of Buttered Beans, a Blue Goblin with a flatulence problem, a funnel, and a robust airtight bottle.*

[760] *If that's the case, what does the Potioneer's Potion of Charm do then? You know what, I don't think I want to know.*

the seal and downs the contents just as the Heartenford Guard approaches, his crossbow already loaded with a second bolt.

Heartenford Guard: "*You there!* What business do you have on the Merchant's Road?"

Inglebold: "Just the usual, looking to trade with the good people of Hearten*f*—*ooooord.*"

From the bushes, I can see the confused look on the Guard's face as he leans over his mount and peers quizzically down at the agitated Potioneer.

Heartenford Guard: "You *alright*, mate?"

Inglebold: "I'm *ooooooooo*—kay*!*"

The Guard shifts uncomfortably in his saddle as if something ails his backside; his trembling finger moves over the trigger of his crossbow. The Potioneer doubles over in pain as his body starts to undulate beneath his robes at an alarming rate.[761]

Heartenford Guard: "What's up with you?"

Inglebold: "N—*ooooooothing! Oh, blast!* I've taken the wr—*ooooooong* ruddy thing!"

The Potioneer writhes on the ground, bellowing with rage.

Inglebold: **"GET O—OOOOOOOOOOOOOOOUT OF HERE!! RUUUUN!!!"**

I watch in horror as Inglebold transforms into an unspeakable monstrosity with bulbous muscles, hungry spider eyes, black tentacle limbs, and needle-like teeth.[762] The Heartenford Guard manages to loosen a second bolt that misses the abominable Potioneer by a mile.[763] The transformed Merchant roars in defiance before leaping at the Guard, knocking him clean off his mount. I bolt from my hiding spot and run without daring to look back at the carnage left in my wake—

---

[761] *This can't be good...*

[762] *I do hate it when I'm right!*

[763] *Making any Goblin and Halfling Archers reading this feel a <u>whole</u> lot better about themselves.*

the sound of a screaming horse and ripping flesh[764] is more than enough to spur on my expeditious retreat.[765]

---

[764] *For any concerned readers out there, no horses were harmed in the making of this interview—the same can't be said for the luckless Guard, however.*

[765] *Who says that you need a potion to run away at great speed? All you really need is the threat of death at the hands (or tentacles/claws/teeth—delete as appropriate) of a monstrous abomination. Although, all this unscheduled exercise is not helping my hangover!*

24. Pilstone, the Guild of Heroes Guildmaster

Behind The Giggling Gnome tavern, in the busy harbour town of Port Ardor, is an outhouse that could uncomfortably fit four Halfling Clerics or one heavily encumbered Human one. So, imagine my surprise when I discover this inconspicuous privy is also the not-so-secret address for a brand new Guild—the Guild of Heroes. I've come to visit the Guildmaster of this newly created association to see how he's faring in the wake of a realm gripped by a Quest Drought—yet filled with heroes desperate to make a name for themselves.

I knock on the privy door and wait for a reply. There's a **'BANG!'** as the red *'occupied'* sign slides open, and a pair of eyes glare intently at me from around groin height—I bend down to greet the scowling eyeballs.

Me: "Hello?"

Glaring Eyes: "Password?"

Me: "*Erm*—I haven't got one."

Glaring Eyes: "What is it you want? Are you a Wizard?"

Me: "*Ah*, no—I'm not... a Wizard. I'm here to meet Pilstone, the *Guildmaster?* I'm Elburn, the *Loremaster*—"

The eye slat slams shut, and I'm left staring blankly at the red *'occupied'* sign once more. I'm now wondering if I've unwittingly stumbled upon the secret entrance to the missing Thieves Guild instead. As I turn to leave, I hear the sound of a bolt sliding free from the lock. The outhouse door creaks open, and a smiling Halfling dressed in scale mail greets me warmly.[766]

Me: "*Erm*, Pilstone?"

Pilstone: "At your service! You must forgive the clandestine nature of our meeting, but it pays never to assume the best in people when it comes to the matter of adventuring or adventurers."

---

[766] *Remembering Inglebold's warning about Halflings and Lucky Potions, I find myself keeping a slightly tighter grip on my bag than usual.*

Me: "Really? I thought adventurers were trustworthy if nothing else."[767]

Pilstone: "*Oh*—I'm sure most adventurers you'll meet are just that. But a few, the darker ones,[768] are wolves in heroic clothing, hunting for their next easy meal."

Me: "What do they want, these dark ones?"

Pilstone: "The usual—power, riches, fame…"[769]

Me: "Isn't that what every adventurer wants?"

The Guildmaster holds my gaze before turning away.

Pilstone: "Can I offer you a beverage? Some tea?"

Me: "That would be most welcomed—thanks."[770]

The Halfling heads deeper into the privy—his discombobulated voice echoes through the darkness.

Pilstone: "It's a privy, Loremaster, not some monster-filled dungeon. Come in before you let all the freshened air out."

Feeling a little foolish, I hurry inside and close the privy door behind me before the potent scent of rose water makes a break for freedom. I immediately find myself descending downwards; arriving at what proves an unfathomable maze of wooden corridors connected in such a haphazard way it's almost impossible to gather my bearings.[771] I feel uncomfortable, as if unseen eyes are watching my every move from the shadows. I try my best to head in the direction of the Guildmaster's footsteps, following the echoes until the passage opens into a small

---

[767] *Although, I'm starting to have serious misgivings that this may not 'actually' be the case…*

[768] *I'm assuming the Halfling here means Dark Elves or Necromancers (or possibly a combination of the two), but I have met a whole ensemble of candidates who could easily fit the bill—including a swear-fuelled Paladin, a kleptomaniacal Sorceress, a talking skull, a sadistic Dungeonmaster, and a Druid with a serious cheese addiction.*

[769] *Or if you're a Necromancer, dead bodies…*

[770] *Although not too hot please!*

[771] *I pity the poor soul who is caught short and has to use this place in an emergency.*

white porcelain-tiled alcove where I find the Halfling lifting a hot kettle from a stove.

Me: "This place is quite disorientating—how long has your Guild been here?"

Pilstone: "About a month. We rent it from the new owner of *The Giggling Gnome*—except on Thursdays when the *Midnight Singers of Perpetuity* use it."[772]

Me: "Isn't that a bit awkward? Where do you go on Thursdays?"

Pilstone: "It's our day off from Guildly duties, so we generally enjoy a quiet drink in the tavern before heading home."

Me: "Hold on—Perpetuity? I've heard that name before. Are they anything to do with the *Sisters of Perpetuity?*"

Pilstone: "Yes! The *Midnight Singers of Perpetuity* is a splinter order who believe they can heal with the power of their song."

Me: "Does it work?"

Pilstone: "To be honest, all they seem to do is make my ears bleed—so make of that what you will."

Me: "Can I ask how many members are in your Guild?"

The Halfling pours milk into the tea and hands the cup to me before taking a seat.[773]

Me: "Thanks."

Pilstone: "We've only been running for a summer, so our active member list is still quite low. Now, let me see... there's Tarquinn

---

[772] *The Giggling Gnome is now run by a pleasant Landlady who is neither gruff nor cantankerous to her patrons; this often confuses heroic visitors, who expect to be growled at for bothering the tavern's patrons as they search for any scraps of adventuring information. Not to be confused with The Giggling Giant tavern, where the Landlord is noticeably flatter and less tolerant...*

[773] *It's brewed to perfection and hasn't had any Wasp's Milk added, thankfully—as I can't detect the familiar bitter after-sting in the taste.*

Vinelord, Wildthorpe Sten, Juliannal Fox, and Othollrad the Unready."[774]

Me: "Only five of you?"

Pilstone: "Permanent members—yes?"

Me: "Permanent?"

Pilstone: "We also offer a *Pay-as-you-slay* membership too."[775]

Me: "*Pay-as-you-slay?* How does that work?"

Pilstone: "You only pay the Guild fees when you complete an adventure—if you don't, then there's nothing owed to us."

Me: "That sounds... actually quite clever..."

Pilstone: "*Really?* I mean, yes—yes, it does."

Me: "So, how many adventurers do you have using your *Pay-as-you-slay* rate?"

Pilstone: "Currently?"

The Guildmaster mulls the question over several times before answering.[776]

Pilstone: "*None*—but that doesn't mean there won't be any in the near future!"[777]

Me: "A Guild like this survives on completing quests—how many adventures have you and your members successfully completed since you opened your door?"[778]

---

[774] So-called because every time Othollrad looked like he was about to venture out on a quest, he would suddenly turn around and hurry back to use the privy one last time. If I'm being perfectly honest, if I were in that adventuring party, I think I would have gone ahead without him and hoped he caught up.

[775] This is quite catchy—Pilstone would be wise to hire the Heralds and use their Arcane Copyright magic to deter others from using it.

[776] Obviously, crunching through some fairly big numbers here.

[777] Oh, my mistake...

[778] Hopefully, with a courtesy flush beforehand or an air-freshening spray spell cast...

The Guildmaster shifts uncomfortably in his seat.

Pilstone: "We've—*ah*, not actually *been* on a quest yet—"

Me: "Not been?"

Pilstone: "You see, none of us can agree on what adventure we should attempt."

Me: "Why not?"

Pilstone: "It's complicated to explain."

Me: "Can you try?"

The Halfling sighs as he puts his tea aside and leans back in his seat; he presses his hands together, almost as if readying himself for prayer.

Pilstone: "We are waiting for the right sort of quest."

Me: "Is there such a thing? How can you know if it's the right adventure unless you *actually* go on one first? Why don't you ease yourself in and attempt a low-level dungeon adventure to test the water?"[779]

Pilstone: "We can't *go* on a dungeon adventure—"

Me: "*What*—why?"

Pilstone: "Tarquinn the Paladin is claustrophobic. He hates the idea of anything set inside.[780] He doesn't even like turning up to our weekly meetings!"

Me: "How do you ever talk to him then?"

Pilstone: "We have an *arrangement*."

Me: "What sort of *arrangement?*"

---

[779] *...without disturbing it—for some strange reason, Halflings have an uncontrollable urge to throw large rocks at any still body of water they encounter purely to disturb anything hiding in its depths. More often than not, their projectiles make a satisfying 'SPLOSH'. Still, on the odd occasion, they'll disturb something in the watery abyss, something that 'had' been quietly watching from afar, something with giant tentacles, sharp teeth, and, coincidentally, a sore head.*

[780] *Which is why Tarquinn is the only Paladin in existence who does not wear any form of plate armour either...*

Pilstone: "We leave notes for one another in a turnip field outside Wendle."

Me: "Why a turnip field?"

Pilstone: "He's partial to the stuff—especially roasted ones."

That slightly disconcerting sensation travels the length of my spine—I can't shake the feeling that someone or *something* is watching our conversation from the shadows—I look around but notice nothing out of the ordinary.

Me: "*Okaaay,* so the countryside appears to be the obvious solution, with nice wide-open spaces outside—"

The Halfling shakes his head in disagreement.

Pilstone: "It wouldn't work. We also have an agoraphobic in the group, Wildthorpe the Ranger—he's scared of being outside."[781]

Me: "*Ah,* which makes it difficult for Wildthorpe and Tarquinn to agree on what quest they should undertake together."

Pilstone: "Precisely."

Me: "What about your other permanent members?"

Pilstone: "Well, Juliannal is a Barbarian who hates any form of conflict."[782]

Me: "Not exactly helpful when you're on a bloody adventure."

The Halfling glares at me reproachfully.

Pilstone: "There's no need to use <u>that</u> kind of language!"

Me: "No—I mean, never mind... what about Othollard?"

---

[781] And bushes, apparently—which is a fundamental flaw for any Ranger to have. Bergenn's leaves would shake in disbelief upon hearing this.

[782] The Barbarian doesn't really lose her temper; she just gets a little melancholy for a while as she swallows her burning rage. This is not a good thing and can only lead to a huge explosive outburst at some point in the near future—she's the walking equivalent of a 'delayed' Fireball spell, just waiting for a good excuse to punch something hard in the face when least expected.

Pilstone: "Othollard the Cleric? He is afraid of wounds. He'd faint at the first sign of a nose bleed."

Me: "That sounds like a critical issue to have as the group's healer. Couldn't you find another Cleric to join you instead?"

Pilstone: "Wouldn't make much difference. You'd be surprised how common it is for Clerics to be scared of *body sauce.* I've yet to meet one who doesn't have a debilitating fear of the stuff."

Me: "Body sauce? That's not a term I've heard used before."[783]

Pilstone: "Unavoidable really, Othollard *also* fears the word *blood.*"

Me: "It sounds like you have quite the collection of heroic misfits within your ranks."

Pilstone: "Now you can see why we've never *actually* managed to adventure together as of yet."

Me: "Yes—but then why don't you all agree to adventure on your own? You know, do some solo questing?"

The Halfling almost chokes as he takes in a mouthful of tea.[784]

Pilstone: "You're kidding, aren't you? We wouldn't last a minute out in the realm on our own. No, we need to wait for the right group of adventurers to turn up. Safety in numbers—you know, like a school of fish or flock of birds."[785]

Me: "Forgive me for saying, but it seems like your current crop of members is doing more harm than good to your Guild."

Pilstone: "They are—but I can't get rid of the only income this Guild has! It would spell the end of the Guild of Heroes; this is all I have in my life now."

Me: "Why? What do you mean all?"

Pilstone: "I've put everything I have into it."

---

[783] *Or ever want to hear again.*

[784] *See how dangerous tea drinking can be?!*

[785] *Also known as the infamous 'I hope someone else here gets eaten instead of me' defence.*

Me: "*Everything?*"

Pilstone: "**Everything**—I sold my home and all my valuables to pay for this."

Me: "You did WHAT?! So you now live—"

Pilstone: "—here, except, of course, on Thursdays, when I have to vacate it for—"

Me: "—the *Midnight Singers of Perpetuity.* Yes, I remember you mentioning them. So, where do you sleep on a Thursday night? You said you went home—but you've just said you sold your home."

Pilstone: "Home is where the heart is.[786] The Landlady of *The Giggling Gnome* kindly allows me to stay in the stables when the weather is inclement."[787]

Me: "If it's not?"

Pilstone: "Then the realm is my bedroll—I can sleep anywhere I like! It's only for one night. I'm sure when a few more members join our ranks, our coffers will be filled with coins—then I'll be able to buy back my home."

Me: "So, how much does it cost to be a permanent member of your Guild?"

Pilstone: "About a gold coin a summer—I believe that's a pretty attractive rate if I say so myself."

Me: "And how much does it cost to rent this place?"

The Guildmaster sucks in his cheeks.

Pilstone: "Around eight gold coins a summer..."

Me: "So, you're not actually—"

Pilstone: "—making any coin. I know..."

---

[786] *Actually, home is where a comfortable bed is.*

[787] *I suspect this arrangement is mildly irritating to the Paladin's haughty steed if it happens to share the stables with the Halfling on the same night.*

Me: "How can you hope to survive?"

Pilstone: "With luck,[788] it's all about taking small steps[789]—*and* a rather large loan I took from the Sharks Guild—"

Me: "The Sharks Guild? Isn't that risky? Doesn't the Sharks Guild have an unpleasant reputation of literally biting chunks out of any debtors who miss a payment?"

The Halfling pats his stomach and laughs.

Pilstone: "I always thought I could do with losing some encumbrance. But seriously, I'm not too concerned. That's all just word of mouth designed to scare debtors into paying up—I'm sure it won't come to that."[790]

Me: "So, when do you have to repay their coin by?"

Pilstone: "I've no idea—but they seemed like reasonable people. It's not as if they'll leave me unable to walk without the aid of a Levitation spell if I miss a payment or anything. I'm sure Shytlock will understand—"

Me: *"Shytlock?"*

The Halfling pulls out a hip flask and adds a large drop of what I hope isn't Dragon's-gin to warm his beverage.

Pilstone: "He's a Rogue, but not the type who likes to skulk in the shadows and backstab you when your back is turned—no, that seems a little beneath him if I'm being honest; Shytlock isn't like that. He has always taken a healthy interest in our Guild, popping in unannounced to see how we're doing and how our finances look. He never seems upset about our losses, quite the opposite—which is surprising for

---

[788] *As much as I feel for the Halfling's situation, I'm not sure even one of Inglebold's Lucky Potions would be enough to solve this coin-losing conundrum.*

[789] *I cannot help but look at Pilstone's feet.*

[790] *Even with the Guildmaster's spirited bravado, I sense a lack of belief in the Halfling's tone.*

someone supposedly in charge of the Sharks Guild."[791]

Me: "Surprising indeed—can I ask you about your Guild's name?"

The Guildmaster grumbles defensively.

Pilstone: "What about it?"

Me: "How have the Heroes Guild reacted to your newly formed Guild of Heroes? Have they taken umbrage at the clever rehashing of their name?"

Pilstone: "Not as far as I know; we checked it with the Heralds Guild when we first came up with it. They approved the use without fear of complaint or reprisal from the Heroes Guild—for their customary fee, of course."

Me: "How much did they charge you for the privilege?"

Pilstone: "Around fifty gold coins for all the parchments to be notarised."[792]

Me: "*Fifty* gold coins? Please tell me you didn't go back to the Sharks Guild to pay for that?"

Pilstone: "Shytlock was more than happy to loan us the extra coin we needed, no questions asked—in fact, he insisted we take it with his blessing."[793]

Me: "That was... *kind* of him..."

Pilstone: "Wasn't it just!"

Me: "Why did you pay the Heralds Guild for the Arcane Copyright spell? Why not just come up with a completely different name for free?"

---

[791] *Alarm bells are ringing loudly inside my head, not unlike the same sound that rang out over Castle Verdale. I'm expecting a blind Monk to appear any minute now and rudely dropkick the Halfling into the privy's trapdoor, only to be dragged to the stinking depths by a hungry Turd Lurker as a consequence.*

[792] *'Notarised' is a Gnomish word meaning 'Make sure you make a bloody note of it—or you'll only end up asking me about it later'.*

[793] *I bet he did!*

Pilstone: "Because I understand the *true* value of a good name. The Guild of Heroes will be on the lips of every hero by next summer[794]— you mark my words, our coffers will finally be overflowing by then!"

Me: "How do you plan to achieve that?"

Pilstone: "Though an aggressive recruitment drive!"

Me: "Recruitment drive?"[795]

Pilstone: "I paid for a small number of Barkers to go from town-to-town broadcasting our need for fresh adventurers."[796]

Me: "Let me guess, Shytlock agreed to cover this for you too?"

Pilstone: "He was most insistent."

Me: "I'm starting to see a pattern forming."[797]

Pilstone: "He also paid for ten thousand call-to-join parchments to be produced too—here, look…"

The Halfling hands me one of the sheets of parchment to read. True enough, the core message appears to be a call-to-join—but I spot one glaring error.

Me: "How do you think the Heroes Guild will react to this parchment?"

Pilstone: "They won't be pleased, I know that—but they have to understand they aren't the only Guild on the lookout for new heroes now."

---

[794] Hopefully not said in passing as a bad joke.

[795] So-called, after the Lord of Barrow's Keep, who had to spend a whole season driving a carriage across his sizeable domain to muster his army—only to discover that he had driven into a neighbouring territory and had mistakenly raised an army that, ironically, invaded *his* kingdom instead.

[796] Unfortunately, as anyone who has used a Barker before knows, the original message is seldom delivered correctly. After some painstaking research, I subsequently discovered that the *final* message from the Guildmaster had morphed from 'Fresh Adventurers' into 'Flesh Dentures'—which had the small but dedicated group of Toothsmiths running for the hills in fright as a result.

[797] A bloody pattern, made from the Halfling's own body sauce…

Me: "I mean, how will they react when they discover you've been promoting their Guild rather than your own?"

The Guildmaster's eyes widen in alarm. Maybe life on the road has sent me mad, but I swear I hear a stifled chuckle from the unseen shadows nearby.

Pilstone: "*What?* What are you talking about?"

Me: "You've written the name of the Heroes Guild at the bottom of this parchment, not the Guild of Heroes—"

Pilstone: "**Where?!**"

The Halfling snatches the parchment sheet from my hand and feverishly reads the sign-off at the bottom. His rosy cheeks rapidly drain of colour.

Pilstone: "That... *bastard!*"

Me: "Who?"

Pilstone: "The Calligrapher! That <u>bastard</u> did it on purpose!"[798]

Me: "Did what on purpose?"

Pilstone: "**HE BLOODY CHANGED OUR GUILD'S NAME TO THEIR GUILD'S NAME! WHAT DO YOU THINK!?**"

Me: "Why would he do that?"

The Halfling frantically checks through the large stack of parchments set to one side, each printed with the exact same error.

Pilstone: "**NO! NO! NO! HE KNEW WHAT HE WAS DOING! THE BLOODY HEROES GUILD GOT TO HIM! THEY MADE HIM CHANGE IT—**"

Me: "Can you go back and get them to amend it for free—I mean, it *was* the Calligrapher's error in the first place?"

---

[798] *As any Loremaster worth their salt will tell you, 'Calligrapher' is a Gnomish word meaning 'great at lettering, but terrible at spelling'.*

Pilstone: "I can't! I signed this off in front of him—I swear it definitely said *Guild of Heroes* at the bottom, unless...."

Me: "Unless?"

The Halfling snaps his fingers together in sudden realisation and sits back in his seat with disbelief.

Pilstone: "That *damn* Wizard!"

Me: "Wizard?"

Pilstone: "I remember the Calligrapher telling me he had just purchased a magical quill from him—he was so proud of it, even let me use it to sign off on the work. It must have been cursed—that's the only explanation that makes any sense!"

Me: "A cursed magical quill? Cursed to do what? Change the words on your parchment?"

The Halfling sits forward in his seat and points at me feverishly.

Pilstone: ***"EXACTLY"***

Me: "Seems a little unlikely."[799]

Pilstone: "Unlikely but not impossible."

Me: "But that still leaves the question—what are you going to do about it?"

Pilstone "What *can* I do? I spent the last of my coin on these *useless* parchments for the wrong Guild—I've got no choice but to go back to the Sharks Guild and ask for more coin so I can get new ones made."[800]

Me: "That doesn't sound like the greatest of ideas."

---

[799] *I know Morgan has a reputation for creating 'cursed' magical items, but a 'cursed' Quill of Signing seems a little unbelievable, even for him.*

[800] *Perhaps ask for a different quill next time, though.*

Pilstone: "Well, if you have any other suggestion—I'm all ears.[801] Say, maybe there *is* something you could help me with—do you have any heroic friends you could persuade to join our cause?"

Me: "Well, I *do* have an older brother—"

Pilstone: "*Really?* What's his name?"

Me: "Aldon—Aldon Barr?"

Pilstone: "Is he an adventurer?"

Me: "Far as I know."

The Guildmaster suddenly brightens.

Pilstone: "You think you can convince him to join us?"

Me: "I wish I could, but I haven't seen him now for ten summers."

Pilstone: "*Ah,* dammit..."

The hope from the Halfling's face crumbles to dust once more.

Me: "But if I do find him, I'll be sure to ask."[802]

Pilstone: "At least that's something... I appreciate it—"

There's a sudden chill in the air as I swear I can hear a menacing melody whispered from the shadows, *dur-da... duuur-daaa... du-du-du-du...*

Unseen Voice: "Well, well, well, Pilstone—I didn't know you were receiving guests. Who is this? A new Wizard you've finally managed to lure through your privy door?"

---

[801] *A saying that sprung up after the discovery of a creature called an 'Eavesdropper', which is made up solely of stolen ears. This dreaded monstrosity hangs from the rafters, listening out for victims before jumping onto them, stealing their ears, and reattaching them to its own body shortly afterwards. Victims are left discombobulated and unable to wear a Gnomish seeing-device without them first falling onto the floor.*

[802] *In the event of an unlikely reunion, this may not be the first thing I ask my brother; it also may not even be the hundredth-and-first thing I ask him either—but I don't think I'll let the Halfling Guildmaster know that.*

From the darkness, a Gnomish figure appears, his sharp eyes twinkling in the dim light; the hood of his cloak rises upwards ominously, forming a narrow point above his head—much like a mountain peak or fin.[803] He wears a grin that is nothing more than a mask concealing his true intentions. The ominous figure pulls down his hood to reveal a mop of dirty blond hair and a badly pockmarked face. He throws his robe dramatically wide as my eyes are immediately drawn to the unmistakable glint of daggers strapped to his chest. Everything about this Gnome screams *trouble*."[804]

Pilstone: "*Shytlock!* I—I wasn't expecting you today—"

Shytlock: "That's because you *never* expect me on *any* day."

Pilstone: "*Ha,* very true…"

The Rogue's eyes are unblinking as they remain fixed on me.

Shytlock: "You seem to have me at a disadvantage…"

The Gnome invites me to finish the sentence for him.

Me: "Elburn, Elburn Barr—I'm a Loremaster."

Shytlock: "And what would a *Loremaster* want with the Heroes Guild?"

The Halfling coughs.

Pilstone: "The Guild of *Heroes*."

The Rogue snarls in the Halfling's direction.

Shytlock: "My mistake—the Guild of… *Heroes*…"[805]

My senses are screaming at me to leave, but I know the Gnome could probably cut me down before I made it to the first wash basin.

Me: "I'm here to interview the Guildmaster."

Shytlock: "Do I look like a fool to you?"

---

[803] A <u>shark</u> fin, to be precise…

[804] Which, coincidentally, is also the Gnomish word for 'an untrustworthy Rogue with lots of sharp daggers'.

[805] I can't miss the thick dollop of sarcasm dropped into this sentence.

Me: "*Erm...* no?"[806]

Shytlock: "Then why are you speaking to me like one?"

Me: "I—I didn't think I was—"

Shytlock: "So, I'm also mistaken as well as a fool, am I?"

I find myself laughing out of nervousness[807]—the Rogue rounds on me, his eyes wild with frenzy.

Shytlock: "What's so funny? Do you find me funny? Do I *amuse* you—like a clown?"[808]

Me: "*Erm... I... I...*"

Pilstone: "Shytlock? *Relax*—he's here to put the Guild of Heroes on this realm's map! This could be the making of us. More adventurers will flock through our doors once the people start reading about the Guild of Heroes. We'll be able to repay the coin we owe you in full—"

The Gnome turns on the Halfling—somehow managing to lean over him with a certain amount of intimidation to boot.[809]

Shytlock: "Relax? **Relax?!** This is **my** business we're talking about—not some Dwarf you met locally and toss about for fun!"[810]

Seizing the opportunity, I quickly pull out the *Lucky Potion* from my bag and quietly crack the seal. Neither Shytlock nor Pilstone has noticed my covert actions.

Pilstone: "There's no need to be like that—I told you would I pay your investment back in full—"

---

[806] *I've a coin-flip's chance of getting this right—or wrong...*

[807] *As Uncle Bevan Barr always said, there's a time to laugh and a time to run like your life depended upon it—which, for my Uncle, was usually after a misplaced racial joke about a group of less-than-impressed Dwarves 'to' a group of less-than-impressed Dwarves.*

[808] *Clowns scare me... Mime Artists on the other hand—they are hilarious!*

[809] *And the literal threat of a well-aimed 'boot' too...*

[810] *It's worth pointing out that Dwarves have a love/hate relationship with 'tossing'. Your average Dwarf hates being tossed or hates anyone asking to toss them, while everyone else absolutely <u>loves</u> seeing a Dwarf tossed—either with or without their consent.*

349

Shytlock: "If I wanted my coin back, I wouldn't have given it to you in the first place! I don't want my coin—I want everything else you have!"

I take a tiny swig of the potion, just enough to see me safe.[811]

Me: "Can I ask why you are so invested in the Guild of Heroes? It's not as if this place looks likely to make any substantial coin—"

Pilstone: "—*Hey!*"

Me: "—and the Guildmaster has already sold everything he owned to afford this place."

The Gnome switches his attention away from the Halfling, back to me.

Shytlock: "Who do you think I am? Some mug that enjoys sharing my plan with strangers?[812] You might be a Loremaster, *Loremaster,* but you're not getting another word on the matter from me—"

Unseen harmonious voice: "*Ahem!?*"

Shytlock, Pilstone, and I turn as one as this new mystery voice joins our conversation. From the shadows of the privy corridor, an older woman steps out into the dim light. She wears a simple white robe with the phases of a golden moon embodied along the hem. The woman's impressively stern gaze puts Shytlock's own glare to shame. Pilstone seems to be edging further away from this confrontation for some curious reason—making me feel compelled to do the same.

Shytlock: "Who are you?"

Older woman: "I am Sister Tabital—"

Pilstone: "*Erm...* Shytlock—?"

Shytlock: "Shut it, Pilstone—well, *Sister* Tabital, you're in the wrong privy—you want the one across the yard, the one that says '*Mind Your Own Business*'—"[813]

---

[811] *Remembering the Potioneer's words, I'm wary of ingesting too much and becoming the ruler of some long-lost forgotten kingdom.*

[812] *'Mug' is a Gnomish word meaning 'Gargantuan nostrils'...*

[813] *This would actually be quite punny for a privy sign; I should make a note of this one and register it with the Heralds Guild later—if there is a 'later', that is.*

Sister Tabital: "I assure you, _I_ am in the right place. It is _you_ who is not welcome here."

The Sharks Guild leader stands nose-to-hairy chin with the Sister. There's an uneasy standoff between the pair—broken only by the strange feeling that we are _all_ being watched.

Shytlock: "You don't know _who_ you're messing with, _Sister_—"

There's the briefest of pauses before the Sister replies.

Sister Tabital: "I think you'll find it's _you_ who does not understand with whom you are messing..."

More movement in the shadows as an entire ensemble of singers now stands behind their Sister—each holding a different musical weapon menacingly[814] as if they are about to launch an attack on a less than appreciative audience.[815]

The Gnome blinks several times and sizes up the overabundance of Sisters looming in front of him—their eyes fixed on the Rogue's every movement. For the first time this evening, I notice a crack of uncertainty in Shytlock's demeanour.

Shytlock: "I—_erm,_ yes, well—I have places to be. I'll be back to resume our conversation another time, Pilstone."

The Rogue snarls with contempt.

Shytlock: "_Loremaster... Sisters..._ I'll see myself out."

Without another word, the Gnome storms out of the privy, his fin firmly tucked between his legs.[816]

Pilstone: "Sister Tabital! What are you doing here?"

---

[814] _There's even a Sister here holding what appears to be a small metal triangle—I hate to think what she could do with __that__ implement if called into action._

[815] _I've been warned the Sisters have an extremely low tolerance for noisy eaters or talkative spectators who continually chatter through one of their performances._

[816] _The privy corridor has a low ceiling—Shytlock would only end up ruining his fin-hat in his hastiness to leave if he kept it on._

Sister Tabital: "What do you think we're doing here, Guildmaster? You know we have an *arrangement* with *The Giggling Gnome* to have this privy every Thursday—"

Pilstone: "B—But forgive me, Sister, it's only Wednesday..."

The Sister looks confused.

Sister Tabital: "Wednesday? *Really?*"

She turns to me for confirmation of this fact.

Me: "I'm afraid he's right."

Sister Tabital: "*Oh well,* my mistake. See you tomorrow, Guildmaster. I trust you'll ensure you've given the privy a good clean before we arrive—I do hate finding a mess."[817]

The Halfling nods in agreement.

Pilstone: "Of course—I'll see to it personally."

Sister Tabital: "Until then, we shall bid you farewell. Goodbye, Guildmaster..."

Me: "*Sister...* and thank you..."

She stops and turns back to regard me with her cold grey eyes.

Sister Tabital: "For what?"

Me: "For turning up on the wrong day when you did."

The Sister stares impassively in return.

Sister Tabital: "Our *bad luck*, it seems."

Me: "But *good luck* for us."

Sister Tabital: "Indeed it was. Farewell, *Loremaster*—I do hope your path continues to be safe."

---

[817] *As does everyone—although some will try to blame it on a particularly stubborn Turd Lurker...*

352

I watch Sister Tabital disappear into the privy corridor's darkness with the rest of her musical troupe. There's a smacking sound as if a pair of tight-fitting breeches have just been stretched around the waist of a heavily encumbered Cleric. I look over my shoulder and see the Guildmaster trying to squeeze himself into a heavy leather gown, complete with gloves, boots and a full leather mask with a breathing tube attached to it.

Me: "What are you doing?"

Pilstone: "Duty calls, I'm afraid—Loremaster. I have a particularly stubborn Turd Lurker to deal with before I leave."[818]

Me: "Good luck."

Pilstone: "Thanks, but I don't need luck—I need a hero or two..."[819]

The Guild Master sets down the passage in the opposite direction, leaving me to find my way out alone...[820] alone... except for the same unshakeable sensation nagging me since I first set foot in this privy— that my movements are somehow *still* being watched.[821]

---

[818] *I KNEW it!*

[819] *With deep pockets and plenty of spare loot to share.*

[820] *I really hope the effects of my Lucky Potion don't run out before I've managed to find the exit...*

[821] *And I don't mean bowel movements!*

25. Shana, the Battle Dancer

I find myself in the humble surroundings of Shady Pastures, a small homestead complete with rolling green hills and picturesque meadows in the distance where wild horses frolic freely. It's also home to The Heroes Hall of Legends, a residence famed for adventurers who have long since hung up their battleaxes and locked their spellbooks away for good—until they embark on their last great adventure.[822]

The Heroes Hall of Legends is where some ex-adventurers hope their heroic path will one day lead them to, my own parents included. So, as I approach the large terracotta building standing proudly amongst an outcrop of smaller terracotta hovels and abodes, I feel like I'm on something of a family scouting quest, as well as pursuing my own agenda. I stroll past meticulously maintained flowerbeds, and thoughtfully placed ornaments, including a detailed collection of life-sized garden Gnomes, dotted around the immaculately cut lawn.[823] A Sister of Perpetuity leads me towards an elderly woman dressed in battle leathers; she's sat in a summer chair admiring the distant view beyond the grounds, blissfully unaware of my presence as she hums peacefully to herself.

Sister of Perpetuity: "Shana is our newest resident at *The Heroes Hall of Legends.*"

Me: "How long has she been here?"

Sister of Perpetuity: "Only a few days—she appeared on our doorstep one evening with a note which had her name poorly scrawled on it; I assumed the Heroes Guild dropped her off."

Me: "*Erm...* I guess that was kind of them."

Sister of Perpetuity: "They always look after their members, even when they're at the end of their usefulness."

---

[822] *For most Humans, this would be towards the Great Beyond; for Elves, this would be the Great Behind; for Dwarves, this would be the Great Beard Halls; for Half-Orcs, this would be the Great Belch; for Gnomes and Halflings, this would be the Great Barrier (that somehow needs to be climbed over, or tunnelled under before access to Nirvana is granted—and they thought death was the end of their problems).*

[823] *Peculiarly, each Gnome statue has a surprised look chiselled upon its face for some unfathomable reason.*

Me: "That makes them sound more of a burden than a benefit."

Sister of Perpetuity: "Believe me, some *are* more of a burden than they realise. But they all need caring for just the same."

As we walk through the garden and pass several more shocked-looking garden Gnomes, the Sister gently puts her hand on my arm.

Sister of Perpetuity: "I should warn you, like many of those who reside here, Shana is prone to bouts of irrational fantasy and delusional behaviour. But pay it little heed—sadly it's common for heroes who are past their prime to recall some of their more *traumatic* adventuring experiences again and again... and Shana is no exception—she certainly likes to keep us on our toes!"

Me: "What do you mean?"

Sister of Perpetuity: "She's convinced we're trying to hurt her."

Me: "Why would she think that?"

Sister of Perpetuity: "Shana struggles to tell the difference between what is real and what is still locked in her mind. Like a lot of our residents, Shana continues to be haunted by whatever monsters she encountered in the wilds."

Me: "That must be a dreadful thing for her to experience, and for you to witness first-hand."

Sister of Perpetuity: "It is—although some carry more scars than others.[824] I'll leave you two to get acquainted. Just call if you need my assistance."

Me: "Thank you—I will."

I watch the Sister depart before approaching the elderly Battle Dancer and taking a seat; she seems oblivious to my presence, still fixated on the horizon as she lovingly strokes something small and silver in the palm of her hand—a Heroes Guild badge.

Me: "Excuse me, *Shana?*"

---

[824] *Such as old Barbarians who have spent their entire life punishing their bodies on an hourly basis, while elderly Clerics still have skin as smooth as the day they were born.*

I wait patiently for my voice to register with the Battle Dancer.

Shana: "It never gets old…"[825]

I take a seat next to her and try to follow her fixed attention.

Me: "What doesn't?"

Shana: "The world… the one beyond these walls… it's always full of promise—of *adventure*."[826]

She turns towards me, smiling sweetly.

Shana: "You look like someone who is searching for something."

Me: "How can you tell?"[827]

Shana: "It's there, behind the eyes—it's that annoying itch you can't quite reach.[828] Have you found whatever it is you are looking for?"

Me: "Not yet—I'm still searching."

The Battle Dancer laughs.

Shana: "I like you—you're funny."[829]

Me: "Thank you, I'll take that as a compliment."

Her eyes suddenly narrow as her voice lowers to a whisper.

Shana: "Not like those Sisters—I don't like them."

---

[825] Unlike the Elf—so much for buying into the myth that they're 'supposedly' immortal.

[826] *And* death—why do you think they sometimes refer to it as a 'breath-taking' view.

[827] Unlike many in the realm, I've never once believed the myth that Elves are able to read minds.

[828] In case you were wondering, if you <u>do</u> have an annoying itch, you can employ the services of a 'Backscratcher', a stick-carrying Halfling, hired to get to those frustratingly hard-to-reach places.

[829] Uncle Bevan Barr would be proud to hear this—if he were still alive and hadn't been on the wrong end of a fatal heart attack brought on by a chasing pack of angry dogs that had been released by a group of less-than-impressed Dwarves who had taken offence at one of his jokes whilst he was performing on stage.

Me: "Why?"

Shana: "They're trying to kill me."

Me: "Kill you? Surely not—they're here to help you."

Shana: "They're evil! Always stopping me from leaving this place."

Me: "Why would you want to leave—this is your home?"

The Battle Dancer shakes her head and glares darkly.

Shana: "Home? This isn't my home. It's my prison."

The Elf's words fill me with dread. I glance over at a few of the other former adventurers relaxing within the grounds of *The Heroes Hall of Legends:* there's a gruff Dwarf who appears engrossed in his precious rock collection; an old Wizard who is having a heated argument with one of the stone garden Gnomes;[830] and an elderly Paladin who seems to be either asleep or dead—it's difficult to tell from this distance.

Me: "This place appears calm and peaceful enough—nobody here looks like they're being held against their will."

Shana: "That's because it has been stripped from them."

Me: "What has?"

The Battle Dancer stares coldly at me through her tired eyes.

Shana: "Their will."

Me: "I still don't understand—"

Shana: "The Sisters, they know why you're here; they know you're a Loremaster—they don't want you going away telling everyone the truth about this place. You'd better watch your back, Loremaster... *if* you know what's good for you. The Sisters of Perpetuity are maintaining an illusion of tranquillity here, while chaos reigns out of sight."

Me: "So, this is all just an illusion—an act?"

---

[830] *I still can't figure out why the sculptor chose to chisel each one with an expression of abject horror.*

Shana: "Yes, created solely for visitors—like you."

I watch from afar as the Sisters quietly go about their business, tending to their elderly charges, bringing them soft biscuits and hot tea. I have a hard time believing the Battle Dancer's words; the Sisters here appear caring and focused on keeping the residents comfortable. I'm starting to suspect the Sister was right—perhaps the Battle Dancer *has* convinced herself of her own delusion.

Me: "Can you tell me about yourself? I've never met a Battle Dancer before."

Shana: "But you *have* met a Mime Warrior before if I'm not mistaken..."[831]

Me: "H—How did you know that?"

Shana: "How did I know *what?*"

Me: "How did you know I've met a Mime Warrior before today?"

The former Battle Dancer stares at me blankly. I sigh and try again with my original line of questioning.[832]

Me: "What's it like being a Battle Dancer?"

The old Elf settles back into her seat as she fondly recalls the memories of her past—happy to shift the conversation without a blink of her eye.

Shana: "*Ah...* to be a Battle Dancer, you must have rhythm. You need to hear the beat calling to you, igniting your soul, lighting a fire that has only one purpose and one purpose alone—to *fight!*"

Me: "*Erm*—don't you mean to dance?"

Shana: "Dancing. Fighting. To me, there are both sides of the same coin."

Me: "How does that work?"

Shana: "Imagine we are two mortal enemies facing off against one another—each of us waiting for the other to make the first move. One steps forward, so the other naturally takes a step back. One moves to

---

[831] Maybe the Elf <u>can</u> read minds—maybe she's reading my mind right now!

[832] I take it back—the Elf has no mind reading abilities to speak of whatsoever...

the left; the other moves to the right. This dance continues until someone misses a step, and only one of them remains standing.[833] Now you tell me, are they fighting or are they dancing?"[834]

Me: "*Hmmm*—I think I'm beginning to understand what you mean. The poetic movement as you match step-for-step with your opponent, searching for an opening to go for the kill."

The Battle Dancer's eyes light up at my reply.

Shana: "*Exactly.* It's the heartbeat that exists within every living thing—*the rhythm of the fight.* It's what every Battle Dancer yearns for."

Me: "You must have had some epic battles in your time—care to share any stories with me?"

Shana: "Stories... *stories*... I know I have one somewhere..."

The Elf scratches her head, trying to recall her past. I wait patiently but find myself distracted again by the Wizard, who is still berating one of the stone garden Gnomes somewhere off to my right. I pity the poor garden ornament and wonder what travesty it had committed to warrant such venomous abuse from the elderly Spellcaster.

Me: "What's up with the Wizard?"

Shana: "*Huh?*"

I motion towards the elderly Spellcaster, who is now pointing an accusing finger at the Gnome statue and shouting obscenities at it.[835]

The Battle Dancer gives the Wizard a terse look and shakes her head disapprovingly.

Shana: "He hates Gnomes."[836]

---

[833] *I assume the loser is dead rather than on the floor holding their foot in pain.*

[834] *I guess it depends upon who is doing the asking.*

[835] *My editor has advised me not to print the foulness being spouted by the Wizard—believe me when I say it would make a Blue Goblin blush in shame.*

[836] *Halfling blood must be running through his family tree somewhere down the ancestral line.*

Me: "Even the garden variety?"

Shana: "Garden variety?"

Me: "Yeah—all these stone Gnomes dotted around the garden?"

I point out several of the statues to the confused Elf.

Shana: "They're not garden Gnomes."

Me: "They're not? What are they then?"

Shana: "Real Gnomes—well, they *were* at some point."

Me: "Real Gnomes!?"

Shana: "They continually plague us, but the Wizard is a sharp one—I told you, he <u>hates</u> Gnomes. He lies in wait to turn them into statues with a handy *Flesh-to-Stone* spell as soon as he spots one sneaking into the garden."

The revelation is a little shocking, to say the least—my own face almost mirrors the same frozen look on the petrified Gnome statues.[837]

Me: "Why do they all come here?"

Shana: "The Dwarf thinks they're after his valuable rock collection—but I know the truth."

Me: "Which is?"

Shana: "The Sisters of Perpetuity."

Me: "What about them? You don't think—"

The Battle Dancer slowly nods with assured knowing.

Shana: "The Sisters are summoning them to torment us—it's like an amusing sport for our captors."

Me: "I can't begin to believe they would—"

Shana: "Look about you, Loremaster—the evidence in this garden is compelling, is it not?"

---

[837] *No doubt this revelation must amuse any Halflings reading this.*

Me: "I guess—if that's true, how are they calling Gnomes to this place?"

Shana: "That, I do not know—they must have some sort of Gnomish contraption under lock and key that calls out to them, or a secret stash of bright red lichen they use as bait—*or* even a Ring of Power..."[838]

I'm keen to steer the conversation away from Gnome infestation conspiracy and back onto the topic of adventurers and adventuring.

Me: "You were going to tell me a story?"

Shana: "*Was I?* What story?"

Me: "It was a story about one of your epic fights—I mean *dances*, sorry... I mean *dancing fights.*"[839]

Shana: "*Oh*, there have been so many, I can't remember them all."

Me: "You don't need to remember them all, just one—maybe you can tell me about your last battle; that must have been a bittersweet day."

Shana: "My... *last*... battle..."

A small tear forms in the corner of the elderly Elf's eye—she wipes it away before composing herself again.[840]

Shana: "I—I remember... a Warrior who wielded an invisible sword. Can you *imagine* it—an *invisible* sword? I thought she was crazy at first—then... then we encountered that infernal Warlock Lich—"

My ears prick up at the mention of a Warlock Lich.[841]

Me: "A Warlock Lich? What happened?"

Shana: "We tried to fight it. I... I remember twirling and dancing around that foul creature; I was too fast for it—too fleet of foot for it to catch

---

[838] As curses go, a ring that calls all Gnomes to it doesn't feel that bad, although I'd imagine some of the lured Gnomes in question would say otherwise.

[839] Not to be confused with 'fight dancing', which usually happens at a Halfling festival after the festival goers have consumed a few too many 'whole' pints...

[840] I find myself getting upset for Shana—curse my sensitive side and insensitive question!

[841] Although I quickly ignore the bit about the crazy Warrior with an imaginary sword, if anyone's crazy around here—it's clearly the confused Battle Dancer.

me. My blade sang as it bit deep into the creature's side. It screamed in frustration—do you know how dangerous a Warlock Lich is?"

Me: "I heard they can drain your life essence if it manages to touch you?"

Shana: "Precisely. So, I couldn't let it near me—I had to keep moving, keep the rhythm flowing through my body, but my sword had wedged in the unholy abomination's armour—"[842]

Me: "What did you do then?"

The Battle Dancer looks at me, suddenly distressed—something is clearly upsetting her.[843]

Me: "Are you okay?"

Shana: "I—I don't know. I *really* don't know. I—I *shouldn't* be here."

I can see she's getting agitated—I know I must tread carefully if I don't want to cause her any further discomfort.

Me: "Where should you be, Shana?"

The Battle Dancer points to the horizon.

Shana: **"*Out there! I should be out there!*"**

Me: "But you've had your time out there. You're much safer here with the Sisters—"

Shana: "**No!** I remember now that fight with the Warlock Lich. It wasn't that long ago—**it wasn't!**"

Me: "Shana? What do you mean it wasn't that long ago?

Shana: "I—I don't know. I—I *can't* remember! Why can't I remember? It was something to do with that unholy creature!"

The Elf grips her wrist tightly as her face turns ashen and drawn.

---

[842] Somehow, I don't think this is an officially recognised dance move.

[843] Something other than the grotesque and horrifying faces frozen on the Gnome statues dotted around the place—or <u>me</u> for that matter!

Shana: "The last thing I remember was a burning coldness..."

Me: "What was it, Shana?"

Shana: "My wrist..."

I look down at where the Elf is covering her arm. She lets go and I spot a partially healed burn of a handprint around her wrist—it still looks relatively 'fresh'.

Me: "That mark—how did you get that?"

The Elf looks down at it, tracing her fingertip around the edge of the wound.

Shana: "That's where it grabbed me..."

Me: "But that makes no sense—"

The Battle Dancer's antics have drawn the attention of one of the Sisters of Perpetuity. She hurries over to see what is vexing the elderly Elf—she glares at me sternly.[844]

Sister of Perpetuity: "Everything okay here, Shana?"

Me: "She has a strange wound on her arm—"

Sister of Perpetuity: "*Oh dear,* maybe she spilt some tea on herself this morning?[845] I'll see to it that a bandage is put on her wrist—"

Shana: "*I—I shouldn't be here!*"

Sister of Perpetuity: "Now, we've spoken about this before. You have to stay with us now, Shana—we're here to take care of you."

Shana: "*NO! NO! NO!*"

Sister of Perpetuity: "I think that's enough for you for one day. I'm afraid I'll have to ask you to leave—"

The Sister doesn't get a chance to finish her sentence before the Battle

---

[844] *I've seen this same stern look before; could this Sister be a relative of Miss Riler?*

[845] *I told you tea could be dangerous! Fortunately, it wasn't Cavern Tea—otherwise, there would be an odd patch of hair growing there instead of a burn mark.*

Dancer is on her toes, leaping over the garden flowers and twirlingaround the surprised-looking stone Gnomes.[846] The Wizard points and laughs at the fleeing Elf as she dodges past two Sisters who throw themselves at her in an effort to stop the Battle Dancer—but just end up knocking each other out cold. The Dwarf claps his hands and shouts words of encouragement from behind his rock collection, waking the Paladin in the process. The former Holy Warrior suddenly lurches to his feet and starts swinging his sword at imaginary foes— cleaving the stone head of the nearest stone Gnome clean off its shoulders whilst bellowing unholy swear words in every direction.[847] But the Battle Dancer doesn't hear them; she keeps spinning and dancing towards the horizon. It's a beautiful spectacle as her youth briefly returns to her old bones. The Sisters of Perpetuity quickly regroup and give chase;[848] even though it's a comedic sight to behold, it's one I secretly hope never ends for the Elf. I'm still unsure how much of what Shana told me was true, but regardless, the sheer delight to see her reliving a moment from her adventuring past warms my soul—*and* guarantees a small mention within the pages of my trusty journal. As I depart, with the Sisters *still* trying and failing to bring Shana back under control, I pass the Wizard, who glares and points accusingly at me.

Wizard: "You're not a Gnome, are you?"

Me: "*Erm...* No, I'm a Wizard—just like you."[849]

The Wizard squints as though searching for the truth within my lie.

Wizard: "Well, just watch out for those pesky Gnomes. If you see one— make sure you let me know, you hear?"

Me: "Perfectly. I—I better be going..."

---

[846] *With their fixed facial expressions that capture this bizarre moment to perfection...*

[847] *Using profanity so vile it would make Redmane blush.*

[848] *With a big Elf-sized net...*

[849] *I cannot believe I just said this!*

I hurry out of the Gnome-filled garden, keen to avoid becoming the latest permanent addition to this place.[850]

---

[850] *When I finally see my parents next, I will tell them The Heroes Hall of Legends is a far stranger place than the glossy parchment scroll suggests.*

26. Bartlet, the Tallyman

I'm slightly nervous about today's meeting, not because of whom I'm interviewing, but because of where the interview is taking place—at the beating heart of the Heroes Guild, in Tronte. I've been told that the person I've arranged to meet is an unassuming Gnome with a keen eye for the smallest of details,[851] and a nose for a tall tale.[852] His formal title is the 'Recorder of Records', but he's more commonly known as a 'Tallyman'—responsible for keeping track of every 'official' adventurer in the realm and every adventure they've attempted.[853]

I'm not sure what to expect when I step through the door of the Heroes Guild for the first time, but I'm immediately greeted by a relaxed and inviting atmosphere,[854] quite at odds with the picture painted by many I've spoken to on my travels. Even before I've had a chance to ask someone for assistance, a smartly dressed Halfling spies me from afar and rushes over to save me from my own awkwardness.

Halfling: "Hello, can I *help* you—are you looking to join up?"

Me: "*Erm,* no—I'm actually here to meet the Tallyman."

The Halfling cocks an eye.

Halfling: "The Tallyman?"

Me: "*Erm—yes?*"

Halfling: "You sure you're in the right place?"

Me: "Yes—why?"

Halfling: "It's just you look more like a Wizard than a member of our Guild. If you need directions to their door, they can be found just a little further along the street—"

---

[851] *Being a Gnome, I assume Bartlet means Halflings here.*

[852] *No doubt an unbelievable yarn spun by a higher than usual High-Elf.*

[853] *By this, I mean 'officially' recognised by the Heroes Guild.*

[854] *So relaxed, some members of the Guild are walking around dressed in complimentary robes and matching Shoes of Comfort as they step in and out of steam-filled rooms.*

Me: "I'm neither with them nor you—I'm a *Loremaster*. I'm here to meet Bartlet. He should be expecting me."

Halfling: "*Hmmm...* A Loremaster, you say? Well, you'd better follow me then..."

The Halfling spins on his heels and leads me through the halls and corridors before opening a door and stepping into a large room filled with towers of stacked parchments. I stare in awe, wondering if these swaying columns will come crashing down at any given moment, literally burying my guide and myself under a mountain of paperwork.[855] We carefully meander through the towering stacks until reaching the centre of this precarious paper acropolis. Sitting at an antediluvian desk is a Gnome in deep discussion with a large plate armour-wearing Paladin opposite him.

Halfling: "Wait here..."

Without giving the Paladin a second look, the Halfling interrupts Bartlet's meeting and speaks quietly into the Tallyman's ear. The Gnome looks up at me and frowns as the Halfling whispers what I hope is a polite introduction.[856] For a moment, I convince myself I'm about to be escorted off the Guild's premises by Enforcers or worse.[857] But the Tallyman brusquely ushers the Halfling away and politely asks the Paladin to leave; he waits until both have safely navigated past the towers of parchment before speaking again.

Bartlet: "That idiot tells me you're the Loremaster I'm supposed to meet today."

Me: "What idiot?"

Bartlet: "The Halfling."

Me: "*Is* he an idiot?"

---

[855] *The irony of a weary hero, who barely survived a death-trap-filled dungeon—only to expire under the crushing weight of ten thousand parchments as they return to the Tallyman, is not lost on me.*

[856] *And not a recommendation to send the nearest tower of parchment, crashing down on me...*

[857] *Enforcers who have had their treasured pamper time rudely interrupted by a most unwelcome Loremaster.*

Bartlet: "He's a Halfling—is he not?"

Me: "Y—Yes?"

Bartlet: "Then he's almost certainly an idiot—what can I do for you, Loremaster?"

Me: "I—I've been documenting heroes, adventures, and everything between—"

Bartlet: "And you believe I fall neatly inside the 'between' category?"

Me: "I'm here to understand what goes on behind the Guild's veil. You hear plenty of tales about heroes and their quests, but never really about the people who toil thanklessly away in the background."

Bartlet: "Is that what you think I do—toil?"

Me: "Forgive me—I didn't mean to offend."

Barlet: "The only way *you* could offend me is if you were a Halfling. Tell me, why do you care about the little people?"[858]

Me: "I'm following the footsteps of my brother."

Bartlet: "Don't you mean *in* your brother's footsteps?"[859]

Me: "No—I'm no hero. I have no desire to tread the same path. The closest I ever want to get is simply understanding what it means to be a hero."

There's an awkward silence as the Tallyman regards me longer than what feels naturally comfortable.

Bartlet: "Very well. My role here is to document every hero's quest regardless if they are successful *or* not."

Me: "Did you always want to become a Tallyman?"

---

[858] Technically, the Gnome could <u>still</u> be talking about Halflings here. However, I'm sure most Halflings would strongly insist the Tallyman is really talking about Gnomes, while Dwarves will be saying it's both of them, and Elves will insist all three should shut up—and start 'growing' up.

[859] Not unless he's been cursed with oversized Titan feet at some point on his travels.

The Gnome shifts in his seat uncomfortably.

Bartlet: "No. I was an adventurer first—but quickly realised I was better suited for the role of a Tallyman."

Me: "*You* were a hero?"

Bartlet: "Don't look so surprised—it was a long time ago."

Me: "What happened?"

Bartlet: "I took a Goblin arrow to the knee on my very first adventure[860]—I never fully recovered."

The Tallyman winces as he gingerly flexes his leg to make both this point and his bone-crunching kneecap heard.

Me: "That must have been incredibly frustrating."

Bartlet: "That's one way of putting it. After spending many months recovering in a chapel run by the Sisters of Perpetuity, it was clear I would never be the same. Fortunately, the Heroes Guild approached me with an offer—they wanted someone good with numbers and who had a keen eye for the little details. I had plenty of time on my hands and still wanted to be involved with the adventuring business in some capacity, so I agreed to take the role as their Tallyman. It wasn't the path I imagined I would walk[861]—but it is an important path nonetheless."

Me: "So, you keep a record of *every* quest attempted?"

The Gnome raises his hands to the mountain range of paperwork and parchments looming over us.

Bartlet: "By those who are members of this Guild? Yes. You need only look about you to find every adventure, every success, and every failure—it's all here, somewhere in these towering monoliths of paper, written down in black and white."

---

860 *There is no way a Goblin Archer made that shot without considerable 'bottled' assistance from one of Inglebold's 'Lucky Potions'—either that or the Goblin Archer was aiming for something completely different, like themselves.*

861 *Or at least hobble as fast as a painful kneecap allows.*

Me: "That's quite an undertaking."

Bartlet: "You have no idea how much of an undertaking it has been. And not just in terms of quillwork; the intricacy of construction that keeps those piles of parchment perfectly stacked would make any Dwarven Builder[862] weak at the knees."[863]

My eyes cannot help but be drawn to the stacks of paper swaying ominously above me.

Me: "They *do* look a touch... precarious."

Bartlet: "Pure illusion—they're sturdier than the cliffs of Antenook."[864]

Me: "I'm in awe of how much paperwork is actually here—"

The Tallyman fixes me with a withering look.

Bartlet: "Do you know how many active heroes there are in the realm?"

Me: "A thousand?"

Bartlet: "Try forty-five thousand."

Me: "*Forty-five thousand?*"

Bartlet: "And that's just the ones we know about—you could probably triple that if I included the non-Guild members. Naturally, that number is constantly fluctuating based on certain variables.[865] But until I enter the exact details of a quest—everything is just a rough estimate."

---

[862] There are many Dwarven Engineers in the realm—but none compare to the legendary Balfour's Beardy, a no-nonsense craftsman who built the Great Dwarven Mall—with its endless rows of specialty 'Rock-Shops'. A Dwarf who is also famed for stroking his impressive beard and noisily sucking in his breath when costing up any new job for a prospective client.

[863] Hopefully, this has <u>nothing</u> to do with a 'lucky' Goblin arrow...

[864] A legendary coastal range that forms part of the Dagger Coast, it is believed to have been fashioned by the bare hands of the Warrior God, Wurtzite Boron. The impressive cliff face is so hard it could stop an unstoppable force in its tracks without breaking a sweat.

[865] Such as heroes dying or Wizards casting duplication spells on themselves to confuse a nearby Barbarian.

Me: "But why the need to document everything in such meticulous detail?"

The Tallyman grins at my words.

Bartlet: "Because the levels are in the details."

Me: "Levels?"

The Gnome nods as he scribbles a signature on the bottom of the page sat in front of him.

Bartlet: "Every adventurer has a level; the higher their level, the more dangerous the quest becomes—but the greater the reward if they are successful..."

Me: "—and in turn, the more the Heroes Guild earns?"

Bartlet: "Adventuring is a perpetual circle. My job is to ensure everything keeps turning—and greasing the wheel does not come cheap."

Me: "How do you decide what level a hero is?"

Bartlet: "Let's take our friend the Paladin as an example—he has returned from completing a quest to secure a precious gemstone from some greedy Dark Dwarves.[866] A simple enough task—one our Paladin is overqualified for."

Me: "Why is he overqualified?"

Bartlet: "Because on our books, he's fifth-level—meaning he can go five dungeon levels deep before he's out of his depth and asking for trouble. The quest he was on was a second-level adventure; it was second-level because there were only two dungeon levels in the quest to navigate through—you follow me?"

Me: "Let me get this right—the number of dungeon levels determines the adventure's difficulty, and who attempts it?"

Bartlet: "Always."

---

[866] Dwarves, by their very nature, are greedy—but Dark Dwarves would steal the 'Elf' out of 'selfish' given half the chance.

Me: "What if there's only one level?"

Bartlet: "I'd say that's pretty obvious—then it is a first-level adventure."

Me: "But what if it has a powerful Evildoer at its end—like a Warlock Lich?"

Bartlet: "Impossible. That would *never* happen."

Me: "How can you be so sure?"

Bartlet: "Because that isn't the way of things! By their very nature, Warlock Liches do not simply frequent a solitary level; it's... *beneath* them."[867]

Me: "Hold on, you're saying a Warlock Lich wouldn't be found in a first-level adventure because their reputation wouldn't allow it?"

Bartlet: "Put it this way, if *you* were a Warlock Lich, would you be happy dealing with annoying first-level adventurers every day?"[868]

Me: "No, I suppose not. Here's another scenario—what if a first-level adventurer got lucky and made it all the way to the end of a high-level dungeon?"

Bartlet: "That is highly improbable."

Me: "But it *could* happen."

The Tallyman's eye twitches in annoyance.

Bartlet: "The fact remains, even if they did make it, they would still have a very surprised and annoyed Warlock Lich to deal with—which would certainly kill them."

Me: "Are you sure?"

The Gnome fixes me with a slightly ominous glare.

---

[867] *Technically, it would be the same level as the one they are on—<u>deeper</u> levels would be beneath them, but I'm splitting hairs here.*

[868] *If I were a Warlock Lich, I think I would choose a better place to reside than a cold, dank dungeon or crypt—something like a lovely little retirement castle by the sea where nobody would bother me.*

Bartlet: "I can *guarantee* it."

Me: "What sort of creatures frequent a first-level dungeon?"

The Tallyman pulls out a small purple book from his desk and starts to flick through the pages.

Bartlet: "Rats, Bats, Cats, Hats,[869] Goblins, Bandits, Goblin Bandits, Orcs, Orc Bandits, Spiders, Spider Bandits—"

Me: "Spider Bandits?"

Bartlet: "After they rob you, they tie you up and leave you dangling from the ceiling."

Me: "Makes sense."

Bartlet: "Now, can you imagine a Warlock Lich wanting to hang around with some Spider Bandits?"

Me: "Depends if they just robbed him or not, I guess..."

The Gnome stares coldly at me once more.[870]

Bartlet: "No—he wouldn't, and for a good reason. Imagine the carnage and confusion that would rain down upon a first-level adventuring party who just encountered a dreaded Warlock Lich in the first room they explored? The fallout from this travesty would rock the foundations of this Guild,[871] not to mention hit us financially in lost adventuring revenue."

Me: "I see—but wouldn't the Heroes Guild do well out of such an unfortunate encounter? I heard the '*Death in Service*' clause would at least ensure the Guild gained the deceased adventurer's entire estate—"

Bartlet: "That's something I cannot comment on. You need to talk to the Guild's Heralds if you want an answer on anything to do with contracts.

---

[869] *Probably a disgruntled 'magical' Sorting Cap, who has given up being a Careersmith and turned their frustration towards adventurers by becoming a grumpy Hat Mimic that angrily breaks wind on any hero foolish enough to place it upon their head.*

[870] *I don't think the Tallyman likes my sense of humour.*

[871] *And possibly knock over some of the monolithic parchment columns in the process.*

But speaking for myself, the retrieval of a fallen hero from any failed quest comes with considerable time, cost, and risk to all those involved with the task. Being a Loremaster of note,[872] I'm sure you're more than aware the '*Death in Service*' clause goes some way to repaying the Guild's debt for a hugely noble service."

Me: "Yes, I'm well aware of the substantial cost and risk involved with retrieving fallen heroes from wherever they fell."[873]

Bartlet: "Good—then you already have an understanding of how much thankless work gets done around here."[874]

Me: "Can I ask you something else—Talbert the Herald mentioned you record the names of every Evildoer your members encounter? Is this true? I'm searching for a particular Warlock Lich..."

Bartlet: "Yes, we used to keep track of all Evildoers—but we stopped."

Me: "Stopped? Why?"

Bartlet: "Toldarn's orders—he also insisted all our historical records detailing Evildoers be destroyed."

Me: "Isn't that a bit strange?"

The Halfling shrugs.

Bartlet: "Saves me some paperwork."

I nod in disappointment.

Me: "How successful was the Paladin you were talking to just now?"

Bartlet: "An unusual question. One I wouldn't normally entertain, but given your profession and the fact the Heroes Guild is always looking for ways to reassure new heroes of their honourable intentions, let me see if I can give you the answer you seek..."

---

[872] *I'm now worried what this 'note' actually says about me—and more importantly, who wrote it!?*

[873] *Unless the adventurer in question 'fell' even before leaving the tavern—then perhaps the actual job of retrieving the body is a lot more straightforward than first thought.*

[874] *Believe me when I say this was said with a huge slice of sarcasm served as Elevenses.*

The Tallyman picks up a sheet of parchment and scans the notes written on it.

Bartlet: "Six Dark Dwarves killed, that's sixty points—"

Me: "Points?"

Bartlet: "We use a point scoring system for everything a hero does on an adventure. The more points accrued, the more levels the hero will attain. But as Dark Dwarves are worth double points, then the Paladin actually gained a respectable one hundred and twenty points—"

Me: "Why are Dark Dwarves worth double points?"

Bartlet: "Because I say they are."

Me: "Is anything else worth double points?"

Bartlet: "Yes—Halflings."

Me: "That's an unusual foe—don't you think?"

Bartlet: "Not particularly, Halflings can be dangerous when cornered."

I stare at the Gnome, wondering if there's an ulterior reason as to why the diminutive Tallyman has such a burning issue with Dwarves and Halflings.

Me: "Had the Paladin accrued enough points to gain a level?"

Bartlet: "Well, he earned another thirty points for killing three Giant Rats and another hundred points for successfully retrieving the gem and returning it to the Heroes Guild—"

Me: "That's two hundred and fifty points—sounds like a lot."

Bartlet: "Yes, but the Paladin is fifth-level, so in the grand scheme of things, it wasn't enough for him to get to sixth-level."

Me: "So, how many points short is he?"

Bartlet: "He needs another two hundred and fifty points."

Me: "So, if he did the adventure again, he'd have enough points to level up?"

Bartlet: "That would seem logical."

Me: "What happened to the gemstone that was recovered?"

Bartlet: "It was placed in our vault for safekeeping. I assume the gem will be returned to the original owner at some point, who will be *encouraged* to make a small donation to the Heroes Guild in gratitude."

Me: "How much did the Paladin earn from this quest?"

Bartlet: "Again, such small details are usually confidential, but I can tell you the Heroes Guild made around a hundred and eighty coins from it."

Me: "That's not a huge amount—how much could the Heroes Guild make from one of its higher-level members?"

Bartlet: "We'd expect to make in the region of ten thousand coins."

Me: "*Ten thousand coins?* From *one* adventure?"

Bartlet: "We're talking about a Category Five adventure for that sort of amount.[875] Only a select few ever manage to reach those dizzy heights. Many will merely taste the dungeons that their level permits. Here at the Heroes Guild, we pour a lot of our time and energy into our members, trying to help them reach their unrealised potential."

Me: "Even the Dwarven and Halfling ones?"

The Gnome Tallyman gives me a stern look as if I've touched a nerve.

Me: "Can I ask, do you have any record of a hero named Aldon Barr?"

Bartlet: "No."

Me: "Wait, do you mean I can't ask, or you don't hold any information on him?"

The Gnome continues to stare emotionlessly at me.

Bartlet: "The latter..."

---

[875] **Loremaster Tip #7:** *It's worth noting there are five different categories for adventures:* **Category One:** *A low-level adventure usually set in cellars, privies, and suspicious wardrobes.* **Category Two:** *A low/mid-level adventure that starts in a tavern—but never leaves.* **Category Three:** *A mid-level adventure that usually has some grumpy outdoor camping involved.* **Category Four:** *A high-level adventure that requires a Cleric who doesn't faint at the sight of blood.* **Category Five:** *The highest-level adventure that usually affects the entire realm—certain death assured. Involves more than one tavern and a double-cross from the Rogue when you least expect it.*

Me: "But you didn't even look him up!"

Bartlet: "I know the names of every member of our Guild."

Me: "All forty-five *thousand* of them?"

Bartlet: "Correct. And to save us both the agony of reciting them all, just take my word for it—that is a name I do not recognise."

Me: "That's unfortunate to hear—he's my brother, you see, and I'm trying to find him. He left home ten summers ago to make his name as a hero, my family and I have heard nothing since."

Bartlet: "Do I look like a Landlord asking about your life quest to you? Let me put this bluntly—I don't hold any information on your brother as he never joined the Guild here in Tronte."

Me: "I see... so there's no record of his adventures, or if he teamed up with any of your members?"

Bartlet: "I don't log the names of non-members. They just pay their dues to the Guild on completion of a mission before moving on."[876]

Me: "They still pay you? Even if they're not affiliated with the Heroes Guild?"

Bartlet: "Naturally, when one of our members joins a quest, it gives that quest a better chance of succeeding—we take a small fee in return for those improved odds, but we don't keep a list of their names. To do so would triple the size of the paperwork you see here."

Me: "Who is the most successful hero within your Guild?"

Bartlet: "Without question, Arin Darkblade."

Me: "What is his level?"

Bartlet: "Eleven."

Me: "Your levels go all the way up to eleven?"

---

[876] *Hopefully not to the Great Beyond, Behind, Beard, Belch, Barrier or whatever afterlife starting with the letter 'B' is believed in at the time.*

Bartlet: "No, we usually stop at ten, but Arin likes to be one better than his peers."[877]

There's a knock at the door behind me as a familiar face pokes his head around a column of parchments—I instantly recognise the smiling features of Dorn the 'Barbarian'.

Dorn: "Hello, Bartlet—I'm back!"

The Gnome seems momentarily perplexed by the 'Barbarian's' impromptu appearance and candid manner.

Bartlet: "So, it seems, and so soon too—*most... impressive...*"

The 'Barbarian' catches sight of me as I wave at him from my seat.

Dorn: "*Oh,* it's *you* again, Loremaster Elburn—funny meeting you here!"

Me: "Hello, Dorn."

Bartlet: "You two *know* each other?"

Me: "Our paths crossed when he first joined the Heroes Guild—"

Dorn: "—and again when I met you in Cloverton, *you remember?*"

Me: "Indeed I do; with Flintlok and Brin—did they create the entrance theme as you hoped?"

Dorn: "Not really. They messed up the Hydra part."

Me: "Messed up? How?"

Dorn: "When I stepped into the tavern for the first time, they summoned a Gorgon instead."

Me: "A *Gorgon?* What happened?"

Dorn: "Let's just say *The Giggling Giant* has a new range of shocked patron statues."[878]

---

[877] Why didn't the Heroes Guild make level ten just a bit harder to attain?

[878] As the Giggling Giant's patrons weren't left wearing bags on their heads, I'm fairly certain Flintlok didn't summon a Gorgon—maybe he summoned a cranky old Wizard from The Heroes Hall of Legends instead?

Me: "I guess you won't be welcomed back there in a hurry."

Dorn: "It's not all bad—fortunately, I was still within my '*Thirty-Day Satisfaction Guaranteed*' clause, so Flintlok & Brin had to pay back the coin they took from me."

Me: "I guess the poor patrons of *The Giggling Giant* have yet to be returned to their former state?"

Dorn: "No, but that's another quest for another day—"

Bartlet: "—and *another* hero."

The 'Barbarian' pulls up a seat next to me and sits with his feet on the Gnome's desk, a manoeuvre that doesn't seem to impress the Tallyman—although the Gnome seems strangely reluctant to challenge the young 'Barbarian' over his relaxed manner.

Bartlet: "So, did you break the Titan of Thunder's Storm Hammer as requested?"

Dorn: "Broke it? I *smashed* it into a thousand pieces—it is no more."

Bartlet: "—and the Titan of Thunder?"

Dorn: "Was torn **asunder!**"[879]

The 'Barbarian' winks at me—pleased with his little jaunty rhyme.

Bartlet: "You *killed* him?"

There's something odd about the Tallyman's question—can I detect a hint of nervousness in his voice?[880]

Dorn: "It's usually hard to remain alive when a head has been cleaved from one's shoulders—don't you think, Bartlet?"[881]

The quill in the Gnome's hand suddenly snaps—he looks down at it, startled.

---

[879] *The 'Barbarian's' booming voice seems to reverberate around the room, causing the parchment columns to sway even more than before.*

[880] *Perhaps he's also noticed the increased swaying of the paper monoliths towering over us.*

[881] *Unless an undead Dragon is the one doing the 'cleaving'...*

Bartlet: "This is *most* irregular—most irregular indeed."

Me: "What's irregular?"

Bartlet: "No—nothing. I—I'm sorry, Elburn Barr—I'm afraid I'm going to have to bring our time here to a close."

Me: "That's a shame; I wanted to see what Dorn scored on his latest adventure."

Dorn: "It's high—I'm certain. I killed a lot of monsters. I'm sure I'll be jumping up a level or two after this!"

Bartlet: "That's... *not* going to happen."

Dorn: "You mean I'm not gaining any levels—?"

Bartlet: "*What?* No, not that. I mean the Loremaster staying to see if you've gained a level or not—*that* is not going to happen."

Me: "Why?"

But the Tallyman doesn't reply.

Dorn: "Catch you around, Loremaster."

I get up to leave and try to say farewell to the Gnome—but he's now too preoccupied with the ink splat steadily spreading over his carefully detailed records. I quietly turn to bid the 'Barbarian' adieu.[882]

Me: "Until next time, Dorn. Stay Safe."

Dorn: "*Safe?* That's not a word a Barbarian knows—unless it's the kind that needs breaking and contains a lot of loot."

The 'Barbarian' takes his feet off the Gnome's table and leans closer to him.

Dorn: "You alright, Bartlet? Or has a *Halfling* got your tongue?"

I catch a sight of the Tallyman's flushed face, his rage silently simmering underneath. The 'Barbarian' bursts into laughter and slaps

---

[882] *'Adieu' is Gnomish for 'Mind your head on the way out'—commonly said to tall visitors as they depart from a Gnome's cave.*

the table hard, causing the mountain of paperwork to rumble ominously—the Tallyman stares upwards in horror.[883]

Dorn: "Tiiiiimber!"[884]

Bartlet: "*Oh, sh—*"

I run as fast as I can as thousands of sheets of paper fall all around me. Looking back through the blanket of white, I search for Dorn and Bartlet, but they are nowhere to be seen. I sprint back down the hall, almost reaching the exit before the avalanche of parchment finally sweeps me off my feet and slides me out through the doors of the Heroes Guild, coming to rest in the courtyard outside. As I stand and brush myself down, I catch a glimpse of someone staring down at me from the Guild's uppermost window. A figure that seems somehow *almost* familiar—a sudden cry of alarm from inside the Guild distracts me. When I glance back up at the window, the figure has vanished.

Halfling: "What happened?"

The same Halfling who welcomed me into the Heroes Guild is now standing in confusion and shock at my feet.

Me: "There was an accident—the Barbarian and the Tallyman were in there when all the stacks fell—"

Halfling: "Dorn the Barbarian is *buried* in there? I'd better get help— _wait_ here!"[885]

The harried Halfling clambers over the piles of paperwork and disappears back into the Heroes Guild.

I wait several seconds before deciding that perhaps it's wiser to leave the fallout of this parchment tsunami now rather than being roped into

---

[883] *An old adage says: 'Too much paperwork will eventually kill you', which could be about to become true in the Tallyman's case.*

[884] *'Timber' is a Gnomish word meaning 'Look out! You're about to become a lot shorter than the shortest Halfling I know!'*

[885] *I can't help but notice the Halfling didn't ask after the Gnome...*

picking it all up later.[886] With a final look at the vacant window, I hurry back into the hustle and bustle of the busy street and what I hope is relative safety.[887]

---

[886] *There's so much paperwork everywhere, it would just take a Fireball-loving Wizard to turn up and the entire Heroes Guild would be no more—lucky then that they <u>don't</u> have any Wizards in their ranks, huh?*

[887] *Right now, I'd happily let a Spider Bandit or Hat-Mimic ambush me rather than face the fury of a paperwork-buried Tallyman.*

27. Elamina Quince, the Greatest Fan of Heroes

Once past the Heartenford Fords, you will come to the last hamlet before the desolate ShadowLands stretches further than the eye can see. The settlement of Undervale often attracts an abundance of pedlars, all keen to make their fortune off those brave souls who are about to set foot into the hostile domain beyond the township's borders. It has become an invaluable stop for adventurers who need one last drink of courage before embarking on their latest quest.[888] But I'm not here to meet confident adventurers, coin-hungry Merchants, or hawkers of dubious potions; I've come to Undervale to meet perhaps the greatest enthusiast in the entire realm, a self-professed 'worshipper' of all those who answer the call to adventure.

I find myself standing in the humble living quarters of Elamina Quince; this *'greatest fan of heroes'* is somewhat of a big deal within the small-but-dedicated adventuring fandom. As I wait for my host to return from the kitchen with refreshments, I stare at the plethora of hero trinkets and paraphernalia covering all four walls. Except for a curious pair of small velvet curtains patterned with hand-stitched gold battleaxes, every inch of shelf space is crammed full of adventuring knick-knacks and goodies. My eyes are drawn to a familiar-looking figurine sitting on a shelf nestled between a smiling treasure chest with large teeth and an authentic 'magical' Sorting Cap.[889] As I step closer, I realise the figurine is none other than Redmane, complete with detailed armour and moveable limbs—it even has the same four S's carefully etched on his miniature pauldron.

Elamina: "—*that's* an original..."

Me: "Excuse me?"

A small Dwarf[890] hurries out of the kitchen area carrying a steaming cup and a plate of Rock-Slate biscuits. She hands me the mug and puts the plate on a nearby table. The Dwarf smiles expectantly at me as I take a sip of the black liquid before launching into a coughing fit as the

---

[888] *If they can <u>actually</u> find a quest, given the current Quest Drought, that is...*

[889] *That appears to be sleeping—given the loud snores coming from its general direction.*

[890] *Shorter than your average Dwarf but not as short as a Halfling, nor a Gnome for that matter...*

strong sooty taste ambushes my taste buds.[891]

Elamina: "It's Cavern Tea—it'll put hairs on your chest."

Me: "—and also on my tongue, so it seems."

The Dwarf laughs and points to the Rock-Slate biscuits as I go to take one; she waits for the exact moment I'm about to take a bite when she chooses to offer some words to the wise.

Elamina: "Just watch your teeth on those things—you're liable to lose one if you're not careful."[892]

I stare at the offending biscuit for a moment before deciding to put it back on my plate—my stomach growls in protest, but I ignore it and turn my attention to the Paladin figurine standing stoically on the shelf.[893]

Me: "I recognise that fellow—"

Elamina: "**Yes!** Redmane the Paladin—it's in perfect condition. Not a single scratch on it. *Unlike* the one Muldoon Stool has in his collection—"

Me: "Muldoon Stool—who's that?"

Elamina: "Muldoon Stool is a rival collector from Tronte, who claims *he's* the realm's *'greatest fan of heroes'*—but Muldoon is an idiot. Anyway, *his* Redmane figurine has a noticeable dent in a left greave. That fool doesn't realise his prized Redmane figurine is practically worthless now."

Me: "Worthless? How much could it be worth if it was in perfect condition?"

Elamina: "We don't call it perfect condition—we call it *mint* condition."

Me: "Why is it called mint condition?"

---

[891] *And demands a ransom for their safe return. I have to say, this tea is probably the most dangerous brew I've ever had the misfortune of tasting!*

[892] *You're also liable to break a toe if you subsequently drop the rocky biscuit beast on your foot while nursing your recently broken tooth.*

[893] *Even in miniature form, Redmane cuts an imposing figure—or should that be _figurine?_*

Elamina: "Because we usually pack away our prized collections in mint-soaked cloths—it helps keep any Heist Moths at bay.[894] Anyway, this is a *Limited Edition Stoic Redmane*[895] in *pristine* condition—it would set you back a few hundred coins at least. The one Muldoon Stool has is probably only worth around ten copper coins, if he's lucky. That's about the same amount you'd pay for one of the poor knock-offs from the Back Market."

Me: "Knock-offs?"

Elamina: "Fake ones are easy to spot; they usually lack the official wax seal on the base—*see.*"

The Dwarf gingerly picks up the figurine and turns it over to show me the small wax stamp carefully applied to the base; I can just make out the letters 'BTM'.

Me: "BTM?"

Elamina: "Balstaff the Merchant."

Me: "I've met Balstaff—I recently visited his store in Port Salvation."

Elamina: "Then you already know he's a great guy. Whenever I travel north to Port Salvation, I always pop in to see what new stock he has."

Me: "Do you often visit Port Salvation? It seems quite an undertaking to go there for a figurine."

Elamina: "*Ah*—you see, that's where *Heroes Guild Tours* comes in handy."

Me: "Heroes Guild *what?*"

Elamina: "Tours."

Me: "I thought that's what you said."

---

[894] *Heist Moths are notorious for stealing small valuables and flying off with them—often to sell on the 'Bug Market', which is an insect version of the 'Back Market' but with more legs and buzzing.*

[895] *I wonder if there's soon to be a Limited Edition Sweary Redmane too...*

Elamina: "They take a group of us to all the popular spots so we can tread on the very footsteps where our heroes have stepped.[896] The tours are awesome: we get to visit the same places adventurers such as Gilva Flamebeard, Axel-Grind, and Dorn the Barbarian have ventured—it's *truly* inspiring. They even have an *arrangement* for a guest hero or two to accompany us on the trip. None of the big names, only a few older adventurers who have had their time out in the field but aren't quite ready to give up on adventuring just yet—"[897]

Me: "Did you say Dorn the 'Barbarian'?"

The Dwarf looks at me, impressed.

Elamina: "You've *heard* of him?"

Me: "Heard of him? Our paths have crossed—on numerous occasions."[898]

Elamina: "You're *so* lucky—I'm his <u>*biggest*</u> fan!"

Me: "He's still fairly new on the hero scene—how can you be his biggest fan?"

The Dwarf grins and reaches across to pull a cord hanging by the wall, the little velvet curtains part and reveal a handsome portrait of Dorn in a thoughtfully heroic pose.[899] Mistaking my look of amazement for enthusiasm, she opens a nearby drawer, which turns out to be filled with even more Dorn memorabilia; everything is here, from a replica battleaxe with the 'Barbarian's' signature scrawled across it to an official Dorn the 'Barbarian' loincloth.[900]

---

[896] Not the 'exact' same steps, not unless you want to end up stepping on a dungeon trap by mistake.

[897] Those who are keen to avoid staring at Gnome garden statues for the remainder of their days.

[898] The last time I saw the 'Barbarian', he was literally buried under a mountain of paperwork.

[899] Or at least a heroically thoughtful pose...

[900] I suspect Dorn wouldn't be happy to learn someone is selling loincloths with his name on them, let alone a picture of his grinning face slapped across the front. This would come as a double-blow as I know first-hand that Dorn isn't the 'only-wears-a-loincloth' type of Barbarian of old.

Elamina: "I've already used the last of my drawers and cupboards for Dorn's souvenirs—I need to find more space to hold all his stuff!"

Me: "He is quite the hero. Even the Tallyman at the Heroes Guild seemed surprised how quickly he was working his way through his quests."

Elamina: "Everyone else says there's a shortage of adventures, but Dorn appears to be the exception. That's why I'm following him—he's *bound* to become a legend in his own lifetime."

Me: "What about Muldoon Stool?"[901]

Elamina: "He's not following Dorn yet—he's still collecting any and all Redmane memorabilia he can get his hands on."

Me: "What's wrong with that?"

Elamina: "Nothing—but the value is going to drop on the Paladin's souvenirs, even my *Limited Edition Stoic Redmane* will lose its worth soon."

Me: "Why?"[902]

Elamina: "He had a slight altercation with some locals in a tavern."

Me: "What tavern?"

Elamina: "Most of them. It has taken some of the shine off his reputation."

Me: "I see..."

Elamina: "Yes, that's why I can't rest on my laurels; I have to be ahead of the competition when it comes to new heroes like Dorn. I don't want Muldoon Stool sneaking in there and stealing my thunder. So, I've been using the local Barkers to keep track of Dorn's achievements."[903]

---

[901] *A point of clarity here, I'm not suggesting Muldoon Stool is going to eclipse what Dorn is doing in the adventuring field.*

[902] *I have a slightly sick feeling in the pit of my stomach that I already know the answer to this.*

[903] *Using Barkers means there's a good chance Dorn's exploits will sound like he defeated a Great Weevil, killed a Chunder Tighten, and retrieved a Ping of Powder—whatever that is!*

The Dwarf pulls out a map and unfurls it before tapping a finger on *The Spit and Spear* tavern circled in red ink.[904]

Elamina: "I've plotted his travels every step of the way from *The Spit and Spear* to places like the Thunder Citadel, home of the Titan of Thunder."

Me: "Hang on, where you have circled the Thunder Citadel on this map, isn't that the Dragon Lord's old citadel?"

Elamina: "Yes, that's right. The Dragon Lord was replaced by the Titan of Thunder, who was subsequently slain by Dorn—"

Me: "I had heard this—do you know *why* the Dragon Lord fled the citadel?"

Elamina: "The word on the street is... *Arin Darkblade* paid the Dragon Lord a *little* visit and encouraged him to leave.[905] Although, I'm not so sure that's true, Arin has been retired from active adventuring for a while now; he's what is politely termed a *desk hero*."

Me: "A desk hero—what's that?"

Elamina: "A desk hero is a hero who works for the Heroes Guild from behind a desk. His days are spent pushing around everything from parchments and paperwork to unreliable Spellcasters[906] and nervous Clerics.[907] Purely for selfish reasons, I'm delighted he's finally decided to hang up his sword."

Me: "Delighted?"

Elamina: "Now he's retired, the value of my extensive Arin Darkblade collection has increased tenfold!"

---

[904] *Unsurprisingly, there are a lot of taverns circled on this map Dorn has frequented—I pity any of those establishments with poor table service.*

[905] *Considering the citadel is an arduous two-week hike into the Doom Mountains, I'd hate to know what a 'big' visit is.*

[906] *A 'reliable' Spellcaster is something of an oxymoron. However, their ability to be unreliable is wholly reliable, which creates something of a paradox.*

[907] *You'd think someone with a Deity on high looking out for them would be a little less nervous in pressured situations—but then who am I to judge?*

The Dwarf opens up a cupboard to what can only be described as a shrine to the legendary adventurer. A myriad of objects and curiosities stare back at me, from flagons and plates to paintings and heraldry flags. Anything you care to think of is probably here with the legendary adventurer's face on it—complete with his trademark eye-patch and grizzled features.[908]

Me: "There's *so* much of it."

Elamina: "I know, right—what do you think?"

On cue, the Dwarf grabs a black cloth object from the shelf, affixes it to her face, and grins at me.

Me: "You look like a miniature Pirate."

Elamina: "Don't let Arin Darkblade hear you say that—he doesn't appreciate being likened to a Pirate."

Me: "I'll keep that in mind."

The Dwarf narrows her eye and glares at me menacingly.

Elamina: "You'd be wise to do so—Arin's thirst for revenge is well-founded."[909]

She removes the eye-patch and gently wipes it clean before carefully placing it back on the shrine's top shelf.

Me: "How did you start all this?"

Elamina: "By accident—it started when my stepfather gave me an official Arin Darkblade dagger to win favour with my mother. It was a beautiful reproduction—even had Wizard's blood on it, supposedly from his last adventure."

---

[908] *It's slightly unnerving to have so many Arin Darkblades glaring back at me in one place with the same sneering look. It's like I've just portal-crashed a secret meeting of Doppelgänger Pirates (Pirates from the Doppelgänger Coast who all dress and wear the same clothes to confuse their enemies, but who usually end up confusing their own crew—usually in the middle of battle).*

[909] *Don't forget he got his revenge on Simply Morgan after the luckless Wizard accidentally knocked the adventurer's drinking arm, causing him to spill a precious drop of ale from his flagon. Arin repaid the Wizard by stealing his shoes and covering the ground with Tickle Thorns—but you know this already, and I'm just needlessly increasing my word count for nothing!*

Me: "Wizard's blood?"

Elamina: "Well, *fake* Wizard's blood. It's well known that Arin doesn't trust Wizards—so I'm guessing someone thought it would be funny to sell replica daggers coated in the stuff."

Me: "Do you still have the dagger?"

Elamina: "Somewhere in a box—it's not a particularly valuable piece. The Blacksmith responsible made a lot of them, so it only holds sentimental value to me these days. But it did light a fire inside that still burns brightly now as it did back then. My collection grew as I sought out highly prized hero souvenirs—before the Back Market caused the price to jump up.[910] Rival collectors like Muldoon quickly appeared on the scene, and I began to lose out on some really exquisite pieces. So, I started seeking heroes who had yet to make a name for themselves—heroes I could start my collection with early, before the Back Market caught on to their growing reputation."

Me: "But your Arin Darkblade collection is almost complete. It must have cost you a fortune to pay for all this!"

Elamina: "Luckily, my mother left me a sizeable collection of precious rocks[911]—the sale covered nearly *every* missing piece of Arin Darkblade memorabilia I was after."

The Dwarf smiles as she stares lovingly at her Arin Darkblade collection, lost in the haze of admiration.

Elamina: "For all its faults, the Back Market helped me find most of the priceless pieces you see on display, but it cost me my mother's entire estate..."[912]

Me: "You said 'nearly'—so what pieces are you missing?"

The Dwarf points to a blank space in the centre of the shrine.

---

[910] *To prices so ridiculous, they may as well have been wearing Boots of Leaping.*

[911] *I suspect any Dwarven rock collector would have snapped up these precious rocks in a heartbeat.*

[912] *If the Heroes Guild ever got wind of this, I'd imagine they'd move quickly to capture this lucrative revenue stream.*

Elamina: "Just one final souvenir…"

Me: "What is it?"

Elamina: "The rarest of them all—imagine the most challenging quest possible. Now double it, no—triple it! That's how difficult it is to get a *Limited Edition Laughing Arin Darkblade* figurine in mint condition. What would I give to hold one in my hands, or just to look at it from afar while in someone els—"

Even before the Dwarf has finished her sentence, I reach into my backpack and withdraw the same souvenir Balstaff gave me.

Me: "You mean this *Limited Edition Laughing Arin Darkblade?*"

The Dwarf's eyeballs almost pop out of her sockets as they lock onto the grinning eye-patch-wearing figurine in my grasp.

Elamina: ***"By the GODS! It can't be—is that—NO?!"***

In disbelief, the Dwarf drops to her knees and stares at the figurine in my hands.

Elamina: "C—Can I *hold* it?"

I nod and pass the Holy Grail of figurines to the trembling Dwarf as she hops on the spot in excitement.

Elamina: "Functioning limbs, removable eye-patch—***YES!*** It even has a head that can be changed to one that's even *meaner* looking[913]—I must have it!"

The Dwarf looks at me with fevered desperation written across her face.

Elamina: "How much?"

Me: "What?"

Elamina: "How much for the figurine?"

Me: "I'm not sure I really want to sell it—"

---

[913] *One with a slightly more pronounced laughing sneer…*

Elamina: *"You... don't... want... to... sell... it...?"*

The Dwarf repeats the words as if struggling to comprehend their meaning.

Me: "I was going to keep it as a memento of my adventures on the road..."[914]

I gesture for the Dwarf to return the figurine to me—Elamina stares at it, unsure if she should comply or not. I can sense the Dwarf playing several scenarios over in her mind.[915] Finally, she relents and hands the figurine back to me before falling back to her knees in defeat.

Elamina: "You take good care of it—you hear?"

Me: "I'll try."[916]

The Dwarf goes to a drawer and opens it, taking out a sheet of paper.

Elamina: "If you're going to start an Arin Darkblade collection of your own, you may as well have something else to go with it..."

Me: "What's this?"

Elamina: "The list of party members for Arin's last known adventure. It's the perfect place to start your collection from."

Me: "I can't accept thi—"

The Dwarf holds up a hand to stop me from speaking.

Elamina: "I insist—you've done a great service by letting me hold that *Limited Edition Laughing Arin Darkblade* figurine. Hand on heart, I never thought I would ever see one, let alone touch it. This is a small gesture of thanks for that."

Me: "Doesn't this lessen your own Arin Darkblade collection?"

---

[914] *I can't fail to notice the Dwarf seems to be clutching her heart in pain at the mention of this.*

[915] *By the look on her face, I'd say the Dwarf, in the Living Quarters, with a Rock-Slate biscuit...*

[916] *The Dwarf winces again in pain at my reply.*

Elamina: "It's nothing really—a duplicate of the original I already own."[917]

I nod as I read through the names listed in Arin's party. The legendary adventurer's name is there at the top, but another name catches my eye. My fingers tremble as they trace over two words... *Ricardo Stagaxe*—it couldn't be him, *could* it?

Me: "When was this list from?"

The Dwarf takes the paper from me and looks at the names in greater detail.

Elamina: "The DeepVale Crypt quest—it was attempted by Arin Darkblade, Morgan the Wizard, Tormane the Paladin, Larpole the Rogue, Sirran the Cleric, and Ricardo Stagaxe the Fighter. Judging by the Guildmaster's signature at the bottom. I'd say this was about eight or nine summers ago—"

The Dwarf notices the shocked look in my eyes.

Elamina: "*Loremaster?* Did I say something wrong?"

Me: "Ricardo Stagaxe... it was the adventuring name he used when we were kids..."

Elamina: "Who did?"

Me: "My brother, Aldon Barr..."

Elamina: "*Really?* Well, aren't *you* full of surprises? He was a first-level fighter—"

I suddenly feel as if a cold hand has a tight hold of my innards and is squeezing for all its worth.

Me: "Wait—What? What do you mean *was?*"[918]

Elamina: "*Oh my*—you *didn't* know... I'm sorry to say, your brother *died* on this particular adventure."

---

[917] *No doubt created by a Wizard's 'Mirror Image' spell...*

[918] *It's now my turn to suddenly clutch at my heart in pain.*

The revelation hits me like a punch-drunk Barbarian,[919] knocking the breath out of my lungs. I stagger forward, searching for something to steady my fall. The Dwarf is quickly by my side to lend me her support.[920]

Elamina: "Let me get you something stronger to drink than Cavern Tea—"

I shake my head, recoiling at the thought of anything stronger than that sooty beverage.

Me: "No, thanks, it's okay. I wasn't expecting… to find out… not like this—it has just come as a bit of a shock…"

Elamina: "I'm *sorry*."

Me: "H—How can you be *sure* he died on this adventure? The information could be wrong—"

Elamina: "I've followed nearly all of Arin's quests when he was active, especially those in his twilight days. Only two people walked away from DeepVale Crypt alive that day—Morgan the Magnificent and Arin Darkblade."

Me: "Morgan mentioned this when I interviewed him; I didn't know my own *brother* was one of those he incinerated with a Fireball too…"

Elamina: "A Fireball? Ouch, *not* a pleasant way to g—"

The Dwarf stops suddenly as she realises what she's saying—I can feel her pity-filled eyes on me.

Elamina: "I know this must be a mortal blow for you. Please, let me pour you a glass of Granite Rum—it'll at least help numb the pain…"[921]

She hurries into her kitchen but carries on talking.

---

[919] *Or should that be drunk-punch Barbarian?*

[920] *Although, I'm not sure the Dwarf appreciates me leaning on her head like that.*

[921] *Granite Rum is an exceedingly heavy drink that can floor a Troll if accidentally knocked off a shelf while the unfortunate creature is unlucky enough to be standing directly beneath it. Suffice to say, one tends to put on a lot of weight after drinking several glasses of the stuff.*

394

Elamina: "Later, I'll dig out the *very* swear box Redmane the Paladin filled up in one blue evening—not *even* Muldoon Stool has one of those!"

I don't wait for Elamina to return. I don't even say goodbye. Instead, I grab my bag—I have to get away from here before deciding what to do next.[922] Before I go, I gently place a gift on the empty spot of the shrine's top shelf—the *Limited Edition Laughing Arin Darkblade figurine,* to thank the Dwarf for perhaps the most valuable piece of information I've gained since starting my journey. A part of me hopes the figurine confirms her position as the realm's greatest hero fan, while another part hopes I never have to set eyes on Arin's laughing face ever again.

---

[922] *Should I go home and face my parents with this devastating news—or continue with my journey and my journal until the last page turn?*

28. Lindelard, the Cleric

Waverdale is an over-populated castle town struggling to find any scrap of free space to grow. Homes and shops are so tightly packed together, the locals are almost bursting out of their abodes like a heavily encumbered Cleric wearing plate armour three sizes too small.[923] Not willing to be constricted by the stone walled corset that encircles Waverdale,[924] the locals have found an ingenious solution to their tight-fitting problem—they have built their town upwards.

As I walk through Waverdale's narrow streets, I find my shoulders scraping against the brickwork on either side of the thoroughfare; more than once, I'm forced to turn and walk sideways or risk losing bare skin to the encroaching structures. A mishmash of gangways and beams support a plethora of buildings above, including an auspicious temple that sits like a star on top of an overdressed Treant that's lost all its leaves for winter.[925] *The Temple of The Enduring Light* is a sanctuary no worshipper in their right mind would ever want to visit— yet it is *this* temple that is my final destination for today.

I try not to notice how dangerous my journey to the entrance is. More than once, a poorly strapped beam works loose in my hand and falls away.[926] But I'm too distracted by the revelation of my brother's death to notice how many times I almost plummet to my own. My mind wanders to my continuing quest, the burning need to document more adventurers and their adventures. I should return home to my parents, but deep down I know Aldon would want me to push on and pursue my quest to its conclusion, just as he did—and that is what I intend to do.

As I step into *The Temple of The Enduring Light,* I'm immediately greeted by a massive candle display encircling a vast central flame pit,

---

[923] *But still insisting everything is fine, even though they've lost all feeling in their extremities.*

[924] *A 'corset' that is barely holding in the bulging structures found within Waverdale's sucked in boundary.*

[925] *An overdressed Treant who has mistakenly stumbled into a Woodcutters' Winter Solstice just as they've run out of wooden logs for their dying fire...*

[926] *Crashing noisily somewhere far below—quickly followed by screams and curses of those unfortunate enough to be caught in the beam's path of destruction.*

which burns furiously. An enormous amount of heat is being generated inside the temple while huge overhead pipes funnel the warmed air back down to the homesteads far below. The smell of burning wax slams into my nose like a blind Monk's fist, striking without sound as the Limeweed and Essence of Rosewart knocks me backwards.[927] There's an uneasy motion beneath my feet—it feels like I'm standing on a ship in the middle of a turbulent storm. The foundations and supports beneath this heavy temple creak and sway with worrying frequency, forcing me to cling onto a nearby pillar for support just as a surprised parishioner slides past in mid-confession.

Unseen Voice: "Are you alright? Does something ail you, brother?"

I turn on my heels to see a concerned-looking Elven Cleric dressed in azure blue armour. His blond locks radiate softly in the candlelight, and a hefty silver mace hangs off his hip.

Me: "Yes, but I don't think it's anything a spell or potion can remedy."

The Elf puts a reassuring hand on my shoulder.

Cleric: "Have faith in *The Enduring Light*. It will be your guide when all other lights have been snuffed out."[928]

Me: "You may be able to help—I'm here to see someone."

Cleric: "Who?"

Me: "Lindelard the Cleric."

The Elf stiffens a little as he releases my shoulder.

Cleric: "What business do you have with Lindelard?"

Me: "I'm Loremaster Elburn; I've got a prior arrangement to meet him."

His face breaks into a relieved, warm grin.

Cleric: "It appears *The Enduring Light* smiles upon you, brother—for *I* am the Elf you seek. *I* am Lindelard."

---

[927] *The pungent aroma reminds me of Elves when they've broken wind after eating something extremely healthy.*

[928] *Or forcefully blown out by a sudden gust of wind from the Great Elven Behind...*

Me: "I—I'm sorry, I should have guessed. It's a pleasure to meet you."

The Elf stares at me as if sizing up the weight that sits heavy on my brow.[929]

Lindelard: "I sense you carry a great pain—release it from your heart and make your peace."

Strangely, I cannot stop myself from unburdening my troubles upon the Cleric.

Me: "It's my brother—"

The Elf opens his arms wide to embrace me.

Lindelard: "We are *all* brothers here—*brother*..."

Me: "No, I mean my *real* brother, he died—"

The Elf stares at me aghast and withdraws slightly.[930]

Lindelard: "*Oh my*... w—what happened to him? It wasn't the pox, was it?"

Me: "No, nothing like that—he fell while on a quest..."

Lindelard: "Falling is fraught with danger—I should know; I have lost a few parishioners to a misplaced step.[931] I'm sure in his final moments, as he hurtled toward the ground, his thoughts were with his loved ones—"[932]

Me: "He didn't die in a fall."

The Elf looks at me in confusion.

---

[929] *Almost as heavy as a heavily encumbered Cleric carrying a heavy backpack filled with heavy stuff and who <u>still</u> insists on wearing plate armour three sizes too small.*

[930] *Out of 'touching' range.*

[931] *Judging by my perilous journey to this place, I'm surprised the Cleric has any parishioners left to preach to.*

[932] *If my brother 'had' died from a fall, his final thoughts wouldn't be of our mother fussing over supper or father snoring in his favourite chair. I'm reasonably positive his last thoughts would have been frantically wishing he and I could somehow swap places with one another.*

Lindelard: "He *didn't?*"

Me: "He fell to a Wizard—"

Lindelard: "He fell *onto...* a Wizard?"

Me: "No—fell <u>to</u> a Wizard!"

The Cleric waves at me to stop.

Lindelard: "Forgive me, I'm confused... *did* he die in a fall, or *didn't* he?"

Me: "He was killed by a wayward Fireball <u>from</u> a Wizard—"

He stares at me as he tries to keep up with the thread.

Lindelard: "I take it he wasn't struck by the infernal thing as he fell to his doom?"

Me: **"NO. HE. WASN'T."**

The Cleric nods before closing his eyes and raising his hand skyward.

Me: "What are you doing?"

Lindelard: "Sending a silent prayer to *The Enduring Light* on behalf of your brother's departed soul, may he rest in peace in whatever '*Beyond*' he believed in."

Me: "I don't think my brother was much of a believer."[933]

The Elf opens his eyes and smiles warmly at me.

Lindelard: "It matters not to *The Enduring Light*—for it believes in *your* brother."

Me: "It believes?"

Lindelard: "*The Enduring Light* believes in *every* living thing—its light shines on all."

Me: "What? *Even* Dwarves?"

---

[933] *The only time my brother mentioned any God was when he was swearing, or promising to send me to the 'Great Beyond' during our many play-fights; I'm not sure that would grant him access to any afterlife with a strict entrance policy at the door.*

Lindelard: "Even them."

Me: "What about Gnomes and Halflings?"

Lindelard: "Them too."

Me: "Orcs, Ogres, and Goblins?"

The Cleric coughs.

Lindelard: "Maybe not *that* lot."[934]

Me: "I see *The Enduring Light* does have some limits, then?"

The Elf's cheeks look slightly flushed as he shifts his feet in agitation.

Lindelard: "I assume you did not come here to discuss your lack of faith?"[935]

It's my turn to shift awkwardly on the spot.

Me: "No—I wanted to talk to you about your adventuring experiences."

Lindelard: "*Ahhh,* adventuring. It can be a double-edged sword—although, as you can see, I prefer to use a mace..."

The Cleric taps the weapon hanging from his hip and waits for my reaction—it's a wait that leaves us both staring at each other a lot longer than what is comfortably acceptable.[936]

Lindelard: "That was a joke."[937]

Me: "What was?"

Lindelard: "The double-edged sword thing."

Me: "I don't follow..."

---

[934] *Funny that.*

[935] *Which I think the Cleric finds 'disturbing'.*

[936] *Not entirely sure what the Cleric expects me to say—nice mace?*

[937] *Uncle Bevan Barr would no doubt be turning in his grave to argue that it wasn't.*

Lindelard: "Because my faith frowns upon those who turn to the sword."

Me: "*Oh, I see...* wasn't there a recent relaxing of the rules surrounding Clerics and their contentious use of swords?"

Lindelard: "This much is true. Although, I prefer to keep with the old traditions rather than embracing new heathen ones—a Cleric should never use a blade of any kind; they should *always* use something blunt, like a sturdy mace."[938]

Me: "Why is that?"

Lindelard: "Because, my child, a Cleric should never have to see the *red stuff.*"[939]

Me: "The red stuff? Don't you mean bloo—?"

The Cleric holds up his hand to stop me from finishing the word.

Lindelard: "Please! *Don't*—I can't stand any mention of the word! It *literally* makes me sick with fright."[940]

Me: "But as a healer, isn't dealing with wounds part of your job? Trying to heal your comrades must be challenging when you're fainting at the mere sight of a scrape."

Lindelard: "It makes it near impossible. It also doesn't help that I'm always the one they turn to when they require healing—not even the Paladins offer to help."

Me: "Why not?"

Lindelard: "They prefer to keep their healing spells for themselves."[941]

---

[938] *Or if you're a High-Elven Cleric—a Halfling-rolled woodbine, maybe?*

[939] *It's worth pointing out that not every creature in the realm has red blood; certain ones have orange, yellow, white, black, and green—some have even been known to have blue blood, although those tend to be really, really, annoyingly logical.*

[940] *I instantly wonder if Lindelard is related to Othollrad, fellow blood-phobe and member of the Guild of Heroes—or should that be, the 'Heroes Guild'?*

[941] *So much for their 'selflessness' and 'sacrifice'—more like 'self-preservation' and 'sod you'...*

Me: "That must be hugely frustrating for you."

Lindelard: "I continually pray for guidance. But, I must *endure*…"

Me: "Much like your Everlasting Light—"

Lindelard: "*Enduring Light!*"

Me: "*Ah yes,* of course, enduring—hence your need to *endure*…."

The Elf eyes me suspiciously.

Linderlard: "Anyway, *The Hammer & Tongs* proprietor personally forged this mighty mace for me. He was also kind enough to offer a hefty discount on it too—"

Me: "You mean Thorde the Forgemaster?"

Lindelard: "*Ah,* you know of him? He's a pleasant enough fellow—even if he is a little gruff, but then aren't all Dwarves?[942] He's also the only Forgemaster in the realm who guarantees *every* weapon he sells. If one should break during an adventure, he promises to give a full refund as long as you can bring the broken weapon back in one piece.[943] It's reassuring to go on an adventure knowing you have that sort of protection to fall back on should things start to go awry."

I stare at the Cleric in confusion as this paradoxical conundrum once again raises its ugly head to torment me. I shoo it away and quickly move the interview on.

Me: "Have you always been a Cleric here?"

The Elf laughs.

Linderlard: "No—I used to be a Nomadic Cleric."

Me: "I've heard of Nomadic Clerics before, but I don't know anything about them."

---

[942] *With their love of ale, coins, and intolerance of people, Dwarves are pretty much identical in every way to the average Landlord or Landlady—except a bit shorter and with more facial hair…*

[943] *There's a clever loophole in the wording of the Forgemaster's guarantee hidden somewhere in plain sight—but for the life of me, I still cannot see it.*

Linderlard: "It's a Cleric who has faith but follows *no* specific God."

Me: "Faith but no specific God—how does that work exactly?"

Linderlard: "Not very well—it's a hard life moving from town-to-town, encouraging locals into prayer, having no idea if anything or anyone is listening at the other end.[944] Although you tend to gain more donated coins from passing locals, probably out of sympathy than devotion."

Me: "What made you turn your back on your Nomadic life and embrace *The Enduring Light?*"[945]

Linderlard: "The lack of a greater *'Being'* can be a little… *distracting.*"

Me: "Distracting? What do you mean?"

The Cleric looks sheepishly at me as his voice drops to a whisper.

Linderlard: "I could entertain a vice without fear of any divine retribution."

Me: "*Oh* really? What vice did you entertain?"

The Elf waits for a wide-eyed acolyte to slide past at speed before answering.

Linderlard: "Gambling—for a while, I worshipped Lady Luck and prayed at her alter of fortune…"[946]

Me: "*Ah*—I bet that was an expensive habit."

The Cleric eyes me suspiciously and drops his voice to a whisper.

Linderlard: *"What do you know about the habit?"*

---

[944] Or if something or someone *is* listening at the other end of a prayer, how do you know it's the 'right' omnipresent recipient and not some 'cross' omnipresent instead?

[945] Metaphorically speaking, unless you want to end up with inner arm burns for your troubles.

[946] Lady Luck is a recognised Deity worshipped by finger-crossed believers who wear various 'lucky' trinkets to curry favour with their fickle Goddess.

Me: "Only that it destroys lives, forcing the hapless to lose their homes, family, and friends—not to mention their dignity."[947]

The Elf breathes a noticeable sigh of relief.

Linderlard: "*Oh,* you mean *that* habit. For a moment, I thought you were talking about the robes I borrowed from the Sisters of Perpetuity—"

Me: "What robes?"

Linderlard: "*Erm*... nothing. Forget I mentioned it—Yes, well, gambling can lead many to lose everything—"

Me: "Is that what happened to you?"

Linderlard: "No, I was lucky—I only lost a dungeon."

Me: "Wait—you have a dungeon?"

Linderlard: "—*had*, yes. It's true; I briefly owned a dungeon for a while. I had big plans for it—I was going to turn it into a training guild for Clerics and Necromancers.[948] That was before I foolishly wagered it in a card game."

Me: "What card game were you playing?"

Linderlard: "Blasphemous.[949] That's when I realised Lady Luck wasn't the right Deity to follow anymore. A word of warning: Never play cards with a Gnome while drunk—they'll take the shirt off your back."[950]

Me: "What happened afterwards?"

Linderlard: "In my post-gambling stupor, I stumbled into the ShadowLands—that's when it hit me."

---

[947] *'Dignity' is a Gnomish word meaning 'to lose all one's clothes'...*

[948] *I'd imagine the Clerics would use their ability to smite the undead. In contrast, Necromancers would use their power to raise them again, thus creating a perpetual cycle of death and reanimation—this would be an ingenious idea if it weren't wholly immoral.*

[949] *A notoriously competitive game of bluffing that often sees the loser launching a tirade of unholy profanities in their shocked Deity's direction.*

[950] *Also known as 'stealing your dignity'.*

Me: "What did?"

Linderlard: "A sign, a *literal* sign, made of wood. Heavy wood I seem to remember—it struck me from above as I wandered aimlessly in the darkness."

Me: "Where did the sign come from?

Linderlard: "Isn't it obvious?"

Me: "*Erm... no?*"

Linderlard: "It came from *The Enduring Light!*"

Me: "Don't you think there's another plausible reason why this particular sign hit you?"

The Cleric scoffs at my doubtfulness.

Linderlard: "I *suppose* you believe a passing Wyvern stole the sign from outside a Merchant's shop and *accidentally* dropped it on me as it flew overhead? Do you honestly think that sounds more plausible than a sign coming from a higher power?"[951]

Me: "I wouldn't know—"

Linderlard: "Well, how can you explain the sign speaking to me—guiding me to where you find this Cleric standing before you now?"

Me: "The sign spoke to you?"

Linderlard: "Well, it didn't literally *speak* to me—no. But there *were* words etched into the sign that called out to me, giving me direction and purpose."

Me: "What did the sign say exactly?"

Linderlard: "There were six simple words that would change the course of my life forever: *Join The Enduring Light in Waverdale.*"

Me: "*Join The Enduring Light in Waverdale?* Does that seem a little...?"

Linderland: "What?"

---

[951] *Admittedly, not my first guess—but way more plausible than the Cleric's explanation.*

Me: "—you know… *specific?*"

Linderlard: "Who are we to question the will of *The Enduring Light?*"[952]

Me: "What did you do afterwards?"

Linderlard: "Once the red stuff from my head wound had stopped *and* the wearisome cycle of vomiting and fainting had subsided enough, I crawled eastward towards Waverdale until I finally found my salvation."

Me: "You crawled all the way here? How far was that?"

Linderlard: "Over three hundred miles as the Dragon flies."[953]

Me: "*Three hundred miles?!* How long did that take you?"

Linderlard: "Nearly the whole summer."

Me: "Why didn't you just walk?"

The Elf stares at me as if I've just reanimated his long-deceased grandmother.

Linderlard: "Because the path to salvation is *never* the easiest. When I finally arrived at the foot of this temple, I was a changed Elf."[954]

Me: "So, how long have you been part of this temple's Holy Order?"

Linderlard: "Over eleven summers have passed since I first crawled through the doors behind you—but time has no meaning anymore. *The Enduring Light* is my life now."

Me: "What makes it enduring—the light, I mean?"

Lindelard: "The flame has never been extinguished by hopelessness; it has never once flickered in the winds of uncertainty—it burns with

---

[952] *Or the subtlety of its recruitment signs…*

[953] *I don't have much knowledge on Dragons, but I would imagine this would include a fair amount of unnecessary loops and several detours to devour the occasional bovine-filled field.*

[954] *This would undoubtedly be the case if the dusty Cleric had crossed paths with Inglebold the Potioneer and drunk any offered elixir in his desperate state.*

unwavering strength, _that_ is what makes it enduring."

Me: "What's it like to adventure as a Cleric of _The Enduring Light_?"

The Elf stares at me as if I've now just propositioned his recently reanimated grandmother.

Linderlard: "W—What do you _mean?_"

Me: "It's just I heard a few stories—"

Linderlard: "Stories? _Who_ has been telling you these stories?"

Me: "Just some of the other heroes I've spoken to... those who have adventured with your kind—"

Linderlard: "Was it a Barbarian by any chance?"

Me: "Excuse me?"

Linderlard: "A Barbarian—have they been spreading poisonous _lies_ about us Clerics again?"

Me: "What makes you think it was a Barbarian?"

Linderlard: "Because it's _always_ a Barbarian."

Me: "Don't you get along with the angry-Warrior types?"

Linderlard: "**Bah!** They are brain-shy oafs who always talk a good fight but are the _first_ to come crying to us when they've been injured. Every last one is a muscle-bound liability!"[955]

Me: "It was a Halfling Rogue, actually."

The Cleric looks at me in surprise.

Lindelard: "A Halfling Rogue? So, what pearls of wisdom did this Halfling _Rogue_ impart upon you?"

Me: "Nothing you haven't already told me—that most Clerics have an inherent problem with blo—erm, _the red stuff_..."

---

[955] _These are brave words from the Cleric—but clearly said out of earshot of any nearby Barbarians._

Linderlard: "Yes, well... I wouldn't pay much heed to what those small idiots say—most are self-serving and only have their greedy eyes fixed on things that don't belong to them.[956] In my humble opinion, they are no better than Barbarians—or Paladins, Druids, Rangers, Necromancers, Wizards, Sorcerers, Monks, or your average Fighter, come to think of it!"

Me: "Do I detect a hint of bitterness towards your adventuring comrades?"

Linderlard: "If that is true, I shall ask *The Enduring Light* for forgiveness. It is a dark thought that must not be allowed to fester."

Me: "Do dark thoughts often plague you?"

Linderlard: "We *all* have dark thoughts—but as a Cleric of *The Enduring Light*, it is my sworn duty to cast any such odious cogitations into the abyss and seek divine illumination. For it is divine illumination that will fill my spirit with strength and resolve to overcome all and any obstacles."[957]

Me: "What other sort of dark thoughts do you find yourself casting out?"

The Elf frowns, clearly uncomfortable with my question.

Linderlard: "There are many dark thoughts that plague the mind—it's not something I'm keen to dwell on for long."

Me: "I understand, but could you at least give me an example of one—no matter how small? Imagine these words reaching a young Cleric who feels the same dark thoughts you are hesitant to describe; a young Cleric who seeks divine illumination from someone with your benevolence. Your words could give them the guidance they desperately seek."

The Cleric stiffens slightly as his sense of duty grows within him.[958]

---

[956] Like Lucky Potions—and after a quick check of my bag, I still have mine, mercifully!

[957] I suspect divine illumination wouldn't help much when dealing with a serious wound—especially if the Cleric was trying to avoid seeing any of the red stuff or body sauce.

[958] At least, I hope it's his sense of duty!

Linderlard: "Very well—for *that* future Cleric, I shall grace your question with an answer."

I nod, waiting for the Elf to take that leap of faith with me.

Linderlard: "Resentment."

Me: "What could you possibly have to resent?"

The Cleric throws his hands up in the air in exasperation.

Linderlard: "Do you know what everyone thinks when they see a Cleric?"

Me: *"Here comes a Holy Warrior priest?"*

Linderlard: "***No!!*** They think, here comes the healer—someone who comes to their aid in the middle of a battle. Well, I like to think that my spells are _not_ just for healing!'

Me: "What other spells can you cast?"

Linderlard: "***Ah!*** Glad you asked. Let me think now... there's Cure Wounds, Cure Serious Wounds, Cure Not So Serious Wounds, Cure Mysterious Itches, Cure Mysterious Stitches, Cure Migraines, Cure Hangovers,[959] Cure Stubbed Toe—"

Me: "That still all sounds very healing-orientated."

Linderlard: "I also can cast Sanctuary."

Me: "I've heard of that spell."

Linderlard: "It's my favourite spell if I'm being honest. I love how it creates a little safe area where I can cast my *other* spells—it also protects me from the extreme cold!"

Me: "I *see...*"

Linderlard: "A small glowing ball of goodness filled with lights and sparkles—not that anyone in my group ever appreciates it."

---

[959] *Undoubtedly, this would be the most frequently called-upon spell in the Cleric's book for any Dwarven Barbarian who is travelling in the same adventuring party as the Holy Warrior.*

Me: "But they could be busy fighting for their lives against some unholy abomination or crying out for aid themselves—"

Linderlard: "**Bah!** All excuses! Would it hurt them to stop what they're doing and take a look around once in a while to admire something as beautiful as my Sanctuary spell?"

Me: "Surely the companion spread-eagled on the floor, in desperate need of healing, has other pressing matters on their mind?"

Linderlard: "Like what?"

Me: "Like trying to staunch the fountain of blood leaking out of them?"

The Cleric's face goes pale as he visibly weakens at the knees. He suddenly lunges forward for support from a nearby stone column.

Me: "Sorry, I forgot."[960]

Linderlard: "It's okay... it'll pass..."

Me: "How do you cope with a nasty injury?"

Linderlard: "I close my eyes—"

Me: "And what? Pray *The Enduring Light* will guide your hands?"

Linderlard: "*No*—I just close my eyes and try to help without looking at anything that will make me vomit; sometimes I ask the companion lying there to help out."

I can sense my mouth is wide open in shock.[961]

Me: "How does *that* work?"

Linderlard: "With great difficulty—I usually feel around a bit and ask a lot of questions."

Me: "What sort of questions?"

---

[960] *Don't judge me, but I wanted to see how Linderlard reacted if I accidentally slipped the 'B-word' into the middle of our conversation—and now I know.*

[961] *Like a Druid that's just been struck by a bolt of lightning...*

Linderlard: "*Oh*, the usual—does *this* hurt? What about if I do *this?* What's *this* hole I can feel? Why aren't you wearing any breeches?[962] What's this sticky stuff on my fingers? Grunt if you're still alive—*that* sort of thing."

Me: "And you've found that works?"

Linderlard: "I have, you know. I haven't lost a single adventurer on my watch—although plenty succumbed to their wounds much later. Adventuring isn't for everyone, as you well know."

Me: "Do I?"

Linderlard: "*Ahem*—your brother?"

A twinge of pain shoots through my chest as the Cleric's words cut deep.

Me: "Yes, of course—you're right."

Linderlard: "You must not grieve for your brother. He died an adventurer's death. Do not allow any dark thoughts in. They will do you no good. Your brother has stepped into *The Enduring Light*—"

Me: "Well, he actually stepped into the path of an oncoming Fireball— but I'm pretty sure the end result was the same."[963]

Linderlard: "Take solace from the fact the searing pain which undoubtedly engulfed your brother and scorched the flesh from his bones, would have been short-lived."

Me: "Thanks—that makes me feel *much* better."

Linderlard: "*Damn Wizards!* You wouldn't catch me being so reckless with my spells—"

Me: "I doubt *Cure Stubbed-Toe* is in any real danger of wiping out your party."

---

[962] *They were undoubtedly lost to a Gnome with an unbeatable hand in 'Blasphemous'.*

[963] *I suspect that may have been a joke too far, even by Uncle Bevan Barr's standards... sorry Aldon.*

Linderlard: "Don't be so sure, brother. I've seen plenty of inexperienced Clerics mess up their healing spell and kill the *very* hero they were supposed to be saving. Do not underestimate the lifesaving work we do on the adventuring frontline."[964]

Me: "My apologies, I didn't mean to offend you—"

Linderlard: "You didn't offend me. *The Enduring Light* is my shield."

A strong wind suddenly whips around the wooden beams that miraculously support the temple's entire weight. There's a wail from the choir as they slide past in panic, rapidly gaining momentum—but impressively, most still manage to stay in tune.[965] I focus on the intricate architecture carved into the ceiling to distract myself long enough for the stomach-churning waves of nausea to subside. The Cleric follows my line of sight upwards as he nods with approval at my admiration for the temple's architecture.

Linderlard: "Is this temple not a marvel of engineering? Do you know there's nearly a thousand wooden stilts holding up the whole structure?"

Me: "Yes, please don't remind me—I'm not good with heights. I nearly turned back several times before finally reaching the temple's doors. Do the foundations of this place not concern you?"

Linderlard: "*Concern?* Nay, this place was built in honour of *The Enduring Light*, and like *The Enduring Light*—it shall forever remain."

Me: "But why build it so high—it even towers above the castle's tallest point?"

Linderlard: "This temple is a beacon against the endless tide of darkness—and like most beacons, it must stand against those who seek its downfall.[966] This temple fills the heart with hope—giving

---

[964] *Calling it the adventuring 'frontline' is perhaps a little generous with the truth—I have it on good authority that most Clerics generally congregate towards the rear of an adventuring group—closest to the nearest exit (in case of an emergency).*

[965] *Singing, somewhat ironically, the hymn 'Be Perfectly Still, In The Presence Of Thy Enduring Light'.*

[966] *I think the Cleric is being literal here—the temple is a 'tempting' target for any rapscallions with opportunity and time in one hand, and a BIG <u>saw</u> in the other.*

strength to those needing to step out of the shadow for themselves. Also, being this high up makes it a lot easier for *The Enduring Light* to hear our prayers."[967]

Me: "A prayer is all well and good—but even the Godless can bring down a God."

The Cleric grins at me as he pulls out a strange spherical object covered with ornate gems and inscriptions. He holds it out for me to examine.

Linderlard: "That is why I always carry one of these—for Godless encounters."

Me: "What *is* that?"

Linderlard: "A Holy *Hand of Grenade.*"

Me: "A Holy what—?"

Linderlard: "*Hand of Grenade.*"

Me: "What's a *Grenade?*"

Linderlard: "Named after the famous Cleric, Isabard Grenade—this is what divine retribution looks like! Who needs *one* Fireball when I hold an item in the palm of my hand that could unleash a force greater than a <u>hundred</u> Fireballs! This Holy weapon can deliver a 'smite' far greater than Isabard himself!"[968]

Me: "Isn't that dangerous to hold?!"

Linderlard: "That is why one must always remember to throw it first— unless one wishes to *endure* no longer."

Me: "Where did you get it from?"

---

[967] *The Cleric's Sky God must be deaf for the temple to be this high.*

[968] *Isabard Grenade was a Cleric of The Enduring Light who lived several hundred summers ago and had a feared reputation for delivering the biggest 'smite' with an open hand. As a strict disciplinarian, any acolytes who were foolish enough to attempt to sneak out of his lessons to smoke a Halfling-rolled woodbine behind the pulpit would inevitably face his stinging right hand of justice as a consequence. The item Linderlard holds tightly in his hand is a stark reminder of the pain Isabard could deliver if he ever caught anyone sloping off for a smoke during his prayer studies.*

Linderlard: "Thorde Ironstein sold it to me".

Me: "Where did he get it from—it seems a little beyond the skills of a simple Forgemaster?"

Linderlard: "Don't let him hear you say that—but you are correct in your assumption. I, too, believe there is an intriguing origin behind the *Hand of Grenade*—but as of yet, the arcane scribes here at the temple have not found the answer to this puzzling mystery."[969]

Me: "How do you know it even works?"

Linderlard: "I have faith it will work—lest you forget, it is covered by the Forgemaster's personal guarantee."[970]

Me: "I suspect, bringing it back in one piece could prove a little tricky in this instance."

Linderlard: "Nonetheless, it is a weapon that should strike fear into the hearts of the Godless—"

I'm both in awe and fear at being so close to a weapon so volatile.

Me: "Can I ask, what makes a weapon like this... *erm*...'Holy'?"

Linderlard: "Well, it's not *actually* 'Holy' just yet..."

Me: "But you said—"

Linderlard: "I *know* what I said, but as luck would have it, we are due to bless the *Hand of Grenade* shortly. Would you like to watch?"

The temple shudders and trembles as dust falls from the ceiling. The Cleric does not bat an eyelid and instead waits for my answer.

Me: "What does this blessing involve?"

Linderlard: "We must trust our faith by placing it in the heart of *The Enduring Light*—"

---

[969] *Although the initials 'S.M.' etched on the base of the Hand of Grenade is a bit of a giveaway.*

[970] *Unless it's magical—but I don't think now is the right time to point out this tiny detail to the Cleric...*

Me: "That doesn't sound exactly *safe*."[971]

Linderlard: "Nonsense! That is because you are faithless and weak."[972]

To my look of horror, the Elf tosses the *Hand of Grenade* into an iron bowl, hanging above the burning fire of *The Enduring Flame*.

Linderlard: "Faith is what empowers a Cleric. It gives us our strength—without it, we may as well be dust blowing in the wind."[973]

Me: "*Erm*—I'll pass if it's all the same to you."

The Cleric's face falls with disappointment.

Linderlard: "*Really?* You have nothing to fear here, brother. *The Enduring Light* protects all—"

The temple foundations rock and shift angrily once more, almost with rage at my defiance. Like a battle-shy Cleric, I feel myself edging towards the exit, keen to leave before the now white-hot *Hand of Grenade* cuts short my time in these worn boots.

Me: "You know—I think I'd better be going. Thank you again for speaking to me today; it's been *illuminating*, to say the least."

Linderlard: "Go peacefully into *The Enduring Light*. I shall pray for both you and your recently departed brother."

Me: "—and may *you* go peacefully into *The Enduring Light* too."[974]

I hurry towards the exit, almost tumbling down the rickety staircase in my haste. Every step I take is a step I fear will be my last. But there's no explosion, no cries of terror or falling masonry raining down from on high[975]—I breathe a deep sigh of relief; perhaps there's something to be said for faith after all.

---

[971] *I'm not entirely convinced this is one bet the Cleric really should be making.*

[972] *Or sensible and cautious—but that's just my biased opinion.*

[973] *Judging by how rapidly the Hand of Grenade is turning orange, this may happen <u>much</u> sooner than the Cleric anticipates.*

[974] *Or should that be '—go in <u>pieces</u> into The Enduring Light too'?*

[975] *Or angry curses from those caught by the fallout far below...*

As I walk through the gates of Waverdale, I look back at *The Enduring Light* burning high above the temple—I can't help wondering if one day the flame will go out forev—

B—OOM!!!

29. Pippo, the Couturier

Located close to the unremarkable town of Coburn, Pippo's Palace is hidden behind a fortified wall that stands at least ten Gnomes high[976]—leaving me to wonder if it has been built to keep undesirables out or to keep something 'remarkable' in. Visitors to Pippo's Palace are by special invitation only; fortunately, the gold-sprinkled letter I'm holding in my hand, stamped with Pippo's official seal, has granted me access to the legendary Gnome's abode. As you can imagine, it's unlikely I'll find any ordinary folk browsing through the Couturier's wares here, for Pippo only caters to the 'extraordinary', such as seasoned adventurers, Kings, and Kingmakers alike.[977]

Gentle music fills the air as I pass a well in the courtyard and ascend the wooden steps leading to Pippo's famous residence. Walking through the doors, I notice several glass-cased mannequins flanking the hallway, each one dressed in some form of extravagant attire—anything from flamboyant armoured corsets to steel-plated cloaks.[978] I'm in the middle of reminding myself that I'm about to meet the realm's leading purveyor of adventuring clothes when a shrill voice suddenly fills the air.

Voice: "Well, well, well—what *doooo* we have here?"

The voice continues to echo around the room before the double doors at the far end of the grand hall swing open with theatrical effect, revealing a beam of light on the floor. I watch mesmerised as a Gnome, dressed in an outrageous yellow sequinned jerkin, yellow tight-fitting shorts, and matching knee-length yellow leather boots, steps out into the spotlight. He spies me through his star-shaped seeing-device and begins to strut dramatically in my general direction.

Me: "P—Pippo?"

---

[976] *Gnomes insist this equates to around 15 Halflings, whilst Halflings insist that this number actually only equates to 9 Halflings—whatever the truth of this matter, everyone agrees the wall is no greater than 7 Dwarves high or one really tall High-Elf on stilts.*

[977] *That's not to say that Kings and Kingmakers are cut from the same cloth—in fact, most Kings will insist that any visiting Kingmakers cannot turn up on the same day in case their Highnesses is suddenly dethroned and replaced by a smug-looking ginger cat.*

[978] *Ideal for stopping backstabs but utterly impractical for keeping safe during a thunderstorm.*

The flamboyant Couturier bows as he reaches my position.

Pippo: "At your service and in the flesh..."

I can sense his eyes lingering on my tired attire; I find myself drawing my cloak around my slender frame, conscious my worn-out clothes appear excruciatingly dull compared to the Gnome's lively apparel.

Pippo: "By the looks of you, I would hazard a guess that you're a *Loremaster*."

Me: "Am I that obvious?"

The Gnome circles around me as he takes in my appearance from every conceivable angle—hand on his chin, his face sour with disapproval.

Pippo: "Well, let's just say you are certainly dressed for comfort, not for an expeditious retreat."[979]

Me: "I freely admit, I've only ever chosen clothes for their practicality."

Pippo: "*Ha!* In that case, I'm not sure you've come to the right place, for my designs are anything *but* practical."

The Couturier claps his hands—from out of nowhere, a harried-troupe of Halfling assistants rush out to place a large, plush seat under Pippo's posterior just before the Gnome sits down. The smiling Couturier continues to regard me from behind his star-covered eyes, clearly revelling in the moment.

Me: "Can you tell me how you came to be the realm's foremost supplier of dungeon-ready garments?"

Pippo: "Please—you make it sound so *seedy*. To answer your question properly, I need to take you back to my humble beginning. Mine was not an idyllic fairy-tale—I grew up in the cold dark caverns of Faldern Moon, scavenging around in the shadows for any Barbed Lichen and Undertoe Fungus—"

Me: "To eat?"

Pippo: "To *eat?* No—to *make* clothes!"

---

[979] *Finally! Someone who <u>doesn't</u> think I'm a bloody Wizard!*

Me: "Barbed Lichen and Undertoe Fungus? That doesn't sound very comfortable to wear."

Pippo: "You are quite correct—they are not. Do you know how itchy Barbed Lichen is, or how much Undertoe Fungus reeks of rotting cheese?"

Me: "I'm guessing it was tough back then."

Pippo: "Tough is an understatement. My skin was constantly sore—I would cry myself to sleep on my giant granite pillow, dreaming of soft silks and crushed velvet bed sheets. I smelt *so* bad I used to attract all manner of Turd Lurkers to my chamber. Do you realise how unsettling it is being woken up by a Recurring Bobber appearing and disappearing from the bottom of a slate-covered sheet?"[980]

There's an awkward silence as I briefly picture the scene in my mind's eye—it makes for grim viewing.[981]

Pippo: "I promised myself I would find a way to wear only the finest of clothes—but I was young and foolish, and I had absolutely no idea where to start."

Me: "What did you do?"

Pippo: "What could I do? I lamented as I endured. It was only by the good grace of Lady Luck that a distant Uncle died and left an old dungeon in his will to me."[982]

Me: "Your Uncle owned a dungeon?"[983]

Pippo: "He was a bit eccentric—fashioned it out of the rock with his

---

[980] I don't, but I suspect it's infinitely better than being woken to find you've been grabbed by a Bunjee Spider and are hurtling towards the cave ceiling faster than a Wizard trying to evade combat.

[981] And smelling.

[982] Although Lady Luck insists she has an alibi around the time of death.

[983] Perhaps he hired it out for parties—by that, I mean the adventuring kind, rather than the kind of 'parties' attended by hyperactive children and their tired parents (who are desperate to feast upon the leftover party food when nobody is looking).

bare hands.[984] My Uncle never had any children of his own, nor did he like anyone from the extended family. But by some quirk of fate, I was gifted the deed to the dungeon when it was time for him to dig his final tunnel under the *Great Barrier.* I have no idea why he chose me—I guess I annoyed him slightly less than any of my other relations. Stepping inside for the first time, I soon discovered my Uncle had filled the dungeon with intricate traps and weird rooms—but it was in disrepair; the traps wouldn't work properly and needed frequent cleaning..."

Me: "Cleaning?"

Pippo: "Of expired adventurers."

Me: "That sounds a little dark."[985]

Pippo: "It was, although it did have *some* benefits."

Me: "Like?"

Pippo: "Clothes—lots of clothes. Of course, I had to repair whatever I found. Most of the previous owners had been impaled, eaten, or crushed. You have no idea the number of holes I had to sew closed or bloodstains I had to boil out—but with time, I was able to amass a small fortune selling on the repaired and steam-pressed garments to new adventurers looking for a bargain."[986]

Me: "From where do you think your love of clothes first sprang?"

Pippo: "It's a passion I've had for as long as I can remember. When I was younger, I used to dress my stone toys in mossy outfits I had designed. My rocks were 'models' and walked—no *strutted,* down my makeshift runway while my family clapped enthusiastically. In those tender childhood days, little could I imagine the wealth of exotic and

---

[984] *Tunnelling rock with his bare hands? It would literally take 'bear hands' to achieve this feat.*

[985] *That can be said of <u>any</u> poorly lit dungeon, filled with deadly traps designed to maim unwary adventurers.*

[986] *'Steam-pressed' usually involves an extremely angry Barbarian hitting the clothes with a very heavy hammer. Needless to say, the whole process is fraught with danger and often ends badly for everyone involved.*

unusual clothes I would acquire every time a hero inevitably fell in my dungeon."

Me: "Inevitably?"

The Gnome grins innocently as if butter wouldn't melt off his yellow hot pants.[987]

Pippo: "I *may* have made a few modifications to the dungeon when I took over."

Me: "Like?"

Pippo: "I thought the Dragon was a nice addition."

Me: "A Dragon? How in the Gods did you manage to get a Dragon inside your dungeon?"

The Gnome doubles over, laughter echoing off the walls—making the Couturier appear immense despite his diminutive form.

Pippo: "It wasn't easy! First, I needed a Potion of Shrinking—fortunately, I knew of a travelling Potioneer who frequently passed our cave on his journey west."

Me: "I see. But wouldn't the Dragon, *you know,* turn you into a charcoal smudge on the floor the instant you uncorked the magical elixir?"

Pippo: "That's where a *Helm of Dragon Control* came in handy."

Me: "And I suppose you just happened to have one sitting around?"

Pippo: "Don't be ridiculous."

Me: "I was about to say that it sounded *highly* implaus—"

Pippo: "I *knew* someone who had one. So, I borrowed it for a while until I found a suitable Dragon I could take back to the dungeon under my complete control."

Me: "Hang on... you *borrowed* a Helm of Dragon control?"

---

[987] *I'm only calling them 'hot pants' because I have a genuine concern they are on the verge of spontaneously combusting at any given moment—they crackle like boar slices on a sizzling pan.*

Pippo: "Yup—from the Dragon Lord. I knew him from when he was a simple Turnip Farmer. Anyway, he seemed more than happy for me to take the Helm of Dragon Control off his hands for a little while—to be honest, I think he really needed a break from all those bloody Dragons..."

Me: "Isn't the Helm of Dragon Control cursed?"

Pippo: "It certainly would've been if anyone I knew had seen me wearing it. Whoever designed the damn thing had all the sartorial sensitivity of a blind-drunk Barbarian—it really didn't do anything for my look. But no, in all seriousness, the rumoured curse gave me little cause for concern—such malign enchantments do not affect Gnomes".[988]

Me: "*Ah*—handy. Let me get this right, so... with the Dragon under your control, you got it to drink the potion... and then *shrunk* it—then what? Did you put the tiny lizard in your pocket before reaching the dungeon and waiting for the potion effects to wear off?"

Pippo: "Sounds about right."

Me: "How did you stop the Dragon from incinerating or tearing any clothes into unrecognisable shreds?"[989]

Pippo: "I used the Helm of Dragon Control to ensure the Dragon didn't overkill any adventurers and ruin their clothes. I also made the Dragon promise it would leave any adventuring garments unspoiled. Most of the time, the Dragon demanded the clothes off a hero in return for sparing their life—you'd be surprised how often that simple request worked."[990]

Me: "And the Dragon did what it was told?"

Pippo: "That Helm of Dragon Control wasn't a novelty item! Although there was one unfortunate *inferno* incident... but, on the whole, the Dragon did whatever I commanded of it—even long after I gave the Helm of Dragon Control back to the Dragon Lord."

---

[988] *Although curses <u>do</u> affect Halflings—much to every Gnome's delight...*

[989] *The same probably can't be said for the hapless hero wearing the clothes in the first place.*

[990] *Leaving the naked hero to 'streak' all the way back to the tavern with their cupped hands held between their legs.*

Me: "And to think, to many, the Dragon Lord is just another Evildoer—"

Pippo: "An Evildoer? No, no, no, not at all. He was trying his best to keep the Dragons from attacking the local farms—<u>he</u> was a hero if you think about it. I remember how I used to repair his worn farming clothes in exchange for some freshly dug-up turnips. It was a damn shame what happened to him."

Me: "You mean with the Titan of Thunder?"

Pippo: "Yeah—I like to think the *Titan of Thunder* let him go home, back to tend to his turnip field."

There's a moment of genuine sadness that washes over the Gnome. But in an instant, it's gone as the Couturier continues with his origin story.[991]

Pippo: "Anyway, the dungeon served its purpose as a stepping-stone to where I find myself today. When I gathered enough materials, armour, and clothes, I sold the dungeon to a Nomadic Cleric for a tidy sum."

Me: "A Nomadic Cleric? What would a Nomadic Cleric want with a dungeon? Where did they get so much coin?"[992]

Pippo: "Only the Gods know, but I wasn't about to look a gifted Hydra in one of its numerous mouths, so I agreed to sell it to him."

Me: "With the Dragon still inside it?"

Pippo: "Buyer beware."[993]

Me: "What did you do with the coin you made from the sale?"

The Gnome gestures towards the room, and we both take in the décor. Between the delicate drapery and the countless works of fine art, I find myself thinking about the number of exposed heroic backsides it took to build this architectural marvel.

---

[991] *I hope it's not an origin story that involves caves filled with bats and Pippo's parents murdered by a psychopathic 'Joker' in oversized boots. That would take the shine off this interview and make my Uncle Bevan Barr's profession seem somewhat unstable.*

[992] *Maybe the Nomadic Cleric couldn't resist using the rather large amount of coin that was just 'resting' in their donation box.*

[993] *Which is Gnomish for 'Bad luck—but there are <u>no</u> refunds'.*

Pippo: "It didn't take long for word to spread of a new Couturier who only catered for the very finest heroes of the realm. I become the most sought-after purveyor of adventuring attire and armour almost overnight. Gilva Flamebeard, Redmane the Paladin, Silvanna the Sorceress,[994] even the legend himself, Arin Darkblade, were *all* invited to wear my creations—and *all* of them came without exception."

Me: "That must have been a humbling experience."

Pippo: "It was—it's *also* one that makes me *very* proud!"

The Gnome claps his hands in excitement. There's a small amount of movement just in my peripheral vision. I turn to see a large contraption being wheeled in my direction by several exhausted Halfling assistants. My eyes fix on the mysterious rectangular box as it towers over me before slowly coming to a halt a few feet from where I'm sitting.[995] Protruding at odd angles from the contraption are red mechanical arms. It looks like a fuming metal arachnid waiting on the doorstep for it's mechanical partner to return home after spending the whole evening *'tinkering'* with some Gnomes. The disjointed configuration of windows gives the apparatus the appearance of a somewhat disapproving sneer. I find myself sinking into my seat with guilt—even though I haven't been near a Gnome-filled tavern for several days.

Me: "What manner of sorcery is this?"

Pippo: "It's not magic—it's *all* mechanical. Please don't concern yourself; the Red Room is anything but dangerous."[996]

One of the Halfling assistants opens the door and politely waves me inside.

Me: "Am I expected to—?"

---

[994] *Although I'll be surprised if the Elf actually 'paid' for any outfit she walked away with.*

[995] *Please don't be a Mimic. Please don't be a Mimic. Please don't be a Mimic...*

[996] *Whenever I'm told not to worry that something isn't dangerous—is precisely the time to worry that something is dangerous (and will probably try to kill me in the near future). Also, the fact this mechanical monstrosity is painted in blood red is not helping matters either...*

Pippo: "Worry not, Loremaster. You will be walking in the footsteps of many exalted clients before you."

Me: "I'm not sure I'm ready for—"

Pippo: "Nonsense! The Red Room is a wonder to behold! You know, it even created invisible armour for a Mime Warrior—although it did take a while for the Improv-Fighter to work out which way round the damn thing went on."

Me: "Invisible armour?"

Pippo: "The Mime Warrior in question wanted an outfit that stood out—I have to say, I think it's one of my favourite creations. The craftsmanship of that piece is something to behold."

Me: "But it's invisible—how can anyone *see* any craftsmanship?"

Pippo: "It's only invisible to the *naked* eye.[997] Anyway, *up, up, up, up*— off you go!"

I try to swallow, but my throat is suddenly bone dry with fear, while my legs feel like a rapscallion has removed them with a big saw and replaced them with two Gelatinous Cube-like stumps instead.[998]

Me: "You really want me to go inside *that?*"

Pippo: "Of course—this is *all* for you!"

Me: "What will it do?"

The Gnome's eyes sparkle with countless possibilities.

Pippo: "It will *transform* you—not with a spell or any of that magical nonsense, but in ways you cannot comprehend. Shall we get started?"

A little nervous, yet eager for a closer inspection of Pippo's contraption, I place the bag containing my journal under my seat and get to my feet. I slowly ascend the ramp toward the Red Room's waiting door of disapproval. Before daring to look inside, I turn one last time to the Couturier looking on with unbridled anticipation.

---

[997] *Ironically.*

[998] *Probably the same rapscallion who'd gleefully cut down the wooden supports from under The Temple of Enduring Light...*

Me: "Is it safe?"

Pippo: "Completely—I've only lost three Halfling assistants to it so far."

Me: "***THR—***"

The Gnome shoves me inside the box and slams the door in my wake. I hear his cheery voice calling to me from outside.

Pippo: "Sacrifices are always required if one wishes to attain perfection."[999]

With an anxious prayer to whatever God listens to non-believers,[1000] I stand alone in the darkness, completely exposed to whatever is about to happen next. The Gnome shouts from the other side of the Red Room's door.

Pippo: "You may feel a weird sensation. That's perfectly normal. Just close your eyes and try to relax. Right, where to begin... I know! *A Paladin!*"

Me: "A Palad—?"

The mechanical arms suddenly whirl into life and begin stripping the clothes from my back like a ripe Gonganana.[1001]

Me: "***WHAT THE—***"

Pippo: "Remember to breathe slowly—*enjoy* this experience!"

Me: "***ENJOY? WHAT'S TO ENJOY? IT'S STEALING THE SHIRT OFF MY BACK!***"[1002]

Pippo: "You'll get it back when we're finished."

---

[999] *I agree sacrifices are often needed; I just wasn't expecting to be the one thrust upon the altar.*

[1000] *This would be the Deity, Agnostic, who isn't even sure of their own existence—which makes it awkward for everyone when they show up unexpectedly at the 'End of Summer Omnipresent Party'.*

[1001] *An exotic fruit found in the humid climates of the Eastern Plains, famed for making an enormous racket when dropping from a tree or stepped on by a clumsy Mime Artist.*

[1002] *It also probably hustles inebriated Clerics with games of 'Blasphemous' in its spare time.*

Before I can reply, I suddenly feel a hundred pounds heavier—as if I'm carrying the world's burdens on my shoulders. A sudden hiss of steam obscures my vision, followed by a blinding light as the door opens again. I stagger out of the red-automaton horror and almost collapse under the weight of my armour. An enthusiastic round of applause erupts from Pippo's Halfling assistants. I stare down at the heavy plate armour covering my torso. It's magnificent to behold, but I'm struggling to raise my arms higher than my hips.[1003]

Pippo: "*Hmmm...* something about this isn't right. Maybe it's the colour or the way it makes you slouch. But I'm not feeling this, *no no no...* forgive me, *Loremaster...* but I don't think a 'Paladin' is really... *ahem...* you..."

Me: "I'll be honest, I'm not into the whole 'standing-silent-looking-stoic' thing either."

The Gnome claps his hands together—I'm suddenly aware the Halfling assistants are slowly turning me on the spot. After several attempted pushes and shoves from the miniature entourage, I make my way back up the ramp at a pace that would make a heavily encumbered ant feel like they're wearing Boots of Speed.

Pippo: "Let's try again—perhaps you're more *Rogue* material?"

There's a loud *'CLUNK'* as the mechanical arms spring into life once more, stripping away the Paladin's armour in the blink of an eye. The door opens, and I'm kicked back into the hall by a heavy iron boot. I find myself dressed in black breeches, tunic, and boots. I also have a belt of wicked-looking daggers strapped across my chest. A menacing scar has been painted across my left cheek,[1004] while the letters B-A-C-K have been tattooed on the digits of my left hand—I look at my right hand and see the letters S-T-A-B inked onto the backs of the fingers. Almost instantly, the Halfling assistants clap enthusiastically at my latest attire, but Pippo remains ominously silent once more.[1005]

[1003] *Which means I can just about make a crude hip-thrust gesture—but little else.*

[1004] *Facial cheek!*

[1005] *I'm starting to suspect Pippo's chorus of pint-sized sycophants is not the toughest of crowds.*

Pippo: "I don't think 'black' is your colour—it makes you look a bad Pirate.[1006]

I stare at my shadowy clothes, wondering when this nightmare will be over.

Me: "I suppose I do prefer a bit more life in my attire—"

Pippo: "More life..."

The Gnome clicks his fingers in sudden realisation.

Pippo: "Yes! I've got it! *A Bard!*"

Before I can utter a word of objection, I'm ushered back towards the infernal apparatus to be subjected to its transformative powers once more. Several painfully awkward moments later, I emerge dressed like a rainbow chicken[1007] sitting at the keys of a portable pipe organ. I grin painfully through the lenses of a crescent-moon seeing-device as a heavy iron hand rudely hurls me out of the box. I rapidly gather speed as I roll down the steep ramp—it's only by the good grace of the Halfling assistants, ready and waiting with a rather large net that I don't go hurtling toward the horizon.[1008]

The Couturier stares at me with complete disdain.

Pippo: "*Oh*—no, no, no, no! This is all wrong. I mean _really_ wrong."

My blank expression masks the screams of endless torture rattling around my brain.

Pippo: "By the Gods, hurry up and get him back in there—this is an abomination to rival Quoth-Shogga, the thousand-headed floating

---

[1006] Contrary to popular culture, there are both 'good' Pirates and 'bad' Pirates. 'Good' Pirates are identical to 'bad' Pirates but still have all their own teeth, wear brighter clothes, and make their prisoners 'dance the plank'.

[1007] Rainbow Chickens are a legendary species of fowl found at the opposite end of a rainbow to the one with the pot of gold. As a result, many Fortune Hunters have cursed their luck when they've trekked across the realm searching for the treasure, only to discover the bemused colourful bird pecking away at the prismatic beams of light hitting the ground.

[1008] —And possible towards the Great Beyond waiting... erm... beyond it...

428

Demon from the White Porcelain Rim!"[1009]

The Halfling assistants puff and groan as they haul the pipe organ, with me still sat at it, back into the mechanical monstrosity. One quick change of clothes later, I now find myself wearing nothing but a padded fur loincloth.

Me: *"Oh my..."*

I raise my arms in an attempt to strike a heroic pose, but my biceps fail to make an appearance. The Gnome stares for a moment in contemplation before clapping his hands with urgency.

Pippo: *"Erm... let us move swiftly on without ever mentioning this hideous mistake ever again."*[1010]

I hear soft sniggering coming from the bemused Halfling assistants watching on. I hurry back into the *Red Box of Woe,* as I'm now starting to call it, for once thankful for its dark embrace. From inside my shelter, I hear the Gnome click his fingers together in a moment of inspiration.

Pippo: *"Aha!* I think I have it—the answer to our prayers."

Me: "Please, *not* a Cleric, *anything* but a Cleric—"

Pippo: "It's *not* a Cleric—it's something far more *magical* than that!"

There's another loud *'CLANG'* of metal as the mechanical arachnid begins to work overtime. Bolts shake in their holes as the entire contraption groans and protests as if *it* were the one being tortured, rather than I. Pipes creak and crack as steam pours from a vent high above me. But the *Red Box of Woe* still thunders and roars to please its diminutive taskmaster.

Me: ***"HELP ME—!"***

Before anyone can come to my aid, I'm suddenly ejected from the box like a bolt of lightning. I tumble down the ramp and land in a heap on

---

[1009] *The Mother God of all Turd Lurkers...*

[1010] *How anyone can wear this attire without some serious questions being asked about their state of mind, is beyond me? Not that anyone other than a muscle-bound Barbarian would ever be seen dead on a dungeon floor whilst wearing it, of course...*

the floor at the Gnome's feet. There's a stunned silence from the nearby Halfling assistants, too nervous to show their hands in case their hard-to-please boss is far from pleased.

As I pick myself up and wipe the dust from my clothes, I can't help but notice I'm wearing a lavish purple robe that covers my entire frame. The hem is lined with arcane symbols carefully embroidered in shades of silver. There's a slight shimmer to the material as I slowly rotate my arm and admire the exquisite craftsmanship.

Pippo: "*Yes! Yes!* **YES!** That's it! Of course, why did I not see it before? You're a Wizard, *Loremaster—**A WIZARD!***"[1011]

As I marvel at the shimmering clothes, I must confess that I feel a strong sense of purpose growing within me—almost as if my whole being is answering a call to adventure. But before I can say another word, a loud *'BANG'* from behind nearly makes me jump out of my new robe in fright. Turning, I see black smoke billowing from the expired mechanical contraption as it threatens to give up on life and shuffle its spider-like metal arms off to the *Great Breaker's Yard.*[1012]

Me: "*Oh… d—did I do that?*"

The Couturier brushes away my concerns with a wave of his hand whilst his Halfling assistants run around one another in a blind panic.

Pippo: "There are *always* casualties in fashion. But please, it was <u>*so*</u> worth it to *finally* find the right outfit for you—besides, my Halfling assistants are more than capable of dealing with this."

I notice an awkward exchange of looks between the Halfling assistants, but none dare say anything to the contrary. Only the automaton offers any protest as it shudders and splutters before finally expiring in a spectacular shower of sparks and flames. The onlooking Halflings, realising the situation is rapidly spiralling out of control, grab nearby

---

[1011] *I do not ruddy-well believe it—<u>you</u> can stop your sniggering too!*

[1012] *'The Great Breakers Yard' is where Gnomes believe their strange mechanical contraptions end up when they inevitably expire—although it's not totally unheard of for some of these automatons to make an unexpected return to the land of the living. When something like that happens, it usually requires the services of a specialist Gnomish Cleric to finally lay the 'Ghost in the Mechanical' to rest.*

wooden pails and run to the well outside.[1013] Pippo is entirely oblivious to the fiery carnage unfurling, still hypnotised by the shimmering robe I'm wearing.

Pippo: "Yes, yes, **YES!** This is more like it! The cut is *perfect*. It fits you like a glove—I even love the colour! You look amazing—like a *true* adventurer!"

Aware I may not be around long enough to enjoy the new attire, I point to the fire that has now engulfed the wall drapes.

Me: "Shouldn't we be worried about that?"

The Gnome turns and stares at the inferno with a strange calmness. He seems unruffled by the line of Halfling assistants frantically passing pails of water at great speed, trying to stop the fire from consuming the entire palace—but it appears that it's too little too late.[1014]

Pippo: "We should leave them to it—they know what they're doing."

Me: "B—But your beautiful building?"

Pippo: "Don't worry—I have enough coin to build this place ten times over…"

A more troubling thought suddenly makes my blood run cold as I remember the bag I stashed just before entering Pippo's accursed *Red Room*.

Me: "*MY JOURNAL!*"

Pippo: "I think we should probably wait outside."

The inferno is now threatening to cut off our only escape from this fiery deathtrap. I briefly contemplate running back into the flames to save the bag containing my precious journal, but the Gnome grabs my hand and hauls me outside. Standing beside the well, we watch from a safe distance as Pippo's Palace burns brighter than *The Enduring Light*.

[1013] *Sadly these particular pails seem to have been acquired for their dainty artisan charm rather than their practicality. Each one might conceivably conceal the modesty of Devlin Stormwind's previous owner, Thimble Groin, but they offer little hope in the face of this growing blaze.*

[1014] *Not that I feel that's a direct reflection of the Halfling assistants' efforts they are making—nor their diminutive size.*

I can see silhouetted figures against the blaze as the Halfling assistants still battle bravely to keep the fire under control—but they may as well be throwing a pitcher of water at an angry Red Dragon with sunstroke on the hottest day of the summer.

Me: "It's gone... it's *all* gone..."

I'm broken... first my brother, now my *journal*—I seem to be losing everything that matters to me. The blaze has robbed me of every scrap of knowledge acquired on this journey, from the most precious secret to the most inane nonsense—putting my quest right back to its start. I find myself glumly wondering if I can muster the will to begin again, even though deep down, I know such a thing is impossible.[1015]

Me: "I should really be giving these back to you—"

I resignedly gesture to the Wizard robes I'm still wearing.

Pippo: "Keep them. Your clothes are pretty much ash now anyway.[1016] What sort of Couturier would I be if I let you loose into the wild *Oh, Natural?* We both know you're not going to fool anyone into thinking you're a Barbarian."

Me: "T—Thank you..."

Pippo: "No, thank *you*—I'm sorry about your gear, but let's be honest, those old clothes were doing nothing for you."[1017]

I'm about to leave and start my long walk home when a soot-covered Halfling assistant comes running out of the smoke and hands a small-blackened bundle to the Couturier.

Pippo: "*Ah*—I think *this* is yours."

Expecting the worse, I carefully break open my baked clothes. An overwhelming wave of relief fills me as I spy my trusty leather bag and, more importantly, my journal almost completely unharmed. I flick through the opening pages to ensure none of my interviews perished

---

[1015] *A fiery ball took my brother, and now a fiery hall stole my journal—the Barr Brothers are cursed!*

[1016] *So much for getting my shirt back.*

[1017] *Apart from keeping me warm and keeping my starkness locked away...*

432

in the inferno and say a silent prayer to whatever God is watching over me.[1018]

Pippo: "Well?"

Me: "I think I got lucky; there's only a hint of fire damage on the cover."

Pippo: "I could always get a *new* cover made for you—I mean, a book jacket is *just* like a regular jacket, only a tiny bit smaller. I could even have it made in a colour to match your Wizard robes."

Me: "Would that involve another one of your strange contraptions?"

The Couturier gives me the broadest of smiles.

Pippo: "Almost certainly!"

As generous as the Gnome's offer is, I don't think I'm brave enough to become his muse—nor risk the safety of my journal again. I politely decline Pippo's offer and bid the Couturier farewell. With my new robes sparkling in the glow of the fire and my journal safely tucked inside the bag on my shoulder, I head with renewed optimism towards my next interview. I may not be a fully-fledged Wizard, but at least I now know what it's like to leave a flaming catastrophe in my wake.[1019]

[1018] *A little disconcerting—but this voyeuristic God <u>has</u> just used a divine hand to save my journal from being turned to ash, so I guess I can't complain too much...*

[1019] *I feel no guilt for what has just transpired—maybe there's more 'Wizard' to me than meets the eye.*

30. Snodgrass, the Goblin Archer

Greenvale Forest has many unpleasant surprises hidden within its emerald foliage. From the rumour of a Goblin infestation that threatens to spill out beyond the Merchant's Road to the Heartenford Guards, who have gained notoriety for allegedly stashing the extra coin they've pressed out of travelling pedlars in secretly marked tree stumps. It is a place where danger lurks behind every bush; a sudden snap of a twig or scampering of feet could be the last thing an unsuspecting adventurer would ever hear[1020] if they're not too careful.

I'm following a secret woodland path, which meanders through Greenvale Forest that, in theory, should lead me to the very gates of Heartenford itself. You may be wondering why I am undertaking this journey, given the unsavoury reputation of this inhospitable place. Hagworl the Gravedigger has come through on his promise and arranged a clandestine meeting with one of the more unusual contacts he has dealings with—namely, a representative who works for an Evildoer.

As I step into a clearing, I hear a rustling in the undergrowth and stop dead in my tracks. I immediately change my laboured breaths into shallow sips, trying hard not to give myself away even though I can hear my heart beating noisily from my chest—but it's to no avail. Whoever or whatever is making the sound up ahead already knows I am here—and is coming straight for me!

A nasty-looking pot-bellied humanoid emerges from the heavy thicket with a bow hooked across its back,[1021] and a wicked-looking scimitar[1022] tucked in its belt. The green-skinned creature brushes the bugs from its shoulders before choosing to eat the juiciest one—this is unmistakably a *Goblin!* My heart leaps in fright at the sight of this fearsome creature as it looks up to see me frozen to the spot.

Me: *"A G—GOBLIN!"*

[1020] *Or a Loremaster wearing a Wizard's robe, pretending to be one...*

[1021] *There's no tangible reason a Goblin would be carrying a bow other than to use it to prod dubious things or scratch a particularly bothersome and hard-to-reach itch (this would be because the Goblin in question has already foolishly eaten the local Halfling Backscratcher).*

[1022] *By this, I mean it looks nasty and could really hurt someone—not that it looks 'excellent'.*

The Goblin panics as it quickly glances in both directions.

Goblin: "Where!? *Oh*—yeah, me... y—yew der Loremaster?"

Me: "Y—Yes?"

Hagworl failed to mention his contact was a Goblin; it would have been nice to know this beforehand in case I needed to bring a little extra protection along.[1023]

Goblin: "I'm Snodgrass... 'Agworl said yew wanted to talk—"

The Goblin makes for a fallen tree trunk and jumps on it to sit down.[1024]

Snodgrass: "—so talk... und if I get bored, I may 'ave to eat ya instead."

A cold shiver runs down my spine. I'm acutely aware I'm in no position to stop this creature from carrying out its threat if it *really* wanted to.[1025]

Snodgrass: "I'm just messin' with ya—I like my food less magical lookin'..."

It momentarily crosses my mind to explain to the creature that I'm not a Wizard, but I think it's probably wiser to keep the facade going, just this once.

Me: "R—Right, well, did Hagworl tell you *why* I asked for this meeting?"

Snodgrass: "'E said yew wanted to know why we keep droppin' off dead 'eroes to 'im—or somefink like dat?"

Me: "Yes—something like dat—I mean '*that*'. I wondered if we could start at the beginning, and by that, I mean the end."

Snodgrass: "Are yew tryin' to be cleva'?"

[1023] Like a Dwarven Barbarian with a VERY big axe, or armour made to look like an archery target...

[1024] A tree trunk with a peculiar marking carved into its bark that looks like the letter 'H' riding a letter 'G'; even Greenvale Forest isn't immune to degenerates wanting to leave their mark wherever they please.

[1025] Which I really hope it doesn't. I'm glad that in a recent poll published in the monthly edition of 'Dungeons & Flagons' Loremasters appeared second to last in the 'How Tasty Is Your Profession To Eat' rankings—one place higher than Gnome Rogues—and those ruffians don't even wash!

I can't help but notice the Goblin resting his hand on the pommel of his scimitar.

Me: "M—My apologies, let me explain myself better. Let's say an adventurer enters your dungeon—"

Snodgrass: "Crypt."

Me: "Sorry?"

Snodgrass: "It *ain't* a dungeon where we live—it's a crypt."

Me: "*Ah,* okay, a crypt. So, this adventurer enters your... *crypt*—"

Snodgrass: "Wot kind of adventurer?"

Me: "I don't know; what does it matter?"

The Goblin glares at me with his sickly yellow eyes.

Snodgrass: "It matters..."

I catch a glimpse of purple from my robes and latch onto a moment of inspiration.

Me: "Okay, let's say this adventurer is a Wizard—"

Snodgrass: "I <u>'ate</u> Wizards; dey're always burnin' me stuff."

Me: "Sorry—you *ate* a Wizard?"

Snodgrass: "Not ate—**'ATE!**"

I'm still confused, but I don't want to end up as the Goblin's main course before I've even had a chance to finish this conversational starter.

Me: "What sort of stuff do they burn?"

Snodgrass: "**ME** stuff—wot do yew fink?!"

I wince in pain as the memory of my brother's fiery demise flashes across my mind. This doesn't go unnoticed by the Goblin.

Snodgrass: "Wot's wron' wiv yew?"

Me: "*Oh,* nothing, probably something I ate that doesn't agree with me."

The Goblin nods in sympathy.

Snodgrass: "I know der feelin'. I ate a Dwarf once who didn't agree wiv me—"[1026]

Me: "A Dwarf?"

Snodgrass: "Yeah, I said I should eat 'im—'e disagreed. Yew wanna know der worst of it? Took foreva to get der taste of stone out of me mouth."[1027]

Me: "Why did he taste of stone?"

Snodgrass: "Because we were arguin' when 'e suddenly went grey 'n' 'ard—"

Me: "Sorry... he went... grey unnard?"

Snodgrass: "Dat's wot I said. Is dere sumfink wron' wiv ya 'earin'?"

Me: "Wrong with my...? But I don't wear an earring—"

Snodgrass: "—'Ells bells! 'Ow someone dim as yew can put one word next to der ova... 'Ooten der 'Orned 'Obgoblin only knows!"

Fearing I'm testing the patience of my subject, I attempt to steer the exchange back towards familiar territory.

Me: "*Ah*—wait a minute, I see! He was *hard* because he had been *turned to stone!* How did that happen?"

Snodgrass: "Might 'ave 'ad somefink to do wiv der stick 'e woz holdin'."

Me: "Stick? *Oh*—you mean a wand—"[1028]

[1026] *To be fair, Dwarves seldom agree with themselves, let alone with anyone else.*

[1027] *I know Dwarves LOVE their stone, but I always thought they'd taste a bit more like ale-soaked boar if you ever had the misfortune of eating one.*

[1028] *What's a Dwarf doing with a wand? This would be like a Wizard pulling out a two-handed sword and charging headfirst into battle before the nearest Barbarian could go red with rage.*

Snodgrass: "I *mean* a <u>stick</u>."[1029]

The Goblin snarls as he *'pops'* the scimitar from its scabbard with an upward thumb flick.

Me: "Stick it is—but you still ate him?"

Snodgrass: "Wozn't about to let a free meal go to waste now—woz I? If yew chipped away at 'im bit by bit, yew could make one nugget last all day."

My stomach nearly leaps out of my mouth in disgust.[1030]

Me: "So, back to our hypothetical Wizard... he enters your 'crypt' and unfortunately dies—"

Snodgrass:" 'Ow did 'e die?"

I stare at the Goblin with unbridled apathy coursing through my veins.

Me: "Painfully..."[1031]

Snodgrass: "Serves der Wizard right for burnin' me stuff."

Me: "Okay, let's just take for granted the Wizard died—then what happens?"

Snodgrass: "'E stops breathin'."

Me: "No—I mean, *after* that..."

Snodgrass: "'E stops burnin' me stuff!"

I feel my patience reaching limits usually reserved for Paladins.[1032]

[1029] *I'm guessing at some point, the Dwarf and this 'stick' had a 'big' falling out—probably over the unhappy wand being used to unblock a nostril, or something else equally repulsive where Dwarves are concerned...*

[1030] *I honestly believe it would crawl away from this clearing of its own volition if it could.*

[1031] *Like a Loremaster having a lengthy conversation with a poorly educated Goblin...*

[1032] *I almost pity any Goblin parent trying to raise their offspring with this level of patience-draining conversation to wade through on a daily basis. Also, I now have a newfound respect for Paladins... well—almost...*

Me: "Forget the stuff he did *or* didn't burn—what happens to the Wizard's body?"

Snodgrass: "We'd kick 'im a few times to make sure 'e's *really* dead. Wizard's 'ave a nasty 'abit of pretendin' to be dead—only to suddenly jump to dere feet und start runnin' around, burnin' me stuff again."

Me: "Why?"

Snodgrass: "Yew fik or somefink? I **told** ya! Wizards like burnin' me stuff—"

Me: "No, I mean, why would he suddenly jump to his feet?"[1033]

Snodgrass: "Depends where we kicked 'im, I suppose."[1034]

Me: "Fine—so after several hours of kicking the poor unfortunate Wizard's corpse without any reaction or consequence, you decide he is indeed *very* dead—what happens after that?"

Snodgrass: "We'd all look around at each ova wonderin' who's gonna be der one to tell der boss."

Me: "Tell the boss?"

Snodgrass: "Yeah, our boss. 'E don't like it when an 'ero dies in our crypt."

Me: "Why? Aren't you supposed to defeat heroes who are foolish enough to enter your dark domain?"

Snodgrass: "It's not dat—der boss 'ates 'avin' to fill in der paperwork."

Me: "Paperwork? Why does he have to fill in any paperwork?"

Snodgrass: "I dunno—'e don't tell me everythin'; I just know 'e 'ates it when a dead 'ero turns up."

Me: "What do you do while your boss fills in the paperwork?"

Snodgrass: "We search der corpse for loot."

[1033] *This wouldn't normally happen, not unless a mischievous Necromancer with pyromaniacal tendencies is nearby...*

[1034] *Although, that would also do it...*

Me: "How do you decide amongst yourselves who gets what?"

Snodgrass: "It all goes to der boss—dat's der rule."

Me: "Wait—you mean you don't even get to keep *anything* you find?"

Snodgrass: "Yew don't ever mess wiv der boss. 'E always wants to see everythin' first before it disappears."[1035]

Me: "Why—what would happen if a Goblin kept something back for themselves and your boss found out?"

Snodgrass: "Den dey'd be put on *Sui-cida Wotcha*—dat's der worst."

Me: "Sui-cida Wotcha—what's that?"

Snodgrass: "Dat's when we are told to guard der crypt—it's called der Sui-cida Wotcha coz yew can end up dead."

Me: "Dead? Why?"

The Goblin spits at the ground angrily.[1036]

Snodgrass: "Because of 'eroes like dat Wizard. 'Dose on Sui-cida Wotcha 'ave to check when an 'ero starts pokin' dere conks in places where it ain't wanted. Dey are der first ones who 'ave to ask to see an 'ero's badge—"

Me: "Wait, hang on—what badge?"

Snodgrass: "An 'Ero's Guild badge; so dey know wot kinda 'ero dey are before decidin' wot to do wiv 'em next."

Me: "What type of badges are there?"

Snodgrass: "Gold, silver or nun…"

[1035] *The Goblin's boss is wise—you don't want to be handling a Ring of Power after it's been inserted into the kind of orifices a Goblin ring-bearing finger will undoubtedly be thrust into.*

[1036] *The globule of phlegm hits the back of a passing slug that slowly turns to stare up in disgust at the creature—the Goblin is none the wiser of this indiscretion.*

Me: "Nun—there are badges for *nuns?* Do nuns adventure that much?"[1037]

Snodgrass: "Not *nuns*—<u>NUNS!</u> Like... **NUF—FINK!**"

Me: "*Oh*—yes, I see... so what do the different badges mean?"

Snodgrass: "Gold ones are okay as long as yew keep out der way—if ya do somefink stupid like gettin' one angry, den yew gonna be dead for sure."

Me: "What about the silver ones?"

Snodgrass: "Anythin' goes with dem—if dey die, dey die. Der 'Eroes Guild don't care about 'em. If dey don't come back alive—nobody minds, least of all der 'Eroes Guild."

Me: "So, you *kill* them?"

The Goblin laughs darkly.

Snodgrass: "We don't kill 'em much—"

Me: "If you don't kill them? Then how do they end up dead in your crypt?"

The Goblin shrugs his shoulders again.

Snodgrass: "Adventurers do stupid stuff dat gets 'em killed all der time—*especially* der silver ones."

Me: "Like what?"

Snodgrass: "Openin' a trapped chest... unlockin' a trapped door... standin' on a trapped floor—"[1038]

Me: "I'm sensing a common theme here."

Snodgrass: "We put signs up tellin' 'em to wotch out—und dey still end up dead. Sum adventurers are born un-cleva'..."

[1037] *Clerics and Paladins aren't the only Holy profession to embrace the adventuring life. Nuns have been known to venture into dungeons armed only with their vows of poverty, obedience, and chastity. You may feel this slightly foolish, but you forget they can call upon the most formidable nun of them all, the much-feared 'Mother Superior', to vanquish any foe.*

[1038] *If you're a Barbarian—sitting on a trapped throne...*

Me: "You put *warning* signs on your traps? Doesn't that defeat the whole purpose of a trap? Not to mention making your crypt relatively safe."

Snodgrass: "Don't ask me, dat's wot der boss said we' 'ave to do."

Me: "Walk me through what happens if a hero with a silver badge walks into your crypt?"

Snodgrass: "Der Sui-cida Wotcha try to chase 'em away. But if dey do get past der Sui-cida Wotcha, den we are allowed to hit 'em until dey don't move anymore, or we can 'ide und 'ope dey die from doin' somefink stupid."

Me: "Like ignoring a warning sign for an impending trap?"

Snodgrass: "Sum don't even do dat. Sum are so fik dey impale demselves on dere own sword or burn demselves up wiv dere own spell…"

Again, the Goblin's words cause the memory of my brother's death to flash across my mind's eye in a blaze of fiery woe.

Snodgrass: "Yew sure ya okay? Yew are makin' dat funny face again."[1039]

Me: "I'm fine. It almost sounds like you're saying the greatest threat to silver-badge wearing adventurers is usually themselves? What if they don't die as expected?

Snodgrass: "Den we 'ave to wait to see if dey leave. If dey don't, den we 'ave no choice… we 'ave to let der boss deal wiv dem…"

Me: "And what does he do?"

Snodgrass: "Wotever it takes. 'E's got dese gauntlets—nasty fings. Steal's ya life before ya very eyes—dat usually does der trick."

Me: "What do you do with the heroes then?"

Snodgrass: "Dey are too old to do any 'arm. We try und drop 'em off at der old 'eroes 'ome."

Me: "And if a hero *without* a badge shows up in your crypt?"

[1039] *Not now, Uncle Bevan Barr, not now.*

Snodgrass: "Dose ones can be tricky."

Me: "Tricky?"

Snodgrass: "'Cos ya don't know wot kind of adventurer ya gonna get, could be an 'armless fighter, could be a dangerous Barbarian..."[1040]

The grinning image of Dorn suddenly pops into my mind's eye.

Me: "Have you come across a Barbarian by any chance?"

It's the Goblin's turn to wince as a painful memory prods annoyingly at his consciousness.[1041]

Snodgrass: "'E should 'ave 'ad a gold badge—stupid silver badger... 'e wozn't supposed to be *dat* good..."

Me: "What did this Barbarian look like?"

Snodgrass: "'E woz a thin and angry 'uman who killed me mates before I 'ad a chance to shout a warnin' to 'em.[1042] All I could do woz drop to der floor und pretend to be dead."

Me: "That must have been awful for you."

Snodgrass: "Dat wozn't der worst of it."

Me: "What can be worse than that?"

Snodgrass: "My face woz pressed up against a dead Goblin's stinkin' crack 'ole while I 'ad to wait for der Barbarian to leave."

Me: "Thanks—that's an image which will haunt me forever."[1043]

[1040] Dungeons and crypts are dangerous places enough to venture 'fully' armed, but to explore one without the ability to hold a sword and shield is either showing off, or asking for trouble...

[1041] With something like a Goblin's bow, or a stick that may or may not be an annoyed wand...

[1042] In true Dorn fashion.

[1043] First, my brother's incineration by a Fireball, now a Goblin's face pressed up against a Goblin's dead posterior—this adventure is certainly giving me a few memories I can do well without!

Snodgrass: "Der smell never leaves yew neither…"

Me: "Did your boss take on the Barbarian himself?"

Snodgrass: "Nah—'e was 'idin' in a big urn und waited in dere until der angry-Warrior got bored und left der crypt. 'E told us to burn der dead und go get some more Goblins to replace dem."

Me: "Sounds like working for your boss is dangerous, so why do it at all? Surely there's something out there you could do without taking so many risks?"

Snodgrass: "Like wot? Dere's not much out dere for Goblins to do. At least we 'ave it better den dose cave-dwellin' Goblins—dem idiots 'ave to go into Greenvale Forest to look for bugs; if dey is lucky, dey will only meet a bandit or two. Dey shouldn't be much of a problem for a Goblin wiv a bow…"[1044]

Me: "And if they're unlucky?"

Snodgrass: "Den, an Elven Ranger leaps out at dem from a bush—messy stuff. At least down 'ere, der boss looks after us. 'E feeds us when we're 'ungry, 'e also gives us a shiny coin—I 'ave a few of 'em now. We even 'ave team-buildin' sessions where we goad each other into pickin' der biggest bogey und eatin' it—it's funny, especially if yew get a real juicy one—"[1045]

Me: "I'll take your word for it."

Snodgrass: "Yew should come to one of 'em—dat's a pretty big conk in der middle of ya face."[1046]

Me: "Thanks, maybe another time. Can I ask who your boss is? You don't ever seem to mention him directly by name."

The Goblin shrugs.

[1044] I guess the Goblin could always throw the said bow at them—it'll probably do a lot more damage than trying to shoot arrows with it.

[1045] I can sense my face scrunching up in the same disgusted look the slug had moments ago—speaking of which, the angry gastropod appears to be slowly charging towards the Goblin like a rage-filled Barbarian running through the Sticky Marshes.

[1046] Who are you calling 'big conk'?

Snodgrass: "Neva' asked—'e's just called der boss."

Me: "How did you meet him?"

The Goblin seems caught out by my question.

Snodgrass: "*Erm*—I woz told to go to der crypt to work for 'im."

Me: "Told? Told by whom?"

The Goblin goes a pale shade of green.

Snodgrass: "I—I can't rememba'..."

Me: "You *can't* remember? Or don't *want* to remember?"

Snodgrass: "Wot's der difference—?"

Me: "Can you at *least* describe what they looked like—this person who told you to work for your boss?

Snodgrass: "Male... 'uman... wozn't 'appy—looked a bit like an angry Pirate..."

My ears prick up at the mention of an all-too-familiar description.

Me: "Was his name *Arin* by any chance—*Arin Darkblade?*"

Snodgrass: "Dunno, could 'ave been—it woz some time ago. My memory ain't wot it used to be..."[1047]

The Goblin probably knows more than he's letting on[1048]—but I don't want him to find an excuse to leave, or *worse*.

Me: "Why did you go to the crypt? Why didn't you stay in your cave or roam free in the forest outside?"

Snodgrass: "I 'ate der cave und I 'ate der forest. But I really '**ate** der bushes.[1049] Der crypt don't 'ave any bushes for dose bush lovin' pointy-

---

[1047] *Goblins have a reputation for being unable to retain critical information. As a result, they seldom leave the safety of a dungeon room, just in case they forget the way back.*

[1048] *Or can remember...*

[1049] *Thankfully, I'm starting to pick up on the Goblin's dialect—otherwise I would be mistaken for thinking the Goblin was into eating some <u>very</u> peculiar things!*

eared Elves to 'ide in—unless dey sneak into der crypt wearin' one when we're not lookin'."[1050]

Me: "If you hate forests and bushes so much, why did you agree to meet here, where they surround us?"

Snodgrass: "'Agworl suggested dis place—it would 'ave been bad for yew if we 'ad met at der crypt. 'E's a smart one dat 'Agworl."

Me: "How do you first meet Hagworl?"

Snodgrass: "When der boss 'ired him to take der dead bodies away for us."

Me: "Does Hagworl venture down into the crypt much?"

Snodgrass: "Nah—der boss 'as a special *arrangement* wiv 'im; we always take der body und leave it near a town. Sumtimes we leave a little note on it too."

Me: "A note—what does it say?"

Snodgrass: "I dunno—can't read. Der boss writes it."

Me: "So, what happens next?"

Snodgrass: "I go back to der crypt wiv der lads—der body is 'Agworl's problem after dat."

Me: "How many adventurers have died in your crypt?"

Snodgrass: "Lots."

Me: "More than ten?"

Snodgrass: "'Ow many is dat?"

I hold up all my fingers—the Goblin nods.

Snodgrass: "Yeah—more dan dat."

There's a low growl coming from the Goblin's gut.

Snodgrass: "Yew got any food?"

[1050] But would stand out like... erm... a sore bush... *cough*... in a dungeon—I mean, crypt...

Me: "No—sorry."

The Goblin licks his lips as he stares at me with an ominous glint in his yellow eyes—his giant nostrils sniff the air in front of me. The disgusting creature suddenly spies the vexed slug charging up his leg and plops it into his mouth with a stomach-turning squelch.[1051]

Snodgrass: "Yew smell like cheese—I like cheese!"[1052]

My mind scrambles to think of a suitable reply—but my mouth has already answered.

Me: "I—I tell you what—you get me a meeting with your boss, and I'll bring you as much food and ale as your stomach can handle."

The Goblin licks his lips at the mention of the promised feast.

Snodgrass: "My belly can 'old a lot."

Me: "Does a whole hog roast and a casket of ale sound acceptable?"

Snodgrass: "Yeah—but *three* 'og roasts und *two* caskets of ale sounds betta'..."

Me: "Two—but *only* if you succeed in arranging a meeting."

Snodgrass: "Alright—yew got a deal."

Me: "I only have the one condition—I have to leave the meeting with your boss—*alive*."

The Goblin grumbles before nodding in agreement.

Snodgrass: "I'll let 'Agworl know der details."

Me: "I look forward to it."[1053]

There's a sudden snap of a twig deeper in the forest. The Goblin's ears twitch in agitation as he listens to the stillness all around us.

[1051] *Farewell, poor slug—you died bravely if a little disgustingly.*

[1052] *I brace myself in case the Goblin transforms into a squirrel and leaps straight for me.*

[1053] *Dammit—I knew I should have added 'and still the same age' to this caveat...*

Snodgrass: *"Pointy-eared-bush-Elf..."*

The Goblin spits out his slug, leaps from the tree trunk, and disappears back into the thicket—moments later, I'm suddenly aware of a new bush sitting conspicuously off to my right. It rustles angrily before a familiar-looking Elf jumps out, yelling a war cry at the top of her voice, her sword drawn and ready to strike.

Bush Elf: **"*DIIIIIEE!* *Oh*,** sorry, my mistake. I thought you were a Gob— *oh*, hello again, Loremaster..."

I almost faint in shock.

Me: "Bergenn? W—What are you doing here?"

Bergenn: "Funny, I was going to ask *you* the same thing."

Me: "Just out for a nice stroll in the woods..."

The Ranger eyes me suspiciously.

Bergenn: "A *stroll?* Greenvale Forest seems a bit off the beaten track for a stroll. Do you know how much danger you're in right now?"

Me: "Danger? *Really?*"[1054]

Bergenn: "I told you before—Goblins infest this part of the forest. You've not seen any around here, have you?"

I shake my head vigorously.

Me: "Nope."

The Ranger checks the ground around the fallen tree trunk and looks back up at me—she traces a finger over the carved letters 'H' and 'G'.

Bergenn: "You're lucky—there's been one here not more than a few minutes ago."

Me: "How can you tell?"

The Elf narrows her eyes as she picks up something black from the ground and sniffs it.

[1054] *I hope someone isn't about to make me drink a large mouthful of scalding hot Cavern tea!*

Bergenn: "I assume you don't eat slugs?"

Me: "*Erm,* no—"

The Ranger sheaths her sword and unslings her bow, notching an arrow in one swift motion.

Bergenn: "Then you'd better follow the path out of here—and *hurry!*"

Me: "Why? What are *you* going to do?"

The Elf turns her back to me and grins mischievously.

Bergenn: "I'm going to hunt *Goblin.*"

The Ranger jumps back into her bush and leaps into the thicket in a blink of an eye. I'm left alone in Greenvale Forest, wondering if my potential meeting with an Evildoer is now in jeopardy. As I turn to leave, something catches my eye—the tree stump with the carved letters now has a gaping hole beneath it that I'm sure wasn't there before. Perplexed, I start to follow the path leading out of the forest—with this new baffling mystery now plaguing my thoughts.[1055]

[1055] *What was in the hole? Who took what was in the hole? Why did they take what was in the hole? How did they take what was in the hole without anyone (me) noticing? Why am I even thinking about this so much? Why is this frustrating me so!? Why does my head hurt!?!* ***ARGGGGHHH!***

31. Tilluga, the Monk

The Pagoda of Tranquillity sits nestled between the peaks of two snow-covered ice glaciers, with a solitary, if slightly slippery, path ending at the temple's frost-covered door. The journey up the precarious icy steps[1056] is a long and arduous one. A careless pilgrim has only a worn hand rope to save them from sliding buttocks first towards their doom.[1057] This frozen temple of solitude is home to a unique Elf, trained in the Way of the Fist rather than the Way of the Sword or Bow. Tilluga is an Elven Monk who teaches her students using the unforgiving frozen peaks in preparation for the hardships found on the adventuring road.

The wind blows angrily around my robes[1058] as the freezing fog slowly rolls down the peaks, threatening to obscure my view completely. I keep my eyes locked on the last few lanterns dotted along the path, which have accompanied me on this fraught journey, guiding my unsteady footsteps towards the tall looming shadow ahead that I pray is the *Pagoda of Tranquillity*. As I slide up the last few steps and reach the door, I spy a large cowbell with a heavy chain. I reach for it, mindful not to let my exposed skin touch any freezing metal as I cover my hand in the cuff of my robe and pull downwards.

A solitary dull **'DONG'** rings out and echoes across both glacial peaks[1059]— I wait patiently, conscious that the biting cold is now threatening to freeze my bones through my robes. There is no God I worship; I find the idea of being held to account by some kind of omnipresent force *quite* absurd. But now, in my moment of desperation, I suddenly find myself saying a silent prayer in the hope that someone answers the door before I become the Pagoda's newest frozen ornament. Mercifully, my pleas are quickly answered;[1060] the heavy iron door open inwards,

---

[1056] *From the recently rebuilt town of Arkatwo far below...*

[1057] *Gracing them with a frostbitten posterior to add final insult to fatal injury.*

[1058] *I wish I still was wearing the Barbarian's furry loincloth under my robes—the cold wind blowing up the inside of my leg is certainly putting the 'oh' into fr-oh-zen...*

[1059] *Answered by a distant rumble as a sizeable avalanche erupts down one side of the glacier toward the soon-to-be-renamed Arkathree...*

[1060] *Although, please don't take this as a sign that I'm now a convert—it's going to take a lot more than that before I start taking orders from a mysterious Sky God with a hidden agenda and a penchant for celestial theatrics...*

and I'm greeted by a calm-looking Elf who welcomes me by thoughtfully throwing a warm fur over my shoulders.

Elf: "It is not often we have visitors to the Pagoda of Tranquillity during the height of the snowy season. But I sense you are not here to train."

Me: "I'm *actually* seeking Tilluga—the Monk."

The Elf turns and smiles. I can't help but notice the unmistakable milky white sheen that covers her pupils[1061]—she is blind.

Tilluga: "I'm pleased to say you've found her, Master *Loremaster*."

Me: "*Erm*—how did you know I was a Loremaster?"

Tilluga: "The ink in your pen is *Soul Squid;* the acrid saltiness is unmistakable. As I couldn't detect the same saltiness on your breath—I wagered you were a user rather than a consumer of the stuff."

Me: "Consume? Who in their right mind would want to drink Soul Squid ink?"

Tilluga: "Pirates. They believe it's good luck to take a swig of Soul Squid before raiding Gnomish Merchant ships carrying valuable wares into Port Salvation[1062]—but then if you *were* a Pirate, you'd already know that..."

Me: "Excuse me for asking, but how can you be so sure I'm not a Pirate? I could be in disguise."

The Monk leans closer and sniffs.

Tilluga: "The distinct lack of any *Yo-Ho-Blow* rum tells me otherwise."[1063]

Me: "Okay, *very* astute, you are correct—I am no Pirate."

[1061] I mean <u>her</u> pupils—not her <u>pupils</u>.

[1062] Although if any of the raided wares belonged to Balstaff the Merchant, then the Pirates would be opening crates filled with collectable Gelatinous Cubes and Mimic figurines rather than untold riches. Although, I'm pretty sure the average Swashbuckler would be blissfully unaware of the eye-watering price these souvenirs could fetch on the Back Market.

[1063] Yo-Ho-Blow rum is a beverage favoured by Pirates and infamous for its explosive reaction to loud singing, making shanty-time on any Buccaneering vessel fraught with danger. It's also worth noting a single bottle could literally blow the 'poop' off a ship's deck.

The Monk leads me away from the main entrance towards what appears to be a large combat arena. A giant wheel hangs from the ceiling, holding at least a hundred burning candles.[1064]

Tilluga: "Though you *are* partial to the company of Goblins."

Me: "How did you—"

Tilluga: "I can detect its foul odour on your robes."

Me: "My robes? That was over five days ago… it—it was *just* an interview."

The Monk holds her hand up to stop me mid-excuse.

Tilluga: "*Know thine enemy*—you owe me no explanation."

There's a faint ringing from a tiny bell in the distance; I'm suddenly reminded that we aren't alone.

Me: "One of your pupils?"

Tilluga: "*Very* perceptive, Loremaster—yes, they reside here until released from my charge to venture out into the realm alone."

Me: "How do you know when they are ready to leave this place for good?"

Tilluga: "There are three disciplines I teach—each one takes a summer to master. After that, they're ready to explore the realm and make a name for themselves, like many who have gone before."

Me: "Where are they now, your students?"

Tilluga: "They should be practising."

I look around, expecting to see the Monk's pupils quietly sparring with one another[1065]—nothing moves bar the gentle swaying of the giant

---

[1064] *A wheel not unlike the Barbarian's Wheel of Pain—but quite a bit brighter and without an angry-Warrior strapped to its middle, soaking the floor with their lamentation juice.*

[1065] *I mean her* pupils*—not* her *pupils.*

452

wheel above us.[1066]

Me: "I can't *see* any—"[1067]

The Monk lifts her head to sniff the air; her face scrunches into a disapproving frown.

Tilluga: "Well, maybe they are meditating in their chambers, or perhaps they're studying the '*Way*'—please, sit."

I realise the Monk is gesturing to a straw mat on the floor. My knees crunch in protest as I try to make myself comfortable. After several painful attempts, I manage to sit cross-legged in front of the Elf. She, by comparison, rests her knees as easily as a Cleric sitting in a comfortable chair by a tavern's roaring fire.[1068] The Elf turns to the small table next to her, picks up an ornate teapot, and pours a hot beverage into the two waiting cups. Filling each just short of the brim, she carefully replaces the teapot and hands me one of the cups.

Me: "Thank you."

The hot tea is a welcome antidote to the cold—chasing the icy chill from my body. I feel myself relaxing more and more with every sip.[1069]

Tilluga: "Your heartbeat is finally returning to normal. I sense exercise is a stranger to your body."[1070]

Me: "Well, *yes*, but I—I have done a fair amount of walking on my travels—"

[1066] *Almost as if the imaginary Barbarian tethered to it decided enough was enough and stormed off in a huff...*

[1067] *That was an unfortunate slip of the tongue.*

[1068] *And who is already starting to nod off after one half-flagon of light ale...*

[1069] *I mean _really_ relaxing... I'm almost in danger of casting my own rendition of 'Stinking Cloud' if I'm not too careful (which would be dangerous for everyone else, rather than me for once)!*

[1070] *Less of a stranger, more of an uninvited guest who keeps showing up when I've other, less physically demanding things that need my urgent attention...*

Tilluga: "So does the boar searching the forest floor for grubs—but that still doesn't mean its rump won't make a tempting target for a Hunter's bow."[1071]

Me: "I guess that really depends on the Hunter's ability to shoot straight."[1072]

The Elf stares at me with her deathly white eyes before blinking and placing her cup back on the table beside her.

Tilluga: "But you did not travel all this way to talk about boar hunting..."

Me: "You're right—I..."

My voice trails away as I catch a hint of movement from the alcove directly behind the Monk. I watch, mesmerised, as a student edges past—his hand holding what appears to be a tiny bell on his belt. He stops at the halfway point and turns to see me staring at him. With panic on his face, he places a trembling finger to his mouth before softly continuing out of sight.

Tilluga: "Well?"

Me: "*Erm,* y—yes... I have some questions—your students, how did you come by them?"

Tilluga: "I did not find them; they found me the same way you did."

Me: "By taking the glacial path?"

Tilluga: "Precisely, the glacial path is the first test."

Me: "The *first* test?"

Tilluga: "Yes—to survive the perilous journey to this temple's door; those who survive are given a temporary place here at the Pagoda of Tranquillity. But, there are many more challenges a prospective candidate must overcome before they are deemed worthy enough to become one of my students."

[1071] *I doubt a bow will damage it; arrows, on the other hand, are lethal in the right hands.*

[1072] *And if the Hunter is a Goblin, or a Halfling—or not...*

Me: "What happens to those candidates who don't make it this far?"

Tilluga: "Then I place a lantern on the path to mark where they fell."[1073]

I try to recall the number of lanterns I passed on my ascent—too many to count; I shiver at the thought of the numerous lives lost journeying to this place.

Me: "You mean *every* lantern I passed marks a failed candidate?"

Tilluga: "*Felled* candidate—yes."[1074]

Me: "But how do you know *if* they fell? Or even *where* they fell? I mean, you're... you're..."

Tilluga: "I'm what—*blind?*"

I shift a little awkwardly on the straw mat.[1075]

Me: "To be blunt about it—yes."

Tilluga: "I may be blind, but it does not mean I cannot see."

I move my hand slowly in front of the Monk's face—she suddenly strikes like a snake, grabbing it in a single motion before I can blink an eye.

Me: *"Wha—!"*

Tilluga: "Do you know how often someone has waved a hand in front of my face after they've discovered I am blind?"

Me: "Forty-five times—?"

Tilluga: "It was a rhetorical question. Instead, you <u>should</u> be asking, how did I know where your hand was to grab it in the first place?"

Me: "Y—Yes... how *did* you know that?"

[1073] *My heart sinks at the thought of so many hopefuls who slid backside first at great speed towards oblivion; the freezing ice must have made it impossible for the helpless souls to clench their buttocks together in their final moments.*

[1074] *This couldn't be any more literal if she had pushed them off the glacier herself—which she may well have done.*

[1075] *My buttocks now feel as numb as those who slipped off the glacial path.*

Tilluga: "This answer comes in two halves. First, my loss of sight has helped hone my other senses. I felt the faint air movements surrounding your fingers as you waved them. I then triangulated that position with the sound of your heartbeat and the shifting weight of your buttocks on the straw mat.[1076] Once I had done that, I had the precise calculation for your hand's exact position to strike."

Me: "That's impressive—but how can you begin to learn something like that?"

Tilluga: "Before I give you my answer, can I offer you some more tea?"[1077]

I look down at my empty cup. Somehow, the Monk had sensed I needed a refill even before I did. I nod in reply, forgetting the Elf cannot see me. Tilluga smiles, suspecting my faux pas,[1078] and begins filling my cup with better accuracy than the Barmaid from *The Blighted Blizzard* tavern back in Arkatwo.[1079]

Me: "Thank you."

The heat of the liquid continues to massage my inner core—filling me with a strange peace that has been lacking since the revelation of my brother's death.

Me: "The taste is unfamiliar—what is this made from?"

Tilluga: "This place is called the Pagoda of Tranquillity for a reason. On the highest slopes of these peaks, you will find one of the scarcest of herbs in the entire realm—*Ice Sativa*."

Me: "Ice Sativa?"

I'm suddenly aware of loud '**THUDDING**' approaching me from behind; it sounds almost like a Rogue's horse has just galloped in to backstab me. I turn to see the smallest of rodents scurrying in my general direction before realising its mistake, swerving left and loudly

---

[1076] *I knew my backside would be behind this betrayal. I've been 'backstabbed' by my own posterior—or butt-stabbed, as we're talking about buttocks here.*

[1077] *I may as well live dangerously and have a second brew!*

[1078] *'Faux pas' is the polite Gnomish way of saying 'F— up!'*

[1079] *Who served most of my breakfast onto the dirty tavern floor this morning.*

retreating out of the combat arena.[1080] Confused, I turn back to the Monk.

Tilluga: "This is the second half of the answer you seek. Ice Sativa heightens the senses beyond normal limitations, allowing those who use it to operate far beyond ordinary constraints. It lets me, for example, catch your hand in mid-air with ease. As you can imagine, this makes the Ice Sativa coveted by those who wish nothing more than to take advantage of this power. My pupils and I are the herb's sworn guardians."[1081]

Me: "I thought the students who came here were learning skills they need to survive an adventure in a far-off dungeon—not to protect a glacial herb from would-be thieves?"

Tilluga: "Those who seek the wisdom of this temple must protect the Ice Sativa as payment for my extensive training.[1082] That debt <u>must</u> be settled before they can embark on their life of adventure."

There's another flash of movement from the alcove beyond the Elf's shoulder. The same student who originally sneaked past has returned, carrying an armful of what looks like small cakes.[1083] As the pupil continues across the alcove, a cake suddenly slips and falls from his grasp. But, in a feat I still can't quite believe, the student rolls forward and catches the plummeting cake with the arch of their foot without making a single sound. What makes this deed even more remarkable is the student is *still* holding on to the tower of cakes in one hand while his other keeps the tiny bell on his belt from ringing. The Monk, sensing something is amiss, turns and stares at the cake-laden pupil, who is now frozen to the spot—their face filled with fear. There's a tense standoff as the blind Elf stares in the direction of the statuesque student. I can see the pupil's muscles trembling in protest at their enforced rigidity, trying to keep their visibility 'invisible' to the Monk's unseeing eyes.

[1080] *Phew, for a moment there I thought Raglan the Druid had tracked me down to this remote mountain sanctuary on the hunt for cheese...*

[1081] *The Elf could mean <u>her</u> pupils, but she could also mean her <u>pupils</u>... best I leave it for now.*

[1082] *This includes bed and breakfast—hopefully not served upon the temple's floor.*

[1083] *From what I also assume is the kitchen area.*

Me: "Are there many who try to steal the Ice Sativa from the glacial peaks?"

The Monk turns away from the statuesque student to reply.

Tilluga: "Yes, many have tried, but all have failed."[1084]

Me: "How do you know they all failed?"

The Monk chuckles and leans forward to whisper.

Tilluga: "*Oh,* I <u>know</u>..."

The hairs on my neck stand up as my senses suddenly teleport to a point back in time where I can only watch helplessly as the Monk shoves untold numbers of would-be Ice Sativa thieves down the glacial path on their posteriors.[1085] Before I can say another word, my senses are catapulted back to the here and now. Feeling slightly alarmed by the disturbing vision I've just witnessed; I quickly change the subject.

Me: "So, how do you use the Ice Sativa? Do you eat it?"

Tilluga: "Eat? You *can't* eat it raw; its potency would render you <u>insane</u>! No, it must first be distilled before hanging up to dry over steaming volcanic stones. After three days of desiccating, the dried leaves are carefully stripped and cut into a fine powder that can be added to tea or baked into cakes."

My thoughts return to the cake-laden pupil in the alcove who is still rooted to the spot like a human-sized cake stand.

Me: "What happens if you were to consume a great quantity of Ice Sativa?"

Tilluga: "Your senses would pass beyond the normal plane of consciousness. You would reach a state of euphoric joy that your mind could never hope to comprehend. But that knowledge would be too much for you to control, and your sanity would fracture into a multitude of pieces, leaving whatever is left to fall into an eternal

---

[1084] *I'd imagine quite a few of these being High Elves, Bards, and High-Elven Bards.*

[1085] *Minus any form of wooden sledge and whoops of joy...*

abyss. You would be lost to the Ice Sativa forever."[1086]

My eyes dart back to the alcove where the cake-laden student has finally tiptoed out of sight.

Me: "Aren't you worried your students could become addicted to the formidable properties held within the Ice Sativa? Isn't there a danger they could develop a craving for the very thing they have sworn to protect?"

Tilluga: "No—part of the training here at the Pagoda of Tranquillity is to temper the body and mind to acclimatise to the Ice Sativa's influence. We achieve this by carefully introducing the Ice Sativa into our meals, slowly building up a resistance until we are blind to its addictive lure.[1087] I'm particularly proud of the Ice Sativa cakes I like to bake—they are exceedingly delicious. Could I tempt you with one?"

Me: "*NO*—I mean, no, *thank* you. The tea is more than enough for me. So, I'd imagine consuming large quantities of these cakes would be ill-advised."

Tilluga: "That would be most reckless. *Ice Sativa* cakes should only be digested after a heavy meal, never on their own."

Me: "I see..."[1088]

Tilluga: "But there is nothing to be concerned about here; I only added a small amount into the tea you enjoyed. Nowhere near enough to cause you any lasting harm."

Me: "That's... reassuring—can I ask you about your adventuring days?"

Tilluga: "You can ask."

There's an awkward pause, broken only by the six students softly sneaking across the alcove, as they head towards the kitchen area—each one holding the bell on their belt as if their lives depended upon it.

[1086] *So probably best it's taken in small nibbles then.*

[1087] *Some are obviously a little <u>more</u> blind to it than others.*

[1088] *I wince, cursing my uncanny ability to put my foot in it...*

Me: "What were those days like?"

Tilluga: "Vivid."

Me: "What do you mean?"

Tilluga: "I could see for a start."

Me: "You could *see?*"

Tilluga: "As clear as day."[1089]

Me: "I know this may be difficult for you to answer, but can I ask how you came to be blind?"

Tilluga: "Simple. It was stolen from me."

Me: "Stolen by whom?"

Tilluga: "No—by *what*. It was stolen by a *Gibbering Goomba*."[1090]

Me: "I've never heard of a—"

Tilluga: "—*Gibbering Goomba*. I know not many have and lived to tell the tale, which is a testament to one's own abilities—if I say so myself."[1091]

Me: "What did it look like?"

Tilluga: "As I recall, it was small with bright blue fur, big eyes, and a devious grin; it looked harmless enough. Foolishly, I thought it was friendly—I was gravely mistaken."

Me: "What happened?"

The Monk gestures to her face.

Tilluga: "The last thing I remember was the Goomba grinning at me before it briefly 'gibbered'—then my whole world was plunged into darkness."

[1089] *Just not a grey foggy day like today, with poor visibility...*

[1090] *I subsequently discovered that Gibbering Goombas bottle the eyesight they steal and sell it on the Back Market to short-sighted Dwarves, so you can imagine how popular their wares are.*

[1091] *Which you do—instantly shattering the illusion that all Monks are meek and humble...*

Me: "That must have been nerve-wracking for you."

Tilluga: "Nerve-wracking is a bit of an understatement—I was *petrified.*[1092] I was in the middle of a hostile dungeon and completely blind. My senses weren't as honed as they are now. I was completely unprepared for a world I had to feel rather than see."

Me: "How did you survive?"

I glance up as the six pupils surreptitiously return from the kitchen area, each one carrying an alarming number of Ice-Sativa cakes in the crook of their arms.

Tilluga: "*Painfully*—I was on an adventure at the time. I hit my head on more door frames and protruding torches than I care to remember. I also fell—sometimes off steps, sometimes into pits. I had to call upon *all* my training just to escape that death-trapped dungeon[1093] in one piece."

Me: "It's a miracle you're still alive to tell the tale. Where did you go once you had escaped the dungeon's depths?"[1094]

Tilluga: "To the nearest town for help—but it took me nearly three days to make what should have been a three-hour journey. When the locals found me, I was a walking mess of cuts and bruises. Fortunately, the *Sisters of Perpetuity* came to my aid and helped me get back on my feet."[1095]

Me: "Yet somehow you managed to adapt quickly to your blindness?"

Tilluga: "I have found a way to cope with my affliction, which allows me to traverse the occasional dungeon or free a town from the iron grip of an unscrupulous Baron."

[1092] *Not strictly true, the Elf had their eyesight stolen—they weren't turned into an oversized garden ornament.*

[1093] *Not to be confused with the 'actual' Deathtrapped Dungeon™—a place not even a Herald dares mention without some serious Arcane Copyright spells beforehand.*

[1094] *Also, not to be confused with the Dungeon of Depths™, which has so many steps it'll make you wish someone had the foresight to install a Gnomish floor-descending device (even if there is a high chance of it spontaneously combusting into a raging inferno while you're stuck inside it).*

[1095] *For the usual 'required' donation...*

Me: "Is that when you first encountered the mysterious properties of Ice Sativa?"

Tilluga: "Yes—as luck would have it, a wandering Potioneer visited me while I was convalescing in the chapel. He was the one who first introduced me to the hidden powers of Ice Sativa. The old Potioneer bequeathed a small sample for me to try—out of eyesight from the ever-watchful Sisters of Perpetuity.[1096] He promised to return the next day to see how I had fared with his newly brewed elixir."

Me: "So, you drank the potion?"

Tilluga: "That *very* night."

Me: "What did it do to you?"

Tilluga: "It let me see."

Me: "It cured your blindness?"

Tilluga: "Not in the way you mean—but it did open my third eye."

There's a pause as I quickly examine the Monk's face.

Tilluga: "What are you doing?"

Me: "*Erm*—nothing…"

Tilluga: "You were looking for a third eye, weren't you?"[1097]

Me: "N—No…"

Tilluga: "It's not a *real* third eye…"

Me: "I wasn't suggesting—"

Tilluga: "The third eye is an unseen perceptive one—which the Ice Sativa heightens enough for my vision to return through it."

Me: "So, you *can* see—"

[1096] And technically, the Elven Monk too…

[1097] If this Potioneer <u>was</u> Inglebold, then there's every chance of a <u>real</u> third eye sprouting in the middle of the Monk's forehead.

Tilluga: "*No*, I am blind. That night, for the first time, I finally made it to the privy without tripping over the bedridden Wizard laid up next to me."[1098]

There's more movement from the alcove behind the Elf as all twelve bell-holding students now silently file past towards the kitchen area—I try my best to ignore whatever clandestine shenanigans are going on back there.

Tilluga: "The next day, the Potioneer returned as promised. As you'd expect, I wanted more of his Ice Sativa—but there was one problem."

Me: "It was highly addictive?"

Tilluga: "Yes, but that wasn't the real issue—the *real* problem was *this* temple; the Pagoda of Tranquillity had fallen into the hands of bandits who were farming the Ice Sativa and selling it at an inflated price on the Back Market. It was only by chance the Potioneer had somehow managed to get his hands on enough of the valuable herb to make a small batch of potions—but it was barely sufficient to see out the week. I had no choice but to act quickly in both our interests."

Me: "So, you struck a deal with the Potioneer?"

Tilluga: "Indeed I did. *He* needed someone who could drive the bandits from the temple and protect the valuable herb from unscrupulous opportunists, while *I* needed the Ice Sativa and its secrets."

Me: "But you were blind—how could you ever hope to defeat a band of heavily armed bandits?"

Tilluga: "The Potioneer gave me the last of his Ice Sativa for the task ahead—those outlaws didn't stand a chance. With my senses heightened to unparalleled levels, I sneaked into the temple and swiftly dealt with them."

Me: "What did you do?"

[1098] *I just want to clarify that the bedridden soul wasn't Regalast the Wizard; it just happened to be 'another' Wizard who got fried by a Dragon—which just goes to show how often this sort of thing happens to Spellcasters.*

Tilluga: "I *encouraged* the bandits to leave this glacial temple and never return."[1099]

Me: "So, the Potioneer got what he wanted from the deal—whilst you got to discover the mysteries of the Ice Sativa's influence."

Tilluga: "Yes, but I didn't just do it for the Potioneer, nor the Ice Sativa's secrets. I realised this small quest had given me a renewed sense of purpose. As the Ice Sativa coursed through my veins, I heard the Pagoda of Tranquillity calling out to me to become the guardian of this place and train those who would seek my wisdom."[1100]

Me: "Which naturally included you taking up residence here."

Tilluga: "I will not let my blindness take control of my life. I was once a Monk who knew no fear, a Monk who would venture into a dangerous dungeon with only their bare hands for a weapon,[1101] a Monk who could pluck a Goblin's arrow out of the air[1102]—but all that changed the second I lost my sight. The Ice Sativa on these glacial peaks has given me a second chance at life. I'm not prepared to let anyone take that away from me—not while I draw breath."

Me: "Are you often called into action to protect the secret that grows on these glacial peaks?"

Tilluga: "There have been many who attempted the hazardous climb here to steal the Ice Sativa—those who didn't slip on their rumps and slide to their doom would find twelve dangerous students and one deadly Master waiting for them."

Me: "How easy is it to recognise friend from foe in the Pagoda?"

[1099] *With a hefty shove in the direction of the glacial path added for good measure, I wager...*

[1100] *Was it the Pagoda who spoke to the Monk, or someone with a twisted sense of humour and an ulterior motive—like an opportunistic Potioneer or a decapitated skull with nothing better to do?*

[1101] *Although after taking one of the Potioneer's potions—the Monk could have really ended up with bear hands...*

[1102] *This is a feat worthy of note, especially as the arrow could be flying in the opposite direction to the Monk's position.*

Tilluga: "All my students have a tiny bell woven into their belts—that way, I can pinpoint their location immediately."

Me: "What if your pupils decided to remove their bells?"

Tilluga: "They wouldn't dare! They know failure to follow my rules to the letter would result in severe punishment. Their continual presence here is at the behest of my good grace. Blind or not, they would *not* take advantage of that."

Me: "How do any of your prospective students find out about your teachings?"

Tilluga; "Word of mouth.[1103] The Potioneer likes to scour the taverns searching for prospective candidates,[1104] especially those he deems worthy of my training in *The Way of the First*."

Me: "Shouldn't that be 'Fist'?"

Tilluga: "Why would it be Fist? No—lesson one is always *The Way of the First*."

Me: "What is *The Way of the First?*"

Tilluga: "It is the art of hitting your opponent before they are ready to attack."

Me: "That sounds suspiciously like a pre-emptive strike."

Tilluga: "Winning a fight is all about learning to hit your opponent early—stealing the wind from their sails before they know what's happened."

Me: "Isn't that a little underhanded?"

[1103] *Not to be confused with 'Word of Moth'—a Holy prophecy, foretold by Cleric Moths who travel from torchlight to torchlight prophesying the end of all Moth-kind via an all-consuming Fireball, cast by a giant Wizard.*

[1104] *And unwittingly creating something of a nemesis out of Kara Rocksplitter along the way...*

Tilluga: "We do not carry weapons into battle[1105]—therefore, we must press home any advantage we can find."

Me: "I see—what lesson follows after *The Way of the First?*"

Tilluga: *"The Way of the Foot."*

Me: "I guess that is all about kicking your opponent—correct?"

Tilluga: "Yes."

Me: "Then am I to assume, after that, comes *The Way of The Fist?*"

Tilluga: "**NO!** We are *not* common Barbarians. We only master *The Way of the First, The Way of the Foot,* and *The Way of the Forehead.* **We do _not_ use a fist! Not _ever!_**"

I sense a tsunami of fury growing inside the Monk—it's a wave that could easily drown an angry-Warrior trying to cool off in the shallows after a rage-filled adventure.

Me: *"What's The Way of the Forehead?"*

Tilluga: "It's our final, most devastating attack—the last lesson all my students must master. When we use our heads, *The Way of the Forehead* can floor the toughest of opponents—but you must make sure they're not wearing a metal helm first."

Me: "Do you use any *other* part of your body against an opponent?"

Tilluga: "There are some *Monks* of ill repute who train in the forbidden *Way of the Middle Finger,*[1106] but those foul-mouthed hooligans are not welcome within these four walls…"

Me: "I meant to ask; do you pay the Potioneer a fee for finding prospective candidates?"

[1105] *My eyes are drawn to the strange white baton hanging from the wall—it does look more like an anaemic stick than a weapon. Perhaps the Monk uses it to navigate around tricky obstacles, although I'd imagine some kind of animal assistant would be better suited to the task—like a highly trained cat.*

[1106] *I'm shocked to learn that the Way of the Middle Finger is not the only forbidden lesson being taught by uncouth Monks—there's also the Way of the Two Fingers, the Way of the Thumb and Forefinger, and the Way of the Rock Sign…*

Tilluga: "He gets an extra sack of Ice Sativa for every successful candidate who passes through our temple door."

Me: "Is that much?"

Tilluga: "On the Back Market, a quantity like that would fetch over five hundred coins."

My eyes widen in awe.

Me: "I can see why many would try to profit from it."[1107]

The briefest moment of silence passes between the Elf and myself.

Tilluga: "Who was it that you lost?"

Me: "Excuse me?"

Tilluga: "The loved one you lost—was it your father?"

I stare in confusion at the Monk; she remains motionless, patiently waiting for an answer.

Me: "A brother, but *how* did you—"

Tilluga: "Another side-effect of the Ice Sativa is I can detect pain and suffering in others. How did he die?"

Me: "H—He fell while adventuring..."

Tilluga: "Climbing is a risk on adventures. One loose handhold and **_SPLAT_**—"

Me: "He wasn't climbing—"

Tilluga: "*Ah,* pits can be deadly—I should know... one missed step and **_SPLAT_**—"

Me: "It wasn't a pit."

The Monk stares with emotionless eyes.

[1107] *This sort of sum could floor a Dwarf—especially if that Dwarf were Kara Rocksplitter.*

Tilluga: "Forgive me, you mean he died while *on* an adventure—not falling to his death on one. So many, like your brother, are to their doom chasing riches and glory. I'm sorry for your loss—my words are useless here, but if you drink some more tea, you will find it will temporarily lighten your suffering and lift your heart."[1108]

As I take another sip from the warm cup,[1109] I find the dull ache surrounding my brother's death diminishing into the background of my consciousness.

Tilluga: "Better?"

I nod, knowing the Ice Satvia's power won't last, but it is welcome, nonetheless.

Tilluga: "I'll ask one of my students to furnish you with a flask of Ice Sativa tea for your descent."

I look up at the exact moment the sneaking pupils walk back across the alcove—each heavily laden with handfuls of cakes. They freeze as the Monk turns to talk in their direction.

Tilluga: ***"STUDENTS!"***

None of them dares move or answer their Master.

Tilluga: "Where *are* those blasted clowns?"

The Monk continues to stare obliviously at the twelve students still standing statuesque like a troupe of acrobats who just caught sight of a Gorgon with a deep-rooted hatred of tumbling.[1110]

Me: "*Really,* there's no need—"

Tilluga: "Of course there is, let me just get you—"

At that exact moment, the cake at the apex of the most teetering heap starts to roll from its precarious position. All the students stare wide-

---

[1108] *I've been told that a really good cup of tea always makes a problem seem better—regardless how dangerous it could potentially be.*

[1109] *I should just say 'no', but the Monk is <u>very</u> persuasive!*

[1110] *Not an overly unreasonable hatred, all things considered. Although watching tumbling acrobats trying to perform while wearing bags on their heads could be quite entertaining!*

eyed in terror as it falls from the pile, hurtling toward the floor. One of the pupils tries to grab the wayward cake, only for their stack of contraband baked confectionary to tumble from their grip—landing noisily on the floor.

Tilluga: "You thieving scoundrels—they're after my cakes again! Well—you know what this means!"

The Monk springs to her feet and immediately adopts a battle pose as she plucks the large white baton hanging from the wall.

Tilluga: "Leave us, Master Loremaster—it appears my students are about to be *painfully* reminded of their obligations to the Pagoda of Tranquillity."

The blind Elf leaps forward with a cry and begins swinging her white baton at her students with almost prophetic precision. It's mesmerising to watch, but time is against me—the snowstorm outside is threatening to make the descent almost impossible, and I don't wish to spend the next few nights listening to the groans of wounded students.

With a last sip of tea to negate the plunging temperature outside, I pull the fur blanket closer around my shoulders and quickly make for the door. I leave behind the chaos of student screams and the sound of the white baton cutting through the air.[1111]

[1111] *Hopefully, I can make it down the mountain safely without making an impromptu backside slide that will undoubtedly accelerate my precarious descent.*

32. Gaudron, the Baron

I've been granted a special audience with Gaudron, an under-pressure Baron of one of the smallest kingdoms in the entire realm—Brundale. Only a single square mile in size and surrounded by four other principalities, Brundale has struggled to protect itself under the rule of Gaudron from its aggressive neighbours. For nearly forty summers now, the four Princes of the bordering principalities have quarrelled for dominance over the tiny territory. Each has claimed ownership over Gaudron's domain on several occasions, yet mysteriously none have ever successfully annexed it. I hope my visit might shed some light on how the Baron has managed to keep the Royal Wolves from his doors.

I join the Baron in his war room as he stares impassively at a table with a map of Brundale spread out over it. I can't help but notice the small number of blue flags pinned to crudely drawn fortifications and towns scattered across his miniature square of land. Running along Brundale's borders sits an imposing number of red, green, orange, and purple flags. Gaudron is so engrossed in the flag-impaled map—he doesn't notice his Steward standing beside him, patiently waiting to announce my arrival. After a protracted moment of silence, the Baron finally acknowledges his Steward's presence and looks up from the table to stare directly at me with his tired grey eyes.

Gaudron: "Is *this* the Wizard?"

Me: "I'm not a *Wiz—*"

Steward: "*M—My Lord,* this is Elburn Barr. He's a *Loremaster.*"

The Baron glares at me with harsh disapproval.

Gaudron: "*Loremaster*? I have no need for Loremasters—I need more damn *heroes!* Find me Wizards, Barbarians, or Paladins—I'd *even* take some Clerics if they were actually of any use!"[1112]

The Baron slams his fist hard on the table, knocking over several of the tiny blue flags.[1113]

[1112] *Harsh—but some will say that's reasonably fair.*

[1113] *And leaving the western border almost defenceless in the process...*

Me: "Forgive my impertinence, My Lord—but I'm actually here to talk to you *about* heroes; I'm following an adventurer's journey, writing up my experiences as I go—"

The Baron's ears prick up at the mere mention of 'heroes'. He gestures for me to take the seat opposite.

Gaudron: "So, you're writing *about* heroes—but you're not *actually* a hero?"

Me: "Yes and no."[1114]

Gaudron: "I assume you are writing this in some kind of book?"[1115]

Me: "*Yes*—a journal."

Gaudron: "And it's safe to reason you are hoping large swathes of people across the realm will read this *journal* of yours?"

Me: "It hadn't crossed my mind if I'm being completely honest with you[1116] —but yes, that would be something safe to assume too."

Gaudron: "Good. Then ask your questions, Loremaster..."

I smile hesitantly, a little unsure of the Baron's true motivations.

Me: "Let's start with the obvious—you mentioned you *need* heroes. Can you explain why?"

The Baron points at the battle map spread out between us.

Gaudron: "Why do you think? Brundale is surrounded! Our enemies are on all sides. This land has been under threat for nearly forty summers now, long before I rose to become Baron of it."

Me: "And am I to understand by '*enemies*' you mean the four Princes who covet this small patch of land?"

[1114] *In that order...*

[1115] *My memory is good—but not <u>that</u> good; notes are a basic necessity rather than a luxury I cannot do without; hence, I always carry my faithful journal by my side.*

[1116] *This is a lie, but I want to appear humble in front of this Baron—or at least humbler than your average blind Monk.*

Gaudron: "Steady on—I wouldn't necessarily say '*small*'—"

Me: "Well, it *is* no more than a square mile in size—even the city of Tronte is larger than you."

Gaudron: "True, but you are only looking at it from one perspective; if we were ambitious enough, we could dig our way into the Underworld or build upwards until we reached the stars—our kingdom could quickly become so much more!"[1117]

Me: "Let me get this right—you're saying, if you kept building upwards or digging downwards, you could claim to be the largest region in the realm?"

Gaudron: "Precisely!"

Me: "So, you need all these heroes to do *what* for you exactly?"

Gaudron: "Simply to keep on visiting our land!"

Me: "Why? What good are heroes against one army—let alone four?"

Gaudron: "I'll tell you why they're important—if the kingdom of Brundale has a *single* official hero adventuring within it, no Prince, no matter how big their army or how much they want this land, will openly invade it."[1118]

Me: "But how is that possible? How can a few scattered heroes stop such an advance from happening?"

Gaudron: "Because even the Princes aren't foolish enough to get on the wrong side of Arin Darkblade or the Heroes Guild—their reputation for fighting fire with fire is well earned."[1119]

My face must betray some emotion at the mention of Arin's name, for I find the Baron regarding me curiously. I hasten to my next question.

[1117] *Although if Gaudron does build upwards, I hope he won't be so foolish as to construct an extremely unstable temple at the summit.*

[1118] *By this, the Baron means a Heroes Guild hero, not the 'other' non-Guild member kind...*

[1119] *Considering the Heroes Guild burnt down the Wizards Guild in revenge for a Wizard turning one of the Heroes Guild's Barbarians into a literal flaming ball of angry rage—I would take this threat very seriously indeed!*

Me: "Why are these four Princes *so* obsessed with Brundale? If you'd forgive my boldness, there seems little strategic value to it, nor does it hold any precious resource of note."

I sense the Baron biting his tongue as he allows my words to stand unchallenged.

Gaudron: "You are correct. We do not have much in the way of export, nor do we hold any strategic advantage for our neighbours. The simple truth is that this land is sought after because they *cannot* have it, and that is more than enough reason for them to want it in the first place."

Me: "How did Brundale come to exist?"

Gaudron: "Over forty summers ago, this small square of land was given to my Grandfather as payment for vanquishing a fearsome Dragon that terrorised the King's prized cows."[1120]

Me: "What King was this?"

Gaudron: "The King of Brindale."

Me: "Brindale? I've not heard of that particular region. Does it lie somewhere to the south?"

Gaudron: "South? *No*—but I'm not surprised you've never heard of Brindale; it was divided into four different territories."

Me: "Wait—you said *four* different territories? You mean—?"

The Baron nods.

Gaudron: "Yes, each of the King's sons were given a quarter of Brindale as their own."

Me: "Surely the King's eldest could assert their right to rule the entire region rather than divide it into quarters?"

Gaudron: "*Ah,* but there lies the problem; it seems all the heirs were born at the *exact* same time—they were identical quadruplets."[1121]

[1120] *Even after forty summers, I see some things never change—not where horny Dragons and bovine herds are concerned anyway.*

[1121] *I pity the poor Queen who had to deliver four Royal babies all at once!*

Me: "So, all four Princes look identical to one another?"

Gaudron: "Unbelievable, I know."[1122]

Me: "I guess they couldn't agree on who was the eldest Prince to inherit the kingdom of Brindale?"

Gaudron: "Not only that, they couldn't even agree who was whom at any one time or another—they kept swapping identities in an attempt to dupe each other for the throne. As you can imagine, it was utter pandemonium."[1123]

Me: "So, the kingdom of Brindale—?"

Gaudron: "—is no more. Instead, we are surrounded by these quarrelling Princes of Brandale, Brondale, Brendale, and Sommerton—"

Me: *"Sommerton?"*

Gaudron: "Seems one of the Princes decided he wanted to be a little more rebellious with his naming convention."[1124]

Me: "—and these Princes have been hostile to Brundale ever since?"

Gaudron: "The problem is Brundale is a crossroads where all four kingdoms meet."

Me: "The tightest of spots for sure."

Gaudron: "If only I could pick up and move this entire region somewhere else—all our worries would disappear overnight."[1125]

Me: "Why did your Grandfather call his land Brundale?"

[1122] *Not to mention hugely confusing for all the Royal servants at family get-togethers.*

[1123] *With plenty of pushing, shoving, angry pointing, and rude gestures...*

[1124] *There's always one Black Prince in every Royal family.*

[1125] *There is a small group of opportunistic Giants who use their immense size and strength to relocate large buildings or areas of land for a competitive fee. These Titans go by the name 'Big Hands Removal'. They have been given a glowing review by every one of their customers—even those who have had their prized crockery broken after a poorly packaged outhouse was clumsily dropped from a great height.*

Gaudron: "My Grandfather had a huge amount of respect for the King of Brindale, so 'Brundale' was chosen to keep the spirit of that admiration alive after the King died.[1126] But perhaps in hindsight, I can see how it may have just stirred up strong emotions, especially amongst the locals of Brandale, Brondale, Brendale, *and* Sommerton."[1127]

Me: "What did the Princes do after the King's death?"

Gaudron: "Before the Gravediggers had lowered the King's lukewarm body into the ground their forces were amassing on our borders."

Me: "Why didn't they just invade straight away?"

Gaudron: "I suppose they were waiting to see if one of the other Princes would make the first move."

Me: "Why? What would happen if one did?"

Gaudron: "What usually happens when there's a dispute over land— war happens, Loremaster, *war*... and none of the Princes want that!"

Me: "I see, so even though you're completely surrounded, their continued presence on your borders means they all stop one another from attacking you..."

Gaudron: "Yes—although recently, the Princes have grown tired of waiting and have started making small night-time advances into Brundale."

Me: "So, there *is* an invasion happening—right now?"

Gaudron: "Technically—yes, but it would be generous to call it that. They only move their pitched tents a few inches beyond our borders each night.[1128] We've started placing posts along our boundaries so we

---

[1126] *Without risking the wrath of the Heralds and their overly complex Arcane Copyright spells...*

[1127] *Who were probably annoyed their principality didn't start with the letter 'B'...*

[1128] *Making it one of the slowest invasions in the history of invasions, though not the slowest of all time; that particular honour belongs to the 'Army of Snailus', which took three summers to reach the privy before spending a further six summers advancing towards the enemy's border, only to turn around after their only Cleric decided he needed the privy again.*

can check the progress of their creeping advance. But our patrols have reported that our posts have also been surreptitiously moved forward along with the advancing armies, making it impossible to track correctly."

Me: "How can you stop it? It seems inevitable they will slowly work their way toward this castle's gate."

Gaudron: "That's where the Heroes Guild come in—we've set about creating hundreds of different quests and scattered them along the borders of our kingdom."

Me: "Quests?"

Gaudron: "Well, *side-quests* really—a plethora of small stuff[1129] that keeps any visiting hero entertained and, more importantly, keeps them within our borders."

Me: "But what good is a side-quest against an army... or four, for that matter?"

Gaudron: "Well, for a start, it can dramatically slow an advance to a veritable death crawl."[1130]

Me: "But how?"

Gaudron: "Moving a post is easy—but moving a crypt, citadel, or a dungeon? That's another thing altogether."

Me: "That's clever—especially as the Princes are no doubt aware they would incur the wrath of the Heroes Guild if they made one tiny error of judgement."

Gaudron: "I know all four of the Princes have held numerous meetings with the Heroes Guild to get them to look the other way. But unbeknownst to the Princes, we already have our own *arrangement* secured with them."

Me: "What sort of *arrangement?*"

[1129] *Not to be confused with 'stuffed-smalls'—which is a quest to locate some stolen Halfling, Gnomish and Dwarven underwear that have been shoved down a Giant's breeches.*

[1130] *The type of desperate crawl reserved for a backstabbed Cleric trying to dramatically claw at the loose coin spilt on the ground from the donation box they've dropped in shock.*

Gaudron: "You are no doubt aware that we are in the grip of the worst *Quest Drought* this realm has ever known."

Me: "I know this is a concerning issue that all heroes face—*yes*..."

Gaudron: "Well, believe it or not, the sum of side-quests within our proudly compact borders outnumbers those found in every corner of the realm combined."

Me: "I don't *believe* it!"[1131]

Gaudron: "That is your prerogative. But I speak the truth."

Me: "What sort of side-quests are we talking about?"

Gaudron: "Let me see, there's the *'Old Hermit's Birthday'*, where the heroes have to travel around Brundale trying to get all the items needed to throw a surprise party for an old cave-dwelling Hermit—"[1132]

Me: "I assume this side-quest is only available once per summer?"

The Baron smiles broadly.

Gaudron: "Age is just a number."

Me: "You mean you've celebrated his birthday more than once per summer? How many times has this side-quest been completed?"

Gaudron: "I've lost count."

The Baron turns to his Steward, who is standing nearby.

Gaudron: "How old is the Hermit now?"

Steward: "Officially? Four thousand and forty-five, *my Lord*."

Gaudron: "There you go—and I have to say he's looking pretty good for his age."

[1131] *Coincidentally, this was a catchphrase my Uncle Bevan Barr would say ad nauseam during his numerous tavern comedy routines. It was also the last words my Uncle ever spoke before his fatal heart attack brought on by an enraged pack of dogs.*

[1132] *There's something paradoxical about an adventuring party 'adventuring' for a party, even if it is only for a Hermit—though I'm positive the recluse still wouldn't appreciate the time, effort, or any gift the heroes finally turned up with (unless it was a magical Ring of Bugger Off And Leave Me Alone).*

I shake my head in disbelief at what I'm hearing.

Me: "Are there any other notable side-quests?"

Gaudron: "*Hmmm*—there's *'Brushing With Death'*."

Me: "*Ah,* now that's more like it—what's that quest about?"

Gaudron: "The heroes have to rescue a local artist who has mysteriously vanished after painting a poor depiction of 'Death'."[1133]

Me: "That sounds a little underwhelming if I'm being honest. Don't you have larger quests that include Dragons in dungeons?"[1134]

Gaudron: "We don't have any room for dungeons *with* Dragons[1135] or *even* Dragons.[1136] Given our limited size, we've had to really scale back on the main quests—they just take up too much space."

Me: "How is it you've managed to create so many side-quests?"

Gaudron: "*Erm*—well... the Heroes Guild have helped a little in that regard..."

Me: "Wait! The Heroes Guild *tells* you what side-quests to set for their *own* heroes?"

Gaudron: "I suppose it is a trifle unusual if one stops to think about it."

Me: "But why would they do that?"

Gaudron: "I don't look a gifted Wizard in his spellbook.[1137] The Heroes Guild have their reasons. All I know is that without their help—we

---

[1133] *Proving once and for all that 'Death' is the harshest of critics...*

[1134] *I can't explain why, but I suddenly felt a jittery Herald was about to suddenly appear as I spoke those last few words—no doubt with a hastily prepared Arcane Copyright spell at the ready.*

[1135] *There's that strange uneasy feeling once again.*

[1136] *But there is always space for dungeons—just without the Dragons.*

[1137] *A 'gifted' Wizard is a Wizard who has completed a high proportion of their quests without an unfortunate 'Fireball' incident.*

wouldn't be able to attract the best heroes to the realm.[1138]

Me: "Why don't the Princes join forces against the Heroes Guild and strike at its heart first?"

Gaudron: "They fear waking the Quakken, so to speak."[1139]

Me: "You have a *Quakken* here? I thought they were just a myth—"

The Baron holds his hands up apologetically.

Gaudron: "No, no, _no_, I didn't mean a *real* Quakken—my Grandfather would be spinning in his grave at the thought! Rather, the Heroes Guild is the *figurative* Quakken,[1140] a terrible creature the Princes would do well to leave well enough alone."

Me: "But that must mean you need heroes to be constantly travelling to and from Brundale? Why don't the Princes stop them from entering your land?"

Gaudron: "The moment word got back to the Heroes Guild that their heroes were being denied entry into our kingdom—there would be uproar, not to mention a lot of sharpening of swords, axes, spears, arrows, and maces.[1141] No—for now, the Princes have no choice but to allow free movement of heroes through their territory. But I cannot rely on that lasting forever. The Princes are growing braver and braver by the day—and that's where *you* come in."

Me: "Me? What can I do against four Princes with land envy?"

Gaudron: "Relax, Loremaster, I'm not going to ask you to do something you're not already doing. I just want you to write something about Brundale in that journal of yours—perhaps paint a picture of our

---

[1138] *Or at least a Heroes Guild one—just _not_ a Guild of Heroes one...*

[1139] *A Quakken is a mythical beast spoken about only as a whisper between frightened Pirates, fearful it will hunt them down on their next voyage. The handful who survive such an encounter all mention hearing a loud mournful duck-quack that echoes across the seas before it strikes without mercy, sinking ships in its giant beak while using mouthfuls of water to soak the wooden masts and hulls.*

[1140] *Soon to have its own figurine range available to purchase from Balstaff in Port Salvation...*

[1141] *Though this last one would probably just be polished within an inch of its life instead.*

kingdom as a thriving hero-friendly community with untamed adventuring potential.[1142] Somewhere danger lurks around every corner, where quests literally fall from the trees. I want you to keep the mystery of our land alive with adventuring possibilities! Brundale should be the must-visit location for every hero in the realm, be they from the Heroes Guild or not..."

Me: "Isn't that a bit misleading? The most dangerous quest you seem to have is looking for a lost book belonging to a forgetful librarian or winning the heart of the Landlord's daughter for the local woodcutter—"

Gaudron: "Landlord's *son*."

Me: "Sorry?"

Gaudron: "It's to win the heart of the Landlord's *son*—not daughter."

Me: "How many times has that side-quest been completed?"

The Baron looks up to his Steward for help.

Steward: "Three hundred and seventy-two times by the last count, *my Lord*..."[1143]

I shake my head in utter disbelief.

Me: "The effort required for this task must be monumental! How do you keep track of where every adventurer is on every adventure? What if two different heroes attempt the same quest minutes after one another?"

Gaudron: "That's why I pay for the finest Gnome Dungeonmasters in the entire realm to keep a record of everything for me. They're surprisingly good at the small stuff[1144]—like the details..."

[1142] *Just don't paint one that includes 'Death'—not unless I want to be on the wrong end of a 'critical scythe'...*

[1143] *They must almost be sick of seeing one another by now, like a married couple that have been together for a summer too long.*

[1144] *Such as antagonising Halflings—especially the adventuring kind...*

Me: "The side-quests, the Heroes Guild, the Dungeonmasters... it must be costing you a small fortune![1145] How are you paying for all this?"

Gaudron: "*Ah*—yes, well, as you can imagine, I'd rather not divulge any financials, you understand—"

Me: "But you can see the problem, can't you? How long before the coffers are bare and you can't keep the Heroes Guild interested in Brundale anymore—?"

The Baron's cheeks go red with rage.

Gaudron: "Now **look** here! I don't want you to print what I'm about to say next, not unless you want to see what an *extremely* upset Arin Darkblade can do to your spleen—am I clear?"[1146]

Me: "Perfectly."

Gaudron: "Well, then, as long as we both recognise there's an *understanding* in place between us, I'll let you in on another little secret. Another Guild resides here, in Brundale... a Guild whose members have a *particular* set of skills..."[1147]

Me: "What sort of skills?"

The Baron seems agitated; he gestures for the Steward to put his fingers in his ears—which he duly does. The Baron's voice drops to a nervous whisper.

Gaudron: "The kind of skills that are good at *loosening* the coin purse of the careless..."

Me: "I didn't know Clerics had Guilds—"

Gaudron: "**What?** No, not Clerics—*thieves!*"

Me: "You mean the Thieves Guild are here? In Brundale?"

The Baron's face goes even redder as he gestures for me to lower my voice.

[1145] *Or a very large fortune if we're still talking in Gnome or Halfling terms...*

[1146] *As clear as a naked Mime Warrior after they've downed a potion of invisibility...*

[1147] *Please—not tumbling acrobats, anyone but those forward-rolling clowns!*

Gaudron: "*Please,* Loremaster—walls have ears.[1148] I have a mutually beneficial *arrangement* with the Thieves Guild. I've permitted them to reside here within a secret underground lair. In return, they've agreed to help us obtain large amounts of coin to keep the Bailiffs from making a castle call."

Me: "Can I ask, what do the thieves do for you?"

Gaudron: "*Oh,* the usual underhanded carry-ons—encourage travellers to donate to our cause via the point of a dagger, steal the coin purse from any unwary rich-looking visitors, use loaded dice to pocket the winnings from bored enemy soldiers camped just within our borders. The Thieves Guild is working hard to ensure this land continues to survive."

Me: "Isn't that a somewhat risky partnership? Even the Heroes Guild frown upon the undesirables found lurking within the Thieves Guild—and they're not the only ones."

Gaudron: "The enemy of my enemy is an acquaintance I want to call a friend, but I don't—I *know* it's not ideal, but the fact remains, the Thieves Guild have been instrumental in keeping our coffers flowing with coin. If that means they have a safe space in exchange for that service, then so be it."

Me: "Are the Heroes Guild aware the Thieves Guild operates out of Brundale?"

Gaudron: "Not fully—only their Guildmaster, Toldarn knows..."

Me: "Why would Toldarn keep something like this from the rest of the Heroes Guild?"

Gaudron: "Toldarn's a shrewd man—he realises there's profit to be made from working with the Thieves Guild rather than against them."

Me: "But he has been using the Heroes Guild to hunt the Thieves Guild, squeezing them until they had no choice but to flee into Brundale?"

Gaudron: "And for good reason..."

[1148] *I've known that some magic walls have mouths—and use them to catcall passing female Stone Golems or curse drunken heroes who unwittingly relieve themselves against their hard cheeks. I've never known a magic wall to have ears, but I'd imagine they'd make excellent listeners if they did.*

I look at the Baron as he patiently waits for me to connect the two broken strands of thought.

Me: "You mean Toldarn has been conspiring to establish the Thieves Guild at the heart of Brundale? To what end?"

Gaudron: "Toldarn believes this *arrangement* will keep a steady stream of coin moving in the Heroes Guild's direction. He knows a single side-quest is far from profitable—but in great numbers, their cut from each successfully completed side-quest would be substantial, to say the least."

Me: "But why not let the rest of the Heroes Guild in on this ruse?"

Gaudron: "It's all about controlling the flow of information—to openly support the Thieves Guild would cause much consternation amongst those searching for any excuse to remove Toldarn from power—that's why only he and I know the truth, not even the Thieves Guild are aware of this particular *arrangement.*"

Me: "But now *I* know..."

Gaudron: "Y—Yes, *well...* I trust you can be discreet with the information I have entrusted you with?"

Me: "Of course, I don't want the fall of this kingdom on my conscience—no matter its size."[1149]

The Baron seems relieved.

Gaudron: "You have my thanks."[1150]

I look at the poor Steward next to me; fingers still wedged deep in his ears.

Me: "Shouldn't you—?"

Gaudron: "I should, but let us leave him like that for a while longer—it amuses me no end."

[1149] *I'm talking about the size of Brundale here, not my conscience.*

[1150] *But not the Baron's sword, axe, or bow... I suppose I cannot expect such a reward for my silence.*

I smile at the Baron's light-heartedness even though the gravity of his predicament seems to weigh heavily on his brow.

Gaudron: "I noticed something about you when I mentioned Arin Darkblade's name earlier—almost as if he had somehow wounded you personally?"[1151]

A flash of pain stings my consciousness again—Arin's name is *always* there, waiting in the shadows at every turn. My brother's burning face forms in my mind's eye before transforming into ash. I rue my decision to leave the *Pagoda of Tranquillity* without a flask of Ice Sativa—I could well do with a relaxing brew right now.

Me: "No—I only know of his foreboding reputation. It alone can strike fear into the bravest of hearts; the Princes are wise to be wary of him."

The Baron nods in agreement.

Gaudron: "No one is brave enough to go toe-to-toe with Arin Darkblade—not just yet. As dangerous a hero as he is, I'm at least thankful he's on our side."[1152]

Me: "I guess you're safe as long as Arin and the Heroes Guild don't change the terms of your *arrangement*."

Gaudron: "I pray they don't..."

Me: "But, if they decide to withdraw their support—?"

Gaudron: "Then nothing would stand in the way of the Princes using our kingdom as a battle arena to settle their scores. Brundale would cease to exist overnight..."

Me: "A sobering thought."

We sit in silence, playing through a visual tapestry of an alternate future—one where neither the Heroes Guild *nor* Arin Darkblade exists. It proves for grim viewing where Brundale is concerned.

Gaudron: "When is your journal being published?"

[1151] *That's because the pain of my brother's death is now forever entwined with his name—thanks for reminding me...*

[1152] *From what I've heard about the man, Arin is only ever on Arin's side.*

Me: "Just as soon as I've stopped writing it."[1153]

The Baron tightens his jaw at my evasive answer.

Gaudron: "Well, I can't sit chatting with you all day. I have an endless supply of side-quests that demand my urgent attention—while you have your journal to finish."

We both rise from our seats and politely shake hands.

Gaudron: "You *will* let me know when it's published, won't you? I do hope it becomes the roaring success I need it to be."

Me: "Of course—I'll even send you a complimentary copy of it."[1154]

Gaudron: "*Excellent!* Do that—*Oh,* and send any heroes you meet my way too. The Gods know we *really* need them, after all!"

Me: "It's the least I can do."

The Baron smiles one more time and turns to the Steward.

Gaudron: "Be a good chap and see the Loremaster to our border, will you?"

The Steward doesn't answer; his fingers are still wedged in his ears, eyes now closed.

Gaudron: "For pity's sake—*see*, this is what I've got to put up with around here, Loremaster."

The Baron shouts again at the Steward.

Gaudron: "**TAKE YOUR BLOODY FINGERS OUT OF YOUR EARS— YOU DOLT!!**"

[1153] *Unfortunately, having a journal accepted by the Publishing Guild is on par with a Category Five adventure. In reality, I'm doomed to spend the next two summers writing enquiry letter after enquiry letter, supplying sample chapters accompanied by a concise synopsis and a blood oath for my first-born, ONLY to hear back three summers later (if ever). If I do get a reply by some miracle, I will be frustratingly told it's a 'pass' (which is a Gnomish word meaning 'I'd rather pass urine on it than consider printing this old twaddle!').*

[1154] *Signed, of course. Although I will <u>not</u> be happy if I discover the Baron later sold it on the Back Market for an obscene amount of coin.*

The Steward doesn't react to the Baron's cries but opens his eyes in surprise as he stares nose-to-nose with an irritated Gaudron.

Steward: **"I can't hear you, *my Lord*—I still have my fingers in my ears!"**

Me: "I'm fine—the border is only a short walk from here."[1155]

The Baron narrows his eyes, unsure if there's a subtle subtext hidden in my reply.

Gaudron: **"TAKE YOUR FINGERS OUT OF YOUR EARS!"**

Steward: **"*Pardon?*"**

Gaudron: **"FOR THE *LOVE* OF THE GODS... I *SAID*—"**

I hurry out of the Baron's war room, keen to leave Gaudron's exasperated shouts and the Steward's deaf ears far behind me.[1156]

[1155] *I can make it to Brundale's border in less than ten minutes as the crow flies—which also includes a quick stop to peck at an unidentified dead critter that may or may not once been a rat from a nearby cellar side-quest (for the crow in question, not me).*

[1156] *I suspect the Steward may be 'trolling' the Baron here, which is a Gnomish word meaning 'To annoy someone to the point of crying'—like any 'actual' Trolls you're unlucky enough to meet...*

33. Zillith, the Herbalist

Suppose you don't trust the unstable magic of Wizards or enjoy testing your luck by downing the mysterious contents sold by eccentric Potioneers. In that case, there's always a <u>third</u> option available for those seeking an adventuring advantage. Zillith Prendergast is a Merchant who specialises in 'Oh, Natural' remedies. A former Ranger, she gave up adventuring to concentrate on her true calling—the foraging and selling of potent herbs. I've decided to drop in unannounced to meet Zillith to learn more about her love of the leaf and how it shapes the life she now leads.

After two days of following the road north from Brundale, I find myself back within the dirt-stained walls of Tronte. The familiar stench of rotting vegetables is unmistakable as I walk along the main street that pierces the Merchants' Quarter, cutting through the shops[1157] like a hot knife in a buttered-up Bard.[1158] I am mesmerised by the pungent aroma that hangs in the air as it solidifies into a semi-physical apparition. It gestures me to follow it along the cobbled thoroughfare like an onion-soaked sea siren luring me towards deadly unseen rocks.[1159] The abnormal smell leads me through a maze of backstreets and ominous alleyways before stopping at an old-fashioned shop with a sign that reads *'Zillith Prendergast: Herbalist To The Heroes'.*[1160] The foul-smelling stench that lured me to this place is joined by a horde of odours, each clambering over the other to attack my senses. With my nasal hairs threatening to leave in search for pastures new, I take a final breath of Tronte 'air' before stepping inside.[1161]

[1157] *There's even a shop that has been physically bisected by the street, making it impossible for the poor Merchant to spot any opportunistic larceny from the hundreds of Tronte citizens wandering through on their way to whatever business lies beyond its threshold.*

[1158] *Bards are notoriously easy to mug; it only takes a couple of free beers, a Halfling-rolled woodbine, an attractive distraction, and several flattering remarks to catch them completely off-guard.*

[1159] *Or in this city, deadly unseen Rogues...*

[1160] *Conspicuous by its absence, there also seems to be an empty section just above the sign where something else stood. Twisted and broken beams are everywhere—as if a powerful force 'ripped' whatever it was out of its very foundations before flying off with it in its claws, to only the Gods know where...*

[1161] *Which is like taking a final breath of noxious gas before heading into an even deadlier stinking cloud.*

Zillith: "What do you want, Wizard? If you're looking for Mandrake Root, you're out of luck; I sold the last of it this morning—you'll have to wait until next week before I have time to forage for some more."

The voice that greets me belongs to an elderly Half-Elf with long curly grey hair and a mischievous glint in her eye. She smiles as she sees me struggling to cope with the overbearing stench that swirls around her shop.

Me: "I'm not a Wiz[1162]—I'm a *Loremaster,* Elburn the Loremaster. I was given your name from a mutual acquaintance."

Zillith: "My name is not yours to take, not without getting to *know* you better first..."

I shift uncomfortably on the spot.

Me: "I didn't mean..."

Zillith: "I *know* what you meant—who was this mutual acquaintance of ours?"

Me: "He said you were in competition with him."

Zillith: "Was it another Wizard?"

Me: "No—"

Zillith: "*Ah,* then it must have been the Potioneer, Inglebold. How *is* the old goat?"

Me: "When I left him, he had just transformed into a hairy monstrosity and half-eaten a Guard on a horse..."[1163]

Zillith: "*Oh,* the usual for him then. To be honest, you got off lightly— the side effects from his potions are unpredictable at best and catastrophic at worst..."

[1162] *I'm starting to think it may just be easier to say I am a Wizard and be done with it, rather than go through this every time I meet someone new. Unless, of course, I'm talking to a Wizard's natural enemy—a Barbarian...*

[1163] *The horse survived—the same can't be said about the unfortunate Heartenford Guard riding it.*

Me: "Really?"[1164]

Zillith: "*Oh yes—so* spill, *Loremaster, what did he have to say about me? I bet it wasn't anything wholesome.*"

Me: "It was... *colourful,* to say the least."[1165]

There's a sudden *'thud'* from the floor above.[1166] The Half-Elf slaps her hand on the counter and points excitedly at me.

Zillith: "**HA!** I *knew* it! He's always been the same, never changes—well, obviously he *does* change, but that's down to his unstable concoctions rather than any learned response. Tell me, Loremaster, does he still keep one eye on the lookout for trouble?"

Me: "He did appear somewhat on edge—do you know why?"

Zillith: "Probably something to do with an ill-advised deal with the Sharks Guild that went awry—he was never very good holding onto his coin... did he tell you he had to leave Tronte in a hurry?"

Me: "No."

Zillith: "Why am I not surprised."

Me: "I get the impression there's an unspoken rivalry between you both; something that's bubbling away under the surface—"

Zillith: "Three of us."

Me: "Three?"[1167]

Zillith: "You left out Morgan."

Me: "Morgan? You mean *Simply* Morgan?"

[1164] *My mind wanders nervously back to the few sips of Lucky Potion I recently downed—I check the palms of my hands for any sign of hair, but thankfully they still remain bare (and not bear).*

[1165] *To be fair to the Potioneer, he only mentioned Zillith and her herbal wares in passing— but I wanted to see how she reacted if I stoked their rivalry a little.*

[1166] *Maybe the Herbalist has a rat infestation problem in her attic?*

[1167] *Has one of the Potioneer's potions accidentally split him into two slightly-smaller-but-doubly-eccentric halves?*

Zillith: "Is that the name he's going by now? Back when I knew him, he was *Morgan the Magnificent*—which, if you ask me, was blowing his own trumpet a little too hard."[1168]

Me: "What happened between the three of you?"

Zillith: "What usually happens between three strong personalities—*jealousy*."

Me: "Professional?"

Zillith: "Personal."

Me: "What do you mean?"

Zillith: "*Oh,* you know, I wasn't *always* this old, Loremaster—and neither were my companions. We were all attractive and full of vim and vigour. We used to adventure together back then, the three of us."

Me: "You used to adventure together? I didn't know that—I mean, they never mentioned it to me."

Zillith: "Probably because it was a long time ago—and time has taken its toll on their failing memories. But, I can recall our many quests like *The Blue Plums Mountain,*[1169] *Peeping on the Shadowlands,*[1170] even really <u>hard</u> adventures like *The Journey to the Huge Angry Cock*[1171]—all satisfying quests in their own right."

Me: "Wait—you mean each adventure is named?"[1172]

[1168] *An all-too-common problem, <u>especially</u> amongst trumpet-carrying Bards...*

[1169] *An adventure to steal a Mountain Giant's cold plums (from his frozen garden).*

[1170] *A quest that includes a lot of secretive 'watching' from a watchtower while no one is looking.*

[1171] *A quest to find a rage-filled cockerel that vanished after moodily crossing the Merchant's Road...*

[1172] *A Quest-Namer is an individual who has the demanding task of naming every adventure in the realm—usually while sitting safely behind a desk. Although it does beg the question, how can a Quest-Namer name a quest without actually having experienced it first? I suspect a lot of 'making it up as we go along' is happening behind the scenes. Quest-Namers are often just Dungeonmasters who have got spare time on their hands and have a twisted sense of humour.*

Zillith: "Of course, each adventure is named! How else are you supposed to keep track of the damn thing for weeks on end? It's not like we carry scraps of parchment and a quill around all day to write this kind of stuff down—no offence to your craft."

Me: "None taken. So, what changed?"

Zillith: "I grew weary of the dungeon-delving drudgery; I longed to live freely amongst flora and fauna. Foraging for herbs was all I cared for— I realised I could make as much coin selling herbs to heroes[1173] as I could from risking life and limb in some forgotten tomb. So, I gave it all up to follow my dream."

Me: "How did Morgan and Inglebold react to your decision?"

Zillith: "*Oh,* true to form, they blamed one another for driving me out of the hero business. I knew that wasn't the case, but I wasn't about to give them the satisfaction of knowing that."

Me: "Why do I suspect that's only half the story?"

Zillith: "My, my, you *are* astute—good, I do like it when one pays *close* attention to me. Inglebold and Morgan were both good-looking young men in their time— and yes, they were my suitors. You have to remember, being a Half-Elf, I'm torn between doing what is expected of me[1174] and doing what I want to do;[1175] I knew deep down I wasn't ready to become a stay-at-home wife of a Potioneer *or* a Wizard, for that matter..."

Me: "So, you and Inglebold were *together?*"

Zillith: "You could say that."

Me: "*And* you were also with Morgan?"

Zillith: "And Morgan."

Me: "At the same time?"

Zillith: "Not exactly the same time. What do you take me for?"

[1173] *Especially High-Elven Bards...*

[1174] *The Elven part...*

[1175] *The Human part...*

I blush awkwardly, realising what I've just implied.

Me: "Sorry! I didn't m—"

The Herbalist chuckles as she enjoys watching me squirm on the spot.

Zillith: "Not at the same time, but the same time period—if that makes you feel any better."[1176]

Me: "What happened between you?"

Zillith: "I doubt you want all the juicy details for your book."[1177]

I squirm again and go a shade of red that doesn't even exist or has been seen by another living soul since the realm was created from the volcanic magma spewed forth by the Dragon God Volcarnos over ten thousand summers ago.

Zillith: "I left Inglebold after his possessiveness got the better of him. It was clear he wasn't ready for a relationship—his moods kept changing as often as he did. He became irritable and cranky, like a bear with a sore head."[1178]

Me: "But you and Morgan didn't last either."

Zillith: "*Ah,* his work got the better of him. He was so engrossed in tinkering with his enchanted items that he didn't notice how unhappy I had become. The magic quickly faded between us, and inevitably we went our separate ways—I haven't seen him since."

Me: "What did you do then?"

There comes a second thump, louder than the first, from the room directly above our heads[1179]—I stare upwards quizzically. The Half-Elf carries on talking, blatantly ignoring the commotion interrupting our conversation.

[1176] *Not really, but I silently thank the Half-Elf for trying.*

[1177] *It's really not that kind of book!*

[1178] *Or an angry Barbarian who has been playing 'Potion Roulette' with a crate of Transformation Potions—and wound up with all-over body hair, a pig 'Familiar', and a monstrous appetite for honey.*

[1179] *A really BIG rat infestation problem…*

Zillith: "*Oh,* my path has led me across the entire realm. I've journeyed from the Ice Wastes of the Northern Territory to the Unforgiving Seas off the Grudge Coast.[1180] I've dedicated my existence to my love of nature. I've curated as many unique herbs as I could find and documented the properties of each one until I was finally ready to open the doors to this shop here in Tronte. That was forty-five summers ago now[1181]—how time flies when you're having fun..."

Me: "You must have some stories to tell—wonders you've witnessed on your travels?"

Zillith: "I have—but they are insignificant now I have my shop. Wondering *who* will be next to walk through my door is more than enough adventure for this Half-Elf."

Me: "What sort of customers frequent your store?"

Zillith: "All sorts, adventurers seeking a herbal aid, opportunistic pedlars looking to make an easy coin or two near a dungeon entrance—even a few locals who want a little *pick-me-up* or two."

Me: "Pick-me-up? What's that?"[1182]

Zillith: "*Oh,* something to keep the passion in the bedroom going.[1183] I have plenty of herbs that can aid and assist those who find their entertaining skills have dwindled of late. I've got a huge selection of herbs *upstairs* to make things go like clockwork *downstairs* if you catch my meaning—do you want to see?"

I can feel my cheeks burning as if a Wizard's Fireball has just slapped them.

Me: "I—I *don't* think—"

[1180] *A sea where every local fisherman takes umbrage at every missed catch, broken line, and 'big one' that got away.*

[1181] *If every ten Elven summers are the equivalent of one Human summer, then it stands to reason that five Half-Elven summers equate to one Human summer. By my calculations, Zillith's shop has been open four and a half Elven summers, which is also equal to nine Half-Elven summers. But really, who's counting?*

[1182] *You'll be surprised to hear that this is <u>not</u> a Gnomish word to describe a 'needy' Halfling...*

[1183] *I guess this, for some, could <u>still</u> be a 'needy' Halfling.*

The Herbalist laughs playfully.

Zillith: "Relax—I'm just playing around with you."[1184]

I laugh nervously along with the Half-Elf.

Zillith: "Unless, of course, you really *do* want to go upstairs?"

Me: "N—No, thank you…"

Zillith: "*Oh,* well, you can't blame an old girl for trying…"[1185]

The thumping above my head suddenly increases in volume[1186]—I swear I can hear a muffled cry for help. The Half-Elf grabs a broom and uses it to jab the ceiling angrily.

Zillith: **"Quiet down!"**

Me: "*Erm…* W—Where do you get your herbs from?"

The Half-Elf's demeanour quickly changes from playful to professional in a blink of a carriage-driving Cyclops' eye.[1187]

Zillith: "From all across the realm. I have it shipped in—Blue Fortuna from the Doom Mountains, Fillomore from the Unmistakable Marshes, Rusnip Weed from the Deadwood Swamps—I've even got a steady supply of Ice Sativa from a secret source."

Me: "Ice Sativa? I thought only a select few know of its whereabouts?"

Zillith: "By select few, I assume you mean *Inglebold?*"

I don't reply—but my face cannot hide precisely what I'm thinking.

[1184] *That's precisely what I'm afraid of.*

[1185] *It's not that I couldn't see myself attracted to the Half-Elf; I just swore never to get involved with someone who is at least five times older than me, and that again, if we're measuring this in Half-Elven summers, or ten times that in Elven summers.*

[1186] *It appears the big rats upstairs are now wearing heavy boots.*

[1187] *There's a little-known fact that a Cyclops has to blink three times faster than a Human, Dwarf or Elf—if they blink any slower, then they risk a moment of utter blindness when their eye is fully closed. So, imagine the sheer terror of any carriage-riding passengers if some grit flew into the eye of their 'Cyclops' Wagonmaster just as they were traversing a perilous canyon pass at the same time.*

Zillith: "Inglebold doesn't like the cold—he *hates* it."

Me: "But why would he venture up a glacial mountain in search of it?"

I catch the Half-Elf smirking at me.

Zillith: "Why would he indeed...?"

The Herbalist winks as she chews on a purple root.

Me: "It wasn't Inglebold—it was _you_!"

Zillith: "Clever, *huh?*"

Me: "How did you do it?"

In an instant, her face morphs into the familiar features I recognise as Inglebold the Potioneer[1188]—the transformation is staggering.

Zillith: "It's a herb called Myriad Leaf[1189]—you just chew on it and think of a face you want to change into."

Me: "Does it last long?"

Zillith: "A few hours—or a few seconds, depending on whether or not you eat some White Bayliss after to counteract the effects."

The Potioneer-looking Herbalist withdraws a hand to reveal a white root sitting snugly in her palm—in a flash she pops the root into her mouth and gnaws away at it. As promised, in a matter of seconds, Inglebold's face morphs back into the smiling face of the Half-Elf.

I'm struggling to figure out if what I've just witnessed is amazing or disturbing.[1190]

Zillith: "—and it's completely 'Oh, Natural' too!"

Me: "Beyond the obvious, why do it?"

[1188] *In human form—not monstrous form...*

[1189] *Not to be confused with a Myriad Loaf—an appearance-changing bread, nor a Myriad Loafer—an appearance-changing creature that sits around doing absolutely nothing all day.*

[1190] *Not to mention hugely immoral! I wonder how Inglebold would feel knowing someone was using his identity to get what they wanted?*

Zillith: "Because an old girl like me still needs to earn their coin—besides, I'm also having *way* too much fun pretending to be that oaf Inglebold. Think about it; I'm getting a cheap price for an expensive herb; I'm getting free tavern drinks *and* an extra sack of Ice Sativa for sending any half-drunk candidate off towards the Pagoda of Tranquillity. What's not to love? Did I mention The Enduring Light is also paying me to put a large sign above my shop advertising their pointless candle religion—I see all this as a positive sign of things to come."[1191]

Me: "Aren't you worried about any repercussions from this?"

The Herbalist bats me away like a half-bored Ogre trying to swat an annoying levitating Halfling Wizard.

Zillith: "There won't be any repercussions, not for me. If anything—they'll be looking for an eccentric old Potioneer ambling along the Merchant's Road, certainly not a carefree and still ravishingly good-looking Herbalist from Tronte."

Me: "What if the blind Monk discovers your ruse and comes looking for you?"

Zillith: "*Pfft...* that's hardly going to happen—is it now?"[1192]

Me: "*Hmmm,* I suppose not, although she *has* a pretty keen sense of smell."

Zillith: "Smell? Really?"

For the first time in our conversation, the Herbalist appears slightly worried.

Zillith: "How good?"

Me: "*Lethally* good."

The Half-Elf is silent for a moment as she plays out a few different scenarios in her head—she eventually gives up, shrugs her shoulders, and bats the thought away as if a second levitating Halfling Wizard just

---

[1191] *I think the Half-Elf will see an 'actual' sign from upon high when she eventually goes outside and looks at the spot where the 'physical' sign upon high used to stand.*

[1192] *Also harsh but true...*

floated past.[1193]

Zillith: "*Nah*—why am I worried? It probably won't happen."

She smiles sweetly enough, but I can tell the thought is still troubling her.

Me: "How popular are your herbs with the adventuring community? Is there a sense of suspicion to the wares you are peddling?"

Zillith: "Suspicion? Not at all! My herbs are exceedingly popular with all adventurers; I've had everyone from Bards and High Elves *to* High Elven Bards pass through my door."[1194]

There's another series of thumps coming from the room upstairs; something fragile shatters as it hits the floor—the Herbalist looks like she's about to launch another attack on the ceiling with her broom but thinks better of it. She waits a moment before turning to talk to me.

Zillith: "The new crop of heroes coming through the ranks are looking for something they can trust, something they know won't let them down in the heat of the moment, something that tastes good and gives them a little lift when they need it most. My herbs guarantee *all* that without the uncomfortable side effects."

Me: "What sort of uncomfortable side effects?"

Zillith: "Unwanted mutations? Miscast spells? Listen, would *you* trust an Elixir concocted with countless unknown substances? Or worse, try on a magical ring with an immoral curse lingering in its depths? Why risk the unknown when you can put your faith in something *Oh, Natural*?"

My eyes are drawn to a painted sign hanging on the wall behind the Herbalist,[1195] just above Zillith's Certificate of Merit for Big Cat Topiary Sculpting—it reads *Natural Remedies For Those Unnatural Moments*. The Half-Elf catches me staring.

Zillith: "That thing? It's just a little slogan I came up with."

[1193] *Although, technically, it 'could' be the same Halfling Wizard, I suppose.*

[1194] *Who quite possibly left even 'higher'.*

[1195] *Fortunately, a sign-hungry Wyvern hasn't stolen this one.*

Me: "Slogan?"[1196]

Zillith: "Something I like to say to my customers when I've sold them a herb or two—I've always felt it struck a chord."[1197]

Me: "It's quite memorable."

Zillith: "*Thanks*—it suddenly came to me when I was on the privy."

My face turns slightly less than my stomach.

Me: "What about your rivals Morgan and Inglebold?"

Zillith: "Yes, I believe they *still* use a privy too, although Inglebold probably just goes in a bush. Which comes with its own dangers, namely Rangers—they love hiding in bushes."[1198]

Me: "No, I mean slogans—do they have their own slogans?"

Zillith: "*Oh,* I see, silly me—I don't think they have a slogan unless '*That wasn't supposed to happen!*' counts?"

Me: "Inglebold believes he will get the lion's share of coin from the new glut of heroes because he's continually moving from town-to-town. While Morgan's magical items are gaining popularity, now he's working directly with the Heroes Guild—do you worry they will run you out of business?"

Zillith: "*Worry*—about those two idiots? One's an unreliable Wizard who never ventures further than the rickety steps leading from his front door. The other is a Potioneer who doesn't know what's actually in his bottles, let alone what they do when consumed. I don't think there's much I need to be concerned with there."

Me: "What about the rumoured Quest-Drought? Has that affected your business at all?"

[1196] *I later looked up this term 'slogan', learning it is an old Gnomish word that roughly translates as 'tricking an idiot into parting with coin and being glad about it'.*

[1197] *'Struck a Chord' is another Gnomish saying that literally means 'hit a Bard—any Bard... HARD...'*

[1198] *I'm guessing Bergenn wouldn't be too pleased to discover the Potioneer using her bush as a makeshift privy—as if the Heartenford Guards alone weren't bad enough...*

Zillith: "Almost certainly. The number of towns and cities between here and the Dagger Coast has doubled. The forests and woodlands have suffered as a result—most have been lost! Now there's a lack of outdoor adventures; the Ranger community is under threat from those who seek to destroy it in the name of '*Progress*'. I blame the axe-loving types who care not for the flora or the fauna[1199]—their only drive is for urban expansion and the quest for more coin. They are cutting down my beloved trees and digging up my secret herbal gardens at an alarming rate. I remember when Tronte was nothing more than a woodland settlement, but now look at it—not a single tree for as far as the eye can see. Instead, fire and smoke sweep across the countryside, choking the life out of my precious herbal business. I'm concerned the *Oh, Natural* realm will soon cease to exist as we know it..."

Me: "I didn't realise you were here when Tronte was a woodland settlement—"

Zillith: "Yes, I know—I'm old. But I'm *still* young enough for a handsome face or two."

The Herbalist gives me a suggestive wink. The thumping noise has now been replaced by an unbearable scratching noise.[1200] I smile awkwardly at the Half-Elf as she continues to ignore the mysterious sound.

Me: "W—What about the Heroes Guild? I've heard their demands for a heavy discount can be quite crippling to a business such as yours."

Zillith: "We are all after more for less in one way or another—I just prefer to do it with a dried leaf rather than by the point of a sharp sword. As for the Heroes Guild, that's nothing but the usual tough negotiations that occur between Merchants and their customers—it's to be expected. However, I will say this—the Heroes Guild *always* insists on their members visiting my shop before heading out into the wilds. If that means they get a bigger discount off the back of it, then so be it. I'll continue to make a profit, even if it does take me a little longer to retire than planned—I *am* a Half-Elf, after all..."

[1199] *To be clear, the Half-Elf doesn't mean Barbarians. Not <u>all</u> Barbarians love an axe, some love a two-handed sword instead. But one thing is for sure... <u>all</u> Barbarians love ale and using their fists.*

[1200] *If it <u>is</u> a rat—it now seems intent on clawing its way down through the floorboards towards us.*

Me: "How long do you think it will take?"

Zillith: "Maybe shy of a hundred summers—"

Me: "A *hundred* summers?"

Zillith: "Remember, time moves differently for Half-Elves. I've still got quite a few more summers left in these old bones. I won't be retiring to a dilapidated old castle by the sea anytime soon."[1201]

Me: "Forgive me—I wasn't suggesting you were past your prime; I was curious to know how long you thought you had left."[1202]

The Herbalist chuckles wistfully.

Zillith: "Who *really* knows the answer to that question—all I *do* know is that I have a lot longer left here in my store than if I were out there, still adventuring."

Me: "Do you miss it—those adventuring days?"

Zillith: "No. Even though growing up, being a hero was *all* that mattered to me. I mean, who starts out wanting to be a boring old Farmer or an ale-stained Barmaid? Nobody... that's because everyone wants to be a hero—the only thing is, they don't realise most people are already one."

Me: "Already one *what?*"

The noise from upstairs seems to have subsided for now.[1203] The Herbalist sighs and pulls out another twig to chew on.

Zillith: "A hero..."

Me: "I don't follow—"

Zillith: "Everyone is a hero in their own right; they don't *need* to venture into a dungeon to prove it. The Farmer getting up before the

---

[1201] *Or enjoying the view while sitting in the Gnome-infested garden of The Heroes Hall of Legends...*

[1202] *Somehow, I've made that sound even <u>worse</u> than I thought possible.*

[1203] *Maybe the heavy boot-wearing rat has given up on the floorboards and finally scurried off...*

sun to till a field is no less noble than a Barbarian charging headfirst to battle a monstrous beast. The Barmaid serving patrons until the early hours[1204] is just as brave as any Wizard stepping into a ten-by-ten room.[1205] Heroes are all around us, in everyone we meet and everything we do."

Me: "Is that why you walked away?"

Zillith: "I knew I was already a hero—I didn't need to put my life on the line to prove it to anyone else."

Me: "I think that's perfectly put. Would you mind if I included it in my book?"

Zillith: "By all means. If my words can bring comfort or peace of mind, that alone will bring me joy beyond what I already possess."

Me: "I'm glad you've found happiness."

The Herbalist catches my eye and smiles as she proudly opens her arms to embrace the ambience of her shop.

Zillith: "I'm always happy because I know I'm where I should be—as should you be."

Me: "What do you mean?"

The Half-Elf smiles at me with a hungry look in her eyes.

Zillith: "Why with *me*, of course."[1206]

There's that familiar mischievous glint in her eyes again—it's a glint that sends a shiver down my spine. An explosion of footsteps running down the stairs breaks the awkward moment as a completely naked and bound Dwarf bolts past at full speed[1207]—a look of sheer terror on his face as he locks eyes with me.

[1204] *Unless that particular Barmaid happens to work at The Spit & Spear tavern...*

[1205] *The most feared four words a Wizard will ever hear outside of 'Hand-to-Hand Combat'.*

[1206] *Okay, that's probably my cue to leave.*

[1207] *This is probably the fastest I've _ever_ seen a Dwarf move.*

Naked Dwarf: ***"For the love of the Gods—GET OUT OF HERE!"***[1208]

I say nothing; I just stare in disbelief as the naked Dwarf disappears into the alley, the sound of surprised shrieks following in his wake. I eventually turn back to the Herbalist, who smiles apologetically at me before offering some of the black herb roots she's started half-chewing on.[1209]

Zillith: "*Ah* well—easy come, easy go. Now, Loremaster, can I tempt you with some Acadia Root? It does *wonders* for the stamina?"

I stare momentarily at the *Oh, Natural* offering before thanking the Herbalist for her time and hastily retreating in the same direction as the naked, bound Dwarf.[1210]

[1208] *And if footnote 1206 wasn't enough of a clue that I should take my leave, then this* <u>should</u> *clear up any remaining ambiguity.*

[1209] *A word to the wise, never accept herbs from a stranger—especially if that stranger is a Half-Elf with a voracious sexual appetite.*

[1210] *Although I'm mindful of escaping without running faster than a brisk walk—I'm not keen to see the Dwarf's small hairy backside again quite so soon.*

34. Lotho, the Bard

Clamford is a small village wedged between the Merchant's Road and the Pilgrim's Pass to the north.[1211] It's a favourite spot for solo adventurers keen to find a reputable party. As a result, the local tavern in Clamford, The Axe & Dwarf, puts on a regular evening called 'Hasty Encounters' where solitary heroes have thirty seconds to greet a continuous rotation of candidates in the hope of finding their ideal adventuring match.[1212] So, with that said, it may surprise you to hear that I've arranged to interview a hero from Clamford who adventures with some<u>thing</u>—rather than some<u>one</u>...

I'm waiting to meet a Bard who has become something of a legend within the Bardic community—that, as you can imagine, is quite an achievement given the stiff competition. But Lotho isn't just *another* Bard with a Halfling-rolled woodbine addiction and a love of himself;[1213] he's a Bard who has turned his back on lutes, mandolins, lyres, and harps—in favour of the unconventional.

As the sun slowly begins its fiery descent towards the horizon, I find myself gazing at the hillside path that leads down to Clamford, no more than an hour's walk away. Watching intently as a strangely shaped figure approaches along the beaten path towards my position. I watch patiently until this oddly angled stranger comes into full view—it's a Halfling carrying a rather large object on his back.

Me: "Lotho—Lotho the *Bard?*"

The Halfling Bard wheezes as he nears and, with some difficulty, hoists the sizeable rectangular object off his back and drops it with a thud on the ground—it squeals noisily, almost in protest. The Halfling rubs his shoulders, trying to massage the life back into them.

[1211] *The Pilgrim's Pass is a lesser-traversed road frequented by the occasional Cleric seeking to avoid the coin-pinching Heartenford Guards who plague the Merchant's Road, or dubious Potioneers promising instant muscles in potion form...*

[1212] *Wizards usually have an unfair advantage over their rivals thanks to a 'Slow' spell or two stuffed up their oversized sleeves, which is why the Landlord of The Axe & Dwarf charges them a higher fee if they want to participate.*

[1213] *Given that Lotho is a Halfling, this would mean he would 'roll' his own (if he was so inclined).*

Lotho: "*Ha,* yeah, that's a weight off my back. Maybe next time I'll arrange for us to meet at the bottom of the hill rather than at the top—that mistake is on me. Right, yes... introductions—Lotho, at your service, and you must be the *Loremaster.* Well met, good Sir..."

The Halfling holds his hand out for me to shake.

Me: "A pleasure."

I gesture to the mysterious monolith behind him.

Me: "I take it *this* is it?"

Lotho: "Indeed, you are correct—you want to take a peek?"

Me: "Is that okay?"

The Bard chuckles to himself.

Lotho: "Be a short conversation if you didn't."

With a flick of his wrist, he pulls the heavy cloth away to reveal a walnut pipe organ, complete with battle scars from the numerous dungeons it has been hauled through[1214]—it is a sight impressive enough to leave me stunned for a few seconds at least.

Me: "It's... *erm*... big."

Lotho: "Want to hear a few notes?"

Me: "I'd be honoured."

The Bard links his fingers together and pushes them out, cracking his knuckles with a satisfying **'CRUNCH'** before kicking the base of the pipe organ to release a plush-looking seat that he takes in one swift movement.

[1214] *There are even the unmistakable black shafts of a Goblin arrow or two jutting out its side. How the incompetent green-skinned archers managed to hit the instrument is almost unfathomable—I can only assume they were aiming for a nearby trumpet-carrying Bard instead.*

Lotho: "Something rousing to warm the spirits, I think, *ah,* yes—I know, *Great Fireballs of Fire!*"[1215]

A cheerful tune suddenly gasps out of the pipe organ as the Halfling hammers away at the keys. The sound is like nothing I have ever heard before, haunting and encouraging at the same time—almost as if several unholy beasts were being slowly squeezed together to make the bellowing sound. I find my spirits lifting and the weight of my brother's passing subsiding even though the song's fiery words should be hitting a nerve. My foot is guiltily tapping along with the tune when it comes to an abrupt end. The Halfling spins on his seat to look expectantly at me.

Me: "That was—*hypnotic.*"

Lotho: "Thank you, I've not completed it yet—it's still a work in progress."

Me: "Do you write all your own songs?"

Lotho: "Not all of them—some of the popular tunes I 'borrow' from other Bards—like Axel-Grind and Evonne Stardust."

Me: "Do they mind you using their songs?"

Lotho: "Probably, but we have an unspoken rule about singing songs that belong to other Bards."

Me: "What's the rule?"

Lotho: "Sing it—but don't ever talk about it."

Me: "Why?"

Lotho: "Because the Heroes Guild has a group of extremely powerful Heralds who are just waiting to unleash their Arcane Copyright spells on those who dare to use their songs without express permission."

Me: "You need *permission* to sing a song?"

Lotho: "Yes... *look,* all the non-Guild Bards have no problem

---

[1215] *Probably 'not' the cheerful tune I wanted to hear, given how emotionally wrought I am with anything associated with fire—and of course, balls. Still, not much I can do but grin and bear it.*

'borrowing' songs from one another; it's kind of accepted—even encouraged. I mean, that's how Bards *used* to work; they would come together, collaborate, and create the most fantastic songs the realm had ever heard. But when the Heroes Guild showed up, they began to attract the best of our kind to their halls[1216]—getting them to sign over all ownership to their tunes for a substantial one-off fee. Once that happened, anyone on an adventure who sang a melody belonging to a Bard from the Heroes Guild suddenly got an unexpected visit from a Fair-Use Ogre or two."

Me: "I've heard a visit from a Fair-Use Ogre can often be followed by a visit from the Pain Fairy."[1217]

Lotho: "Just pray *Thump*[1218] doesn't turn up at your door; he's a huge lumbering knucklehead who would keep breaking your arms and legs until you coughed up the owed coin. Take my word for it—most of his debtors pay up immediately after a limb's first **'SNAP'** is heard."

Me: "Sounds like you've had a run-in with this Ogre before."

Lotho: "I have—fortunately, I'm too quick for Thump."

Me: "Even with a huge organ strapped to your back?"

Lotho: "You'd be surprised how handy this organ can be in a tight spot."[1219]

[1216] *If not the best—then certainly the most popular if Axel-Grind is anything to go by.*

[1217] *Remember when you stepped on something sharp or stubbed your toe on a chair?* <u>*That's*</u> *the Pain Fairy at work—they are mischievous creatures designed to cause maximum pain with minimum effort. They're also sadistic voyeurs who enjoy nothing more than watching the fruits of their labour unfold while eating a box of cooked corn ears.*

[1218] *In case you weren't paying attention before, Ogres name their offspring after the first noise the newborn hears at the time of birth. I can only imagine 'Thump' was so-called after hearing his mother's fist slamming into his father's face—probably for putting her through the agony of childbirth in the first place.*

[1219] *Although I suspect the pipe organ would be a bit of a hindrance in an* <u>*actual*</u> *tight spot. I can picture the Bard stuck in a stairwell repeatedly shouting 'Pivot!' to himself at the top of his voice.*

A glint in the Halfling's eye suggests there's more to that answer than meets the eye.[1220]

Me: "Funny enough, you're not the first Bard I've seen who favours an unconventional instrument."

Lotho: "*Really?* I thought I was the only one. Who was the other?"

Me: "*Brin of Cloverton*—although he's retired now, so I'm not sure it counts."

Lotho: "That's good; I can't have another Bard doing what I'm doing, even if he is miles away in Cloverton—it'll only confuse both of our loyal fans."[1221]

Me: "Does it bother you that some of your peers, like Axel-Grind and Evonne Stardust have become members of the Heroes Guild?"[1222]

Lotho: "No, it's their choice what they do and who they join at the end of the day. But then, they're not really seen as *official* members anyway..."

Me: "Why?"

Lotho: "Bards aren't like boring old Fighters, nor are they like accident-prone Wizards, or weapon-shy Monks, or donation-hungry Clerics, dead-loving Necromancers, kleptomaniacal Sorceresses, or short-tempered Barbarians—we're different. All those other professions secretly yearn to be what we are. We have a reputation to uphold, a spontaneous upbeat one filled with sexual tension and unbridled passion. We are perceived as free spirits who play hard and sleep with anything with a pulse[1223]. Bards like Axel-Grind will always look to rock the establishment, even establishments like the Heroes Guild—it's in

---

[1220] *Although I'm unsure whose eye 'I' would be meeting—I just hope it's not some big floating eye with teeth, tentacles, and a burning desire to start a staring contest.*

[1221] *I fail to see the problem—Lotho and Brin couldn't be more unalike if they tried. One is three feet taller, and separated in age by at least _forty_ summers—or does Lotho mean the pair only have two fans to share between them?*

[1222] *Dammit! _Now_ I remember the question I was going to ask Axel-Grind in our previous meeting.*

[1223] *A consensual pulse!*

their nature. We don't like *following* rules because we are supposedly born to *break* the rules—Axel-Grind included. Although, personally speaking, I'm happiest when I'm at home enjoying a nice quiet mug of Cavern Tea."[1224]

Me: "Have you ever broken the rules?"

Lotho: "The only rule I've ever broken is the one about having fun and ensuring everyone else in the party is having fun—that's difficult when you're the only one on an adventure. *Oh,* that and the rule about not 'borrowing' songs from Bards who are *unofficial* members of the Heroes Guild of course..."

Me: "So, you'll continue to 'borrow' songs from unofficial members— but without ever telling them you did?"

Lotho: "You got it! See, when we go on an adventure without a member, we're free to sing any of their songs—we just make sure the Heroes Guild never finds out."

Me: "Let me ask you something else; why do you choose to adventure alone?"

The Halfling sits on the fence and stares wistfully across the picturesque horizon, letting the wind gently push his wavy mid-length hair off his face.

Lotho: "Where do I start? I can't *stand* all the bickering about who's getting the points for killing some poor Goblin minding their own business.[1225] The amount of time I've seen wasted arguing over *who* should become the leader defies belief. Quests have been lost thanks to the mind-numbing quarrels over a +3 magical sword the group just found. I mean, come on—*grow up!* I've witnessed Clerics declare they're trap-disarming specialists, only to be impaled on a device a blind Monk could have avoided.[1226] Not to mention the constant fear of being backstabbed by the treacherous Rogue in the group or smote by the Paladin for suggesting they secretly desire to sleep with a

---

[1224] *A paradoxical impossibility where Cavern Tea is concerned...*

[1225] *No doubt innocently searching for a misfired arrow or two.*

[1226] *Though having recently enjoyed the company of a blind Monk, I am left in no uncertain terms they could avoid even the most fiendishly intricate of traps if called upon.*

Dragon—I think I'd rather take my chances alone. At least if I *am* on my own, I know I'm safe from any 'companion' giving me an unexpected shove towards the Great Barrier."[1227]

Me: "I've learned much about the perils attendant to the adventurer's life. But I never suspected a bigger party would make it even *more* dangerous."

Lotho: "Dangerous is putting it mildly—it's practically lethal."

Maybe it's all this talk of danger—but in that instant, I feel suddenly compelled to touch the deep sword scar carved into the pipe organ's side. But as I do, the Halfling growls at me to stop. My hand hovers, suspended in the air as I freeze on the spot.

Lotho: "You *really* don't want to do that."

Me: "I'm sorry—I... I should have asked permission first. I know some Bards consider instruments to be family members—"[1228]

Lotho: "It's not that—I just don't want you to lose any of your fingers."

I stare in panic at the Halfling as I quickly withdraw my hand.

Me: "You'd cut my fingers off for touching it?"

The Bard laughs as if I've just told him the funniest joke in the realm.[1229] Tears roll down his cheek as he wipes them on the sleeve of his jerkin.

Lotho: "*Hahaha!* Gods no, not me—*him*."

I continue to stare at the Halfling, slightly perplexed.

Me: "Him?"

Lotho stows the seat away and slowly beckons me to come closer. As quiet as a Wizard trying to sneak past a cheese-obsessed squirrel with

---

[1227] *Without supplying a ladder or a spade—just to add insult to injury...*

[1228] *Like a favoured Grandparent who always encourages you to have a 'proper' drink when your parents aren't looking...*

[1229] *Which Uncle Bevan Barr insisted went something like this, '...the other day, the Landlord of my local tavern asked why I always carried a sword? Mimics, I growled in reply. I laughed, the Landlord laughed, the flagon laughed. I killed the flagon... good times!'*

a plate of cheese, the Bard lifts the pipe organ's lid and nods for me to peer inside. With fear caught in my throat, I stare down at what can only be described as a slavering maw of sharp teeth surrounded by pink ooze—my body instinctively leaps backwards in shock.

Me: "What *the*—!"

The Halfling puts a finger to his lips and quietly closes the pipe organ's lid once more.

Lotho: "Bet you weren't expecting that!"[1230]

Me: "What *is* it, exactly?"

Lotho: "*He,* not it, is a Mimic."[1231]

Me: "A wha—Mimic? Aren't they d—dangerous?"

Lotho: "Extremely—but *Chester* has become more of a companion than anything else."

Me: "Chester?"

Lotho: "That's what I chose to call him; I thought it was a name that suited him well."

Me: "Where did you find him?"

There's a sudden growl of disapproval coming from deep inside the organ.

Lotho: "In one of my first dungeon adventures, his chest had been smashed open by a treasure-hungry Barbarian. Chester had been left in a bad way when I came across him—something deep inside told me I

[1230] *The Halfling is quite correct—which is why I'm such a poor gambler.*

[1231] *Not to be confused with a 'Copycat', which is a feline predator that likes to impersonate its prey before ambushing it. Mimics would rather avoid that level of effort—preferring instead to hide inside everyday objects, like chests, cupboards, Holy donation boxes, and flagons of ale...*

couldn't leave him like that, so I helped him into a nearby pipe organ and slowly nursed him back to health."[1232]

I stare in a mixture of awe and fear at the rumbling pipe organ.

Me: "How do you nurse a Mimic back to health?"

Lotho: "Usually by feeding him Goblins—he loves the way their bellies **'POP'** in his maw."[1233]

The Halfling grins at me.

Me: "What about your music? Doesn't it make playing your instrument somewhat problematic? What if you hit a wrong note and injure him by accident—or worse, enrage him?"

Lotho: "It's strange, but old Chester here actually *enjoys* the pipe organ keys hammering away—I suspect it's like having a relaxing body massage while in the comfort of your own home. He never seems to complain anyway."

Me: "Not even when the deafening sound starts to wail through the pipes?"

Lotho: "Mimics have no ears."

Me: "So, he can't hear?"

Lotho: "Not in the way you and I hear—Mimics listen by sensing movement and vibrations in the air."[1234]

I start slowly edging away from the ominous oversized instrument.

Me: "So, does he eat everything he can sense?"

[1232] *Something deep inside? Has Seymour been up to his old external, internal monologue tricks again? Also, what kind of narcissistic Evildoer keeps a pipe organ in their dungeon? It's the sort of thing I'd imagine some twisted Warlock would do—moodily hammering out tunes while wearing half a mask just to annoy any nearby adventuring heroes trying to catch up on some much-needed sleep.*

[1233] *Hopefully 'Chester' doesn't have a taste for nervous Loremasters or ones mistakenly dressed as Wizards.*

[1234] *I'd imagine a Mimic would be deafened if it had the misfortune of encountering a Dwarven adventuring party who had just eaten their entire stash of Buttered Beans.*

The Halfling notices my slow retreat and grins wickedly once more.

Lotho: "Not *everything*—only 'things' that threaten me. You'll find Chester an extremely loyal and protective companion."

Me: "That's quite handy, given you're a hero who frequently has to brave the unknown in the name of adventure."

Lotho: "*Ha,* yeah—he's good to have around for sure. Chester has saved my skin more than once, but I don't ever take him for granted; I know he'll eventually leave me."

Me: "Leave you? Why?"[1235]

Lotho: "Mimics are solitary creatures—and even though he's become the closest thing I can call a 'companion', I can't deny his true calling.[1236] When that urge becomes too much, I know I'll turn around one day, and he'll be gone. But I like to think he and I met for a reason."

Me: "What reason is that?"

Lotho: "To help me become the Bard I had always dreamed of becoming—I wasn't always the confident hero you see before you now. When I first stepped into the adventuring arena, I was a nervous wreck, I didn't enjoy exploring the unknown alone, but I also despised being in a party of personalities. Thinking back on it, without Chester, I probably would have ended up singing for spare change from passing strangers while stood in front of an upturned leather helm."

Me: "Where do you think he'll go when he finally leaves your side?"

Lotho: "Part of me hopes he finds another Bard to travel around with."

Me: "Why?"

Lotho: "I think it's his calling—turning up to help struggling Bards reach their potential at the precise moment they need him most; I know I'm grateful he showed up when he did."

Me: "You think he'll do that forever?"

[1235] *Perhaps 'Chester' will move on to occupy another instrument, like a Bardic trumpet...*

[1236] *What is a Mimic's true calling? Isn't it to 'actually' be the thing they are mimicking?*

Lotho: "No, I know one day he'll want to settle down, but until that day comes, he'll just keep moving on[1237]—I mean, the whole realm is his home."[1238]

There's a tear visibly forming in the Bard's eye—he wipes it away and quickly composes himself.

Lotho: "But he's still *here*; he's still *my* Chester."

The Bard lovingly pats the top of the pipe organ, which purrs with contentment at the Halfling's touch.

Me: "Do you carry this huge pipe organ—I mean '*Chester*', everywhere on your back?"

Lotho: "Not always, sometimes he likes to walk around himself—certainly makes things easier for me when it comes to negotiating dungeon stairs."[1239]

Me: "He can *walk?*"[1240]

Lotho: "Yes—it's something special to see him moving in the wild; he's actually quite graceful when he wants to be."[1241]

I cautiously bend down to examine the foot of the pipe organ, trying to see how the Mimic would achieve such a feat.

The Halfling catches me staring.

[1237] *Not long after my encounter with Lotho, I recalled these words of wisdom when learning of another nomadic Mimic—a very tiny one, which had also made its home inside a musical instrument—the 'littlest oboe' it was known as.*

[1238] *That's actually kind of catchy—the Bard should turn that into a little tune.*

[1239] *Mind you, I can imagine with a hefty 'shove', Chester could easily find himself at the bottom of the dungeon stairs in no time.*

[1240] *If 'Chester' can walk, it stands to reason he can run. If he can run, it also stands to reason he can chase. I'm now wondering if I can outpace a hungry pipe organ if called upon.*

[1241] *'Graceful' is not quite the adjective I would have picked to describe a hungry Mimic running after you—'Terrifying' maybe...*

Lotho: "He cut some holes in the base where his tentacle-like feet can push through."[1242]

Me: "If he can walk, why doesn't he walk all the time—it would at least spare you from a serious back injury?"

Lotho: "Chester only likes walking on cold, damp dungeon floors. He hates the outdoors—he especially dislikes travelling on a forest path."[1243]

I stare at the blanket of lush green grass bristling in the breeze for as far as the eye can see.

Me: "So, you *always* have to carry him when you're outside a dungeon?"

The Halfling begins to wrap the pipe organ up in the cloth once more.

Lotho: "I don't mind doing the heavy lifting on an adventure—it strengthens both the body and the mind."

Me: "That pipe organ looks *really* heavy to carry."

The Halfling fastens the ends of cloth together before uncorking a hip flask and taking a deep swig. The Bard winks at me as I see the muscles suddenly bulge in his neck and arms.

Lotho: "Most of the time I manage fine—but sometimes, a quick swig from a *Potion of Strength* helps too."

Even though the Halfling is visibly growing in power, I cannot help but also notice the abnormal amounts of black body hair suddenly sprouting out of his flesh.

Me: "You didn't happen to get that potion from a slightly eccentric Potioneer, did you?"

Lotho: "Yes—how did you know?"

[1242] *Cut? What with? A knife? This is sounding worse by the minute.*

[1243] *Given that I know the Heartenford Guards make frequent 'relief' stops along the path when caught short, I understand this loathing of a forest road* perfectly—*it's not unlike a Cleric's hatred of a seemingly innocent-looking dungeon floor, only to find it trapped. If I'm being honest, I don't know what unexpected stepped-on surprise is worse.*

Me: "Just a wild guess—I—I should probably make a move. I wish you and... 'Chester' safe onwards travel... T-Thank you for talking to me today."

More black hair erupts across the Halfling's body—I fear I already know what's coming next.[1244]

Lotho: "My pleasure, *Loooooremaster*—and remember, if you ever encounter a Mimic in the wild, give it a second *looooook*. It *might* be friendlier than you think.[1245] Right, back to *Clamfoooooord* to get a well-earned drink."[1246]

The hairy Halfling hoists the pipe organ onto his back and settles it between his muscular shoulder blades before beginning his hike down the hill, back towards Clamford.

Lotho: *"Cheeriooooo!"*

With a sense of relief, I watch the Bard march away into the distance—although before he finally vanishes from view, I swear I can just make out a pair of yellow eyes staring back at me from the depths of the pipe organ's interior.

[1244] *And this time, there's no mounted Heartenford Guard to munch on.*

[1245] *Or not...*

[1246] *I fear Clamford's 'Hasty Encounters' event may have an unexpected wandering monster or two, first crashing—then consuming, their party of singletons...*

35. The 'Head' of the Thieves Guild

This wasn't exactly how I envisaged the current interview starting—but after innocently answering a polite knock at my inn room's door, this is precisely how it began. I recall looking up at two burly hooded thugs carrying a sack before one of the gruesome twosomes brought his fist down toward my head, and all sensation was instantly submerged in a sea of blackness. I awoke to find myself being dragged through what seemed to be a maze of steps and stench-filled tunnels. My skull throbbed with pain, not just from the initial knockout blow but also from my captors' inattentive propensity for 'accidentally' smacking me against any low-slung doorways through which we passed. With the sound of a key turning in a lock and a final grunt of exertion, I was thrown rudely into a chair and made to wait—the heavy sack still wholly obscuring my vision. I didn't know what to expect or why I had been taken. I imagined every unspeakable horror waiting for me, from the unseen executioner eager to plunge a cold blade into my body and end my life, to a giant Gelatinous Cube slowly creeping towards me.[1247] Out of desperation, I tried to make conversation with the room, blindly hoping to connect with one of my captors—yet my words were met with stone-cold silence.

Even though I have no idea how long I've been sitting here, I can gradually feel my senses returning. I hear the faint sound of dripping water landing in a small puddle somewhere off to my right.[1248] There's also a strong smell of damp mixed in with the unmistakable stench of rotting bowels that nearly turns my stomach. The dull throbbing in my head has started to subside, replaced by a burning pain in my wrists, still tightly bound together behind my back.

Me: "*Hello?* Can someone tell me what I'm doing here?"

Unidentified Voice: "**Who** have you been speaking to, Loremaster?"

The stern voice echoes ominously around me, bouncing sharply off the chamber walls—causing my heart to jump in fright.

Me: "I—I don't understand. I'm a Loremaster; I'm supposed to talk to *everybody*—"

[1247] *With the skeletal remains of the last Loremaster still trapped inside, their flesh-cleaned bones locked in a frozen state of shock, next to a floating quill, Soul Squid ink and a half-finished journal punctuated with the occasional grammatical mistake.*

[1248] *Or at least I hope it is water and not blood—or worse, my blood...*

Unidentified Voice: "**Silence!** Do not play games with me; you know very well **who** you've been talking to."

Me: "Whoever you are—can you at least give me a clue? Help me narrow the field a little?"

There's an awkward pause as I suspect the voice is contemplating what to do next. What's even more perplexing is that I'm *sure* I've heard this voice before, somewhere on my travels.

Unidentified Voice: "Where to start? Let me see—you know what, this would be a lot easier if we could remove the sack."

Worried that knowing my captor's identity would put me in serious jeopardy, I feel I must try my hardest to keep the makeshift hood firmly in place.[1249]

Me: "That's okay; I'm fine to keep it on. Really, don't feel you have to take it off on my account—"

I feel rough hands grab the top of the sack and sharply pull it free from my head.[1250] The blackness is replaced by a dimness that's marginally better than what I've had to endure. I crane my neck and instantly congratulate my senses for correctly identifying that I am indeed in a sewer system. My eyes slowly adjust enough to the poor light to notice a hooded figure sitting opposite in a heavy cloak. Flanked on either side of this mysterious figure are the same two burly thugs who jumped me outside my room.[1251]

Me: "Where am I?"

Unidentified Voice: "Underground."[1252]

Me: "And who are you?"

[1249] *Even though it does make me feel like someone who came off second best in a Gorgon encounter.*

[1250] **OUCH!** *Taking with it a fair few hairs in the process too.*

[1251] *Or at least I* assume *they are the same two—it's hard to tell just by looking at their hoods.*

[1252] *Ask a stupid question...*

Unidentified Voice: "So many questions for someone who is not in a position to ask questions."[1253]

Me: "Sorry, a force of habit. Can you at least tell me who I'm conversing with?"

Unidentified Voice: "Who do you think you're conversing with? Who captured you with such swiftness? Who could blind you with such masterly misdirection? Who could—?"

Me: "The Thieves Guild?"

Unidentified Voice: "**Dammit**—I was just building up to that!"

An annoying itch continues to scratch at my consciousness—a familiarity in the voice that is only now starting to form in a distant corner of my mind's eye.

Me: "So, can I assume I'm talking to the Head of the Thieves Guild for all the Rogues in the *entire* realm?"

Head of the Thieves Guild: "Yes, you are, *of sorts*—look, it's complicated. Rogues, in general, don't like obeying rules on the best of days;[1254] but enough about that, you are *still* asking your questions."

Me: "*Ah*—sorry, forgive me; what was it you wanted to know?"

Head of the Thieves Guild: "Who have you been speaking to?"

Me: "Do you want a list? It's pretty long, let me think; there was the Wizard, Dorn the Barbarian—"

Head of the Thieves Guild: "No—I mean, who have you been talking to about *us* in particular?"

[1253] I *am* a Loremaster, after all—we're supposed to ask a lot of questions... granted, we may not like some of the answers we get, but that's not the point I'm making here. As a Loremaster, it's my sworn duty to ask questions regardless of the position I find myself in. In fact, we're heartily encouraged by our mentors to get ourselves into difficult situations and ask challenging questions, which occasionally makes me wonder if our mentors never really liked us as much as students.

[1254] I sense attempting to run the Thieves Guild efficiently is like trying to herd invisible cats—impossible and fraught with danger. Maybe they need to hire the services of a Mime Warrior? Mind you, I'd rather deal with Rogues than Bards—that lot sound like a nightmare!

Me: "Can you give me any more clues?"

I can detect a faint whiff of exasperation in the air.[1255]

Head of the Thieves Guild: "You've been speaking to a *particular* Baron—"

Me: "A Baron—do you mean *Gaudron?*"

The figure nods slowly.[1256]

Head of the Thieves Guild: "What did you two talk about?"

Me: "We chatted about his problem with the four troublesome Princes—"

Head of the Thieves Guild: "Did he mention the Thieves Guild specifically?"

Me: "I don't think we talked about i—"

Head of the Thieves Guild: "Let me try again. You talked about us, *didn't you?*"

Me: "I didn't mention you by name; it was the Baron—"

Head of the Thieves Guild: "What did he say *exactly?* I advise you not to scrimp on the details."

Me: "He mentioned you had come to a mutual *arrangement,* one where you could operate freely and safely within Brundale's borders in exchange for certain financial benefits—you know what, this would be a lot easier if I could actually see you—"

Head of the Thieves Guild: "Out of the question. Our identities are shrouded in mystery, known only to those bound by our blood oath; they must remain unknown to the likes of you—"

A sudden flash of recognition hits me straight between the eyes.

Me: "S—Seymour? Is that *you?*"

[1255] *Although that may be coming from one of the burly Guards...*

[1256] *I should have been more impressed by this than I currently am—for reasons that will soon become painfully clear.*

A heavy, sighed reply comes from the mysterious figure in front of me.

Head of the Thieves Guild: "Unmask me..."

I watch, mesmerised, as one of the burly thugs dutifully pulls the hood back and throws the cloak off the figure. Suddenly I'm staring eye-to-empty eye socket of an all-too-familiar skull propped up by an anatomically correct body-shaped plinth. I'm also slightly alarmed by the supreme level of detail the doubtless-skilled craftsperson has brought to all areas of this wooden construction, including the groinal region now staring back at me.[1257]

Seymour: "Magnificent, *isn't it?*"

Me: "*Erm—*"

I can't seem to remove my eyes from the statue's sizeable stones.

Seymour: "I got Thorde Ironstein to fashion this body throne from Treant wood[1258]—it's very comfortable and almost identical to the body I had when I was still flesh and bone."[1259]

Me: "It's certainly impressive craftsmanship. B—But what is it *and* you, doing in this sewer?"

Seymour: "Surprise. I'm not just a Head of a Necromancer[1260]—I'm *also* the Head of the Thieves Guild—"

Me: "But you *are* just a 'head'."

Seymour: "Nice—do you *also* kick defenceless Warhound pups, *Loremaster?* I bet you enjoy telling Dwarves, Gnomes, and Halflings to grow up too?"[1261]

[1257] *That's one 'member' of the Thieves Guild I could have done without seeing.*

[1258] *That's probably a little too much information than I needed to know—I can only assume a cruel Woodcutter must have ambushed the creature mid-gratification—obviously not the happy ending it clearly deserved...*

[1259] *Now, sadly, minus the 'flesh' bit.*

[1260] *He's also the head of a former, wholesome Rogue.*

[1261] *Only if they were the unruly offspring of a Dwarf, Halfling, or Gnome—who had been caught trying to steal my mother's delicious Blue Beret pie!*

Me: "Sorry—that sounded insensitive. Can I ask how you came to be the *'Head'* of this place?"

Seymour: *"Loremaster..."*

Me: "What?"

Seymour: "I see you still enjoy trampling over people's lives with your endless questions—"

Me: "That was an honest mistake—wait a moment, does Holtar know about all this?"

Seymour: "Holtar only cares about dead things..."

Me: "But—you *are* dead?"

Seymour: "My, my, you are on fire today.[1262] The Necromancer is only interested in things that are deader than me."

Me: "Where is Holtar now?"

Seymour: "Probably digging up another lukewarm corpse from a nearby graveyard..."[1263]

My eyes are irresistibly drawn back to the protrusion watching me from between the legs of the sculpted body, which the grinning skull sits proudly atop.

Seymour: "What's wrong with you?"

Me: "No offence, but I think I can only cope with <u>one</u> head staring at me."

The skull looks around in confusion before following my eyes to his crotch area.

Seymour: "Wha—*oh*, guys, come on! How long have I been like that? Can I get a little dignity, please?"

[1262] *I hope not. I don't want to end up like my brother.*

[1263] *While trying his best to avoid any eagle-eyed Mort-Men keeping watch...*

One of the smirking burly thugs throws Seymour's hooded cloak back over the offending appendage.[1264]

Me: "Thanks..."

Seymour: "Sorry about that—for both our sakes."

Me: "Shouldn't you be with Holtar rather than here?"

Seymour: "Why? Holtar's not my keeper; I can come and go as I please."[1265]

An awkward silence falls between us, yet I can't stop myself from asking the obvious burning question.

Me: "How—?"

Seymour: "With *great* difficulty—<u>next</u> question!"[1266]

The soreness in my wrists reminds me I'm still a prisoner of the grinning skull—and his burly thugs.

Me: "Could you be good enough to free my bonds? I can't feel my hands anymore."

Seymour: "Welcome to my world."

The former Rogue follows up his comment with a deathly stare. I'm not sure if the skull is toying with me or not—but mercifully, Seymour shows a moment of compassion for my predicament.

Seymour: "Release him."

I feel the cold metal of a blade against my skin as one of the burly thugs neatly cuts the cord restraining me—I hastily rub the life back into my wrists.

Me: "Thanks—"

Seymour: "Don't mention it."

[1264] *It looks like there's now a tent pitched on the skull's faux groin area or a sheet-covered 'ghoulie'...*

[1265] *I <u>must</u> not ask 'how'... I must not ask 'how'...*

[1266] *I <u>must</u> listen to my own advice... I <u>must</u> listen to my own advice...*

There's another awkward pause as I catch Seymour staring at me coldly once more.

Seymour: "I mean it—don't *ever* mention *it*."

Me: "By *it*, am I to assume you mean *you?*"

Seymour: "Me, this place, my body plinth, the Thieves Guild, Gaudron, Brundale, our *arrangement*—all of it. Don't ever mention it. I like you, Loremaster. I really don't want to see you floating facedown in this cesspit with the Turd Lurkers..."

I glance at the ominous body of water that flows slowly past, crammed with dubious brown objects bobbing on the surface[1267]—keen not to be an unhappy floating addition to the stream of excrement. I shake my head vigorously.

Me: "I—I won't say a word—*I promise!*"

Seymour: "I'm glad we can come to an understanding."

Me: "Where is this sewer?"

Seymour: "Deep under the tavern you were staying at. Every tavern's privy is connected to one another by a complicated system of sewers—we use them to move around the realm. It's a lot safer than travelling the Merchant's Road."[1268]

Me: "Each privy is connected to one another? What happens if one happens to be occupied at the time?"

Seymour: "Then both of us are in for an unwelcome surprise. In all seriousness, we have peepholes to ensure the privy space is vacated before stepping out from behind a secret trapdoor."[1269]

Me: "That's somewhat disconcerting."

[1267] *For the briefest of moments, I swear I can see the hungry sweetcorn-filled grin of a Turd Lurker staring back at me.*

[1268] *And possibly less smelly given the Heartenford Guards' reputation for leaving their mark for others to find—or possibly step in...*

[1269] *Now I understand why Rogues fondly refer to privies as 'traps'.*

Seymour: "You have no idea—you've never had to wait for a Half-Orc to finish their business after a serious bout of bowel-ache. That's one stench that can make your eyes bleed, that's for sure—makes me thankful I don't have mine anymore."[1270]

Me: "I'll endeavour to watch my back next time I dare to set foot inside a tavern's privy."[1271]

Seymour: "It's fine—nothing we haven't all seen before at least a dozen times. Just remember to give any *'trap'* door a courtesy knock before going in—that way, any nearby Rogues traversing along the privy system are given fair warning."[1272]

Me: "Can I ask about your *arrangement* with the Baron, strictly off the Record?"[1273]

Seymour: "Isn't it obvious? The Heroes Guild has made it hard for our Guild to exist peacefully—across the realm, they have been actively hunting and destroying our secret hideouts. We had no choice but to flee to Brundale and ask the Baron for his protection. Through hard negotiation, we have finally agreed to a mutually beneficial deal with Gaudron—we can go about our business in Brundale without fear of discovery or persecution, and all we have to do is help fill the Baron's war coffers in return."

Me: "But we're not currently in Brundale—"

Seymour: "No, you are correct. This is one of numerous 'burner' locations established by the Thieves Guild."

Me: "Burner location—what's that?"

Seymour: "They are temporary safe havens for our members. They allow us to operate safely beyond Brundale's borders."

[1270] Now I'm curious to know how Seymour 'sees' exactly, but I don't want to risk an impromptu swimming lesson with the Turd Lurkers, so I think better of it.

[1271] Because I know a voyeuristic Rogue will <u>certainly</u> be watching mine.

[1272] To avoid an embarrassingly awkward 'squatting' encounter...

[1273] 'Off the Record' is a Gnomish saying, meaning 'I'm going to tell you a secret—and if you tell a soul about it, I'm going to hire the Gnomish Barbarian 'Record the Red' to batter you, until you end up shorter than any Halfling in existence.

Me: "Why only temporary?"

Seymour: "Because we know it's only a matter of time before one of their 'unofficial' Wizards will turn up[1274]—then you can *guarantee* everything will end in flames. Wizards love casting Fireball spells in small, enclosed spaces,[1275] especially those working for the Heroes Guild—"

I wince in pain as I'm suddenly reminded of my brother's death.

Seymour: "That's why we need somewhere permanent, a secret hideout where the Heroes Guild can't find us."

Me: "But isn't the Baron trying to entice every hero from the Heroes Guild to his cause? Aren't you worried they'll eventually track your organisation back to Brundale and shut it down for good?"

Seymour: "Who do you think creates all the quests in Brundale—the Baron? No—*we* do. We carefully construct every side-quest to ensure it keeps the Heroes Guild away from our secret lair."

I give the skull a quizzical look.

Me: "I thought the Baron's Dungeonmasters created all the quests?"

Seymour: "The Gnomes? You really believe they do it all? Those idiots just keep whatever quests we create restocked and working properly. The Gnomes are glorified dungeon caretakers—*we're* the ones who do all the real work, pulling all the strings[1276] to ensure Brundale has enough adventures to keep it busy."

Me: "I see. So, you use quests as a way to keep the Heroes Guild from discovering you by distracting their heroes."

[1274] I subsequently discovered that any 'unofficial' Wizards employed by the Heroes Guild can't be reasoned with, can't be bargained with, show no pity, remorse, or fear—and they absolutely will not stop until every Thieves Guild member is a smoking pile of ash.

[1275] Ouch! <u>Again</u> with the Fireball reference! What I would give for someone to reference a non-Fireball-type spell when mentioning a Spellcaster in the same breath...

[1276] If I remember right, it's actually the Gnomes who do all the string-pulling—especially where clueless Barbarians and trapped thrones are concerned.

Seymour: "Much like a litter of bored Goblin offspring,[1277] we keep them entertained with the pretty stuff that makes a lot of noise. Side-quests are perfect for that—they allow us to continue operating undetected."

Me: "What do you do to obtain wealth?"

Seymour: "Are you asking the Thieves Guild—or me personally?"

Me: "*Erm*—just the Thieves Guild."

Seymour: "There's the Merchant's Road. We charge anyone who uses it—just a nominal fee, but it all adds up."

Me: "That must be difficult, what with the constant patrols by the Heartenford Guards."

Seymour: "Not really. All the Heartenford Guards work for us. We take a fee from whatever they earn; the rest they can keep. The more Merchants they encounter and fine, the more coin we both make—it's a win-win *arrangement* for everyone."[1278]

Me: "What about those Rogues who operate within the towns and cities?"

Seymour: "We have two different methods there—first is your basic shakedown of locals, with a thinly veiled threat of violence if they fail to donate to our cause."

Me: "And the other?"

Seymour: "We like to think of it as *opportunity knocks*[1279]—pickpocketing, mugging, general thievery, that sort of thing."

[1277] *Who have had all their bows and arrows taken away from them by a weary pincushion-impersonating older family member who keeps standing in the wrong place at the wrong time.*

[1278] *Everyone <u>except</u> the Merchant, who just had a substantial amount of wealth freed from their coin purse.*

[1279] *Gnomish for 'a Rogue with a talent for gaining coin using a menacing look and a heavy cosh'...*

Me: "Doesn't that come with certain risks? What if you target a hero by mistake? There's plenty of them wandering around—especially in towns and cities."[1280]

Seymour: "You're right, of course, which is why we never engage in random larceny. Every potential target is checked and double-checked before we make a move.[1281] We turn our attention elsewhere if we feel the risk is *too* great."

Me: "I can't condone what you're doing—but it certainly sounds methodical."

Seymour: "That's why I'm the brains of the Thieves Guild."

Me: "S—Surely you don't—?"

Seymour: "Nope! That damn reanimated Dragon sucked it out through my nasal cavity. It's something I wouldn't wish on a Paladin—I *never* want to relive that, I can tell you."

Me: "Sounds painful."

Seymour: "It was. I thought stepping on a caltrop was the worst pain I had ever experienced; how wrong was I…"

Me: "Speaking of pain, how much of a problem have the Sharks Guild been to you?"

The skull spits on the ground in disgust—it's an impressive feat that doesn't go unnoticed by everyone else in the room.

Seymour: "A bunch of no-good crooks who used to be part of the Thieves Guild until their leader, Shytlock, decided to go it alone. Sure,

---

[1280] *It's a well-known fact that you're never more than ten feet (or one wayward Fireball spell) from a hero at any given time.*

[1281] *This means ensuring any potential target isn't carrying a giant sword, axe, longbow, spellbook, or is wearing full plate armour, robes, or is naked but for a fur loincloth. Although, if the potential target is a Mime Warrior, there's ZERO chance an opportunistic Rogue will spot any of these things until it's far too late.*

we've had a few run-ins, but we're more than capable of dealing with those clowns."[1282]

Me: "Why did they go it alone?"

Seymour: "They didn't care for the traditions of our Guild, all they cared about was lending whatever coin we had just stolen *back* to those who we just stole it from."

Me: "Sounds like a noble, if not slightly misguided, ethos."

Seymour: "Except as both you and I know, Shytlock and his fin-heads don't have a noble bone between them. They're eager to lend coin to those who they *know* will struggle to pay the extortionate interest.[1283] Then when the poor soul defaults on any repayments, the Sharks Guild smells blood and goes in for the kill."

Me: "They *kill* those who can't pay?!"

Seymour: "What—*no!* I was just, you know, keeping the shark metaphor going. They actually go in and lay claim to any property before breaking a few legs—although, I must admit, not many *actual* sharks do that in real life."

Me: "It sounds like *they're* the ones knocking at opportunity's door."

Seymour: "Where's the honour in that? There's no skill, no craft; they're just targeting the poor and desperate. That's not right—<u>*we're*</u> the poor and desperate! That's why we set up the Thieves Guild in the first place. Shytlock is taking advantage of misfortune rather than being a master of it—unlike those you find within the Thieves Guild. What's more, they don't even go on any adventures!"

Me: "So, those in the Thieves Guild still go on quests and adventures with other heroes?"

[1282] *I've heard of Clown Fish before, but never Clown Sharks. Not to be confused with 'actual' Clowns, who belong to a totally different Guild altogether—and who go around in colourful groups terrorizing locals with their bright red 'honking' noses, oversized boots, and rubberized mallets.*

[1283] *'Interest' is a Gnomish word meaning 'more coin than you will ever earn'—<u>not</u> to be confused with the <u>other</u> meaning for the word 'Interest', which is <u>also</u> a Gnomish word meaning 'pretending to show'...*

Seymour: "Obviously not any quests *we* designed—what would be the point of that? As a general rule,[1284] we only go on quests where the rewards are great, and the risks are minimal.[1285] I don't want any of our members returning to our fold looking like they're my long-lost identical twin..."

Me: "*Huh? Oh*—I see! Yes, well, that's understandable. Nobody really wants to return without a body."

The skull's eye sockets remain unnervingly fixed on mine.

Me: "Let me ask you something else... how did you end up as the... 'Head' of the Thieves Guild?"

Seymour: "I had the three *M's*—"

Me: "Mouth, Molars, and a Mandible?"

The decapitated Thief regards me with his empty eye sockets once more.

Seymour: "Means, Motive, and a Murder Weapon..."

Me: "*Erm,* can you elaborate more on that for me?"

The skull sighs deeply.

Seymour: "You can only become the 'Head' of the Thieves Guild if you successfully assassinate the current incumbent. Then by Rogue's Law—the one who did the deed can become the new 'Head' in charge and rightfully claim the recently vacated position."[1286]

Me: "So, you assassinated the last 'Head' and took over?"

Seymour: "Yup."

Me: "Was this before or after you became a living skull?"

[1284] *Which, as we're already established, Rogues seldom pay attention to.*

[1285] *This sounds like something a Cleric would say.*

[1286] *Hopefully, remembering to clean down the recently vacated seat of spilt bodily fluids first.*

Seymour: "After."[1287]

There's another uneasy silence between us.

Me: "How—"

Seymour: "With *extreme* difficulty—next question!"[1288]

I give the two burly thugs standing on either side of Seymour the briefest of glances.

Me: "Aren't you worried that someone in the Thieves Guild will do the same to you?"

Seymour: "How are they *ever* going to do it—backstab? I don't even have a back to stab! They can't even poison me—you know why? **I'm undead!**"[1289]

Me: "Seems being undead has some positives after all."

Seymour: "It's the perfect anti-assassination solution."

Me: "How long do you plan to remain in charge of the Thieves Guild?"

Seymour: "*Oooo*... let me see, I don't know—maybe forever?"

Me: "—Unless someone manages to kill that Dragon Holtar reanimated, of course."

I catch the two burly thugs exchanging looks with one another.[1290]

Seymour: "L—Let's just forget all about that *Dragon* business, *shall we—*"

_____

[1287] *I <u>must</u> not ask how... I must not ask how...*

[1288] *Will I <u>never</u> learn!*

[1289] *Plus, any liquid would spill out onto the floor when the skull took a single drop.*

[1290] *I could tell that even <u>with</u> their hoods on.*

Me: "Aren't you worried someone might go looking for the reanimated Dragon? I mean I know it's not at the Dragon Lord's citadel anymore,[1291] but how hard can it be to find a Dragon that's made up of nothing but rotting flesh and exposed bone, I mean, it's probably going to stand out like a Ranger's bush on a dungeon adventure—"[1292]

Seymour: "**I SAID—SHALL WE!!!**"

I sense Seymour's patience is wearing thin. I just make out what appears to be a few beads of sweat trickling from the skull's brow.[1293]

Me: "Sorry, I didn't mean to put you in an awk—"

Seymour: "<u>Okay</u>, it has been a *real* pleasure to meet you again, Loremaster. But it's time you were leaving. The sack—**THE SACK NOW, PLEASE!**"

I cannot stop a burly thug from pulling the black hood down over my head as my world is plunged back into darkness once more.

Me: "W—What's going to happen to me?!"

Seymour: "Nothing, as long as you can keep a silent tongue in your mouth."[1294]

Before I can reply, I'm suddenly hoisted to my feet and led away—the skull's final warning echoing in my wake.

Seymour: "Remember, the Thieves Guild is *always* watching, Loremaster—**ALWAYS!**"[1295]

[1291] *The same citadel that once belonged to the Dragon Lord before the Titan of Thunder briefly took up residency—and before Dorn cut the Titan of Thunder's head clean off with what I can only assume was a very sharp axe. As to <u>who</u> the next unfortunate occupant will be is anyone's guess—but whoever it is, I hope they don't start making themselves too comfortable.*

[1292] *Fortunately for Seymour, the Dragon's whereabouts is <u>still</u> unknown—although I suspect it's relatively easy to spot even if it <u>is</u> wearing a fake Dwarven-haired 'bushy' moustache.*

[1293] *Or it could be a drip that has fallen from the sewer's dank ceiling—I wouldn't like to hazard a guess either way.*

[1294] *Although he didn't mention a noisy quill scratching this all down on some parchment...*

[1295] *Especially when you're using a tavern's privy!*

I can feel myself being dragged through the maze of tunnels and small doorways again,[1296] to what I hope is my bedroom and not the nearest and deepest foul-smelling body of water...

[1296] *This time remembering to duck...*

36. Dorn, again...

I'm not often brimming with confidence before an interview—most are undertaken with a hint of trepidation, unsure of what I'm stepping into.[1297] But my next meeting is with someone who holds no such fear for me— because this time, I'm catching up with Dorn the 'Barbarian' once more. It's been a genuine pleasure watching this young man rise rapidly through the hero ranks to become a legend in his own lifetime. As I approach an impressive-looking castle set against the backdrop of the Blackrock Falls, twenty miles west of Tronte, I get the impression that fame and fortune have been kind to the 'Barbarian' in a relatively short amount of 'hero' time. The sheer amount of completed quests that must have been needed to afford such a formidable stronghold defies belief. Yet, somehow, Dorn the 'Barbarian' has achieved this with ease—and quite possibly a significant amount more.

There's a loud grating sound of metal on metal as the heavy portcullis protests as it slowly rises, its chains groaning under the gate's immense weight. I look up at the empty battlements towering overhead—nothing moves. There's no sign of any crossbow-happy Guards,[1298] no scraping of armour on stone as the castle's defenders hurry to take up defensive positions along the battlements.[1299] The only thing moving is a solitary flag bearing the crest depicting a *'Wheel of Pain'* symbol being pushed by a skinny man in a loincloth, fluttering in the wind.[1300] Inside is no different; the courtyard is eerily quiet—there isn't even a scrawny chicken wandering about the place on the lookout for scattered grain as if it were an all-consuming life-quest.[1301]

[1297] *Like a trapped dungeon floor or a Greenvale Forest bush that's a popular spot with the patrolling Heartenford Guards...*

[1298] *I've subsequently learnt that prospective Guards are only hired if they have an 'itchy-trigger finger'—which sounds suspiciously like a bothersome ailment that needs a thick layer of Wyvern cream to remedy.*

[1299] *But which could also be the sound of a Paladin in plate armour, struggling to scale the fortifications in search of a despicable Evildoer to smite...*

[1300] *The flag—not the loincloth...*

[1301] *Thankfully it's not a rainbow chicken; otherwise, I'd imagine there would be a few slightly miffed Fortune Hunters about to make an impromptu appearance in the courtyard soon.*

'BOOM!'[1302]

The portcullis slams into the ground, cutting off any chance of escape. Dust kicks up from the dry earth as the creaking chains slow to a stop somewhere off to my right. My mind's eye leaps to imagine a plethora of unseen dangers now that I find myself helplessly trapped like a rat.[1303] But I move swiftly to banish such paralysing thoughts and instead focus on the task at hand—finding the 'Barbarian'. With a renewed sense of purpose, I head inside towards the main hall where I hope to find—

Me: **"DORN?"**

My voice reverberates along the stone corridor as I explore room after room without success. With concern growing, I head up the steps to the next level and immediately spy an orange glow flickering from under a set of heavy doors at the far end of the passageway. I carefully step closer—unsure if I will discover friend or foe waiting beyond. As I slowly push one of the doors inwards and peer past the gap, what greets me almost takes my breath away.[1304]

The room is vast, filled with enormous wealth—coins, rubies, and diamonds... the value is incomprehensible to all but the most dedicated of Tallymen. The riches glisten and glint in the ambience of the burning torches that line the walls. But *that* isn't the most remarkable sight to greet my eyes. What dominates my attention is sitting in the middle of this immeasurable wealth—a bearded Dorn. The 'Barbarian' is wearing little more than a heavy fur cloak, while an impressive-looking crown sits neatly on his brow. In his right hand is an oversized golden spear— the point of which is continuously highlighted by the room's flickering light. Dorn stares at me without recognition as I cautiously approach his golden throne, my hands held out in front of me to show I mean him no harm.[1305]

[1302] *I nearly jump out of my skin, thinking a Holy Hand of Grenade had just exploded behind me!*

[1303] *In a cellar infested by hat-wearing cats...*

[1304] *Which would result in my agonising death—so I'm grateful I still have air in my lungs.*

[1305] *Ha! As if I could ever hurt someone like Dorn the 'Barbarian'—the only way that could happen is if I were to 'Troll' him by sending hurtful messages delivered by a spiteful Troll 'Barker'.*

Me: "*Dorn...?*"

The angry-Warrior's stoic face regards me for a few moments. I can sense he's still deciding if I'm a threat or not. Thankfully, his grim outlook breaks into the broadest of smiles.

Dorn: **"*Loremaster!*"**

The adventurer lets his oversized spear clatter to the ground as he rushes toward me like I'm a Landlord who's just called last orders.[1306] Dorn hoists me into the air to warmly greet me like his long-lost brother[1307]—my ribs, however, scream like a heavily encumbered Cleric *still* stuck in their extremely tight-fitting plate armour. I wince and try to ignore the burning pain in my chest as I'm reunited with the 'Barbarian' again. I cannot fail to notice that he has aged somewhat since our last meeting; there is an unmistakable weariness behind his eyes, almost as if he's seen too much for one so young. Perhaps the countless quests have taken a greater toll on his physical and mental state than first thought? I know becoming a hero has changed Dorn... but I feel a burning desire to know whether it has changed him for the better.

Me: "How have you been?"

Dorn: "*Oh*, you know—*busy,* as you can see."

The 'Barbarian' sweeps an arm, inviting me to stare in awe at the waves of treasure that threatens to come crashing down on us.[1308]

Me: "This is an impressive haul—how did you accrue so much so quickly?"

Dorn: "I kept completing adventure after adventure—I couldn't stop. The more I did, the more I wanted. The Heroes Guild kept giving me tougher and tougher quests—but they provided little in the way of a challenge. By the end of the first month, I had enough coin to buy the

---

[1306] *And needing to get in a round of twenty (or so) flagons of ale before the bell is rung for the evening...*

[1307] *I would happily allow my ribs to be broken if I could be hugged like this by Aldon one last time.*

[1308] *I have visions of the falling parchment towers that nearly crushed us the last time we met.*

castle you find yourself standing in. By the end of the second month, I had enough wealth to retire and live in luxury for the remainder of my days."[1309]

Me: "But you don't look happy—what's wrong?"

The frustrated 'Barbarian' looks at his feet as he kicks a precious ruby out of view.

Dorn: "I was forced to retire from questing."

Me: "What? *Forced?* By whom?"

Dorn: "Who do you think? The Heroes Guild."

Me: "What? I don't believe it! *Why?* If you were so successful, surely that can only be good for the Heroes Guild—and their coffers?"

Dorn: "I know—but they said something about a technicality with my contract and demanded I stopped adventuring altogether."

Me: "What did you do?"

Dorn: "I got angry, broke a few chairs, swore a bit—I even punched the Guildmaster... I think—"

Me: "You *think?*"

Dorn: "Well, once the red mist descends, it's tough to know exactly what I'm doing—or what I've done."

Me: "How did the Heroes Guild react to your violent outburst?"

Dorn: "They revoked my membership with immediate effect."

Me: "They threw you out of the Heroes Guild? What did you do then?"

Dorn: "What could I do? I was in the heart of the Heroes Guild—not

---

[1309] *By the looks of it, he could even afford to buy any castle on offer and then hire 'Big Hands Removal' to relocate it elsewhere, even perhaps by the sea (and* still *have enough change left over to live without needing to get angry with anyone ever again).*

exactly where I wanted to be, so I retreated to my castle to stew in my fury."[1310]

Me: "And you've been here ever since?"

Dorn: "Yup."

Me: "Alone?"

Dorn: "I'm not great around people when I'm spoiling for a fight—so I gave everyone the rest of the summer off. Fully paid, of course. I believe they have all departed to see Axel-Grind perform in Cloverton to celebrate their recent good fortune."

Me: "I saw Axel in Silver Pond with his Bardettes."

Dorn: "I heard he's an excellent singer who loves hitting those high notes."[1311]

Me: "Why didn't you go along with them to see Axel—you look like you could do with letting your hair down a little?"[1312]

Dorn: "Trust me, when I'm lamenting, it's probably best I'm left on my own. I have a strong urge to crush the nearest enemy and hear the wails of their women."[1313]

Me: "So, what's next for the mighty Dorn?"

Dorn: "I don't know—I'm not the same Barbarian you met back in *The Spit & Spear* those many moons ago. I was young, inexperienced, wide-eyed, and naïve to the extreme. I thought *this* was what I wanted—what I *always* yearned for."

Me: "Isn't it?"

[1310] *Judging by Dorn's red face, I'd say the Barbarian is about ready to be dished up and served with a hot breaded roll.*

[1311] <u>*Really*</u> *'high' notes...*

[1312] *Or at least getting it cut by a reputable Hairsmith...*

[1313] *Being a Barbarian, crushing the nearest enemy doesn't sound reckless enough— drunkenly driving over them in a stolen cart, on the other hand...*

Dorn: "I mean, *yes*—the coin is welcome and affords me a certain amount of comfort."[1314]

Me: "Do I sense a weariness about the riches you have amassed?"

Dorn: "You're right. I may be a 'Barbarian'—but I'm no Mercenary. Coin does make life easier, but it hasn't made me any happier."

Me: "So, what *does* make you happy?"

Dorn: "Crushing things."[1315]

The 'Barbarian' grins wistfully at the thought.

Me: "Why don't you go out into the realm and find some random stuff to crush? You've enough coin to buy an entire town and raise it to the ground if you so desired."[1316]

Dorn: "Where's the enjoyment in that?"

Me: "I don't understand—?"

Dorn: "It would be like buying a warhorse and leaving it behind to charge into battle on your own."[1317]

Me: "*Ah*—I see. I guess it's not a real challenge if you have to pay for it yourself."

The 'Barbarian' nods in agreement.

Me: "If it's all about the thrill of the fight, why not just go on another quest? Adventuring doesn't begin and end with the Heroes Guild.[1318] Especially now as you're not beholden to them anymore—"

[1314] *Although a throne literally made out of coins is probably not one of those 'comforts'.*

[1315] *(See footnote 1313)* <u>Definitely</u> *in a stolen cart.*

[1316] *Minus any of the residents, of course—otherwise, somebody is going to be rudely woken to find a rampaging Barbarian smashing through their bedroom door...*

[1317] *Much to the disbelief of the warhorse watching on from afar...*

[1318] *Unless you've signed a contract with them—then their Heralds may take umbrage with you on this particular point and send a rather large Ogre to remind you of your 'legal' obligations.*

Dorn: **"NO!"**

The 'Barbarian' shakes in anger and overturns a nearby jewel-encrusted table in the wrong place at the wrong time.

Me: "I—I'm sorry, I didn't mean to—"

The short-tempered adventurer softens his gruff demeanour slightly as he spies the fear now locked in my eyes.

Dorn: "No—*I'm* sorry, I didn't mean to lose my temper. It's just *hard...* I've spent my entire life trying to join the Heroes Guild so I could become a legendary hero... and—and they've tossed me aside like an empty *Potion of Healing.*[1319] It's left me feeling so empty; I'm not sure I want to go out into the realm in search of new adventures anymore..."

Me: "What about Arin Darkblade?"

Dorn: "What about him?"

Me: "Aren't you worried the Heroes Guild will send Arin after you? Especially as you punched their Guildmaster in the face—and the small fact you own enough riches to embarrass a Gold Dragon."[1320]

Dorn: "*Pfft!* I'm not scared of Arin."

Me: "I guess your reputation offers you some level of protection—"

Dorn: "It's not that—Arin has changed;[1321] he's lost his edge. He's certainly not the intimidating adventurer who would, in the past, cut your tongue out solely to save him the effort of using his own to lick a note closed."

[1319] *Or a full Potion of Stamina—the end result is pretty much the same...*

[1320] *Indeed, Gold Dragons can <u>only</u> fall asleep on piles of golden coins. Given how difficult it is for these overgrown shiny lizards to come by such wealth, it probably means quite a few sleep-deprived Gold Dragons are flying around with extremely short attention spans and sizeable tempers to match. It should then come as no surprise that Silver Dragons can only sleep on silver, and Copper Dragons can only sleep on copper—so spare a thought for the poor old Battle Dragon, who can only sleep while a colossal brawl is going on around it.*

[1321] *'Changed' but not in a Potioneeer or Druid kind of way—at least, I hope not!*

Me: "How do you know?"[1322]

Dorn: "Because I've *met* him—and he has always been polite and respectful the few times our paths have crossed."

Me: "That doesn't sound like Arin Darkbalde—are you sure it was him?"

Dorn: "Know anyone else at the Heroes Guild who wears an eye-patch?[1323] No, he's definitely mellowed since retiring from the adventuring scene. Personally, I think Arin Darkblade is a really nice guy once you get to know him."

Me: "This is far from the picture everyone else has painted of him. Most have expressed his desire to get physical[1324]—especially when it comes to matters surrounding the Heroes Guild."

Dorn: "I've never witnessed anything like that. But then who truly knows what people are like behind closed heavy doors?"[1325]

Me: "Okay—if *not* Arin Darkblade, perhaps the Heroes Guild will task some of their more seasoned heroes to hunt you down?"

Dorn: "Let them come—they'll find out this Barbarian is not for turning."[1326]

Me: "Perhaps your reputation will make the Heroes Guild think twice about taking you on?"

Dorn: "I doubt it—there isn't much that scares them.[1327] No, our paths will inevitably cross again—and not for the better."

[1322] *The 'changed' bit—not the 'tongue' bit.*

[1323] *I'm sure there are a few Pirate-like heroes at the Guild waiting for a sea-worthy quest or two...*

[1324] *And _not_ in an amorous way...*

[1325] *Or heavy portcullises...*

[1326] *I don't think even the Heroes Guild would be foolish enough to send a Cleric after the Barbarian—and besides, Dorn is currently unkempt, _not_ undead.*

[1327] *Except maybe an overly enthusiastic hero who is completing quests a helluva lot faster than they are being created...*

Me: "The Heroes Guild aside, what's next on the horizon for the great Dorn?"

The 'Barbarian' slumps into a pile of coins and stares at me in defeat—for the first time, the short-tempered Warrior looks lost.

Dorn: "I have *no* idea..."

A small fortune suddenly cascades down the gold mountain as I sit down beside the 'Barbarian' on what looks a little like a stool made from coins.[1328]

Me: "Come on, Dorn... imagine the freedom you have at your fingertips! You've been presented with the opportunity of a lifetime—to finally quest without the Heroes Guild breathing down your neck and immediately demanding their cut as you emerge victorious from the depths of a Category Five adventure."

Dorn: "It's funny, but I miss that part the most. Having someone to return to—even if it *was* only the Tallyman at the Heroes Guild. I loved sitting down with Bartlet and regaling him with my adventuring exploits before working out the final numbers and hitting the local tavern."[1329]

Me: "What about finding a *new* tavern to frequent, a tavern similar to *The Spit & Spear?* Why not become a heroic regular who performs side-quests for locals?[1330] You could even regale them with your tales of adventure and epic swordplay?"

Dorn: "Sadly, most locals suffer from what's known as—*Hero Fatigue.*"

Me: "Hero Fatigue? What's that?"

Dorn: "It's the eyeball-rolling moment you get when you first step into a tavern, and everyone instantly recognises who you are, what you do, and why you're there. It even got to the point where patrons would turn their backs on me as soon as they saw my silver 'HG' badge, making it impossible to get any useful information out of them."

[1328] *Not to be confused with a coin stool—which is something that brings tears to my eyes just by thinking about it.*

[1329] *Meant both figuratively and literally.*

[1330] *Lost dog finding and rat infestations ahoy!*

Me: "Information?"

Dorn: "Quest information; every hero knows that a Landlord and their patrons have loose lips and know exactly what's going on at a local level—although these days, it takes a lot more coin than usual for them to divulge any word of note. Taverns were once the best way to get a sniff of an adventure—that was until the Heroes Guild's recent recruitment drives made wannabe heroes out of every first, second and fourth tavern patron.[1331] Sadly, these days, heroes are seen as an irritant rather than a potential source of income."

Me: "That must be hard to take."

Dorn: "Hard is an understatement—you know, I've probably saved their lives more times than I care to recall. But with the arrival of these *new* heroes, I guess we're about as welcome as an invading Orc army.[1332] Locals just want a quiet drink without some heavily-armoured oaf bragging about the latest unholy abomination they've recently 'smote' in the ear."[1333]

Me: "So, where does that leave you now?"

The 'Barbarian' sighs.

Dorn: "I don't know—this isn't the '*happy ending*' I was promised."[1334]

Me: "Do you regret any of it? The Heroes Guild, I mean?"

Dorn: "That's a difficult question to answer. I've regretted everything that has unfolded *since* my expulsion—that's for sure. But I enjoyed my time with the Heroes Guild as a fully-fledged member. I have also tasted fame, fortune, and the adoration from my fans—and begrudgingly, I have the Heroes Guild to thank for that."

[1331] *I guess heroes don't come in threes.*

[1332] *Ironically, the shortsighted Seers of Tavastock were one such community who welcomed an invading Orc army with open arms—if only they had heeded the warnings from their prophecies, they would have avoided the tortuous arm removal that followed.*

[1333] *'Smiting' is most effective when delivered to the two most sensitive places on the body— the ear and the rear.*

[1334] *So much for the Heroes Guild 'loving you' for a long time...*

Me: "If you could go back to those early days, what would you do differently?"

Dorn: "I'd read the small print *very* carefully for starters—that's for sure."

Me: "You mentioned something about a *technicality* with your contract before—what exactly did you mean by that?"

Dorn: "I wasn't aware of the *'Termination'* clause written into my contract, a clause that would only activate *if* I suddenly found myself on the wrong side of the Heroes Guild..."

Me: "Termination clause?"

Dorn: "The actual name for it is a *'Forfeit' clause.* The moment I was kicked out, everything I had earned during my time with the Heroes Guild now *officially* belonged to them."[1335]

An uneasy silence falls between us.

Me: "So... this place and *all* this treasure—?"

Dorn: "Isn't mine. Every coin in this room is theirs—*including* the small pile you're sitting on."[1336]

Me: "Surely they can't force you to forfeit *all* your wealth?"

Dorn: "*Oh*—they are welcome to *try*, but I'm not going to roll over and let them take it. If they want a fight—they can have a fight; I can handle myself no matter who they send. They'll soon discover <u>I'</u>m the one who put the *'Barb'* into *Barbarian*..."

Me: "Even if it *is* the dreaded Arin Darkblade they send after you?"[1337]

Dorn: "I've lived by the sword long enough to realise I may die by the sword one day."

[1335] *Damn those Heralds and their arcane 'Red Tape of Binding'.*

[1336] *Which is ironic, given the uncomfortable small pile I'm currently sitting on has probably just given me a larger pile of my own to worry about.*

[1337] *Or <u>not</u> so dreaded, depending if you're Dorn the 'Barbarian' or not.*

Me: "Can't you go back to your home? I seem to remember your family owned a sizeable estate on the far side of the Evergreen Forest."

Dorn: "The Heroes Guild have already claimed it as their rightful property—my family were forced to find another place to call home."

Me: "Wait—your parents lost their ancestral home?"

Dorn: "They sent my parents a legal parchment[1338]—the Heroes Guild moved in and removed them hours after I was expelled from their ranks. Supposedly all this was in the small print—I just didn't see it or didn't want to see it."

Me: "Are you going to help your parents get your home back?"

Dorn: "I will—but not yet. I have some unfinished business here first."

The 'Barbarian' cocks his head to one side, listening intently. He springs to his feet, letting the crown fall from his head as he rushes back to his golden throne to pick up his oversized spear. He feels the weapon's weight in his hands—nodding with approval at its craftsmanship.[1339] He stops and looks up suddenly as he drops into a combat pose, his muscles tensed and at the ready.

Me: *"Dorn?"*

The angry-Warrior thuds the foot of the spear into a stone panel on the throne—there's a deep rumble coming from somewhere behind us[1340] as a section of the wall opens up to reveal steps leading down into darkness.

Dorn: *"Hurry!* Follow this secret passage to the end; it'll take you to a path that leads underneath the castle—you'll emerge from the Blackrock Falls. You'll be safe there."[1341]

[1338] *Probably a 'Scroll of Eviction' sent by those pesky Arcane Heralds.*

[1339] *I'd wager this spear could be at least a +10—perhaps even a +11 (if Thorde Ironstein had anything to do with its forging).*

[1340] *Hopefully, the rumbling sound isn't Dorn's internal gases after recently consuming an extra-large portion of Buttered Beans.*

[1341] *Albeit a considerable amount wetter...*

I can hear the sound of heavy footsteps outside in the corridor, approaching Dorn's throne room.

Me: "Who is it?"

Dorn: "You mean who are *they?*"

Me: "Alright—who are *they?*"

Dorn: "They are some of the meanest Warriors on the Heroes Guild payroll[1342]—*Enforcers*. They're the ones who love getting their hands dirty when no one is looking..."[1343]

I hear the unmistakable sound of a multitude of blades being drawn from their scabbards.

Me: "Dorn, come with me! You can't hope to defeat them all! At least this way, you have a chance to live—"

The 'Barbarian' turns with a grin.

Dorn: "I'm not a Wizard—I don't run from a fight.[1344] You forget I'm a Barbarian; *this* is what Barbarians live for.[1345] Fighting is in my blood. Get out of here while you can, Loremaster; I'll buy you some time..."

I hurry towards the secret passage, stopping only for a moment to look back at the 'Barbarian' as he leans against the heavy throne room doors—his lithe frame straining as he somehow manages to keep the Enforcers from bursting through.

Dorn: "It's been an honour... knowing you... my *friend*..."

I nod, eager to say more but aware there is no time to waste. I beat a hasty retreat. As I rush down the damp steps of the secret passage, an unseen mechanism causes the wall to close behind me. Descending into the hewed rocky corridor, I hear the sounds of steel-on-steel and

---

[1342] *'Mean' as in 'Ooooo, they're a bit hard', not 'Ooooo they're a bit cruel for mocking that Halfling's height'—although I'm pretty sure they'd cruelly mock any Halfling given half a chance.*

[1343] *What is it with these unscrupulous types who seem to lack a basic hand wash routine?*

[1344] *Or a Cleric...*

[1345] *And, in some cases, die from...*

blood-curdling screams from above, finally diminishing as I put greater distance between the throne room and myself. My thoughts go to the happy-go-lucky Dorn, who now seems to have paid the ultimate price of pursuing his adventuring dream, much like my poor brother before him.[1346]

[1346] *Minus a flaming Fireball...*

37. Hilden Coldsmith, the Museum Curator

The circular city of Heartenford is a sight to behold; its smooth white fortifications starkly contrast the overgrown trees and bushes of Greenvale Forest that stretch beyond it. Heartenford consists of four white-walled levels stacked upon one another, each slightly smaller than the last; it's not unlike an enormous Orcish Wedding Cake.[1347] Heartenford is a city that takes itself far too seriously, and as a result, it is often the target of ridicule from its 'inferior' neighbours.[1348]

I follow the street as it slowly curves to my left, marvelling at how pristine everything is—even the gutters have an iridescent shine to them.[1349] I wonder if the silver coins I've been relieved of by the City Guards at the main gate have gone towards paying for Heartenford's spotless streets—although, I suspect, a fair amount will still end up in the hands of the Thieves Guild. I climb the polished white steps leading to the Heartenford Museum, an auspicious building carved from the purest marble and dedicated to the realm's greatest heroes. As I push open the bronze doors, I see a smartly dressed Dwarf wearing a bronze badge with the words '*Hilden Coldsmith, Museum Curator*' carved into the surface—she greets me with the warmest of smiles and introduces herself.

Hilden: "I've been expecting you, Loremaster."

Me: "Well met—I must say, this place is simply stunning!"

[1347] *Minus the axe-wielding Bride and kidnapped Groom figurine screaming as he's hoisted over the Bride's shoulder. Despite their savage reputation, it's worth noting that Orcs are more than capable of mastering such intricacies as baking an extravagant wedding cake. In fact, when they're not rampaging across the realm, Orcs like nothing more than spending their free time in the kitchen cooking up anything from finger nibbles to lavish banquets. However, before you start tucking into the nearest Orcish delicacy, a word to the wise, ingredients favoured by Orcish chefs include pickled lung, boiled spleen, and suspicious sausage-shaped lumps of flesh—If that doesn't put you off trying a morsel, keep in mind the Gnomish saying: 'Eat with your eyes, just don't eat anything **with** an eye'.*

[1348] *Heartenford is frequently plagued by 'Barker Coughs'—a form of trolling, instigated by mischievous locals from rival towns who arrive at the city gate to cough a mumbled message then run away again before someone asks them what they said.*

[1349] *The Heartenford beggars must be the envy of all other beggars in the realm—so clean are the alleyways and pathways, you could practically eat your dinner off them.*

Hilden: "For as long as I can remember, we have been regarded as the finest city in the entire realm—we've won awards for it.[1350] Do you want to know what our secret is?"[1351]

I nod—feigning curiosity.

Hilden: "Well, *every* resident must do their bit to ensure Heartenford remains at the pinnacle of cleanliness. We do this by putting every resident's name on a rota. When it's their turn, they must take to the streets with a bucket and a Gelatinous Sponge—we find this initiative does wonders to help remove any stubborn vagabonds."

Me: "Vagabonds?"

Hilden: "Yes, vagabonds, beggars, the poor—we cannot allow them to fester within our great walls. So, our residents have set up a community group who patrol the city at night, searching for any *undesirables* who are sleeping rough on our beloved streets."

Me: "What do they do when they find these undesirables?"

Hilden: "We soak our Gelatinous Sponges in our buckets before launching them in the vagabond's direction—they *hate* the idea of an impromptu wash. You should see them run; it's highly amusing."[1352]

Me: "But doesn't every city have a poor quarter somewhere?"

Hilden: "Not ours—the hard work of our locals has helped clear the deprived and removed the stench of rotting turnips from within our walls.[1353] These selfless citizens are safeguarding the integrity of our fair city and ensuring we continue to be held in the highest regard by all others."[1354]

[1350] *Awards that only the residents of Heartenford can vote on. It should come as no surprise that the city constantly wins every single category—even 'The Best City that's not Heartenford' award.*

[1351] *A biased awards jury and a lack of any other nominees?*

[1352] *The vagabond in question would undoubtedly disagree here.*

[1353] *It can't be any worse than the pong coming from a rotting Dragon in an overcooked turnip field.*

[1354] *I guess the Heartenford beggars aren't being spoilt after all—just soaked…*

Me: "Except by the poor souls who have just been forced out beyond the walls by an army of sponge-throwing volunteers."

Hilden: "Out of sight, out of mind—I say… *shall we?*"

Our steps reverberate around the domed ceiling of the museum's alcove high above. I stop and look aloft in admiration; my eyes are drawn to the beautiful art painted on the concave architecture; I marvel at the frieze that runs around the base of the curved dome.[1355] The Dwarf sidles over and whispers into my ear as I continue to stare upwards in awe.

Hilden: "Beautiful, *isn't it?*"

Me: "It's breathtaking—who created it?"

Hilden: "It was fashioned from stone by the talented hand of the Baron of Heartenford's personal artist no less—although, for the life of me, I can't recall her name."

Me: "I wonder how much she was paid to create this masterpiece?"

The Museum Curator looks at me aghast.

Hilden: "She *wasn't* paid. No, no, no—she did this for the *exposure.*"

Me: "Exposure?"[1356]

Hilden: "Yes—this piece, which I understand took over three summers to complete, was done so she could earn more work later in her career. Reputation can be a powerful thing."[1357]

Me: "But you don't even remember her name?"

[1355] *Detailing a party of adventurers who are surrounded by a tide of monsters. The artist has painted a Wizard launching a Fireball that's too big for the room, a Cleric who has passed out from the sight of blood, and a Barbarian who looks like he's getting angry with the Rogue for stealing his fur loincloth. Predictably, the Paladin appears to be depicted as the only one in the party doing any actual 'adventuring' work.*

[1356] *I hope 'exposure' doesn't mean the poor artist paid by being cast out into the frozen tundra without any clothes on.*

[1357] *Though it does little to fill a hungry stomach or keep the Snow Wolves from your door…*

Hilden: "Look—I can't be expected to remember *everyone* associated with this museum.[1358] *Ahem...* anyway, if you look closely, you'll see the artist has even chiseled the Baron's face on the Paladin."

Me: "Is the Baron *really* a Paladin?"

Hilden: "No—but then the Baron did give us the use of his artist for free[1359]—as long as we agreed to feature his likeness somewhere prominently within the frieze. I believe the Baron was delighted with the final result."

Me: "It was a small price to pay—all things considered."[1360]

Hilden: "Indeed... this way, follow me..."

We leave the frieze behind and walk into the next antechamber, filled with all manner of weapons, armour, trinkets, and mysterious-looking objects.[1361]

Hilden: "All the items on display have been generously donated to us by heroes both past and present."

Me: "Why do you think heroes are so willing to hand over their hard-earned spoils or personal effects to you?"

Hilden: "I believe every hero strives to be remembered for as long as possible—even after their adventuring flame has blown out."

Me: "They want recognition?"

Hilden: "They already have recognition—what they *really* want is

---

[1358] *Actually, being the Curator of this place, I would expect <u>exactly</u> that...*

[1359] *I bet the artist didn't think that agreement would also mean 'her' services would go without payment too.*

[1360] *But a monumental price for the artist left destitute by the commission.*

[1361] *The exhibits are either sat on white plinths and encased in glass or firmly secured to the museum's walls. Little plaques sit next to every item with tiny words written upon them— I'm not entirely sure why each plaque is so small (one can only assume that, in addition to spotless streets, the people of Heartenford are also blessed with hawklike eyesight).*

immortality. This museum is their best chance of achieving that."[1362]

Me: "Surely their daring deeds affords them the immortality they crave?"

Hilden: "Perhaps a generation ago, that would have been good enough, but times have changed. Heroes have changed. How do you stand out from the crowd? Slay a Dragon? Three different adventurers did that last week—five the week before that. Noble acts and completed quests simply don't cut the mustard any longer.[1363] The commoner wants something tangible, something they can see and feel, not hear second-hand from the Landlord of the nearest tavern."

Me: "And I suppose that's where all these exhibits play their part. With so many adventurers operating across the realm,[1364] how do you decide what stays and what gets 'politely' declined?"

Hilden: "Any hero who donates something of theirs to us must first have their credentials reviewed and *verified* by our team of heroic registrars."[1365]

Me: "Verified? How does that work?"

Hilden: "It's quite straightforward. Each hero needs a document of identification, signed by a reputable Herald. They also need to list six completed adventures in the past month—and we're not talking Brundale-level side-quests here. Only the greatest acts of valour are allowed—anything less is not worth our time. We also run the usual

---

[1362] *I'd argue the Pool of Eternal Youth is probably a better bet for immortality—although you will have to endure those 'difficult' teenage summers for all of eternity... that and wet feet.*

[1363] *Gnomish for 'that doesn't impress me much'—a saying that originated after the Gnomish Barbarian, Jonta Mustard, attempted to push the 'Wheel of Blades' completely naked, only to end up leaving thirteen small fleshy chunks on the floor...*

[1364] *Around forty-five thousand 'official' heroes by Bartlet's reckoning...*

[1365] *'Heroic' in the sense that they deal with the endless paperwork from heroes, not that the actual act of processing paperwork is heroic—unless we're talking about towering monolithic stacks of paperwork that would make a Tallyman weep in despair.*

checks with a Heroes Guild Tallyman. Once we're satisfied, a hero can expect to receive a highly desirable *'Blue Tick'* from us."[1366]

Me: "You mentioned a Tallyman. Can I assume you only accept donations from Heroes Guild members?"

Hilden: "You are quite correct."

Me: "Why is that?"

Hilden: "From the moment we opened our doors, the Heroes Guild has been an enthusiastic supporter of our museum's collection—it's only right *their* members are the ones displayed and celebrated within these auspicious walls. We only display artefacts from those the Heroes Guild suggests are worthy enough."

Me: "So, any non-Guild members—"

Hilden: "Are automatically rejected out of principle. There are just *too* many amateurs and chancers out there—almost four amateurs for every 'official' hero. Those 'official' members have at least been trained *by* the best to *be* the best; why would we settle for a lesser donation?"

Me: "Have any non-Guild members ever tried to be featured here?"

Hilden: "Undoubtedly, but our registrars are very thorough. As of yet, no undesirables have pulled the wool over our eyes. But it still won't deter them from trying."

Me: "I thought the vagrants were the undesirable ones?"

Hilden: "The poor... non-Guild members... to me, they are one and the same. They all need to be expunged[1367] from our city with anything else

---

[1366] Somewhat disappointingly, a 'Blue Tick' isn't a naked insect that tells rude jokes to a buzzing audience—but is, in fact, a certificate awarded by the Museum of Heartenford to those heroes deemed 'worthy' enough to be included. Many heroes regard the certificate approval process to be one of the hardest quests in existence. A 'Blue Tick' is never handed out to anyone without at least a thousand fans following every adventuring step. Now, imagine if the realm's richest Gnome came along and purchased the Museum, fired most of the staff, then started charging 8 gold pieces for **any** hero to own a 'Blue Tick'—the ensuing chaos and fallout would be felt throughout the realm. Thankfully, the chances of something like that <u>ever</u> happening are infinitely small.

[1367] 'Expunged' is Gnomish for 'you are going to be hit in the face with a soggy Gelatinous Sponge until you have been removed from my vicinity'.

unsightly, like those annoying Mime Artists who constantly pretend they're stuck in some kind of invisible room,[1368] or Potioneers with their dubious bottled concoctions."[1369]

Me: "There must be many who dream of having their name put alongside the greats who reside within these pristine walls."

Hilden: "I understand their need; honestly, I do. I don't blame them—it's natural to want recognition from one's peers, but they are blinded to the truth."

Me: "What truth is that?"

Hilden: "They are simply not cut out to be hero material."[1370]

I nod in thought—but not in agreement.

Hilden: "*Oh*, I know it sounds harsh. But the city of Heartenford and this museum, in particular, are magnificent because we *insist* upon the highest of standards; and that begins with those we let in. The museum, for example, employs only the finest crews of Gnome workers to assemble and disassemble our many exhibits, owing to the uniquely delicate touch they have in such matters."[1371]

Me: "Can you show me some of these exhibits?"

Hilden: "Of course, it would be my pleasure."

The Museum Curator leads me to where a suit of plate armour is inside a glass case; a familiar-looking emblem on the pauldron catches my eye.

Me: "Redmane the Paladin wore something similar to this."

[1368] *Or even a Mine Warrior stuck in an Unexpected Maze...*

[1369] *I guess Inglebold won't be welcomed in Heartenford anytime soon.*

[1370] *I'm sure there are a few heroes I've interviewed in my travels that would take umbrage at this.*

[1371] *It's true; Gnomes are considered the greatest engineers in the entire realm—this is much to the annoyance of the Dwarves, who feel their perfect geometric stonework always gets overlooked. The truth of the matter is that Dwarven artistry is mostly buried deep underground, far from admiring eyes. As my Uncle Bevan Barr would often say: if you tell the funniest joke and nobody ever hears it—the joke is on YOU.*

Hilden: "*Ah*—you know your *'Manes'*. This one belonged to his grandfather, Greymane the Paladin."

Me: "It seems to be covered in the most exquisite etched scripture?"[1372]

Hilden: "*The Paladin's Oath*—he had it engraved into his armour so he wouldn't forget it in the heat of battle."[1373]

Me: "Impressive. I know three of those four interlocking 'S's on the pauldron: *Stoicism, Sacrifice,* and *Selflessness.* But what does the fourth 'S' stand for?"

Hilden: "Silence."

I clench my teeth together and keep quiet, waiting patiently for the Museum Curator to speak again. The Dwarf looks at me quizzically as I stand beside her in absolute silence.

Hilden: "W—What <u>are</u> you doing?"

Me: "Me? Keeping quiet as you asked..."

Hilden: "Why?"

Me: "Because you said—"

The Museum Curator suddenly catches on.

Hilden: "*Ahhh,* no—I meant the fourth 'S' <u>*is*</u> 'Silence'; it was the answer to your question, not a command."[1374]

I chuckle at my mistake.

Me: "*Oh,* I'm such a fool—"

The Dwarf eyes me suspiciously.

Hilden: "I shall <u>not</u> disagree with you there."

[1372] *I can't understand what any of the words say, but I'm sure whatever message they're intended to convey is important and not a list of mundane supplies Greymane's 'wife' asked him to get from the local market.*

[1373] *It does beg the question, what oath could you break while in the middle of battle? Maybe 'Thou shalt not kick thine enemy in the happy-sacks?'*

[1374] *Finally—that's one mystery solved!*

A sudden revelation hits me.

Me: "That's probably why Redmane was so irked by my question—"

Hilden: "Am I to understand you have met him *personally?*"

Me: "Our paths have crossed—*why?*"

Hilden: "He was tipped to continue his family's legacy and become one of the realm's greatest Paladins by signing up for the Heroes Guild."

Me: "Was?"

Hilden: "Sadly, it appears he chose to abandon his father's watchtower—the last we heard of his whereabouts, he was getting drunk in a tavern near the ShadowLands border."[1375]

Me: "He was drunk? *Really?* Are you sure it was him?"

Hilden: "Positive, I'm afraid—eyewitnesses spoke of a heavily armoured man wearing a helm with a giant plume of Oric feathers sprouting out the top of his head, swearing rudely at anyone in cussing range."[1376]

A pang of guilt falls over me.

Me: "Have they any idea what happened to him?"

Hilden: "It appears he fell off the *moral wagon*. I must say I'm surprised; Paladins are usually a little more resilient than most when it comes to the matter of temptation.[1377] But when something like this does happen—Paladins become a bit of a target for all the other classes."[1378]

[1375] *Oops.*

[1376] *Yup—that sounds like Redmane unless he foolishly lost his helm and armour in a terrible hand of 'Blasphemous' to a swear-filled Gnome.*

[1377] *In case you were wondering, vices for Paladins include uninhibited pride (drink-induced), wounded pride (Barbarian-induced), procrastinating pride (Cleric-induced), uncaring pride (Rogue-induced), pious pride (rival Paladin-induced), gloating pride (rival Paladin has left the party-induced), and sulking pride (rival Paladin has returned and taken command of the adventuring-party-induced).*

[1378] *Especially from Rogues who enjoy daubing rude words on the back of their armour whenever the Holy Warrior is stoically looking the other way...*

Me: "Do you think he will ever return to his former glory?"

Hilden: "Who knows? Paladins bottle up so many of their emotions—they're crying out to be released.[1379] Those who fall from grace seldom rise again to become the Holy Warrior they were before. I fear we may have lost Redmane for good..."

Me: "That's awful—so he'll never adventure or quest again?"

Hilden: "*Oh*—I'm sure he will return to the hero-fold in some form, but it won't be as a Paladin, nor will he be allowed to proudly wear his family armour. A few former Paladins are still adventuring, but they are just plain-old Fighters now. To that end, Redmane will never grace our halls."[1380]

My nagging guilt is keen to move us on from this particular exhibit quickly.

Me: "What's that?"

I point to a white fur robe dressed around a short mannequin. The Museum Curator smiles as we both walk towards it.

Hilden: "*Ah*—this robe once belonged to the Dwarven Cleric, Gilva Flamebeard."

Me: "What's it made from?"

Hilden: "Snow Wolf. The legend goes that she was out in the Western Peninsular when she came across a stranded traveller who had fallen into a crevice. Gilva had to endure the biting cold for three days and three nights whilst staving off a pack of hungry Snow Wolves. On the morning of the fourth day, the pair emerged wrapped in the furs of the recently slain beasts. Upon hearing about this tale, Gilva kindly sent her robe to be displayed here, at our museum's request."

Me: "I've heard this story before—weren't the pair forced to lay naked next to one another for warmth during their shared ordeal?"

[1379] *Or sold by an opportunistic Potioneer and labelled as a Potion of Holy Rage.*

[1380] *Unless he turned up in person, of course—good luck removing that particular undesirable.*

Hilden: "I hadn't heard *that* part of the story, but I would imagine it was bitterly cold in that crevice, so yes—it wouldn't surprise me; we are warmer than we look."[1381]

There's a banging noise coming from the next room—curious; I find myself searching for the source of the racket. Through the marble archway, I see several Gnomes on ladders starting to dismantle a statue of a slim man in a loincloth.[1382] I look closely at the rage-filled face and immediately recognise its gaunt features.

Me: "Why—isn't that Dorn the 'Barbarian'?"

The Museum Curator wears a heavy frown.

Hilden: "*Was*—sadly Dorn is no longer welcome in this museum. We are dismantling his statue, returning the two-handed sword he had donated to us, *and* handing his fur loincloth back to him."[1383]

I watch as one of the Gnomes carefully pulls down the Barbarian's fur loincloth with a pair of heavy metal tongs without letting it touch their skin—the disgusted look on the Gnome's face says it all.

Me: "I'd heard he and the Heroes Guild had suffered a parting of ways."

Hilden: "That's not common knowledge yet... but yes, his membership has been revoked—and as I mentioned before, *only* Heroes Guild members can be displayed within our museum's walls. So, sadly, that means he's got to go."

Me: "But he's done so much good—his deeds speak for themselves. Surely a misunderstanding with the Heroes Guild shouldn't jeopardise his place here?"

There's a sudden commotion as the heavy tong-using Gnome manages to ping the freed fur loincloth into the face of a Gnome colleague standing next to him.

[1381] —and hairier, unlike Gnomes, who are just cold, damp, and smooth all over—or so I've been told.

[1382] These particular Gnomes look unusually hot and bothered, as if working under immense pressure.

[1383] I'm not a hundred per cent sure, but I don't think those hairy 'smalls' _ever_ belonged to Dorn.

Hilden: "If it were my decision alone, I would keep Dorn's exhibit on display in a quiet corner somewhere, like a privy[1384]—but I have my orders, and I don't want to upset the Heroes Guild."

There's something unbelievably sad about Dorn's statue being dismantled before my very eyes—the Barbarian may not stand proud anymore, but he's still a hero to many, even if the Heroes Guild has turned their back on its former star.

Me: "Goodbye, Dorn, you're gone but not forgot—"

'BANG!'

There's a loud **'CRASH'** as one of the Gnomes carrying Dorn's sword slams into the glass display containing a flame-etched lute that once belonged to Axel-Grind. The glass shatters, sending the instrument tumbling to the floor.

Hilden: **"No! Not the lute! Not the lute! You clumsy oafs!"**

The Museum Curator carefully reaches down to pick up the instrument from the debris; bits of broken glass slide off as she examines it for damage.

Me: "Is it broken?"

Hilden: "No, *thankfully*—"

'PING!'

One of the lute's strings suddenly snaps, curling over itself like a comical moustache.[1385] The Museum Curator stares accusingly at the nearest Gnome, who, in turn, starts to shuffle out of sight and unwittingly bumps into a ladder in the process. The Gnome turns in horror and can only watch helplessly as the ladder falls backwards through the glass case containing Greymane's suit of armour, which is sent crashing to the ground like a felled steel tree.

Hilden: **"NOT AGAIN!"**

[1384] *Where Dorn's semi-naked statue can keep an eye out for any unexpected Rogue appearances.*

[1385] *Not too dissimilar to the fake one Uncle Bevan Barr used to wear.*

I am mesmerised as the impact loosens an enormous spear from its moorings on the wall behind us. It suddenly shoots forward—impaling the Museum Curator's foot, pinning it to the ground.

Hilden: *"AAAARGGGHH! MY FOOT! MY FOOT!"*

The Museum Curator flails in pain, catching a loaded crossbow on the plinth next to her,[1386] suddenly releasing its deadly payload blindly toward the antechamber. The bolt hits a black shield[1387] and ricochets skywards at an impossible angle—embedding into the face of the Paladin on the painstakingly created frieze. The Dwarf limps towards the museum entrance and falls to her knees in disbelief as she stares upwards.[1388]

Hilden: *"What have you done?"*

The Dwarf's echoed cries are answered by a low rumbling noise from above as a large crack suddenly appears overhead—it stalls for the briefest of moments before rapidly snaking across the entire length of the once beautiful artwork. The Museum Curator shrieks in horror and almost passes out from the blood loss. A Sister of Perpetuity appears out of nowhere and rushes to her aid—a large bandage at the ready.[1389] As the Sister tends to Hilden's injured foot, another loud *'CRASH'* comes from the Gnome dismantling crew—causing the Museum Curator to wail in hopelessness. I give the impaled Dwarf an apologetic shrug before hurrying out of the museum and away from the next wave of exhibit-falling chaos.

[1386] *The very same crossbow crafted by Thorde Ironstein and fired by the legendary Fighter, Raynard Levin, at a pesky Wyvern that had been stealing large signs from outside various Merchant shop fronts from Tronte to all the way to Woverton.*

[1387] *Which belonged to Arin Darkblade—funny, he never seemed the shield-carrying type.*

[1388] *The Museum Curator is bleeding rather badly; somebody better call for a Cleric—on second thoughts, there's probably way too much 'body sauce' on display here for a Holy Warrior Priest to stomach.*

[1389] *As the Gnomish saying goes—'Nobody expects a Sister of Perpetuity'.*

38. Thunk, the Book Merchant

In the trading town of Meepvale, you'll find an impressive-looking bookshop situated at the heart of the main intersection where the Great North Road meets the Great East Road.[1390] Built over three floors, the 'Magnum Opus Emporium' is owned by one of the most unlikely Merchants you'll ever find inside a bookshop—a former Barbarian. I'm here to discover why the angry-Warrior swapped the 'rage' for the 'page'.

There's a gentle *'tinkle'* from the bell that greets me as I step inside the shop; I immediately find myself in awe as I stare at the vast number of dusty tomes crammed into every available bookshelf. The only thing that moves is the gently swaying sign above the counter that reads **'SHHH! QUIET! OR I <u>WILL</u> CRUSH YOU!'**

The ceiling creaks as heavy footsteps descend the spiral staircase. Suddenly I'm nose-to-oiled-chest-pec with a half-naked, half-asleep Half-Orc. I gulp slightly and stare up into his olive-green eyes; the Half-Orc half-mountain yawns and scratches his backside.

Barbarian: "*Yeah?*"

Me: "Are you the proprietor of this place?"

The Half-Orc looks me up and down.

Barbarian: "I'm der owner…"

Me: "I'm *Elburn*—"

I hold my hand out for him to shake; the Half-Orc just sneers at it.

Me: "—erm, the *Loremaster*."

The Half-Orc picks at his giant nostril and wipes it on a nearby open book.

Barbarian: "You *sure* you, Loremaster? You look like *pointy hat*—but without der pointy hat."[1391]

[1390] *Although, ask any resident of Meepvale, and they'll insist it's actually where the Great <u>South</u> Road meets the Great <u>West</u> Road.*

[1391] *I'm now grateful Pippo didn't insist on a 'pointy hat' to go with my robed attire.*

Me: "No, I assure you, I *am* a Loremaster!"

Easily satisfied, the Barbarian hits his chest with his fist.[1392]

Barbarian: "Me, Thunk."[1393]

Me: "Well met, *Thunk*—it's quite a place you have here. How did you come by it?"

Thunk: "Thunk use many coins from adventures—buy from old man who owned shop before Thunk. Thunk got bargain for der shop."[1394]

Me: "You used the funds from your adventures to buy this place? So, why did you choose Meepvale?"

Thunk: "Thunk like town, has good tavern, serves good ale.[1395] Thunk decide to stay, retire from der hero-life."

Me: "But a bookshop? It seems a strange choice for—*erm...*"

A low growl begins to grow in the Barbarian's throat.

Me: "...an adventurer?"

The Half-Orc glares at me for a split second before nodding in reply.

Thunk: "Thunk smart—pick up lots of magic books on many adventures. Thunk knows books hold pointy hat magic. Thunk sells books here in Thunk's shop."

Me: "That's pretty clever—"

[1392] *To the uninitiated, it's worth remembering that most Barbarians rely on their fist to do the 'talking' for them. A heavy fist speaks volumes, from simple introductions and directions giving to fly swatting and argument settling.*

[1393] *Not to be confused with 'Thump' the Fair-Use Ogre. Orcs (and even Half-Orcs) hate Ogres—but they hate being <u>mistaken</u> for Ogres even more. Unlike Orcs, Ogres should <u>never</u> be allowed near a kitchen, especially as they have an annoying habit of removing the head chef's head, instead of the fish they're supposed to be preparing.*

[1394] *I'm pretty sure the former owner never imagined selling his bookshop so cheaply, but who in their right mind is ever going to argue with a screaming Half-Orc Barbarian who negotiates with a battleaxe in one fist and the owner's chest hair in the other. To be honest, I wouldn't be surprised if 'Thunk' came out of it considerably richer than when he first went in.*

[1395] *Ale <u>always</u> tastes good when you never have to pay for it.*

The Barbarian appears to grow in stature and looms over me.

Thunk: "You think Thunk stupid?"

Me: "N—No, no, no, no, I was just saying it was *clever* of you to keep all the spellbooks you found on your adventures. I'd imagine *most* Warrior-types would simply ignore them—preferring to pick up a randomly dropped pair of boots[1396] or a slightly inferior sword instead."[1397]

The Barbarian taps his temple and grins.

Thunk: "Dis Half-Orc smarter dan der other Half-Orcs—and a lot smarter dan Full-Orcs too."[1398]

It's hard to argue with the Barbarian's pragmatic logic, especially as I find myself surrounded by so many rare and valuable books for sale.

Me: "Did you find all these tomes on your adventures?"

Thunk: "Once Thunk realised books were valuable, Thunk took *every* book he found. Even took books from der pointy-hat people when dey weren't looking."

Me: "Wait—you mean you stole books from the Wizards Guild?"

The Half-Orc shrugs.

Thunk: "Point hats weren't using dem—too busy putting out big fire in small room."[1399]

Me: "Wasn't that, you know, dangerous? Wizards don't really like it when people start stealing their beloved spellbooks; it usually brings the worst out of them."[1400]

[1396] Why is it that *every* pair of boots discovered on a quest *always* fits the adventurer who found it, regardless if they are a Half-Orc or a Halfling?

[1397] Maybe one of Thorde Ironstein's misplaced +1 swords that finally washed up...

[1398] I later discovered that 'Full-Orcs' are Orcs who had eaten too much of their own culinary delights.

[1399] A near-daily occurrence where Wizards are concerned...

[1400] An old Gnomish joke goes something like this: What's worse than a Wizard casting a Fireball at you? A Wizard casting TWO Fireballs at you!

Thunk: "Thunk has pointy hat on der inside. Thunk gives pointy hat coin for any books he has."

Me: "That's very shrewd of you—makes me wonder if the other half of you is Elf!"

The Barbarian stares at me suspiciously.

Thunk: "Thunk thinks der Loremaster is making fun of him. Thunk doesn't like being made fun of—Thunk knows a 'shrewd' is a kind of rat."

Me: "No, no—shrewd means to be smart!"

A rather fearsome vein throbs in the Half-Orc's temple—encouraging me to think on my feet.

Me: "What's the most valuable book you've found on your adventures?"

The Barbarian slams his fist down on a heavy tome bound by an even heavier chain fastened to the counter.[1401]

Thunk: **"Dis one!"**

I stare in shock at the book beneath the Half-Orc's clenched fist. From what I can tell, it looks ancient—possibly predates *even* the Thieves Guild.[1402] A thick layer of dust begins to settle back on the brown leather and gold-leaf cover after being disturbed by the green-skinned meat sledgehammer sat on top of it.

Me: "May I?"

I gesture towards the book—the Half-Orc growls and slides his fist away, allowing me to investigate the tome further. The pages are edged with gold, designed to give each carefully leafed turn a suitably impressive shimmer.[1403] I examine the inside front cover, where I can just make out a scrawled name written in faded ink. Most of the letters

---

[1401] *I guess that fist is the Barbarian's attempt at 'pointing' at something.*

[1402] *The Thieves Guild is one of the oldest Guilds in the realm—they have been around since coin-filled pockets were invented, and locals started locking their doors.*

[1403] *They are actually 'sprayed' with gold spittle from a venerable and toothless Gold Dragon before being dried, collated, and bound together.*

have vanished, but I can still distinguish the beginning 'F' and middle 'T' before the rest disappears into the paper.

Me: "Where did you find this?"

Thunk: "*Hmmm...* Thunk found book deep in der Warbling Caves. Was sandwiched between two dead Goblins—lucky find."[1404]

Me: "Dead Goblins? Did you kill them?"

Thunk: "Thunk kill many Goblins, but not dese two idiots—dese two already dead when Thunk found 'em."

Me: "What do you think happened to the wretched creatures?"

The former Barbarian shakes his head.

Thunk: "Dunno, maybe dey had a big ruck over who was gonna use it as privy paper first. Whatever it was, it saved Thunk der trouble of hitting dem with a big fist."[1405]

The Half-Orc slams the book shut and slides it back under the counter, the chain clattering as it's hauled after it.[1406]

Me: "Why do you keep it locked up—the book, I mean?"

Thunk: "Book means a lot to Thunk. Dis first book Thunk finds. Thunk does not want to lose it, be angry if book gone."

Me: "Are there those who want to steal it?"

Thunk: "Pointy hat people—dey worse dan Rogues."

Me: "The Wizards? Why would they want to steal it?"

Thunk: "Pointy hat friend of Thunk says book is special—worth lots and lots of coins. Pointy hat friend tells Thunk to keep it under lock and

---

[1404] *Not for the dead Goblins.*

[1405] *Goblins are pretty easy to kill; the average Barbarian doesn't even bother with a sword or an axe—a well-aimed slap is usually enough to get the job done.*

[1406] *I know the book is valuable, but the heavy chain seems like overkill. Just the Half-Orc's presence alone should be enough to deter any would-be thieves!*

key. So, Thunk put big heavy Dragon Chain on it[1407]—nobody takes book now!"

Me: "Has anyone tried?"

Thunk: "Just one—small hairy kid."

Me: "A small hairy kid? You mean a *Halfling?*"

Thunk: "Looked like small hairy kid to Thunk."[1408]

Me: "What happened?"

Thunk: "Thunk caught him trying to pick der lock on der chain."

Me: "Ha! You probably scared the life out of him."

Thunk: "Not as much as der wall did."

Me: "Wall? *Wait*—what wall?"

The Half-Orc moves to one side and points down a long corridor of bookshelves. My eyes follow in the direction of the Barbarian's fist, stopping at a small humanoid-shaped impact crater in the brickwork.

Thunk: "**Dat** wall."

I walk over to the spread-eagled hole and examine the broken bricks.

Me: "That looks pretty painful. Did he die?"

Thunk: "Nah—der small child crawled out of here when he woke up."

Me: "Woke up? How long was he out?"

The Barbarian thinks hard—*so* hard I can almost see the Human half of his Half-Orc brain cogs turning slowly in his consciousness.

[1407] *Dragon Chain is renowned for being the only chain strong enough to hold back a horny Dragon who has just caught the scent of a nearby farmer's cow. Few Forgemasters in the realm claim they can forge Dragon Chain, and even fewer can actually prove their Dragon chains can do the job of restraining a hungry and amorous overgrown lizard. This fact still hasn't stopped Thorde Ironstein from guaranteeing his Dragon Chains are the strongest in the realm or your coin back—as long as you return the <u>entire</u> chain intact.*

[1408] *To be fair to the Barbarian, it's an easy mistake to make—or it 'could' be a small hairy kid (if so, I'd wager a Dwarven kid, probably).*

Thunk: "Two... maybe *three* days."

Me: "Two or three DAYS!?"

Thunk: "Thunk not good at counting—maybe it was four days..."

Me: "He lay there for four days?"

The Barbarian shrugs.

Thunk: "Small hairy child looked peaceful—Thunk didn't want to disturb him."

Me: "Didn't any of your customers say anything?"

Thunk: "Customers used to people laying around shop. Pointy hat books make customers sleepy. If Thunk finds a customer sleeping, Thunk leaves 'em to sleep—unless dey are snoring."

Me: "Then what?"

Thunk: "Den Thunk gets angry."

Me: "What happens when you get angry?"[1409]

Thunk: "Bad fings happen—you won't **LIKE** Thunk when Thunk is angry."

I notice the Barbarian's muscles tensing up underneath his green skin—like a coiled snake ready to strike.[1410]

Me: "No—No, I wouldn't."

I know I'm dicing with potential death asking the following question—but something inside compels me to ask anyway.

Me: "Do you get angry much?"

The Half-Orc's brow furrows into a frown.

Thunk: "Not anymore—not like before."

[1409] *Thunk is a Half-Orc ex-Barbarian—not entirely sure <u>what</u> answer I'm expecting here beyond the obvious one.*

[1410] *A very annoyed coiled snake that can't get any sleep because of the unholy racket being made.*

Me: "Before?"

Thunk: "When Thunk was adventurer—Thunk was angry all der time. Hit fings... smashed fings..."

The Barbarian looks almost sad.

Me: "What's wrong?"

Thunk: "As much as Thunk enjoys selling books, Thunk misses old days... Thunk *enjoyed* hitting fings and smashing fings[1411]—getting angry *made* Thunk happy."

Me: "Why not give this up and go back to adventuring?"

The Barbarian slams his fist angrily on the counter.

Thunk: ***"THUNK CAN'T GO ADVENTURING! THUNK HAS BOOK SHOP NOW!"***

Me: "What about hiring an assistant to help you?"

The Half-Orc rubs his chin in confusion.

Thunk: "What's dat?"

Me: "What's an assistant?"

Thunk: "Yeah, *ass*-istant?"

I know picking a Half-Orc Barbarian up on their pronunciation is a task more likely to yield frustration than any potential reward. Yet I still feel I should try.

Me: "Not *ass*-istant. Just assistant."

Thunk: "*Ass*-istant."

I smile politely, but inside I'm bubbling with grammatically imbued rage.[1412]

[1411] *And killing 'fings'...*

[1412] *If you ever want to witness Loremaster rage, then just use the wrong their/there/they're in a sentence—then you'll see first-hand what an angry Loremaster looks like.*

Me: "Close enough. An *assistant* is someone who can help you run your bookshop—leaving you free to adventure."

The Barbarian stares at me in confusion.

Thunk: "That sounds like somefink one of dose pointy hat people would say to steal Thunk's books—you not trying to steal Thunk's books, _are_ you?"

Me: "Why would I want to steal your books? Do I look like a Wizard?"

The Barbarian stares hard at my robes.

Me: "You know what—don't answer that. I'm *not* a Wizard, I'm a Loremaster dressed a little *like* a Wizard. But I digress. Honestly, I don't think there's a Merchant out there who *doesn't* use an assistant from time to time. Just imagine all the adventuring you could do while they're looking after your shop. You could go off and find even *more* spellbooks. I bet there's an entire Wizard's library's worth to be found. It makes perfect sense to me—and it can only increase your coin in the long run."

A smile breaks across the Half-Orc's face as the idea is slowly absorbed.[1413]

Thunk: "Thunk like! Thunk wants to adventure again, but Thunk also wants to run der shop—Thunk thinks he needs *ass*-istant!"

The Barbarian's face darkens once more.

Thunk: "But Thunk not know where to find *ass*-istant... maybe *you* can be Thunk's *ass*-istant?"

A cold shiver runs down my body as if death had just patted me on the back with its characteristically cold hand. I raise my own hands in objection—mindful to keep my fists closed.

Me: "No, no... I don't think that would be a good idea."

Thunk: "You write. You read. You like books—"

Me: "Yup, yup, and yup; I really can't fault your logic here—"

Thunk: "Den <u>you</u> become Thunk's *ass*-istant!"

[1413] *Like a Gelatinous Cube who just digested a drunk Clerics-only party—and is now everyone's best friend...*

I try to think fast, but all my brain can conjure is images of Thunk's customers being slowly peeled off the shop's décor—or me sweeping around the unconscious ones.

Me: "I'm not really good working the front of a shop; I don't seem to connect with customers for some reason. Perhaps I think they think I'm a Wiz—I mean, a pointy hat..."

Thunk: "*Hmmm*... But Loremaster speaking to Thunk now? Thunk fink you sound smart. Thunk's customers like smart."

Me: "Yes—but... *but*..."

The Barbarian stares at me, his nostrils flaring in confused agitation.

Thunk: "Thunk finks Loremaster not being honest. Thunk finks Loremaster does not want to be Thunk's *ass*-istant!"

Me: "What? *Well*... I—I..."

Thunk: "Honesty important to Thunk... maybe you shouldn't be Thunk's *ass*-istant after all... maybe Thunk doesn't trust Loremaster..."

I can sense the Half-Orc's green-skinned muscles tensing as if he's about to wind up and unleash a hefty punch in my direction. I close my eyes and brace myself to be the first Loremaster in living history to pass through a solid brick wall without the aid of a spell—when a moment of inspiration pops into my head.

Me: "You need a sign outside your shop!"[1414]

Thunk: "Sign? Thunk <u>not</u> religious."

Me: "No! Not *that* sort of sign—a sign you can *read*. Think of it as a call to arms."

The Half-Orc's face suddenly brightens at the thought of a weapon-carrying assistant working behind the counter, but as quickly as the Barbarian's smile appears, it is replaced by a pained grimace.

Thunk: "Thunk like dis idea—but Thunk cannot write..."

The irony of someone owning a bookshop that cannot read or write is

---

[1414] *Hopefully, out of view of any sign-hungry Wyverns.*

not lost on me. I feel pity for the short-tempered Warrior but sense a chance to use my craft to help someone who could easily rip my arm from my socket if the mood took him. Determined to help the former Barbarian, even if it places me in harm's way—I draw out a piece of parchment, a quill, and a pot of ink from my bag.

Thunk: "You help Thunk?"

Me: "Sure, it's not a problem—"

I find myself suddenly lifted off my feet as the Half-Orc almost squeezes my morning's breakfast out of me in gratitude.

Thunk: "You and Thunk good friends!"

Me: "*C—Can't breathe—*"

The Barbarian looks into my red face as I feel the world spinning and the cold hand of death reaching for me once more.

Thunk: "Why you go a funny colour—?"

I'm finally released from the Half-Orc's grip, and my airways gratefully expand as I gulp in huge mouthfuls of air. I'm relieved I can breathe once more and take a few more cautious gasps to ensure there's no lasting internal damage.

Me: "I—It's okay, I'll be back to normal... give me a moment..."

With my body still trying to recover, I shakily pick up the quill, dip it into my ink pot and start scribbling away.

Me: "H—How much... are you willing to pay an assistant... for their time?"

Thunk: "Pay?"

Me: "You have to pay them for working here; nobody does anything for free—"[1415]

Thunk: "Thunk adventured for free—sometimes clean out dungeon

---

[1415] *Unless you happen to be the Baron of Heartenford's unappreciated personal artist, of course...*

without being asked first."[1416]

Me: "That's very generous of you—I'm sure somebody would have paid you if you found a nearby local who needed that dungeon cleaning.[1417] How much do you want to give them—this potential assistant of yours?"

Thunk: "How much does Thunk have to pay for an *ass*—istant?"

Me: "That depends on how much coin you can pay them."

The Barbarian scratches his head in thought.

Thunk: "A hundred silver coins a day?"

I cough in shock.

Me: "A *hundred* silver coins—? I think that might be too generous. Why not go a little lower? I'll put down one silver coin a day—*okay*? See if anyone answers the call. If you don't get any takers, we can always revisit the pay a little and raise it again—that sound like a plan?"[1418]

Thunk: "You der Loremaster."

Me: "That I am..."

In a matter of moments, and much to the Half-Orc's delight, I write up a rudimentary 'Ass-istant Wanted' sign and position it in the front window.

Me: "All done!"

The Half-Orc hammers my back in gratitude; I swear I hear one of my ribs crack from the 'friendly' blow. He reaches under his counter and brings out a small stack of coins.

Thunk: "Thunk wants to pay Loremaster—"

[1416] *Not to be confused with a Gnomish mother's level of dungeon cleaning—which would see every stone turned over and picked clean of lichen and fungus.*

[1417] *Is it poor etiquette to clean out a dungeon before actually being asked to do it?*

[1418] *I mean, if the Barbarian is willing to pay* that *much for an assistant, maybe I should give up the position of Loremaster...*

I hold my hands up to stop him.

Me: "There's really no need. Your time today has been more than enough payment."

He looks at me, slightly crestfallen.

Thunk: "But Thunk wanted to give his new best friend a gift…"

Me: "Honestly, it was nothing—"

I see a spark of an idea in the Half-Orc's face as he pulls out the tome still securely fastened to the counter by the Dragon Chain.

Thunk: "Thunk give you **dis** book!"

Me: "What—no, I can't accept this. It means everything to you—"

The Barbarian laughs loudly, his booming voice alone sending a few heavy books tumbling from the top shelf."[1419]

Thunk: "Thunk can go get more books now!"

'CHINK!'

He pulls hard at the Dragon Chain, and it snaps easily apart. He hands the tome over to me.[1420]

Thunk: "It's yours now."

I go to protest once more, but there's a '*tinkle*' from the bell over the door. We both turn to see who has stepped into the bookshop. Standing there is a timid female Half-Orc looking to speak to someone in charge. She spies me and assumes that I somehow fit the bill.

Female Half-Orc: "*Erm*, I came about the sign in the window?"[1421]

[1419] *Books with dubious titles such as 'Necromancy Erections—Getting a Rise out of the Dead' and 'Confessions of a Kleptomaniacal Sorceress'.*

[1420] *Difficult to tell if that was down to the Half-Orc's immense strength or the Dwarven Forgemaster's shoddy craftsmanship.*

[1421] *It may come as no surprise that female Half-Orcs usually have a better vocabulary than their male counterparts.*

I find myself caught off guard by the eloquence of her speech, especially after conversing for such a length of time with 'Thunk'.

Me: "I'm not the owner—"

The Female Half-Orc blushes.

Female Half-Orc: "Forgive me, I just assumed—what with the spellbook you're carrying in your hands—"

Me: "This? *Oh* no, this is a gift from… *from*—"

I turn and gesture towards 'Thunk', hoping he'll step up to say something. But instead, the Barbarian seems unable to muster a word—stunned into silence by the female Half-Orc standing before him.

Me: *"Thunk…?"*

Thunk: *"Huh?"*

I elbow the Barbarian in the ribs in an attempt to bring him out of his silent stupor.[1422] The Half-Orc desperately searches his mind for something sensible to say but fails…

Thunk: "<u>Thunk!</u>"

Female Half-Orc: "I'm Brizu, pleased to make your acquaintance."

She turns to me.

Brizu: "And you are?"

Feeling like a Paladin on a Barbarian-only quest,[1423] I smile as I tuck the spellbook into my bag and head for the door.

Me: *"Just leaving*—I think you two have a lot to discuss."

I turn back to the former Barbarian and bid him a fond farewell.

Me: "Good luck with everything, Thunk."

[1422] *A move that does more damage to my elbow than the Half-Orc's ribcage…*

[1423] *Who returns a swear-fuelled Paladin with a love of fur loincloths and bawdy jokes about Clerics…*

The Barbarian cannot tear his eyes away from the smiling Half-Orc standing in front of him, just asking to be his *ass*-istant. As I exit, I hear Thunk's booming voice one last time, conversing with Brizu.

Thunk: "You <u>like</u> books? Thunk <u>like</u> books!"

As I head out of Meepvale, a huge grin spreads across my face. I find my spirits lifted by the small part I've just played in the Book Merchant's immediate future.[1424]

[1424] *If I fail to make my fortune as a Loremaster, I could always forge a new career as a Signsmith—just as long as a passing Wyvern doesn't take a fancy to my handiwork...*

39. The 'Dark Power' in the south

As I step into the metaphorical Dragon's Den, my footfalls reverberate around stone walls. There's a distant low growl coming from the darkness ahead, reminding me of Pippo the Merchant and the Dragon he 'borrowed'. But I tell myself that I'm here at the behest of another; a crudely written note signed by Snodgrass the Goblin, has somehow found its way into my possession.[1425] It's a mystery how the resourceful creature achieved this feat undetected, but I'm grateful nonetheless.[1426] I wouldn't usually put myself in such a precarious position, but the promise of this meeting is too hard to resist. I've been granted an audience with Snodgrass's 'boss', a dreaded Warlock Lich who has been plaguing the realm and bringing untold misery to the locals in the area[1427]— the 'Dark Power' in the south, as this Evildoer has come to be known as...

I descend deeper into the crypt,[1428] having followed the note's directions to the poorly scrawled letter.[1429] My consciousness pleads with me to leave this unholy sanctum as the smell of death grows stronger with every step[1430]. You already know, dear reader, that I'm not the religious type, but I still find myself mumbling a prayer to the spirit of my recently departed brother, urging him to protect me from whatever malevolent force lies in this abyss. When I reach a blackened wall,[1431] a terrifying scream stops me in my tracks, followed by a

---

[1425] *I suddenly remember Snodgrass claimed he couldn't read or write—so either the Goblin is lying about his literacy skills, or I'm potentially walking into a trap...*

[1426] *Even if it will cost me 3 hog roasts and 2 caskets of ale...*

[1427] *Details of this exact misery are thin on the ground—but whatever it is, I can't imagine the Warlock Lich has been sneaking into a local's home to steal a favourite dress or two.*

[1428] *Calling it a 'crypt' is somewhat generous—this tomb appears deceptively small; I can't imagine it would house a dead Halfling or Gnome without considerable effort and a large saw...*

[1429] *This letter must be the Goblin equivalent of a 'Barker'—I'm lucky I haven't traversed to the other side of the realm by mistake.*

[1430] *The only thing that would make my predicament worse is if a clown were to suddenly leap out of the shadows.*

[1431] *A wall with a strange human-shaped mark scorched into it.*

wicked voice that calls out from the gloom.[1432]

Disembodied Voice: "I hear you're the one asking all the questions?"

The voice is cold and brittle, freezing the blood in my veins.

Me: "Y—Yes... I'm Elburn... *E—Elburn Barr,* the L—Lore—"

Disembodied Voice: ***"Fool! I know who you are—for I am the one who wrote the note, inviting you here into my dark domain!"***[1433]

I start to half-turn, my legs urging the rest of my trailing body to bolt for the exit. The voice senses my overwhelming desire to flee.

Disembodied Voice: "You have nothing to fear, Loremaster... there are no Goblins, Giant Spiders, or Gelatinous Cubes[1434] here to trouble you.[1435] You'll be pleased to learn I gave them the night off so we can be alone together..."[1436]

Me: "C—Can I at least know your n—name?"

Disembodied Voice: "Of course, where are my manners—I am *Derrick.*"

Me: "Derrick?"

Derrick: "Yes, Derrick... what's *wrong* with Derrick?"

Me: "N—Nothing... I—I was just expecting something a little... *darker...*"

Derrick: "That was my given name from a life now long forgotten..."

Me: "I—I take it you're the Warlock Lich I've heard so much about?"

[1432] *'Wicked' is also a Gnomish word for something being rather good. However, I think I'll stick with the non-Gnomish meaning in this context.*

[1433] *Aha! I knew Snodgrass didn't write it!*

[1434] *What about their smaller distant cousin, the Gelatinous Sponge?*

[1435] *What do Goblins, Giant Spiders, and Gelatinous Cubes do to let off some steam? I'm envisaging some kind of bizarre bouncing orgy with lots of misplaced arrows zipping around the place and plenty of hanging around.*

[1436] *I'm not entirely convinced this has made me feel any safer.*

There's laughter, not deep, booming and foreboding—but something else: lighter, fragile, with a hint of nervousness thrown in for good measure.

Derrick: "The Goblin told me you wanted to talk—*so talk...*"

Me: "Y—Yes... I'm writing a j—journal of sorts. It's about heroes—"

Derrick: "**Ha!** Heroes..."

I can't miss the thick slice of resentment the Warlock Lich just served up.

Me: "Well, not *just* heroes, but everything to do with them too. How they come to be, not just what drives them but also who drives them."

Derrick: "What do you mean by *who* drives them?"[1437]

Me: "Across my travels, I've discovered a shadow that surrounds many heroes. Almost as if someone or *something* else is working in the background."

Derrick: "And I suppose you have a good idea who this shadowy someone *or* something is?"

I pause for a moment, unsure if I should be revealing my information to a Warlock Lich. However, something tells me the rebellious 'magical' Sorting Cap is well and truly out of the Bag of Holding.[1438] I have little choice unless I want to witness my life force being sucked out of me like a weary parishioner listening to a Cleric's lengthy sermon.

Me: "It's... t—the H—Heroes Guild."

A wall of silence greets my reply.

Me: "H—Hello?"

Derrick: "Interesting—pray tell, what do *you* make of this Heroes Guild?"

[1437] *I hope the Warlock Lich isn't after the name of a reputable carriage driver—they are harder to find than any lost Ring of Power.*

[1438] *Punishment for telling a bunch of should-be Wizards they're destined to become Barbarians...*

Me: "I—I don't understand the question—?"

A hiss of displeasure escapes the unseen Warlock Lich's lips.

Derrick: "It is a simple enough question—are you <u>for</u> or <u>against</u> this Guild of Heroes?"[1439]

A bead of sweat trickles down my temple. I realise now that my life hangs in the balance. If I'm to continue in my current form, I must answer this question promptly <u>and</u> correctly...

Derrick: "Well?"

Me: "They're unscrupulous, dishonest, possibly a touch narcissistic too. They say they support *all* heroes, but they appear only interested in those who can make them a lot of coin—"[1440]

Derrick: "So, you do not approve of them then?"

Me: "If coin is all they care about—then no, I don't approve of them."

I know the Heroes Guilds' influence stretches far—even to unholy places such as this crypt. But right now, alone in this god-awful place, I'm not sure which side of the coin the Warlock Lich will land on. I brace myself for a sudden jolt of pain, silently praying again to any non-existent deity listening that my death be a swift one.[1441] As I do, a figure slowly approaches from the darkness—dressed in black plate armour, a black cloak, and wearing a terrifying iron skull helm; the Warlock Lich holds out a gauntleted hand and points an ominous finger at the centre of my soul.

Derrick: "Am I to assume nobody knows you are here—not *even* the Heroes Guild?"

Me: "N—No—nobody beyond you, me, and Snodgrass."

Derrick: "Snodgrass?"

[1439] *To be clear, I'm <u>against</u> the Heroes Guild and <u>for</u> the Guild of Heroes, even if they do operate out of a tavern's privy (except on Thursdays).*

[1440] *And a sizeable family estate to claim when things inevitably take a dive—sometimes literally off the rickety steps of a rundown castle by the sea...*

[1441] *Although, I'm sure the omnipresent in question is probably too busy existing within nothingness to answer.*

Me: "The Goblin who supposedly set this all up."

Derrick: "They have names?"

Me: "You mean you didn't know?"

Derrick: "I'll be honest with you—getting to know a Goblin personally doesn't rank high on my to-do list."

The Evildoer grabs his iron skull helm and begins to lift it free from his head. I avert my eyes, not entirely sure I want to look into the undead sockets of a Lich—especially one who is also a Warlock.[1442]

Me: "*Really*, there's no need to do that—"

There's a heavy **'CLANK'** as the helm hits the crypt floor.

Derrick: **"Gaze upon my flesh, mortal..."**

With my whole body shaking, I slowly dare to stare at this Evildoer. But instead of being greeted by a rotting abomination, I see a sight that takes my breath away for a completely different reason.

Derrick: "I'm just a normal man!"

Me: "What do you mean you're a normal man?"

Derrick: "I'm just an innocent man!"

The Warlock Lich lurches forward and is about to grip my shoulders with his heavy black gauntlets when he stops short and withdraws them.

Derrick: **"I'M NOT SUPPOSED TO BE HERE! YOU'VE GOT TO DO SOMETHING! YOU'VE GOT TO HELP ME!"**

[1442] *What makes a Warlock—a Warlock and a Wizard—a Wizard? The average commoner would assume it has something to do with their magic—perhaps one uses a spellbook, while the other can recall their magic from memory alone? Or maybe one prefers their magic to be raw rather than relying on a powerful entity? The actual truth of the matter boils down to how they wear their beards. Wizards love letting their whiskers grow wildly out of control and never use any dyes on their greying hairs; Warlocks, on the other hand, prefer a neatly trimmed chinstrap beard and pencil-thin moustache that they dye on a near-hourly basis. Warlocks are also prone to chuckling evilly from time to time, while Wizards just 'tut'... a lot...*

Me: "*What?* I—I don't understand. You're not what I was expecting from a Warlock Lich—"

Derrick: "That's because I'm **not** a bloody Warlock Lich! There hasn't been one in living memory!"

My eyes narrow with suspicion.

Me: "Is this some kind of test?"

Derrick: "*WHAT? A TEST!? NO! THIS ISN'T A TEST, YOU FOOL! WHY WOULD I TEST YOU—LOOK, YOU'VE GOT TO BELIEVE ME! I'M <u>NOT</u> A WARLOCK LICH!*"

Me: "If you're not a Warlock Lich, why are you dressed like one?"

Derrick: "Are you a Wizard?"

Me: "Okay—you got me there. But that still doesn't answer why you're pretending to be a Warlock Lich."

Derrick: "Because that's what I've been <u>told</u> to do!"

Me: "Told? Told by *whom?*"

I can't help but notice that the identity-challenged Warlock Lich is jumping up and down on the spot in agitation.

Derrick: "The Heroes Guild—who else do you think?!"

Me: "What? Why? If I'm being honest with you, that sounds a little unbelievable—are you *sure* you're not undead, and you just don't realise it?"[1443]

The Warlock Lich curls his metal fingers into claws and shakes them in frustration.

Derrick: "Let me make this easier for you. One of the fundamental requirements of being an undead Warlock Lich is that they <u>need</u> to be undead[1444]—*do I look undead to you!?*"

[1443] *It's not uncommon for the recently undead to believe they are still 'alive'—which can make for some awkward moments, especially if they turn up at their local tavern for a swift half and end up 'downing' a fast-moving Halfling.*

[1444] *And a Lich—and probably a Warlock too...*

Me: "Well, you *do* look a tad pale, if I'm being completely honest."

It's the Warlock's turn to narrow his eyes.

Derrick: "So would _you_ be if you were forced to live down here in the gloom without ever seeing daylight. Have you *any* idea how cold it is in this crypt? I have to sleep in the same room as the stinking Goblins just to coax what little warmth I can find into my bones!"

Me: "Why not head to the nearest tavern and order yourself the hottest broth and enjoy the comforts of a soft, warm bed?"

The pretend Warlock Lich hisses in frustration at my question. I flinch, still wary that this meeting could go wrong at a moment's notice.

Derrick: "*Oh*, who I'd <u>kill</u> for a hot meal and a decent night's sleep. But it's not as if I have any *choice* in the matter—the bloody Heroes Guild made sure of that. They even task that noisy Bard of theirs to turn up at my crypt unannounced and warble loudly into the abyss, just to make sure I'm not sleeping on the job!"

Me: "If the Heroes Guild are supposedly responsible for you being here, what can they do to stop you from leaving? I mean, it's not as if they are watching us right now."[1445]

The pretend Warlock Lich laughs a little too manically for my liking.

Derrick: "You're joking, aren't you? They can do a **<u>LOT</u>**—I suppose you know of their Enforcers? They're the best bloodhounds in the tracking business and could hunt a Cleric down just by sniffing their empty collection box."[1446]

Me: "What possible hold does the Heroes Guild have over you?"

Derrick: "A legal one—they tricked me into signing one of their accursed contracts. I now *'unofficially'* work for them. Although 'work' is a little generous because that implies I'll earn some much-needed coin somewhere along the line."

Me: "Doing what?"

[1445] *Although, I do feel as if unseen eyes are watching from the crypt's privy that sits inconspicuously in the furthest corner.*

[1446] *That's another image that won't leave my memory anytime soon.*

The fictional Warlock Lich opens his arms wide and smiles ironically.

Derrick: *"Ta—daaaa!"*

The realisation hits me as if an unexpected lightning bolt had just shot from the magical wand of an inebriated Wizard during an impromptu and slightly provocative pole dance routine.[1447]

Me: "Wait—you're *paid* to be an Evildoer by the Heroes Guild—?"

Derrick: "And *finally*, the solitary coin drops into the Bard's upturned leather helm..."[1448]

Me: "But why would the Heroes Guild hire someone to pretend to be an Evildoer? It doesn't make any sense? They're in the business of vanquishing Evildoers—not creating them!"

Derrick: "You don't get it yet, do you? The Heroes Guild runs everything, from start to finish, from one end to the other—everything from A *to* Z. The quests, the Evildoers, the monsters— the Heroes Guild are at the heart of it all, quietly pulling strings in the background[1449] while the rest of the realm stares doe-eyed at the next hero they kick out onto the adventuring scene."

Me: "What do they hope to achieve by doing this?"

Derrick: "Total control; quests are at the heart of everything, calling out to adventurers and alike—luring them from every corner of the realm. Wherever heroes go, the coin inevitably follows. Did you know some of us even used to *be* adventurers?"

Me: "What?"

Derrick: "Yup."

Me: "Wait—*you* were a hero?"

[1447] **Loremaster Tip #8:** <u>Never</u> *let a Wizard get drunk whilst carrying a Wand of Lightning Bolts.*

[1448] *Perhaps the unfortunate Bard in question is playing all the right notes, just all in the wrong order?*

[1449] *However, if we're talking 'dungeon' strings, then that task is the responsibility of the Gnomish Dungeonmaster running things in the background.*

Derrick: "I was a Paladin until the quests dried up, as did the promise of coin. I had nowhere to turn to; everything I had earned had been given away to those who needed it the most. Unfortunately, I realised too late that I was the one who needed it the most. That's when the Heroes Guild is at their most dangerous—when you are at your lowest. I was offered this temporary role in exchange for a trough of riches that never materialised. I was an utter fool, but it was too late; I was in too deep—trapped by one of their infernal *'binding'* contracts and the overarching fear of what the Heroes Guild would do to me if I reneged on our *arrangement.*"

Me: "That sounds almost unbelievable—so, you're telling me you're *forced* to run this place for them now? If true—what's it like being an Evildoer?"

Derrick: "*Oh,* you know—it's a living nightmare. The Goblins are a pain in the backside; they <u>never</u> do anything asked of them—and don't even get me started on their stench and lack of basic hygiene. But that's not the worst..."

Me: "You mean there's something worse than the stench of Goblins?"

Derrick: "One word... paperwork."[1450]

Me: "I'll be perfectly honest; paperwork wasn't *exactly* the answer I was expecting."

Derrick: "*No?* Well, it is. The Tallymen are quite insistent all external paperwork aligns correctly with their internal paperwork. It's worse if a hero actually *dies* on our watch—then all manner of reports and forms need to be written up and countersigned."

Me: "I thought the Heroes Guild tried their best to *avoid* hero deaths? Assigning quests to adventurers based on their level of experience? If they run everything in the background as you say they do, surely they'd *know* if an adventurer is likely to die attempting it?"

The fake Lich gives me a knowing gaze.

Me: "They <u>do</u> know... which means... they <u>want</u> them to fail."

Derrick: "It all depends on the adventurer in question and how rich

----

[1450] *Which are two words pounded together...*

they are."

Me: "Rich—I don't follow?"

Derrick: "I assume you're aware that each adventurer signs a *'Death in Service'* clause when they first join?"

Me: "Yes, I'm aware..."

Derrick: "Then you must also be aware that if any of their heroes were to... *ahem...* expire whilst on an adventure, then their entire fortune and any family estate is taken by the Heroes Guild?"

Me: "I know of this—yes, it *does* sound a little mercenary, but surely they're entitled to protect their investment—"

Derrick: "*Pfft...* Investment... it's really quite simple; the wealthier a hero is, the more likely they are to die quickly and quietly mid-quest so the Heroes Guild can cash in on that clause."[1451]

My thoughts immediately spring to Dorn, his family estate, and his untimely expulsion from the Heroes Guild.

Me: "What if that doesn't work?"

The sham Warlock sucks in his breath and blows out his cheeks.

Derrick: "Then that adventurer can expect a visit from the Heroes Guild Enforcers; they are more than versed with tidying up any loose ends."

Me: "Loose ends—such as a hero unexpectedly surviving a quest?"

Derrick: "Loose ends *exactly* like a hero unexpectedly surviving a quest..."

Me: "So, you're stuck down here playing Evildoer for the Heroes Guild—"

The mock Warlock Lich fires a threatening glare in my direction.

[1451] *I remember something Hagworl said to me about how a large portion of heroes aren't slain by monsters or even by ex-Paladins masquerading as Evildoers—most 'conveniently' die as a direct result of their own inexperience or stupidity, which must suit the Heroes Guild down to the ground (or at least until the hero in question is buried in it).*

Derrick: "Choose your next words wisely, Loremaster—I may not be undead, but these gauntlets can <u>still</u> rob you of your life."

I back away nervously from the black plate gauntlets, conscious of remaining beyond the lethal reach of the pale man.

Me: "What's so deadly about them?"

Derrick: "Absolutely <u>everything</u>! That damn Wizard gave me these to wear."

My ears prick up as I suddenly recall another crucial piece of information.[1452]

Me: "This Wizard didn't also try to fry you with a Fireball, *did he?*"

The weekend Warlock goes red with embarrassment.

Derrick: "*Ah*—so you know about the *incident* then?"

Me: "Yes, but I'd like to hear your version of events..."

Derrick: "It was all a bit of a misunderstanding—the Wizard was expecting payment for the gauntlets, whereas I was expecting someone else to have handled that particular *arrangement.*"

Me: "By that, I wager you mean the Heroes Guild?"

Derrick: "It doesn't matter who—what <u>does</u> matter is that super-heated words were exchanged, quickly followed by a super-heated ball of fire."

Me: "What did you do?"

Derrick: "What could I do? I'm not trained to go toe-to-toe with a bunch of short-tempered heroes, so I ran for my life. The last thing I remember was the screams coming from the unlucky souls caught in the Wizard's blast radius—why do you ask?"

I shift my feet uncomfortably.

Me: "I think my brother was one of those *unlucky* souls..."

[1452] *That surprisingly has nothing to do with remembering where the nearest exit is...*

Derrick: "*Oh...* I'm so sorry about your brother—I didn't know. When it was safe to return, the only sign they were ever there was the scorched wall over yonder."

As I follow the phoney Warlock's pointing gauntlet to the human-shaped blast mark on the wall opposite, an awkward silence falls between us.[1453]

Me: "It's not your fault—it was just one of those things..."[1454]

The sham Warlock nods slowly.

Me: "What were your gauntlets supposed to do?"

Derrick: "I was told they would grant the wearer immortality and protection from a specific weapon type.[1455] But the moment I put them both on, the curse activated—instead of holding back the summers, they rapidly aged anyone I touched."

Me: "Aged anyone you touched? That sounds like a frightful power!"

Derrick: "You have <u>no</u> idea."

The bogus Lich nods towards the privy in the far corner.

Derrick: "Do you know how fraught with danger every visit I make is? One misplaced wipe and I'm suddenly ten summers older than when I first stepped inside."[1456]

Me: "Why not just take the gauntlets off?"

Derrick: "What a **good** idea!"

Me: "Is it?"

[1453] *I'm still struggling with the realisation that my brother died because of a misunderstanding over a sale of goods transaction—and not any 'good' goods to that end either.*

[1454] *This is a Gnomish saying that means, 'It's one of those unfortunate things that happened to me—when I'd rather it had happened to you.'*

[1455] *I later found out the specific weapon type was a Halfling sling. Which, as weapons go, is perhaps the most ridiculed of all the weapon types.*

[1456] *That's probably a little more information than I needed to know—although it would undoubtedly cause any watching Rogues to avert their eyes in horror.*

Derrick: "**NO, YOU DULLARD!** Don't you think I've *tried* that already? I can't remove the gauntlets without touching them—and any Goblin I order to help me has found itself accelerating towards old age faster than a Wizard trying to evade guard duty. Nobody wants to risk becoming a shambling wreck with nothing to look forward to—except maybe Halfling Bingo."[1457]

Me: "Have you ever t—"

Derrick: "—touched a hero, sure... *yeah,* I have."

Me: "Who?"

Derrick: "There was this Battle Dancer, a lovely Elf—full of spirit and life. She crept into the crypt one evening and surprised me as I tried to find a warm Goblin to snuggle up to. The Elf immediately drew her blade and began rapidly spinning toward me."

Me: "What did you do?"

Derrick: "I was mesmerised by her constant twirling and nifty footwork. I—I just stood there, entranced by the Battle Dancer's intricate dance routine."

Me: "This Battle Dancer... she wasn't accompanied by someone wielding an 'invisible' sword, was she?"

Derrick: "No—she was alone; why do you ask?"[1458]

Me: "No reason—just curious,[1459] ignore me... anyway, you were saying?"

Derrick: "Before I could do or say anything, her sword was suddenly jutting out of my side. Fortunately, my armour is pretty thick, so it just

---

[1457] *'Halfling Bingo' is a highly entertaining pastime within small-folk communities where locals have numbers painted onto their foreheads before being stuffed inside a huge Gnomish tombola. The Draw Master then cracks a whip as a herd of oxen, tethered to the mechanical drum, start swishing around the Halflings inside until one dizzy occupant is released at random. This continues until someone in the watching crowd with the matching numbers printed on a parchment shouts 'Bingo' or until one of the tombola-tumbling Halflings starts violently throwing up.*

[1458] *The Mime Warrior probably got stuck trying to escape an Unexpected Maze...*

[1459] *...or fell fighting Goblins from the Halgorn Crags with a weapon that only existed in her imagination...*

got stuck. I went to pull it out at the exact same time as she did—and accidentally grabbed her wrist. I'll never forget the look of confusion written across her face as she withered and aged before my very eyes. It was heart-wrenching to watch."[1460]

Me: "That's terrible!"

Derrick: "You want to know something else? She was a Heroes Guild Member, so I was expected to complete all the appropriate paperwork detailing the events leading up to the incident."

Me: "What did this frail Elf do?"

Derrick: "She just started shuffling around the crypt trying to stroke my cat—"[1461]

Me: "Wait—you have a *cat?*"

Derrick: "Had—to be honest, I think it adopted *me.*"

Me: "Had?"

The pretend Warlock Lich holds up his gauntlets to remind me of the curse locked within them.[1462]

Me: "What did you do about the elderly Battle Dancer?"

Derrick: "I ordered my minions to drop the confused Elf off at the Heroes Hall of Legends."

Me: "I know of this place."

Derrick: "Good; saves me explaining to you that it's a retirement home for adventurers who are too frail to adventure any longer.[1463] The Sisters of Perpetuity run it—"

Me: "I've *been* there."

[1460] *But probably way worse to experience first-hand...*

[1461] *(See footnote 643) I knew it!*

[1462] *Nine lives are obviously no match for cursed life-sucking gauntlets...*

[1463] *Which the faux Warlock Lich just did anyway...*

Derrick: "*Ah*—then chances are you may have encountered this Battle Dancer."

Me: "*Shana...*"

Derrick: "Excuse me?"

Me: "Her name is Shana..."

Derrick: "A lovely name—how is she?"

Me: "She moved on..."

The fake Warlock Lich looks crestfallen.

Derrick: "She was very old. I guess it was her time."[1464]

Me: "No—I mean, she really *did* move on. The last I saw of the Battle Dancer, she was twirling like mad for the hills."

Derrick: "I bet that was a beautiful sight."

Me: "Beautiful isn't quite the word I would use—*bizarre* maybe."

Derrick: "Why bizarre?"

Me: "I think being hotly pursued by the Sisters of Perpetuity had something to do with it."

The phoney Warlock chuckles at the image burning in his mind's eye.

Me: "How long have you been doing this—evildoing, I mean?"

Derrick: "Too long—I can barely recall when I was doing anything else."

An awkward silence leaves us both focused on the guttural growls coming from another part of the crypt.

Me: "Can you remember much of your old adventuring life?"

Derrick: "I catch small flashes but nothing that makes much sense anymore: an unremarkable dungeon,[1465] a chained up and slightly

---

[1464] *'Time' that the imitation Warlock Lich accidentally stole.*

[1465] *Aren't all dungeons, by default, unremarkable?*

miffed Dragon, the odd Fireball or Goblin arrow flying past your nose[1466]—
it all seems to roll into one these days. All my time is spent running this
place. I don't have the energy to dream of days of yore."

Me: "Who, from the Heroes Guild, tells you what to do?"

Derrick: "Nobody—not directly anyway. I receive my weekly orders
from a Barker,[1467] who usually forewarns me of any heroes assigned to
my crypt—and what to do with them."

Me: "How do you know these orders are from the Heroes Guild?"

Derrick: "Because who else, in their right mind, would send a *Barker*
into my domain?"[1468]

Me: "And these orders tell you who to allow through and who to... kill?"

Derrick: "Yes—but I'll be honest with you, that has never sat well with
me. I prefer to find ways to spare souls rather than taking them."

Me: "What do you mean?"

Derrick: "I usually attempt to persuade a visiting hero to adventure
somewhere *less* fatal to them."

Me: "Does it work?"

Derrick: "For some—for others, it's too late. They are too trusting of
the Heroes Guild to heed my words."

Me: "What do you do for those who agree to turn their backs on their
masters?"

Derrick: "*Ah,* they need a bit more help to pull the wool over the Heroes
Guild's eyes. For that to work, we have to fake their death—which
involves paying Hagworl to dig up a corpse for us to use. I'm not saying
I'm *entirely* happy desecrating a deceased adventurer's corpse—but
needs must when the Heroes Guild is snapping at your heels."

[1466] *The Goblin Arrow I would expect to miss—but a Fireball will probably singe more than
a few overgrown nasal hairs as it roared past.*

[1467] *No doubt to be told of an approaching Writer, Manger, Drunk, and Eric...*

[1468] *Maybe someone with a 'Barker' grudge to settle after receiving the umpteenth
misspoken word.*

Me: "How can you achieve all this without being discovered by the Guild's Tallymen?"

Derrick: "With great difficulty. But Hagworl is good at switching the identity of one hero and giving it to another—it also helps he has a large number of unidentified dead adventurers to choose from."[1469]

Me: "I suppose you're aware of the dark rumours circulating about you."

Derrick: "Why do you think I agreed to this meeting in the first place?"

Me: "I don't follow—"

Derrick: "—I want you to help me."

Me: "*What?* How?"

Derrick: "By exposing the truth about the Heroes Guild—I need you to let the realm know what's happening here—that I'm not the real threat. If everyone opened their eyes, perhaps they'll see the Heroes Guild for what they really are—then we can all be free from their iron grip."

Me: "We?"

Derrick: "You don't think I'm the only unfortunate 'Evildoer' the Heroes Guild has under their control? There must be hundreds of us, if not thousands—all trapped in this endless existence, all desperately searching for a way out—*do this for them, Loremaster!*"[1470]

Me: "H—How can I? I'm just one normal man—?"

Derrick: "One normal man, who is writing a journal—don't you see? You hold more power in your quill than I do in these accursed gauntlets.[1471] Your words will free us if you are brave enough to share the truth."

[1469] *I think I'm starting to understand the relevance of the Phoenix symbols now...*

[1470] *Not sure how I feel about doing the bidding of Evildoers—even if it is for a 'good' reason.*

[1471] *Erm... others, like a certain Battle Dancer, may say otherwise...*

I stare at my hands, imagining them holding the quill as it writes the words that might yet set the fictitious Warlock Lich free.

Me: "I—I'll try..."

Derrick: "Do you want to know *why* there's a dark rumour circulating about me?"

Me: "Because you're up to no good?"

The inauthentic Warlock Lich stares at me emotionlessly.

Derrick: "No. I think the Heroes Guild may suspect I'm trying to expose them. So, they have concocted a Cockatrice and Minotaur[1472] story that I'm building an unholy army to unleash upon the realm!"

Me: "Why would they do that?"

Derrick: "Why do you think? Ask yourself, what do they gain by sending *every* adventurer in the realm to my crypt?"

Me: "*Erm...* they're hoping... that one of them... will eventually vanquish you?"

Derrick: "Precisely!"

The ersatz Warlock drops to his knees and clasps his gauntleted hands in mock prayer.

Derrick: **"PLEASE, LOREMASTER! I'M RUNNING OUT OF TIME! I CAN'T TAKE ANOTHER NIGHT WITH THESE FOUL GOBLINS, STINKING FLATULENCE, _AND_ THEIR CONSTANT NEED TO PRACTICE ARCHERY IN THE DARK—"**

Tears fill the pale man's eyes.

Me: "I—I will... I'll try and do my best to help you..."

Derrick: "*T—Thank you!* **THANK YOU!!** You don't know what it means to hear you say that."

[1472] *The Cockatrice and Minotaur story is a legendary tale about two mythical beasts who were close friends—but betrayed one another after arguing over dungeon wandering rights. Consequently, the Minotaur and his ball of twine were turned to stone, while the Cockatrice was forever lost in a Maze without hope of escaping. There's a moral to this story somewhere, but not even the Great Unwashed Oracle, Columbow could unravel it...*

My ears detect the sound of running footsteps coming from deeper within the crypt—the made-up Warlock Lich quickly gathers to his feet and picks up his dark helm off the stone floor.

Goblin: "*Boss?*"[1473]

Derrick: "*YUP—JUST GIVE ME A MOMENT!*"

The Goblin cowers in fear and slinks away as Derrick quickly wipes his eyes with the hem of his cloak before replacing his iron skull.

Derrick: "Well, back to work. I'm counting on you to do this, Loremaster... we all are."

I nod and instinctively go to shake the former Warlock Lich's hand.

Derrick: "*Ah*—forgive me if I don't..."

I curse myself for a moment of stupidity.

Derrick: "No harm done—*this* time. One last thing, I suggest we don't meet again—the Heroes Guild has spies everywhere."

I watch as the imitation Warlock Lich turns and disappears into the darkness. I'm not sure what to make of this revelation—perhaps I have been told the cold truth about the Heroes Guild, or maybe this is just a clever ploy to discredit the Heroes Guild by a Warlock Lich who really is a Warlock Lich. A sudden growl in the distance snaps my attention back to the now.

Me: "*H—Hello?*"

The faux Warlock Lich calls out from the darkness.

Derrick: "You'll have to forgive me, but it's probably not a good look if I simply *allow* you to walk out of this crypt unharmed. I must continue the ruse for now, you do understand—it's nothing personal..."

Me: "*Erm—?*"

Derrick: "I'll tell you what, I'll count to ten before releasing the undead cat—does that seem fair to you?[1474] Okay... *one... two—*"

[1473] *Obviously 'this' Goblin didn't read the fake Warlock Lich's memo about staying away...*

[1474] *I guess you can't steal the life from an undead cat!*

I don't hear a *three* because I'm already on my way, hurrying past the spot where my brother died, before bolting for the exit and relative safety beyond.

40. Toldarn, the Heroes Guild Guildmaster

I can say with near certainty the following interview will be one of the most intimidating I've ever attended.[1475] I find my usual optimism diminishing under the intense glare of the stern-looking Dwarf sitting opposite me. His face is a smoking battlefield, etched with the scars of every near-death he has experienced.[1476] This is Toldarn, the highest-ranking Guildmaster found within the Heroes Guild—an imposing Dwarf who mysteriously requested a private audience with me.[1477] I'm trying my best to remain calm, knowing that any weakness, any sign of fear, could potentially have mortal consequences for this particular Loremaster.

Toldarn has regarded me in silence for the past five minutes; who knows what unstable emotion is fermenting under his uncommunicative mask. I feel myself subconsciously trying to read into his posture, examining his calloused hands for any clue of his intent. Examining the heavy ornate ring on his finger—his sign of power. Nothing is welcoming about this Dwarf; even the black eye he's sporting feels like an omen of the animosity he must hold towards me. I finally muster the courage to speak—but the Guildmaster slices through my words like an unsteady Beardsmith's cutthroat.

Toldarn: "Loremaster Elburn, it's a *pleasure* to finally meet you..."

Me: "How did you know my n—?"

Toldarn: "I make it my business to know any and all matters where the Heroes Guild is concerned—*and* if necessary, take the appropriate action."

[1475] *Even more so than my recent meeting with Derrick (maybe he is or maybe he isn't), the Warlock Lich...*

[1476] *This information comes third-hand from a drunk Cleric I met in the local tavern—Toldarn's scars could be the result of an unfortunate meeting with the realm's worst Beardsmith, for all I know.*

[1477] *Although perhaps 'requested' is putting it mildly, a giant Enforcer 'encouraged' me to visit Toldarn moments after stepping out of The Spit & Spear Tavern. The muscle-mountain placed a sizeable cold hand around my neck and escorted me to where I now find myself currently sitting.*

I glance behind at the heavily armoured muscle-mountain barring the only way out of the Guildmaster's room.[1478]

Me: "By that, you mean your Enforcers, I assume?"

Toldarn: "It pays to have a strong arm, Loremaster."[1479]

Me: "For when you need to pry a Barbarian's fortune out of his castle?"

I notice a slight sneer curl from the corner of the Guildmaster's mouth.

Toldarn: "*Ahhh,* I see you know about our short-tempered friend. It seems Dorn took his expulsion from the Heroes Guild rather badly. Shame really—he had so much potential."

Me: "Can I ask what happened between you both?"

Toldarn: "It's quite simple, we discovered he had been less than honest with us."

Me: "He lied to you?"

Toldarn: "He claimed he came from coin and that his family held a significant amount of land. He was perhaps more than a little generous with the truth—and his estate was considerably smaller upon closer inspection."[1480]

Me: "Why do you think he did it?"

Toldarn: "Some are born liars, others just can't help themselves—they chase a fool's dream of adventuring and will say or do anything to be a hero in their own lifetime. On reflection, Dorn was no different—he desperately yearned for something he was never destined for. When we realised the extent of his deception, we had little choice but to rescind his membership with our Guild with immediate effect."

Me: "I think that's a little harsh. Having met Dorn several times, I wouldn't say he was a fool or a malicious liar. So, he inflated his

---

[1478] *The same muscle-mountain that moved me here...*

[1479] *Although two strong arms are undeniably better than one...*

[1480] *Remember, it's not the size of one's estate—but what you erect upon it.*

credentials on some past paperwork—haven't we all oversold ourselves at some point in our lifetime?"[1481]

Toldarn: "That matters not—a lie is a lie."

Me: "But can a lie not sometimes be a close bedfellow of truth?"

Toldarn: Truth? *Bah,* Dorn can't *handle* the truth. If Truth-Handler were an adventuring class, he'd be bottom of the dung heap."

Me: "But he *is* a hero to so many!"

Toldarn: "<u>That</u> is irrelevant—Dorn will no longer be regarded as a hero in name nor by any past, present, or future actions here within these Guild's halls."[1482]

Me: "But wasn't he the most successful hero to rise through your ranks?"

Toldarn: "*Aye,* I admit he was hugely fruitful as an adventurer[1483]—and it is not a decision the Guild have reached lightly, but, truth be told, he had become a problem for us."

Me: "A problem? How?"

Toldarn: "Dorn was completing far too many quests far too quickly."

Me: "Wait—aren't *all* quests supposed to be completed with great haste? In some instances, the realm's survival <u>depends</u> upon a speedy resolution."

Toldarn: "Yes and no. It really rests on *who* is attempting the quest in the first place. Some of our heroes need to spend more time in the field to earn their experience rather than speed-running through to a

---

[1481] *I admit I have once or twice oversold myself to curry favour with a quill and parchment Merchant to gain a hefty discount (don't judge me, Soul Squid ink does not come cheap!).*

[1482] *Nor within the halls of the Heartenford Museum... or what's left of it.*

[1483] *I'm now unsure how the Heroes Guild measures a hero's success. Is it the number of quests completed, the amount of coin earned or the number of Goblins slaughtered—who knows?*

dungeon's end.[1484] There is a natural balance to the adventuring world, with heroes on one side and quests on the other. Our job is to ensure both adventurer and quest are aligned perfectly—we can't have strong heroes taking on weaker quests, and likewise, we cannot have weak heroes taking on stronger quests. But with so many '*unofficial*' heroes out there, the scales of balance have been shifted—we have seen a noticeable decline in available adventures. Now *everyone* feels they have the right to take on *any* quest they see fit—<u>that</u> is a big problem."

The Guildmaster lets out a deep sigh and sits back in his seat.

Toldarn: "It's all about supply and demand in our game—there are just too many adventurers kicking their heels and fighting amongst themselves for whatever scraps come their way. It's been financially devastating for us; running the Heroes Guild does not come without a sizeable burden placed upon our coffers. We have made the tough decision to cut back on our numbers to maintain the equilibrium. But heroes never want to go quietly—they always take it badly when it's their head on the executioner's block."

Me: "So, Dorn was one of those who did not want to go quietly?"

Toldarn: "I can't blame him—but regardless of what adventure we gave him, he always returned far too quickly, unscathed and eager for the next one. In any other circumstance, he would have become a *legend* amongst his peers—but instead, his actions have enabled this Quest Drought. To speak plainly, Dorn was literally sucking the coin out of our coffers, and something <u>had</u> to be done."[1485]

Me: "You mean he was too good at his job?"

Toldarn: "To start with, even <u>I</u> had to admit his results were quite impressive. But once the Tallymen did their calculations, they quickly realised that left unchecked, Dorn would cause irreparable long-term

---

[1484] '*Speed-running*' has become hugely popular amongst the Wizard and Cleric classes. Rumour is they ply themselves with numerous Potions of Haste and wear as many Boots, Helms, and Socks of Speed as possible to complete an adventure before the first encountered Goblin has the chance to fire a wayward arrow into the ceiling.

[1485] I doubt he was '*literally*' sucking the coin out of the Heroes Guild vaults, not unless he was really a 'Coin-Lurker' in disguise (Which is a precious-metal-hungry critter that enjoys sucking down piles of coin). It may come as no surprise to learn that Coin-Lurkers are a frequent thorn in the side of Clerics who have an overflowing collection box hidden about their person.

damage to the Heroes Guild."

Me: "Surely your cut from Dorn's successes would have been substantial? I've even sat on the wealth Dorn accrued. I know how much you would have earned…"

Toldarn: "Even the coin from Dorn's completed quests wouldn't have kept us from falling into financial ruin. We need heroes to fail as well as succeed. Dorn was simply making it impossible for that to happen."

Me: "And I suppose you had to find a way to get rid of him—I mean, it wasn't likely he would fall mid-quest…"

Toldarn: "Dorn's falsification of his estate gave us the perfect opportunity to act."

Me: "Perfect *excuse,* you mean."

Toldarn: "Your words, Loremaster, not mine—look, we tried everything to discourage Dorn from completing his quests so fast. We kept the richest, most lucrative adventures from him, deliberately leaving the poorer ones free for the Barbarian to attempt at his leisure. But Dorn didn't take the bait—he somehow kept turning up and completing our highly prized quests too. We even employed our Enforcers to patrol the quest areas to keep him at bay—but it was to no avail; he just beat them into submission without breaking into a sweat. I seriously underestimated how formidable a hero he had become."

Me: "Were these the same Enforcers who turned up at Dorn's castle?"

Toldarn: "Yes—we lost twelve good men that day. Men that left behind grieving wives and sobbing children.[1486] Merrick there, standing behind you, lost three of his brothers."[1487]

Me: "I—I'm sorry for his loss—I recently learned how it feels to lose a brother. I feel your pain, Merrick."

The Enforcer growls at me in reply, wearing a look that suggests if I carry on talking to him, I <u>really</u> will feel his pain—courtesy of his fists.

[1486] *And possibly a few lamenting Barmaids on the side too…*

[1487] *I can almost hear my father's chiding words, 'to lose one brother is unfortunate—to lose three is just plain stupid'…*

Toldarn: "It was a regrettable incident—one I gravely miscalculated. Their deaths will forever haunt me."

Me: "And what of Dorn himself?"

Toldarn: "Missing—but we will find him <u>and</u> his errant coin."

Me: "What did you expect? Dorn was protecting what he had risked life and limb to earn. Surely you can see why he took up arms to defend himself?"

The Dwarf clenches his jaw; I sense the Guildmaster is fast running out of patience with me. He stands to unroll a realm map and throws it across his desk. The Dwarf taps one of the quests marked on the landscape. I look into the Guildmaster's eyes—including the one still black and puffy where it had been on the wrong end of an angry fist.

Toldarn: "Look at this map. Do you see how many adventures and quests are marked? Impressive—no? Last summer, it was **twice** that number..."

Me: "What happened?"

Toldarn: "What do you <u>think</u> happened?! <u>Dorn</u> happened! The Heroes Guild survives on two absolutes—some heroes <u>will</u> live while others <u>will</u> die. The loss of our members is inevitable. That's where the '*Death in Service*' clause comes in handy—"

Me: "Wait a minute—you *wanted* Dorn to die?"

Toldarn: "All our members understand and accept that not every hero with a silver badge makes it out of a dungeon alive. Those who fall are often a stepping-stone in the development of the golden stars who rise. Legends are built on the foundations of their fallen brothers and sisters."

Me: "So, you <u>need</u> heroes to die so you can lay claim to their estate in the event of their death..."

Toldarn: "It's not cheap retrieving a fallen hero from a dangerous quest. So, yes, the '*Death in Service*' clause covers all post-death expenses if the unfortunate <u>should</u> occur mid-adventure."

Me: "Even the ones you have helped create?"

The Guildmaster's eyes momentarily flick to the Enforcer standing behind me.

Toldarn: "My, my—whom *have* you been talking to?"

Me: "People."

Toldarn: "Don't be coy, Loremaster; you're amongst friends[1488]—give me a name."

Me: "I'd rather not reveal my source."

The Dwarf regards me for what seems like an age—but in truth, it's only about the same amount of time it would take for the Enforcer to quickly and quietly snap my neck. Fortunately, the muscle-mountain remains standing stoically at the door—although I can feel the heat from his glaring eyeballs burning a small hole in the back of my neck.[1489] The Guildmaster absentmindedly twiddles with a heavy ornate ring on his finger, a ring that could easily have been given to him by a Wizard on the coast.

Toldarn: "You, out of all of us, know that you cannot trust everything you hear. The Heroes Guild has many enemies—your own endeavours could be fuelling this false narrative they seek to push, creating a picture of disharmony and dishonesty that would tarnish our good name."

Me: "So, you're saying you're <u>not</u> creating quests, *nor* employing Evildoers?"

The Guildmaster belly laughs at my words as he continues to fiddle with his ring of power.

Toldarn: "Evildoers and quests? Someone has been feeding you a line, Loremaster—and like a Gullible fish, you have taken the bait."[1490]

[1488] *That's not how you spell 'fiends'...*

[1489] *No doubt, a future Paladin in the making—one with an unholy love of neck-snapping...*

[1490] *A Gullible fish is a fish common to the shallows of the Dauntless Sea. As its name suggests, it is one of the easiest fish to catch—and can often be persuaded to leap out of the ocean, straight into a sizzling frying pan sitting on a roaring fire with nothing more than the promise of a hook-free life.*

Me: "Fair enough—but you <u>are</u> taking fortunes and estates from your deceased members. Why the need for a '*Death in Service*' clause? Why not just take a bigger cut from your heroes and let their family keep their assets? Dorn had amassed a haul of coin that would make a Gold Dragon break out in a cold sweat."[1491]

Toldarn: "That would only cause more consternation amongst our heroes—they already feel our cut is deep enough; to ask for more would be to risk unrest. Need I remind you, we are also competing against non-Guilders, those who pay nothing for the privilege of adventure; that means the Heroes Guild needs to handle things carefully to ensure our members feel well looked after. We have found that most heroes are more than happy giving up their family's estate rather than handing over a larger slice of their hard-earned coin. As for Dorn's riches, he took his spoils with him when he disappeared..."

Me: "That's quite a feat considering its size—not to mention rather inconvenient for your Guild given the amount lost."

The Guildmaster sits back in his chair and smiles at me; the prolonged silence is arduous to endure. Finally, he sits forward to speak once more.

Toldarn: "Dorn can and will spend his riches as he pleases. He can fritter it away on the finest wines, ales, or pleasures of the flesh.[1492] He can buy the most *extravagant* clothes from Pippo the Clothesmith or the *mightiest* weapon from the Forgemaster, Thorde Ironstein—and he can do so with our blessing. Do you want to know *why?* Because *all* that coin is fated to find its way back into our coffers one way or another."

Me: "Yet you still consider Dorn a thorn in the Heroes Guild side?"

Toldarn: "He will be dealt with in time. Our main focus now is sharing the remaining quests we have left between our active heroes so we can slowly rebuild the coin Dorn has inadvertently taken from us with his adventuring exploits..."

[1491] *Gold Dragons are the most kleptomaniacal of all fantastic creatures in the realm (even more so than Elven Sorceresses); they're also die-hard completists who are hungry for every coin of every denomination of every race that has ever been minted. Maybe they like putting them into a coin book collection for the other Dragons to pore over with envy... or scorn. As you can imagine, Gold Dragons do not play well with Coin-Lurkers...*

[1492] *To a Barbarian, this means eating as much hog roast as possible until they pass out.*

Me: "I cannot believe the Heroes Guild is only motivated by wealth—"

There's another wry smile on the Guildmaster's face—something I've *missed*... something on the map... something under the surface of what's already there—I don't know. I stare again at the chart spread out over the desk, following the contours of the land with my eyes, tracing each territory's borders, and noting the principalities shaded to identify each specific ruler. A moment of clarity finds a gap through the fog of my confusion.

Me: "But this <u>isn't</u> about wealth—*is it*... coin comes and goes easily within the Heroes Guild, and as you say, it will *all* come back to you eventually—especially when you have the realm's Forgemasters, Landlords, and Merchants lining your pocket. This is a power grab— you're after your <u>own</u> territory. You're taking principalities not with sword and shield but by the quill and parchment."

The Dwarf continues to stare, letting me stew in the juices of my own rationale.

Toldarn: "Principalities are *not* worth our time."

Me: "No, you're right... principalities *aren't* worth your time—they have boundaries and neighbours who need to be treated with respect. You don't want a principality—you want the **<u>entire</u>** realm..."

The Guildmaster says nothing for a moment, as he continues to stare at me while spinning the heavy ornate ring on his finger with his thumb.

Toldarn: "That's an interesting theory you have there—probably a result of an overactive imagination. I can assure you our <u>only</u> motivation is the creation of the best heroes this realm has *ever* seen—"

Me: "Maybe that's how it looks on the outside. But in reality, you have all these heroes on your books who collectively hold small amounts of land around the realm—every ill-fated quest is placing more and more of their territory under your control."[1493]

Toldarn: "Let's entertain this fantasy a little longer—do go on..."

[1493] *Suddenly all these tiny pieces are beginning to fall into place. I feel like the Great Unwashed Oracle, Columbow—who always wore the same robes regardless of the occasion and ended every prophecy with the infamous words: 'There's just one more thing...'*

Me: "This '*Dark Power*' in the south that is supposedly rising? I believe there is no Warlock Lich. I believe the unholy creature is nothing more than a former Paladin *forced* to become an Evildoer by your Guild to do your bidding. He's not the only one—I suspect there are others, like the Dragon Lord you had to replace after you discovered he was loaning Dragons out on the side[1494]—"

Toldarn: "That's quite a revelation—do you have any evidence to back this up?"

Me: "*Well*—I know where the Warlock Lich's dungeon is, for starters."

Toldarn: "Bravo—but you'll find it's *actually* a crypt."

Me: "Excuse me?"

Toldarn: "I think you meant to say it's a crypt—or at least, it *was* a crypt; if you were to revisit it again, I'm sure you'd be pleased to discover it has been cleared of its unholy residents; they are mercifully no longer a threat to the good people of this realm."

My eyes widen in shock.

Me: "You—"

The Dwarf smiles wickedly.

Toldarn: "Before you make a fool of yourself, we had nothing to do with it—seems a non-Guild adventurer entered the crypt and successfully cleared it out—maybe it was our favourite 'Barbarian' doing the Heroes Guild an *unexpected* favour."

Me: What happened to the Goblins and the Warlock Lich who resided there?"

Toldarn: "Permanently removed, I suspect. *Which* reminds me—"

The Dwarf scratches out the crypt's name on the map with a black-inked quill.

Me: "Very convenient."

[1494] *It's like I've been possessed by the spirit of the Great Unwashed Oracle, Columbow! I also feel the hairs on the back of my neck standing up—almost as if they can sense the Enforcer behind me, sizing my neck up for an extremely tight 'fitting'.*

Toldarn: "Luck more like.[1495] Whoever it was, they kindly dealt with a danger that threatened the entire realm—I have it under good authority that the Warlock Lich was calling Goblins down from the Halgorn Crags to raise a huge army."[1496]

Me: "That is not true—he told me he just wanted his nightmare to end and be released from his torment—"

Toldarn: "*Ah,* so the plot thickens! So, you actually *spoke* to him... well, I'm sure the Warlock Lich was given the quick release he so desperately yearned for."

Me: "You heartless bast—!"

Toldarn: "Please—you do not need a heart to run this place, Loremaster... you need a brain and balls of steel..."[1497]

Me: "This *isn't* a Heroes Guild—it's a Guild of Lies.[1498] You're pulling the wool over the eyes of the entire realm!"

The Dwarf ignores my anger as he sits and unrolls a scroll next to him.

Toldarn: "I heard *Aldon* was a former hero—"

The sudden mention of my brother's name steals the wind from my sails.[1499]

Me: "My *brother...?*"

The Guildmaster picks up the scroll and quickly scans its contents.

Toldarn: "It says here he fell attempting an adventure."

[1495] *The kind of luck that <u>only</u> comes out of a bottle.*

[1496] *As most of them were armed with bows, I doubt there was little chance this Goblin army would do much harm to anyone but themselves or a nearby Treant minding its own business.*

[1497] *I've heard so much about this exotic weapon—I must ask Thorde Ironstein to show me his (if he has any hanging around, of course).*

[1498] *Admittedly, that's less catchy than the name they already have.*

[1499] *The words rock me like a Pirate who just drank several barrels of Yo-Ho-Blow rum and quickly followed it up by singing a rather jolly shanty...*

Me: "Y—Yes, it was a Fireball..."[1500]

Toldarn: "Unfortunate... I'm sorry for your loss; truly, I am. Had he been a member of the Heroes Guild, he would *undoubtedly* still have been with us—"[1501]

A hot flash of anger and pain crosses my brow. I sense the Enforcer behind me, tightening his imaginary grip around my neck.

Me: "Forgive me, but I doubt he would have willingly joined a Guild like this."

Toldarn: "Perhaps, but at least if he had, we would have given Aldon a quest that suited his experience level, rather than allowing him to attempt a quest that robbed him of his life so easily—"

I can feel the anger rising from the pit of my stomach, the acrid taste of bile in my mouth as I clench and unclench my fists.

Me: "Please... don't **ever** mention my brother's name again."

The Guildmaster finally ceases tinkering with his ring and leans forward menacingly.

Toldarn: "The pain you carry is clouding your judgement, Loremaster—creating ghosts and conspiracies where there are none. You have manifested this fantastic scenario to mask your own guilt of being less of a brother than Aldon deserved."

Me: "It seems *pain* is a familiar friend to you..."

The Guildmaster touches his black eye and smirks.

Toldarn: "This? *This thing?* It wasn't painful—it was business. It's always just business. It's never personal. But I will make exceptions for those who continue to be a thorn in this Guild's side."[1502]

[1500] *Technically, it was a Fireball, but it wasn't the Fireball's fault; it was only doing what it was created to do; if anyone is to blame, then it's the Wizard who cast the infernal spell in the first place. Seriously—who chooses to cast a Fireball in a ten-foot square room anyway? You know what, don't answer that.*

[1501] *Obviously, my family's estate isn't worth that much to the Heroes Guild...*

[1502] *Barbarians and Loremasters alike...*

Me: "Is that a threat?"

Toldarn: "This personal quest of yours is at an end, Loremaster—go home, be with your family. Leave this world of heroes far behind and forget all you have spoken to."

Me: "And if I don't?"

The Guildmaster's features darken as he leans closer to me.

Toldarn: "There are many inside the walls of this Guild who can cause you untold misery and suffering—but I *need* only one."

Me: "Merrick?"

Toldarn: "No you fool—*Arin Darkblade!*"

Me: "Arin Darkblade? I heard he retired—he is now nothing more than a glorified parchment-pusher."[1503]

Toldarn: "He has indeed stepped back from day-to-day adventuring, but he is as dangerous as ever. I believe his retirement made him even hungrier for action. I'd imagine he would relish an opportunity to meet you in person..."

Me: "I do not bow to threats."

The Guildmaster's eyes fall on the bag hanging from my shoulder.

Toldarn: "I know you keep a journal with you."

I instinctively clutch it tighter to my body.

Me: "You cannot take it—"

The Guildmaster raises his hands defensively.

Toldarn: "Why do you recoil? I am no thief![1504] I never said I wanted it, did I? But let me ask you this—what do <u>you</u> intend to do with it once it is finished?"

[1503] *Who has nothing left but to spend his days raiding the supplies desk for a treasure trove of quills, parchments, and Soul Squid ink...*

[1504] *By the look of him, I'm positive the Dwarf would say differently if this were one of the many Rings of Power in circulation rather than an ordinary-looking journal...*

Me: "*This?* I—It's for my parents. Initially, I wanted to chart my adventures for other reasons. Then when I discovered my brother, their son, had died—I realised I could use it to honour his memory for them. This journal is a way for my parents to find closure."

The Guildmaster sits back in his chair and smiles, his arms held wide as if granting me back my freedom.

Toldarn: "Then go home, take your journal, and bring an end to your questing. You have what you need, the answers you seek. But do not prod the Hydra's nest any more than you already have—you do understand what I'm saying—*don't you, Loremaster?*"

Me: "And if I don't?"[1505]

The Guildmaster points to my clothes.

Toldarn: "Then I fear the realm will lose another Wizard mid-quest."[1506]

There's an awkward silence as we stare intently at one another.

Toldarn: "Was there anything else you wanted to know?"

My mind flashes to the conversation I recently had with Gaudron, but I resist the urge to ask the Guildmaster just *one* more thing...

Me: "I think I have everything I need, thank you."

The Dwarf nods in agreement.

Toldarn: "Then I wish you safe travels, Loremaster Elburn—may your journey home be swift and free from physical and lasting harm."

The Dwarf holds his hand out for me to shake; I refuse to take it, preferring instead to turn on my heels and walk straight out past the snarling features of Merrick, the Enforcer. I don't know if the Heroes Guild will follow through with their threats against me—but for now, I had best be on my guard.[1507]

[1505] *I meant the prodding of the Hydra's nest bit, not the understanding or not understanding bit—you understand?*

[1506] *What Wiz—? Oh, very funny...*

[1507] *Meaning I will be sleeping with my Lucky Potion under my pillow from now on!*

41. Enolin, the Curse Keeper

The rain hammers on the poorly maintained roof tiles above my head, which are failing to stop the odd drop from trickling through. There's a scraping of wood on stone as a bucket is hastily deposited to catch the next drip before it splashes on the red flagstone floor. I'm standing in a gloomy shop, admiring a plethora of exotic paraphernalia that adorns the wooden shelves and wall displays; I can't help but notice each curious object has a handwritten tag hanging from it.[1508] A new drop of water bounces off my ear and onto my shoulder; rough hands suddenly shove my hips aside as a second bucket lands on the floor where I stood only moments ago. Officially speaking, Enolin Grey is a Gnomish 'Evaluator', an appraiser of magical items, but I've been told she prefers to be referred to as a 'Curse Keeper'—Enolin also has a leaky roof, which she refuses to repair.

The gaily-attired Gnome waits as she checks her ceiling for any new leaks. Satisfied her growing bucket army is capturing all the watery invaders, she shuffles back behind a low counter tailored to her diminutive size and smiles a knowing smile.

Enolin: "Forgive my directness, but I have to act fast when it rains or risk the water reaching one of my many magical artefacts."

Me: "Is that much of a problem?"

Enolin: "That all depends on the artefact in question."[1509]

Me: "Why not simply fix the roof?"

Enolin: "Do you know how much I've spent on that roof? *Too much!* I'm not wasting another coin on it until I'm convinced it needs replacing."

Me: "Judging by the numerous leaks, I'd say that time has come—"

[1508] *Worryingly, each tag appears to have a number of stars etched onto it—from what I understand, the more stars an item has, the worse the curse held inside the damned object is.*

[1509] *(See footnote 1513…)*

Enolin: "*This?* This is nothing—it would take a tsunami to get me to call in a reputable Roofsmith."[1510]

Me: "Let's hope it doesn't come to that—I can't swim."

My eyes are drawn towards a smooth white wand on display—the tip glows with a steady pulse.[1511] My hand reaches out to touch the ornate lightning bolt carved into the handle when the Gnome suddenly shouts a warning to—

Enolin: "**STOP!**"

I freeze on the spot—almost as if I'm a Gremlin caught in the act of sabotage.

Enolin: "It would be unwise to touch a cursed Lightning Wand while standing in a pool of water."[1512]

I look down and lift a boot. Sure enough, there's a small puddle beneath my feet.

Me: "Why—what would happen?"

Enolin: "**ZAP!**"[1513]

The Gnome abruptly claps her hands, scaring the life out of me.[1514]

Enolin: "You'd be gone in a flash! That wand has a love-hate relationship with water—trust me, you *really* don't want to come between them."

[1510] *Roofsmiths are infamous labourers who are notoriously evasive when asked to cost up a job. They're also well known for taking on a task, demanding payment upfront, and never turning up to work—as a result, Roofsmiths are often called the 'Thieves of the Tiles'. So, as you can imagine, finding a 'reputable' one is a Category Five quest all of its own.*

[1511] *It also has five ominous little stars scribed onto the tag—so I'd best have my wits about me.*

[1512] *Maybe this particular wand has a somewhat cantankerous personality and takes umbrage at anyone leaving wet footprints everywhere.*

[1513] *(See footnote 1509...)*

[1514] *Well, at the very least, temporarily deafening me...*

I recoil at the thought as I step out of the puddle and carefully move a safe distance away from the irritable **BOOM**-stick.

Me: "Perhaps it's wiser to keep such an item in a glass case?"[1515]

Enolin: "Why?"

Me: "Because it's dangerous!?"

The Curse Keeper laughs at the naivety of my comment.

Enolin: "My dear boy, *everything* in this place could probably kill if you let it."

I glance around at the cursed objects in the shop, feeling as though each of them is trying to reach out and vaporise my being in the blink of an eye. The Gnome notices my discomfort and tries to calm my nerves.

Enolin: "But nothing will hurt you while I'm here. Just breathe—try to relax..."

I nod in the direction of the five star-tagged wand.

Me: "I also guess using that lightning wand in the rain would be a bad idea?"[1516]

Enolin: "<u>Fatally</u> bad—but then it wouldn't be much of a curse if it wasn't."

Me: "Funny, it doesn't look cursed."[1517]

Enolin: "That's the beauty of curses. You never know they're there until it's too late—if a cursed object <u>looked</u> like a cursed object, you wouldn't dare pick it up in the first place, would you?"

[1515] *I feel I may be shouting this question a little too loudly.*

[1516] *I was later told by a badly scorched Wizard that, cursed or not, it's NEVER a good idea to use a Wand of Lightning Bolts when it's raining outside... **or** when standing under a tree... **or** standing next to someone wearing metal armour...*

[1517] *I'm not exactly sure what to expect from a cursed object—I guess I imagined something eviler looking.*

Me: "I suppose not; there does seem to be a sizeable risk attached to these unstable artefacts—why do you deal in them? Why not sell something less perilous?"[1518]

Enolin: "Where's the fun in that? Honestly, who needs another Merchant selling poorly crafted weapons that snap on the first swing, armour with inbuilt design flaws,[1519] or threadbare clothes that wouldn't keep a beggar warm? I've always believed there's good coin to be made out of bad curses."

Me: "But who would want a cursed item?"

The Curse Keeper taps her nose and winks.

Enolin: "Who indeed—ask yourself this, who would want an item that could potentially kill or, at the very least, make life exceedingly difficult for any unsuspecting hero who stumbled upon it?"

Me: "*Ah,* I don't know—*Evildoers* maybe?"

Enolin: "There you go—you got it on your first try. You're not so stupid after all!"

Me: "What? I was joking—do Evildoers *really* come in here to buy your wares?"

I look over my shoulder, half expecting a Warlock Lich to be there, browsing the aisles in a bid to find something slightly less cursed than a pair of life-sapping gauntlets.

Enolin: "That would be exceedingly reckless, not to mention potentially fatal—for the both of us. No, I offer an *Order & Delivery*™ service to any of my more treacherous patrons."

Me: "Order & Delivery?"

Enolin: "You forgot to say '™' after that…"

Me: "'™'?"

[1518] *Like quills, Soul Squid ink, and reams of blank parchment…*

[1519] *Such as plate armour with a small but highly vulnerable rear-exhaust port that a small-yet-determined Halfling Rogue Leader could exploit…*

Enolin: "Yup! I own the words 'Order & Delivery'—nobody else in the entire realm is allowed to mention that phrase without saying '™' after it."

Me: "So, if I say 'Order & Delivery'—"

Enolin: "—You have to '™' after it—yes."

The Gnome looks at me expectantly.

Me: "What happens if I *don't* say '™' at the end?"

The Curse Keeper pulls a face that can only be described as a mixture of disbelief and shock.[1520]

Enolin: "Then a Fair-Use Ogre will undoubtedly pay you a visit."

Me: "*Thump?*"

Enolin: "I'm sure the brute will hit you if you keep forgetting to say Order & Delivery's name correctly.[1521] I paid good coin for the Heralds to make this all official; I have the paperwork around here somewhere—so everyone can start **damn-well** saying it right."

The Gnome starts to dig through a large stack of papers under her counter.[1522] I try my best to steer the Curse Keeper back towards my original question.

Me: "S—So, what *is* Order & Delivery... *erm*...'™' exactly then?"

Enolin: "Good, you're a fast learner—Order & Delivery™ is a new business model I've invented; it's quite simple. I write down on a piece of parchment all the details of the magical wares I have on offer, together with a description of the curse and its star rating—then I leave it at the entrance of an Evildoer's domain. The following morning, I return to the same location and collect the parchment to see if they've circled any items they're interested in—*and*, more importantly, left any

---

[1520] *In keeping with the '™' theme currently being discussed with the Curse Keeper, I have taken the first two letters of 'Disbelief' and the last two letters of 'Shock' to create a new name for this unique facial expression I've just witnessed. Rest assured, I shall be '™'—ing this brand new gurn with the Heralds Guild at the earliest opportunity.*

[1521] *Wait a minute—shouldn't that be Order & Delivery™?*

[1522] *This is a tiny stack if we're talking in Tallyman sizes.*

coin in payment. I return the day after that and leave the purchased item they've requested in the same spot—the transaction is quite safe and profitable. Evildoers are all too willing to pay over the odds for a cursed item, which more than covers the expense and effort in the first place while *still* leaving enough profit for a slap-up meal at *The Hog & Roast* tavern too!"[1523]

Me: "Why do these Evildoers want cursed items? Don't they realise there's a hex on these wares? Isn't there a chance of serious harm if they try to use any of these items against an intruding adventurer?"

The Curse Keeper shakes her head.

Enolin: "They're not *using* them against the heroes—they're *giving* them away."

Me: "Giving them away—you mean for *free*?"

Enolin: "Yes, for free—okay, they're not personally handing them out; that would be foolish too.[1524] Instead, they leave the cursed item at a convenient spot for any unsuspecting hero to find and hopefully take."

Me: "So, an adventurer won't realise they're picking up a cursed item."

Enolin: "You are quite correct—unless there's a particularly shrewd Wizard in the party. Then there's always the chance they'll spot the accursed item for what it really is."[1525]

Me: "Does that happen much?"

Enolin: "From time to time, but the chances of that happening are pretty slim. Your average Wizard can barely dress themselves these days—no offence."

The Gnome gestures toward my magical-looking clothes.

Me: "*Huh?* Wha—? *Oh*—no, I'm not a Wizard, my other clothes were burnt... in... a... fire—"

[1523] *Ironically, The Hog & Roast is the only non-meat serving tavern in the realm; avoided by Barbarians and Dwarves everywhere...*

[1524] *Not to mention a bit weird...*

[1525] *That's when they're not incinerating the rest of a party in a dungeon room the size of a privy.*

Enolin: "—*ball* spell was it?"

The Curse Keeper winks and taps her nose again.

Enolin: "Say no more..."

Me: "What? No, it <u>wasn't</u> a Fireball; I can't even <u>cast</u> a spell! You have to believe me—I lost my clothes in a fire that <u>wasn't</u> of my own making!"

Enolin: "I'm just messing with you—you may look like a Wizard, but you sure don't *talk* like one. You don't have a crazy white beard, for starters."[1526]

Me: "That's because I'm a *Loremaster*."

Enolin: "*Ah*—<u>that</u> explains all the funny little questions."

Me: "Without having the expertise of a Wizard around, at what point would your average hero realise they own a cursed item?"[1527]

Enolin: "Some never do—they just carry on using their accursed object as if it's bad luck that's continually tripping them up.[1528] Others finally realise the truth only after they've fluffed their umpteenth attempt at whatever they're trying to do and start looking for answers. On the rare occasion or two, a smarter hero will notice something isn't quite right with their recently obtained sword or trinket."[1529]

Me: "Then what happens?"

[1526] *It's worth noting that the size of a Wizard's beard directly correlates to the size of that particular Wizard's spellbook. The bigger the beard, the more spells a Wizard will have in their magic tome. It's also worth mentioning that a Wizard should only ever have a white beard. If you meet a Wizard with a grey beard, you can safely assume they recently had it burnt by a wayward Fireball spell, while a Wizard with a black beard is a Warlock— regardless of what they say to the contrary.*

[1527] *An average hero like a Fighter—also referred to as the 'mediocre', 'vanilla', or 'yawn' class...*

[1528] *I feel the Gnome is talking about every magic item-carrying Barbarian and Cleric in existence.*

[1529] *Such as a longbow that keeps hitting the Cleric in the group no matter where they're hiding. Although, I suspect you could create a cursed infinite loop by giving the Cleric-hunting longbow to a Goblin and instructing them to fire an arrow at the Holy Warrior.*

Enolin: "Depends on the hero in question—some will spend all their time trying to find out exactly what the problem is. When they've exhausted all logical possibilities, some eventually point '*The Finger of Suspicion*' on the cursed item.[1530] The clever ones save themselves a lot of pain and heartache by seeking out my services. Others will blame the Rogue for all their misery."[1531]

Me: "If they're aware of it, why don't they simply try to get rid of the accursed item themselves? They could throw it away or leave it for some other unfortunate adventurer to stumble across?"

The Gnome sucks in a mouthful of air through her teeth in disbelief— almost creating a second unique facial *gurn* I'm tempted to '™'.

Enolin: "You *really* don't know how curses work, do you? Once it's attached to a hero, there's no easy way of getting rid of it. *Oh*, sure— you can throw the offending object away, of course. Or even try to destroy it[1532]—but it always comes back to the curse-bearer—and in perfect condition too."

Me: "How do heroes know to seek you out?"

Enolin: "Word of mouth—some Barker or another usually shouts directions toward my shop.[1533] As far as I know, I'm the only Merchant in the entire realm who specialises in cursed items. If the hero in question hasn't found some way to remove the cursed object themselves, then it's more than likely they'll turn up at my door, asking for my help."

Me: "By help, I guess you mean the removal of the offending curse—"

[1530] *'The Finger of Suspicion' is the gnarled mummified finger of a long-dead Necromancer that was turned into a novelty magic wand. When asked, the unholy wand has the unerring knack of uncurling and pointing at anyone or anything guilty of the specified crime. It's especially good at settling the 'who smelt it, dealt it' argument once and for all.*

[1531] *Which is also a valid assumption—especially in the 'Who denied it, supplied it' argument.*

[1532] *There have been reports of a foolish Halfling Rogue or two trying to throw a cursed Ring of Power into the fires of a volcano used to create it. As you can imagine, it didn't end well for the poor Rogues who found themselves trapped on a large boulder only to be devoured by a hungry Giant Eagle who happened to be flying past.*

[1533] *Either the heroes in question were standing really, really, really, close to the first Barker who held the correct information—or this never happened.*

There's a vigorous shake of the head from the Gnome.

Enolin: "*Oh,* no, no—I don't *remove* curses."

Me: "I don't understand; if you don't remove curses, then what <u>do</u> you do?"

Enolin: "I remove the cursed bond <u>between</u> the item and the hero carrying the cursed trinket—freeing them of the annoying object so they can continue adventuring unhindered."

Me: "I see, so they don't get to keep the accursed item them—I mean, it is technically theirs?"

Enolin: "You jest—do you think they <u>want</u> to carry around a cursed object all day? *No*—they'd rather pay through the nose for me to take the troublesome item off their hands."

Me: "They pay you *and* give you the cursed item to keep?"

Enolin: "Wonderful, isn't it? If you think about it, I make coin at both ends of this whole exchange. In addition, I get the cursed object back too—how perfect is that?"

Me: "It's an infinite cursed loop[1534]—that's clever!"

Enolin: "I *knew* that would impress you."

Me: "I'm curious; how can you tell if an item is actually cursed?"[1535]

There's a rattle from a drawer under the counter as the Curse Keeper fishes out a multi-lensed, multi-coloured seeing-device and places it on the bridge of her nose.

Enolin: "With these."

Me: "What are they? I—I mean, I know they're a seeing-device, but what do they do?"

[1534] *(See footnote #1509 and #1513) This is an example of a cursed loop admit it, you thought I had made a footnote error—didn't you!*

[1535] *Beyond the obvious clues—like your palms are suddenly very hairy or you've sprouted another head, which then tries to coerce you into asking an angry Barbarian about their 'Wheel of Lame'.*

The Gnome flicks several levers on the arm of the seeing-device—I watch in amazement as a different-coloured lens flips down before sliding in front of the Curse Keeper's eye.

Enolin: "Each one contains a magical essence that can detect the individual signature of a particular curse."

Me: "Individual signature? I thought a curse was just a curse—"

Enolin: "That's a common misconception. There are actually *hundreds* of curse types in existence—all sitting at a different point on the *Curse Spectrum*. They're invisible to the naked eye, but these—"

The Gnome taps the seeing-device on her nose reassuringly once more.

Enolin: "—let me pinpoint exactly where that curse sits on the *Curse Spectrum*—and that in turn tells me what type of curse I'm dealing with."

Me: "Can you show me how that works?"

Enolin: "Sure—"

There's a click as a blue lens flips into place.

Enolin: "This lens lets me see any curse that affects the average intelligence."[1536]

There's a second click as a blue lens slides away, and a red lens moves into its place.

Enolin: "This one can identify *transformative* curses. Those can be pretty amusing—especially when it affects a stuck-up Paladin and turns them into an ass with pointed ears."[1537]

A horrendous image of a foul-mouthed Redmane with big ears pops into my consciousness. I quickly banish it to the farthest corner of my mind, where I hope it remains forever.

Me: "Has that ever happened?"

The Curse Keeper chuckles to herself.

[1536] *Generally, curses such as this do not affect Barbarians.*

[1537] *Which is one of many Gnomish ways of saying 'Elf'...*

618

Enolin: "No—but I'm allowed to dream."

There's a third click as an orange lens flips into place.

Enolin: "And this one—"

There's a weird pause as she stares at my hands.

Me: "W—What? What is it?"

Enolin: "Give me your hand."

As I offer my right hand, I can't stop it from shaking with nervous anticipation.

The Gnome slaps it hard.

Enolin: "The *other* hand, you dolt!"

Me: "*Oh—*"

The Curse Keeper grabs my left hand and examines the ring on my finger[1538]—the same ring Simply Morgan gave me at the beginning of my journey.

Enolin: "Interesting, <u>very</u> interesting…"

Me: "W—What is it?"

The Gnome doesn't look up as she continues to pore over the ring in meticulous detail—studying all aspects of it from every angle possible.[1539]

Enolin: "Do you *always* wear a cursed ring?"

Me: "*What?!* **Cursed?!** I thought it was a Ring of Water Breathing?!"

In shock, I pull my hand away and try to yank the ring from my finger—it doesn't budge. A wave of panic grips me as I feel the world spinning away.

Me: ***WHY WON'T IT COME OFF?"***

Enolin: "Relax—"

[1538] *On my 'ring' finger, to be precise, unsurprisingly…*

[1539] *And a few angles my hand doesn't appreciate being put in.*

Me: **"RELAX!? YOU'RE NOT THE ONE WEARING A CURSED RING!"**

Enolin: "I mean, relax—it's not one of the bad curses... it could be worse, a <u>lot</u> worse."

Me: "How <u>bad</u> is *not bad?*"

Enolin: "It's a *Projection* Curse."

Me: "What's that?"

Enolin: "There are two main curse groups—"

Me: "Wait—I thought you said there were *hundreds* of curse types?"

Enolin: "I did—but they all sit within two main groups. Curses that affect the wearer; we call that an *Impact Curse.* Or there's a *Projection Curse* that affects others. What you have here is a *Projection Curse.*"[1540]

Me: "S—So, *how* does this ring affect others e—exactly?"

Enolin: "If you can keep still—I'll take a closer look and maybe get to the bottom of this for you."

Several more coloured lenses flip into place on her seeing-device, changing the colour of the Gnome's eyes from orange to purple.

Enolin: "*Ha!* This one actually *influences* them."

Me: "Influence how?"

Enolin: "I just need to modify the lens—give me a moment..."

A second, smaller orange lens slides across the purple lens, creating a russet hue.

Enolin: "Interesting, it appears this ring holds a *Curse of Parley!*"

Me: "What's that?"

Enolin: "Have you noticed how easy it has been to talk to <u>everyone</u> you've encountered—even those who don't *really* want to speak to you?"

[1540] *There's actually a third, lesser-known group—called the 'Blue Curse', which features a lot of swearing, nudity, and embarrassment for everyone involved.*

Me: "I—I thought that was just *me* being *me*—"

Enolin: "Sorry to break it to you—but it was the ring's doing, not your infectious personality."

I stare down at the silver ring on my finger.

Me: "That doesn't sound like much of a curse."

Enolin: "Really? What if you heard something you didn't want to hear? A secret that needed to remain buried—but the ring dug it out? The truth can hurt; sometimes it can be <u>fatal</u>."

Me: "So, it's <u>not</u> a Ring of Water Breathing?"

Enolin: "*Hmmm*—yes, it is, in theory."

Me: "In theory?"

Enolin: "Well, have you tried breathing underwater yet to see if it works?"

Me: "No—not yet anyway..."[1541]

I feel a flash of anger at the thought of myself wearing this cursed ring for so long.

Me: "That bloody Wizard!"[1542]

Enolin: "You want me to get rid of it for you? I can take it off your hands—well, your finger, for a nominal fee—"

I pull my hand away. The ring has been an ally in my quest for so long that I'm unsure if I'm ready to part with it just yet.[1543]

Me: "Thanks for the offer... but unless you can give me a good reason, I think I'd like to keep it for now."

Enolin: "Fair enough. Be warned, though, the curse will continue to influence others. If you're happy hearing the truth, whether you want

---

[1541] *And long may it remain that way!*

[1542] *I should be grateful it's not a Ring of Goblin Arrow Attraction, Fireballs Attraction, or even Goblin's Balls of Fire Arrow Attraction...*

[1543] *Even though it's cursed, it's still precious—<u>my</u> precious!*

to or not, then good luck to you. Remember, the ring <u>only</u> works on Humans, Half-Elves, Elves, and High-Elves, Dwarves, Halflings, Goblins and Half-Orcs."

Me: "But not Gnomes?"

Enolin: "We're naturally resistant."[1544]

Me: "You could have saved yourself time and just said it doesn't work on Gnomes."

Enolin: "I could have—but unluckily for you, I didn't. It also doesn't work if the person you're speaking to is wearing a *Dwarven Ring of Curse Immunity*—but there aren't many of those kicking around in the realm, thankfully. You *sure* you want to keep it?"

Me: "Yes, you never know; it might come in handy. It has gotten me this far. I may as well let it carry me through to the end."[1545]

Enolin: "No problem at all. You know where I am if you change your mind."

Me: "Thanks."

The Gnome seems distracted by something or someone behind me as she glances over my shoulder.

Enolin: "A friend of yours?"

Me: *"Huh?"*

I turn around, expecting to see someone standing behind me in the shop—but it's empty.

Enolin: "Across the street—there was someone watching you."

Me: "What did they look like?"

Enolin: "Human... tall, dark, grizzled..."

[1544] *I'm curious to know what natural immunity Gnomes have that affords them protection from Curses. Perhaps there's something to be said for growing up in caves and living off a diet of lichen and fungus, after all...*

[1545] *Hopefully, not the kind of 'end' that sees me inhabiting the grave plot Hagworl has kindly put to one side for me.*

Me: "Anything else?"

At this, the Gnome smiles slyly and places a hand over her right eye. A cold chill of fear shoots down my spine.

Me: "He was wearing an eye-patch!?"

Enolin: "He looked like a Pirate who had lost his frigate and didn't seem happy about it."[1546]

I look at the Gnome in desperation.

Me: "I have to get away—**far away!**"

Enolin: "I assume without being spotted?"

Me: "**Yes!** Can you help me?"

Enolin: "I might have something out back—*wait here.*"

The Curse Keeper pats my hand and hurries out of sight. I glance over my shoulder; the street outside is eerily empty of life. My heart thumps as I wonder whether the presence spotted by Enolin has taken their leave or if they are inching closer to where I stand, poised to strike? I hear the Gnome digging through piles of boxes somewhere deep in the recess of the backroom; I silently urge her to hurry.

Enolin: "*Aha*—here we go! This should do the trick."

The Curse Keeper returns with an ornate chalice. She grabs a water urn from the desk and pours some clear liquid into it, filling the cup to the brim.

Enolin: "This is supposed to give the user eternal life. But in reality it teleports them somewhere else."

Me: "Where?"

Enolin: "*Oh,* just *closer* to death—"

Me: "**To <u>WHAT</u>—?!** *HOW IS THAT BETTER?!*"

I glance over my shoulder—and stare straight at Arin Darkblade, standing on the other side of the shop window, his one good eye locked

---

[1546] *No doubt filled with 'Pieces of Hate'...*

on me.[1547] I quickly look back at the Gnome, cold fingers of fear closing around my heart, even as she blithely prattles on.

Enolin: "Not your *literal* death, that would be particularly unfortunate—but it <u>will</u> put you on your path towards your *eventual* death. But as everyone will die anyway, you have to ask yourself if that's really as bad as the present alternative?"[1548]

There's a creak as the door opens. Slow, thudding footsteps fill the anxious void; I daren't turn around—the Curse Keeper peers over my shoulder and smiles at the ominous figure I know is looming right behind me.

Enolin: *"Be with you in a minute."*

Dark Voice: **"I came for the Wizard—"**

I instinctively snatch the chalice from the Gnome and press it to my lips. The Curse Keeper's eyes widen in horror.

Enolin: ***"NO! DON'T DRINK IT <u>ALL</u>—"***

There's an immediate flash of light as my world slides away into whiteness.[1549]

[1547] *Perilous danger, Ahoy!*

[1548] *Better the Demon you <u>don't</u> know, I guess…*

[1549] *Is this the Great Beyond I've been told about? I hope it's not the Great Barrier—and definitely not the Great Behind; that would be awful!*

42. Gilva Flamebeard, the Cleric

The white swirling sensation stops abruptly as I find myself catapulted from the bleached abyss—and straight into another bleached abyss. A freezing wind hits me as I plough headfirst into a crisp blanket of snow; the Gnome's cursed chalice has fired me into the middle of nowhere! Enolin Grey's shop has completely vanished, but so mercifully has Arin Darkblade. Hope rises in my heart; not even the want-to-be-Pirate could track me to this unforgiving tundra. The Curse Keeper's chillingly prophetic last words echo through the blowing maelstrom: "it will put you on your path towards your eventual death".[1550] I frantically look around for any sign of life in this lonely expanse, but there is only ice and snow for as far as the eye can see. Part of me suspects the Gnome's prophecy is moments away from coming true—this place could be the last I ever see. The cold has already cut through what little warmth my robes can muster,[1551] and I can't feel the tips of my fingers or my toes.[1552]

I start to walk in one direction—but I become quickly disorientated. Before long, I find myself stepping in my own footprints once more. My situation is rapidly becoming desperate; I realise I'm doomed to perish here. All I can do now is pray for my death to be quick, but I curse as I remind myself that I am <u>still</u> not the religious type and no God would answer my plea.[1553] I can sense a familiar presence—my old friend, Death, is nearby as the driving snow forces me to the ground.[1554] I hug my body tightly and wait for the inevitable mortality knell to ring time on my life. But the absolute darkness does not slide over me—instead, a golden ray breaks through the snowy haze, singling me out in this

---

[1550] *If we're being precise, her last words were, "No! Don't drink it all—" but that doesn't make for a dramatic opening to this interview.*

[1551] *Oh, the irony, what I would give for a close shave with a Fireball spell right now, or even a Barbarian's well-worn fur loincloth.*

[1552] *As I can't feel with the tips of my fingers, it's highly unlikely that I'll be able to feel my toes with them either...*

[1553] *You'd think with all the Gods I have dismissed so readily, at least one would be chomping at the bit to prove my heathen soul wrong—I guess this just goes to show there is no such thing as Gods, or if there were, then they are really, <u>really</u>, sulky omnipresent beings.*

[1554] *Probably sitting there with an extremely hot cup of tea, enjoying the last few gasps of my life.*

deathly place.[1555] Warmth fills my heart, expelling the enduring chill that threatened to overwhelm my core. I look up to see a figure, silhouetted in the light—small yet stocky. I shield my eyes, trying to catch a glimpse of whomever this mysterious being is. Could I be delirious, imagining a messenger from the Gods welcoming me to whatever afterlife I never believed existed? Confused and panicked, I call out to this most welcome figure.

Me: "Who are you? Are you real? Am I dead?"

The silhouetted figure comes into view; I can see the features of a battle-hardened Dwarf dressed in wolf furs and holding a mighty warhammer in her grip.[1556]

Dwarf: "You're a long way from the Wizard's Guild, aren't you?"

Me: "H—Huh?"

Dwarf: "Your robes. They're not exactly the attire best for this weather—"[1557]

Me: "Oh, yes, I mean no—I'm no W—Wizard."

Dwarf: "Not a Wizard? You could have fooled me. Still, I guess a real Wizard would never let a Cleric save them. That is if you do want to be saved?"

Me: "I—I'm sorry, w—who are you? You're not a God, are you?"[1558]

The Cleric laughs as she holds out a gloved hand for me to take.

Dwarf: "A God? No, there is no God in this godforsaken place. Allow me to introduce myself; I'm Gilva Flamebeard—"

[1555] I take that back; they have answered my desperate calls! Praise be to the Gods—whichever benevolent one has decided to make a timely appearance!

[1556] Whoever it is, they're a little short for an all-powerful, omnipresent being—unless I'm about to discover that a hammer-wielding Dwarven God rules our realm (which would be unfortunate for me considering the amount of tongue-in-cheek comments I've peppered throughout these footnotes at their expense).

[1557] Oh great, it's a 'comedic' hammer-wielding Dwarven God—Uncle Bevan Barr would be rolling with laughter at this revelation.

[1558] A noted God-busting Warrior once observed that if someone asks you whether you're a God—you say YES!!

Me: "G—Gilva Flamebeard? I—I've heard of you—"

Gilva: "All good, I hope."

Me: "W—Where are w—we?"

Gilva: "Two days from Port Salvation, deep in the Western Peninsular—but you're in no fit state to make the journey just yet. Come on, put this on; my place isn't far from here."

The Dwarf unravels a heavy wolf-pelt from her backpack and throws it at me. I hastily wrap my freezing frame in the heavy fur, grateful for the warmth it provides.[1559]

Gilva: "Don't worry about the previous owner; they died quickly."[1560]

We walk the short distance to a pitched snow tent, built inside a glowing sphere of light, complete with a campfire and Ice Chicken slowly roasting on a spit[1561]—all seemingly immune to the raging snowstorm around it. The Dwarf catches me staring and gives me a nudge forward.

Gilva: "You going to gawp all day? Or do you want to get out of this cold?"

I nod and follow the Dwarf through the shimmering sphere into the warm interior. A strange aroma fills the air inside the Sanctuary, like a cat that's been at the local nip.[1562]

Me: "What is this place?"

The Cleric removes her fur gloves and kicks off her boots, letting her

---

[1559] Although it still smells of wet dog—but I don't want to look a gift...erm... wolf... in the mouth, which I can do given the wolf's surprised-looking head is still attached to the pelt.

[1560] Which explains the frozen surprised look on the wolf...

[1561] An extremely tough breed of bird, Ice Chickens are only found in the coldest and harshest of wastelands. Given they lay ice eggs on a near-daily basis, they have a reputation of having the warmest of posteriors and are often used by Halflings as gloves (while still alive).

[1562] 'Nip' is a Gnomish brew that's strangely moreish—best enjoyed with salted snacks while watching a Wizard and a Barbarian battle one another on the far side of the tavern.

bare feet breathe in the open air[1563]—seemingly unaffected by the cold snow underfoot.

Gilva: "It's my Sanctuary—a safe place that cannot be penetrated by the harsh elements outside, nor any opportunistic hostiles who happen to wander by."[1564]

Me: "That's handy—perks of being a Cleric, I suppose?"

Gilva: "Well, we have to grab what few advantages we have—it's not like you Wizards with your Fireball spells. Although, as strange as it may seem, a Fireball wouldn't be much use out here; it would fizzle out long before it had a chance to incinerate anything... it's too cold and too vast to be effective."[1565]

Me: "I'm not a Wizard!"[1566]

The Dwarf rubs her luscious red beard and eyes me with suspicion.

Gilva: "If you're not a Wizard, what are you then—a Rogue? Someone who steals Wizard robes for fun while running around pretending they can cast spells?"

Me: "They were given to me after my own clothes got... *erm*... lost..."

Gilva: "Lost?"

Me: "...in a fire..."

The Cleric points to my bag.

Gilva: "And I guess that's not a spellbook either?"

I look down in horror at the magical tome peeking like a rebellious

---

[1563] Or should that be 'bear' feet—given the Dwarf has extremely hairy ones? I've never met a barefooted Dwarf before, but I have heard how warm and cosy they can be from Balstaff the Merchant—especially this Dwarf in particular...

[1564] I need one of these to keep one certain Mr. A. Darkblade at bay...

[1565] Although, I'm pretty confident it would be useful for turning a hairy Cleric into an impromptu bonfire for a while...

[1566] I fear these words will be etched forever on my gravestone—that or an ominous Phoenix symbol.

'magical' Sorting Cap out of a Bag of Holding.[1567] I quickly bury the spellbook into the bag's depths and pull out my journal instead.

Me: "I'm a Loremaster—see, <u>this</u> is a journal of my travels; you can read it—"

Gilva: "Right, so you're a Loremaster who dresses like a Wizard but *isn't* a Wizard, who has a spellbook that's *not* a spellbook but a journal... who also appeared out of thin air in the most inhospitable of places—a bit *like* a Wizard..."

Me: "I know how this looks. I'm only here because of a cursed chalice... I—I was trying to escape someone... it teleported me here unexpectedly—I didn't know what it would do! You <u>have</u> to believe me; I'm <u>not</u> a Wizard!"

The Cleric chuckles as I flap like a Gullible fish that's just been convinced there's a shark after them, and their only chance of survival is to leap into a nearby sizzling frying pan.

Gilva: "Forgive me—the frozen wastes have skewed my sense of humour. It matters not if you are a Wizard or Loremaster to me. Who was it you were trying to escape?"

Me: "Arin Darkblade—you know of him?"

Gilva: "I've been out of the hero-loop for many summers now—but that name does strike a familiar chord. Perhaps he was one of the new recruits tasked with polishing my warhammer?"[1568]

Me: "I don't think Arin is the polishing type."

Gilva: "Well, regardless—he won't find you in this frozen wasteland."

Me: "*You* found me easily enough..."

Gilva: "I had some help from your teleportation spell—it left a faint trace of magic; a residue of essence that some can see—"

[1567] That 'had' been happily dozing but now wants to see what idiot had the gall to disturb it.

[1568] No doubt this will be a bitter disappointment to any Bard reading this, but to 'polish' one's warhammer is not a euphemism. New heroic recruits are expected to clean and polish the weapons belonging to seasoned adventurers on a near-daily basis (after signing a waiver in case of accidental and unexpected impaling, poisoning or disintegration).

Me: "Some?"

Gilva: "Races such as Dwarves, Elves, Halflings, and Gnomes—but sadly not humans. Your type appears to lack the ability to notice the *sparkly* stuff."[1569]

I grin ruefully.

Me: "Not even Human Wizards?"

Gilva: "Okay, you got me there. Maybe Human Wizards—but only the *really* good ones, of which there are few and who don't include you."

Me: "So, you detected the spell's essence and followed it to my location?"

Gilva: "Exactly. Nobody teleports to this frozen limbo without good reason—I suspected someone like you required some *Divine Intervention*."[1570]

Me: "But why are you out here—in this inhospitable place?"

The Dwarf cuts a piece off the cooked Ice Chicken and hands it to me.[1571]

Gilva: "I'm taking a well-earned break from questing."

Me: "A well-earned break? But you've been missing for numerous summers. That's a long time to be away from the adventuring life."

Gilva: "Time has no meaning anymore. Out here, nobody bothers me. Nobody makes demands of me—in this icy tundra, I'm free of the responsibility of others, and I love it."

Me: "I don't understand."

[1569] *So-called because Dwarves, Elves, Halflings, and Gnomes continually 'claim' to see sparkly stuff when magic is used—usually to the annoyance of any humans within earshot who just stare blankly into the void, hoping to catch a glimpse of whatever everyone else is staring at.*

[1570] *'Divine Intervention' isn't a voyeuristic God who decides to step in when things go wrong but a Gnomish phrase for 'saving your skin when you're neck-deep in Turd Lurkers...'*

[1571] *It's surprisingly nice—and as you can imagine, tastes a lot like regular chicken just with a sprinkle of more vim—also, rather strangely, it's making my posterior extremely warm.*

The Cleric sighs wearily and puts her hot plate of Ice Chicken down on the snowy ground, which slowly begins to melt down deeper into the packed ice.

Gilva: "I got tired of being a hero; I found it was becoming meaningless. I didn't want to storm castles or raid dungeons. I felt I was being used and manipulated into doing bigger and bigger quests that made no difference to a single soul in the realm beyond certain benefactors. I wasn't making the locals any safer—but I <u>was</u> making a select few richer."

Me: "Certain benefactors?"

Gilva: "You may know them as the Heroes Guild."

Me: "I'm well-versed with this Guild and their less-than-honourable treatment of those they claim to champion."

Gilva: "You speak as though you've suffered personally at their hands."

Me: "That's how I wound up out here in the first place. Their attack dog,[1572] Arin Darkblade, had been sent to dispose of me as they do with all their loose ends."

Gilva: "Then you're lucky to be alive. Once you cross swords with the Guild, you're as good as dead to them. More often than not, *actually* dead once they've finished with you."

Me: "But I've seen your legendary Snow Wolf robe in the Heartenford Museum! You must still be considered part of the Heroes Guild for it to be featured there?"

The Cleric looks a little sheepishly in my direction.

Gilva: "It's true—I may disapprove of the Heroes Guild, but I'm not foolish enough to poke it in the eye and risk its wrath. I simply asked for some time away to get my head straight. The Heroes Guild wasn't happy but understanding enough to give me what I wanted without expelling me completely. They sent messages using a chain of Barkers for a while to see if I was ready to return. But they never seemed to understand my reply."

Me: "Which was?"

[1572] *Or should that be scurvy sea-dog?*

Gilva: "No."[1573]

Me: "How did they react to that?"

Gilva: "They didn't—one summer, the Barkers simply stopped coming. I haven't seen or heard from the Heroes Guild since. I assumed I had been expelled in my absence—but it's nice to know my memory still stands in the Heartenford Museum for all to see."[1574]

A cold blast of air briefly pierces the boundary of the Sanctuary, forcing me to momentarily draw my robes tighter around my body for warmth.

Me: "H—How can you live out here i—in this frozen tundra?"

Gilva: "You get used to it after a while. Sure, the isolation and unforgiving conditions push your body and mind to the limit—*but* I still like to call it home."

Me: "I cannot summon a Sanctuary to keep me safe from the digit-freezing elements. So, what else could I do to survive?"

Gilva: "Without shelter and the means to keep warm—I'd wager you'd perish before you've walked the first mile."[1575]

Me: "I guess I'm fortunate you found me, Gilva."

My saviour offers no reply; she has undoubtedly heard such platitudes before. Instead, the Cleric gazes out through the luminous sphere, her features forming into a pensive expression.

Gilva: "It's getting dark. The Sanctuary won't be able to protect us when the sun drops below the horizon. It's a strong spell—but even *it* has its limits."

[1573] *There's more than a good chance this message returned to the Heroes Guild as 'Snow'— which would have been a perplexing reply to receive unless you were asking about the weather.*

[1574] *Although knowing how fastidious the Museum Curator is about non-Heroes Guild members being featured in her Museum, I wouldn't be surprised to see this exhibit disappear in the near future if the truth surrounding Gilva's 'unofficial' retirement ever saw the light of day—my heart goes out to those unlucky enough to be caught in the blast radius of the Gnomish 'dismantling' operation if that ever happens!*

[1575] *Not a wager I'm overly keen to take the Dwarf up on.*

Me: "What can we do?"

The Dwarf looks awkwardly at her hairy feet.

Gilva: "Well... you could always spend the night with me in my tent? I—I don't mean for any *funny business.*[1576] I could do with having some welcome company for a change—I only have myself and the *Snowy People* to talk to around here."

My cheeks flush red as the Cleric's suggestion catches me off guard—I hastily change the subject.

Me: "Snowy People?"[1577]

The Cleric points towards some figures carved out of the ice, sitting a short distance from the Sanctuary. With the swirling blizzard still raging outside, their presence had completely escaped me.

Me: "Were they... *erm*... real?"

I'm slightly concerned the Dwarf is suffering from snow-madness as she laughs maniacally and almost falls backwards off her fur-lined stool in the process.[1578]

Gilva: "*Real?* I made these! Although I admit the facial work perhaps isn't my finest, I'm relatively happy with the final result."

I stare closer at one of the figures—a wave of familiarity washes over me; I know this soul, but I cannot remember why. An awkward cough from the Dwarf snaps my attention back to the here and now. I can't help but notice the Cleric's demeanour has stiffened slightly.

[1576] *That would be Uncle Bevan Barr's department (the Gods watch over his soul) unless the Cleric means something else, which in that case, my dearly departed Uncle Bevan would be the last person you'd want to see rising...*

[1577] *No relation to the 'Sandy People', a race of short-tempered scavengers living in the Endless Desert; they usually complain bitterly about the amount of grit that gets into everything they own, including bedrolls, breeches, boots—even their vacuum sealed sandwiches.*

[1578] *Snow madness is a terrible affliction that leaves the sufferer gripped with an insatiable need to throw snowballs at everything they see—especially mythical Snilloks and their legendary swarms.*

Gilva: "When this blizzard finally lifts, we'll head straight for Port Salvation. Well, *you will*—I'll probably leave you just before we reach the main gate. I don't really want anyone to see me."

Me: "Why won't you go into town? Wouldn't the locals be thrilled to witness the return of so lauded a hero?"

Gilva: "*No—no*—it's just... I swore I would leave that part of me behind. I'm not sure I'm ready to return to it just yet. Besides, nobody is waiting for me to reemerge from this frozen nightmare."

I glance again over at the snow carving; a bolt of lightning suddenly fizzes through my brain with recognition.

Me: "Not even a *certain* Merchant?"

Gilva: "What? Who?"

Me: "Balstaff. He fell through the ice on the Western Peninsular—he told me how you saved him from a pack of ravenous Snow Wolves."

The Dwarf's face softens as she recalls a tender moment from her past.

Gilva: "*Ah,* he was lovely. He made me laugh with his grand plans for his business. I often wonder what had become of him."

Me: "As far as I know, he stayed in Port Salvation—by all accounts, you made quite the impression on him too. Your selfless actions inspired him to make a career out of heroes by honouring them with their own range of figurines. He even made a range of heroes based on your shared experiences."

Gilva: "He made *what?*"

Me: "Figurines."

Gilva: "Lifesized?"

Me: "No, miniature[1579]—they're so small you could carry them in one hand."[1580]

[1579] *And not out of snow either.*

[1580] *Which, surprisingly, is 'almost' possible with a regular-sized Halfling or Gnome— especially if you're an Ogre or a Storm Giant.*

The Dwarf looks visibly stunned by this revelation.

Me: "Unbelievable—I know, *right?* I guess he wanted to thank you for saving his life by dedicating it to this unique range of heroic figurines.[1581] You want to know something else?"

Gilva: "What?"

Me: "I think deep down he misses you."

Gilva: "Misses me? Don't be ridiculous—why would he miss me?"

Me: "Three days stranded alone together; I understand you two became rather *close*..."[1582]

The Cleric almost falls off her fur-lined stool for a second time.

Gilva: "What? Close? Nothing happened! He was the perfect gentleman!"

Me: "I—I *wasn't* suggesting—"

The Dwarf quickly waves away my protests.

Gilva: "Did he... Did he make a figurine of *me?*"

Me: "Lots—yes, let me see if I can remember them all; there was *Rescuer Gilva, Sanctuary Gilva, Snow-Wolf Slayer Gilva, Brow-Kiss Gilva, Warm Bedroll Gilva*—"[1583]

The Cleric's face noticeably darkens.

Gilva: "*Warm Bedroll Gilva?*"[1584]

[1581] *I suspect I may be slightly exaggerating the point here. I'm sure Balstaff's intentions were noble at the start of his adventure, but the reality of most noble gestures is they seldom put food on the table nor keep the bailiffs from kicking down your shop door for non-payment of rent.*

[1582] *For survival purposes!*

[1583] *But, surprisingly, not 'Looking pissed off to discover they have a miniature figurine range Gilva'...*

[1584] *Which is a marked improvement on 'Warm Breadroll Gilva'...*

Me: "*Oh*, I'm sure it was just one he made for himself—a one-off, so to speak."

Gilva: "Warm. *Bedroll.* Gilva."

Me: "It wasn't anything to worry about; they are all tastefully done, especially *Hairy Gilva*—"

Gilva: "Excuse me—Hairy *what?*"

Me: "Gilva."

In anger, the Cleric stomps her feet and hammers at the sphere's surface.[1585] Suddenly, being trapped in this anger bubble in the middle of a white death-land with the Dwarf for the next few days seems decidedly foolish.

Me: "He did it because he loves you!"

The Dwarf stops mid-hammer and looks at me quizzically.

Gilva: "He *what?* Why would you say that?"[1586]

Me: "Because it's true—he <u>must</u> love you! If he didn't, he wouldn't have created the figurines of you or made it possible for the commoner to own a little replica of their favourite hero."

The Cleric stops and thinks for a moment.

Gilva: "He loves... *me?*"

Me: "I—I think so, but there's only one way to know for certain. Why not come with me to Port Salvation and talk to him?"

Gilva: "But what if he says no? What if this is just something you've misinterpreted? What if it's all just a huge mistake?"

Me: "Well, being a Loremaster—this is what I'm good at, getting to the truth of the matter. Besides, ask yourself, what if I'm right and you never do anything about it?"

[1585] *Thankfully without her 'actual' warhammer in hand...*

[1586] *This 'could' be true, or this also 'could' just be me trying to stop the Dwarf from switching professions from a 'calm' Cleric to a 'rage-fuelled' Barbarian in the middle of the night.*

Gilva: "Balstaff..."

The Dwarf looks wistfully at the snow carving of Balstaff—for a split second, I swear the snowy Merchant is smiling back at her.

Me: "Do you feel the same?"

I sense there's still a degree of uncertainty within the Cleric.

Gilva: "I—I don't know *what* I feel for him. I've not articulated this to anyone in a very long time... it's all very confusing."[1587]

Me: "What have you got to lose? If he rejects you, you could always disappear back into the tundra again; no one would ever be the wiser."[1588]

The Cleric slowly nods, thinking through my suggestion, playing out the scenario multiple times in her head.

Gilva: "Maybe I will... maybe it's time for Gilva Flamebeard to step out of the cold and back into the warm embrace of life."

Me: "That sounds like an <u>excellent</u> idea."

The Dwarf smiles at me.

Gilva: "You might be a useless Wizard, but you're a pretty good listener."

I smile back at the Cleric.

Me: "Thanks, I'll take that."

Gilva: "It's twenty miles to Port Salvation; we can reach it tomorrow—"

I glance at the solitary wolf-skin bedroll unfurled on the ground.

Me: "—or we could travel to Port Salvation right now."

Gilva: "That's a perilous journey to make—why not wait until dawn when it's safer?"

[1587] Like an unexpected Barker message that perplexingly says, 'I glove yew.'

[1588] Although Balstaff would probably make a new Gilva figurine to capture the embarrassing moment to sell to every fan in the entire realm—he would probably call the new figurine 'Wrong End Of The Stick Gilva' or something equally humiliating (it's best I didn't mention this to the Dwarf).

Me: "Love should never be kept waiting. I'm prepared to take the chance—besides, with the legendary *Gilva Flamebeard* by my side, how can we fail?"

The Cleric thinks for a moment and nods.

Gilva: "I'll start packing."

Me: "Excellent—I'll help."[1589]

As we start to pack, the Cleric turns to speak to me once more.

Gilva: "What about Arin Darkblade—doesn't going back to civilisation mean your paths will inevitably cross?"

Me: "I've made it this far. I'm confident I can look after myself."[1590]

Gilva: "But what if he finds you?"

Me: "Perhaps we need to meet for my story to find its end."

Gilva: "It just may not be the end you were looking for..."

Me: "True—but like love, sometimes you need to leap into the unknown to know you're alive."

Gilva: "Although, I don't think there's much chance of being impaled on a sword if things don't go the way you intended..."[1591]

Me: "True—but a metaphoric stab to the heart can be just as fatal as any blade."[1592]

The Cleric smiles as she grabs two cups and uncorks a bottle of mead that has been warming by the fire. She pours out a drink and hands it to me.

Gilva: "Here's to leaping into the unknown..."

[1589] *Starting by quickly rolling that wolf-skin bedroll up and stowing it well out of sight.*

[1590] *Who is this fearless Loremaster? What have you done with the real Elburn Barr?*

[1591] *Unless, of course, you've attempted to woo a Battle Dancer who has taken an immediate dislike to your advances...*

[1592] *Although, those stabbed through the heart may disagree with this point—both figuratively and literally...*

Me: "...*leaping into the unknown...*"

Our cups meet with a satisfying **'*CLINK*'**—but as much as the mead warms my soul, I can feel a deathly chill hanging in the air; I fear the worst is yet to come.[1593]

[1593] *And I don't mean an evening spent snuggled up with the Cleric in her wolf-skin bedroll, with her hairy feet rubbing up against mine.*

43. Rillirum Woodstack, the Guide of the Tour

Scattered about the realm, you will find a handful of individuals who belong to an order called the 'Guides of the Tour', who specialise in 'Hero' walks—a unique service offering the chance to follow in the footsteps of past heroes. With the rise of adventurers across the realm the tours have become hugely popular with locals and travellers desperate to traverse the same path as their favorite sword-wielding champion.[1594] One such tour operates from the village of Hangmoor, a two-week ride south of Port Salvation.[1595] Yet as I arrive, I am shocked to see the town has been reduced to ashes. The tavern is smouldering, the stable is absent, and the few shops are in ruins. I know I should be keeping an eye out for the one-eyed pirate impersonator, Arin Darkblade—but I'm also curious to discover what unfortunate 'incident' changed the town's fortune for the worse.

I stand next to a handwritten sign: *Rillirum Woodstack, Guide of the Tour Extraordinaire,* where five gold stars sit under Rillirum's name,[1596] and a further quote boldly states: **'THE BEST HERO TOUR IN THE ENTIRE REALM'**—attributed to Elamina Quince. I stare past the sign and block out the glare of the sun with my hand; it has only been in the sky for a few hours, but already the heat is rising to a level that would make a Red Dragon sweat. I'm grateful for the occasional chill breeze that sweeps down from the highest peaks of the Doom Mountains in the distance, cooling my brow in the process.

Voice: *"Hooeee*—Yes, Sir! It will be a **HOT** one today, that's for sure!"

I turn to see the beaming face of a grinning Halfling—the woman wears a bright blue tunic and carries a long pole[1597] with a large plume of Oric feathers hanging from the tip.[1598]

[1594] *And even a few dagger or mace-carrying runner-ups.*

[1595] *Where the weather and locals are noticeably less frosty.*

[1596] *I hope that doesn't mean the Halfling or her tours are cursed.*

[1597] *The Halfling reminds me of a 'Backscratcher'—offering to scratch hard-to-reach places for a nominal fee.*

[1598] *So extravagant is the pole; I swear the Halfling has just prized it out of the cold dead hands of Pippo the Gnome—either that or she's just vanquished a sweary Paladin and claimed the feathers from his helm as her trophy.*

Me: "Rillirum Woodstack?"

Rillirum: "That's the name on the sign, isn't it? You're a little early if you're here to join my tour—it doesn't start for a while yet."

Me: "*Ah*—not quite; I'm a *Loremaster*. I'm here to talk to you about heroes and your role in their story."

The Halfling looks pleasantly surprised.

Rillirum: "A Loremaster? Are you sure? It's just you look more like a—"

The Guide of the Tour stops as she notices a slight grimace forming in the corner of my mouth.

Me: "Please... don't... don't do that—I'm *not* kidding. I assure you, I *am* a Loremaster. I'm here to talk to you about your part in all this."

Rillirum: "M—My part? I'm honoured, b—but I'm just a *'Guide of the Tour'*—certainly not anyone of importance."

Me: "Everyone has a role to play, no matter how small."[1599]

I wince slightly as the last word leaves my lips—the Halfling continues, oblivious to my faux pas.

Rillirum: "Well... what is it you want to know?"

I hold my hand to shield my eyes as the sunlight slowly beats me into submission.

Me: "Can we move out of this heat?"

The Guide of the Tour nods and leads me to some welcome shade thrown by a sizeable solitary oak—the only thing still living in this town.[1600] We sit on a low circle wall and gaze outwards as several figures approach the Halfling's booth.

Me: "They're keen—more customers?"

[1599] *What is wrong with me? Perhaps I've also been cursed with putting my foot in it all the time?*

[1600] *If a small smattering of leaves constitutes 'living'—this tree looks like the kind of tree a Necromancer just raised from the dead after being cut down by a Woodcutting Elf with a very large axe.*

Rillirum: "They are the ever-faithful *early birds.*"

I watch the heavily laden locals dump their belongings at the front of the booth and begin setting up a basic campsite.

Me: "Early birds?"

Rillirum: "Yup. Those fans desperate to be first in line when a tour starts—they are the masters of knowing how to wait. They also turn up with enough food to last an entire week."[1601]

The early birds have somehow summoned several chairs out of thin air[1602] and are now sitting in a circle in front of the booth, tucking into copious amounts of cheese and bread from a net sack.[1603]

Me: "Are they really going to wait that long—in this stifling heat?"

Rillirum: "They're renowned as the most dedicated group of hero fans for good reason; they have all sworn to follow their favourite adventurer to the end of that hero's life or their own—whichever comes first. Also, an early bird <u>always</u> wants to be at the front of the queue when a tour starts—it's all that matters to them. Coming second is unthinkable and usually draws harsh stares and filthy looks."

Me: "Which legendary hero do you follow?"

Rillirum: "Redmane the Paladin."

The Halfling catches a hint of recognition behind my eyes.

Rillirum: "I assume you've heard of him, of course…"

Me: "Our paths have crossed."[1604]

The Halfling looks surprised.

[1601] *I hope the poor souls waiting in line won't still be there when the supplies and tempers become considerably shorter.*

[1602] *They have obviously made some dark pact with another being from another dimension for some poorly crafted furniture in exchange for eternal damnation.*

[1603] *There's so much cheese being passed around I'm surprised a cheese-obsessed Druid-cum-squirrel hasn't made an unexpected appearance yet—drawn by the pungent cheesy aroma…*

[1604] *I seem to remember the Paladin left rather cross too…*

Rillirum: "*Oh*—you've actually *met* him!? This is perfect! Perhaps I can convince you to join the tour and talk to the fans about your experiences of the great Paladin. It'd be good to get some insights into his fall from grace. It's tragic, really; he had everything going for him—he was at the top of his profession, regarded as one of the brightest stars in the realm. He shall be missed by many."[1605]

Me: "Why do I detect a large number of past tenses in that statement?"

Rillirum: "That's because when that Paladin finally left Hangmoor, Redmane ceased to be what you and I would call a *hero*."

Me: "Why?"

The Guide turns to regard the smashed walls and shattered beams surrounding us.

Rillirum: "What do you think happened here? Dragons? Powerful Spells?"

I stare at the skeleton of this smouldering town, trying to imagine it full with the hustle and bustle of life.

Me: "He did this—*all* of it?"

The Halfling laughs.

Rillirum: "He probably caused more destruction in one drunken evening than a rampaging Goblin Horde could achieve in ten summers.[1606] Redmane brought with him such thunderous fury; he could make the realm's angriest Barbarian look like a doe-eyed Cleric by comparison..."

Me: "But why? How?"

Rillirum: "I don't know, but something or someone had whipped him into this unnatural rage—you know what I mean?"

Me: "N—No... not at all. Can you talk me through what happened when he first reached Hangmoor?"

[1605] Including Goblin Archers and easily impressed Barmaids...

[1606] To be fair, most of the Goblin Archers in the horde would have undoubtedly wiped out the rest of the horde with their opening volley...

Rillirum: "Well, the information I have is somewhat fragmented. There were a lot of locals running around screaming that day—and finding any surviving eyewitness is as rare as a sword-wielding Wizard or Cleric heading into the unexplored dungeon room first.[1607] What I do know is that as soon as he was in the square, Redmane headed straight for the nearest tavern, the one that once sat over yonder—*The Phoenix and Phalanx.*"[1608]

I stare at what remains of the tavern in question; the roof has almost been stripped bare of its tiles. Most of the brickwork is now just a huge pile of broken rubble and fire-scorched beams.

Me: "I'm guessing it wasn't always like that?"

The Halfling gives me an unfathomable look—as if I've just asked the most stupid question of all questions.[1609]

Rillirum: "No—you should have seen it in its former glory. Beautiful crisp white walls, purple flower boxes, exposed black beams on the ceiling—"

I point to the charred wooden beams in the roof, now laid bare to the elements like the bones of a decaying carcass.

Me: "I guess technically, it *still* has exposed black beams."

The Halfling shakes her head sadly, completely missing my joke.[1610]

Rillirum: "Yeah, that Paladin, he was bad news. He burst into the bar like a pissed-off Banshee, swearing at everyone and everything. I mean, he even cussed the flagon he was drinking from; can you believe that— the *flagon?!*"[1611]

Me: "Paladins are usually quite restrained and stoic."

[1607] *So, practically unheard of...*

[1608] *Often mistakenly referred to by Barkers as 'The Flea Nicks Hand Phallic'.*

[1609] *Sometimes I really let the Loremaster profession down.*

[1610] *Sometimes I really let the memory of Uncle Bevan Barr down.*

[1611] *This is completely unacceptable unless the flagon in question was really a Mimic flagon with an unhealthy appetite for adventurous tongues—in that case, cuss away, Holy Warrior, CUSS AWAY!*

Rillirum: "Completely, I've never heard anything quite like it in my lifetime. Something must have pushed him over the edge, and he just—"

The Guide of the Tour suddenly clicks her fingers together noisily.

Rillirum: **"SNAPPED!"**

Me: "*Ah—erm*—it must have been something *considerable*. But that doesn't quite explain the tavern's demise."

Rillirum: "It was a perfect storm; a Fireball-loving Wizard <u>and</u> an even shorter-tempered-than-usual Barbarian. I believe the foul-mouthed Paladin swore at the Barbarian, who took immediate offence at the slur on his mother and threw a punch in retaliation. The punch missed and landed squarely on the nose of a Wizard, who immediately cast a Fireball spell at the Barbarian in defence. But wouldn't you believe it? He missed with his flaming ball of death and instead incinerated the bar and gave some Elves who were minding their own business, a rather healthy tan. The Paladin tried to extinguish the fire by 'smiting' the life out of it—instead, he somehow slammed the Barbarian through the main support beam, bringing down the entire tavern in the process."

I look nervously over at the pile of rubble.

Me: "Did anyone—?"

Rillirum: "Die? No idea. But they do say the Barbarian is <u>still</u> buried beneath the ruins."

Me: "Buried? Surely he's not alive? Nobody could survive <u>that</u>—not even a Barbarian!"

Rillirum: "I hope not—otherwise, he will be in the foulest of moods when he eventually claws his way out.[1612] Anyway, when the building collapsed, everyone ran for their lives. I believe even before the dust settled, the Paladin had walked into a nearby Provisions shop where he

---

[1612] *Without extensive training and summers of research, it's difficult to understand the sliding scale of rage the average Barbarian can reach. Most simply hit the first level of rage, which is generally a point where a Barbarian will hit everything else. But higher levels include foaming at the mouth, spitting, roaring with rage, feet stamping, swearing, and farting with extreme fury on rare occasions.*

insulted a Cleric, punched a Gnome,[1613] and slapped a Monk who had been waiting for their cured meat in a bap to be made."

Me: "What happened to the Wizard?"

Rillirum: "He vanished—probably cast a teleportation spell to avoid the fallout."[1614]

Me: "Fallout?"

Rillirum: "From the Heroes Guild, they weren't going to be pleased when they discovered a Wizard had a hand in turning a perfectly good recruitment tavern into a deconstructed recruitment tavern with a side order of chaos."

Me: "A recruitment tavern, *here*—in Hangmoor?"

Rillirum: "Don't sound so surprised—the Heroes Guild has Scouts everywhere. If you ask me, the Wizard was wise to make a run for it when he could. The Heroes Guild has a long memory and even longer reach when it comes to payback."

Me: "I can't believe a Paladin could cause so much devastation."

Rillirum: "The Holy Warrior's repressed anger was probably fuelling his destructive path, much like a woo-avoiding Battle Dancer—nothing could stop him. After the Provisions shop, he somehow managed to set fire to the stables and damaged the local market area so badly it was impossible to identify any of the *Back Market* wares the vendors were peddling at a hugely inflated price.[1615] When the sun finally set on that terrible day, Hangmoor was left in such a state most knew it would be impossible to rebuild it back to its former glory—so those still able to walk under their own volition simply left..."

Me: "That's awful—couldn't the townsfolk do anything?"

[1613] *I can't help but detect a hint of pleasure in the Halfling's voice as she informs me of this fact.*

[1614] *No doubt teleporting to the furthest point from Hangmoor, which ironically is slap-bang in the middle of the Dauntless Sea...*

[1615] *Although, if the Merchants were canny enough, they could still sell their charcoaled wares on the Black Market...*

Rillirum: "What could they do? They'd just seen a profanity-spouting Paladin literally bury a Barbarian and decimate their beloved town. It soon became obvious that starting afresh elsewhere would be easier rather than wasting time and effort clearing up the smoking remains that was once Hangmoor."

Me: "And Redmane?"

Rillirum: "He disappeared shortly afterwards and hasn't been seen since."

Me: "What do you think happened to him?"

Rillirum: "I heard a rumour he fell out with a Necromancer and got turned into a Deaf Knight as a consequence."

Me: "A *Death Knight?*"

Rillirum: "No—a *Deaf* Knight."

Me: "What's a Deaf Knight?"

Rillirum: "A Paladin who has committed an act so heinous it literally binds their soul to their armour—making them deaf in the process.[1616] It's really nasty stuff, especially when a Necromancer is involved, and we all know they love getting a rise out of the dead."[1617]

Me: "I hate to think of Redmane as an undead Warrior, doomed to wander the realm with his soul locked inside a rusting suit of armour."[1618]

Rillirum: "No, that certainly doesn't sound like a deserving end for poor Redmane—personally, I like to think he's living in a cave somewhere, seeking atonement for his mistakes with self-imposed exile and time spent helping the local community. Perhaps one day, when he's come to terms with his actions, Redmane will return and rise once more to

---

[1616] *They also experience their own 'death' during this transformational process, so I suppose, technically, that makes them a Deaf-Death Knight. It's worth noting that Deaf Knights go around saying 'pardon' a lot; no one can be sure if the unholy Warriors are asking for forgiveness, or asking you to repeat what was just said—but a bit louder...*

[1617] *Although most Necromancers insist this is just a normal, healthy 'professional' obsession of theirs.*

[1618] *Who can't hear a thing—like opportunistic Rogues sneaking up on them to daub rude messages on their backs...*

become the Paladin we all deserve."[1619]

Me: "If the Paladin's story ends so poorly, why have you organised one of your infamous 'tours' about him?"

The Halfling points to the steadily growing queue waiting by her stall.

Rillirum: "You're joking, aren't you? Redmane is *more* popular than he has ever been. Before, he was just a Paladin—now he's a Paladin with a tragic backstory! It's practically priceless. This incident has done more for him than slaying any number of Dragons, Dragon Lords, or even staring stoically from the top of a watchtower.[1620] Now everyone wants to visit the places Redmane destroyed so they can breathe in the ashes of his fury—and ponder his subsequent downfall."

Me: "Why do you think so many fans are drawn to his tale?"

Rillirum: "Nobody is interested in the usual, run-of-the-mill heroes these days. Everyone wants a hero with an edge, or as I like to call them, *anti*-heroes."[1621]

Me: "What's an anti-hero."

Rillirum: "An anti-hero can be someone doing the right thing for the wrong reason or doing the wrong thing for the right reason. But whichever way their cloth is cut, they are guaranteed coin-makers for yours truly. My patrons can't get enough of my *anti*-hero tours! They're always booked out, with a huge waiting list if anyone drops out at the last moment—not that they ever do."

Me: "How expensive is it to join your tour exactly?"

Rillirum: "Forty-five gold pieces for the day—that includes us ending up in the *Troll's Tooth* tavern not far from the Southern Pass. The tavern has an excellent selection of overpriced pies and ales that are sold to my tour—with a share of the takings going to my pocket."

[1619] *Well, return as a Fighter who swears a lot less than before, at the very least.*

[1620] *No doubt looking for Dragons or their Dragon Lords...*

[1621] *Not to be confused with 'Aunty-Heroes', a distant relative and general busybody of regular heroes. She's also someone who can't resist spreading a bit of juicy gossip about why the latest dungeon adventure went wrong or how the Cleric has been secretly stealing from the temple's collection box.*

Me: "But you start here, in Hangmoor?"

Rillirum: "Yes. We work backwards until eventually finishing our journey at the steps of the great watchtower overlooking the ShadowLands. It's quite a walk but, in my honest opinion, worth the sore feet, blisters and the occasional Sand Worm encounter.[1622] Once the tour is over, I lead my patrons towards the *Troll's Tooth* tavern for an evening's entertainment provided by the Halfling Bard, Lotho, and his enormous pipe organ."

The Halfling shakes the feathered pole with joyous vigour. The bells at the tip ring above the silence, causing several of the early birds to turn around expectantly.

Me: "I meant to ask—what's with the ornate pole?"

The Guide of the Tour stares upwards, mesmerised by the feathers softly shaking in the breeze.

Rillirum: "This thing?"

Me: "It doesn't look much of a weapon."[1623]

Rillirum: "That's because it's not—it's a *totem.*"

Me: "A totem? A totem for what?"

Rillirum: "Not what—for *whom.*"

The Halfling gestures to the massive line of people that now snakes its way from the booth, twisting around the burnt stables until it disappears behind the ruins of abandoned shops.

Me: "Is it magical? Do you use it to summon them?"[1624]

Rillirum: "*Haha!* If only! That would be quite something... no, this is to ensure my customers always have sight of me—even when I'm knee-

---

[1622] *Contrary to popular myth, Sand Worms are not gigantic beasts that tunnel beneath the dunes as if they were crashing through the waves of the Dauntless Sea. Instead, they are tiny worms that emit a highly amusing shriek when accidentally trod on, making for a comedic musical interlude if you suddenly step on a nest of them.*

[1623] *Unless you consider a +2 Stick of Tickling a 'weapon'...*

[1624] *Which would explain how the Guide of the Tour's line has suddenly increased tenfold.*

deep in a crowd. It can get quite busy, and as you've already noticed, I'm not the tallest—although I <u>am</u> taller than your average Gnome.[1625] This handy pole makes it easy for my patrons to keep sight of me."

Me: "That's clever."

Rillirum: "Thanks—it's my invention. I may try and get it patented with the Heralds Guild to stop the other Guides of the Tour from stealing the idea for themselves."

Me: "You think any of the other Guides of the Tour would do that? Steal your idea, I mean?"

Rillirum: "For sure, there's a huge rivalry between us Guides—and I want to ensure I'm top of *The League* when the summer ends."

Me: "The League?"

Rillirum: "You've not heard of *The League of Guides?* It's a competition to see which one of us has the highest turnout of patrons attending our tours. The winner claims the highly sought-after realm map as their prize."

There's a rumbling deep beneath the smoking ruins of the tavern, as if a underground void suddenly filled with rubble.

Me: "A realm map? The sounds pretty unimpressive as a reward—"

Rillirum: "You'd be gravely mistaken—that map holds detailed information of *every* quest any hero has <u>ever</u> undertaken since records began. In the hands of a Guide, it's practically priceless."

Me: "<u>Every</u> quest? That map must be **huge!**"

Rillirum: "Huge is an understatement. It would take a day just to traverse from one corner to the opposite corner. I've even heard it's so immense, it would keep a Storm Giant warm on a bitterly cold night."[1626]

Me: "Given Redmane's popularity, I'm surprised you've not won it already."

[1625] *I know plenty of Gnomes who would brashly claim otherwise.*

[1626] *Without the need to use a lovestruck hairy Dwarf as a makeshift hot water bottle...*

Rillirum: "I've been close a couple of times, but I keep getting beaten by Willard Vanes, an irritating Gnome who takes his patrons into the inhospitable wastes beyond the Western Peninsular."

Me: "I've been to the Western Peninsular—why would he organise a tour of that frozen tundra?"

Rillirum: "To follow in the footsteps of *Gilva Flamebeard,* of course— she still commands a sizeable following, perhaps even one to rival that of Redmane."[1627]

Me: "I see. So, are you concerned about your rival, Willard?"

The Guide of the Tour looks at the queue as it spirals out of view. There's another ominous rumble beneath the remains of the tavern, as the last of the burnt roof tiles come crashing to the floor in reply.

Rillirum: "Do I look worried to you? Once I have this latest group of paying patrons under my belt, that map is as good as mine."

The Halfling gets up from her seat on the wall and shakes my hand as she leaves. Her eyes light up as she spots something in my half-open bag.

Rillirum: "I thought you said you *weren't* a Wizard?"

Me: "I—I'm not—"

Rillirum: "Then why are you carrying one of those?"

The Guide points at the curious spellbook, which is once more poking its nose where it's not wanted.[1628]

Me: "This thing? *Ah,* it was a gift..."

Rillirum: "*May I?*"

[1627] *I'm not sure Gilva would be happy seeing a tour group turning up at the exact moment when she finally mustered the courage to declare her true feelings to Balstaff the Merchant—although, it may inspire a new 'Going red with rage, Gilva' figurine.*

[1628] *If this spellbook had a nose, it would be the largest nose in existence—even putting the sizeable 'conk' of a Benoser to shame.*

I nod as I hand the magical tome over to the Halfling to examine—she sniffs the edges before gingerly creaking open the cover with the lightest of touches.

Rillirum: "This is a first edition if I'm not mistaken."

Me: "A *first* edition?"

Rillirum: "A Wizard's first spellbook—very rare."

Me: "Why rare?"

Rillirum: "Because most spellbooks are accidentally incinerated long before a Wizard can master their art.[1629] The average seasoned Wizard would be on their fourth or fifth edition by the time they've reached the end of their first summer in the field.[1630] How much do you want for it?"

Me: "What?"

Rillirum: "How much?"

Me: "It's not for sale—"

Rillirum: "One-hundred coins, no—two-hundred!"

Me: "I'm sorry, but I'm not looking to sell."

The Halfling wags her finger at me knowingly.

Rillirum: "You drive a hard bargain—five-hundred coins, and that's my final offer!"

My gaze drifts down from the Guide's eager face to the hefty tome held in her hands. I have almost no use for it—and I can't deny the Halfling's offer is extremely generous—but I can't bring myself to part with the item. I shake my head. As tempting as the promise of coin is, I don't think I'm ready to part with the spellbook just yet.

Me: "Sorry..."

The Halfling sighs and nods her head in resignation.

───────────────────────

[1629] *No surprise there, really...*

[1630] *Not a turnip field.*

Rillirum: "Fair enough, but if you ever decide to part with it—you *promise* to seek me out first?"

Me: "Agreed."

Rillirum: "Fair enough…"

The Guide of the Tour looks over at the long line of patiently waiting patrons. Some are beginning to noticeably sway under the punishing heat.

Rillirum: "Well, I know it's early, but I'd better open up my stall and start the tour. I don't want anyone fainting and squirming out of the entrance fee. Especially when a legendary map is at stake—I don't think I could live with myself if that bloody Gnome pips me to the post again."[1631]

Me: "Thanks—and good luck."

The Guide of the Tour gives me the warmest of smiles.

Rillirum: "Luck isn't something I need."[1632]

The Halfling's words are cut short by a muffled bellow coming from *The Phoenix and Phalanx* ruins. A pile of nearby bricks erupts as a Barbarian's hand suddenly punches into the air. The hand is quickly followed by his arm, shoulder, bellowing face, and finally, by a furious fart. The Barbarian's angry bottom-burp is replaced by the screams coming from the Tour's waiting line, who are watching on in disbelief. I can only stare open-mouthed in shock as the throng of locals suddenly breaks rank in fright. Even the die-hard early birds bolt for their lives—keen to avoid the wrath of the rumbling berserker who seems desperate to hit anything or anyone in his path. Rillirum, showing admirable commitment to her duties,[1633] reacts to the unfolding chaos by putting herself directly in the way of the onrushing hero fans.

[1631] *'Pips me to the post' is a saying that came about after a luckless Gnome named 'Pip' was beaten by his neighbour in a summer-long game of 'Fellowship'. So enraged was the Gnome at this defeat, he tied his conqueror to a wooden post and left him there for a hungry eagle to find…*

[1632] *That's handy because I'm not prepared to hand over the last of my Lucky Potion to the Halfling—no matter how much she's prepared to pay.*

[1633] *Or desperation to beat that pesky Gnome, Willard Vanes, whatever the cost…*

Rillirum: *"**NO WAIT! PLEASE! <u>DON'T GO!</u> STAY!**"*

But it's hopeless: the Halfling is quickly swept away by a sea of bodies, her feathered pole briefly bobbing above the wave of screaming heads before finally sinking without a trace. Conscious that I don't want to be mistaken for the Barbarian's mortal enemy, I grab my belongings and flee as fast as my legs can carry me. Not for the first time, I'm left wishing I had the magical means to vanish instantly, rather than testing my luck and hoping the Barbarian doesn't spot this particular *faux* Wizard through the panicked mob.[1634]

[1634] *I still carry the last of my Lucky Potion in my bag, although I don't think now is the right time to polish it off.*

44. Stanlorp, the Hermit—

Ascension Falls is the highest waterfall in the realm, running off the peaks of the Dragon-laden Doom Mountains. The ice-cold waters take over a minute to descend from the highest point to the wide-flowing Elkar River far below.[1635] It's an impressive sight, one I'm pleased to admire while taking a much-needed break on my enduring quest to discover the truth about adventuring life. I reflect upon the myriad of folk I've met on the road[1636]—each one eager to share their story with me.[1637] My mind wanders to the thought of home and my parents. I can picture my mother in the kitchen, cooking a delicious Blue Beret pie,[1638] while my father is in his workshop, busily sharpening one of his old swords and secretly hoping the call to adventure comes knocking at his door once more. But while such tender scenes play out on the stage provided by my imagination, I know the reality of my return home would swiftly become a nightmare. The news of my brother's passing would change the light in my parents forever—could I really do that to them? Would I be wrong to stay away and pretend Aldon is still alive? Could I live with myself knowing I had forever denied their fondest wish by exposing the true fate of their eldest son? Or would that cruel mercy result in my parents losing both of their sons? I watch the glistening warm waters of the Elkar River; my next-arranged interview is with Stanlorp, the Hermit, a recluse and former quest-giver who had to go into hiding after making a significant numerical error with the proposed reward that bankrupted his Baron and caused a bloody uprising[1639] in his kingdom as a consequen—

Unseen Voice: "You're a difficult man to track down, *Loremaster...*"

The shade of strength and severity colouring the voice leaves me with little doubt about its owner. Who else would have reason to track me

---

[1635] *It's worth noting that the sun warms the falling waters on a hot day, making the Elkar River a pleasure to soak in, not that I can swim to enjoy such a thing.*

[1636] *Or in a tavern, watchtower, castle, forest, shop, sewer, unstable temple or dubious-looking bush...*

[1637] *I finally understand why as I stare accusingly at the accursed ring on my finger.*

[1638] *Blue Beret pie isn't some kind of rude edible hat, but a pie made using Blue Berets, which confusingly is a fruit that looks like it's wearing a hat to impress any non-hat wearing fruits within a 10-foot radius.*

[1639] *Meaning a lot of 'body sauce' was spilt, not that it was an uprising that was a 'bit annoying'—although that was probably true too.*

to this quiet corner of the realm? I slowly turn, the quiver in my stomach hardening to icy fear as I find myself gazing upon the grim face of Arin Darkblade. His solitary eye glares at me intently.[1640] The former adventurer doesn't draw a blade nor throw an expected punch—instead, he points to the empty space opposite me.

Arin: "May I?"

I nod—knowing it doesn't matter what I say, the one-eyed adventurer will do whatever he pleases with or without my permission.

Me: "I take it there is no Stanlorp or meeting?"

Arin: "There's still a meeting for sure, just not with a Hermit…"[1641]

Me: "How did you find me?"

Arin: "It wasn't hard, really—there aren't many Loremasters travelling from town-to-town asking about heroes these days. Like you, I found people are more than willing to tell me what I want to hear with the *right* amount of persuasion."[1642]

Me: "So, you've been following me for a while? Why wait until now? You could have caught me at the Curse Keeper's shop."

Arin: "I could have, easily—but first I wanted to speak to you alone."

Me: "Why alone?"

Arin: "You've been an interesting distraction from the mundane rigours of Guild life. Spending your days behind a desk is not the fitting end for <u>any</u> adventurer, especially one as renowned as Arin Darkblade. So, I persuaded the Guildmaster that it was in the Guild's interest to make *you* my quest, and to your credit, you have played your part to perfection—you have been a most exceptional quarry."

[1640] *Looking like a Pirate who just discovered this Loremaster sitting in what remains of the poop deck, surrounded by empty bottles of Yo-Ho-Blow rum…*

[1641] *Somehow, I don't think Arin is here to tell me he's giving up his role at the Heroes Guild to live alone in the wilds, never to be seen by civilization ever again—still, one can dream.*

[1642] *I suppose what I can achieve with a cursed ring, Arin can achieve with a solitary eye stare and the threat of organ removal—and by that, I don't mean Lotho's beloved musical companion.*

Me: "But, like all hunts, it must come to its inevitable conclusion, I suppose?"

Arin: "One end is just the beginning of another. We <u>all</u> must face our final arrow sometime or another.[1643] But before you face yours, tell me, Loremaster, look me in the eye—*what* do you see?"

If this is to be my last, I shall go out with the mightiest of roars rather than a mouse-like whimper.

Me: "I see the Heroes Guild's muscle—a tired and jaded attack dog. Sent to clean up whatever mess your paymasters need sweeping away, silencing anyone with a bad word to say about the Heroes Guild or who are a threat to their self-serving interests. You crave adventure but are nothing more than the one-eyed and worn-out bog brush of an overused tavern privy."[1644]

Arin: "So, <u>not</u> a hero then?"

Me: "I thought a hero was someone remarkable, someone pure— someone *noble*. But I've discovered heroes come in many curious, contradictory, and unpleasant varieties like any other walk of life. One thing is for certain, you are no hero to me, but if you are—perhaps the people of this realm have the heroes they *truly* deserve."

The former adventurer nods, slowly contemplating my words as if they were a particularly fatty cut of meat.[1645]

Me: "Now that you have me—what do you intend to do with me?"

Arin: "That all depends on you—what do *you* intend to do?"

Me: "I don't understand?"

The one-eyed adventurer chuckles darkly.

[1643] *Unless the executioner in question is a Goblin or Halfling Archer, then I'm afraid you will be clinging to life for a considerable amount of time.*

[1644] *Frequented by a Half-Orc who opted to polish off the leftovers from a spoiled roast hog and who now severely regrets that decision—much to the horror of the voyeuristic Rogue waiting for the 'trap' to be vacated and whose eyes are bleeding from the nostril-melting stench coming from the Half-Orc's repugnant behind.*

[1645] *I 'may' have put a bit of weight on during my travels—but I'm not <u>that</u> heavily encumbered.*

Arin: "You certainly stirred the hornet's nest, didn't you?"[1646]

Me: "You wouldn't be here if I hadn't."

Arin: "All those questions, all those answers. I ask you—_what_ has it achieved?"

Me: "The truth—that's what it achieved. I know your _precious_ Heroes Guild isn't the glistening beacon of hope it claims to be."

Arin: "The Heroes Guild is just a business—"

Me: "_Just_ a business? The Merchant selling hero figurines _is_ a business. The Potioneer peddling his wares from town-to-town _is_ a business— but the Heroes Guild? It's an empire slowly stretching across the realm, grabbing every piece of land for itself. It's an occupying army welcomed with open arms by the populace, hiding behind heroes and their heroic feats. But it's all a ruse; the whole thing is one big damn **lie**—and that's why you're here, to end my life and keep this truth from ever seeing the light of day."

The former adventurer nods once more as he listens to each and every word without interruption or snide comment—finally, he points to the bag slung about my shoulders.

Arin: "I take it that contains all your notes from your travels?"

I instinctively cover my bag, trying to keep it from view.

Arin: "You know the Heroes Guild have tasked me with securing your journal from you."

Me: "I know—but this is too important to give up; there are too many stories in here that need to be told."

Arin: "I realise that—but what if I were to tell you there's a party of Enforcers headed this way who will be less likely to engage in light conversation with you? They _will_ catch you—and when they do, I can guarantee they _will_ kill you and take your precious journal back to their paymaster, Toldarn."

[1646] _This is a Gnomish saying that sprung from an infamous incident whereby a mischievous Gnome decided to stir an actual hornet's nest before launching it into the middle of a party of half-naked Halfling Barbarians. Needless to say, since that painful day, Halfling Barbarians have worn a lot more than tight-fitting furry loincloths._

I stare at Arin in confusion.

Me: "I thought that was why <u>you</u> were here?"

The one-eyed adventurer winks and runs his fingers through his dark hair.[1647]

Arin: "I am many things—but I am no assassin, nor a thief."[1648]

Me: "What *are* you then?"

Arin: "Why are you dressed like a Wizard if you're a Loremaster?"

Me: "I lost my clothes—"

The pretend Pirate roars with laughter at my obvious expense.

Arin: "Really? You *lost* your clothes? How did you manage that?"

Me: "They were incinerated when this infernal Gnomish contraption I was in caught fire—"

The one-eyed adventurer roars with laughter again, almost falling backwards in hysterics—he holds his hands up defensively.

Arin: "***Stop! Stop!*** I'll do myself a critical![1649] That's the funniest thing I've heard in a long time. Gnomes and their love of the mechanical—I'd rather trust my luck to my sword than any of their highly-combustible devices."

Me: "This wasn't a weapon—it was supposed to change my attire."

Arin: "Your attire?"

Me: "I was trying out different hero clothes."

Arin: "Why?"

[1647] *This would've been an opportune moment to sock Arin in the knackers, grab my bag and make a mad dash for freedom. Alas, the plate steel of his codpiece warns me of the futility of such an assault.*

[1648] *Although he could still be a Pirate—which is a type of Rogue who likes to backstab unsuspecting swimmers.*

[1649] *'Critical' is a Gnomish word meaning 'to do oneself an injury'—an injury so bad that it would take a natural roll of a '20' on a twenty-sided dice for it to occur.*

Me: "I wanted to know what it felt like to *be* a hero."

Arin: "So, what <u>does</u> it feel like?"

Me: "I—I don't know... the whole thing caught fire before I could find out for myself, but one thing is for certain—I'm no hero."

Arin: "What makes you say that?"

Me: "I've not delved into a dungeon—"

Arin: "But you *have* explored a crypt and faced a Warlock Lich."[1650]

Me: "I was interviewing him, not vanquishing him."

Arin: "So, you faced him without a weapon by your side—I'd say that's pretty heroic."

Me: "I'm not the hero in the family; my—my brother was the hero."

Arin: "Your brother?"

Me: "He left home to become a hero, but..."

Arin: "But?"

Me: "He died."

Arin: "How?"[1651]

I furrow my brow in pain—has he already pushed this incident far from his mind?

Me: "Unfortunately."

Arin: "Unfortunate indeed."

There's an awkward moment where neither of us says anything—we just sit silently in each other's company staring at the warm vapour rising from the surface of the Elkar River.

Arin: "So, you thought you would follow in his footsteps and try to become a hero?"

[1650] *Albeit a pretend one...*

[1651] *You should know! You was there!*

Me: "Yes... no... *I don't know.* I wanted to know what it felt like to be held in high regard."

Arin: "Held in high regard? By strangers you have never met?"

Me: "By my parents... they—they thought the world of my brother. They poured all their hopes into him. I wanted to know what that felt like, to understand why he was the hero to them... and I... I wasn't..."

Arin: "You honestly believe that?"

Me: "I—I don't know what to believe anymore. I just know I have to tell my parents the truth."

Arin: "Which is?"

Me: "I failed them... I failed to bring home their son safely..."

The one-eyed weekend Pirate falls silent, deep in thought.

Me: "Why are you saying this? What does any of this matter to you?"

Arin: "I see you still wear that cursed ring."

I instinctively cover my hand, hiding the troubling trinket from view.

Me: "How did you know?"

Arin: "Our last encounter—I persuaded the Curse Keeper to tell me everything about your conversation with her, including the one about your ring.[1652] Why didn't you remove it when you had the chance?"

Me: "I guess I didn't mind a curse that helped me get to the truth."

Arin: "Even if that truth could get you *killed?*"

Me: "This ring has helped me in more ways than I care to mention... but more importantly, it revealed to me how my brother died at the hands of a Wizard—"

Arin: "—*Morgan the Magnificent.*"

Me: "He doesn't use that name anymore."

[1652] *I hope Arin wasn't too tough on Enolin—she has enough problems keeping the rain off her wares to worry about being harassed by a landlocked Pirate.*

Arin: "Really?"

Me: "It's *Simply* Morgan now—he gave up on his full name after…"

My voice falls away as the death of my brother fills my consciousness.

Arin: "…the Fireball accident."

Me: "So, you <u>do</u> remember."

Arin: "That day has been seared into my consciousness forever."[1653]

Me: "W—Was it quick? His death, I mean—I hope he didn't suffer. Can you tell me anything about his last day?"[1654]

The former adventurer shakes his head.

Arin: "You are better off not knowing."

Me: "Please, I have to know. I hate to think how scared he must have been in the face of death. Did he say anything? Were his final words calling out for those he loved? I know it's an impossible wish, but nobody should ever die alone. I feared telling my parents without being able to answer their questions. You could give me those answers. You <u>owe</u> me that."

Arin: "I owe you *nothing*…"

I can sense Arin's patience wearing thin—but I'm too close to the truth to give up now.

Me: "M—My brother… he was my world, my idol. I just wish I could tell him one last time how much he mattered to me, that I didn't mean to be jealous."

The one-eyed adventurer stares at me in cold contemplation.

Arin: "So, you <u>really</u> want to know what happened on that fateful day?"

Me: "Yes…"

[1653] *Much like my brother's outline that's now baked into a crypt's wall…*

[1654] *But not stuff like what he ate for breakfast—or if he still liked to fart loudly when he woke up in the morning (which was <u>one</u> way to be woken in the morning).*

Arin: "Even if knowing could lead to your own grave?"[1655]

Me: "Before I answer, I ask only one thing—that you send word to my parents; they deserve to know the fates of both their sons."

The grizzled adventurer thinks a second before answering.

Arin: "I can do that."

Me: "If my life is the price I must pay—then *so* be it."

My eyes are burning brightly with a steely determination of their own.

Arin: "As you wish..."

The part-time Pirate begins to unfasten his eye-patch.

Me: "W—What are you doing?"

Arin: "Giving you the truth—you're not the only one who wears something that makes them what they are not..."

I watch on in silence, partially curious, partially horrified to witness whatever lies beneath Arin's eye-patch.[1656]

Me: "You don't have to do that—"

Arin: "*Oh*, but I *do*, Loremaster..."

I'm ill-prepared for the unfathomable truth that now sits staring proudly back at me—it's a perfectly normal eyeball![1657]

Me: "I don't understand. Why do you wear an eye-patch if you have a good eye?"

Arin: "I'll ask this again—look at me, what do you see?"[1658]

[1655] *Carefully prepared by Hagworl and shaded beneath the branches of a mighty oak tree.*

[1656] *Please don't be a hole. Please don't be a hole...*

[1657] *Okay, that was unexpected. It's not even a milky-white eyeball, but a perfectly healthy one!*

[1658] *This feels like the type of question that ends with the one of us who doesn't wear an eye-patch being punched very hard in the face.*

663

Believing I'm being set up for a horrendous gag, I double blink in exasperation.

Me: "What do you *think* I see? I see Arin Darkblade—"

Arin: "Look again."

I stare hard into Arin's cold eyes.

Me: "I don't—"

I stop mid-sentence; there's a flicker of confusion in the fake Pirate's face—for a moment, I swear I spy something warm and familiar about the features looking straight back at me—features that once belonged to my now-deceased brother!

Me: "I'll be a Troll's Auntie—what is this?! Are you so heartless that you must mock the memory of my brother with cheap conjuring tricks?"

I jump to my feet and take an uncertain step backwards towards the bank's edge, where it falls away into the waters of the Elkar River below.

Aldon: "No tricks, little brother—it <u>is</u> me, in the flesh."

Me: "But this cannot be—you are supposed to be **dead!**"

Aldon: "It takes more than a wayward Fireball to get the better of a Barr."[1659]

I step forward, my hands shaking as they trace the contours of my brother's face. Tears of unbridled joy fill my eyes as I throw my arms around Aldon's muscular frame.

Me: "It's you—it's <u>really</u> you!"

As we embrace, we share relieved smiles.

Aldon: "Pray tell me, Elburn—how is mother? I miss her constant questioning of my daily adventuring life—even though my answer was pretty much the same from one day to the next."

[1659] *This feels like the start of a joke where the punchline is: 'Two wayward Fireballs!'*

Me: "After you left, she quickly turned her line of enquiry towards me—wondering when I would write the greatest book the realm had never seen."

Aldon: "Forgive me for that, brother—it's just mother's way of showing she cares. Is she still baking pies filled with fashion-conscious berries?"

Me: "She has been baking one every week without fail, just in case you returned unexpectedly."

My smile fades from my face as soon as the words escape my lips.

Me: "But you *never* did..."[1660]

Aldon: "I know... it's not that I didn't want to—but I couldn't..."

Me: "Why? Father has gone grey with worry.[1661] He would deny it, of course, but you can tell it has taken a toll on him both physically and mentally."

Aldon: "Father understood more than anyone the dangers of an adventurer's path—why do you think he encouraged you to study books and not pick up a sword?"

Me: "I was never cut out for a life of adventure—"

Aldon: "Don't forget you're a Barr—you're born to adventure. It's in your blood, as it has been in our family for many generations. Father didn't want you to follow in his or my footsteps because he wanted you to be better than that..."

Me: "All this time... I thought *you* were his favourite..."

Aldon: "We are both his favourites, Elburn. He just couldn't stop me from following the same path he trod. On the other hand, you were always destined for something far greater..."

Me: "But I believed there was no higher honour than being a hero."

[1660] At this exact point, I felt a sadness fill my soul—as if a more significant entity that controls everything I do and everything I write used me as a conduit for their grief. I don't know who this mysterious omnipresent lost, but whomever it was—they were hugely important to them, like a mother...

[1661] Father is bald, so I'm talking about his skin colour here—not the hue of his locks.

Aldon: "I also thought being an adventurer was what everyone expected of me—to continue following the family's tradition. I didn't realise the harder path would have been to turn my back on it all—the way you did…"

I can hear the sound of rolling thunder on the horizon.

Aldon: "We don't have much time. The Heroes Guild Enforcers are almost upon us, little brother…"

I can see a giant ball of dust rising in the distance—I'm suddenly aware that it's not thunder I can hear but the sound of heavy hooves on the road.[1662]

Me: "Then with haste, brother—tell me what happened to you!"

Aldon: "I died—well, my *name* did. Morgan's Fireball didn't kill me— but it *did* slay the real Arin Darkblade. I was the one that survived—not he."

This revelation rocks me to the core.[1663]

Me: "Arin's dead—but how is it you appear as he?"

My brother holds up Arin's trademarked eye-patch.[1664]

Aldon: "You're not the only one with a cursed item."

Me: "But how…?"

My voice trails away as the answer suddenly appears as clear as a Paladin's conscience.[1665]

Me: "Morgan!"

[1662] By this, I mean a large number of horses, not just a heavily encumbered one…

[1663] It also makes me secretly pleased—which is a little unnerving, to say the least.

[1664] I subsequently discovered the design of this particular eye-patch has been logged with both the Heralds and the Heroes Guild. I wonder what would happen if the Arcane Heralds found out about the one Elamina Quince has in her possession—or the one Balstaff had made for his Arin figurine.

[1665] Obviously, not a sweary one…

Aldon: "He knew he was in trouble when he incinerated Arin. The Heroes Guild wasn't going to rest until they had answers—we had no choice but to concoct a ruse. It was a way for Arin to appear alive and spare us both from the wrath of the Heroes Guild. So, he created an eye-patch that could change my appearance into that of Arin Darkblade..."

Me: "But Morgan, either by design or dim-wittedness, creates cursed items!"

Aldon: "I know... well, I know now. But by then, it was too late. The ruse had worked, and we were both in too deep to do anything about it."

Me: "Yet I hear you work these days from behind a desk?!"

Aldon: "You have the curse to thank for that—the eye-patch indeed changed me into Arin, but it also stripped me of any desire to adventure.[1666] It was a hefty price to pay—but one that would ensure our family's safety nonetheless..."

Me: "Safety? How?"

Aldon: "Who do you think keeps the Enforcers from our family's door? I have my hands full, pulling the strings from within, ensuring the Barr name is protected from the Guild's greedy fingers."

Me: "I understand, but surely you've done enough to come home now? Our parents are sick with worry and cling to hope that you are still alive—why prolong their agony like this? Come with me to them and return not as a hero, but as their son..."

Aldon: "I want nothing less, but it is not as simple as that, little brother. Believe me when I say, if I were to reveal myself, our family would lose everything—I have to remain in place to protect everyone I care about..."

Dark riders appear on the horizon; the Enforcers are closing on our position—fast.

Me: "How did they find me so quickly?"

[1666] *Not too bad a curse then—one that would at least keep you safe from being dissolved by some giant jelly-like cube, unless you were really unlucky and was jumped by one as you opened the door to the pantry.*

Aldon: "I <u>told</u> them…"

Me: "Wait! You <u>led</u> them to me?! You do realise they'll probably kill me!"

Aldon: "Yes, but they won't—"

Me: "That's a relief—"

Aldon: "—because <u>I'm</u> going to kill you instead, little brother."[1667]

Me: "***WAIT! <u>WHAT!?</u>***"

Aldon: "Trust me, Elburn, this is for the best."

Before I can say another word, there's a **'*CLUNK*'** of metal as my brother puts me in manacles.[1668] But I don't try to struggle or break free—instead, I place my life in Aldon's hands.

Me: "D—Do what you must."

The Enforcers from the Heroes Guild are almost upon the pair of us—I can see the horses snorting out steam from their flared nostrils. Aldon opens the bag around my shoulders and takes out my journal.

Me: "That's mine!"

Aldon: "Yes—and now it's *mine*."

My brother gives me a firm shove backwards, causing me to fall towards the fast-flowing river behind me.

Me: "***<u>Wha</u>—!***"

I jolt painfully as Aldon snaps a hand out and stops my sudden descent. I look up in sheer terror at Arin Darkblade's snarling face once more.

Me: "I—I <u>can't</u> swim!"

Arin: "I don't <u>need</u> you to swim—I <u>need</u> you to sink…"

[1667] *I admit this is one plot twist I didn't see coming…*

[1668] *My brother's sleight-of-hand has improved from our childhood days—where did he get these manacles from? Who carries manacles around anyway? I have so many questions and so little time!*

Me: "Please <u>don't</u> do this!"

Arin: "I'm sorry, Elburn. I have no choice. I <u>have</u> to do this."

Enforcer: ***"STOP! STOP IN THE NAME OF THE HEROES GUILD—!"***

Suddenly my brother releases his grip, and I find myself tumbling backwards. I hit the water hard as my manacles immediately drag me beneath the surface. I briefly struggle, kicking for all my worth—but the weight of my bonds pulls me deeper. I can see Arin Darkblade staring down at me as sheer panic takes hold. I notice several figures standing next to my brother as my vision vanishes into the gloom.

I feel the overwhelming desire to take a breath; my lungs scream in protest—forcing my mouth open to gasp for the non-existent air. But strangely, nothing happens. I don't feel the warm waters of the Elkar filling my lungs. It becomes immediately clear to me that I'm not drowning—that I am, in fact, stepping into the unknown. I look around, perplexed as I find I'm breathing as if taking in the air from the idyllic countryside. Fish swim past—curious to see what exactly I am.[1669] They circle me several times before darting away for safety as I slowly stand up in the mushy riverbed.

I look upwards, my eyes adjusting to the gloom. I can't tell if the figures are still there or if they have moved away—satisfied I've met a watery end. I wait for what seems an eternity before deciding not to press my unnatural luck any further and find a way out of my bizarre predicament.[1670] I slowly trudge along the riverbed for several hundred paces before noticing the ground lifting sharply—inviting me to the surface.

The dry ground is a welcome relief as I collapse onto the grass bank and laugh at the absurdity of my situation. I spy the cursed Ring of Water Breathing on the finger of my manacled hand and kiss it in gratitude.[1671]

Me: "Wherever you are, *Morgan the Magnificent,* I thank you kindly for your cursed craftsmanship..."

[1669] *Wondering if I'm rather large bait on a rather large hook.*

[1670] *I'm not sure 'exactly' how long this ring's ability will last—so best I don't 'test my luck' any further than necessary.*

[1671] *My one and only time I will <u>ever</u> kiss a ring.*

Unseen Voice: "Seems you're in a bit of a soggy bind, Loremaster."

A slim but muscular figure appears above me, blocking out the sunlight. I manage to half sit up, my body tensed, fearing the Heroes Guild Enforcers. It takes several more blinks for the figure to come into view; I grin in disbelief as it finally dawns upon me who I'm looking at.

Me: **_"DORN!"_**

The 'Barbarian' kneels and unlocks the manacles. My chains **_'CLINK'_** together as they land heavily on the ground, and I appreciatively rub the life back into my wrists.

Me: "How did you—?"

Dorn: "Your brother."

Me: "My brother? You <u>know</u> him?"

Dorn: "Yes—but I'll explain on the way. We have to leave here in case the Enforcers come back to fish your body from the river's depths."[1672]

Me: "Why would they want to do that?"

Dorn: "For proof that you're _really_ dead."

I stare at the 'Barbarian', still a little in shock.

Me: "T—Thank you—"

Dorn: "You have your brother to thank. He's the one who came up with this idea. I told him that it wouldn't work. But he insisted it would—I'm glad to say he proved me wrong."

Me: "Where is he?"

Dorn: "He's gone, Loremaster—back to the Heroes Guild."

Me: "So, what happens now?"

Dorn leads me through the bushes to where two tethered horses are waiting patiently. The 'Barbarian' picks the larger of the two and hauls himself into the saddle.

[1672] _Using another large hook minus the bait._

Dorn: "*Now?* Now we have some decisions to make."

Me: "What decisions?"

The 'Barbarian' kicks the flanks of his steed, and it trots away along the path.

Dorn: "All in good time, Loremaster... *all in good time.*"[1673]

[1673] *Sounds ominous...*

45. Devlin Stormwind, the Wizard

It's been twenty-four hours since the incident on the banks of the Elkar River. Twenty-four hours since I was soaked to the skin and in need of a tavern of repute's roaring fire.[1674] Twenty-four hours since I discovered my brother is alive. Twenty-four hours since I found out my brother is the true identity behind the formidable reputation of Arin Darkblade. Twenty-four hours since I lost my journal...

Dorn has been steadily leading us westward towards an unknown destination, riding fast with a strong wind whipping at our tails. We've not seen a single person since the banks of the Elkar River—when we left my brother in our dust-filled wake. Thankfully my robes have dried fast in the heat of the sun and the warm air coming off the ShadowLands far off to the south. Even though we have put some distance between the Enforcers and ourselves, my saddle-sore rear threatens to annex itself from my body unless we stop to rest soon.

I draw level with the 'Barbarian', who has been unusually quiet for much of our journey together so far. I have been waiting for Dorn to speak first about the incident with my brother—not wanting to drown the 'Barbarian' in a colossal wave of questions.[1675] But his continued stoic silence has only increased the intensity of my wanting to know.[1676] The sun is starting to descend towards the western horizon, acting like a beacon hovering over our final destination—wherever that may lay.

Me: "We should stop and make camp soon. Our horses could do with the rest—as could my battered posterior."

The 'Barbarian' points further along the path ahead, where a second path cuts across it.

Dorn: "There's a river after the next crossroads—we can stop and make camp beside it for the night."

[1674] *Three taverns can be considered 'reputable': The Saint & Saintly, run by the Sisters of Perpetuity, who give away a hangover cure with <u>every</u> drink they sell—The Tea & Total, which is a tavern that insists on only serving water, which, as you can imagine is an establishment popular with the Elven Monks, but little else—and The Hog & Roast, which despite the name, does not serve up a single slice of meat whatsoever—much to the disgust of Barbarians, Dwarves, and Dwarven Barbarians everywhere.*

[1675] *A rather unfortunate turn of phrase considering how close I came to a watery grave...*

[1676] *A silence that would put any watchtower-standing Paladin to shame...*

Me: "Great, *another* river..."[1677]

We ride in silence and peel away from the path as we finally stop by the banks of an unremarkable stream. Dismounting, I water the horses in the shallows while Dorn begins setting up camp.[1678] By the time we've finished, the sun has dipped below the hillside, and the first starlight begins to break through the spreading darkness. I settle down on a bedroll as Dorn hands me some dried meat to eat.[1679]

Me: "Thanks."

The 'Barbarian' nods in reply but offers little else in the way of conversation. I can no longer bear the awkward silence and decide to test the waters.[1680]

Me: "I've wanted to ask you something..."

Dorn: "Then ask..."

Me: "The last time I saw you, you were fighting for your life against a tide of Enforcers."[1681]

Dorn: "That was a good day—I lost count of how many of their numbers ended up impaled upon my spear."[1682]

Me: "What did you do afterwards?"

Dorn: "I waited."

Me: "Waited? Waited for what?"

Dorn: "Your brother—*well*, Arin Darkblade to be precise. I waited for him to show up at my castle. I knew he would come, but I'll be

---

[1677] Hopefully, this is one river I don't end up at the bottom of.

[1678] Which includes removing the surrounding area of brambles and rabbit droppings.

[1679] I hope the 'Barbarian' remembered to wash his rabbit-dropping covered fingers before handing the unidentifiable meat to me.

[1680] Why do I feel the need to remind myself of my recent aquatic misadventure within my prose?

[1681] (See footnote 1680) I rest my case...

[1682] Creating a macabre Enforcer-kebab that would be hard for any Titan or Giant to resist.

completely honest with you, I was expecting a fight—Arin's reputation for brutality is well-founded.[1683] I didn't realise his connection to you until he removed his eye-patch…"

Me: "How did you react?"

Dorn: "I almost punched him. I mean, I wasn't expecting his face to move and change like that—I thought I was dealing with a shapeshifting monster."[1684]

Me: "Yeah—that bit *was* unexpected…"

Dorn: "Your brother explained his desperate situation to me—you know, he cares deeply for you and your parents. It's warming to see such devotion to one's family; he reminded me how much I missed the lush trees of the Evergreen Forest… how much I missed my own parents… how much I missed home…"[1685]

Me: "He has a funny way of showing his devotion—he pushed me into a river!"

The 'Barbarian' chuckles to himself.

Dorn: "Yeah, that was a late addition to the plan—"

Me: "Plan? What plan?"

Dorn: "The plan to save you from the wrath of the Heroes Guild. Your burning desire to uncover the truth nearly led you to wake a sleeping Dragon—and the beast was hungry to taste fresh Loremaster."[1686]

Me: "So, my brother *pushing* me into the river was intentional?"

Dorn: "What do you think? You're lucky—originally, your brother wanted to shove you off a cliff then use a Gnomish contraption to catch

---

[1683] *Although, I'd like to point out this was long before my brother took over the 'Arin' persona.*

[1684] *Or another luckless customer who had been suffering the side effects of one of Inglebold's unstable potions…*

[1685] *Now I'm filled with a longing to return home—curse you, 'Barbarian'!*

[1686] *After it had presumably stretched a bit and broke wind—as do all creatures that wake from a deep slumber.*

you as you fell. But, as you know, Gnomish contraptions can be a little... *unreliable.*"[1687]

Me: "Trust me when I say this—I'm *exceedingly* grateful you didn't go through with that original plan."

Dorn: "You can thank the Curse Keeper for that. When your brother found out about that cursed ring on your finger, we realised we had been given the perfect opportunity to hide your escape using the depths of the Elkar River."

Me: "A river which I sank to the bottom of!"

Dorn: "Good job you <u>did</u>—if you hadn't, we'd probably be taking your corpse to a graveyard about now. You got lucky, Loremaster—*real* lucky."[1688]

Me: "Why did my brother come to <u>you</u> with his plan?"

Dorn: "For it to work, he needed the best. He knew I could keep you safe in the wilds—I had already proved I was more than capable of handling anything the realm could throw at me. All I had to do was give him *everything*—the castle, the riches, and the treasure—all of it. But, in return, I would get a second chance—a quest like no other."

Me: "What quest?"

The 'Barbarian' grins at me through a mouthful of dried meat.

Dorn: "You, Loremaster... <u>you</u>..."

Me: "What? <u>I'm</u> your quest? You gave up everything you had for <u>me</u>?"

Dorn: "Your brother offered something I yearned for—the chance to experience one last great adventure, a quest that wasn't just another boring dungeon-run, and even though the offer meant giving up everything I had... it was a price worth paying."

Me: "I—I don't know what to say."

Dorn: "Maybe *thank you?*"

[1687] *I wince as I recall the inferno caused by Pippo's unreliable Red Box of Woe.*

[1688] *And all done without needing to use the last of my Lucky Potion too...*

Me: "Y—Yes, of course—*thank you!*"

Dorn: "I'm joking, Loremaster—it is I who should be thanking *you*. You've given this weary Barbarian a hunger for adventure again."[1689]

Me: "What did Arin—*Ah,* I mean, Aldon, do with your substantial wealth?"

Dorn: "What do you think? To keep up the ruse, your brother said he had to give it to the Heroes Guild. I imagine it would have taken them considerable time to move the loot back to their vaults safely[1690]—time we needed to prepare your escape."

Me: "So, what do we do now I'm *'officially'* dead?"[1691]

Dorn: "That's up to you…"

Me: "My whole adventure has been about my journal, documenting everyone I had come across in my travels. But my brother took it before I found myself at the bottom of the Elkar—I'm unlikely to see it again.[1692] It's forever lost to the Heroes Guild."

Dorn: "Your brother said you'd say that."

The 'Barbarian' reaches into a sack and pulls out a large book-shaped object wrapped in a cloth. As the angry-Warrior peels back the folds, a huge wave of relief rushes through my entire body—it's my journal!

Me: "It cannot be!"

Dorn: "You brother thought it would be a travesty if you lost your book. He hid it on the path for me to find."

Me: "I—I didn't think I would ever see this again!"

With my hands shaking, I gratefully accept the book from the

[1689] *And given Dorn's currently eating something unidentifiable—I'm sure that is a good thing.*

[1690] *No doubt hiring the services of 'Big Hands Removal' to lend… erm… a big hand or two…*

[1691] *I suddenly feel like I've been given a second chance at life—minus the chuckling Necromancer in the background.*

[1692] *The journal, not the bottom of the Elkar—I never want to see that again…*

'Barbarian'. It's comforting to feel the familiar touch of scorched Wyvern leather,[1693] with its faint yet unmistakable aroma.[1694] I sit quietly opposite Dorn, flicking through the numerous transcribed interviews held inside, checking the tome for any missing pages. The last hint of daylight diminishes behind the horizon, replaced by a blanket of stars that spread out across the night sky.

Dorn: "It's all there—not a *single* page is out of place."

Me: "You have no idea what this means to me; this book changes *everything* in the entire realm—*forever*. It's going to give my parents the answers they desperately seek—"

Dorn: "Change the realm *forever?* You sound like an Evildoer rather than a Loremaster—are you *sure* you're ready to wield that much power?"

Me: "What do you mean?"

Dorn: "That journal of yours will undoubtedly bring down the Heroes Guild—but it will also affect the lives of many in this realm—for some it will not be for the better."

I stare at my journal. It has taken on a new, darker form, morphing into a cursed object—no different to the trinkets fashioned by Simply Morgan or those found on the shelves of Enolin, the Curse Keeper.

Me: "So, what do I do? If the first-hand accounts held within these pages never see the light of day, then nothing will ever change—and the Heroes Guild wins."[1695]

Dorn: "Thankfully, that's a decision that rests on <u>your</u> shoulders—not mine. I'm just here for the ride..."

I stare at the battered cover of my journal; it's a journal that's been with me every step of the way—be it in the light or the shadows...

[1693] *Made from the skin of a Wyvern slain by a Merchant who had taken umbrage at his expensive sign continuously being ripped out by the beast, so took matters into his own hands. The journal's cover still has several scorch marks on it where the flames that claimed Pippo's Palace (and possibly a handful of Halflings too) left its mark...*

[1694] *Of arrow shaft and barbecued Halfling...*

[1695] *Albeit a <u>really</u> slow win that will feel like a loss to everyone else...*

Me: "I thought this thing would be filled with wondrous tales of heroism and heroes."

Dorn: "*Heroes...* I'm not sure what that word means anymore."

I look at the glum-faced 'Barbarian' as I sense his words playing on his mind.

Me: "If there's one thing I've learnt since starting this adventure, it's that a hero is no more important than a father who raises the kids while the mother guards the citizens as they sleep soundly at night. The *real* heroes are those without a sword, a spellbook or a badge on their jerkin. Everyone has the right to be called a 'hero', but we only notice those who go around slaying Dragons or bringing home a Quest-Orb or two... not the ones who put bread and ale on our table or keep a roof over our heads."[1696]

The angry-Warrior sits up and grabs a nearby stick to jab into the campfire; making the flames spark with every robust poke he gives it.[1697]

Dorn: "Get some sleep—we have a long ride tomorrow."

Me: "Where are we going?"

The 'Barbarian' doesn't look up to reply, preferring to carry on prodding the fire with such ferocity that I'm half expecting the hearth to suddenly turn on the angry Warrior and start poking him back.

Dorn: "You'll see..."

My sleep is filled with the most vivid of dreams. I saw my country home, my parents waiting at the door to welcome me as a returning hero—my brother by my side, nodding with approval as I regale everyone with my *extraordinary* exploits. But the dream quickly morphed into a living nightmare as an eye-patch-wearing giant serpent reared up to stare at me with its solitary eye, before baring its fangs and leaping to strike.

[1696] *Hopefully not a leaky roof recently constructed by a work-shy Roofsmith...*

[1697] *The flames dance and leap like an enraged Battle Dancer whirling their way towards freedom.*

I'm jolted awake by the smell of mouth-watering slices and eggs sizzling on a frying pan.[1698] I blink several times to see Dorn preparing us both a hearty meal to start the new day on the right foot.

Dorn: "Morning—sleep well?"

Me: "I—I think so."

Dorn: "You snored like the warthog I killed to make this."[1699]

The 'Barbarian' gestures toward the slices sizzling away in the frying pan.

Me: "I—I *don't* snore."

Dorn: "*No?* Tell that to the rest of your valley—I don't know how your noises didn't attract a wandering monster or two."[1700]

The aroma of cooking meat quickly banishes any thought of wandering or wondering monsters.

Me: "That smells <u>really</u> good."

The 'Barbarian' grins at me.

Dorn: "A breakfast fit for a hero."

I can't help but chuckle along with his joke. Dorn's breakfast delivers on its promise, a meal that satisfies a hungry stomach. We finish our food in contented silence, mopping the last bits up with pieces of bread before washing our plates in the river and refilling our waterskins. Dorn kicks the fire to death before mounting his horse.[1701] We slowly ride back onto the road and reach the crossroads when the 'Barbarian' suddenly stops and turns to me.

Dorn: "This is it, Loremaster—this is where we choose our path."

[1698] *That I hope are warthog rashers and not Hobgoblin ones...*

[1699] *Phew! Glad my nose is still on song, even if my snoring isn't.*

[1700] *Or should that be 'wondering monster'—as in 'I wonder what is making that God-awful racket?'*

[1701] *I guess that means the 'Barbarian' won that flaming duel...*

I stare at the angry-Warrior in confusion.

Me: "What path?"

Dorn: "*Devlin Stormwind.*"

Me: "Excuse me?"

Dorn: "I snuck a peek at the parchment you carry with you in your bag—it appears your hero name is *Devlin Stormwind...*"

Me: "It wasn't serious. The Herald gave it to me as a gift. It runs out in a few days unless I pay a hundred coins, and that is never going to happen, so—"

Dorn: "It's a good name... a strong name. Probably wasted on a Wizard, though, but then you can't have everything..."

Me: "But I'm not a Wizard—"

Dorn: "And I'm *not* supposed to be a 'Barbarian', but I still lose my temper, get drunk and punch anyone who *really* annoys me."[1702]

Me: "What are you saying?"

Dorn: "We are at a crossroads."[1703]

Me: "Go on."

The 'Barbarian' fishes out a hefty leather tome from a sack and flicks through the pages.

Me: "Hey! That's *my* spellbook!"

Dorn: "So, you *are* a Wizard..."[1704]

Me: "It was a gi—"

[1702] *Like a Barmaid-impressing Paladin...*

[1703] *Nothing gets past this 'Barbarian'!*

[1704] *Sometimes I'm my own worst enemy.*

Dorn: "A gift—I know. Funny how you've been given all the things you need to be a hero… almost as if fate is *trying* to tell you something…"[1705]

Me: "What? That I <u>should</u> be a hero?"

Dorn: "Why not?"

Me: "The realm is already overrun with them, for one thing."

Dorn: "No. The realm is overrun with those *seeking* an easy dose of fame and fortune—but <u>true</u> heroes? Those are in as short supply as ever."

Me: "I—I wouldn't last a <u>day</u>!"

Dorn: "Alone, you're right—you wouldn't last five minutes."[1706]

My heart sags slightly as Dorn's words charge headfirst into me without mercy.

Me: "Thanks for softening the blow for me."

Dorn: "Sometimes, Loremaster, it's better to speak plainly—without pulling punches."[1707]

The angry-Warrior stares towards the western horizon before turning to speak to me once more.

Dorn: "The way I see it, you have two choices. Choice one: you burn the journal with all its secrets. The Heroes Guild stays the course, and we forever live our lives in their shadow, knowing we did nothing but let fate decide our outcome."

Me: "Not very encouraging. What's choice two?"

The 'Barbarian' hands me back my spellbook.

Dorn: "You learn to read this…"

Me: "You mean… *become* a hero?"

[1705] *Probably that I should stop accepting gifts from strangers…*

[1706] *A little unfair—I'd give myself at least ten minutes before I'd expire.*

[1707] *Spoken like a true 'Barbarian'.*

Dorn: "*Whoa* there, take some smaller steps, Loremaster—let's try *being* a Wizard first; we can work towards the 'hero' bit later..."

Me: "But I know <u>nothing</u> about being a Wizard!"

Dorn: "Can you read?"

Me: "Of course I can read."

Dorn: "Then you can read spells. And if you can read spells, you can <u>cast</u> spells..."

I find it hard to fault the angry-Warrior's logic as I stare at the spellbook in my left hand. I reach into my bag and draw out my journal, holding it in my right.

Me: "What about the Quest-Drought?"

The 'Barbarian' opens his arms wide as if <u>he</u> is the only answer here that makes sense.

Dorn: "You're speaking to the one hero in the entire realm who <u>never</u> runs out of quests. Do you honestly think a Quest-Drought is going to slow me down? Besides, I've already made a few *'arrangements'* of my own and rustled up a side-quest or two to for us to try."[1708]

Me: "Why go to all this trouble? To what end?"

Dorn: "The Heroes Guild's end, of course..."

Me: "We're going to take on the Heroes Guild? Are you <u>mad</u>?"

Dorn: "Quite possibly—but what a tale it would make! The quest of all quests—the adventure only the bravest of heroes would ever attempt!"

Me: "I've already said I'm <u>not</u> a hero!"[1709]

Dorn: "Then, isn't it about time you became one?"

The angry-Warrior's words rock me to my very core. I stare at the two books I'm holding in either hand—feeling the heavy weight and burden of picking one over the other. With a resolute nod, I finally place my

---

[1708] *As long as it's not clearing a rat-infested cellar—I've got to draw the line somewhere!*

[1709] *Numerous times!*

journal back in my bag and open the spellbook. I flick through several pages before stopping to tear out one particular one.

Dorn: "What are you doing?"

Me: "There's a spell in here that I <u>never</u> want to cast…"[1710]

I scrunch the page up into a ball and throw it to the ground, where it briefly flames before burning itself out.

The 'Barbarian' laughs.

Dorn: "Where to next then, Wizard?"

I think for a moment before a wry smile spreads across my lips.

Me: "There's a Publishers Guild in Tronte—is there not? I think they're overdue a visit…"[1711]

The 'Barbarian' grins as he spurs his horse into a gallop and heads westwards—shouting behind him.

Dorn: ***"TRONTE IT IS, WIZARD! TRONTE IT IS!"***

I watch the 'Barbarian' disappear in a cloud of dust before patting my faithful bag that has accompanied me this far on my journey. It holds my precious journal, a Fireball-less spellbook, and a half-used Lucky Potion[1712]—what more do I need?[1713] I spur my horse on and give chase.

Me: **"Wait for me, Dorn! *WAIT FOR <u>ME</u>!*"**[1714]

[1710] *No experience points for guessing which particular spell I'm talking about here.*

[1711] *With Dorn the 'Barbarian' by my side—I feel supremely confident the Publishers Guild are going to give me a book deal that will shake the very foundations of this realm.*

[1712] *That I still feel every Halfling in a three-mile radius can somehow sense is in my possession.*

[1713] *Maybe a long white beard, a white staff, and a white horse—then again, maybe not right away…*

[1714] *I certainly don't want to be adventuring without Dorn's sword by my side—even if it is only forty-five paces away from me at this given moment!*

So ends the adventures of Elburn Barr, Loremaster, and thus begins the adventures of Dorn the Barbarian[1715] and Devlin Stormwind the *ahem*...Wizard...[1716]

The End.[1717]

[1715] *You know what, I think Dorn has earned the right to be called 'Barbarian'—erm... I mean Barbarian...*

[1716] *If you can't beat them...*

[1717] *For now... although, I suspect there's an exciting book in the near future—maybe something suitably titled like 'The Hero Diaries'.*

About the Author

Andi Ewington is a writer who has written numerous comic titles including Forty-Five45, S6X, Sunflower, Red Dog, Dark Souls II, Just Cause 3, Freeway Fighter, Vikings, and Campaigns & Companions. Andi lives in Surrey, England with a plethora of childhood RPGs and 'Choose Your Own Adventure' gamebooks he refuses to part with.

Twitter: @AndiEwington

First published by Forty-Five Limited 2022

First edition

Cover art by Conor Nolan. Editing by Paul Martin.

Printed in Great Britain
by Amazon

23197494R00383